SHACKLED SOULS

BOOKS 1-3 WITH BONUS NOVELLA

HEATHER LONG

Welcome to the Shackled Souls Omnibus collection which includes the completed trilogy of Succubus Chained, Succubus Unchained, and Succubus Blessed as well as a special bonus novella just for the Fiona fans among us.

To say that I have never had a character like Fiona would be an understatement of epic proportions. When I was initially invited to join this collection of paranormal prison tales, I immediately thought back to a blurb I'd written years ago.

The tale of a succubus inadvertently turned into a vampire. I'd wanted to write this book for *years,* but it never seemed the right time. This trilogy is the reason why. Fiona wanted to wait for this moment, this setting, this story and I'm thrilled to be able to share this scorching hot tale.

Fair warning, this book is probably hotter than any I've ever written and the heroes are downright swoon worthy when they aren't being assholes (Fiona's words, not mine!)

I'd like to take a moment to thank C.R. Jane, Mila Young, Rebecca Royce, Lexi Foss, Lacey Carter Andersen, Ripley Proserpina, Autumn Reed, Katie May, K. Webster, Jennifer

Thorn, Coralee June, Ivy Asher, and Raven Kennedy. These amazing authors have been a blast to share this journey with. Also hats off to my Heathens, Lysanne Therrien, Blake Blessing (who kept changing her mind on who her favorite hero was) and Sara Vermillion. Then there's my #girlgang, you're always here for me.

Finally, just a couple of housekeeping notes!

For those of you who have never read a reverse harem before, thanks for picking this up and giving it a shot. A reverse harem means the heroine will not make a choice in this book or any other between the guys in her life. It may take her a while to reach that conclusion, but it's the journey that drives it. There are many ways to frame this kind of relationship, currently reverse harem fits it very well.

I'm not going to give you the song and dance about cliffhangers with a happy ending at the end, because you're holding the whole kit, or in this case Fi, and caboodle right in your hot little hands. I advise that you hydrate, kick back, and get ready to laugh.

Fiona is a character like no other and she is hands down one of the few that I can honestly say I never know what is going to come out of her mouth next.

xoxo

Heather

Sometimes, I don't know what to say. Funny when I'm the author, right? Except, here, this is very true. Almost a year ago, I was invited to participate in a collection of paranormal prison stories along with a few other authors. Initially, I wasn't sure what I would do. Then I remembered a blurb I'd written like five or six years ago.

True story, I can't write a book without having a title and blurb for it. Even if I ultimately end up changing them, I need to have them beforehand so I can make space for them on my mental bookshelf. I also need the blurb to intrigue me so I *want* to write it, a lot like how blurbs invite us as readers to want to read the book.

But I digress.

The thing was, I had this blurb I'd written years earlier, but never used. Oddly, I had the heroine and the villains pretty nailed down, but nothing else. Literally twenty minutes after I was invited to the project, Fiona's guys crystalized for me.

Yep, I'd had Fiona in my head for years, but never her

whole story or where she was going. But from the moment Fin, Maddox, Rogue, and Alfred appeared, I had it.

When I started writing, Fiona was so loud and maybe a little obnoxious. All right, no maybe about it, but damn I love her. I don't think I'll ever have another character as brassy, bold, snarky, and without an ounce of self-preservation. Her journey has taken her from prison to transition to anger to running away to coming back and fighting and somewhere along the way she fell in love.

It's not a feeling a succubus is terrifically comfortable with, but then, she's not really a succubus anymore. She's changed and this has very much been her story.

Now that we dive into this third and final book, I worried it would be bittersweet and I would not want to let her go.

But just like she came into my world, she's leaving it the same way: on her terms.

Thanks for coming on this trip with us. Now buckle up, because like Fiona says, here she comes.

Warning, this book contains aggressively snarky characters, a bit of twisted humor and a lot of passion.

— HEATHER LONG

USA TODAY BESTSELLING AUTHOR
HEATHER LONG
SHACKLED SOULS BOOK 1
SUCCUBUS
CHAINED
NP
PARANORMAL
PRISON

SHACKLED SOULS BOOK 1

SUCCUBUS CHAINED

SHACKLED SOULS BOOK 1

Nightmare Penitentiary

I bet you're asking yourself, why am I here? What happened that landed me in this cell? Trust me, you aren't the only one.

Who am I?

You'd do better to ask what I am.

You know it's going to be a bad day when you wake up in the wrong man's bed, your favorite leather outfit is completely shredded, your best Manolo Blahniks are broken, and your eighty-dollar manicure is ruined.

But would you believe me if I said that's just the tip of the shit storm?

My name is Fiona MacRieve, and I'm a succubus...or I was. I seduced a vampire and we had a fantastic time, until he drained me almost to death. Which wouldn't have been so bad if he hadn't forced his blood down my throat thinking it would heal me.

Yeah, it didn't.

Cause that's not how I heal.

So not only did I wake up to losing my best outfit, I woke up dead.

Now I'm a vampire.

Some shit you just can't make up.

Oh…and my favorite part? I'm under arrest.

CHAPTER 1

"Of all the things you choose in life, you don't get to choose what your nightmares are. You don't pick them; they pick you" - John Irving

I didn't want to be a damn vampire. The screams echoed off the stone. The sound distant, yet anguished. It must be that time. In the two weeks since I'd been dumped into this place, I'd tracked the routine by when those screams began.

It marked the death and birth of a new day. The chill in the room barely touched me. I wouldn't have minded better accommodations. Despite my expensive tastes, the damp, stone cell with its single hard bed, a sink that allowed water for washing, and a toilet in the corner they'd actually let me clean before I touched it—look, a girl has to have some standards—was empty.

I was also the only one in this wing, so the wrought iron door, reinforced with its magical protections and salted to boot, didn't even provide me a view of the emptiness beyond. It was all shadows. The sconces in the corners lit up in the "morning" and extinguished at "night."

I'd destroyed them twice.

The little bastards always popped back up.

Still, it was something to do when the mental retail therapy grew stale. Currently, I debated between a pair of Louboutins that were last season and the Stuart Weitzman that were just perfectly classic and provocative. Both had stellar heels and would definitely work for my ass. The red-bottomed Louboutins had gotten a little too common. Everyone wanted to be seen in them.

The screams climbed in volume. It would be nice if he could arrive without the serenade. The noise was hardly conducive to mood.

Still, if I went for the Weitzman, what would I pair them with? I was still mentally scrolling through the dress racks when I considered ditching the heels for thigh high boots and a mini-skirt. I had fabulously long legs, and I knew how to work them. Thigh highs screamed 'come and get me.'

Heat and hunger vied for my attention as I shifted on the bed. The problem was that my fabulously toned legs were looking a little too slender. The thigh highs would hide the loss of tone.

Thigh highs it was.

The door grated open, and I didn't bother rising as he suddenly filled the space. The shadows deepened, darkening the already pitch space. Seeing in the dark had never been my talent, yet I could make him out as easily as if the sconces were lit. Tall, rangy, and gorgeous, despite the mean streak in him.

"Fiona," he greeted me as he closed the door and made his way across the cell. Not like he had far to travel.

"Dorran," I mocked his deep, husky tone as I crossed one

leg over the other. I wore the equivalent of a polyester jump suit in the most horrid shade of gray. The color was so drab, it blended with the walls around me.

Chuckling, he held out a hand as he stood in front of me. "You haven't been eating."

I rolled my eyes and ignored his hand. "I don't survive on blood."

"You used to not need it," he reminded me, as if I could forget. Even the mention of it had my teeth sharpening. The canines weren't quite as pronounced as most vampires. I hadn't been born one or even turned like they sometimes chose with the human cattle they kept close to them. I certainly shouldn't be one now.

Stupid. Fucking. Dimitri.

When I got out of here—and I would—I planned to gut Dimitri and hang him by his entrails. When he healed, I'd do it again.

A few centuries of that, and I might be willing to let bygones be bygones, or simply rip his head totally off.

That would be nice.

The lust for blood sent another wave of heat and hunger to balloon through me. It didn't help to have him looming over me, flushed with a lust of his own, and it wasn't just lust for me, though that was definitely present. Dorran had been feeding, and it practically coiled around him, a dark energy that licked at my skin, even if he wasn't touching me.

Demons, after all, understood other demons.

With a growl, he clasped my hand and yanked me to my feet. The moment his mouth crashed down on mine, I gave in to the need to feed. Blood may be among my cravings now, but it wasn't what I needed to survive.

With hot heavy hands, he shoved up my top, even as I pulled at his vestments. His tongue tangled with mine, and he tasted of coffee, cake, and passion. Someone had been dining well this evening. When he pulled back to yank my shirt up and over, I got his jacket off.

The clothes hit the floor with a thump. Other prisoners might try to purloin something from his pockets or steal from him. I wanted what was under the clothes. The power eddying over his skin stroked mine, and the shadows began to sink into me before he looped an arm around my bare waist and dragged me back.

Mouth on mine, he began to feast. The despair and aggravation in my blood churned as he sought to suck it out of me. Fisting his hair, I hiked my thighs to his hips. He had one hand on my ass, lifting me, and I began to writhe against the hard length of cock pressed right against my pussy.

Fuck, his lust magnified. Even as he dragged the despair out of me, I began to feast on the hunger in him. It was a magnificent loop.

After four days of denying him, I was starved for it. He drove me back against the wall, and I fisted him into position. The rough stone scraped at my back. Without waiting or warning, he slammed into me. Eyes rolling back, I tipped my head away. The pistoning of his hips jolted me right between pleasure and pain, a seesawing effect that only heightened his wanton desire.

When he bit against my throat, I bucked back at him. Fucker loved to mark me, even if he didn't require blood. The thrust of darkness teased against my anus. It was his turn to fist my hair, and he dragged my gaze to him.

A scream broke free as he began to prod the tight rosette, his lust magnified, and a choked laugh broke out of me.

"It's that or you feed on blood," he ordered me, and his whole body vibrated against mine. Not once did he stop drilling into me. My breasts scrapped against the sweaty heat of his chest, the hairs there prickling my nipples. His power thickened as he began to breach the puckered opening, and another shudder raced through me.

He wanted me so bad, and it flooded my starved senses.

"Fiona," he snarled my name, and I clenched my teeth in a grimace as his thrusts grew more ferocious. Every glorious slam he ground against my clit. The hot slide of his cock through me only ratcheted the temperature in my body higher. My blood thundered as his lust filled me.

"You want me," I snarled at him, digging my nails into his bare shoulders. "Then take it."

The flare of surprise followed by a swelling in both in his cock and his need threatened to tip me over. The shadows went hazy as he pummeled me, and my parched soul soaked up every drop. The first thrust of shadows filling my anus sent pain splintering through the pleasure, and he lapped it up even as he stilled his thrusting. Impaled on both his body and his power, I met his gaze. Heat roiled around me, in me, and him.

A testing probe, he eased the shadow thrust back and slammed his cock into me.

Fuck.

I forgot how to speak as he began to drive all thoughts from my head.

"That's it." He ground out the words somehow as he ramped his pace up. Every thrust of him stretched me. What pain his abrupt penetration caused faded as his lust spilled over onto everything. He could have carved me up right now, and I'd have orgasmed from the knife.

The scent of copper flickered across my drunken mind, and then he had my face pressed against his throat, and the first sticky drops hit my tongue. Instinct had me sinking my teeth in.

The hot flow of blood hit my mouth, rich in spice and power. The first gulp was like ice-cold water in the boiling desert. It made me desperate for more. As soon as I latched on, he began to rock his hips again. Thrust, counterthrust, he kept my body full as I gluttoned on his lust and blood.

When he began to nail that sweet spot with every hammer home, I screamed against his throat but I kept drinking. I needed it so bad. I needed everything he had, and he let out a roar as he came. We leaned there, him buried in me and panting as he emptied himself, and I kept lapping at his throat, wanting more of the power rich blood.

Gradually, the tension of his hand lighting my scalp up as he tugged on my hair pulled me free from feeding, and I met his gleaming gaze a split second before his smirking mouth closed over mine.

Too drunk to care, I cradled him and let him hold me against the wall until his cock finally slipped free. He didn't knot, but it took him time after release to soften enough to leave me.

Then he turned me from the wall and dropped me on the bed. Naked. Spent. And floating on a haze of it.

"Do not wait so long next time," he told me as he drew a finger down my cheek to my breast. "You are not dying on my watch, Fiona."

The possession in his voice should worry me, but fuck, it would hardly be the first time a lover—even one as casual as he was—decided I was something to be collected. Part of the reason I was stuck here in the first place.

"Fuck you, Dorran," I managed to slur. Why did he have to taste so good? I hated the need for blood, and it was that loathing that he began to soak up as he knelt down and latched his mouth over a nipple. Instead of pushing him away, I gripped his head and kept him there, until his shadows thrust into my pussy this time and tumbled me over the precipice into a deep, drunken stupor.

Nothing left of me to worry about.

It was the only reason I had to have imagined him smoothing the sweat-dampened hair from my face and the almost chaste kiss he left on my forehead.

"When I send you blood tomorrow," he whispered at my ear. "You will drink."

In my dream, I flipped him off, but he'd already pulled on his clothes after folding mine neatly and setting them at the foot of the bed. Then the warden was gone. I didn't even hear the rattle and slam of the door.

The screams continued after that, but I drifted on a lazy river of sensation. I barely twitched when the sconces lit, marking a new day. Replete and flushed with energy and vigor, I was like a cat who wanted to stretch out in the sun.

Except there was no sun.

And I was still in prison for the crime of being impossible.

I was a succubus, but a vampire turned me after he drained me to the point of death.

Idiot.

When I woke, I was living yet not. I was a succubus, yet also a vampire. My favorite outfit had been trashed, and my best shoes broken. My creator also panicked and fled, sticking me with the hotel room bill.

Do you have any idea what it costs to clean blood out of carpet?

Worse still, when I went to the city's vampires for some assistance in finding the asshat who'd fucked up my life, I ended up here.

In prison.

Yep.

So if you wanted to know how I got here, that's it.

For the last two weeks, these four stone walls have housed me and the warden—he told me to call him Dorran—

has been my only visitor. He wants me to feed. But I don't survive on blood alone.

I wish I didn't need the blood at all.

Four times now, he's had to force the issue.

Totally worth it by the way, because I won't touch that bagged stuff, and if the only way to feed my lust was to get him to show up, then I still wouldn't touch the bags.

I shifted against the bed, aware of every scratchy inch of the blanket and the uncomfortable, almost slab-like surface the too thin mattress covered. Nothing else here offered even a little bit of pleasure. Dorran, on the other hand, definitely filled a need.

Lazing through the day, I barely rose by evening to clean myself up at the sink and to get some water to drink. I could actually eat real food, not that they brought me any.

When the bags of blood arrived through the slot in the door, I was already back to leaning against my wall, dressed in the drab gray with my damp hair drying slowly. At least I could wash.

Instead of thigh-high boots, I decided I'd shop for jewelry tonight. Even if I was almost full to the brim, I wouldn't be opposed to my sometime visitor.

It gave me something to do while I wasn't allowed to rot away in here.

The funny thing was, if they didn't want the world to know about me, why would they want to keep me alive?

Why not just stake me or burn me alive or something?

Hell, cut off my head. Chop chop, and we're done.

Rolling my eyes, I jerked my attention back to virtual shopping.

My name is Fiona MacRieve. Always good to remember that part.

I was a succubus.

Or I used to be.

Now?

I didn't know what I'd become.

But as long as they planned on keeping me alive, they better hope they could keep me in here, because my lust for vengeance grew by the hour, and I could feed on that, too.

Just saying.

"A lion's work hours are only when he's hungry; once he's satisfied, the predator and prey live peacefully together." - Chuck Jones

The next week passed much as the first two here had. I'd finally begun to decorate my new vacation house. The one I hadn't purchased yet, but would be on my list when I got out of here. I used to have this really great loft apartment that overlooked a river. Some nights, when there were fireworks, I could lie in bed and watch them go off.

My new place would be high up, too. Something with lots of windows…whether I could take the sun or not was semantics. I hadn't actually tested the theory. I'd pretty much woken up trashed, dead, and sporting some semi-fangs that weren't as nice as those you could buy at a costume shop.

Then I was here.

In this *hole* at the bottom of the world.

Focus. The mental chastisement pulled me back to the target. Cliff house, maybe something sitting up on a bluff. I wanted to look out over the ocean this time, not just a river, and I didn't want city lights in the distance…or did I?

Compromise. Put a secondary deck on the opposite side that would let me look at a city in the distance. That would work, but I wanted my bedroom open to the ocean. I wanted to be able to throw open the windows and let in the breeze. I wanted to taste fresh, salty air and feel the sun warm my skin.

A clang in the hall jerked me out of my building. Irritated, I sat up on the bed as the first clang was followed by a second. Then the unrelenting clanging grew in force and volume. My head began to pulse in time to the banging, and I scowled.

It was too early for Dorran to come calling. He'd only come twice in the last seven days. Both times because I'd refused to feed. The last time had been the night before. My hunger and my body were both well-sated. I usually enjoyed a lovely period of hazy daydreaming in the first couple of days after glutting myself.

As distasteful as drinking blood was, I had begun craving his. Probably why the fresh blood bags they'd delivered at first light still lay right next to the door. I wasn't touching them. I didn't even like how they smelled.

The racket outside increased in volume until it seemed the pound right through my body, splintering any focus I tried to rebuild. Glaring at the door, I waited. *This* was a departure in my routine.

After three weeks of staring at walls punctuated by nightly screaming and the regular visits of the warden for some bouts of fucking and feeding, *this* stood out.

The clanging stopped abruptly a split-second before the metal of my door screeched a complaint when it was hauled open. It didn't open inward, no, that would allow me to block it. It swung out, so they could also barricade me in.

A guard filled the doorway. Well, maybe it was a guard. He was dressed in a heavy black uniform with tight leather breeches that were doing fabulous things for his thighs. His ferocious expression betrayed nothing.

Dude had *mastered* resting dick face.

Awesome.

The piercing frost of his almost silver eyes bored right through me. "Fiona MacRieve?"

Rolling my shoulders back, I gave him a bored look. "Depends."

"On what?" he barked in a growly voice, something like shock creeping across his scruffed face. The straight edged nose above his very full lips added to the overall appeal. He didn't belong in this dark, dank place. The flickering light from the sconces played over his face and warmed him a fraction.

Course, that could just be a trick of the light.

He took a single step inside, but I didn't respond. Instead, I just watched him. The sudden shift in routine offered me an opportunity. The question was what kind opportunity.

"Answer the question, woman," he growled, then his nostrils flared as he studied me. Another deep inhale, and he frowned even deeper.

One moment, he was at the door, and the next, he was in front of me. The flash of movement so swift, I didn't have time to escape before he hauled me up by the arms. "Are you Fiona MacRieve?"

"Well, like I said," I drawled slowly. "That depends on who's asking." Poor fool. This close, I could taste the desire and lust simmering under his fierce exterior. The ice in those eyes cloaked a much deeper fire. The male reminded me of the warden in some ways. Rich, powerful, and intoxicating in his wantonness—funnily enough, it wasn't my body pulling at him at the moment. The lust wasn't physical.

But it was primal.

I could work with that.

Ignoring his bruising grip on my arms, I lifted a hand to test the roughness of his face. "Who are you, sugar?"

His nostrils flared even as his pupils expanded then constricted to pinpricks. That was also different.

And not in a good way.

"Yes, you're her," he answered his own question instead of mine. When he thrust his face at my throat, I slammed my knee up between his very sexy thighs. Those gorgeous leather breeches really did him justice.

Unfortunately—for him anyway—he wasn't wearing a cup. Across nearly all creatures shadowy and otherwise, the male of the species was very vulnerable to attacks on their genitals, provoked or not.

Though, arguably, if someone slammed their leg up against my pussy like that, I would be in similar pain. His grimace at the blow promised me I'd landed it true, but he didn't release me.

I repeated the gesture, and this time, I slammed my head forward at the same time. That beautiful nose I'd been admiring crunched gorgeously, and his pained gasp accompanied the sudden release of my arms. As he swayed, I shoved him backward. The head butting left me seeing stars, but I'd stumbled out of plenty of bars drunk off my ass riding the lustful wave of humanity, I didn't need to see clearly to move.

Once out in the hall, I swung my gaze left and then right. Fantastic, it was all rough-hewn stone, and both directions looked exactly the same.

Fine, I went right.

I passed by other iron doors, locked and barricaded. I didn't bother to try them. They opened out. The door to get out of here would open also open out, but I would be on the inside of it.

Jogging, I thrilled to the fact Dorran had fed me so well, even if he'd left me sore and achy in all the right ways. But I was full, and I had strength. The hallway seemed to elongate or stretch on to infinity. There were no bends or curves.

That wasn't good. If I couldn't find a corner to turn soon, there was every chance my surprise visitor would catch me up. He definitely had fit and virile going on for him, even if I'd left him breathless and cupping his nuts like a little bitch.

Served him right.

I'd barely found the door I could push outward when the scuff of a step on stone reached my ears.

Dammit.

Risking a magical shock, I shoved the door open. The racket clanged up the hallway. The volume jolted me.

All the doors I'd passed…

Dick boy—fine, man—had opened every door along the hall on his way to me. That explained the clanging racket. Not good. No one had stopped him, that meant the guard had either been dispatched down here to fetch me for something nefarious or more likely to just kill me.

Stumbling out into a stairwell, I growled to myself. The door slammed shut behind me with tremendous force. Yeah, no one would miss the gong of that.

Up?

Down?

Damn good question.

The obvious answer would be up, because I'd been in the pit, right? No windows, sealed inside a stone coffin that just happened to be room-sized. I didn't have time to debate this in a committee of me, myself, and I. I flipped a mental coin.

Fine.

Down it was.

If up was the obvious answer, then down would be the correct route.

Descending the stone steps, I kept close to the wall. The smell of musk grew stronger the lower I went. Wet animals. Maybe dog.

Wolf.

Ugh.

Howling echoed behind the first set of doors I reached. Yeah, not opening the door to find the big, oversized floof-balls who wanted to rip out my throat. Last time I checked, vamps and wolves weren't exactly kissing cousins.

More like spitting, snarling, and teeth gnashing. Though my bestie had been a wolf. Hopefully, he hadn't heard about the latest and greatest. It'd be a real bitch to have to throw down with Elias.

Man could make a smoked brisket better than anyone I'd ever known, and I'd be really pissed if I never got invited over for dinner anymore. Continuing the down-ward trajectory, I listened for the raucous noise of the door opening above. Hopefully, when dick man got there, he'd go up.

Up made sense.

Why the fuck had I thought going down made more sense?

It was three more flights before I found another door of any kind. Was I about to knock on Hell's back door?

Like the door from my floor to the stairwell, this one opened away from the hall. I extended a hand to test the magical protections. I was on the outside, so they should be geared toward keeping stuff in, not out?

Then again, I went down—look, it seemed reasonable at the time, and I might still be a little drunk on Dorran—so what did I know?

Energy licked against my fingers, and the vaguest of hums

touched my ears. Dammit. Definitely warded. Warded to what? Give a sweet tickle, or blow someone's head off?

Last I checked, those spells were actually in the same category. Don't look at me like that, succubus here, not a witch. They do some messed up stuff.

A hush of breath was my only warning before powerful hands seized me, hauled me backward, and slammed me against the wall.

"Oh," I drawled after I caught my breath again. Having it all knocked out of me was a point in my favor. Fucking vampires didn't need to breathe. I did.

Score one for me. Take that you twisted fucks.

Still, I stared up at the now bloodied face of my erstwhile visitor and his very, excuse me, extremely pissed off face. Resting dick face had taken active to a whole new level.

"You are a pain in the ass," he snarled.

"Look who's talking, jackass," I retorted. "I was minding my own business in that cell when you got all handsy." For evidence I glanced at those huge paws he called hands currently pinning me to the wall. In fact, most of him was pinning me to the wall, and it was hot.

His lustful fragrance swarmed me, and I wanted to take hits off of it. I might need the extra boost, but I didn't need to go into a stupor, so I kept it to the mouth breathing.

For. The. Moment.

"Why do you smell like a man?"

"Because you're a little whacked. Trust me, no penis here. Currrently."

I smirked at my response.

"Need to check?" I widened my stance a little. It took some wiggling, but it ground me against him and the now very thick evidence of *his* penis. "I can feel yours, seems only fair you check out mine or the lack thereof."

His growl vibrated right through me, and fuck, that felt

good. Okay, first, I didn't need to feed, so stop it. Second, growling boy might want to eat me and not even in a nice way, so *focus*.

Tilting my head to the side, I considered licking him just to see what he would do.

Could be fun.

Might get me killed.

Both were definitely more than I had to do an hour ago.

"Also, kudos for the erection, man. I was pretty sure two slams of my knee would have knocked your balls into your throat."

Poor baby was not amused.

"Who touched you?" Each word came out on a spikey, near guttural sound, swallowing the vowels.

Kind of sexy in a primitive caveman way.

"At the moment, hot stuff, that would be you."

He shook me once. This close to the wall, it only served to knock my skull against the stone. Great, the stars I'd still been seeing since earlier now had do-si-do partners to dance with.

"Who *fucked* you?"

Oh.

That.

"Do you really want to know?" I asked, more curious than anything for his response.

"Yes," he rasped.

"Let's see—that would be 'none' and 'of' along side 'your fucking' and wait for it, 'business.'"

His brows pulled together. "You'll tell me, and I'll deal with it."

"Yeah, okay, this isn't entertaining anymore. We need to communicate in more than grunts." When he pushed his hips at me again, I debated his reaction if I slammed my knee up once more. He was pretty hard. "Thanks for the offer, by the way, I'm not hungry."

A puzzled look crossed his face for a split second, then he did something utterly unexpected.

He laughed. What the fuck?

Before I could verbalize the question, he closed his exceptionally large hand around my throat. While he didn't squeeze, the strength there couldn't be denied. "I wasn't offering you my blood, Fiona," he told me.

"I didn't think you were, since it's all in your cock," I countered.

He snorted. "Thank you for confirming you're Fiona."

"Discussing your dick does not make me Fiona."

Frustration filled his eyes. "Why are you being difficult?"

Was he for real?

"Um…look around," I pointed out. "What do you see?"

"You descending to the darkest parts of the penitentiary, where even the most dangerous hunters would be loathe to go."

"Cool, you run along then." Dammit, I knew I should have gone up.

He let out aggrieved sigh. "Not without you."

"Excuse me?"

"I'm here to rescue you."

Rescue. Me.

"Why the fuck didn't you say that upstairs instead of getting all monosyllabic and snarly?"

"Because you smell like another man, he's been all over you." He tilted my head to the side and then stroked his thumb over my throat. Told you Dorran liked to mark me. "He's done it recently, too. Are you sure you won't tell me who?"

"Nope," I said. "I don't fuck and tell. Rules of the game."

Not really, but I didn't know this guy, and rescue or not, I was not in the mood for this crap.

His lips compressed into a thin line, and he dropped his hand from my throat. When he backed up a single step and gave me room to breathe, I narrowed my eyes. That was an unexpected twist. Reaching behind him, he pulled out a pair of shackles, and I glared at him.

"No." I was not going in chains.

"You have to," he said. "I'm a guard. I can get you out if I *escort* you. But prisoners are not allowed to roam freely."

"No." I folded my arms. I was not going to put those on willing.

"I will take them off, Fiona. I promise." The growl underscoring each syllable didn't inspire confidence. Besides…

"I don't even know you, why would your promise mean shit to me?"

"My name is Maddox." He intoned it so formally, like I would recognize him by the moniker alone. Was it like Madonna or Cher? If so, 'fraid it was lost on me. "I'm here to see you to safety."

"Define safety," I challenged. "And why I should believe you just because of your name, which for the record, doesn't mean anything to me."

Surprise crystalized in his expression edged by real frustration.

Yeah, I had a gift.

"Woman, I don't care if you believe me. I'll carry you out of here kicking and screaming. I can knock you out if I have to." He dragged my arm out and slammed one of the shackles on. It burned as it snapped around my wrist. "I'm rescuing you whether you want to go or not."

Why the fuck would I not want to go?

I just wanted to know whether I was going somewhere better or not.

He wrestled me into the second shackle, and I let out a frustrated scream as it closed on my free wrist. They were spelled. The magic in them burned where they rested against my flesh. Dick face—Maddox—stared down as my skin began to blister and smoke.

"That should not be happening."

Oh.

That was it.

This guy?

I was killing him first.

Shackled wrists and all, I clenched my fists together and struck both at his bloody nose.

If I didn't break it the first time, I was damn well going to break it now. Unfortunately, he caught the slender chain locking my wrists together and hauled my arms up to slam them against the wall before he boxed me against it again.

"Stop fighting me," he ordered. "The shackles have a spell."

"No shit."

"The spell is to help us get you out."

Us.

Wait.

Gritting my teeth against the blistering sensation crawling over my skin and scalding it, I asked, "Who's us?"

A flash of teeth. "You'll find out. When you come with me."

I hated this man.

Alarms began to sound and doors above opened with a clang. His expression turned furious. When he turned that glare on me, I gave him a little shrug. Or at least, as much as I could manage pinned to the wall in his murder bracelets.

"Oops?"

CHAPTER 3

Maddox

*I*f he didn't want to kill her, Maddox might end up liking her. As it was, she fought like a hellion, blooded him, and managed to evade him by persistently doing the unexpected. As more doors opened above, he clenched his jaw. Then again, if he managed to get both of them to safety before this was over, he might just kill her himself and to hell with what Fin wanted.

Cutting his attention back to her red and blistering wrists, he ground his teeth together. The wild, erratic path had taken them far from the mapped exit. More guards would be upon them at any minute.

"Take them off," she ordered, and his cock pulsed with

every word spilling from her lips. The fact that she reeked of another male did him no favors. He waxed and waned between homicidal rage that someone had touched her while she'd been trapped here, and the very distinct urge to override that scent with his own.

Neither was useful in their current situation. A situation, he might add, that was her *fault*.

Shooting a look behind him at the door to the unknown level, he gripped the chain between the shackles and tugged her from the wall. Her hiss of pain dragged his attention to the blistered and reddened skin of her wrists. The spelled shackles shouldn't be reacting to either her succubus nature or her vampiric side.

Then again, she was a baby vamp.

Fuck, he'd have to take them off. He didn't want her suffering. Gripping the door, he wrenched it open and glared through the opening. The shadowed hall looked identical to the one he'd pursued her from her cell to the stairwell in the first place.

Fuck Fin and his fired hurry to get in here. They should have tracked her together, gotten her out together.

Better, he should have just let Maddox do it himself. Hunting was his thing. Dragging her with him, he strode down the hall. The sealed cells all looked the same, but the magic on them was different.

Something he'd noticed on her level. The unoccupied cells didn't have a metallic taint to the spell work on the doors. Something charged one of the doors they past and hit it hard enough to shake the whole frame. Magic flared, and yowl pierced the air.

That would probably leave a mark.

"Where are you going?"

"Be quiet," he ordered. The last thing he needed was for

his body and instincts to riot and override his common sense. The urge to strip her naked and sink his teeth into her grew with every passing moment. To his surprise, she cooperated and went silent. Instead of forcing him to drag her, she moved up alongside.

For exactly three more doors, then she clasped his forearm. The weight of her slender fingers gave him little warning for when she twisted the chain from his grasp while wrenching his arm up against his back. She tried to drive him into the wall.

Nice attempt.

Sexy little kitten.

Strong, too.

But he was stronger. He bore back on the force of her arms, not needing the leverage. Her little gasp as he whirled and caught her by the throat as he successfully slammed her against the wall did all sorts of things to his libido.

"Stop fighting me," he ordered. "I don't want to hurt you." Quite the contrary, he wanted to lick her from one end of her body to the other, until he satisfied this wild craving she'd evoked.

"That's not going to happen." The stunning amber of her eyes dared him to retaliate. Most newborns boasted blood-red eyes their first couple of years. Something about the tissue in their body and how it adapted to the need to feed. Barely weeks old, Fiona's eyes were as unique as she was.

Narrowing the distance, he forced himself to breathe through his mouth, though that did little to mute the stench of her lover or her far more provocative nature beneath it. Rage kindled in his blood, racing through his system with claws and teeth. Maddox wouldn't forget that scent. "Fiona," he focused on her eyes as he mouthed her name. *This* particular trick wasn't his specialty. "You have to cooperate until we're secure. Then I'll remove the shackles. Tell me you understand."

She laughed in his face, and Maddox snarled. The beast inside of him lunged forward until they were nose to nose. The humor in her expression drained away, but not the murder she promised him in her eyes.

"You want to kill me, kitten. You're going to have to live long enough to do that. I could snap your neck and leave your corpse here as I made my way out. You'd wake up back in your cell, and you'd never find me."

Her upper lip curled. "Fine," she conceded. "But as long as we're clear on the fact that I am going to fucking kill you."

Maddox snorted, then licked her cheek from the curve of her jaw to the corner of her eye. It was a stupidly possessive and territorial gesture, but he did it anyway. "I'm pretty clear on the facts, kitten," he whispered before jerking her away from the wall and gripping the chain once more.

"Blegh," she grimaced. "Dick."

"You wound me, kitten," he snarked. Braced for any further attempts, he resumed his mad dash to find them a place to ride out the security breach. Twelve doors later, he found what he wanted. Gripping the door, he yanked it open and ignored the racket it made. Just another lovely feature of the supernatural roach motel they called Nightmare Penitentiary.

Empty.

Hauling her inside, he released her in the direction of the empty cot in the corner. This room was actually smaller than the one he'd found her in, but it would do. Pulling the door closed, he put a palm against the handle and muttered three words. Now to see if the cost of those syllables had been worth it. The spells flared, and his nose burned at the sudden icy metallic stink wafting at him. Retreating a few steps, he settled into a stance as he listened.

To his continued surprise, Fiona didn't interrupt or say a word. It wasn't long before the shuffle of footsteps reached his ears. Even the sound dampeners of the too thick walls and their magic infused layers could muffle it fully.

The drag and thud wasn't shifter or troll. Sentinel.

They'd loosed them in the prison.

Not an unusual occurrence.

Fin. Hear me.

He waited a beat, but got no response. Telepathy wasn't in his wheelhouse of skills either. That was all Fin. If the little fucker listened for him, he would be able to respond. Then again, it might be the prison itself. He was a few levels lower than planned, and escapes usually triggered stronger defenses.

Fin was on his own.

Clever bastard could figure it out.

The shuffling steps continued along the hall, but Maddox held off facing his charge until after the sentinel's steps faded in the distance.

They'd have to sit it out for a few hours at least.

Pivoting, he met the baleful glare of his charge. Instead of saying anything, she merely raised her eyebrows, then held out her wrists. The rich tang of copper hit his nose at the same instant, and saliva flooded his mouth. Concern drenched his earlier rage as the blood ran in rivulets from her savaged wrists.

"Fuck," he swore and reached for the first shackle. Pressure applied in the right spot should release them, but they refused to budge. The metal itself had begun to sink into her wrists.

Lips compressed to a thin white line, she stared at him with fiery retribution in her eyes. The shackle didn't release as he continued to press into it, and the blood slicking her arms began to pool on the floor. The overwhelming fragrance with its sensuous notes of bourbon soaked vanilla stoked a hunger he hadn't experienced in well over five hundred years.

The magic in the shackles wouldn't release. Renewed anger flooded him. So far, this retrieval had turned into a clusterfuck. "You shouldn't have run," he growled at her, and she shifted her fingers, curling three of them and her thumb, leaving only her middle fingers extended at him. "Very cute, Kitten."

"Stop calling me that."

He considered it for a beat before he gave her a smile that was more grimace than grin. "Sorry, Kitten, no can do." He didn't mean the apology about her name but about the fact he had to grip and tear the shackles. The metal screamed and fought him as he wrenched the first one open. The magic zapped along his arms, and the unpleasant odor of singed hair polluted the air.

Fiona didn't make a sound as he ripped the first shackle off. The horror of her flesh would haunt him for a while. Blood dripped steadily, even after he removed it. Fortunately the second one didn't fight him and responded to the correct pressure points, popping open.

"What the fuck are those things?"

Maddox stared at the dwarven-forged cuffs. They'd cost him his weight in gold and had held everything from a mad troll to a wild vampire in a feeding frenzy without ever breaking.

And he'd had to use the fact they were keyed to him to destroy them.

"It doesn't matter," he said, tossing them into the sink to be cleaned. Maybe he could fix the other cuff later. Doubtful, but worth a try. He went to take her hands and lift her bloodied wrists to his lips, but she pulled free.

"Let me help," he ordered, and she rolled her eyes.

"I've had enough of your help. You know, I was having a really lovely day before you showed up with your bitching, snarling, and moaning—not to mention your murder bracelets. I don't mind kink, hot stuff, but I draw the line at fire games."

Fire...

"They weren't fire-infused, but cold forged. They shouldn't have done that." They'd never responded to any thing or person he'd shackled before like that. "If you won't let me lick them, Kitten, then you should."

"Why the fuck am I going to lick my bloody and mangled wrists?"

Because they were still bleeding, even if sluggishly, and she had grown paler. The puddle grew wider as well as deeper. Done with the argument—all the arguments—he pounced. Tossing her onto the narrow cot, he dropped down to pin her, even as her eyes blazed. He narrowly caught her forearms before she clawed him with her hooked fingers.

Running his tongue over her ravaged flesh, he damn near moaned aloud. Despite the stench of the other male, her blood tasted sweeter than nectar and twice as potent. Even the lingering hints of magical steel decorating the wounds couldn't detract from its potency.

Hunger ripped through his beast with a kind of ferocity he hadn't experienced since he'd settled into his first true transformation. Man, animal, and vampire lived in harmony, but right now, both vampire and beast fought to lap up every drop. Her musk deepened, grew more refined, and even as the wounds closed on one wrist, he turned to suck gently against the other.

Cock painfully swollen, he ground his hips at hers, and she arched her head back as a low moan vibrated from her throat. Fierce desire fisted him, and he gazed at the slender column of her throat as he cleaned her wrists and hands of every drop and scrap of blood. He sucked on her fingers, and she let out another of those delicious moans that vibrated from her throat like a true purr.

Definitely his kitten. Only when her hands and wrists were clean and the skin shiny and pink from fusing closed, did he push her arms up and shackle her wrists with his hands this time—one hand to be precise. With his free hand, he caught her chin and tilted her face so he could see the color in her lips. Still too pale, but there.

She opened her eyes. The amber color of them drowned out by fat, blown pupils, and her scent grew all the more intoxicating.

"You need to feed." His voice came out too animalistic, rough, and raw. The rumble of his beast stalking through each word.

"No," she husked the word, and he reared his head back. Her languid smile taunted him. "I don't. Trust me, I'm well-sated."

He'd kill the bastard. It wasn't just about territory anymore. Whoever that male was, he'd never live to whisper about having touched her, much less think about it. The only one who would be sating her from now on would be him.

When her purr turned to a laugh, he glared at her. "You might have been sated." He refused to use the word 'well.' "But you're still a newborn. Blood is vital to you, you need to drink plenty and often. The stronger the blood, the less you'll have to feed."

"I'm not a vampire," she informed him. "I'm a succubus. I've always been a succubus. I don't feed on blood."

She hitched her thighs around his hips, and one minute, he blanketed her, and the next, he was on his back on the hard stone floor. His skull rapped against the surface with a blow that stunned him. His kitten straddled him, grinding against his aching cock even as she gave him a vicious smile.

When he would have gripped her hips, she smirked and then stood. His whole body shook with want of her. Not even the other male's stench was a deterrent. More, it served as enticement to remove it and replace it with his own, until he branded her with it.

His beast snarled as she looked down at him, her expression almost disdainful.

"Your lust is a magnificent thing, hot stuff. But as I said earlier, I'm full." Then she casually stepped over him like he wasn't even there. Skirting the pool of blood she paced over to the sink where she lifted the shackles up and out with two fingers and dropped them on the floor like they were a distasteful.

Disbelief rocked through him as she cranked on the water and began to wash her hands. Before he could growl or even summon his language skills, she stripped off her top, giving him an eyeful of her slender back and the fresh bruises littering her flesh.

His mind stuttered to a halt as she raised her damp hands to her wild tumble of red hair and then began to twist it up, tucking it into itself in a knot.

The fact that she shed her pants nearly made him swallow his tongue. What fresh hell was this? With cupped hands, she splashed water over herself, and he tracked every droplet as it skated over her soft flesh.

Until he zeroed in on the very present, deeply imbedded handprints bruising those hips he'd wanted to hold while he fucked into her.

Their presence doused his lust in ice water.

The hot rage turned cold. Every little thing he learned just made him want to kill this asshole more. But now...now he wanted to make him suffer while he died. He'd put his hands on what was not his.

"You should stop growling so much," she commented in that low, sex-drenched voice. "It's very unattractive."

Maddox snorted. He didn't need any of his senses to confirm the mistruth. "Liar."

She glanced over her shoulder as she worked water down her arms, sluicing away any last minute traces of the blood—and his saliva. Still, Maddox sat up and didn't move to interfere.

The show was definitely worth it, and if she managed to rinse herself of that stench, it would be much better for both of them. He didn't need to be battling with his urges to erase it himself, and it would settle his beast. His vampire had given up trying.

Not many understood the clear lines of distinction he experienced with his aspects. It was a delicate balance, one he'd maintained for centuries.

Until today.

The hellion utterly ignoring him as she bathed from the sink captivated him in a way he'd never experienced. Instead of plotting their way out, he debated the different ways he could lure her back over to the bed. Dominating her was definitely one way, but she had too much fight in her to submit to him yet.

Begging wasn't an option.

He would never take without permission, no matter how badly he wanted her. Even aware she'd stripped for the sole purpose of punishing him wouldn't make him breach that inviolable wall.

He murdered men who did that.

No, Maddox had only one choice. He would have to seduce her and earn her trust. Then convince her she wanted to submit to him. That she wanted him to claim her. It would be much sweeter for both of them that way.

He was a hunter, and he'd never failed to get his prey.

They couldn't hide her deep enough in this dungeon turned prison to escape him. He could be patient.

It would have been nice to know before the shackles, though.

His beast settled, and his vampire surged, even as the man took his place at the peak of the pyramid. Once they had the nature of the hunt, nothing stopped them.

"You're smiling," Fiona said, half-turned and revealing the spectacular curve of her breasts. They were crowned with strawberry shaded nipples that made him hungry for summer.

"I'm enjoying the view, Kitten," he told her honestly.

She rolled her eyes and turned away, leaving him with her glorious ass on display and the occasional glimpse of pink lips when she bent over. Yes, he had the taste of this hunt, and while she might think she was denying him, he would lap up every single moment.

Where are you? Fin's voice pinged against him.

It was about damn time. *In Hell with a nymph. Where the fuck are you?*

Where I'm supposed to be. Why haven't you rendezvoused? The guards are everywhere, and they're about to let out the warden's corspesnare.

That could be bad.

Course, it also meant they'd just have to stay in this cell.

Are you safe?

His only response was a mental snort followed by *Do you have her?*

Not quite yet. *Yes.*

We'll adjust the plan.

They were going to have to.

"You're still smiling," Fiona challenged as she faced him a split-second before she pulled her top back on. The color didn't suit her in the least, and yet, she turned the drab fabric into something glorious because it touched her skin.

"We might be here a while," he said as he rose and then sprawled on the cot, stretching out. He'd slept on stone that was more comfortable. Even with his eyelids half-lowered, he didn't miss her stepping into her pants and pulling them up.

No panties.

At all.

He approved.

"So you're just going to nap?"

He patted the cot next to him. "Plenty of room, you can sleep on me if you like."

"Generous," she deadpanned.

"I can be."

Arms folded, she glanced from him to the door. "Some rescue plan."

"Not done yet, Kitten. Now sheathe your claws and come give us a cuddle."

She flipped him off and moved to the far corner where she sat down with her back to the wall and her eyes half-closed.

Eh, it was worth a try.

Maddox? Fin reached out.

Hmm?

Is it true? Hope and anticipation curled in Fin's mental voice.

Was she a hybrid like them?

Yes. He confirmed. *She's ours.*

Fin didn't respond in words, but the enormous satisfaction swelling through the connection made Maddox smile again.

"Keep smiling over there, hot stuff. You're still in a cell."

"I know," he answered. "You're still with me."

"Yay." The single dry syllable enticed him to laugh all over again.

She didn't like him.

But she also didn't know him.

Not yet.

CHAPTER 4

"The first step towards getting somewhere is to decide that you are not going to stay where you are." - Unknown

Twelve or so hours after the male interrupted my mental building, I finally managed to get the house's construction perfect. The bluff it would sit upon was somewhere along the California coast. It would make for spectacular sunsets in the evening over the water. The deck above would allow me to greet the sun in the mornings.

I really missed the sun. Weird to think about the things you lose. No, not because of that idiot vampire, but because I'd landed up here, consigned to the Nightmare Penitentiary for the crime of fucking up someone's idea of what was natural.

Hybrids couldn't possibly exist. On that note, I agreed with them. I wasn't a vampire. I'd died—theoretically—then woken up to whatever these physiological changes were I'd undergone. The transformation left me exhausted, starving, and really, really irritated.

How had Elias described me once?

Oh, right, Psychotic Monster Syndrome.

The humming leftover buzz—what little of it remained from Dorran's visit—had waned. The lightheadedness began with the blood pouring out of my wounded wrists. Before my latest captor decided to get all finger, wrist, and hand licking good with cleaning me up. The fact the wounds closed explained the shivers of awareness rippling through my system, and it had nothing at all to do with the intensity in his eyes as he worked to repair what his nasty little toys had done.

Nothing at all.

The torches had gone out in the corners. If this level were like my own, then night had fallen. The time for Dorran's potential visit approached. Only there would be no visit because I wasn't on my level—probably not even then. It hadn't been a full twenty-four hours since his last call. He rarely came two nights in a row. In the beginning? Yes. Not anymore.

I'd been well fed.

Emphasis on the past tense.

The blood loss also explained the electric need to roll around in the lust roiling off the snarl-monkey currently sprawled on the bed like some over-sized lazy ass cat, expanding to take up all the room.

I eyed him, then the door. He'd done something to it, but I hadn't tested it—yet. Not as long as sentinels shuffled in the hall. It had been a few hours, though. Maybe they'd moved on.

Could be they hadn't noticed my absence. The only person I'd seen since my arrival *was* Dorran. Even the blood bags arrived through a slot in the door.

I sighed.

"Something wrong, Kitten?"

I didn't bother to answer.

My name wasn't fucking *Kitten*.

Back to the house...

"You know," he said, almost idly. "I'm here to help you."

...I wanted something hedonistic in the bathroom. A huge tub, something I could practically swim in, as well as just languish and soak. When was the last time I had a *real* shower much less a bath? One upside to the vamp blood, I supposed, was the lack of body hair growth. This long without a real chance to groom, and I should look like Bigfoot.

I could stand the hair on the legs, not the hair in my pits. Nope. Just made me itch thinking about it.

But the lack of even the appearance of stubble was definitely an upside.

"You are a stubborn little hellion, aren't you?" The amusement curving through the words wasn't remotely sexy. "*Kitten.*"

Definitely a big tub, jets, too. I could do bubble baths, or crank it up to something churning.

Oh. A splash guard would be—

From indolent to action, Maddox suddenly loomed over me in my corner, his eyes blazing. When hot fingers cupped my chin and yanked my gaze up to his, I curled my fingers. I did not give him permission to touch me. "You go ahead and claw at me if you need to," he told me in a raspy voice. "You can scowl, you can even kick me in the balls—though I'd prefer not to repeat that experience—what you don't get to do is ignore me."

I snorted. The weight of his thumb along my jaw sent heat curling through my system. It was colder on this level than it had been on mine. Maybe it was just the fact that I'd been sitting against the stone for hours and it had leached all the heat from my body. Not that it mattered. I wasn't in any danger of freezing to death. My eyes had adjusted fine to the near-total darkness the extinguishing torches plummeted us into. But I didn't need the night sight to make him out.

The son of a bitch's eyes glowed.

"You know, Kitten, it's rude to withhold your tongue. Even if all it has to say are scathing things."

"Are you bored?" I asked abruptly, and surprise flickered through his eyes.

"No," he answered after a beat, keeping his hand firm on my jaw.

"Neither am I. Now fuck off."

A growl rumbled in his chest, but I flicked my gaze to the left of his and let my eyes go unfocused. The bathroom could be done in blue tones…

The grip on my jaw tightened and then released abruptly. I kept my gaze trained elsewhere, but the jerk of him scooping me off the floor yanked my attention to the present. "Are you impaired in some way?" I demanded, ignoring the hard chest he cradled me against or the fact that heat from his body licked across mine like a cheerful fire crackling in the fireplace.

His snort seemed to echo mine from earlier, but he didn't answer as he stood and carried me back over to the bed he'd been occupying. When he settled, he didn't lie down so much as sit with his back braced against the wall and me in his lap.

The very hard cock beneath my ass wasn't remotely comfortable. Maybe I should have kicked him harder.

"Get some sleep, Kitten," he rumbled. "If you can."

"Did anyone ask you?" I flattened a hand against his chest to shove away, but it was like being bound in steel. The heat seemed to rise off of him in shimmering waves, chasing away the stone chill buried in my bones.

"No," he murmured, almost agreeably before he nuzzled his face against my hair.

"If you start licking me again, I'm going to tie a knot in your dick so tight, you'll be screaming when you take a piss."

Dead silence greeted my proclamation. Then he began to shake. The soft vibration and huffs of barely suppressed laughter rocked him. Since he had me all wrapped up in the steel bands of his arms and curled against his too hot, too hard body, it rocked me, too.

"Kitten," he said in between growling chuckles. "You're a delight."

Oh, just fucking kill me.

I rolled my eyes and tipped my head back, uncaring if he thought I bared my throat to him. For the record, I wasn't, but what I debated was whether I should slam my head into his face again. I still had a headache from earlier, but it would be worth it to shut him up.

When he dragged his nose along my throat, however, I froze. Every instinct I possessed began to scream. I curled my fingers at the first deep inhale he took, and tried to ignore the way my skin pebbled and my pussy clenched when he exhaled and the warmth of his breath eddied over my flesh.

Liquid warmth spilled through my system, chasing the chill from my veins, and I squirmed to find a more comfortable place to sit than the hard cock jabbing me right in the ass. He pressed his lips right over my pulse point, but at my next wriggle, his teeth grazed the skin and I scowled.

"You bite me, and I will end you."

His laughter huffed against my skin, even as he began to move his mouth along my throat in a half caress, half nibbling motion. His teeth added just the promise of sting, and I wasn't clenching my ass or my pussy in anticipation of that bite.

No, I absolutely wasn't.

"The last son of a bitch who bit me nearly drained me to death," I said in as icy a controlled tone as I could manage given the conflicting messages of 'no' and 'oh fuck yes' my body seemed to be giving out. The musk of his desire scented the air heavily around me, a cloud of choking testosterone and something so very decadently other that I had to fight against sucking it in greedily.

Whatever he was, he smelled divine.

It, I mentally corrected. It. Not he.

A pause, then a soft kiss and the rasp of his stubble against my flesh like he was rubbing his cheek against my throat. Fuck me, that actually felt good.

"What was his name?" The question slid through me, inviting me to answer, beckoning as surely as if he'd slid his fingers into my wet pussy and crooked them until I saw stars.

Stop it.

My traitorous body needed to shitcan those thoughts right now. I was *not* hungry, and contrary to all the lovely rumors about my kind, I didn't just spread my legs for every dick I met.

Not even hard, hot dicks that would probably take some effort to engulf and would likely drill me until I saw stars.

Nope, not doing it.

What was the name of the fucker who drained me to the brink of death then force-fed me his blood? Not happening.

When I caught up to him—and I would—I planned to break his legs and then every other joint in his body, give him just enough blood to heal, then start over.

A few centuries of that, and I might get bored.

Asshole.

"You can tell me, Kitten," Maddox invited in that sexy baritone. "I promise to share, but I'd rather end your maker before he recalls the persuasive power he might have over you."

That made me laugh. "He can't control me."

The idea was so patently ridiculous, I couldn't stop the chuckles shaking me. He lifted his head abruptly as I ran a hand over my face trying to suppress the mirth. The riveted stare suggested he'd never heard a woman laugh before.

How sad for him.

"All vampires can control their get, at least in the beginning. It's how baby vamps are kept from going absolutely mad and slaughtering whole villages." Then he seemed to consider it and shrugged. "Unless, of course, that's what you want to happen. Beyond that, only the most powerful can control another vamp."

"The prince of the city couldn't control me, sugar, trust me. My so-called maker couldn't either. Probably because, wait for it, I'm *not* a vampire."

The gentlest stroke of his fingers eased beneath the hem of my shirt and caressed the flesh there. It was pleasant, not provocative, so I didn't break his hand. "Are you sure about that?"

"Yes." No doubt existed in me on that front at all. "Ugh, why am I talking to you? I have a bathroom to build."

"Perhaps because I'm here," Maddox suggested. "And you're not shivering from the cold anymore."

I hadn't been shivering before.

"It could also be, I'm on your side and came to rescue you."

"Well, you're doing a bang-up job so far," I remarked. "How's that going for you?"

"Challenging," he admitted. "Yet, you won't hear me complaining about the time together."

I rolled my eyes. Not charmed.

"Then what was all that growling and shackling earlier, hmmm?" Yeah, wiggle out of that one.

"The shackles, I apologized for," he said, catching my hand and lifting it to press his lips against my wrist.

"Not that I heard."

"No?" A tease.

"No." I kept my tone flat.

"Hmm." Another kiss placed right over my pulse point that had absolutely nothing to do with the tautness in my core. I wasn't hungry.

Why was I getting all soft and cuddly?

Ugh.

I would not be one of *those* women.

Or even one of those succubi.

"Then please accept my apologies, Kitten," he murmured against my skin, the vibrations sending little shocks racing up my arm. "The intention was never to harm you."

"Huh."

He lifted his head, and his eyes shimmered as he stared at me. Interesting. All pretense of humanity abandoned those slitted eyes.

"What are you?" I asked before I could think better of opening that door.

"Curious, Kitten?"

I jerked my wrist from his clasp and slapped his chest. "Stop. Calling. Me. That."

"No," he answered with too much of a smile in his voice. He cradled me closer as though he wanted to tuck my head against his shoulder. I didn't want to get much closer than I already was. The man's scent seemed everywhere, like a cloud that wanted to hug me.

"Why not?"

"Because you're sharp toothed and clawed, like a kitten," he murmured, then pressed a kiss to my forehead. When I jerked my head back, he didn't seem remotely perturbed by the action. "You're impulsive and headstrong. You're doing things without an ounce of consideration for the fact that you're alone with a much older, much stronger, and far more dangerous being than yourself." His voice dropped an octave as he reached the end of his not-threat.

"Far more dangerous than me?" I almost purred—fuck that analogy, really, but I did it anyway—and narrowed the distance to his face myself this time. I cupped his cheek, the rasp of stubble prickling my palm. His slitted eyes constricted, but the glow behind them intensified. Shifting until his lips were a breath from mine, I met his stare unblinking. His body went taut, and the band of steel around my back tightened further as his fingers dug into my side. "I don't know about that," I whispered. His sharp intake of breath made me smile. "I'll give you old and cranky," I said after a pregnant pause. "But dangerous? Hardly."

The split-second between his pupils' constriction and sudden expansion warned me of his intention, and as soon as he darted his head forward to claim my lips, I wrenched his head sideways.

I didn't snap his neck, but the action promised I could have, and I held his head tight, not releasing my grip even when his own turned bruising.

"Don't presume you know me," I whispered through clenched teeth. "I didn't ask for your help. I didn't ask for you to come here. You don't own me. No one does."

"Fuck, that's hot," a new voice said from behind me, startling the fuck out of me. I scrambled to disentangle myself from resting dick face. Not that I needed to bother, he'd already risen and tossed me behind him on the cot as he lunged to put himself between me and our new arrival.

Instead of an immediate fight, Maddox laughed. "You always did know how to make an entrance."

"Been here a few minutes," the new voice said, though I couldn't make out more than a faint outline of negative space in the dark. "But you two were being all cuddly, I didn't want to step on your moment. Should have known better, brute. Your lack of charm seems to have rubbed our lady the wrong way."

The possessiveness in that last sentence irked. With a light slap, the owner of the voice sidestepped Maddox and then seemed to hover over me. Top notes of ginger, grapefruit, and cardamom teased a clean, almost playful essence, but the vetiver, cedar, and the rich loam of freshly turned earth cautioned me.

"Has Maddox been being his normal, boorish self?" Sympathy and humor weaved through his voice. "He means well, he really does."

"Fuck off, Fin," Maddox growled. "Kitten, this is Fin. Our ticket out. Fin, this is Kitten."

"Kitten?" 'Fin' sounded almost insulted. "Maddox, the lovely lady has a name. Don't you, darling?"

The sweetness in his voice threatened to choke me, or maybe send me to a dentist. Instead of answering, I turned my glare on where Maddox stood. "Why are there now two of you?"

"Ignore her, she's been in here too long," Maddox stated. "Has the breach calmed down?"

"No," Fin said before he dropped to sit next to me on the cot. Only—there was an absolute absence of warmth. If Maddox was the sun, this guy was the cold, dark void. How did he have such a powerful scent and absolutely no heat?

And why couldn't I be left alone to design my house?

"In fact, it's worse," Fin sounded almost cheerful about the fact. "The warden's pacing the levels, going one by one. Did you know he's a shadow demon?"

Maddox growled.

Fin leaned toward me. "Don't mind him, he gets a little grouchy about demons of all kinds. Present company excepted, of course."

"She's not a demon," tall, dark, and growly snarled. He said it with almost the same amount of force I'd used when I told him I wasn't a vampire.

Weird.

"Anyway," Fin said, with a wave of his hand. I couldn't quite make him out, even this close. My night vision was good, even with the absence of light, but it was like he was undefined. "They're really hot to find her. That, or they're just having a dick measuring contest with how much security they can throw out there. The corpsesnare is wandering, Sentinals are out, there's like three times the number of normal guards at all the exits, and I almost ran into Brina."

He gave an indelicate shudder on the last.

"We should be fine here for a couple of days," Maddox said, and despite the definitiveness of the statement, his tone didn't suggest the same.

"Maybe," Fin said. "Maybe not. I sent for Rogue."

"Why the fuck did you do that?" Oh, that pissed him off. His anger flooded the room with so much delicious heat, I sighed and stretched. I swore his eyes glowed even brighter, enough to give more definition to the room, but not to Fin.

"He sounds really pissy, but he's just frustrated," Fin told me, head tilted toward me as if confiding state secrets. "Rogue's not a people person anymore, but he's also more than capable of creating the distraction we need to get out of here." The last he directed at Maddox. "So just simmer down and cool the fire breathing."

Fire breathing?

A growl resonated through the room. "Fin, Rogue won't just cause a *distraction*. We haven't summoned him in over a century."

"So?"

"So, do you recall the *last* time we had to call him?"

"Yeah but that was totally different," Fin countered. "One, we had no way of knowing what those trolls were hiding, and two, if the scouts hadn't shot first and tried to ask questions later, he wouldn't have slaughtered them."

I had to admit, I was getting more curious by the minute.

"And to be totally fair," Fin continued. "We were this close to getting our heads chopped off."

"That's because *someone* doesn't know how to follow a plan." That someone was clearly Fin. I'd just met him, and the fact he had impulse issues couldn't be clearer if he'd taken out a neon advertising sign.

"Oh, I know how to follow a plan," Fin argued in a smooth tone, then leaned toward me. "I definitely know how to follow a plan, it's just that when it's a stupid plan, I like to get creative."

His shoulder brushed mine, and the sense of nothingness hit me. My palms itched to reach out and put a hand on him.

"Fin," Maddox growled. "When did you send for Rogue?"

"About an hour before we left." The cheerfulness in his voice pulled a reluctant smile from me. The fact Maddox actually exhaled the most put upon sigh so heavily made me laugh.

The chuckle worked its way up from my belly, and I shook from it. I *almost* felt sorry for Maddox.

Almost.

But really, fucking with his day? Couldn't happen to a nicer guy.

"She thinks I'm funny," Fin said with a grin in his voice. "You like me best, don't you?"

Still chuckling, I almost answered in the affirmative, in spite of the fact that I would rather be back on my rather monotonous routine if I had to be stuck in this place. Probably better to *not* encourage them. Then again, Maddox's derisive snort made me rethink that. Dropping my hand onto Fin's thigh, I said, "I absolutely do like you better."

Not best.

But better.

There, suck on that dick face.

I didn't really get to savor Maddox's response though, because that sense of nothingness regarding Fin only intensified. No heat. No pulse. No sense of him being *there*, and yet, I could touch him.

"You're astral projecting." Shock rippled through me.

"Very good, beautiful," Fin complimented me. "I was supposed to meet you hours ago, but apparently, Maddox doesn't know his ups from his downs and totally screwed the pooch on the introductions. I didn't want to wait a couple more days, so—voila. Here I am, and not too soon, if you don't mind me bragging."

Another aggrieved sigh from Maddox made me smile wider. Fin could really push his buttons.

Still…

"To be fair, he could have been out of here, but he insisted on following me." I shrugged. "I'm the one who came down the stairs instead of up. Oops."

"It's all right, anyone could get turned around in here. Sometimes down is the way to go. Who knows, by the time Rogue gets here, you might have to go down to get up, and then we'll go right to get left. It'll be a whole thing. But we'll both be here to help Maddox out so he doesn't get lost."

"You really aren't helping," Maddox said, his tone bland and bored before he moved back to the cot. When he dropped to sit right on top of Fin, I expected more of a protest than an exasperated sigh.

Then the shadow disconnected itself from him and stood. "You know I hate it when you do that."

"Amazing the things we do that we know will irritate the other."

"True," Fin admitted. "I'm guilty of that." Then he turned to me again, and the shadowy hand came to rest against my thigh this time as he knelt. "I'm honored to meet you, Fiona MacRieve, I don't know if I said that earlier."

"No," I told him. "Not really. But I'll bite, why are you honored?"

"You're the—"

"Fin." Maddox's snarl cut him off. "Later. For now, find us a route out of here preferably *before* Rogue arrives. This is an extraction, not a war."

"Eh," Fin, said. "It's kind of both. Even you have to admit that. With the lovely Fiona here the prize at the center of the maze. We just have to get through all the mini-bosses to the big boss, and boom, we get the girl."

"Okay," I said, removing his shadowy hand off my thigh with two fingers. "Bored now."

"Ha." You could practically taste the smirk in Maddox' tone.

"First, no one asked for rescue. Second, I'm not some helpless damsel. Third, I'm nobody's fucking prize."

"I can't wait to lay my real eyes on you when we rescue you," Fin said. "You're *delightful.*"

Then he vanished, and it took everything I had not to scream.

"Do either of you actually listen?" I demanded.

Maddox shrugged before he looped an arm around my shoulders and dragged me against the furnace of his body. If I really were a kitten, I'd sink in my claws and shred him before I sprawled out to doze in the heat. I'd almost forgotten what it was like to be surrounded by this much warmth. The only heat I'd had came when Dorran...

"Oh." Fin popped back in and gave Maddox a start. His

jerk betrayed his surprise, which I'd bet on my best pair of shoes—well, second best at any rate, since my best ones got trashed in the same incident that landed me here. "Don't believe a word Maddox says about me. He really does love me, he just doesn't know how to show emotions. He's very sixteenth century in his affections."

Then Fin vanished again, and I chuckled.

"You really do like him," Maddox stated, and I couldn't tell if he was disgusted or pleased by that revelation.

"Don't be jealous," I advised. "I haven't really *met him* met him yet."

"True." That seemed to please him way too much though.

"Then again, I like him more than you—so that's something."

A rumbling growl was his only answer, and I tipped my head to rest against his shoulder and went back to designing my house. Better to not get attached to anything. 'Cause the first opportunity I had, hasta la vista, grumpstiltskin, and his nutty buddy, Fin.

"Reality doesn't impress me. I only believe in intoxication, in ecstasy, and when ordinary life shackles me, I escape, one way or another. No more walls." - Anais Nin

The sudden tension cording the arm I dozed against as the torches whooshed to life in the corners of the room woke me. "It's morning," I told him, then let my eyes fall closed again. The heat rolling off him probably shimmered the air, but I wasn't going to complain.

"That's the only marker for time shifts?" Dislike crackled between the words.

"Well, I ordered the turn down service and breakfast in bed, but the service here is you get what you get and you don't throw a fit." A yawn elongated the last word.

When he rumbled a growl, I leaned away and began to stretch. Fine, if he was awake, it was hard to justify using him as a pillow. Though to be fair, I didn't think he'd actually slept. It was more like he'd just been quiet, and I could sleep without remorse for using him as a pillow.

The arm he had around me tightened, and he dragged me back with a huff. "You don't have to move," he said, then pressed his chin to the top of my head. He was a big dude, but I wasn't a damn doll.

"If you're talking, you're up," I told him, and peeled his hand away from my waist as I stood. The room swayed, but I locked my legs to keep from falling on my ass. The last thing I wanted was to give Mad Dog Twenty there a chance to scoop me up.

As soon as I was sure I wouldn't collapse, I made my way to the toilet in the corner. Dropping my drawers, I took a seat and emptied my bladder. Some people would be put off by being on display. Me? Not so much. I didn't invite him. He was just lucky I didn't have to crap. I had no problems with giving him a stink bomb he would remember.

Finishing, I flushed the evidence then stripped out of the top and pants to begin my daily wipe down. The water from the sink was always cold. But it was clean, and there was no taint to it. The ache in my wrists served as the only reminder of the damage the shackles had done. He'd done a very effective job cleaning the injuries. Had he healed them or just sealed the injuries? I'd certainly burned enough resources in the recovery, so it was a fifty-fifty debate on who owed what to whom.

The items in question were no longer on the floor. He must have recovered them when his friend beamed in for a visit. Ignoring the chill, I wiped down the best I could with what passed for soap. What I wouldn't give to wash my hair in a real shower. So far, I'd made do with washing it in the sink, but there was no conditioner, and even my hair needed something. Dipping my head, I twisted to get it under the water.

A pained groan issued from behind me, and I rolled my eyes.

"Don't look if you can't handle it," I told him.

"Oh, I can handle you just fine," Maddox informed me. "Though you're lucky it's me and not someone else. Not everyone would be so restrained."

I snorted. "No one takes anything from me," I reminded him as I worked the soap through my hair. Eyes closed, I massaged my scalp. "And intentions matter."

"Fair." The single grunt was his only response. I appreciated his lack of challenging the assertion. All things being equal, I didn't need to deal with another flood of choking testosterone. That said, I didn't question the fact he wouldn't try to take what hadn't been offered to him.

Like I said, intentions mattered. His lust hung over him like a cloud of electricity, buzzing the air with its presence. But he also hadn't moved from his spot on the cot, nor had his focus lasered on to me. After rinsing the soap out, I wrung the hair as best I could, then straightened.

I almost objected to putting the clothes back on, but I didn't have anything else to wear, so clean or dirty, the ugly drab gray would have to do. The top clung to me in places, and my dripping hair soaked the back. The chill raced over my flesh, but I ignored it as I stepped into the pants.

Unsurprisingly there were no blood bags on the floor. That was a nice change of pace. I never touched the damn things anyway. Finished, I headed for the corner I'd sat in the day before when Maddox released a warning growl and stood. The cell suddenly seemed far too small for the two of us as his presence billowed out, carrying heat with it that chased away my chill.

"Sit."

"Not a dog."

The baleful look he sent me promised a hell of a fight,

then he exhaled. "Kitten…*don't* provoke me. This whole situation is grating on my nerves. I do not want to take it out on you."

The request surprised me. It wasn't an order. The fact that he asked followed by the explanation pleased me on a level I wasn't going to examine at the moment. Instead, I had a counter offer. "Answer a question for me?"

If my response surprised him, he gave no indication. In the light from the torches, he seemed even bigger than he had the day before. His shadow stretched even further across the walls, even as his eyes reflected the flickering flames. They weren't slitted at the moment, but more normal. The hazel-green a pretty enough color. Almost simple.

Yet nothing about Maddox was at it appeared.

That much I didn't doubt.

He shrugged. "Ask."

"Why are you here? I mean really. Why come to get me? You don't know me. We've never met before." I'd have remembered him. "So why risk it to get in here?" This place was legend. Most who were consigned within its walls never returned. Those rare few who had? Well, it was said they weren't the same.

Granted, rumors and urban legends weren't precisely facts, but they were all I had to work with.

"Because what you are isn't a crime," he said simply. "And we take care of our own."

While vastly unspecific, it was an answer. Before I could press the point, a shuffle and scrape from the hallway seemed to echo in the silence. We both stilled, but Maddox went from looming over the bed to next to the door in the blink of an eye.

That shit was unnerving.

If he could move that fast, how had I outrun him?

Oh. I nailed him in the balls.

Right.

Even supergrunt there needed time to catch his breath.

Good to know.

"We'll get you out of here, Kitten," he continued when I said nothing. "You may trust that if you trust nothing else."

I trusted very little, but sure, why not? Shrugging, I moved back to the bed and took a seat. Crossing my legs, I leaned back against the wall and let my eyes drop half-closed. I was far more tired than I wanted to tell him. The lost blood volume wasn't a problem. Maybe if I hadn't fed so well before, but I was still weary.

Even though I wasn't looking at him, the weight of his stare settled on me like a tangible presence. Finally, he moved to the sink, and from beneath my lashes, I caught the flash of golden skin as he shed his shirt and then washed his face and chest.

The ripple of muscle didn't surprise me. Having been gripped to that steely body, I wouldn't expect anything else. When he finished, he ducked his head under the water, and slicked back his sandy brown hair away from his face. It just gave him a more angular look, not that it was a bad look.

When he turned to use the toilet, I closed my eyes and let him have his privacy.

See, I had manners, unlike some people.

The image of my house flickered to life, and I began to do some rearranging in the room I'd make my bedroom. I wanted it to be as spacious as possible, no walls to hem me in. Having floor to ceiling windows all along one side would help.

Unless the sun turns you into a pile of ashes, then you better invest in a good vacuum for the next residents.

Shoving that wordy bitch out of my head, I debated the color scheme. I wanted blues in the bathroom. The sea and the seashore were good themes. But the bedroom? Soft creams, maybe, nothing too bold. I wanted it to be restful.

Heat settled next to me, and an arm slid around me. I didn't fight the tug as he settled me right against him. I'd actually gotten chilled after the cold wash and the fact that my hair was still wet.

"What are you thinking about so hard you have a tiny frown right here?" He traced a finger between my eyebrows, and I flicked my eyes open to find him studying me intensely. His shirt was back in place, and his damp hair had already begun to dry. Guess all that heat he put off took care of that quick.

The words 'none of your business' lingered on my tongue. Not that what I was doing was really a state secret. "I'm building a house."

Surprise reflected in his narrowed eyes. "A house?"

I nodded. "A retreat. Some place just for me. I'm building it from the ground up, so it's exactly what I want and where I want it."

Closing my eyes, I went back to my room and studied it from floors to ceiling. Carpets, definitely. I might do wood floors or tile in the main body of the house, but I wanted the good carpet in here. Did I want a fireplace?

Yes. Images of a stone fireplace flickered to life, then river rock, I kept shifting the construction.

"Can you show me?"

The voice intruded, and I slid him a look. "What?"

"Show me your house."

"No. I'm not done with it yet."

Despite his seeming repose, nothing about Maddox was relaxed. Likely, he tracked any sound in the hall, though there had been none since the earlier shuffle step. In theory, no one was supposed to be in this cell. We could languish here without detection unless they happened to open it up for a new occupant.

Well, then we were fucked.

"Tell me about it then." The soft invitation in his voice came at a direct contrast to his aggravating and entitled tone of the day before.

"No."

"Well that's rude," he chided me. "We're alone. We have time. You could get to know me."

"Or you could shut up and let me build my house. I've been working on it for weeks. By the time I get out of here, I'll be ready to build it."

To my absolute surprise, he went quiet. I half-waited for him to interrupt again. My focus divided between the half-formed nebulous bedroom and the very much present male currently binding me to his side. When his silence continued, I settled into the work of carpet selection, fireplace construction, and where the bed would go. The room would be open, not cluttered. There would clothing storage in the enormous walk-in. Plenty of space for my clothes and shoes without taking up the bedroom. I wanted nothing to obstruct the walls.

Maybe one of them could be painted with a scene. A mountain glen came to mind—trees, grass, and a crystal lake. It was absolutely stunning and pristine in how untouched it was. I could escape all of humanity there. The peace twisted into my veins, and the lust for it flooded me.

The water was cool, even on the warmest days of summer. The woods and the surrounding mountains boasted plenty of game. The location, tucked away so high, wasn't near any crossroads or passes. To ascend to it would require master climbers and a sure knowledge of the way.

It was the perfect escape from everything and everyone. The longer I stood there, the more I realized it was a very real place. This was no simple painting. I drew back from it until I stood only in my room again, and the wall stretched before me beckoned like a gateway.

Almost as if it were saying, *You know you want to come through. Come, play with me.*

Snapping my eyes open, I glared at Maddox. He was absolutely still next to me, his eyes closed and his breathing deep and regular.

He wasn't asleep though.

"Afraid, Kitten?"

"How are you doing that?"

"He's not," Fin announced in a cheerful voice. "That would be me."

Of course it was.

"Fin," Maddox growled. "Have they reduced their security?"

"Nope," Fin stated. Even in the torchlight, I couldn't quite make him out. The blurring seemed to take him just out of focus. Understanding that he wasn't truly present helped, but it was equal parts irritating to focus on him and intriguing to discover how he pulled it off. "They've increased it."

Maddox let out a growl.

"What was that? 'Oh, thank you, Fin. You're right, Rogue was the perfect one to summon for this situation,'" he mimed the answer to himself, pitching his voice almost perfectly into Maddox's deep rumble. "No problem, Mad. You know, I've only got our best interests at heart." He waved off the make believe gratitude with the air of a cocky grin. "'You're too humble, Fin, it doesn't suit you. You were right, and I was, and yes, I know you don't hear this often, but you should. I was wrong.' Hey, it takes a big man to admit something like that, my friend. Have no worries, I won't lord it over you, much."

A snicker escaped as Maddox snorted. "Keep patting yourself on the back."

"Someone has to," Fin said easily, and I could have sworn he winked at me. "Hang on a little bit longer for us, beautiful Fiona. Rogue will be here at nightfall, then you two move and I'll meet you. Between us, we'll get you out."

"You sound very confident," I told him.

"That would be because Rogue knows what they're hiding here, he won't let them say no. While he's making a lot noise, we'll slip out unnoticed. It's a whole thing. Just trust me."

"She doesn't trust easily," Maddox warned, not that I needed him to answer for me.

"But we've already got a connection, Fi and me," Fin argued. "You just sit over there and be all grumpy in your grumpiness, and let me handle this."

Granted, he was kind of cute and amusing, but Maddox wasn't so bad when he wasn't talking. He definitely made the air warmer.

See, I was using my positive people skills. They did actually exist.

A yawn split my jaw before I could say anything though, and both went a little quiet.

"You feeling okay, Kitten?" Maddox pressed his nose to my hair and took a deep breath.

"She looks a little pale, course, you both do. Firelight's not exactly ideal lighting for determining coloring…" Fin drifted closer. I hadn't really paid attention to his movement the night before. Course, it had also been dark. He didn't quite touch the floor as he moved.

How much effort did it take to do that? Not to mention, what was he that he could do it at all? Astral projection was a rare talent, and most who possessed it didn't advertise it. They made the best spies and, under certain circumstances, excellent assassins.

"She lost a lot of blood yesterday." He motioned to the dark stain on the stone. Yeah, I wasn't going to comment on the fact the stone had all but absorbed all that blood. The dark brownish stain was all that remained of my pooled blood.

"Then feed her, asshole," Fin said abruptly, all trace of playfulness gone from his tone. "You can certainly spare a pint."

"I'm not hungry," I said before Maddox could snarl. The fact that the arm he had around me tensed and the rest of him seemed to vibrate suggested his rather vehement response to the accusation.

Fin jerked his gaze to me.

"And I don't heal that way anyway."

Head tilted, he stared at me. "You do realize you're part vampire, right?"

"You do realize that's an oxymoron, right?" What was it with people telling me what I was? "There's no such thing as a part-vampire." Hybrids didn't exist. Do join the party line. Why else was I in this prison? Oh yeah, because I'd broken some covenant by existing.

Right.

"Agitation. Pallor. Exhaustion. Dissociation, bloodlust, and madness follow. Baby vamps have to eat." He ticked each item off like I was five.

Yeah, my estimation of Fin began to drop by several points. "I'm a succubus," I reminded him. "That's not how I heal." Or feed.

"Well, I'm pretty sure Maddox still remembers how that works, just let him…"

"Fin," Maddox snapped. "She already told you she wasn't hungry. Leave her alone."

Oh ho, he was defending me now? The flip-flop was enough to make anyone a little dizzy.

"Yeah, but she's going to need her strength, and if she's waning after only a day in your company, what's she going to be like tonight?" He folded his arms, and I swore I could almost hear the tapping of his foot, even if it wasn't audible.

"We'll be fine," Maddox stated smoothly. "Speaking of conserving energy, you should."

"Says the one who gets to spend time with her while I lay here under the stone floor with a mouse for company," Fin grumbled.

"Stop bitching and go away," Maddox said in an aggrieved tone. "We'll head up when the torches go out."

"Fine. But she sleeps with me tomorrow." He blew me a kiss before focusing on Maddox again. "You got two days. Fair is fair." Then he was gone before my companion could respond.

"Still like him better, Kitten?"

"Not so much."

He chuckled, then slid his hand up to massage my nape. "He's not wrong. You do need some fresh blood. Feeding your dual nature needs to be something you get used to."

"If that's your polite way of saying 'bite me,' no thank you." I really didn't want blood. The image of Dorran cutting himself so the blood trickled out flashed through my mind, accompanying the hot flavor of it on my tongue.

I shuddered and curled my toes as I closed my eyes. I did not want to want it. I wasn't a vampire.

"The hardest part of the transition is accepting your needs have also transitioned," Maddox said, drawing circles against my shoulder with his thumb. "You have to feed both."

"Or what?" I asked, in spite of my intentions of focusing on my house.

"Or bloodlust will set in. The need to sate yourself on whatever you can get your hands on, and you won't mind killing to get what you need."

I didn't mind killing so much now.

"And you won't be able to tell friend from foe."

That part bugged me a little.

"For those who truly deny themselves, they may lose the thread of who they are entirely. Minds have broken in transition before, it is why those who are turned are carefully curated." He was almost likeable as he handled this conversationally, without his domineering and orders.

"Too bad I missed that memo," I told him, though maybe that was another reason Dorran had taken such an interest in me, particularly when I wouldn't feed. It could also be he just wanted to have a good time. Though it was something to consider on both fronts.

"I'll give you some latitude, Kitten, if I hadn't put the shackles on you—you wouldn't be half-starved now." Before I could deny it, he gave my shoulder a squeeze. "Deny you're hungry all you want, but your body betrays you. You can't stay warm, can you? It's why you're letting me hold you."

I would have wrenched away, but he had an iron grip on me. I debated and discarded a half-dozen responses, then settled for just ignoring him.

"Fine, don't answer. But I know the truth, and deep down, so do you. I will not force you, but if it comes down to a choice between risking your sanity or your fury...well, I'll take your rage, and you will feed. Fin was right, I can more than spare the blood, and it's old enough that it will sate you."

"Confident, aren't you?"

He chuckled. "Very."

"Hmm. Are you done?"

"For the moment."

Nodding, I closed my eyes and returned to my house building. I must have drifted off again because he woke me with a gentle shake, and I snapped my eyes open to find myself not just leaning against him, but curled up in his lap like a slutty cat absorbing all that heat.

Okay, I never said I wasn't a slutty cat.

"Is it time?" I asked, and my voice came out a croak. The torches were out, but as with the night before, his eyes glowed.

"Nearly. Fin said five minutes and we move."

Extracting myself from his lap, I nodded. He set me on my feet, bracing me as my head swam. Yeah. That wasn't a good sign. Fuck, I did not want to drink his blood. Once I was out of here, I'd ditch them and go find some cheerful fucker and seduce him. Then I'd find that asshole vampire and rip his spleen out.

Maybe the so-called prince, too.

I was an equal opportunity bitch slapper.

Maddox said nothing as I made my way over to the sink. I splashed a little water on my face to chase away the sleep. I'd slept a good portion of the day. Then I drank down a couple of palmfuls to wet my throat.

"When we get out there," Maddox said. "You'll stick close to me."

Ah, there he was, the autocratic jerk who issued orders. I'd started to worry he'd been replaced by a kinder, gentler Maddox. No one would want that.

"You will do it," he continued. "Don't make me have to drag you out of here kicking and screaming."

I chuckled. "I already kicked, and you have to be really good to make me scream."

The abrupt silence made me smile wider. Never play the game with me. Turning from the sink, I stared across the void toward the glowing eyes regarding me from their narrow slits.

"Kitten, are you going to cooperate?"

That question was pregnant with all kinds of possibilities.

Then again, so was my answer.

"What's in it for me?"

"Your ticket out of here," he promised. "And a long conversation, a real one, with communication on both sides. After that, you're free to go wherever you like."

Sounded too good to be true.

Probably was just a lure to get me to agree. Once we were out, he could focus on containing me. He also had allies waiting for him, the irascible Fin and the mysterious Rogue.

Not that I couldn't handle multiple men, the more the merrier actually. Still…

"Neutral location for the conversation," I said. "No secret fortress with security in place for my 'protection.'"

"Done."

"And if I say no," I continued crossing toward him slowly. "I'll mean 'no.'"

"Understood. But you'll listen to all of it," he countered. "Not just the opening lines before you cut me off to go build your house."

I could live with that.

"Then you have a deal." I held out my hand. One conversation, and I was free? Yeah, I'd take that deal.

His rough palm glided against mine as he closed his fingers over mine. "Stay with me." With a gentle tug, he pulled me to him then set my hand to his belt. "Grip back here, stay there. No matter what happens, do not get in front of me."

"Even if someone is going to try and skewer you from behind?" I mean really, if he wanted to set explicit terms. "Because if they have to stab me to get to you, I'm probably going to move."

Silence. "Fine. You may take out anyone who comes at us from behind."

"Lover here, RDF, not fighter."

"Now that," he said slowly, his face suddenly close to mine. "Is the first true lie you've told me. I have faith in those claws, Kitten."

A beat.

"It's time. Save all debates, discussions, and arguments for once we're out. Just remember, we have a deal."

"Sir," I purred. "Yes, sir."

He shuddered, and I smiled. When everything has been taken from you and all you have left was revenge, there wasn't much you wouldn't do.

Even take jabs at the so-called rescuer who inserted himself into your problems.

The door clanged open, and we were moving. The hall had more light, which helped.

It also had a very large, very angry looking corpsesnare, who whirled at our presence and stared right at *me*, salivating.

"Maddox?" I said lightly when he stared the other way.

"Just stay with me."

"Yes, well, I just wanted to point out that we might have a problem."

Turning his head, he paused.

The corpsesnare's jaw was open, showing his row of shiny teeth and letting bits of saliva fall to the stone below.

"Hi, Puppy," I greeted him. "Who's a good dog?"

It snarled.

"Kitten?"

"Hmm?"

"What are you doing?"

"Saying hi to the puppy."

"*That* is not a puppy."

Yeah well, I wasn't a kitten either. But we did what we did with what we had. The corpsesnare began to approach, a low growl rumbling from him like an avalanche of rocks tumbling down the mountainside.

I could seduce a lot of things, but I'd never tried it against something so…impressively oversized and radiating barely suppressed rage.

Maddox turned abruptly. "Stay behind me."

No problem. If it ate him, I'd use that as a distraction. Maddox gave me heartburn, and I hadn't even had a bite.

Bracing himself, Maddox seemed to flicker as the corpsesnare continued to approach, his pace deliberate and measured, hackles up and a constant growl rising in volume.

When he was nearly in snapping range, he roared.

Ugh.

Someone needed to give him a breath mint.

CHAPTER 6

"It simply isn't an adventure worth telling if there aren't dragons."
- J.R.R. Tolkien

The corpsesnare's roar redoubled along the hallway and set most of the hair on my body standing on end, including the wild tangle of curls falling from my head. While I would have loved a blow dryer earlier, this was not what I had in mind. Not even close.

For his part, Maddox hadn't moved, not so much as rocked in the face of fetid breath, razor sharp teeth, and a salivating tongue. Even with my hand on his belt, Maddox didn't seem solid, and yet, his presence swelled. The corpsesnare roared again, but he didn't charge.

That was good.

The only lust he displayed at the moment was bloodlust, and it rolled off of him in stomach-curdling waves along with his rotten breath. All at once, Maddox shifted and the air grew hotter, heavier, and…holy shit.

Yeah, I blew that hold onto his belt promise, dropping it like a hot potato as I backed off from the dragon pushing at the walls around us. The stone began to shred as his wings extended. His size was massive, however, far more than the corpsesnare.

Puppy went for another growl, then retreated a step. He didn't give up much ground, snarling and snapping with each motion of withdrawal he took.

Me? I didn't hesitate, I was almost to the stairwell when the corpsesnare lunged and fire flooded the hallway.

I winced at the yelping shriek from the oversized beast. Hands pressed firmly over my ears, I dropped when fire flared down the hallway, and the smell of singed hair burned my nostrils. Oh. That was nasty.

The roar vibrating me to my bones wasn't coming from the corpsesnare. I almost felt sorry for the oversized beasty, particularly when he yelped and pounded away in the opposite direction. All he'd wanted to do was chow down on some prisoner escapees, not his fault one of them turned out to be a damn dragon.

Seriously? Maddox's arrival had turned my day upside down, too. So I got it.

The dragon in the hallway—yes, that sentence actually passed through my head—twisted around, eyes glaring to find me.

Amidst the smoke and haze of debris, I really didn't have time to consider the color of his scales. But those slitted eyes glowing me? I'd know them anywhere. He opened his mouth, displaying an impressive array of teeth. Here was hoping we weren't going to test his morning breath, because how about no?

Still twisting, he knocked more bricks loose, and a metal door screamed as his tail lashed against it, knocking it open.

The explosion of magic lit the hallway up like a Fourth of July bonfire gone wrong.

I had to be honest here, something ran out of that cell he'd just carelessly torn open with his *tail* as it lashed about. His maneuvering that bulk through a hallway nowhere near big enough for him to spread out, not to mention his wings, kicked up more debris. But that thing or person or whatever that ran out of that room?

It made it three steps in my direction when hot stuff there gave me an up-close look at hungry, hungry dragon. The chomp followed by the crunch of bones was both awesome in its display of power and utterly disgusting.

No sooner had he done it and *swallowed* did he look at me. Lowering my hands, I met that stare. "One, if you belch right now, you will find a dick shaped hole where your cock used to be. You might be big and scaley at the moment, but you gotta play shrinky dinky sooner or later." Head cocked, the dragon stared at me, his inner eyelids blinked once. "Second, you better gargle with like industrial strength bleach before you try to bring your mouth anywhere near me."

Just. Saying.

Ugh.

I had never been so utterly turned on and repulsed by the same action.

What? I was complicated. Suck it.

For the most part, Mad-Dragon—that name was totally sticking—huffed a sound that might have been laughter, even as a hint of fire burst from his nose. Was that the dragon equivalent of a giggle-snort? He continued toward me, showering more debris down from above, and his eyes shifted imperceptibly. The air around him shimmered like a desert mirage.

The temperature in the hallway left me sweating, but I could live with it. Deodorant would have been nice. But who was going to complain? Right, Mad-Dragon of flaming breath and questionable eating habits—I wasn't going to worry about that. He began to draw back to his original size. The flicker of surprise on his face had me twisting and whirling just as a boot scraped the stone not far from me.

Guard uniforms.

I didn't wait for whoever this was to identify themselves, I struck. Fortunately for me—yes, I said I was weird—they were also mid-strike as they swung the equivalent of a glowing billy club in my direction.

Catching his wrist as he was mid-downswing, I twisted and lunged forward, slamming the heel of my hand right at his crotch. Armor or not, the impact sent a jolt up my arm, but he still hissed, and his grip on the billy club of doom faltered. I didn't wait for it to fall as I slid right into him. The lust wafting from him was also tinged with fear. He didn't want me so much as he wanted desperately to contain me.

Too.

Fucking.

Bad.

As the billy club hit the floor, I clasped his face and yanked it down for a kiss. Shock turned him rigid as I soaked in even his watered down lust. It wasn't much, more like the soggy French fry at the bottom of the bag. It filled the hole, but lacked any kind of satisfaction. The guy sagged, and no sooner had I begun to feed, then he was yanked away. I hissed, but Maddox glared at me as he snapped the guy's neck. The man dropped without another word.

"You want to feed, you feed on me. Until then, we're moving."

Well. Fuck you, too.

"Jealousy doesn't look good on you, Dragon Boy M," I told him, but when he snagged me close to him, two things hit me in the same breath.

If I'd thought he was warm in the cell, he was a thousand times hotter in the hall. His skin should be steaming, he was so hot. The second thing? He was naked. Absolutely, gloriously, one hundred percent naked. He was definitely sexy with a capital damn.

The weight of his cock poked at the too thin fabric of my so-called uniform, and I had to tilt my head to meet his gaze. Yeah, there might have been the vaguest amount of drool involved.

Vaguest.

Possibly.

A few drops.

Fuck. Me.

Why did he have to do this now when we were leaving the enforced isolation with the very tiny bed?

As if reading my mind—or maybe my body, 'cause it got there several seconds before my brain did—Maddox dipped his head. Laser focused on that sensuous mouth, it took me a whole extra-half a heartbeat to put my hand over it before he got too close.

He just ate someone or something.

Right.

Big crunch.

Gross. Hot.

"Gargle. With. Bleach." At the reminder, his eyes crinkled and his smirk pressed against my palm. Catching my hand, he bit down on my palm. Not enough to break skin, but enough that the pressure of his teeth sent an answering pulse straight to my pussy.

Really not the time.

Course, now I was hungry, and he'd killed off my limp noodle of a snack. Maybe I'd make him make it up to me later.

No limp noodle here.

No sirree.

After he released my hand, he retrieved a bag I hadn't even noticed him carrying. He had to bend for it, and let me just add, the view going was almost as good as the view of him returning.

Almost.

He dragged a dark shirt on and then pulled on some pants.

Pity.

His boots were gone, as was his belt. Didn't do a damn thing to turn me off, though. Honestly. He looked even better all disheveled, hair askew and shirt hanging open. He slung the bag over his shoulder, and it lay crosswise over his torso.

Yeah, how had I not noticed that?

"Coming?" He gave me an expectant look, and it was my turn to smirk.

"Until I was so rudely blocked?" I let that suggestion hang out there for a minute before I slapped his chest on my way past. "Not even."

His rough chuckle chased after me as we moved in tandem toward the door. "Grip the strap," he ordered before pushing the metal door outward. It gave him some minor resistance, but the door buckled under the force he exerted.

Yep, that just set all kinds of things fluttering. Though brute strength wasn't a turn on by itself. Fuck, I was hungry.

Once in the hall though, all thoughts of eating took a sharp right turn. A dozen guards swarmed toward us.

"Stay with me," Maddox snarled as he waded in.

Yeah. Sure. No problem.

He moved hella fast, and the first jerk forward nearly pulled my arm out of the socket. Yeah, that wasn't working for me. The first guard who tried to drag me away, however, ate my elbow in his teeth. They were mostly shifters. Not that it slowed Maddox down. I was pretty sure these were wolves. They had that eau de wet dog going on for them.

It was all fun and games until one of the bastards bit me. To be honest, when asked about it later, I had no idea what I did so much as I whirled. Letting go of Maddox, I landed on the bastard, all teeth and claws. The first drag of hot blood on my tongue, and I latched. I consumed every drop, the lust for blood he'd been simmering in along with the blood in his veins.

When this prey was ripped away from me, I whirled, intent on clawing out eyes, only to come face to face with a pair of nearly pitch-black eyes with the barest ring of gray around them, dark hair, and a face like an angel.

"Bad for the digestion, Beautiful."

Oh, I knew that voice.

"That's it. Focus on me."

I was focused on him.

"You about done there, Maddox? This is a lot of fighting for the sweet baby."

Then Maddox was there, he had a hold of my arm and turned me slightly. "Fucker tore right through her shoulder."

Oh. Yeah. Someone bit me. I turned to go after said fucker, when Fin caught my free arm.

"Nope, he's very dead, Beautiful. I promise. Time to go though." Everything but the two of them seemed to be coming from a great distance.

"You're overdoing it," Maddox snarled.

"I can't help it if she's more naturally drawn to me," Fin said smoothly, giving me a charming smile. My heart gave a distinct double-thump. He really was gorgeous, and his voice was buttery soft. I gave into the impulse to lean toward him, but Maddox's grip on my arm kept me from going too far.

Pain lit up along my shoulder and raced across my skin.

"None of that," Fin murmured, pressing a kiss to my wrist. "Nothing hurts. We're going to get out of here, okay?"

I exhaled a long breath. "Okay." That really did sound like a great idea.

"Let's go, straight up," Fin ordered. "Ten levels." He swept me up into his arms, and it made Maddox release me. The poor Mad-Dragon let out a very disgruntled sound. "You first, we need to move fast. I doubt she can keep up with either of us, so let's go."

The world blurred past. The throb in my shoulder returned, and bit-by-bit, the foggy cloud muffling the sounds of combat around me faded. The sheer volume of bodies lying around us should have made my gorge rise, but as it was, I could barely muster the interest.

When had we gotten up here?

I vaguely remembered getting to the stairwell and the fight there. The man holding me, swung around and stared. That was it—just *stared* at the guy rushing us. The guard switched directions abruptly and ran into a wall.

Not kidding. Slammed himself bodily into a wall, and the crunch of breaking bone hearkened back to Mad-Dragon's hallway snack.

Okay, that turned my stomach a little and had my pussy clenching.

Seriously, don't look at me like that. I said I was complicated.

"Like that, did you?" Fin asked, his lips against my ear. A delicious shiver worked its way down my spine. The guy looked like an angel and smelled like one. We might be surrounded by blood and gore, but pressed up to him, all I could scent was this deep, masculine flavor and something that reminded me of fresh brewed coffee. The perfect scent to start the day.

Fuck, I hadn't had coffee in weeks.

My hunger redoubled, and I nuzzled at his throat.

"Oh, so tempting, Beautiful," Fin chided with the faintest of groans. "But a little busy at the moment. Just hold that thought."

A familiar growl echoed behind me. "Don't you dare."

"Temper, temper. I told you she liked me best."

A dull roar echoed through the great stone chamber we were in. And really, it was huge. The ceiling stretched up at least three or four stories. Mad-Dragon could really stretch out in here.

"Trolls," Fin said abruptly, and Maddox swore. "A lot of trolls."

"What is it with you and trolls?"

"My sparkling personality?" Fin quipped. A giggle escaped, he was so blasé about it. Not all doom, gloom, and scowls like Maddox. Though to be perfectly fair, Maddox was hot.

Fin adjusted his stance, and I started to wiggle to have him put me down, but he gave my hip a squeeze.

"Stay put, Beautiful. We're going to get an opening any minute, and you're safer right where you are."

A pull, dark, luscious, and full of familiar lust tugged at me, and I snapped my head to the side.

Dorran.

The shadows around him thickened, and despite the herd of trolls storming toward us, it was Dorran who held all my focus. Hunger cramped my side, and I strained to pull away from Fin. The languidness weighing down my limbs evaporated. As much as the warden irked me, he could slake my thirst and quench my hunger.

"Fuck," Fin snapped. "Maddox get over here."

A growl reverberated as Maddox stepped into my line of sight, blocking Dorran. No, this wasn't right. I needed him. I didn't know this insane pair, and as charming as they might be—better the devil I knew.

The air around us darkened, even as Fin's grip on me turned to stone. He had my arms locked down, and the grip around my legs didn't let me do more than wiggle my feet. Not even the sweet attraction of his scent could dissuade me. A clash of bodies exploded in front of us as Maddox let loose with another roar.

Even though the twisting was in vain, I glared at Fin. Unfortunately, he ignored me in favor of narrowing his eyes at the troll looming over us. Maddox had vanished into the darkness, though the sounds of his battle roars and the collision of fleshy impacts added to the cacophony of battle. The troll bellowed with all of his stinky might, and the distraction loosened Fin's grip on me just enough to slip free.

He swore and then barely got his hands up in time to block the troll's huge and heavy fist. To my surprise, though really why *anything* surprised me at this point I couldn't say, Fin not only caught the monstrous arm that was easily thicker than his whole body, but he stopped it. Then struck with his own fist, sending the troll sliding backward.

Okay.

That was hot.

Astral-Boy had skills.

Fiona...

The whisper of Dorran's voice curved around me, and Fin's lovely face vanished as the shadows closed around me. Edging right up against pain and frustration, I turned into the darkness. It had never held any fear for me. My fingers had just brushed the warden's, when the darkness recoiled and a hard body slammed into me.

Bright light pierced the shadows, and my eyes watered at the burn. I hit the hard stone floor as the shadows whipped backwards, the tangle of them leaving me, and suddenly, all the throb of my shoulder head butted against the hunger pangs wrenching my sides, and I fucking hurt.

Seriously fucking hurt.

Legs obscured my view, and I canted my head back to find a Viking like figure standing over me. With hands that looked like they'd been dipped in blood and an expression so full of vicious wrath, he was a nightmare incarnate. Still, the warden retreated, even as tendrils of his darkness lashed out and slapped against the light, only to sizzle, pop, and burn.

I couldn't look away. It was kind of like staring into the sun during an eclipse. I was probably frying my retinas, but what was one more agony atop all the rest? A troll shrieked at the newcomer, and Viking-guy literally tore the guy in half and then ripped off one of his arms to beat another one.

"Well, better late than never," Fin said cheerfully as he hooked his hands under my armpits and dragged me upward. With my back against his chest, he bound me with his arms around me, even as…

"That's Rogue." The two disparate pieces of information snapped together like a puzzle slotting into place.

"Yup," Fin said, then nipped my ear. "We'll discuss you being shadow-addicted later, it's time to go."

The sting of his teeth scraping my earlobe sent an answering wave to all my other hurts. Somewhere along the way, I'd torn up my palms. There were gouges in my side that oozed blood, and I was pretty sure I'd bitten the inside of my lip. The blood welling up just added to my starvation.

Maddox emerged from the dust clouds and darkness, coated in gray ash with blood running in rivulets through it. Filthy, but alive.

It was a good look. Somewhere, he'd lost his shirt, but his pants held up despite being utterly shredded from one thigh down.

This was a man who could easily walk around in a loincloth and totally get away with it. To be honest, he should absolutely be encouraged.

Then the noise just kind of faded. Maddox stared at me, chest heaving and eyes furious. What the fuck did he have to be so pissed about? I wasn't the one who started all of this. If anything, I'd gotten dragged up those stairs.

Oh. Rescue effort.

Right.

I shook my head a little to try and clear more of the fog. Why it was so hard to focus all of a sudden, I didn't know. To be honest, it was like being drunk and fighting a hangover in the same breath, without any of the fun stuff—you know, like alcohol.

Our latest arrival spun, and if he wasn't a gruesome sight, I didn't know what was. The light around him had at least dimmed to not eye-popping bright anymore. But what held my attention now wasn't the gore on him or the light he'd extinguished, but the ferocity in those too blue eyes. They pinned me in place like an insect on a pegboard.

"He's been feeding on her," he said in a voice so rusty with disuse, it came out even deeper than Maddox's. "She won't leave willingly."

"We noticed," Fin stated almost idly. "Why do you think we've been trying to hang onto her?"

"Give her to me," Rogue ordered, but rather than release me, Fin actually backed up a step dragging me with him.

"Fight over her later," Maddox ordered. "We need to go now. The path is clear, but he'll bring back reinforcements."

"Let him," Rogue said with so much arrogance, I believed he would relish the opportunity. "Killing him would be one way to free her."

"While I don't mind the fight, I'd rather get Kitten to somewhere secure and let her feed. She's hungry."

Thank you.

I almost said it aloud, but then thought better of it when Rogue seemed intent on boring his way into my soul, and the longer he stared, the more uneasy I became.

Mad-Dragon I got.

Astral-Boy? Him, too. Mostly.

Even Dorran—longing punched through me. I'd been so close to feeding, and now he was absent. If I followed through with their insane plan, I'd be out of his reach.

That was what I wanted, right?

I wanted out of that cell.

Out of this prison.

I wanted what remnants of my life were left to me.

All of those things were true. But so was the sudden anxiety swarming me. If we left, I'd never see Dorran again. I might…

What, Fi? What might I do? Die?

The thought was so patently ridiculous, I snorted, and yet the ever tautening ball of anxiety in my chest began to compress my lungs.

"Give her to me," Rogue said taking a step toward us.

"No," Fin began, but whatever else he might have said was lost in a whoosh of motion as Rogue suddenly wrenched Fin's arms away from me and slid one of his gross, bloody hands to my waist. I slammed against him, and if Fin and Maddox were steely, Rogue was damn near diamond in his surface tension. No give. At all.

It was like being stabbed and cradled in equal measure.

Pleasure and pain.

His hunger?

It was absent.

Except…

The lust unfurled like a slow moving avalanche that gained force and speed as it rolled downward to me.

"I wasn't asking," Rogue finished his sentence, and then

the air whistled past us. I had to hold on for dear life and even managed to get my legs around his hips. He never so much as let me slip, but the wind hitting my back cut at me.

It must have sliced my shirt half to ribbons, or maybe that was my flesh. I barely had time to process Maddox's furious expression or Fin's shocked one before they were gone.

The race through the night seemed to stretch into infinity. Time ceased to have real meaning, and if not for the definitive squeeze of Rogue's hand to my ass, I might have written this off as a bad dream.

Nightmares. I had been known to have them.

I'd been stuck in one for weeks now. They even called it Nightmare Penitentiary.

The sudden stop would have cracked my neck, but Rogue had a hand against my hair. My gratitude for the thoughtfulness died a swift death when he pulled the hand away and my hair clung to the bloody debris decorating his fingers.

Yeah.

Gross.

Stomach lurching, I swallowed back the bile as the raw coppery scents from too many different bodies hit me at once. Troll. Shifter. Pretty sure a couple were vampires, too. And at least four or five others that I didn't know and really didn't want to know.

Instead of putting me down, Rogue pinned me to a wall and leaned his hips into mine. There was no heavy cock shoving its way at me, so that wasn't what he wanted.

Good—

The thought stuttered as he sliced at his throat just above where his neck joined his shoulder. Ancient blood slid out of the wound, fresh, hot, and so pungently sweet and savory, my mouth watered.

"Feed, little *svàss*." The order settled into my bones, and unlike Maddox or Fin, I wanted to obey this one even if a small part of me continued to rebel. I didn't even know this guy.

"I'm not a vampire," I argued.

"I don't care," he retaliated, and then cupped my head and pulled my mouth to the injury.

Yeah, that argument wasn't really working for me either.

The first brush of his blood to my lips, and I latched on without a second thought. Decadence exploded across my tongue, and I closed my eyes as a throaty moan vibrated in my throat.

Sinking my teeth into the wound, I worked it wider, and then it took active sucking to pull more blood from him. I applied myself, because I wanted more. Tightening my thighs against his hips, he rewarded every pull with a grind against me, and where he'd been lacking an erection before, one nudged at me now.

More, the crater of lust simmering beneath the surface cracked wide open, and then it swallowed me hole.

Fuck.

Me.

Maybe there was something to this vampire schtick.

"'I don't believe in magic,' the young boy said. The old man smiled. 'You will when you see her.'" - Atticus

Fin

"*D*roch chrích ort." Fin glared at the gaping hole in the wall through which Rogue vanished with their prize.

Maddox kicked a body away from him as he followed Fin's stare, then scowled at Fin.

"It's not my fault," Fin argued.

"No?" Maddox half-growled, half-rumbled. "Whose idea was it to bring him into the middle of this?"

"I stand by that idea." With a wave of his hand to the stacks of bodies around him, Fin paused, then pulled a handkerchief out of his inner pocket and began to clean the blood from his fingers as they made their way out. "It worked, didn't it?"

For his part, the surly dragon just grunted. "Where did he take her?"

Concentrating, Fin focused on the feel of his brother and where he might have gone. At the moment, there was a blankness to his presence. Out there, but just beyond perception. Rogue didn't want to be found immediately.

Probably protecting their prize. They'd only waited a few hundred years for her to be found, and the first word they get of her, she's trapped in a prison with a shadow demon feeding on her.

Not ideal.

Still…

The white square turned crimson as he continued cleaning his hands. They met no resistance as they made their way down the mountain. Finding vulnerable access points to the prison warded by magic and layered with the power of far too many dimensions to sit in just one had required all of Maddox's skills. Dragons kept their hoards in similar pockets, so he'd at least had a starting point.

Fin had been the one to confirm the vulnerability after Maddox located it. Maddox wasn't in a rush, if Fin didn't know better, he would suspect him of wanting the warden and his guards to pursue them here.

The prison might very well restore some of them. If they decided to follow, they wouldn't recover so easily if at all.

"Well?" Maddox demanded.

"He's blocking me at the moment." As much as he didn't want to admit it.

"Of course, he is. I made that woman a promise." The last came out through gritted teeth.

"How do you think I feel?" Fin turned it back on him. "She was supposed to sleep with me tonight." That, and she was hurting from lack of sustenance. The shadow addiction needed to be dealt with as well. Though Fin didn't doubt for an instant that Rogue couldn't handle her need to feed.

Conversation, on the other hand? Yeah, he wouldn't place any bets on that.

"He'd take her to the keep."

"No one goes to the keep anymore," Maddox argued. "We abandoned it fifty years after I turned."

"Which is why he would take her there."

Maddox understood hunting others, but he'd never had to hunt the rest of them. Why would he? They'd been friends, allies, and occasionally competitors for centuries. Time wore away the harsher edge of their disagreements, and they learned to seek each other out when they wanted the company and to ignore each other when they didn't. "Rogue always liked the keep. It's defensible. High in the mountains. We still own all of the land and the territory. It's never been developed. Urban expansionism won't reach there. The villages on the other side of the mountain are well tended and looked after. They have no reason to come looking for us."

There was another reason Rogue would have taken her there. If Maddox put away his rage for a few minutes, that would hit him, too.

"That's halfway around the world," he argued. "She was already weak."

"And craving," Fin confirmed. They were nearly a mile down the mountainside, and there was no sign of pursuit. A fact Maddox had obviously noticed as his agitation increased. "Rogue can feed her, *dearthair*. Even he understands how important it would be for a baby vamp to eat. His blood is older than ours."

"Not by much," Maddox snarled, but some of the heat drained from his tone, and the scorching air around them cooled. "*If* he took her there..."

"He did." Of that much, Fin was certain.

"You think he's going to try and wake Alfred."

"I would," Fin admitted, and Maddox glared at him. "Look, Alfred went to sleep because the world had worn him out. He'd tired of waiting. We were as safe as we could be, and we didn't need him to look after us. But when he went to ground, Rogue..." Rogue turned away from them.

Even when Fin would try to lure him out, Rogue never stayed. He always came. He'd never let them down, not once. But when he finished his task, he vanished again. Try as he might, Fin hadn't been able to keep him with them. Maddox no longer bothered and acted like it was a crime to even try and lure Rogue out of his self-imposed exile.

"She isn't ready for Alfred."

"I doubt she's ready for any of us," Fin said with a shrug. "It's our job to protect her and make her ready. Besides, she's got spunk. You're already a little crazy about her, aren't you?"

Never had he been so jealous of and thrilled for the dragon in equal measure. Fiona MacRieve was the answer to so much. All they had to do was save her from the insanity of vampire politics, keep the shadow demon away, and show her that being a hybrid was destiny.

"She's a stubborn wench," Maddox grunted. "Fierce, too. I could live without her need to fuck the stupid out of people."

Eyebrows raised, Fin eyed him. "She needed to feed, and I don't think she planned to hop on and ride the guys."

"The shadow demon's been fucking her."

"Well, that was before she met us." Fin kept it philosophical. They'd hardly been monks. Well, Maddox might have been, there was no telling with him. He didn't share much, and Alfred probably wouldn't know a date if it woke up and bit him. Rogue? Yeah, Fin wouldn't place money there either.

Fine, Fin hadn't been a monk.

Course, if the warden had been paying her visits, that would explain the shadow addiction. They could keep her away until they cleansed her system.

"You up for transporting two of us?" Maddox asked abruptly, and Fin didn't bother to hide his smirk.

"Already eager to see her again?"

"I made her a deal," Maddox gritted out. "She'd listen to the whole story, then she was free to go if she wanted."

"That's a terrible deal, why would you offer her that?" Fin stared at him.

"Because she wants nothing to do with us, and she's still fighting the fact she was turned. She needs a sense of control." Then Maddox gave him a firm look. "I plan on honoring my word."

Of course, he did.

Dragons had honor for miles. Sometimes for days.

Why had the species begun to die out? Oh right, they *honored* their treaties when so many others didn't.

"Well, good for us, I made no such promises." He clapped Maddox's shoulder and then focused. Inside him, the magic unlocked. Portal magic wasn't difficult. If anything, it was one of the first mysteries he'd trained in as a young druid. Trees linked the world, their root systems tangling deep beneath the earth and creating routes that those who developed the art could slip along.

Even when a tree had been uprooted, the memory of its pathways remained, which meant even wooden structures couldn't keep him out if he could find the right one. It was knowing how to read the myriad of pathways and follow them. Taking passengers along was slightly more difficult.

But only slightly.

Maddox didn't block him out as he wrapped his power around him. If anything, the dragon allowed Fin access to his own strength, not that this simple transport required it. The world whooshed past them as he found the route they needed and followed it home.

Coinnigh an Rí, King's Keep, had been the center of

Alfred's domain for years beyond counting. They'd all called it home at one point or another. Granted, it was a monolith built almost completely from cut stones hauled miles from their natural habitat and put together.

Magic infused some of the stones, but the rest of it? They'd held it with strength, skill, and wit. When that wasn't enough, a few good slaughters had at least been entertaining. The factions left them alone. But they'd begun to fade from common memory. A choice, really, if the majority didn't think about them, they didn't have to fend off the occasional glory seeker.

The problem, however, was the reckoning Fiona faced. The turning of other species besides human into a vampire was considered impossible, improbable, and socially unacceptable. The legends around so-called hybrids had painted them as monsters.

Well, at least they got that part right.

While rare, hybrids existed in a delicate balance. One Fin, Maddox, Rogue, and Alfred maintained. They were all hybrids. Some of the first.

Currently, the only ones beyond Fiona.

They'd waited a long time for her.

Too long.

Whisking along the paths, he slowed them as they neared the ancient oaks bordering the fields nearest the keep's location. With a pop, he stepped out and yanked Maddox with him. The dragon looked vaguely green, and Fin chuckled as he patted him once and left him to catch his breath. It was a testament to how much Maddox wanted to see *her* again that he'd not objected to transporting on the ancient pathways.

He preferred to fly, but the keep was halfway around the world from where they'd penetrated Nightmare Penitentiary's defenses. It would have taken him a while to get there, and that meant leaving the beautiful Fiona to Fin and Rogue.

Huh. Maybe he should have let Maddox fly on his own.

The sight of smoke curling toward the sky from one of the chimney flues had Fin smirking. He smacked Maddox's arm again. "See, I told you he would bring her here."

The defenses were still active, but they had nothing to worry about. They passed harmlessly through the magical field that would send up an alarm to them no matter where they were of possible invasion. Once inside, Fin took a cleansing breath.

It had been a long time since he'd come home. The air was cool and damp, but the clouds had already parted to let watery sunshine reach the wet earth. They'd just missed the rain. While it had been night where they made their escape, it was nearly midday here.

The wood smoke was almost an invitation to a fire roaring in one of the man-sized hearths that decorated the halls. In the old days, there would be casks of ale and pots of honeyed mead. The food and drink would be free flowing. Artists and musicians often brought in from far and wide would provide the entertainment before Fin left them with pleasant memories and they were sent on their way, purses laden with coin.

The good old days.

Course, now they had internet and access to all types of entertainment at the press of a button. But there wasn't wi-fi up here.

He'd have to fix that if they settled in for the next few decades while Fiona adjusted. The main doors groaned as Maddox got ahead of him and pushed them open. Heavy steel doors needed a winch for most to open, but they weren't so similarly burdened. Inside, he gave Maddox a hand in shutting them both.

Memories echoed against the walls, filling the silence with images from other times. How many times had Alfred shoved these great doors open to allow his men to enter? How often had Rogue followed right in his shadow, a silent sentinel? At times, Fin and Maddox had also been there, always welcome. A brotherhood formed out of necessity, unity, and transition. They were the only ones of their kind to survive.

"The baths." Maddox's words seemed to hang in the air as he vanished. The disturbed dust marked his passage. Fin followed at a more sedate pace. Like Maddox, he was also eager to see Fiona again. He'd only gotten to hold her for a brief time. Clouding her mind to ease her compliance for their flight had backfired when the shadow demon arrived.

In the future, Fin wouldn't make that mistake again.

Ascending the stairs, he followed the sound of the water. The old boilers and piping through the walls used a system of cisterns and aqueducts built through the mountain itself to bring fresh water in, heat it, and then fill the pools in the bathing chamber. That, along with fires laid at each end, made it the warmest and steamiest room in the keep.

It had been the height of convenience hundreds of years earlier, and he couldn't say he would mind a bath himself. Blood had dried on his skin and left him itchy.

Maddox's aggravated voice tickled at his ears as Fin followed the long hall toward the bathing rooms. The bedrooms were all on the floor above, and while hot baths could be pulled there, the old bathhouse idea had still been popular when Alfred settled the keep.

Stripping off his coat, Fin let himself into the oversized chamber. Five pools placed strategically around the room with varying levels to each pool afforded bathers with a place to wash, a place to soak, and a place to steam by ascending the levels.

Unsurprisingly, Fiona was sprawled in a soaker pool, her arms hooked against the sides as she half-floated. Her eyes were closed and expression blissful. Across from her, Rogue sat, naked and cleaned. His dirty blond hair had been recently washed and hung halfway down his back. He flicked his gaze at Fin as he approached the pool.

Like Rogue, Fiona was also naked, but she didn't seem remotely aware of them. Flushed with color, her gorgeous red hair clung to her skin, though in places, it had begun to curl away. The tips of her breasts were just barely visible. While Fin looked forward to exploring her with great detail, he focused on the necessities for the moment.

The vicious bite in her shoulder was almost closed, the angry black lines radiating out from it the last bits of venom being decimated by her body.

"Why the fuck did you just take her?" Maddox demanded. Not waiting for Rogue to answer, he continued, "I had a deal with her. She would hear us out, then if she chose to go, I wouldn't stop her."

Lifting a flask, Rogue took a long drink, then held it out to Maddox wordlessly. The dragon scowled and accepted it.

"Fin shouldn't have dragged you into it, we had it covered." He took a long pull from the flask himself, then passed it back before he stripped off his own clothes and sank down into the lower pool. The water went crimson and streaked as the blood, dust, and soot worked free of his skin. "The point," he persisted. "You weren't aware of the rest of the plan, and you just kidnapped her. That completely contravenes *my* word. Now I have to make up for that lost honor."

Fin met Rogue's bemused gaze, and the other just shrugged. Unfortunately for Maddox, neither Fin nor Rogue shared his honor system.

Nor had they made her any promises. Well, Fin had more or less suggested his word in getting her out.

"You fed her?" he checked with Rogue. The blond nodded

once, then motioned to his throat. There was a fading wound there, likely inflicted by himself. Breaking his skin was damn hard and many had tried.

Crouching, Fin used careful fingers to tilt her head to look at her throat. No other bite marks marred her skin saved for the one faded scar that would likely always remain. The mark of her maker. Lashes lifting, she stared up at him with ruby colored eyes, though they weren't as blood-red as they'd been when he found her and Maddox in the hall. The barest hint of green surrounded them.

"Hmm, getting better at that astral projection," she murmured.

He chuckled. "Rest, Beautiful." He punched just a bit of compulsion into the command, and she let out a sigh, head tipped back and throat vulnerable as she sank under again. Yeah, that wouldn't hold.

Maddox growled at him. "Don't take advantage."

"Actually, I'm just making sure she's in one piece and doesn't try to escape on us before I've had a bath. Just because you need to chain women up to get them to stick around, doesn't mean I have to."

Rogue snorted, but the weight of Maddox's cold stare was even more impressive than his growls. Tossing a glance toward him, Fin gave him a little chin dip. Some lines weren't worth crossing.

Hardly mollified, the dragon went back to his bath, and Fin finally stepped down to shed his own blood-marked and shredded clothing. The fight had been impressive. They'd mustered their defenses, but it was hard to take on a druid and a dragon individually, much less together. Throw in a warrior, and they were really outmatched.

When the king awoke...

Fin paused, eyes closing for a moment as he searched the keep mentally. Alfred hadn't stirred yet. There was no mistaking his influence once he left his sleep. It was a crackle of energy in the air, a weight that draped everything, his power and his protection. The absence of it was just as keen.

They had so much to show him when he did rouse. The world would fascinate him. At least it had gotten interesting since the last time he was awake, anyway.

The water stung Fin's skin as he slid into it. The temperature higher than the air around them, Maddox had already moved up to sit in the soaking pool. Fin ducked himself into the water, then scrubbed the last flakes of blood and debris off. Having spent hours tucked under a stone floor, he could use the scrub.

Finished, he ascended and settled into the hotter water. Rogue turned a bland eye on him, then nodded toward Fiona.

Her closed eyes and serene expression were not something Fin wanted to disturb. "It can wait," he said quietly.

Maddox scowled.

"She's exhausted. All of our intelligence says she was dumped there within hours of her first waking. I can't imagine transitioning in there was very easy."

"No," Maddox admitted as he wrapped an arm around her and pulled her against his side. She let out a little sound that Fin swore was a purr. Her lashes moved faintly, and then she seemed to recognize Maddox and curled right up against him.

Jealousy painted bloody stripes through him, especially when Maddox's expression turned smug. Yeah, she was probably sleeping with Maddox again that night.

Fine.

Fin would lure her away the next day.

"Don't fight," Rogue ordered, and Fin wasn't the only one who jerked a look to the silent sentinel. The fact that he'd spoken at all when he took Fiona from the prison had been a collection of more words than they'd heard from him in a long time. At his quizzical look, Rogue shrugged. "If you fight over her, I'll end her."

Fin blinked and Maddox scowled, his arms closing around her, and between one blink and the next, it was the dragon staring at Rogue. If he worried about the dragon's rage, the other didn't show it.

"We didn't wait all these years for her for you to just throw that out there," Fin argued, choosing his words carefully. "We're not fighting."

"You're jealous, and he's possessive." Rogue didn't sound like he cared, but it would be a mistake to believe he was cavalier. If he truly didn't give a damn, he wouldn't even be broaching the topic. To Maddox, Rogue said, "You hate that she fed from me and that she is replete because I made sure to give her enough."

The dragon still scowled, but the recrimination seemed to turn inward.

Not to leave him out, Rogue switched his attention to Fin. "You resent she already has comfort with him. You want to claim what he's already found."

"You're not wrong," Fin agreed. "But I can be jealous because I want to know her, too. I've dreamt about her for centuries. Unlike the rest of you, I knew she was coming. I never broke faith."

"Lust-filled dreams about her breasts are not what I would call prophetic," Maddox stated drily, and Rogue gave a half-laugh.

"Oh, if I'd dreamed about those tits, trust me, I'd have found her a whole lot sooner." As it was, the little succubus hadn't even been on his radar until the day she awoke changed. Then the whole world had seemed to ring with her presence. He couldn't not leave immediately on a quest to find her.

The mental anguish alone would have drawn him like a beacon, but it was the raw and primal fury that kept him on target. He'd arrived a day after the sense of her all but muted. It had only taken him interrogating a half-dozen vampires in Dallas to find out where she'd gone.

He knew the name of her maker. The vampire was in hiding at the moment. When he brought his head above ground, Fin would deliver it to her on a platter. Though in truth, they owed him—it was a bumbling and idiotic attempt on the vampire's part to try and turn her in the first place.

By all rights, it should have killed her.

Fiona let out a little sigh. "You know, if you want to talk and keep me awake, you could discuss something more interesting than my breasts. Like, why I'm here and what this great plan was that I had to listen to before I could take off?"

With a slow shake of his head, Rogue slid down into the water. "You need more rest."

The fact that he addressed her directly sent Maddox's eyebrows skyward, even as Fin raised his own.

"Uh huh," Fiona elongated the two syllables even as she stretched. The action shifted her away from Maddox and brought her glorious breasts above the water. They really were quite spectacular. While slighter than he generally preferred in his women, Fiona's curves might also be lacking because of her half-starved state. The denial of her nature and her reliance on a shadow demon meant she might be alive, but she wasn't as healthy as she could be.

Rogue's blood had made a great deal of difference.

"Look," she continued, glancing from Rogue to Fin and finally to Maddox. Fin was almost disappointed he hadn't rated a longer look. Almost. Though the narrowing of her sleepy eyes gave her a harsher appearance. "We had a deal, right, Mad-Dragon?"

"We did," Maddox confirmed, not even batting an eyelash at what she called him. "I have not forgotten, Kitten."

"Good. I'd hate to think of you as an oath breaker. But we're going to put a little clock on this. I've been stuck in a cell for weeks, and this girl has places to go and people to kill. So let's cut to the chase. Why did you bust me out of that place, and what is it you're expecting in payment?"

"No payment would ever be asked," Fin told her smoothly. It had been their privilege to retrieve her, and pleasure. Or at least, it would be to all their pleasure.

"Wasn't asking you, Astral-Boy," she retorted, though the flash of her glance in his direction had him sitting up. "Though you are pretty, I will give you that."

He grinned.

"But I was talking to tall, dark, and ruthless over here." She jerked her thumb at Maddox.

Rogue chuckled.

"What are you laughing at?" Fin demanded, but the blond lifted his hands, palms out, as if saying not his problem.

With a sigh, Fin focused on Fiona, but she stared at Maddox and his dragon stared back at her.

"You're a hybrid," Maddox said finally, almost reluctantly. "You were right when you said vampires cannot turn other supernaturals, right in as much as that's all current thought holds to it. However, what they know and what is fact are two vastly different things."

Fiona stared at him for a bit, her lips pursed. Keen intelligence flickered in her eyes as she studied him. "So I'm a vampire-succubus."

"Yes."

"I need to feed on lust and blood."

"Also yes."

"Well. Aren't I special?"

"Very," Fin exhaled. "More special than you realize."

"Oh? And how is that?"

Ignoring Maddox's warning look, Fin told her the truth. "You're the only female hybrid to ever transition. You're also ours. Our mate. Perfect for us in every way." And she was.

Maddox sighed, even as Rogue just shook his head, but Fiona's response puzzled him the most.

She burst out laughing.

"Oh, honey, I'm a succubus," she said in between gasps. "I'm pretty much perfect for everyone."

Oh.

Fin hadn't really thought of it that way, and the dark look on Maddox's face promised he had, but it was the speculation filling Rogue's expression that worried him all of a sudden.

Wiping at her eyes, Fiona shook her head. "Sorry, I just needed that laugh. Like I said, Astral-Boy, you really are pretty. But you shouldn't bet on me. As soon as this little confab is over, I'm out of here. Like I said, places to go and people to kill." The she muttered something about how destiny could bite her.

"We'll see," he murmured, even as Maddox let out an aggrieved sigh.

"You will need to stay with us long enough to master your bloodlust," Maddox informed her. "And until we can deal with your sire. You do not want him to try and control you."

From the look on her face, Fiona had no intentions of letting anyone control her.

But she might have missed the point. Destiny had already bitten *all* of them. But as long as they were naked, he didn't mind the argument at all.

It would help when they got to the makeup part.

Which they would need in three…

Two…

"I don't care what Maddox promised you," Rogue stated. "You're not leaving, little *sváss*."

Now.

Her eyes flashed, and Maddox growled.

Fin settled back against the ledge to soak and let Maddox and Rogue debate this one.

Then Fin could swoop in with the reasonable compromise and settle it all.

When she stood up abruptly, hands on her hips, he damn near swallowed his tongue.

She really was quite perfect.

And it didn't matter if everyone else wanted her.

They didn't get to have her.

Fiona was theirs.

CHAPTER 8

"I don't believe in love at first sight. You fall in lust with what your eyes see, and in love with what your heart sees." - Unknown

Maybe it was the amount of blood I'd consumed or the age of it, but focusing had become a real bitch. What had been promised as a conversation and explanation had turned into a dictation and argument.

Specifically, Maddox argued, Rogue dictated, and Fin leaned back, arms stretched out, looking enormously satisfied. A certain amount of smugness rolled off Astral-Boy, and fuck, he was so pretty. I'd be jealous, but I wasn't that shallow.

I also really didn't give a damn about beauty except to admire it. Maddox was ripped, powerful, and yes, the fact that he could turn into a dragon was really impressive. But he wasn't *pretty*. Strong. Fierce. Proud. These all applied. Handsome, in his own way, but no, Fin had pretty all tied up.

"You can't just give her that order," Maddox snarled. It was really sweet, and I should probably calm him down, but to be honest, I didn't really care what *Rogue* had decided. The fact that he'd tasted divine and fed me both his blood and his lust had left me floating. He hadn't turned it into sex, not that I'd been remotely opposed, despite the varying levels of grossness decorating both of us. And by that, I meant him, not me. I did not look or *smell* anywhere near that bad.

But the stoic male sitting across the hot bath—really, these weren't baths so much as actual pools, and they were more like hot rock tubs. While they were carved out of actual stone, they were smooth and comfortable. Maddox kept trying to settle me back into leaning against him even if I didn't want to sit yet. Finally, I sat because it was warmer *in* the water. When he tugged me against him again I elbowed him.

Hated to let him know he wasn't any softer than the rocks we sat against. Not that I examined why I was loath to let him know. Anyway, back to the stoic over there.

Him, I couldn't pin down. Fierce? Yes. Beautiful? In a cold and kind of deadly way. There was an ancient power lurking there, something that might possibly be more dangerous than the dragon at my side.

Maybe.

That?

That was sexy as fuck.

"I think I just did," Rogue replied, his tone serene. He just did what? Oh, right. Gave me an order. "If you didn't want her, you wouldn't have gone into the prison in the first place. You wouldn't have given them the chance to shackle you."

"They can't hold me." Maddox glanced at me. "They wouldn't be able to hold me, and I wouldn't let them keep you. This is not something you need to concern yourself about."

"Are you talking to me or to tall, blond, and tasty over there?"

Maddox opened his mouth to respond, then paused, a puzzled look sliding through his expression before he finally said, "His name is Rogue."

"Yeah, I'm all caught up on that part, not that I care." I slanted a look toward the god lounging in the water. "Not that I don't appreciate the fact you got me off and fed me. Seriously enjoyed that. No lie."

"You're welcome. I take guesting seriously. You will not go hungry while you are here." Well, that was *almost* sweet. "You will be here for a while." That was not.

Eyes narrowed, I studied him. "Maddox and I had a deal."

"Exactly," Maddox stated, slinging an arm around me. Now, while I wasn't opposed to the skin on skin contact, I also wasn't interested in the distraction right now. "I gave her my word."

"I didn't," Rogue stated, as though that ended the discussion.

"Fin," Maddox snarled.

"Sorry, big guy," Fin said without opening his eyes, and a smile curved his lips. "I'm on Rogue's side in this. I didn't give her my word either. I said we'd get her out. Which we did. I said we'd feed her, which Rogue has handled this evening." Those beautiful brown eyes opened, and he latched his heated gaze onto me. "FYI, I'll be helping out with the feeding, too. It will be easier on you if you just feed from all of us."

Easier on me. Well that was mighty damn *autocratic* of him and probably had nothing to do with the want in his eyes.

"You know," I drawled sliding away from the dragon. Dragon.

Fuck me.

Yeah, focus.

Rising from the steaming water, I moved toward the side.

"You should soak for a little while longer," Fin suggested. "You're still buzzing from feeding."

And you're fighting the bliss.

The fact that his words flashed against the inside of my mind had me turning. Searching for his access point, I focused on pushing him back out. He studied me with the most patient of puzzled frowns.

Harmonics I'd learned young danced through my mind. One perk of being well-fed, I was also well-armed.

A vampiric succubus. It was an oxymoron.

Elias was going to kill me.

"Who would Elias be?" Fin asked. The sudden resonance of three gazes slamming into me had me rolling my eyes. "Because you can forget him along with Dorran."

Unimpressed, I chuckled. "Elias falls into the category of 'none of your fucking business,'" I informed him. "And Dorran kept me alive."

"Dorran is a the name the shadow demon gave you?" Unlike Fin's playful tone or Maddox's near constant growl, Rogue's voice was more indolent, but power crackled in every syllable. This was not a being who tolerated being ignored.

What he was precisely, I hadn't figured out yet.

Vampires.

Hybrids.

Oh, and how had Fin put it? My mates.

I snorted. Folding my arms, I leaned against the side. The air above the water was much cooler, and goosebumps rippled over my skin and turned my nipples taut. It was a good reminder that I wasn't here for sex and games.

You could be... Fin's teasing remark stroked across my mind like a caress. Bad vampire. I slapped his mental fingers with a slam of shutting off his access. The harmonics kept witches out of my head. One perk to having known a witch singer, those same harmonics kept other magic users out, too.

He gave a little jerk of surprise, his lazy air dissipating as he stared at me with blown pupils. "That… How did you do that?"

"Ask me no questions, and I'll tell you no lies," I chastised him.

Maddox snarled, "Stop poking in her head. We're supposed to be convincing her, not chasing her away."

Well, that was useful knowledge.

"I was playing," Fin argued. "Besides, she thinks I'm pretty. So suck it."

The corner of my mouth kicked up as Maddox surged to his feet, his glare fixed on Fin. There was something really—the thought didn't finish because the icy air around me sucked all the breath out of me. The bathing room was gone as were the sexy brutes about to argue over me.

I barely had time to process Rogue's hands on me before he dropped me in the middle of a bed in a dark, really fucking cold room. My teeth chattered before I could stop them.

"Stay," he ordered with a single gesture in my direction. Like me, he was still naked but the cold—fuck, were we in Siberia?—didn't seem to affect him. Or maybe he was just a better actor. Crossing the room, he moved a flap then struck a match. The smell of sulphur tinged the air, and a minute later, a fire bloomed in the hearth. It wasn't quite as large as the huge furnaces he called fireplaces in the bathing room, but the heat licked at the icy air around us.

"Do I look like a dog?" At least a plume of dust hadn't floated up into the air when I hit the comforter. Speaking of which, the fabric was softer than any I'd felt in days.

"You look like exactly what you are," Rogue informed me

as he lifted a heavy blanket from a chest and carried it over toward me. It wasn't just a blanket…it was a fur.

He snapped it out, and the wash of icy air sent a shudder down my spine. The fur settled over me like a heavy cloud. A heavy *warm* cloud. My still damp hair didn't offer much warmth, but tracing the way the water droplets slid down his skin seemed to be plenty of distraction. When we'd been in the bath, I hadn't really paid attention to the black ink scrawled over his skin or the patterns it made.

"I'm sure there's an insult in there somewhere," I murmured, skimming my gaze down to the half-hard cock stirring despite the brittle cold. Even though I expected it, when he slid beneath the fur with me, surprise still skated along my flesh. "What I'm uncertain about is whether you're trying to offend me or…"

Undeterred by my comments, he levered across the bed, shifting the fur to drape both of us, and then he dragged my legs apart.

Really, like just gripped and spread. With one tug, he had me on my back and his shoulders wedged between my thighs. "Fiona," he said, staring up at me with eyes gone shimmering blue. "Shut up."

"Excuse you?"

My next thought completely stuttered however as his hot breath passed right over my pussy to the inside of my thigh and then his teeth sank in. Rage kindled in my blood, but desire stomped right over it as his lust boiled over again. Lust to taste me, to feed himself, and to fuck me.

As full as I already was, his wild need shouldn't be pounding into my veins and taking over my pulse. Not that I was even remotely struggling against his hold.

What? I liked dominant men. Especially those who just went for what they wanted. It beat the hell out of the guys who tried to *lure* me in with pretty promises.

The hot pull of his mouth seemed to absorb all my focus, and with every tug, there was an answering pulse in my pussy. Fuck. I was going to be soaked in no time. I clenched at the blanket or the sheets. Anything to hang on because the orgasm he sent crashing through me shattered any arguments.

Two fingers—stiff like marble but hot like lava—speared into me, and I wanted to roll my hips and ride, but his fierce grip kept my lower body still, impaled and pinned beneath fingers and fangs. Toes curling, I dug them against his back as he sucked down more, and the vibrant buzz along my flesh doubled, then redoubled until he crooked his fingers and I came again.

The wrench of reality faded as I floated on a sea of sensation with his hot need sizzling into my soul. I was almost too full, I couldn't consume more, and yet, more was what I got. Still, he continued to suck, pulling and draining me. Feeding one beast, he starved the other.

The lazy seal of his tongue stroking the bite mark sent little eddies of fresh pleasure through me. His fingers were still sheathed in my pussy, even as my inner walls fluttered and clenched against them.

"Better," he murmured before he began to lick along the seam of my labia. Blood loss left me pliant. He hadn't drained me completely, but weakness invaded my limbs as he began to suck against my clit. The storm that unleashed made me twitch.

"Much better," he continued as the room flashed from color to black and white, then back again. Everything was hazy. "You have two natures," he informed me as he tugged his fingers free from my pulsating flesh, and I whimpered.

Fucking. Whimpered.

Oh. Hell. No.

Even as I rejected the need swelling through me, I couldn't deny the pleasure still quaking under my skin.

"They both need to be fed," he continued lazily before he latched onto a nipple and began to suck. The sting of his teeth came a second later, and he began to drink again. The haze at the edge of my vision darkened further.

How much was he going to take? The errant thought drifted through my mind, but couldn't light or take purchase. A lick and a kiss, then he was at my throat, and the drag of his chest rasped against my nipples, twining pain and pleasure.

Hovering above me, he nestled his hips against mine, even as he slid a hand down to grip my thigh and drag it upward. "Now," he murmured, his breath hot against my lips. "You need to feed."

"Asshole," I whispered. "I didn't need it before you did that."

"No," he said, simply. "You need it more than you know. The shadow demon fed on you constantly, Fiona. He chomped away at pieces of your soul, pieces you could restore because you fed on him."

So? But the challenge died unspoken.

"And he's going to call you because his blood is in you."

I almost laughed. "Pretty sure it's in you…" His cock teased at my entrance, and it wasn't half-hard anymore. No, it was thicker and far stiffer than his fingers had been. Rogue didn't kiss me, though his nose brushed mine. Licking my lips, I fought the gradual darkening of my vision. "I fed on you once," I argued.

"Yes, and you're going to do it again," Rogue ordered. "You'll feed on all of us. We're going to feed on you until we clean him out of you."

I laughed. My fangs grazed against the inside of my lips as I smiled. "Demanding fucker, aren't you?"

With one hand, he clamped it against my chin. "Tell me your objections."

"To being fucked?" I shrugged. "Not many. Though a girl does like to be asked before she's thrown on a bed in an icy room and tongued to orgasm. Or in your case..." I licked my lips again. "Fanged and fingered."

He chuckled. "You don't want to be asked."

No, I really didn't.

"You just don't want to be a vampire."

Nope. I didn't want that either.

"But you are."

Asshole.

"More, you're a hybrid."

Yeah, I got that. Flicking my gaze from him, I stared at the shadowed ceiling.

"How did he feed you, little *sváss*?"

What the fuck was a *sváss*?

"Tell me," he commanded.

"Blood bags were how they tried." It was an answer without being an answer.

His fingers tightened against my jaw in warning. His cock nestled right against my labia, the tip pressing against my clit, but his absolute lack of motion meant if I wanted anything more I'd have to grind.

Well, two could play the denial game, fuck you very much. I might not have the strength to move after he bit me so intensely—that had felt ridiculously good—but he didn't control me.

No one controlled me.

"Disgusting."

I glanced back up to find those too blue eyes still glowing as he stared at me. "Agreed."

"You didn't drink from them?"

I would have shaken my head, but I couldn't move it.

Okay, the restraint game had potential, but this was getting old. His lust still licked over me, fanning against my bloated soul like I needed more, and fuck if I wasn't absorbing it. It wasn't quite enough to edge the need above empty where his draining had left me.

"But you drank from the demon?"

"Don't judge me."

Rogue snorted. "I'm not. I'm judging them. Did you drink from the demon or not?"

I shrugged as much as I was able. I'd half-expected Fin or Maddox to have tracked me down by now, but apparently not. Maybe I wasn't even in Castle Numbskull or wherever it was Rogue had dragged me off to.

"Are you planning to fuck me or just interrogate me?"

"Feeling restless, little *sváss?*" He ran his nose along my cheek to my throat. My heart clenched at the first scrape of his teeth. Fight surged into my veins. If he wanted to bite my thighs or my breasts, fine. I didn't want him at my throat. Strength surged through me, and I reached for the lust he had on simmer.

One beautiful thing about being a succubus, I might feed on lust, but I could also fan it. While I had no idea what the hell Rogue was in addition to being a vampire, three facts were distinctly clear.

He was a vampire.

He was old.

He was *very* male.

His cock stiffened further at the first surge hitting his system. He snapped his head up and his teeth away from my throat. The flare of his nostrils and the shift in his eyes told me that I'd found the right circuit.

"*Sváss,*" he warned me. Jaw clenched, he ground his hips into mine, and the slide of his cock against my clit threatened my concentration, but I just added that fuel to the fire. A shudder overcame him, then another. "You should stop."

"You first," I pointed out. I wasn't the one who threw my naked ass on this bed and went down on me without so much as a *may I*. I wasn't the one who kidnapped me out of a prison—granted, I was glad to be out, but I refused to trade one cell and keeper for another.

Rogue began to shake, but his grip on me didn't loosen. When his eyes flared from blue to pure white, it was my turn to shiver. Nothing natural inhabited that brilliant gaze of pure white light. The shadows in the room retreated, and even the glow from the fire seemed insignificant in comparison to the pure light escaping him.

"What are you?" I had to ask.

"Dangerous," he replied, and then his mouth clamped down on mine and all that power surged back into me. My lust. His. Like a feedback loop, and I stopped squirming to wrap my arms around him. At some point, he fisted his cock and then pushed into me, and I dragged my other leg up until I had them both locked around his hips.

The piston of his hips slamming into mine should have brought pain, but fuck, it was exactly what I needed and wanted. He filled me with every thrust, the friction generating more heat if possible, until what breath escaped his punishing kiss fogged in the air. His tongue matched his cock for lashes inside my mouth, and I dug my nails into his shoulders. When he ripped his mouth upward, his whole expression was one of tortured need, and I didn't shy from it, arching up to meet the rock of his hips.

The feel of him working through me lit me up. Fucking and I were old friends, but this was different. This was... I couldn't hold on to the spiraling thought. When he yanked out of me, I hissed, but the fur fell away as he rose up on his knees and slammed me back when I would have followed him. I got one brief glance at his cock, straining out toward me, thick, curved, and seeming to pulsate.

Oh, mama was intrigued. With one grip of my legs, he flipped me over onto my stomach and dragged my hips up. When he impaled me again, I didn't bother to hold back the scream or the need to claw at the covers. He wrapped my hair around his fist and anchored one hip with his hand, and then he began to drive every thought out of my head.

The flood of lust filling me redoubled, and I had to send it back to him. His cock seemed to swell, and it took real effort for him to work it into me over and over again. Every drag and push against my pussy lit me up more, and when he yanked me up and back, then slid his hand down to flick my clit, I came apart. His teeth sank into my throat, and his own orgasm flooded me as he roared.

Life suspended on a rocky precipice, pleasure and pain pulling me taut as raw power filled me until it spilled over, leaving only bliss as he pumped inside of me and drained me at the same time.

The world splintered, and I sank into a haze of pure pleasure.

"Fuck," Maddox's voice weaved through the brilliant darkness holding me. "Stop."

I wasn't doing anything, just riding out orgasm after orgasm as it detonated in my system. My clit hurt, Rogue had teased it so much at this point, and yet even that pain sent eddies of pleasure to drown me. The darkness pulled me down.

"I said *stop.*" The roar punched down to me and dragged me back to the surface.

Dragon.

Right.

Then hot hands were on my face, and another mouth claimed mine. Where Rogue tasted like ice, Maddox was all fire. The heat flamed through me, even as ice coated my back. The bruising force of Rogue's grip was still in my hair and skating along my chest to my breasts, and despite his own orgasm, he was still thick and buried deep.

Some distant part of my mind wondered at the fact he could still stretch me so tight.

"Feed her," another voice penetrated the floating haze. "I can't believe he fucking drained her." Fin.

Right. Astral-Boy was there.

Astral-Boy.

Dragon.

Wild Dick.

Yeah, that last name really applied because I wanted to rock against that dick still impaling me, and at the same time, I wanted to feel him moving again. What did it say about me that I wanted this sexy combo of desire and torture?

"Kitten," Maddox said in a harsh voice, and cupped my face. The weight of his thumbs worked my mouth wider. "You need to feed."

"Oh..." I husked out another laugh as fresh lust crashed into me. I was feeding. The words weren't forming. My tongue was too thick...

"You asshole," Maddox snarled. Not really the way to romance a lady, but I didn't have it in me to care. "What the hell were you thinking?"

"He's lust drunk, what do you think he was thinking?" Fin snapped. "Just feed her. He's all knotted up inside her and not moving for a while."

Oh, that was nice. I was now a glorified cock warmer.

"Drink," Maddox urged me in a much softer voice. Better.

He cupped my head, straining against the hand already wrapped in my hair, and my breasts impacted his hot chest. Oh. Sandwich. Then blood trickled against my lips, and I swallowed.

Sweet.

Hot.

Spicy.

I latched on to the slender cut and worked it wider. If Rogue had been decadence, Maddox was pure gratification. The tingling in my lips spread down my throat as he both quenched the raw emptiness and set it on fire. I clutched at him, moaning as I drank more, and he swore again. Every gulp had me clenching, and Rogue let out a strangled groan.

"Fuck," Fin whispered, and really, what could I do but agree?

Maddox kept my face planted to his throat, and I writhed between him and Rogue, glutting myself on the blood and pleasure they offered.

Behind me, Rogue finally loosened and slipped away. The chill at my back when he released me had me shaking. Then Maddox forced my head up and away, and I growled.

Actually growled. I wanted more.

"Shh, Beautiful." Fin had his arms around me, and then he tucked my face to his throat and the scent of his blood hit me. Forests and sunlight and sumptuous spring days, and I clamped down on the cut waiting for me. An orgasm shattered me even as I fed, and what few splinters of the world I'd held onto slid right through my fingers.

"Why the fuck did you do that?" Maddox demanded from somewhere as Fin dragged the fur around me and tucked me against his hard naked body. I kept feeding, content to be right where I was.

"Because I pushed her," Rogue admitted. "And she pushed back."

Damn right I did.

"Shh," Fin whispered again as his mind tumbled over mine. "We have you."

Fine, I'd sleep.

But he better not get used to this.

He smoothed a hand over my ass. "What if I want to?"

I'd think about it.

"That's all we're asking." A shudder passed from him to me as I took another hard pull. Liar. They were asking for more, but I wanted more, too. How much would I drink before this aching need would be gone?

"We'll figure it out," Fin assured me. When the darkness stretched up to tug me in this time, I didn't bother to fight it, just lapped at the cut as I withdrew my teeth and drifted at the edge of sleep with my senses full of all three of them.

Something was missing though.

But I couldn't quite put my finger on it.

A hot hand stroked my spine, even as Fin caressed my ass. Interest spiked through the drunken laziness.

"Sleep," Maddox ordered in a rough voice. Movement in the bed, and then he was pressed against me. Another move, and Rogue's scent filled my nostrils and he pressed an almost chaste kiss to my bloodstained lips.

"She is dangerous," he murmured, but I couldn't hold onto the words.

"But she's *ours*," Maddox argued.

"Yes," Fin said without reservation.

"This is a terrible idea," Rogue muttered.

Yeah well, fuck you, too.

Fin chuckled.

I'd have to figure it out later.

Then sleep swallowed me whole.

CHAPTER 9

"She's got the eyes of innocence; the face of an angel. A personality of a dreamer and a smile that hides more pain than you can ever imagine." - Unknown

The hard body beneath mine shifted enough that the arm tossed over me slid down until the dead weight rested on my bladder. Nothing said fuck off to sleep faster than needing to pee. Well, that or the gagging sound a cat made right before it coughed up a hairball.

I peeled one eye open. The shadowy darkness had a couple streaks of sunlight piercing it. The dust floating in those streams made me think of fairies. A fanciful notion because fairies were annoying little pricks and should be swatted with the same efficiency used to clear mosquitoes.

Shafts of sunlight.

At least, I was pretty sure it was sunlight. I hadn't seen anything close to it in far too long. The body beneath me shifted again, and I glanced to my left. Maddox lay on his stomach, one arm flung across me and the other under a pillow. The air might be cool, but the fur left his bare back exposed. Not that he seemed remotely cold. The bed was very warm.

To my right, Rogue sprawled on his back, his expression utterly devoid of any expression and out cold. Only the faintest rise and fall of his chest betrayed he was alive.

That meant Fin had to be my mattress and the owner of the stiff cock wedged against my ass. Fair enough. Maddox dragged his arm up my body, the weight of his elbow digging against my bladder again before he cupped a breast.

Typical.

I needed to piss, and I needed to stretch. Everything hurt. My mouth tasted like ass.

Considering I'd fed on two of them—all three if you included the feasting Rogue gave me when he first dragged me here—that actually fit. Removing Maddox's hand was easier than sliding off Fin. He still had an arm around me, and every movement I made ground his cock more firmly against my ass.

The idea had potential. Later.

Right now, I had to take a piss. Focusing, I peeled his arm away and settled his hand on Rogue's thigh. I sat up as Maddox shifted to fling his arm out again. Narrowly avoiding the trap, I grinned over my shoulder at Maddox cuddling Fin. They were adorable.

With care, I extracted myself from the pile of vampire Jenga and shivered once I hit the cooler air of the room. The fire was down to ashes in the fireplace, and the room was wildly empty of anything definitive. The bed. A chest. A low bench sat near the fireplace. That was it, almost monk-like in its austerity.

Hell, there were still sconces in the walls. It was like an unsubtle upgrade on the prison. Fun.

I studied the shafts of light though. There were windows placed higher up, thin, angular ones. They had coverings over them, a part in the cover was what let the light through. I was tempted to slide my fingers into the light to see if I caught on fire.

Still, I'd wait for that particular trick until *after* I peed. If I planned to go out like a succubus flambé, I wasn't going to do it pissing myself.

That said, the bathroom wasn't immediately evident. The only visible doors led *out* of the room presumably, not that I got a tour the night before. I limped my way to the door. There wasn't even a dressing gown or something to throw on to ward off the chill. Fuck, I moved funny. I ached in all the best ways from my thighs to my breasts to my throat. I put a hand up to the raw mark on my neck, and it was rough under my fingers, closed but puffy. Like it hadn't wanted to heal all the way.

Turning, I glanced back at the bed. Monk-like in the decorating choices, but definitely not in the sheets. All three males slept, sprawled together, not quite cuddling, and yet adorable.

It was amazing what a lack of talking did for a guy. Although to be fair, Maddox had at least *attempted* to honor his agreement.

Yeah. I wasn't that fair.

He was a dragon. He could have attempted a lot harder.

Fin was either a witch or a druid. Druid more likely. What that meant Rogue was, I had no idea.

And fuck, I had to pee. I shifted my weight from foot to foot, I gripped the heavy circular handle and yanked the door open. Fuck, what had they built these things out of? Thankfully, it didn't creak like something out of a horror movie.

The brush of icy air from beyond the big ass door hit like a sledgehammer. Fuck, it would be more comfortable to try and take a piss in an ice storm. I stole a look back at the fur blanket on the bed. I was tempted to steal it.

But I wasn't an asshole.

Most days.

Clenching my teeth against chattering, I hobbled out and pulled the door closed to keep from freezing them to death. The hallway had one long shadowy crypt like feeling going on. The shudders wracking my spine had nothing to do with the cold. It was old here. Too old.

Ancient whispers drifted along the hallway.

Yeah, that wasn't creepy.

Arms folded over my breasts even if my nipples could probably cut diamonds they were so stiff, I tossed a mental coin. Pivoting left, I hurried along. The place had a bathing room. Maybe the toilets were there.

The heavy fucking doors were all through this section. Some gave with a good shove, others just held like they were made of iron. I found two more bedrooms, no bathrooms.

Okay. Think Fi.

I couldn't feel the bottoms of my feet anymore, which was probably good, hopefully my bladder would freeze before I peed. It was bad enough I was running around bare-ass naked covered in spunk and flecks of dried blood. At the thought of the dried come, I swore my pussy flexed.

"Enough of that," I informed myself. "You should be nursing a pulled muscle after all of that. Or three." It certainly felt like I was. Not that I was complaining. At the end of the hall, I pushed open the last door and nearly wept.

It wasn't quite the porcelain altar of the Ritz with a fancy French bidet, but it was a working toilet with a tile floor, and rough amenities. There was even a shower stall. I flushed the toilet once to make sure it worked.

Since my breath kept fogging, I was surprised the pipes

weren't frozen. The water swirled away, and I grimaced as I settled on the seat.

Nope. Fuck that.

Too cold. I squatted.

I don't care how unattractive it might look or how much my core complained. At least the prison had access to a toilet without walking through the wilderness of a keep to find it.

A keep in the wilderness.

A sudden longing for my house on the cliff with its floor to ceiling windows and ocean views flooded me. Southern California was so temperate. Getting cold there would take some serious effort.

Unlike this gothic monolithic nightmare.

A long sigh escaped me as I relieved myself. Seriously, it took me a while to pee. I would probably be dehydrated at this rate. It didn't matter, the relief was so profound, it was nearly orgasmic.

Eh.

Maybe not that good.

Still, it was damn nice.

Finished, I cleaned up and flushed again, then moved to the sink. What were the chances of hot water in here? As much as I ached, I'd rather go find that hedonistic bathing chamber I'd been in the day before.

I'd also like some damn privacy.

I debated finding my way back to the guys or striking out to explore. The rest of me was rapidly growing numb, too. How long did it take frostbite to kick in?

There was no mirror over the sink. Well, I didn't really care what I looked like at the moment. Probably better not to scare myself. I did, however, rinse out my mouth. No toothpaste or even a toothbrush—not that I would borrow one of their toothbrushes. Suck their dick? No problem. Use their toothbrush? Gag.

With a finger, I scrubbed at my teeth, then wet my mouth and spit a few times. Not great, but between the icy water and my finger, it helped.

Top of the list, toiletries.

Second item on that list, clothes preferably, including a fucking parka.

Where was this asinine place anyway?

Once in the hall, I stared back the way I came then cocked my head toward the stairs.

Vampires were supposed to have really sharp hearing, right?

So I focused.

Yeah.

I couldn't hear much more than the faint whistle of wind from somewhere and the sound of my own breathing. Yeah. Impressive I was not. The lack of emotion was also telling. Every living thing possessed some form of lust. A lust for life, a lust for food, sometimes a lust for their next breath. Even the most devout possessed a lust for something. Shockingly enough, a lust for charity and a lust to do good things could exist. Granted, it was like having a plain potato chip with zero flavor and no seasoning—it could fill the hole, but it lacked any real satisfaction.

Still, the only hints of it I could detect came from behind me.

The guys.

So…we were alone.

Fine by me.

I descended the steps to start my hunt. Baths and clothes. Maybe just clothes, and I could get the hell out of here and make my way back to where I belonged. Then I could hunt down Dimitri and shove a cactus up his ass. I had stilettos thicker than his dick. Maybe I would start with one of them and work my way up to the cactus.

The heavy stone walls threatened to close in on me as I made my way down the steps. The lack of natural or artificial light wasn't doing much for the mood. I half-expected to Dr. Frankenfurter to pop out and start singing in his teddy.

Lips curling at the mental image, I tried to cast Grumpilstilskin, Dick Face, or Astral-Boy in the role.

Astral-Boy for sure. He had that angelic look and the body I'd been sleeping on would definitely look fine in or out of a teddy.

I descended two full flights of stairs before I found another set of doors. These things were big enough that Maddox would be able to fit through them maybe.

Huh, maybe that was why the place was so tall and wide. They'd had a dragon hanging out, probably saved money on the repair bills. Dragon would be nice right about now, at least he was his own heat source.

The door opened into a huge hall. Three steps led down into a sunken floor area. Columns lined it, and there were even larger gated doors to my right. I'd bet all the non-existent money in my invisible clothes those went outside. Based on their height and construction, they had likely been built with Maddox in mind.

Joy.

Twisting, I glanced at the huge receiving hall. It was like something out of the Middle Ages—right down to the throne on a dais toward the end. There were a few seats around it, but the throne was definitely that. Maybe not ornate, but definitely elevated.

So which of them was the master of the keep?

My money was on Rogue. He had that arrogance to him. In fact, he kind of made Maddox look like a pussy cat.

A grumpy pussycat, sure, but still a kitty dragon.

The idea made me snicker despite the gloom of the place. The ancient whisper drifted against me like an errant breeze.

Another shiver worked its way through me. Yeah, I wanted the mansion on the cliffs over the beach, not the old-world keep in the assback of nowhere.

Back up for the baths, or maybe down?

Wait. This was the receiving hall. Most of the stuff on this level would likely be for public access. I glanced back at the stairs. Those pools had heated water coming from somewhere; old world construction would use cisterns and aqueducts.

Downstairs it was.

It took me another thirty minutes of hunting, but I found it by following the smell of dampness, and it was tucked on a lower level on the far side of another huge open space. This one wasn't as decorative, but I could almost hear the clang of steel and the rustle of leather. A training room?

That kind of made sense.

I couldn't feel anything anymore. Once I shoved the door open, warm moist air hit me like a slap to the face, and I sighed in absolute relief.

Shoving the door closed, I leaned against it. It was hardly a workout to walk all over the place, but I was bone-deep tired. I headed over to the first pool and slid into it. The hot water stung my icy flesh, and I hissed, teeth clenching as the shivering and teeth chattering hit me all over again. I needed to wash, but I couldn't get my fingers to cooperate.

"If you'd wanted a bath," Fin said idly. "You should have just asked me."

Hypothermia kept me from letting out a startled scream or jumping like one of those girls in a horror movie this place would make the great set for. However, I did spin and punch him square in the nose. The sudden motion sent pins and needles raking through my frozen limbs, but the numbness protected my hand when a couple of the bones crunched at the blow.

Fin winced and put a hand to his face, even if the blow barely rocked him. A real smile curved the corners of his mouth. "Maddox said you were a fighter."

"Fuck you."

"I won't say no." His grin grew more teasing, and I rolled my eyes as I sank into the water. Sobering, he shook his head, then shed a heavy robe before following me into the water. "Come here."

"Why?" Hostility rolled off the word, but it didn't slow Fin down. He grasped my arm and hauled me over to him.

"Because you're freezing, Beautiful. And I can help warm you up." He pulled me right to him, one arm around my waist and the other hooked around my shoulders.

The hot water swirled around me, but he was warmer still, and his hands were like brands where they rested against me. He sank us down to sit so my shoulders were under the water. My tangled hair was soaked from the mid-length down, but I didn't care.

"If you knew I was up and looking, why didn't you just tell me where the bathing room was?"

"I didn't know you were looking for it," Fin told me, then kissed my nose. "My apologies, Beautiful."

I stared at him. "You thought I was wandering around this frigid ass mausoleum naked for kicks?"

A grin flashed across his face. "I didn't know what you were doing, Beautiful, but since you didn't come back to bed, I thought I'd watch and see. I figured if you wanted us, you would have at least come and woken us up."

Yeah, that was too reasonable.

I scowled. "Spying is kind of creepy."

"If I were spying, I would agree with you. I think of it more as advanced protection detail. You get your privacy, and I get to look after your gorgeous ass." He cupped his hand against my ass. "Speaking of which…"

"I'm sore, you can wait."

He blinked at the rejection, but his smile only grew. "Good to know, we'll be sure to take better care of you. Rogue didn't mean to be so rough, you know. It's just been a while."

And I'd had him on a lust loop. "The rough was fine, he's very talented," I said with a shrug. "Just I'm definitely sore in a lot of places." I lifted a hand to finger the puffy bite at my neck. I didn't want their teeth at my throat, but Rogue had bitten into me while he fucked me stupid, and I hadn't said a damn thing.

"Why the hell did he drain me?"

Fin snapped his focus from my breasts back to me. No, I hadn't missed the way he'd zeroed in on them after my comment about liking it rough. Pretty boy here probably didn't know what really rough was like. I could show him—after I no longer felt like I was straddling a bowling ball.

What the hell was Rogue that he'd knotted up in me like that, too?

Did they all knot like that?

Studying me from beneath half-lowered lashes, Fin traced his fingers up to the spot and a shudder went through me as he circled the bite. "You fed off the warden."

"So?"

"So, shadow demons have powerful blood, don't get me wrong. The more of them you take in, the more access they have to you. You probably had a craving for him, he came to you often, then started stretching it out. Making you wait a little bit longer each time."

Eyes narrowed, I nodded. "I figured he just didn't think I needed as much. He definitely fed me well."

"I'd keep that last part to yourself where Maddox is concerned. He already wants to kill the guy. If he finds out he was marking you too, it could be bad."

I rolled my eyes. "Back to the draining part."

Fin sighed. "Rogue drained you because we all need to. We need to drain and feed you back up. Your transition was sloppily done, and then giving you nothing but a shadow demon to feed off of is a terrible idea. You're vulnerable. We'll make sure you're not."

"Uh huh, you know what I hear you saying?" Despite my irritation, I relaxed more and more as feeling surged through my limbs. The hot water melted away the chill. "We want to make sure the only ones marking you are us."

"Not denying it," Fin said easily. "We can feed both sides of you quite easily, but we need to balance you out. I should have gotten to you sooner, Beautiful. I missed you by mere hours."

No skin off my nose. "I'm not staying here."

"A discussion for another day," Fin told me, then pressed his lips just below that spot on my neck, and I would have rocked off his lap, but he gripped me tighter. "Not going to bite. You've made it clear you don't want us there." Another kiss. "Was that where Dimitri bit you?"

Fingers curling, I glared at him. "Don't dig around in my head."

"Can't help it if you projected those thoughts of vengeance so loudly, Beautiful. I have no problem helping you remove his spine one vertebrae at a time."

Oh. That was a provocative image.

"Or we could nail him to the floor," Fin continued kissing a path to my shoulder. "Nail guns are really neat. We could start with his penis and work our way out to all his extremities."

"Vicious," I approved. "I like it."

His lips curved against me, then he kissed my biceps and glanced up me. "Bloodthirst is very normal in a baby vamp."

"It's not his blood I crave."

"No, it's his suffering because he took something from you that wasn't his."

Precisely. "And he's a moron."

Which was almost worse than if he'd done it out of some evil nefarious purpose.

"Does that bother you more because of his choice, or because you fucked him?" Genuine curiosity lived in that question.

I shrugged. "Probably a little bit of both. I just needed to feed, and I figured it was an even exchange. The sex wasn't even that great." Hell, I hadn't even gotten off at first. No, I had come later. He had though.

Twice.

Asshole.

I'd also died later, too.

Good times.

"Oh, we'll definitely start with his dick then," Fin told me cheerfully. "Not pleasing you was his first mistake."

Okay, I laughed. That was funny.

Fin's eyes twinkled as he grinned. "Feel better?"

"A little bit."

"Good." He pulled my hand from the water and kissed my palm. "The soaking pool is much warmer."

"It was warmer when there were big ass bonfires lit in the hearths, too." Neither of which were burning right now.

"I can fix that if you like, Beautiful." The offer came with another kiss, this time to my fingers. "Would you like a fire?"

I studied him. "Are you trying to seduce me?"

"Is it working?" He raised his brows and then ruined the effect with a laugh.

"Not really." Though he didn't need to try that hard. He really was very pretty.

"Thank you." This time, he dropped the kiss on my lips. "But no, I'm not trying to seduce you. Not yet anyway." With care, he stood and then carried me through the water to the steps before climbing to the second pools. Even though we were in the chilly air for a moment, I barely felt it and steam rolled up from our skin.

Oh, I groaned as he waded us into the hotter pool. Tension I hadn't even realized I was carrying faded away.

He set me down against the carved spots in the stone that made for a perfect cradle, then knelt between my thighs before he kissed me again. This time, it wasn't just a peck, but a genuine, open-mouth, tongue flicking, toe curling, pussy-clenching kiss that had me fisting his hair. When he lifted his head, he licked his lips.

"I'll get the fires started, then I'll go fetch you a breakfast."

Real food.

My stomach growled and did a little flip-flop.

"I really can still eat regular food?" It was such an idiotic question. I didn't want to be a vampire. But all they'd given me at the prison were bags of blood that I wouldn't touch. No other food. I hadn't had anything except water in weeks.

"Yes, Beautiful," Fin promised me. "You can have anything you want. Tell me, and I'll make it happen."

I eyed him for a long moment. Things that sounded too good to be true often were. "What will it cost me?"

"Nothing," he said, frowning, his playful expression turning fierce. "I *want* to take care of you."

And I wanted to believe that...

If he heard that thought, he didn't comment on it.

"Tell me what I can bring you to make you smile." The quiet plea there touched me, even if I didn't want to admit it. That, and he really hadn't made a move to get me to ride his cock. Impressive, since most guys wanted in me within a few minutes of talking to me. But he and Maddox had both handled it well. Rogue had too, really, until I lashed out at him.

Worth it.

"Coffee," I told him honestly. "I'd kill for fresh coffee, a gallon, I like it with a little sugar and cream. Bacon. I haven't had bacon in weeks." My mouth watered at the thought of it. "Real British fry-up actually, the bacon, the eggs, the English muffin, some pork and beans, and sausages." My stomach growled vociferously, and Fin's smile grew. "And clothes, my clothes, something I can put on because it's so cold here."

Lips quirking, he said, "I will bring you back all that you have asked for, though I might work on a way to heat the place. I like watching you walk around naked. Your body is spectacular."

I snorted. "If I'm naked, then so is everyone else."

"Deal," Fin said with a wink. Then he vanished from the water. Vanished from the whole room. I pivoted to look around for him, but he wasn't there. Suddenly, fire boomed in one of the fireplaces, then the other. The roar of two miniature explosions made me laugh.

"Nice," I called out. "Very nice."

You're welcome, Beautiful. I'll be back soon. Relax and stay warm. I'd like that soreness to go away so I can show you just how much I'd like to please you.

Okay.

That was hot.

I heard that...

Dick.

Heard that, too.

I laughed.

Well, I'd give them this.

They weren't boring.

"Seduce my mind and you can have my body. Find my soul and I'm yours forever." - Anonymous

As promised, Fin wasn't gone long at all. Long enough, I tired of soaking in the water. I'd dropped back into the washing pool and actually washed my hair and cleaned up before returning to the soaking pool. Conveniently, Fin had left an oversized robe that reached my ankles and had sleeves that went past my hands, but it was warm and thick.

Wrapped up in it, I headed over to one of the benches in front of the huge fire. Granted, the stone wasn't the most comfortable piece of furniture—would it kill them to invest in something less Dark Ages? At this point, I'd take eighteenth or nineteenth century.

Still, I was finger combing my hair while basking in the heat when Fin returned with a ripple of air and a distinctive 'pop.' The scent of the coffee hit me first, and I was on him faster than a one-night stand at Mardi Gras. He chuckled as he surrendered the first large cup to my eager hands.

I took a deep breath, and I swore I orgasmed right there. It was like manna from heaven. Or at least something like that, not that I'd ever had manna. Yeah, that didn't work. Here, just picture waking up every day for weeks to shitty circumstances, and to top it off, you get no coffee. Now, the really sexy druid not only brought coffee, he brought bacon.

I was so sucking him off after all this.

The first sip hit my taste buds, and I moaned. Oh, it was the perfect dark blend. Strong enough to fuel the fantasies with just enough sugar and cream to tie you up in silken ropes so it could have its way with you.

"You really like coffee," Fin commented softly, and I cut my gaze to him on the next sip. His lips were wet like he'd been licking them, and I didn't bother to contain my next moan.

"You have no idea," I whispered after I swallowed the next mouthful. "Bacon?" My stomach had begun to growl and gurgle. It really hadn't in weeks; I thought it had given up on me ever eating real food again, like a lost cause. I know I had. But this…this was better than sex or escape. This was perfection.

"I brought you everything you asked for," he promised, and turned to the rolling table that looked so horribly out of place here.

"Did you steal that from a hotel?"

That would be hilarious. Go to a hotel, order room service, just bring the whole thing here.

Wait, if we could do that, why couldn't I just go to the hotel?

"Not quite," Fin retorted, dispelling my fanciful ideas. Reaching for one of the silver tray lids, he added, "For now, let's just—"

The doors to the hall slammed open with a crashing force, and I damn near spilled my coffee jerking around as a rush of icy air flooded what had actually finally started to warm up. Dressed in only a pair of jeans and barefoot, Maddox strode across to us.

His fierce expression seemed on the edge of barely restrained rage.

"Someone woke up on the wrong side of the bed," I muttered. "Rogue not a good cuddler, DF?"

He drew up short with a hitch in his step. "DF?"

"Dick face," Fin supplied for me in an oh so helpful tone. "I'm Astral-Boy. I think he'd prefer Mad-Dragon, Beautiful. But it's all the same to me."

Maddox glared at me, then at Fin. "Why the fuck did you drag her down here? We're supposed to be together, where we can all protect her."

"Yes, because that long walk from Rogue's bedroom to here is rife with pitfalls as we waded through the swamp of despair to reach the hall of gloom and finally the lava pits of Marwen."

The dry look and tone were perfect. Letting them hash it out, I took another drink of the decadent coffee and hummed happily. On the plate were all the foods I'd asked for. Maddox reached for one of my slices of bacon and then let out a harsh yell when I put a knife right through his hand.

"What the fuck?" He glared from me to where his hand was now impaled on the table, and Fin bit back a smile. A circle of crimson stained the white linen as his wound bled.

"Don't touch my bacon," I said without missing a beat. "I'm starving, and Fin got it for me, not you. I'm sucking you off for that later, by the way," I told Fin. Then focused on Maddox. In truth, I hadn't intended to put the knife all the way through his hand, but the blade had been there and I really was hungry.

Without comment, Maddox yanked the blade out of his hand and nodded curtly.

Wait.

That was it?

Just a nod?

"As I was saying, Beautiful, before we were so rudely interrupted by your Grumpilstiltskin."

I burst out laughing as Maddox favored both of us with a surly look. He really was a grumpilstiltskin. Poor baby. I popped a slice of bacon into my mouth, and the first salty crunch had me moaning all over again.

Gurgling stomach gnawing on my backbone, I scooted forward to snatch up another piece. Fin said something about the food and where he got it, but I barely heard anything. All of my focus lasered onto the food as I took bite after bite. I was torn between eating the bacon or using the muffin to mop up some of the egg yolk. The potatoes were perfectly crispy, and even when my stomach hurt from how much I'd eaten, I didn't slow until I'd cleared the plate and drained the coffee.

I groaned happily as I sprawled back on the bench. The fire, the hot bath, and now a fully tummy.

I could die happy.

"Fuck," Maddox exhaled.

"More or less," Fin murmured in agreement, and I slanted a look at the two boys I'd half-forgotten were there. Oops. "No need to apologize, Beautiful," Fin assured me. "That was practically a religious experience, watching you eat. And it's been a long time since I had one of those."

Maddox gripped his cock and adjusted it until it stretched down against one of his thighs. I trailed my gaze over the thickness appreciatively. Not that I wanted to do much with it at the moment, but he had a very nice piece of equipment. One should always admire these things.

Males liked it.

And so did I.

Fin chuckled. "You know, when I said I couldn't wait to put my real eyes on you because you were a delight, I had no idea how delightful you really are."

"Oh, she's wonderful." Maddox made it sound far more sarcastic, but I settled for flipping him off.

"You don't need to compliment me, Fin. I'm totally making good on my promise as soon as I can move. You deserve it after that feast." My eyes were half-closed, and I wanted to curl up like Maddox's kitten and go to sleep.

"I'm very patient," Fin promised me as he smoothed my hair away from my face. "I brought you some clothes, but I think you're ready to go back to bed."

"I don't want to move," I admitted. The fire felt really good.

Crouching down, Fin tilted my head until I was looking at him. "We can take care of that, but we need you to answer something for us right now."

"Ugh, no twenty questions, just a little nap, and then I'll suck you off so hard, you'll think you came three times."

The corners of his mouth curved. "I'm sure, but one of us needs to drain you, and after last night, I thought it would only be fair to let you decide which of us it would be."

Fuck.

"You were serious about that?"

"'Fraid so," Fin assured me. "It'll be easier on you now. You won't be so hungry, and there's more coffee," he offered, like a temptation. "After you're drained, we'll all feed you again."

I closed my eyes and dragged an arm up to cover them. "Can't it wait? You're totally spoiling my good mood."

"Kitten," Maddox growled. "He should have done it first thing this morning as soon as you were up and moving. We need to flush that demon out of you completely. He doesn't get to have even a piece of you." His grip on my ankle was hot and possessive.

Pretty much described the dragon in a nutshell. I shifted and slid my other foot toward him, and he caught it then lifted them so he could sit with my legs over his lap.

"You both seem so sure they can control me…"

"It happens," Fin told me. "We want to make sure it doesn't."

"You know that's why the prince of the city threw me in there, right?" I flicked a glance from Fin to Maddox and then back. "He tried to compel me, and it worked as well as a pair of Jimmy Choos at a square dance."

Fin frowned. "Not seeing that analogy, but shadow demons are different. And killing your sire is really no trouble at all."

"Definitely," Maddox said, stroking my leg. "He should have every bone in his body broken for abandoning you."

Well, the guy had been running for his life and probably to keep his dick attached. Not that I planned to let him get away with it. Still…

"So if we don't do this thing right away, what's the downside?"

"The shadow demon tries to track you," Fin suggested. "Or call you like he did at the prison."

I narrowed my eyes. A lot of that escape was still somewhat fuzzy, not that I wanted to admit that. "You tried to compel me, or at least muddled me enough to make me cooperative."

"I did," Fin admitted. "We were in something of a time crunch, Beautiful. I will happily let you argue all you want right now."

"I won't," Maddox stated, but he smiled as he continued

his lazy stroking of my leg. It was kind of nice, especially since my feet were all toasty tucked up to him.

"But we want you safe," Fin continued. "Your transition isn't complete."

"Wait…it's not?"

They both shook their heads.

"Baby vamps need a lot of blood in the beginning," Maddox said. "For us? Hybrids? We need even more. It can't just be any blood."

"No," Fin picked up the thread. "It needs to be powerful blood. Your disdain for those blood bags wasn't just personal taste. I guarantee you they probably smelled like the weakass shit they were."

Fin didn't smell weak, neither did Maddox.

Nor had Dorran for that matter.

And the less you think about him, the better. Fin's voice slid right through my mind. No less possessive than Maddox, despite the lighter tone. He was still crouched near me, so I stretched out a hand to run up his thigh. "Fine, Maddox can bite me after I take care of you."

Fair was fair. He had brought me coffee.

"As sinfully delicious as that offer is, Beautiful," Fin murmured before he kissed me. "You first." He loosened the tie of the robe, and I would have complained about the chillier air, but he ran his very warm fingers over my skin. "And I remember," he promised as he began to massage a breast. "You're sore."

I really was, but I had begun to care less and less, especially when Maddox began to kiss his way up my leg, leaving a trail of fire in his wake. Their lust, carefully banked all morning, swirled up to surface. The languid satisfaction sprawling through me gave way to a familiar tug of desire that began to coil in my center.

Fin caught one nipple between his thumb and forefinger,

and began to pinch and twist. Arching up at the contact, I dragged his head down for a kiss. The first sweep of his tongue against mine, and I moaned. All sense of being replete fled, and I just wanted.

The wanton need didn't match my hunger at all. I wasn't hungry. I didn't need to feed on their lust, I just wanted to roll in it. Maddox nudged my thighs apart, and his breath was hot as he traced his tongue along the seam of my labia.

Fuck. The hot flat edge of his tongue seemed to wrap around my clit once before sweeping downward, and I was instantly soaked. The soreness evaporated as my pussy clenched at emptiness. His growling moan vibrated right to my core, and I tried to push my hips up even as I fought to wrap my legs around him.

Asshole kept my legs spread and my hips pinned as he begun to fuck me with his tongue. Fin swallowed every sound escaping my throat as he nearly matched Maddox's pace with his tongue flicking against mine. Dragging my hands down his sides, I found the snap to his jeans and pulled it open, then tugged the zipper down.

Fin cursed against my mouth as I got my hand around him, and I nearly screamed as Maddox moved back to my clit and began to suck against it. I thought he was supposed to be draining me, not fucking me.

Not that I was complaining. The heat of his mouth was next level out of this world, and he had my thighs over his shoulders as he feasted on me. Every hard pull of his mouth ratcheted the tension higher, and I ripped away from Fin's kiss. He threw his head back, panting as I stroked him from tip to base and then back up. His cock was long, full, and the vein along the bottom throbbed.

The musk of his desire clung to my nostrils, and I twisted, angling away from Maddox, even as he added his fingers to the fucking and teased his thumb against my ass. Hips rolling, I met him thrust for thrust. Fin pressed a thumb against my lips, and I sucked on it.

He groaned again, then replaced it with his cock, the first brush of it against my lips had me sampling the drops of pre-cum. I opened wider, and he pushed past my lips, and I moaned. Maddox let out a hard breath and pulled his fingers out. His clothes rustled as they vanished, and he dragged me downward. We all moved, Fin staying with me as he gripped my hair and began to thrust into my mouth.

The heavy weight of him on my tongue and the dribbles of pre-cum were doing all kinds of things to my system. It was like a heavy ambrosia, and I just wanted more. Then Maddox was between my thighs again, a hand stroking down my abdomen.

"Is this all right, Kitten?" The roughness of his voice had me soaking more. Raw, hot, and needy. What the fuck were these vampires doing to me?

Another pinch of my nipple, the one Fin wasn't caressing, and Maddox's hot cock was right up at my entrance. What the fuck was he waiting for?

Oh… Fin's cock bumped against the back of my throat, and I swallowed against it, pulling him deeper as I dug my fingers into his thighs.

Maddox was waiting for me.

I wiggled and pushed down on Maddox's thick cock myself. The head was fatter and took more effort, but at the first breach, he thrust home and an orgasm rattled through me. Then they were both groaning.

All three of us really.

They fucked me back and forth between them. Fin's hand tightened in my hair as he began to thrust. Maddox's grip on my hip was equally bruising as he slammed into me and his balls slapped against my ass. I flexed and squeezed around him as he pulled orgasm after orgasm with his clever fingers against my clit.

He came first, his shout ricocheting off the ceiling as he pushed in, and then the hot jets of him filling me sent another moaning orgasm through my system. Fin came second, and I choked as I swallowed as much as I could as the aftershocks kept rattling through me. Maddox swelled inside of me as he came, and I swore my eyes rolled back in my head.

Fin barely pulled out when the first graze of Maddox's teeth stroked the curve of my breast, and then he struck. The first pierce a sting, a hot tear before riots of pleasure exploded through my system. Still impaled on his cock, the thickness leaving me so full I could barely breath, he began to suck.

It was like he pulled me out with every sensuous jerk of his mouth. The soft gulps echoed through me, and I swore I tightened up on him or he swelled more. The world faded as he kept drinking, and I found myself anticipating each swallow. When he slid his fingers down to caress my clit, I detonated again, and the world faded entirely.

I must have blacked out because I woke to my mouth latched onto Fin as I drank, and he was trying to ease me away, and Rogue was there.

I had no idea when he showed up, but the shallow gash on his throat pulled me like a siren song, and I closed my mouth over his icy hot blood and drank like a woman dying of thirst. Maddox's cock wasn't buried in me anymore, and I floated on a sea of sex and pheromones and holy fuck bacon and coffee.

What a day.

Fin's soft chuckle wrapped around me like a caress, and vaguely, it occurred to me it was his hand stroking my back.

Rogue had slid his hand down between my thighs, and greedy bitch that I was, I had no problem when he started finger fucking me. I might have made a mess of him, but I pumped my hips in time to the thrust of his fingers as I drank.

Pleasure washed over me, and the next time I roused, I was straddling Maddox's lap, my mouth against his throat as he rocked me while I fed. Nobody was in me, which was nice, just hands petting me.

I floated there.

A girl could get used to this.

"You'll have to drain her next," Rogue said.

"I know," Fin murmured. "She's struggling still."

"We'll get her through it," Maddox rumbled, and his voice vibrated right through me. Fuck I wanted to ride him again, and there was a chuckle as he gathered my hair. "She's already getting stronger."

When I began to writhe against him, a hand smoothed over my ass, and then he lifted me up. The cock thrusting into me wasn't his, but I could feel his tip brushing against my clit. Oh fuck, I wanted to see this, but my eyes were already closing as the cock pistoning into me settled me like a lullaby.

Lust and blood.

Life's nectar.

The next time I woke, I was back in the hot steamy bath, sprawled against Maddox's chest as the hot water soothed my aching muscles.

If I thought I'd pulled my pussy the day before? Well, I think they'd totally wrecked it today.

"You'll heal," Fin said with a near blissful smile on his face. He sat opposite us, and I reached a hand up to pet Maddox's cheek. He kissed my fingertips.

"I don't mind," I confessed. "Totally worth it."

"Not hating being a vampire so much now?" Maddox teased.

"Undecided, but the fucking is extraordinary." It was a compliment, they should accept it. Particularly because I'd wanted, and I hadn't been remotely hungry. Sex filled a biological imperative for me, it was a currency I exchanged for feeding on lust. Getting drunk on their lust could be addicting.

Wanting them without needing to feed?

That was dangerous. I tucked that errant thought away before it could escape.

"Where's Rogue?" I hadn't imagined that, he was here earlier, right? I swore I could taste him on my tongue still. I could taste all of them, individually distinctive and heady.

"He's doing some things," Fin said with an airy wave. "Just rest, Beautiful. After you've napped, you can look at the things I bought you."

Oh, clothes. Right.

"Hmm. We're spending a lot of time in the bath."

"Complaining?" Maddox asked as he nipped my ear. I could barely work up the energy to swat him.

"Nope. Just this frigid mausoleum has to have more than two interesting rooms." Granted, I really hadn't done much more in that bedroom than get gloriously laid and sleep. Could say the same thing about the bathing room for that matter.

"We've got to open it back up," Maddox rumbled. "It will take some time. Just indulge us for now. I promise, we won't let you get bored." He stroked his hand over my belly and up to cup a breast.

No, boredom would not be an issue. Desire stirred, even as he began to toy with my nipple. Seriously, what the hell? I covered his hand with mine and tugged it away.

"Sore, Kitten?" Laughter underscored his concern, and he

shifted his hands to resting on my thighs. The swirls of hot water were definitely helping, still…

"Yes," I said. While true, it wasn't totally true. I could quite happily straddle another one of their cocks. The fact I wanted to bugged the ever-loving shit out of me though. Fin studied me from half-closed eyes, but he didn't call me on my comment. So either I wasn't projecting, or he was letting me get away with my white lie.

The brush of Maddox's cock against my ass sent another curl of desire to stir through me, and I pushed off his lap. I half-expected him to drag me back, but he didn't. Instead, he draped his arms against the side as I moved to another seat.

They were both relaxed, comfortable with the fact they'd drained me for a second time and I'd fed off all three of them. More than comfortable, I was almost looking forward to Fin having his turn to feed on me.

And enough of that. I rose and climbed out of the water, ignoring the sting of cooler air against my thoroughly ravaged pussy. And yes, out of the water, it made sure to let me know it had been well-used and stretched.

The tingle of desire grew as I padded, dripping, over to the fire and reclaimed the heavy robe. Dragging it on, I stared at the flames. Getting comfortable here would be a mistake.

The table was still there, the food definitely absent, but a thermos sat in the middle, and when I popped it open, the scent of still hot coffee filled my nostrils. Oh, good.

I needed to wash the taste of them out. Playing along and letting them get relaxed while I worked out my next step made the most logical sense. They were powerful allies, but they showed every sign that they wanted to *keep* me, and I was no one's pet or prize.

Despite Fin's claims when he visited in my cell and Maddox's insistence on calling me Kitten, I refused to be *owned*. Even if the nickname had begun to grow on me. I'd known them what? Three days? Maybe four? I'd lost all track of time, first in the prison and now here. After taking a swallow of coffee, I looked up and around. There were no windows in this room.

That made sense, it was below ground.

Was it even still daytime out there?

How long had I actually been fucking them and getting fed on before they fed me?

Would the sun still be up?

"Beautiful," Fin said quietly. "What's going on in that head of yours?"

Not glancing over my shoulder, I focused on the fire. "Can't you tell?"

"At the moment?" Something different shifted in his voice. "No. But you're concentrating very hard."

Good. As fun as he was, I didn't want to fall for that charm. There was no place for it in my world. Once I got this sorted out, I had to go.

Long-term things just weren't my jam. A weird little seesaw tug pulled in my belly at the thought of leaving.

"I was just wondering if I could go see the sun…I haven't seen it in weeks."

Then I held my breath, not sure what I wanted the answer to be, but that disquieting sensation over leaving them? Yeah, that could fuck right off.

They weren't mine, and I wasn't theirs.

"Deadly is the tongue that only curls and doesn't stab." - Unknown

Rogue

Pulling open the heavy iron doors, Rogue let himself inside before sealing the entrance behind him. Fin and Maddox had the female in the bathing room. It was warmest there for now. He often forgot about the temperatures here, so after he'd let her feed on him and he'd satisfied her demanding need to fuck her—and his own need to do it for that matter—he'd left her in their hands while he took care of getting the keep more habitable.

Fin would bring in furnishings and had already summoned several pieces from his place on the isles. It was enough to add to the bedroom. They were using his for now, but he would pull the other pieces from storage, including their own beds. No need to sleep in a pile once they smoothed her transition through.

The faint taint of shadow demon lingered on her. The

beast had pounded himself into her cells. Hybrids scared most of the vampire lines. They traced their lineages by how close they were to the seven, the original seven. The closer the links to the seven sires who made all vampires, the more important they considered themselves.

Pompous jackasses, the lot of them.

Hybrids were myths as far as most of them were concerned. Rogue, Fin, Maddox, and Alfred had long since faded from the public. They kept to themselves, and those that decided to hunt myths were usually never seen again. Descending the long flight into the hold buried within the mountain, Rogue didn't need torches to light his way.

This whole cavern boasted hints of ice along the rocks lining the way. Mid-winter, the temperatures were sub-zero. Maddox hated it down here, but Fin didn't mind it so much, though neither ventured too deep anymore.

It had been more than a hundred years since Alfred went to sleep again after only being awake a year. The oldest of them all, he had grown weary of the world, the politics among the councils, and the foolishness of young vampires wanting to cut their teeth on other species.

Old pacts and alliances lay in half-forgotten tatters as younger generations jockeyed for position. Rogue could care less, but it was those same politics that landed the turned succubus in Nightmare Penitentiary and right into the hands of a shadow demon.

At the end of the long cavern, he ran his fingers around the edging of the door, removing the ice locking it closed before he pumped the handle and pulled the door open. Inside the shadowed chamber, he paused.

Nothing moved. The heart beating inside beat sluggishly. One beat for every few minutes. Legend said vampires slept in coffins. Stories to delight and horrify the masses. While they didn't actually sleep in a coffin, those who went to ground often buried themselves far away from civilization, to avoid the sights, the sounds, and the distractions that might wake them early.

Deep in the hold beneath the keep, they were as far from others as they could get. If Rogue tilted his head and focused, he could catch the three beating hearts above. Fiona's beat far faster than Maddox's or Fin's. It had been racing when he sank into her earlier while she fed on Maddox. Rogue's own body had thrummed with renewed vigor since draining her. The shadow taint wouldn't survive within him, just as it wouldn't in the others.

They were old enough in his case, magical enough in Fin's, and just pure stubborn in Maddox's, that it couldn't warp them as it would and had been in her. So far, she'd impressed Rogue with her willfulness and independence. He supposed she'd needed those traits to survive, as her kind were often dismissed as hedonists. It might make fitting her into their lives a challenge.

Fin put too much stock in old prophecies and tales told over many cups of ale. She might not even survive her transition in the long-run.

The reason hybrids were so rare was they often died, a victim to their own dual natures tearing each other apart.

Quieting his mind, he pulled from that darkened pathway and focused on the draped chamber ahead of him where Alfred slept.

"Fin believes she's here," he told him.

There was no response, not that he expected one. The heart pulsed once, then went quiet again.

"I am only telling you because she was in Nightmare," Rogue said quietly, aware his words would echo back to Alfred when he woke. "She may not survive her transition. We may not have gotten to her in time. If they come for her, we will lead them away. If we must flee the keep, they will never get in here, but you will find us in Fin's lands."

The chances they couldn't hold the keep were slim. They would likely have a much harder time holding on to her. Maddox and Fin might be lost in their lust for the red-haired, red-eyed vixen, but Rogue understood the need to assert authority flaring within her.

She would run.

Everyone ran.

Maddox had, though he may not remember it anymore.

As had Fin.

They'd actively sought to become hybrids.

Well, Maddox had. His had been a conscious choice. Fin's had been a matter of his survival.

Still—they all ran.

"We'll protect her," he said finally. "Rest well, brother."

With those words, he turned and left the room, sealing it behind him before he began the long walk back to the stairs and up.

He closed off the iron doors again, then returned to the baths. She'd been out again when he'd left them. Her words reached him just as he got to the doors.

"I was just wondering if I could go see the sun…I haven't seen it in weeks."

The sun didn't affect all vampires. The naturally born had some immunity, but the turned? They all tolerated to varying levels. It was the longing in her voice that tugged at Rogue. She'd fed on all three of them for a second and in some cases a third time. The blood in her was older now, hurrying the transition along.

Did the sun bother succubi in general? Unfortunately, he knew little about the species.

"Maybe not yet," Fin answered into the silence. "It's better if we take the next steps slowly."

"There are places we can go that you can see it," Maddox added, though neither sounded certain.

Rogue scowled at her slow sigh. Disappointment curved through the sound. They weren't giving her definitive answers. Fin had definitely hedged his in uncertainty while Maddox immediately sought a way to soothe her. She required neither coddling nor lies.

Fin didn't know the answer nor did Maddox. The only way to know was to go into the sun and find out what it did. Hauling the door open, Rogue strode inside. The hot humid air billowing in the room wrapped around him. While he preferred it cooler, the heat was also tolerable.

Fiona stood near one of the large hearths, backlit by the flames. Though damp, her rich, red hair seemed to glow as it curled at the ends. A large dressing gown dwarfed her figure, and even though she was backlit, there was no mistaking her crimson eyes for anything other than her transitioning state. They were brighter though.

That was at least a positive.

"Come with me, little *sváss*," he ordered.

"Woah," Fin said as he stood. "Rogue..."

Maddox was already sloshing out of the pool. If Rogue possessed more patience, he would have rolled his eyes. As it was, he met the rebellion in Fiona's gaze head on. "Unless you want to wait for them to decide what you can or can't do."

Predictable. She pursed her lips, shot a glance toward the others, then to him. Weighing. Measuring. Who was the greater threat?

Who could she get what she wanted out of?

Did she even know what she wanted?

Fiona took a step toward him as Maddox cleared the edge of the pool. Uncaring of their nudity, they were across the room to catch her, but not before Rogue swept her up and then he raced her away.

Their curses followed him.

He really didn't want to have the argument with them. As it was, the armful of soft curves cuddled up to them had already brought them more than her weight in trouble. The keep's layout was oblong, tucked against a mountainside and preeminently defensible. A barrier wall and proud gates along with natural obstacles made them difficult to approach overland.

Most of their enemies who would seek them out were not human, however, and those defenses were mostly for show.

The true defenses were soaked into the stones and grown in the cracks between when they'd built the fortress. Magic, power, and blood inlaid all of the spellwork. From the most complicated and delicate to the most basic and plain spells for discouragement, the keep warded them against those who didn't belong with a giant *fuck off* essentially that turned away all but the most determined.

Hence the message he'd left for Alfred. Fiona had already begun to corrupt his brothers, even as she aroused Rogue in a manner he'd *never* experienced before. Already, the craving for her had begun to wind its insidious grip through him. He could still resist the influence.

Maddox and Fin hadn't even tried.

Still, the keep also had two courtyards. The outer near the main walls and the inner, where Alfred had once cultivated a garden. It was to that one he took Fiona. When the keep was closed up, most of the exterior windows were sealed and shuttered. Eventually, they might concede to install the generator Fin wanted to add, but for now, torches and candles more than sufficed his need for any light.

Fiona scowled at him when he stopped before the garden doors.

"Fuck that's cold," she complained, and he glanced down to see her bare feet against the stone.

If the stone was cold, the garden would likely be even worse. It was still late winter in the mountains. Frigid, even when the sun was high.

With one hand braced to keep the doors closed, he reached down and removed one of his boots, then the other, and set them in front of her.

Carelessly pushing a lock of her hair behind an ear, Fiona glanced from him to the boots, then back. Rogue said nothing, he only waited.

It was her move.

Touching her tongue to her teeth, she put a hand on the door for balance, then picked up one far too delicate foot and shoved it into one boot. It dwarfed her, so she would be hard pressed to move in those.

Might make running a little more challenging for her.

Intrigued, he waited until she had the second boot on and shuffled a step. A snorting laugh escaped her. "You know what they say about men with big feet."

"No," he said plainly. "I don't. What do they say?"

Amusement flickered across her face as she tilted her head up. Intrigued, Rogue studied her, uncertain of what her next words might be.

"They have huge shoes," she murmured, almost daring him to dispute her.

"That's not what they say." But he wasn't going to ask her to tell him. She had to learn to trust one way or the other. For now, he gripped the handle of the door and yanked it open. Cold air rushed in, and he straightened at the rush of fresh coolness. Fiona tucked the robe tighter against her naked body and shuddered.

The sudden wash of wintry sunlight blinded him momentarily. The light itself didn't quite reach inside the door, though the radiance brightened the gloom so intensely, he almost found himself reconsidering the generator idea of Fin's. Maybe more light would make Fiona more comfortable. While she would run, perhaps they could delay it.

She started forward a step, and he gripped the doorframe, blocking her. "Be aware," he told her. "It may burn."

Suspicion roused in her narrow-eyed gaze. "May?"

"May."

"That's very non-specific."

"As are we all," he reminded her.

"Oh, so you're a hybrid, too?" A smirk flirted with her mouth. "Vampire and what?"

"Older." It wasn't the answer she wanted, and the perfect symmetry of her face coupled with the husky laughter as she shook her head teased him. There was just a hint of green circling her red irises. They had likely been the color of a forest in full spring. Green, rich, and verdant… The sound of his brothers approaching reached him. If he wanted to test the baby vamp's survival skills, now was the time to do it before her erstwhile and self-appointed protectors arrived.

Removing his hand, he straightened and then motioned for her to precede him. He was fast enough to snatch her back inside if she began to burn. Unlike the ridiculous films Fin took him to see, they did not fall to ash in seconds. Burning someone alive took considerably more effort.

Most of them could survive it, even if it wasn't pleasant. And only someone suicidal or an idiot stayed where they were on fire without trying to put it out.

Instead of rushing through the open door, she hesitated.

Smart.

His admiration climbed a notch.

"What's the catch?"

Leaning against the open door, he folded his arms. "You wanted to know if you could see the sun. There it is."

"But it may hurt."

Another nod.

"You don't know if it will burn me or not."

He shook his head.

"You're very not hyper-verbal."

"I say what I need to say. Your lips are going to turn blue, are you going out or not?"

The shivers had been subtle at first, but she fisted her hands and folded her arms, hiding them. The cold air pouring in was not doing her any favors. She'd end up back in the bathing room until they chased away the chill.

"Wait," Fin called.

"Too late," Rogue murmured. "Your keepers are here." It was an unkind jab, but instead of rushing out to flout the possessiveness of his assessment and acting predictably, she glanced from him to where Fin and Maddox had slowed only a few steps away. The pair had taken the time to find clothing, though Maddox skipped any boots and Fin had found his coat.

"Kitten," Maddox said, almost placating. "We weren't trying to hide anything from you. But everyone reacts to sunlight differently. It may do nothing. It might burn. It might just be uncomfortable."

"But we don't know," Fin picked up the thread. "Throwing you out there without any idea is dangerous. You're still in transition, and some people should remember how precarious that is."

"I oversaw both of yours," Rogue told him without taking his gaze off of Fiona. "I think I'm well aware." They might want to patronize her, but they wouldn't with him.

"We know," Maddox growled. "You have to stop just taking her without waiting for us."

"Or what?" Genuinely curious, he slanted a look toward

him. Would Maddox truly challenge him over Fiona? That could almost be interesting.

"Stop running your heads together like bulls vying for her attention," Fin stated dryly. "This isn't about *us*." *And really, Rogue? You're baiting Maddox right now?*

Rogue didn't have to bait the dragon. The dragon had already begun to stake its claim, and it would fight for its territory whether the man or the vampire realized it yet.

Trouble.

She might not fit with them the way they so clearly wanted her to, and no matter how much she intrigued him, Rogue couldn't allow her to tear his brothers apart.

Still, she looked from them to the open door then back.

"Please, Kitten? If you get burned too badly…"

"I get burned," she said with an almost careless shrug. "The fact that I'm half-vampire or whatever it is I'm becoming is not set in stone."

No. She might yet die for real, and there would be nothing they could do to stop it. Her body either made the transition or it didn't. The fact that she'd survived this long was a positive sign, but caution was the better choice.

"Also, I want real clothes." She swept a hand down at herself. "I look like a reject from a redneck survivor convention."

Rogue had no idea what that was, but the disgust in her tone suggested it wasn't a good thing.

"You don't have to wear the boots," he offered, and she rolled her eyes. Then stepped outside. Rogue barely got his arm up in time to stop Maddox from snatching her back, but Fin vanished from inside to appear ahead of her near the thornier vines, cold and dark with winter's frost.

The lack of smoking was a good sign. Pushing Maddox back a step, Rogue slipped through the door to follow her. The snow on the ground crunched beneath his bare feet. She held up her hand toward the sun, though the light of it already highlighted the glorious streaks of red in her hair. It wasn't just one shade, but multiple hues of red.

If the garden's roses were in bloom, she'd stand out amongst them as even more startling in color.

A sigh escaped her, and she tilted her head back, face up and eyes closed. Maddox came to an abrupt stop, and a muscle began to tick in Fin's jaw. Rapture was the closest Rogue could come to describing her expression as the sun shone against her faintly golden-toned skin. Out in the light, he could see where she'd enjoyed sun the before, though her color had faded dramatically.

Dying and being hidden away in a prison would do that to a person. Still, she looked almost—happy.

More, her heart, which had been racing, began to slow as she took deeper and deeper breaths.

"It's so fucking cold, but I don't want to go back inside."

Maddox brushed past him and slid right up behind her. Wrapping his arms around her, he settled his chin against her head. She seemed to melt into him, and Rogue didn't comment on the curl of irritation working its way through his gut.

The dragon shed heat easily, and the faint blue around her lips receded to pink and plump again as she ran her tongue over it. "Okay, that's really nice."

"Glad I'm still around then, Kitten?" At his tease, she opened her eyes enough to roll them, and Fin snickered.

"She's happy to have all of us around, she just hasn't decided on it yet." Confidence had never been Fin's weakness. Though overconfidence could be a flaw.

Rogue said nothing, though she flicked a look at him.

She didn't burn.

That was good.

They stood there for another ten minutes, saying nothing as she soaked in the sunlight.

"The library," Rogue said abruptly. The sun hurt none of them, so they could open the shutters on that room. Like the bathing room, the library also boasted two large hearths. It could be warmed appropriately, and the windows on both sides allowed the most sunlight all day.

"I'll take care of it." Fin brushed his knuckles down her cheek. "Don't linger out here too long, Beautiful. You still have clothes to try on."

"Did you really bring me clothes?" she asked, looking at him almost sleepily.

"I did."

"Real clothes, or dress me up like a doll clothes?"

The smirk he wore was real, and Rogue rolled his eyes this time. She wasn't wrong. Fin had likely gotten her something easy to remove or very little at all. It wasn't like they wouldn't be fucking her regularly, so why block access? The fact that Rogue was already wondering how long it would be until she needed one of them inside of her again and calculating how often had nothing to do with it.

"You'll see," he said with an unrepentant grin. A bird's cry yanked Fin's attention upward and Maddox's. A murder of crows descended on the inner garden, some of them alighting on the thorny vines while others took to the walls, and still a pair circled around she and Maddox lazily.

None of them moved as the crows drifted closer, then away. Those flying landed and sent others up into the air.

"Take her inside," Rogue said, watching the crows.

"They're birds," she argued. "And we just got out here."

He was very well aware of what they were.

As Maddox started to usher her toward the door, a pair of the crows broke off and cut between them and Rogue, then circled back.

Alfred?

Rogue shook his head. It wasn't unusual for him to summon birds to be his eyes. But he hadn't roused when Rogue had gone downstairs. Others used crows and ravens, too.

"Inside, little *sváss*. You will see the sun again."

Her mutinous expression gave way as she started forward. He didn't assume that meant she trusted him, though when one of the crows dove at her hair, Maddox snapped a hand out and knocked the bird away. They wouldn't kill them, because it wasn't their fault someone used their eyes, but they also wouldn't let them touch her.

Rogue blocked the next one as Maddox got her inside, and then Rogue pulled the door closed, leaving he and Fin to face them.

The crows rose up as one cloud of black. There had to be a dozen, if not more. Then they circled overhead and through the garden once more before ascending to disappear.

"Just letting them go?" Fin asked, tracking their progress with his hands raised and likely a spell or three at the ready.

"We don't know who they are being used by. So for now, we keep her inside, and you should check the wards."

"They aren't meant to keep out animals."

"Let's change that for now." It may already be too late. "After you get the library open, prepare the house on the isle."

"You want to take her to Oileán na Carraige?" His tone didn't convey approval.

"No, but we need a fall back point."

Fin frowned. "You think they are coming for her." It wasn't a question.

"You've had her, would you let someone take her from you?" They'd ripped her from the shadow demon, and soon, very soon, they would have driven him out of her fully.

Expression growing cold and dangerous, Fin said, "No."

"Then expect they won't either. Defend against what you would do, and know that your enemies might do worse."

"She's ours, Rogue."

"That," he reminded his brother. "That remains to be seen. She has to survive first."

"You don't think I know that?"

Still scanning the skies, Rogue shrugged. "I think you and Maddox have decided she is the one, and if she doesn't survive, you may end up joining Alfred in sleep."

When his brother didn't deny it, Rogue nodded once.

"That is why I remain skeptical. One of us has to."

A shudder rippled through the air as though someone tossed a stone into a placid pool and disturbed it.

"That was…"

Rogue was already moving, pausing only long enough to secure the doors before he raced to the hold below the keep. The doors were still sealed, but even as he listened, the heartbeat below had increased its pace.

Do you still want me to go to the isle?

Fin stood a half-dozen steps away.

Rogue nodded. *It will take him time to awake fully.*

I'll hurry.

Then Fin was gone, and Rogue touched the doors. "Easy, brother," he said. "No one has taken her yet."

Still, the crows and now this?

They needed to know before Alfred woke fully.

With Fin preoccupied, Rogue made his way to the library and found Fiona standing in the center of it where two beams of sunlight crossed. Maddox already had most of the windows open and fires going in the hearths. She was still dressed in the oversized robes and Rogue's boots.

The expression of pleasure she still wore flashed through him. The dust was heavy in the room, and it would take some time to clean it up, but she didn't seem to notice them as she soaked in the light.

Fiona belonged in the light.

For her sake, he was glad she could tolerate the sun.

It would help settle her…they could hope anyway.

Though it also meant one less barrier to prevent her escape.

Well, they would just have to give her reasons to stay that outweighed the primal desire to flee.

Or chain her up.

What a sight she'd make for them.

The image threatened to stagger him, and Rogue scowled.

The last thing they needed was for him to fall prey to her, too.

One of them needed to keep his head.

CHAPTER 12

"A cage made of gold and silk is still a cage." - Unknown

The next few hours passed in relative peace. Fin left and returned with food. Maddox and Rogue opened the library, and I didn't want to leave the windows, even after the light waned from the setting sun. Torches and candles illuminated the room. They really were trapped in some other century.

I'd kill for a big screen television and a marathon of *Property Brothers*. Or maybe *Fixer Upper*. Anything. Even focusing on my house on the cliffs seemed too distant to achieve. While I consumed the saffron rice and curried chicken Fin had returned with, he'd gone down to fetch the bags of clothes he'd bought me.

The first two outfits barely qualified as clothes, unless I planned to be the main attraction as a stripper in Vegas, right down to the floss and feathers. The fact that Rogue rolled his eyes at the second outfit made me actually consider it for thirty seconds.

The third and fourth were moderately better, but both were dresses. Cute.

Not my thing.

I preferred clothes I could move in and wouldn't likely tangle around my legs. Also, call me quirky, but I also liked dressing myself. The whole 'guys put a woman in what they want to see her in' thing just squicked me out. I wasn't a possession or a prize. I dressed for exactly one person.

Me.

"No," I said again and again in between bites as he held them up. The way he deflated with each rejection almost made me feel bad for him. Almost. If we weren't in a dusty library that smelled of old books, woodsmoke, and age, I might have. But we were, and they had zero intention of letting me leave.

The minute I said something about going to pick out my own stuff, Fin told me to give him a list and he'd get it exact.

The fact that all three had been right on me when I went out into the sun earlier suggested I'd merely upgraded one prison for another. Color me not shocked.

Down to the last outfit, I studied it musingly. Not bad. Tight leather pants, a black camisole top, and a leather jacket to throw over the top.

"Sold," I told him. "For now, I'll wear that."

He looked so earnestly crestfallen that Maddox chuckled. "You've disappointed him. He truly thought you'd like the peasant dresses he bought."

"You mean the itty bitty 'look at my ass' dresses that would work for a striptease if I didn't want to have to take anything off?"

Rogue smirked and Fin scowled. "They weren't that bad."

"No," Rogue said blandly, lifting a mug of ale he'd been

drinking slowly while I ate my weight in curry. The food was amazing, the flavors intense and sharp on my tongue. "They were much worse. She's not a prostitute."

Maddox and Fin both wheeled on him, and I hid my own smile. "No," Maddox snarled. "She isn't, and those clothes didn't suggest otherwise. A lot of women wear them these days."

With a shrug, Rogue said, "She's not a lot of women, and clearly she doesn't think much of the outfits."

Fin opened his mouth to argue, then seemed to think better of it. Finally, he glanced at me.

"If you don't want me going to stores, do you get the internet in this backwater of time and space, or is that still a few centuries off?"

The corners of Fin's lips twitched. "Make me a list. I have your sizes." Or he could just go get my own things. "I would," he continued. "Get your own things, that is, but they were collected when you were sent to Nightmare Penitentiary. I have no idea where they are."

With the way my luck had been going? Probably burned.

Food finished, I rose and slid my feet out of Rogue's boots. The fact that I'd worn the ginormous things even after we'd retreated inside meant nothing. It was a bit like having clown feet. If clowns had sexy, large feet that matched their rather well-endowed physics. Hard to miss the latter anyway. The minute I started moving, I had their attention.

"Before I get dressed, is there going to be draining going on tonight?" I put a hand on my hip because I really wanted real clothes on, but I wasn't an idiot. If they started on me, I was gonna end up riding all of them again.

Hey, if you couldn't be honest with yourself, who could you be honest with? As it was, Fin studied me.

"It is my turn," he said softly.

"And you need it," Maddox added, but the flash of heat in his suddenly slitted eyes had nothing to do with me feeding.

For some reason, I expected both answers from them. Yes, they wanted to help. They'd made that *abundantly* clear. But they were both rather fond of my body, and they'd made no pretense of wanting their hands on me.

Not complaining. Just an observation.

The one still keeping his distance, at least at the moment, however, was the one I focused on.

"You need to rest. Tomorrow is soon enough."

You could almost taste the surprise in the room, and I nodded. Worked for me. Crossing over to the clothes Fin had stacked on another table, I dropped the robe without a second thought. The bite on my neck was still puffy and more than a little sore. The one on my breast had gone the same way as had the one on my thigh. Wherever they drained me from, it would seem, had grown inflamed in some way. The fact that Rogue had done it twice was also not lost on me.

The dead silence as I flipped through the clothes for underthings had me glancing over my shoulder. All three gazes were pinned on me. "Oh please. All three of you have gone down on me, and I know at least two of you were under me when another of you was in me. This is not a new sight."

I stepped into the panties and tugged them up. They were pure lace and blood red.

Subtle.

I didn't care, since leather pants over a bare pussy was gonna pinch and sweat. I'd pass. The lack of bra also didn't faze me. I didn't like the damn things anyway. I tugged the black camisole on, but when I reached for the leather pants, Fin pressed up behind me.

"Are you planning to sleep in them?" The question whispered against my ear sent a shudder skating over my skin. It didn't help that he'd slid an arm around me and rested his hand on the thin sliver of flesh between the edge of the camisole and my panties. "It's getting late, and you still need to rest."

The invitation rolled through me like spring storm. Leaning my head back against his shoulder, I cut my gaze upward to find him smiling at me. Maddox was rugged, tough, and now that I knew about his dragon, I could see it in how he moved and spoke. He was a creature used to control.

Rogue? I still had no idea what he was, but powerful didn't begin to describe. The elements didn't touch him. He'd walked out into the snow in the garden without flinching. He moved faster than I could perceive. His demeanor? Quiet, reserved, and far from the argumentative and playful natures of Maddox and Fin respectively. The tattoos scrawled over Rogue's biceps and shoulders meant something, but I didn't know what.

But Fin was just adorable. Sexy. Beautiful. It hadn't taken me long to figure out his gifts. Druid. There was something just utterly compelling about him.

Thank you.

"Bite me," I teased, and elbowed him. He brushed his nose against my cheek as he slid his hand along my torso.

"Do not bite her," Rogue ordered abruptly, and Fin made a little huffing noise.

"He's a killjoy."

"You know, I already figured that out for myself."

Maddox chuckled as I untangled myself from Fin's grip. He gave me a hint of a pout as I faced him. The fires burning on either end of the library had turned the room toasty. Still dusty, but definitely warmer. Or the fact that Maddox was a little bonfire all by himself helped, too.

The fact that desire had already begun to curl in my

stomach irked me. I wasn't *hungry* at all. In fact, I was full and replete. Oddly, the blissed out sensation from the prison was missing though. I was *comfortable*. Not that I probably couldn't snuggle up in one of their laps or even on a chair by myself and doze. Be better with one of them.

Shaking my head, I wrinkled my nose when Fin beckoned with a curl of his fingers as he dropped into one of the armchairs. The little poof of dust that went up when he did that though utterly ruined the effect.

Laughing, I shook my head. "I think I'll pass. Or we'll end up back in the bath."

"You say that like it's a bad thing," Fin teased, his grin growing. He twirled his fingers, and a little dust storm rose up around him as it collected the fluttering particles in a swirl of air and then whooshed over to the fire. "See? All better." He patted his lap.

"Subtle," Maddox growled as he prowled forward and dragged a bench over to me. Snagging my abandoned—well, Fin's anyway—robe, he held it up. "You want this Kitten or shall I keep you warm?"

Tempting.

Fuck.

Too tempting. The pair of them.

Not throwing his hat into the ring, however, was Rogue. He merely refilled his mug with more ale and poured a second one that he nudged toward me. "We should talk."

Fin groaned, and Maddox scowled.

Biting back another smile, I set the leather pants down. Apparently, they were fine with panties and a top, but I snagged the robe anyway because unlike these three beasts, the cold did bother me. Dragging it on, I didn't bother with tying it. Ale claimed, I settled on the top of the table where I'd eaten—alone, thank you very much—and crossed my legs.

"Talking would be good."

No, my body didn't want to talk. It protested with the same pout reflected on Fin's too pretty face and with the same force in Maddox's scowl.

Lifting the ale, I had a hard time containing another laugh. They did not like it when they didn't get their own way.

Awareness crept over me as I took a swallow. The sensation of being watched, but the guys weren't looking at me so much as exchanging long silent glances with each other. Well, probably not so silent. Fin could do his little mental hoowah and let them have a private conversation.

Downing another mouthful of the ale, I considered the drink. It was darker in shade, a rich copper without the metallic taste of blood. Toasty and almost nutty, there were hints of malt with a touch of caramel and nuances of fig. As I ran the ale over my tongue and sampled it, the different flavors grew more distinctive.

Like the saffron rice and curry earlier, the different textures and tastes fascinated me. Another deep mouthful, and I swirled it around my tongue. There was definitely raisin in it.

"Fiona!" Rogue's voice jerked me back to the present.

"I'm right here," I told him almost languidly. "You don't have to snap." Despite the harsh crack in his tone, it hadn't really bothered me. I'd rather just poke holes in his reserve. That man had let loose with me and then acted like it didn't affect him at all.

Game on.

"Were you paying attention to the discussion about hybrids last night?"

"Hmm…I don't know, was that before or after you fucked me again? Or was that this morning? It's all sort of running together."

Maddox rumbled, but when I raised my eyebrows at him, he shook his head quickly. What? A warning?

Be careful, Beautiful. Rogue is not Maddox or me. He doesn't play like that.

I snorted, then took another swallow of the ale. All of them played like that. Or had Fin already forgotten the fact that Rogue had gotten me off before they even made it back from the prison?

"Hybrids," Rogue said, as though my comment hadn't registered, "transition differently."

"Right, I have to feed enough to finish it, but we have to flush the shadow demon out of me." I shrugged. "You've all said, hence the draining and me feeding on all three of you."

"There will be four soon," Fin added, the earlier teasing vacating his voice. "When he's awake, we have to have you ready."

"Wait—there are four of you assholes?" I motioned to the three of them.

"Yes, Kitten. There are four of us. Alfred's been asleep for a long time. He hasn't fed in a long time. When he wakes, you'll likely feel his teeth first. He'll need to drain you."

"Well, whoopee. Glad I'm turning into a glorified blood bag slash sex doll for you folks. Let me guess, I'll need to warm his cock up for him, too? Get all the kink out."

Fin winced, then tugged at his ear. "It's not like that, Beautiful."

"Little *svåss*, have a care. They are besotted with you," Rogue warned. "I'm not."

I met his cool-eyed gaze and smirked. "Liar."

It'd be better if he didn't care. Maddox and Fin already tugged at me in ways that didn't make me comfortable. Their lust was glorious to feed on, and I already enjoyed their blood.

There was a thought I never believed I'd give voice to

internally much less externally. Still...if Rogue were my enemy, this would be so much easier.

"There are four of us, Alfred is waking," Rogue continued. "It can be a process. We're only telling you because once he is awake, he will come for you."

"Any minute now *The Twilight Zone* theme is going to start playing. That, or *Psycho*. Are you trying to terrify me, Rogue?" Also, what the hell kind of name was Rogue anyway?

Beautiful. Fin's mental voice strained, but Maddox chuckled. "You are so absolutely irreverent. I am not sure whether to kiss you or spank you."

"Who says you can't do both?" Still, even as the comment rolled off my tongue, I raised my eyebrows in challenge. I could do with more ale, but I drained what was left in my mug.

Maddox grinned. "Good to know you'd enjoy that."

"Succubus, Mad-Dragon. I pretty much enjoy everything if it packs a lust-filled punch." Not entirely true, but I had a part to play, and they were getting all sorts of attached. I had clothes, and I could go out in the sun. I'd already managed to wake before them once.

First thing tomorrow, I was the hell out of here.

The thought of leaving twisted something uncomfortably in my gut. Time to cut out that infection before it sank in too deep. I couldn't afford to get attached. Succubi were not made for long-term relationships. Speaking of which... "Anyway, your point was we need to clear the shadow demon out, Fin needs to drain me, then we can have another magnificent round robin of ride the cock while I feed off of each of you. But you want to wait until tomorrow morning?"

With my new plan in mind, that didn't work for me. The more I glutted, the more likely I could keep on the move.

Particularly since I needed to travel from the dark ages back to the real world.

"Crudely put," Fin said, his scolding very present in his voice. "But it's safer for you. We're hybrids, our blood will sustain you like no one else's will."

"Dorran's seemed to be working for me." Even stoned me out. "Didn't mind his dick too much either."

Yes, I was absolutely pushing, and the black look crossing Maddox's face said I'd definitely achieved aggravation. So what if I never wanted it until I was starving? That wasn't the point. I needed them to let go.

"Little *sváss*, I warned you," Rogue stated. "Maybe we should just press ahead tonight. Eradicate the shadow demon's influence. You seem healthy enough."

A muscle ticked in Maddox's jaw.

"Oh please," I continued, baiting the hook. Or in this case, baiting the dragon, the druid, and whatever the fuck Rogue was. "I was hardly a virgin when I got here. A fact of which you should be grateful. You two knotting up and getting stuck inside of a girl could freak a normal person out. You're all lucky that I'm very not normal."

Fin chuckled. "And you very much want us angry, Beautiful. Despite what he says, Rogue isn't going to hurt you. None of us are."

Maddox surged to his feet, irritation vibrating off of him in waves. "Or is the point to push us away, to make us act rashly?"

I shrugged. "None of this is my plan. I was happily whiling away my time in a cell when you showed up."

"We will move this to the bedroom, save us the trouble of having to carry you when you collapse," Rogue stated. "Clean up in here, Maddox." The dragon was a foot from me, his eyes incandescent when Rogue stopped him in a single order.

"Fin, take her and feed on her until she's silent. We could all use the peace."

"Yeah, fuck you, too." Asshole.

"Oh, you will, little *sváss*." Rogue was suddenly right there, in my space, his mouth mere centimeters from mine. "You will be begging for it as you have each time." With one finger, he stroked my cheek.

"I don't beg." Ever.

His soft chuckle raked over me like a bad rash. Then he bit my lower lip. Not a loving kiss or teasing nip, but full on bite, and it fucking hurt. When I would have jerked away, he locked my head in place, his hand at my nape, and he bit down and then sucked at the blood welling up.

Not an ounce of pleasure stroked through me, nor was his lust even a stir. This was punishment, pure and simple. Pain for being a pain.

He was definitely an asshole. When he released me, the flood of copper in my mouth had me swallowing convulsively. He ran his tongue over his own lips, now stained with my blood.

"You taste better with each sip," Rogue said. "If only you didn't still taste of him. That is what we will remove."

There was just enough distaste curdling his words that fury roused in me. "You don't like it, fuck off. No one asked you."

Instead of responding, he turned away and moved. The speed of his departure took me a moment to process, but one moment, he was in front of me, and next, he was at the fire—with all my newly acquired clothing. From the irritating floss to the semi-decent leather pants, he had everything but the camisole, panties, and robe I was wearing.

He threw them all into the flames.

"You son of a bi—" The word broke off as Fin hoisted me and stepped. My stomach plummeted as the world wrenched around me, and we went from the warm, if dusty library with its roaring fires, to the cold bedroom. I landed on my back on the bed, and a fire burst into being in the hearth.

Shoving upward, I halted as Fin pivoted to face me, his expression dark and severe.

"Stop it, Fiona," he said, his tone unforgiving and without the teasing lilt of every earlier interaction. "You are trying to make us fight you."

Considering I could still taste blood in my mouth, I'd say I'd done a damn good job of it. "Or what?" Because I was tired of these assholes hauling me around like I was their fucking toy or fuck toy. Whatever.

"Or you will make this situation far more difficult than it needs to be for you. For us."

"Well, the gods forbid I make this situation difficult for you. Really wouldn't want that…"

Fin sighed, face turned heavenward. "I love your mouth," he said abruptly. "I love the way you smile. I love how it felt on my cock."

Shocker.

Not.

"I also love the sass you spill so swiftly and without mercy." He faced me then. "You're perfect."

I snorted. "Hardly."

"No, you're perfect." He took a step toward the bed and then slid onto the end of it. "I need you to listen to me, Fi— do you mind if I call you Fi?"

It was the first time any of them actually asked me if I minded one part of this whole thing. "It's fine," I said. "Only Elias calls me Fi, but I don't mind it so much."

"And Elias would be?"

"A friend." A real one. Did he think I was dead? I hoped not. We'd been close for a long time, he would be pissed enough that I'd fucked a vampire much less turned into one.

But that was a problem for *another* day.

"Interesting." He actually sounded like he meant that. "But will you listen to me, Fi?"

"I've been listening, Fin."

His smile was sudden and bright. Yeah, yeah, I used his name. Whatever. He'd been polite to me, why not show a little of the same back to him?

"Yes, you have, but have you heard us?"

"Pretty much. Also rather getting that you all think you get to make these decisions for me. The arrogance is rather off-putting. The magnificent sex does help in that department, but not so much I just forget you're all assholes who stole me from one prison to lock me into another."

Sighing, he nodded. "That's not an unfair assessment."

"Thank you."

"You're welcome." Another small smile. "Fiona, the world as you know it has changed."

No shit, Sherlock. Though I kept that last bit to myself and waited. If this was another 'oh, I was a hybrid and special, la-dee-dah,' I might cut myself just to get on to the feeding and fucking portion of the evening.

My pussy ached at the very thought, but damn if she wasn't already wet thinking about it. They seemed to enjoy wrecking me almost as much as I was enjoying being wrecked.

Like I'd said a few times now, I was definitely twisted.

"You're more than just a hybrid."

I snorted, but at his frown, I raised my hands in surrender and then flopped back against the bed. If I was going to listen to this epistle, I might as well be comfortable.

"I saw you in a vision," Fin continued. "Several centuries ago."

I rolled my eyes.

"You were the most beautiful female I had ever seen, one I

knew was perfect for us. *All* of us. You would fit with us and be our fifth. You would also be a hybrid."

"Well yay you?"

Fin levered himself over me, and I met his gaze.

"Fi, I'm not making this up. I've waited hundreds of years for you. Maddox has, too. Rogue…Rogue will come around. He's more cautious, but he's welcomed you here, and he wants you here."

I studied him. He really was serious.

"You belong to us," he continued, and I clamped my teeth together. I didn't belong to anyone. "When Alfred wakes up…you'll see. The balance is shaky right now. Without Alfred, Rogue feels like he has to look after us, and he and Maddox both think I'm too impetuous."

Well, I couldn't fault that assessment.

He cupped my face, and against my better judgment, I leaned into the contact. "I get that this is a lot. You didn't ask for any of this."

No, I really hadn't.

"But we can make you happy." Then he nuzzled a kiss to the corner of my mouth before laving his tongue against the cut on my lower lip left by Rogue's teeth. It was a soothing gesture, healing the bite. Too sweet. I swallowed. "You don't have to trust us yet, even if you kind of are. You don't have to believe everything, though I wish you would…"

Fuck. Me. "Then what are you asking me for?" Dammit. Pretty boys were like my kryptonite. Especially when they were sweet and wore their hearts on their sleeves.

"Time," he whispered, and then he kissed his way down to my chest, not hesitating or pausing near my throat. When he nudged the robe wider and the camisole up, I sighed. The heat of his mouth on one nipple fanned the flames of languid heat. "Can you give us time?"

When he sank his teeth into my breast, I closed my eyes

and arched. The first hot pull had my brand new panties soaking, and I cried out when he slid his hand beneath the band.

Time, Fi. Just give us time.

Dammit.

I couldn't see him, but his mental smile burst through me, and then he thrust two fingers inside as he began to rub the heel of his hand to my clit. The draining, the finger-fucking, and the smile—a devastating combo.

"A little while," I gasped. I'd give them a little while. Everything else faded as he kept feeding and sent me tumbling toward my first orgasm of the evening.

But it would certainly not be the last.

Not that I was even a little bit hungry.

This was all just for me.

Dammit.

I was so fucked.

Literally and figuratively.

"More is planted in the garden than flowers and food. Hope. Freedom. Joy. They need to be tended, too." - Unknown

Some sixty hours after telling Fin I'd give them some time, I found myself chewing on the jerky of regret. I'd woken in the same pile of limbs we'd slept in since my first night. This morning, I'd been sleeping on Rogue, straddling his half-hard cock still half in me. Face pressed against his throat, I could still taste his blood in my mouth. That part hadn't really bothered me. Nor had the fact that Maddox had a territorial hand on my ass while he draped alongside me or that Fin held one of my hands to his chest.

I'd woken to sleeping on all of them. Despite how large the bed was, apparently I didn't get my own spot. Maddox seemed my usual mattress, but I probably gravitated to him out of heat. Fin though tended to fold around me when I slept on him, but Rogue and I were not friends no matter how good he felt.

No, the physical dimensions of playing human twister with all their naked limbs and their refreshing lack of any kind of concern where their bare skin encountered each other, these I enjoyed.

No, my problem was that morning, I hadn't wanted to move. Awake, aware, and intimately settled, I hadn't wanted the distance I needed to regain each day. I'd kissed the spot over Rogue's throat where I had been feeding. The skin wasn't puffy or swollen like their bites were on me. The fact that they hadn't healed had worried them.

None of them said as much, but I'd caught Fin studying those marks with an intensity that bordered on dangerous. And apparently, Fin draining me to near empty before I fed up on all of them wasn't the last time it happened. He did it again the following night, and the night before it had been Rogue who'd done it after he'd gone down on me.

The man had an extremely talented gift with his mouth, when he wasn't being stoic and distant.

The minute I realized I didn't want to move, I levered myself out of the bed and off of Rogue. His cock had already been stirring, as had a fresh pool of desire, and what the fuck was up with that I had no idea.

My panties and camisole hadn't survived that first night. I was back down to bare-assed naked and the robe I'd claimed. They always had clothes—assholes—and I hadn't figured out where they hid them. This morning though, I'd purloined the t-shirt Maddox had worn the day before. It draped me like a dress, and then I dragged the robe over it. At least I had slippers—a concession I was sure to the fact none of them liked my icy feet on them.

Well, none except Rogue. I don't think he even noticed them.

All we'd done was eat—Fin always left and returned with

the most decadent meals. He brought food from all over the world. So, my life could be tougher.

Sex. So much sex.

Even I don't think I'd ever had as much as I got from them. The fact that I was so full my body hummed constantly hadn't been lost on me. Then the biting and the draining, and none of them touched my neck. Not since that first night. Whether Fin told them why or not, I didn't know and I didn't ask.

Honestly, I didn't care as long as they stayed away from my throat. The fact that asshole's face popped to mind when their mouths brushed past on their way to what had to be their second favorite feeding area—my breasts—bugged me. The fact that he was still out there somewhere, alive and probably going about his normal life bugged me more.

I should have long-since gutted him. Leaving them to sleep, I made my way to the bathing room and made quick work of washing. While it was tempting to linger in the hot water, I needed time to think. The whole keep had begun to transform over the last couple of days.

It started in the bedroom—though I hadn't noticed when Fin stole away with me there. I hadn't until the next morning. In addition to the bed, there was a huge shaped sofa framing the large hearth. They'd added hangings to the wall, thick and colorful. Some depicted scenes of knights on horseback, others were of glades in the forest, another of the mountains, and one of the ocean with the skies turning crimson and orange as the sun set into the sea.

That one was for me. They said nothing, but it was the view I'd wanted from the bedroom of my house on the cliffs. Of course it was for me.

The chilly confines weren't so icy anymore. As I pulled the robe tight and slid my feet into the slippers, I wouldn't freeze as I made my way up to the library. I tried to go there most mornings. It was now dust free with more comfortable seating, and Fin had found an old style record player and a collection of records. The lack of actual electricity required we put batteries in the record player, but I was not bitching.

I missed the modern world. I kept half-expecting one of them to tell me not only had they stolen me from prison, they'd stolen me out of time. But I was too damn chicken to confirm that.

The idea that I'd never see a Starbuck's again or find out who Jeanette picked on *Match Me* was just too damn depressing. There were a couple of blankets in the library now, too. The side table was always stocked with something to eat. Usually breads and cheese. Sometimes meat. And as of today, apparently, jams. I had a sweet tooth that I hadn't been able to indulge, so I spread marmalade heavily on three pieces of bread, then worked my way through eating those while sipping water and staring out at the sun rising over the hills in the distance.

There was another oddity. Vampire or not? I was awake before the sun. Every day since I'd gotten to see it again, I didn't sleep past its rising. Whether I had in the prison or not, I had no idea. I'd been something of a morning person before, but not like this.

It also didn't seem to matter if I got hours of sleep or minutes. By the time I reached the library, the sun would be rising and I could stare out at the kiss of light as it flooded the world.

The marmalade tasted tart and sweet on my tongue. I should probably light the fires, but I wasn't that cold. My initial plan to leave had been shelved when Fin asked me to stay. To give them time. The longer I stayed though, the more I didn't *want* to leave. No matter what Fin believed, I couldn't just stay here.

Stay with them.

I sighed and leaned my head against the cool stone as I stared out the window.

A whoosh in the fireplaces told me someone was awake. The heat wrapping around me as strong arms slid around my waist told me it was Maddox.

"You should have lit the fires, Kitten," he rumbled. "I left them stacked for you."

"I wasn't that cold," I assured him. When he rubbed his bristly cheek to my temple, I closed my eyes and sank back against him.

"No?" Was that hope in his voice?

"No," I admitted. "Took a bath, came up here, got some food. Not really cold. Probably these fuzzy slippers that Fin found me." Fuzzy kitten slippers. No, I hadn't commented on them at the time. They were warm, that was all I cared about. Maddox chuckled, he liked them.

"Good." Satisfaction unfolded in his tone, and he slid a hand inside the robe. "You're wearing my shirt."

Yeah, I didn't ask how he knew whose shirt it was. "You didn't need it," I told him instead.

When he slid his fingers under the shirt, I laughed as he teased down to my thighs and then up. "I like you smelling like me." Then he nipped at my ear before stroking my hair to one side. It was still damp, but he hesitated when he bared my neck and I stilled. "May I kiss you here?" He stroked a single finger along the side of my neck. "I won't bite. I give you my word."

Something unfamiliar unfurled at the solemnity of his promise. Truth resonated in each word, and I bit my lip to keep from groaning. The hammer of my heart though, I couldn't control that.

"I promise, Kitten," he whispered, close but not actually brushing my neck with his lips. The little puffs of his breath tightened the coils in my belly. "I won't bite you. No one will ever bite you there again if you don't wish it." His voice darkened toward the end. "I'll kill anyone who tries."

The promise of death shouldn't turn me on so much, but fuck if it didn't. Tilting my head back to his shoulder I looked up to meet his gaze. The slitted eyes of his dragon stared back at me solemnly. He meant every single word.

A shudder rolled up my spine. I believed him.

Blowing out a breath, I eased forward. He loosened his hold but didn't remove the cage of his arms fully, and for that, I was grateful.

I didn't want him to move away. Shrugging out of the robe, I let it fall to pool at our feet. With one hand, I gathered my hair and pulled it all over one shoulder and then turned my head enough to bare that part of my neck.

"No teeth." The words came out trembling and without an ounce of the confidence I usually injected into my voice.

"No teeth," he assured me, and then pressed his lips to the base of my neck where it joined my shoulder. The pressure sent little shocks pulsing from my skin to my pussy and back up again. The gentle nudge of his leg sliding between mine had me adjusting my stance.

With care, he began to nuzzle kisses along my neck, inching higher with each one. The hum in my system began to ratchet higher. Maddox settled his hands on my bare hips and pushed his shirt up. I had on nothing below it, and the fact that he ground against my ass sent liquid heat to dampen my thighs.

I reached behind me as he reached a pulse point and sucked gently, just his lips and mouth and the sensuous trace of his tongue. Terror and pleasure twinned as the erotic tease continued. He wore jeans, but they weren't zipped or buttoned. I slid a hand in to wrap around his cock easily. It was thick, pulsing, and hotter than the rest of him.

"Kitten," he whispered. "You feel good."

The barest scrape of his teeth to my earlobe, and then he went back to kissing along my throat. My head was all the way back now, baring it for him as he ran his hands up beneath my shirt to cup my breasts. The first pinch of his fingers to my nipples, and I couldn't hold back the groan anymore.

He thrust against my hand, but that wasn't what either of us wanted. I twisted in his hold, then pushed down against his jeans. Without a word, he released me and shoved them down to his feet before stepping free. Meeting his gaze, I hooked my hands to the hem of his shirt and pulled it off.

Bites littered my chest, and he dipped his eyes to trace each one with his gaze. Fuck, I could feel it as if he were touching me. When he cupped my chin and tilted my head up, I parted my lips, anticipating the kiss before he even claimed my mouth. I fisted his hair and wrapped myself around him. The heat of his whole body scorched me, and I wanted that fire.

The rough, cold stone at my back was a perfect counterpoint to the hot, corded muscle pressing into me. He savaged my mouth, every stroke of his tongue had me arching. When he lifted me, I reached between us, and like we'd choreographed it, I stroked him from base to tip, then teased his fat, mushroomed head against my labia until I'd lined him up.

Maddox broke the kiss, his gaze fixed on mine as he hovered there, just barely nudging inside of me. Licking the taste of him on my lips, I gathered every ounce of my courage and tipped my head back to bare my throat. He promised no teeth. His moan reverberated through me as he thrust in one, long relentless push. The girth stretched me as he pressed his lips to the most vulnerable spot, the puffy bite left by Rogue, and when he traced his tongue around the edges of it, I clenched down on him.

He held inside of me as I fluttered and squeezed, all the

while nuzzling my throat. System zinging from the contact, I ran my hands all over his shoulders and then into his hair. At the first touch of my nails to his scalp, he began to rock his hips. Then we writhed together, grinding and arching. He kissed my throat, my chin, my cheek, and then his mouth was on mine again as we moved.

This wasn't a frenzy or heat. It wasn't hunger or feeding. It was dancing. It was loving. It was terrifying. It was wonderful. He lifted my thigh higher and changed his angle, and then every thrust struck a spot inside of me that had me seeing sparks. I clung to him, the sweat adding to the friction as the stone scraped at my back and his chest rasped against my nipples. Then I spiraled, ambushed by an orgasm that detonated in my whole system.

His shout pleased me on a level so primitive, I didn't even understand it. He was swelling inside of me, knotting deep as he came, and then he had my mouth pressed to his throat. "Bite me," he pleaded, and it was a plea. I didn't make him beg. No one should. I needed to bite him, so I sank my teeth in, and he jerked as he came in hot shooting jets that lit me up inside.

We hung there, clinging together for what seemed like an eternity. Locked inside of me, Maddox groaned in between panting explosive breaths as I licked the wound I'd made closed. The mark was deep, deeper than any I'd left on him before. They'd all cut themselves to let me drink. Always opening themselves up for me to feed.

Not this time.

As I laved my tongue against it, I shuddered and clamped down around him again. I'd broken his skin myself. I'd bitten him, sharp and deep, and something unlocked within me that should never have been opened.

Beyond Maddox's shoulder, I met Fin's beatific gaze and warm smile before darting mine away, only to collide with

Rogue's icy blue eyes and satisfied nod. How fucking long had they been standing there?

The fact that I had Maddox balls deep and knotted inside of me still only made their fixation on me hotter. Maddox murmured something against my ear, and I closed my eyes. The depth of feeling when he said Kitten had me closing my eyes. They saw too much.

I wanted too much.

THE MORNING PASSED IN A BLISSFUL HAZE MUCH TO MY OWN disgust. Maddox didn't lord it over me that I'd let him kiss my throat or how we'd been knotted together for nearly an hour before he finally softened enough to slip free. He'd carried me down to the bath, and we'd drowsed there for another hour in the languid heat. By the time we returned to the library, Fin had fetched fresh food, including fruit, and I ended up napping in Maddox's lap like the kitten he'd labeled me.

By afternoon, Rogue had vanished and no one said where. Maddox had left me to sit in a chair by the fire without him as he went to deal with chores. The regret when he kissed me had been as tangible as the gentleness in his voice when he'd whispered against me earlier.

I still wouldn't acknowledge what he'd said. The words branding themselves deep inside of me, burrowing into places where they didn't belong. Fin came and went, all three of them busy with their tasks. Probably getting the keep ready for Alfred. Even as my thoughts turned to him, I scowled.

He would come for me when he woke. That was a cheery thought. Beyond those words of wisdom, they hadn't spoken about him at all. While there wasn't some digital clock ticking down somewhere, I could feel one. It seemed to flicker in my soul, an awareness that each passing second drew us closer to when the mysterious Alfred would awake.

I couldn't tell if they were excited by the prospect or worried. The amount of time they were spending on fixing the keep up suggested a little bit of both. The interior began to look more homey and less like a tomb. So I supposed that was an improvement. There was a set of windows in Rogue's bedroom—the room we'd been using—and Maddox promised he would get those opened today. That way, I didn't have to leave the bedroom to see the sunrise.

That wasn't the only reason I left the bedroom, but I didn't bother to correct him. Guilt wormed its way through me, like a cat scratching its way to the surface. Fin and Maddox had been amazing, and even if he wasn't exactly *warm*, Rogue had been a generous enough companion.

He certainly held nothing back in bed, even if he was far more reserved during waking hours.

Fuck, I was getting attached. It was bad enough they were attached. I couldn't get attached. Succubi didn't settle down, it never worked out. The need to feed coupled with how others responded to us...it was a recipe for disaster. Possessiveness. Fights. There were already rumbles between the three of them, and the enigmatic Alfred hadn't arrived.

What then?

Head resting against the chair, I stared at the fire. Music played on the record player—something bluesy and jazzy. It was nice. At least that suggested a more modern sensibility than some of the hand-inked tomes stored in the library. They had a lot of books. I'd looked for something to read that second day we'd been in here.

I gave up when most of them turned out to be written in Latin or Greek. Though Maddox swore that one was Aramaic.

Whatever. They weren't languages I knew.

Fin offered to read one of the Gaelic ones to me. Selfishly, I'd let him, and we were about halfway through the tale of the Fae who lost his way. Rogue rolled his eyes at the first few words of the book, but neither he nor Maddox left when Fin read to me.

I wanted to know what happened. That was another reason I put off leaving.

How much time was enough?

It had been a few days, and I hadn't been hungry in any fashion. They fed my body, my soul, and my mind. Too comfortable.

Sitting forward, I glared at the kitten slippers on my feet. I could still feel Maddox inside of me like was he buried to the hilt. Not that I had any trouble imagining Fin or Rogue in the same spot. I knew all of them, my body really knew them.

And I was getting warmer the longer I sat there, my body softening and growing damp.

Fuck, they weren't even present and I wanted them.

This was a problem.

Enough with the library and musing about their bodies. They were busy, and I needed something else to do. Sitting idle wasn't how I normally went through my days. Once upon a time, I'd actually had a job. I worked in a shop, I got to see people come and go. It hadn't been glamorous, but I enjoyed helping tourists find the perfect crystal and teasing real witches when they had to make nice with them.

It had been a good space to feed, too. There was always someone lusting after something in the Rising Phoenix. Always some young buck wanting the ingredients for a sex spell to enhance his performance or a silly twat on the hunt for a 'make him love me' potion. The first was possible to a point, the second was ridiculous. Bending someone's will to make them love you? Well, it *could* be done. If you didn't mind the homicidal rage it would trigger, the obsessive behavior, and the fact that the object of the spell would likely turn on you and murder you in your sleep to keep you with them forever.

Sure, no problem.

Nothing said love like a knife in the intestines.

Just saying…

Dragging the robe on, I headed for the doors. A walk to the garden maybe. It would let me get outside, and I could get some fresh air. I'd go to the interior one because if I found the front doors, I'd probably be tempted to keep running.

A pause rocked through me as I reached the gallery leading to the garden doors. Why not just go? It was what I wanted, right? It was what I'd been wanting since I woke up in the prison. I wanted out.

So why stay here? Maybe the shackles were sex and blood, but they were still shackles.

I glanced back toward the hall and the way I'd come. The scent of dust and disuse in the gallery was missing. There were more wall hangings up and wood piled into the large hearths ready to be lit. There was also a long table and chairs set up along the front of the room, and the shutters on the windows had been removed, though they were all frosted panes in different colors. The light coming in was muted, and yet still lovely.

Shaking my head at the inane thoughts, I gripped the door and yanked. It gave a hollow sound and a wrenching creak of noise when I pulled it open. Both comforted me, because until the moment it gave, I half-expected to find it as impossible to open as the cell door in the prison.

The rush of cool air brushed against my face. The sun was on the back half of the garden, not the front. The tangle of dark vines still had snow all over them, and the ground was thick with it. I hesitated. If I walked out there in my slippers, they'd get soaked.

That would be shame.

Making a face, I tugged them off and nudged them to the side. Bracing myself with a breath, I stepped out into the snow. It was cold, but not frigid. Maybe spring was coming soon to wherever the fuck we were. Still, I tied the robe a little tighter. The snow crunched under my feet as I tugged the door closed, not all the way, but to a crack.

Picking my way carefully passed the thorns and ducking below some, I found some patches of rock free of the snow and sitting right in the sun. Perfect.

Climbing up to sit on one, I turned my face upward. There was a distinct difference between the light coming through a window and feeling its actual caress on my skin.

It wasn't warm, and yet, it warmed me at the same time. My breath fogged in the air, but I closed my eyes, savoring the kiss of the sun and the fresh wash of frozen air. I sat there long enough that I should have been shivering, but I wasn't. More, I'd sat there long enough one of my keepers should have come looking.

But they left me alone.

Pleasure bloomed at the show of trust.

Or maybe they hadn't noticed my absence. Either way, it was nice to just have this time...

A bird called. Then another. Cracking an eyelid open, I shaded them as I squinted to scan the skies. A flock—yes, I know they're called a murder—of crows wound its way over the roof to fly through the garden. Weird. I hadn't seen them since my last trip outside. Not even when I looked out the windows the library.

Some alighted on vines, others soared back up to the rooftop. But they were all there.

And all of them were looking at me.

Hello Paranoia, your name just became Fiona.

Ignoring them, I closed my eyes again. I wasn't worried about birds.

The crunch of snow, however, sent apprehension shivering up my spine. One could be a fluke.

The second?

Eyes open, I twisted on the rock and faced the stranger standing in the center of the garden. Deep, dark eyes stared back at me from a bearded face shrouded by messy hair that hung to his shoulders. His skin was darker, almost tanned, like he'd been sun worshipping.

It was the absolute lack of expression that had my stomach bottoming out. That, and the very real sensation of power crackling the air—not a whiff of lust rolled off of him, yet he stared at me like he weighed and measured me.

Maybe for a coffin.

Licking my lips, I pushed off the rock to face him. "Take a picture," I told him with a hell of a lot more bravado than I was suddenly feeling. "It'll last longer."

Maddox growled and snarled, but he hadn't worried me. Nor did Fin, who made me laugh and could be irreverent and playful. Rogue, for all his reserve, infuriated me more than terrified me.

This guy?

The fact that I was half-naked and considerably isolated and lacking any kind of weapon hit me like an avalanche of bricks.

At my statement, however, the corners of his mouth tipped upward. It was the only change in his expression.

"Fiona," he said in a raspy voice. But it was more than just shaping his lips around my name, it was like he intoned all of me in those three simple syllables, and his gaze kept me pinned in spot like a butterfly on a board.

"Yep," I said, warier. "That's my name. Don't wear it out."

He cocked his head.

One moment, he was over there, the next, he was in front of me.

Right in front of me.

I hadn't blinked.

Holy.

Shit.

"Fiona," he said again, then tilted his head and struck. I had zero time to react. One moment, he was looking at me, and the next, he sank his teeth into my throat, directly over the spot where Dimitri had bitten me.

I was pretty sure I screamed.

Or maybe I just froze.

But the brand of his bite rocked all the way down to my soul, and then the world shifted as he began to drink.

Fuck.

Hello, Alfred. Some distant part of my brain offered the introduction as my life pumped out of me, and all I could do was cling to him.

Really not nice to meet you...

Asshole.

CHAPTER 14

"Clip her wings if you dare. She will grow new ones." - Unknown

Alfred

The first whispers reached him when Fin came to see Rogue.

"She's there, I know it's her." Always optimistic and profound in his faith.

"You can't know it's her." Always the skeptic, warier and cautious.

"I do know," Fin insisted. "She's a succubus, or she was. Some idiot drained her while screwing her, and instead of letting her heal naturally, he panicked."

Rogue's sigh carried the weight of the ages. "He force fed her blood?"

"Far as I can tell. A lot of people don't want to talk about it. Their prince has ordered silence. I got there an hour after they took her. She went right for him—the prince and the asshole."

"Where's the asshole now?"

Yes, he would like to know this, too.

"In the wind." Frustration etched Fin's words. "I'll find him, or Maddox will. For now, we need to get to her. The prince sent her to Nightmare Penitentiary. He's determined to cover this up before the American council learns about her. Hybrids are myths after all."

A snort. "You want to go after her."

Then silence.

"Fin."

"Maddox is on his way in. It took me time to track an access point. They've improved their spellkeepers on the gates. Not that much, but he's on his way in. I'm going after him."

"And you're telling me because you want me to come…"

"Just back up. If you haven't heard from us…"

The words faded as they argued. Rogue would go. He wouldn't leave their brothers alone, not if they asked for him.

He drifted.

"Rogue…why the hell did you do that?" Maddox's snarl ripped through his sleep.

"Because she stinks of shadow demon, and if you hadn't noticed, he can already call her."

"I was blocking him," Fin argued.

"She's not even through transition." The disgust curling in Rogue's tone roused him further. "We'll need to drain her, repeatedly. Lance the shadow from her, break the addiction, then infuse her with our blood."

"That will save her?" Hope crept into Maddox's tone. A hope that hadn't been present in so long, Alfred had forgotten the last time he heard it. He was one of the last of his kind. Maybe the very last.

They'd saved him from the hunters who came for him. He and Rogue had both protected the wounded beast and found a friend.

A brother.

"There are no guarantees, Maddox," Rogue told him, and no one but Alfred would have heard the sympathy in his tone. "We'll try."

"What about Alfred?" Fin said. "We should wake him. She's the one."

"We don't know she is," Rogue reprimanded him. "Alfred will wake when he's ready."

Was he even truly asleep?

They seemed to have it in hand.

The slam of a rapid heart and screams of ecstasy ricocheted off the walls. A scent tickled at his nostrils.

"...you're not wrong," Fin agreed. "But I can be jealous because I want to know her, too. I've dreamt about her for centuries. Unlike the rest of you, I knew she was coming. I never broke faith."

"Lust-filled dreams about her breasts are not what I would call prophetic," Maddox stated drily, and Rogue gave a half-laugh.

He dozed.

"Ask me no questions, and I'll tell you no lies." Her husky voice wrapped around him like a lure.

Maddox snarled, "Stop poking in her head. We're supposed to be convincing her, not chasing her away."

"I was playing," Fin argued. "Besides, she thinks I'm pretty. So suck it."

Flashes of impatience from Rogue. The boys argued. They always had. It was good for them. It kept them alive.

"...what the fuck were you thinking?"

"He's lust drunk, what do you think he was thinking?" Fin snapped. "Just feed her. He's all knotted up inside her and not moving for a while."

Quiet again.

Movement roused him. Movement and pain. He tried to

focus on it. The stranger moving about the keep. Her light steps landed like warning thuds. Change eddied in the air. Change he hadn't tasted in generations.

It wasn't time yet.

"…shadow demon…"

Hmm. What was that about a shadow demon? Demons kept their distance. They knew better than to disturb him or his.

The thread faded away.

"…Fin believes she's here." Rogue. "I am only telling you because she was in Nightmare Penitentiary. She may not survive her transition. We may not have gotten to her in time. If they come for her, we will lead them away. If we must flee the keep, they will never get in here, but you will find us in Fin's lands."

If *they* come for her?

Someone hunted her?

His sleeping mind turned the information over.

Shadow demon.

Prison.

Yes. They might try to come for her.

No one invaded his lands.

"I was just wondering if I could go see the sun…I haven't seen it in weeks."

Her voice whispered to him, beckoning, and he listened to the shift in her heartbeat. To the discussion from the boys wanting her to not risk it. Vampires in transition were particularly vulnerable. If the transition wasn't taking, the sun was the fastest way to end their suffering.

Not all vampires could walk in the sun. The bloodlines had begun to weaken. The natural born retained some of the skill, but the turned? More and more, they faded too quickly. Power and hunger had made selection an open market rather than a chosen few carefully shepherded.

Selfish bastards.

Movement against his wards had him stirring.

Crows.

They swarmed toward his garden. Another power touched their minds, and he dislodged it easily. This was his keep. His land. Everything on it was his. The interloper fled at the first brush. An image scorched against his mind, a challenge.

Then he stared into the garden through the eyes of the many. Red hair snagged his attention, full lips and pale golden skin.

The red eyes pulled all his focus, and her pout when they insisted she return inside. He agreed, he didn't want her to go, but then she was gone, and Rogue stared at the crows with a warning on his face.

It had been a long time since he'd lain eyes on his brothers. Rogue didn't know it was him, he worried it was the other.

Then they were gone, and Alfred let his mind wander as the crows flew. Time had marched on. How much had passed, he wasn't certain. He needed to find out.

Anger.

Rebellion.

Lust.

The scent of it permeated the keep. Fiona.

Her name was Fiona.

Maddox called her Kitten.

Fin labeled her Beautiful.

But it was Rogue's nickname that pulled at him. Little *svÃ¡ss*.

Little Beloved.

His heart rate began to increase. They were courting her. Draining her. Feeding her. Fin pled with her for more time. The little hellion wanted to leave. They always ran. But it had been a few days, and she was still in the keep. She still fed from them, and her signature and scent grew stronger every day.

Alfred wanted to see her

Wanted to test her.

Taste her.

Awareness rippled through the keep as a door opened and she left. Her heartbeat grew more distant. He'd been listening to it for days now, the cadence of her heart. When it sped, when it slowed, when it pumped furiously as one of his brothers pleasured her. He understood each rhythm. It slowed and grew fainter as she left the safety of the interior for the sun.

The crows came at his summoning. At his first glimpse of the firebrand's hair, his pulse quickened. The chamber opened with a single wave of his hand, and he stepped out. Hunger assailed him.

Hunger and need.

Like a ghost, he moved through the keep. The locks fell away at his presence. The spells infused into the stone had also used his blood. Outside, the sun warmed his skin and blinded him, but he didn't need his own eyes. The crows gave him all the angles he needed. Her tousled curls. Her full lips. The fact that she wore only a robe and her feet were bare despite the snow.

The flush to her cheeks.

Life suffused the hellion. Life and power.

The first whiff of her stroked through him as he took a deep breath, filling his lungs with the musky femininity. All of his brothers had marked her. The breeze shifted her hair, baring the bite mark on her neck. The puffiness of it hadn't faded. The transition wasn't complete.

They'd kept her alive.

There, just below the sweetness of her perfume and the

overlays of his brothers blanketing her scent, was the taint of shadow. It was still there, like a dark invader lurking beneath her skin.

The demon had done more than just mark blood and her body. He'd marked her soul. It was as much a declaration of property as it was of war. Alfred met her gaze when she jerked to look at him.

Red eyes blazed back at him. But they hadn't always been red. No, that color belonged to his hellion's hair, not her eyes. She needed to complete the transition, to let go of the dual ties and sink into the place she belonged.

Fin might be right about her.

While he'd shared the vision, Alfred had never seen the woman's face. Only her hair.

The same scarlet hair now blowing in the wind. A wind that shifted and flooded him with her scent. Hers, theirs, and the shadow demon's.

Hunger assailed him.

She ran her tongue over her lips, trapping his attention on her luscious mouth. "Take a picture," she challenged as she pushed up from the rock to face him. "It'll last longer."

Amusement curved through him. Defiant.

No wonder his brothers couldn't get enough of her.

She had spirit.

"Fiona," he tested her name on his tongue. Everything about her seemed encapsulated in her name. Queen and demon. Lover and threat. Friend and enemy. Fiona was far more dangerous than she realized.

Dangerous.

Beautiful.

Intoxicating.

"Yep," she replied, brazen in her challenge. Not once did she dip her eyes. Most vampires couldn't meet his gaze head on. Most couldn't even look in his direction. Fiona? She raised that chin and straightened her spine. "That's my name. Don't wear it out."

Lust punched through him. Burrowing beneath his skin to arouse a hunger he hadn't experienced...*ever.*

He closed the distance. The need to touch her overrode everything.

"Fiona," he whispered the hellion's name with the reverence she deserved. The fact that the shadow demon's taint still stained her incensed him. No more. His brothers had tried to erase it. Alfred would remove it entirely. His eyes narrowed on the mark on her throat. Unlike the others, it had faded to a near scar. It was the first one. The one that would remain, even after the others cleared from transition.

It was the mark of the one who made her.

Quiet fury suddenly bubbled in his sluggish system, quickening the pace of his heart and flushing him from inaction to reaction. No one else was allowed to mark her. Not the shadow demon.

Not the bastard vampire.

The need to obliterate their marks and replace it with his own surged like electricity through his blood. He sank his teeth into that mark, his arms locked around her to keep her still. The last thing he wanted to do was tear out her throat. The soft vulnerable column was not a match for the pierce of his teeth as he sank into her sweet flesh.

The first dribble of her blood over his tongue, and he locked his lips to suck deeply. The hot liquid quenched his parched throat, sating both his desire and starving him for more. Every flash of hot decadence rolling around his tongue let him taste her. Her whole body softened against him, the sweet tang of her need adding to the spice on his tongue.

Hello, Alfred. Her biting words lashed at him, even as she gripped his shoulders, clinging to him though she was in no danger of falling. He had her. *Really not nice to meet you...* *Asshole.*

He plunged deeper, drawing it from her. All of it.

All of her.

"You're new," the male said as he slid onto the stool next to me. New? Really? What a tired line. I slanted a look at him without turning. The mirror behind the bar gave me a good visual.

He was lean, dark-brown eyes and hair. He possessed a boyish kind of charm, and his appearance was impeccable. His clothing was upscale and expensive. He'd shaved recently, and his fingers were long and slender. They reminded me of a musician's hands. Beyond all of that, his lust was a potent force, shimmering off of him in waves. All of it focused on me.

I'd been hungry for the last three days, and despite wandering the various bars, I'd yet to find someone I could feast on that I wouldn't hurt. My fault for waiting too long between feedings. I'd been leaching a little here and there to stave off the overriding need. But with full moon and the partying pagans gathering along with a huge influx of supernatural over the last two weeks, I had to play it safer.

Elias would have helped out, but we were friends, and fucking friends was usually a no-no in my book. The very last friend I'd fucked to feed on had grown obsessed, and our friendship died in the ashes of his lust.

No, I kept my feeding separate from the rest of my life. Just so much easier.

This guy...he wasn't human. If I had to guess, I'd say vampire. He was almost too pretty to be anything else. Still...vampires were usually no gos. They wanted more than fucking, and while they could be amazing in bed, Elias had a real problem anytime I indulged my more dangerous fantasies.

Still, beggars couldn't be choosers, and I was so damn hungry.

"Hello," I answered, leaning in to let his lust lick over my skin. Oh, it was delicious, and his pupils dilated as he narrowed the distance even further. I wasn't the only one who was hungry.

Oh, this could work out.

One drink, and we were in a private booth and I had his cock halfway down my throat as he thrust up, desperate for the release as I stroked his balls. The feverish grip of his fingers in my hair pushed me to take him deeper, even as his lust swelled like his cock. When he came, it was a burst of salty bitterness and sweet satisfaction. The wildness of it swarmed through me with a punch more potent than the liquor he'd ordered for me.

His whole body shuddered as he dragged me up, and then his mouth was on mine. The fact that I could still taste his spunk—which meant he could too—amused me on some level, but it didn't deter him in the slightest. If anything, it amplified his need.

When he shredded my panties and I climbed on him in the booth, it was a quick and furious coupling magnified by the beat of music around us. I loved the outfit, the leather dress and the sexy heels. The leather massaged my nipples as I moved, the buttery softness a fantastic counterpoint to the hardness of the cock he slammed me down on.

The guy's technique was lacking, but fuck if he didn't make up for it with enthusiasm. He bit my wrist after the second set of orgasms. His, not mine. He didn't last long enough for mine, but I wasn't here to get off so much as to just feed, and yeah, I was more than a little drunk on him.

The lust rolling off him grew more potent rather than diminishing. When he bit down on my wrist and fingered my clit until I came, I blissed out. Probably explained why I left with him, his come still sticky on my thighs, and why I let him take me back to his place.

Well that, and I wasn't inviting him to my shitty little apartment. It might be small and cramped, but it was mine. I was saving *everything to build my perfect place. I could see where I wanted it and how I wanted it to be. I was always redesigning it.*

His place was much nicer and a penthouse.

Yeah, this dude was loaded.

We were three steps in the door when he was on me again, and fuck if I didn't just go down for all that fierce snarling. He slammed me against a wall—yeah, it was kind of hot, and he had the dress pushed up as he fucked into me. When he bit my neck, I didn't think anything about it.

Fair was fair. I was drowning in his lust, and he was getting off. But a guy had to eat. I'd just wait until the bite marks healed before seeing Elias.

Even after he came again, I was still feeling it. Fuck, it would be nice to be able to feed and get off at the same time. Pants open, he carried me into his room. It was so fucking over the top melodramatic, I started laughing.

Literally, black silk sheets, black wall hangings, black walls—if he'd had a coffin shaped bed, it would have fit right in with the aesthetic.

"What the fuck are you laughing at?" he demanded as he dumped me on the bed.

"Aww, poor baby, did I hurt you feelings?" Okay, so I was a little drunk, pointing one of my heeled feet at him and mocking him just a little. It was no reason to rip the shoe off and snap the heel.

Those were my best pair of shoes.

"I think you have too much energy," he growled. "You need to remember who you're here to serve."

Really?

I slugged him.

It broke my hand, but whatever. When he ripped the dress open though, oh it was on. The problem was that I was already lust drunk, and the more I fought, the more it fanned his lust. Fuck, I didn't care how rough he made it. Or that he half strangled me when he mounted me. The moment his teeth sank into my throat, I was groaning. I came over and over, but more from the lust pounding into me than his body.

Then the world darkened as he wouldn't let go, and the pain pierced the pleasure. I fought to get his teeth out of me, but all he did was moan and suck harder, his hips pistoning until the world blotted out.

Then I was choking on blood. So much blood. It was pouring down my throat until I gagged.

I didn't want it.

Didn't he understand...

Terror clawed at me when I woke.

Blood coated my mouth.

The room was wrecked.

My clothes shredded.

Dimitri was gone. No sign of him anywhere.

I staggered into the bathroom and stared at the red eyes staring back at me.

What the fuck had he done?

Terror turned to rage.

I was going to kill me a vampire.

He'd wrecked my favorite outfit. Broken my favorite pair of shoes. Beyond all that, he'd poured his blood down my throat.

I couldn't be a vampire, but my noodle like limbs and weakness decried all of that.

I didn't heal from blood.

I didn't...

ALFRED LIFTED HIS HEAD. SHE'D GONE UTTERLY LIMP IN HIS arms. Images kept flashing through his mind. Her confrontation with Isaac, her city's prince. That shit stain could die. Her internment. The warden. Dimitri's face and name were imprinted. That was another shit stain. He'd tasted her power and wanted it, that was why he'd brutalized her. Taken and taken until she'd nearly died, the last of her heartbeats so sluggish, she should have, and then he'd fed her blood.

Cupping her face, Alfred murmured, "You will have your vengeance, hellion. I give you my word."

Then he lifted her and carried her inside. Her heart beat so slow. Almost too slow. But he had time. He had to get her right to the very brink to break the last shadow chain. His brothers had done their best, but they didn't fully comprehend demons—or the fact that they tangled deeper than blood.

"Alfred," Fin called him as he passed by, striding toward the stairs to his own wing.

"Not now," he answered. Not while he had her on his tongue and in his mind. He saw every moment from her death to her awakening to her confrontations to when Maddox arrived in her cell.

The warden's visits were particularly colorful, and he planned to remove every inch of his taint. Of course, he'd known what she was, he couldn't have mistaken her for anything else. To control one like her would have given him enormous power.

"You drained her?" Maddox was in his way. The dragon's eyes furious, battle-readiness etched into his every muscle. Rogue stepped between them, but he couldn't contain the dragon's growl. "She wasn't ready for that."

"Later, Maddox," Alfred ordered him. "She's mine now."

His until he purged the taint, then his brothers could have at her again. The danger to them was more real than they'd realized. They'd done well to split her blood between them, to flush her with theirs. Smart.

The blood had sustained her. But the taint, no matter how minute, was still there.

Maddox lunged forward, and Rogue barely caught him. "Hold off," Rogue told him. "He's helping her."

"She's mine," Maddox challenged him, and the dragon's eyes were incensed. Cradling Fiona to him, Alfred met his stare and waited. The dragon was powerful. Had always been among one of the strongest creatures he'd ever encountered.

But he would fight his brother and his brother's fire if he demanded it. "I am not taking her from you forever," he told him. "You know this. Control yourself."

The dragon shuddered as he dropped his gaze to the woman in Alfred's arms and then up again. The mark on his throat drew Alfred like a laser.

"You bit her throat," Maddox snarled. "She doesn't want anyone at her throat."

He understood. "It was necessary."

"You scared her."

"I do not have time for this argument." Her heart grew more sluggish with each passing second. The brink of death drew closer. "I will speak to you all later." He nodded to Rogue, then continued.

Whatever debate occurred between the others, he tuned out. His focus was solely on the way her heart beat.

His rooms were open, a fire burning in the hearth and the bed made. The windows had been unshuttered, and everything aired out. Fresh furniture filled in the open spaces.

It was not the black coffin of Dimitri.

Satisfied with Rogue's choices, Alfred set her on the bed and then stripped away the robe that smelled of Fin and his brothers. Bite marks littered her chest. Two more on her thighs. They had been thorough in their choices.

Divesting his own clothes, he ignored the dust on them and then examined his skin. He needed a bath, but it would have to wait. He bit down on his wrist to get the blood flowing before he slid onto the bed and pulled her limp form into his lap. Her mouth opened as he drew his wrist closer, the scent of his blood rousing her.

When her heart beat stuttered and finally faded, only then did he press his wrist to her mouth. Maddox's roar punched through the near silence in the keep. Fin's mind reached out to him, but Alfred batted it away. Of the three, only Rogue didn't question him, yet his concern was there, a palpable force.

For all that he had held himself in reserve, the frost elf had already succumbed to the attraction. Hardly surprising, and Alfred wouldn't fight the need to be there. At first, nothing happened, but he waited as his blood trickled between her lips.

The silence. The absolute lack of a heartbeat.

Death hung like a curtain.

Then it shredded as she gripped his arm, and her mouth closed over the wound. The scrape of her teeth forced at his skin, trying to widen the slash. Stroking her hair away from her face, Alfred smiled down at her. "Feed, little hellion," he murmured. His whole body stirred to the contact with hers, but he focused on the gulps she took and the way color flushed across her breasts.

Life suffused her, and her scent curled around him until he wanted to sink his teeth into her again. But he had patience, he had to let her drain him, then he would drain her again.

More and more, she sucked, pulling harder, and his cock grew stiffer with every healthy pull. It defied logic, but then the idea that a mate existed for all four of them had always defied it.

When she fluttered open her lashes and looked up at him with near green eyes, Alfred smiled.

A queen.

Finally.

CHAPTER 15

"You have escaped the cage. Your wings are stretched out. Now fly."
- Rumi

In its purest form, the act of retribution offered symmetry. It offered payment for a crime. The danger, however, was that retaliation often only furthered the cycle of violence. Yet, what else could I do when the greater offense would be to let a crime go unpunished?

Those thoughts filtered through my foggy brain as I roused to the taste of aged blood. The flavor was beyond anything I'd ever experienced. The effervescence of Fin, the spice of Maddox, and the cool fire of Rogue had become somewhat familiar to me. I wouldn't say I craved their blood, so much as I craved them.

This? The flavor sent spots of gold flickering like a flip-book of images played on fast forward. Intense aromas of brown sugar, toffee, and lime teased my palate as I rode horses, raced armies, faced the sun, and conquered my enemies. Battle and I were old friends, but I was always alone.

Others wanted to follow me, and I allowed it, but I never encouraged it. When Rogue came into my life, he had his own agenda. He fit, and when battle nearly took him, I saved his life. He did not thank me for it.

No, quite the opposite, he tried to kill me. It says something for our friendship that he tried to kill me for five years before he considered forgiving me.

He has been my friend ever since. My constant companion.

The images raced away, almost too fast for me to hold onto. I gasped when he pulled his wrist from my mouth and then tucked his face down to my throat.

"No," I tried to squirm, but his arms locked around me.

"Yes, my hellion. I am removing all trace of him from you." The rasp of his voice was a dark promise all its own, and my whole body seemed to go liquid. Then his teeth sank in, and I wanted to scream. Panic clawed its way up, but he didn't tear away or rend. His arms tightened, a hug not pinning me down, and with care, he began to stroke my hair.

I was in the shop. I loved this shop so much. We'd worked hard to cultivate the clientele. Mundane and supernatural, they all came to us. I didn't own the place, no, I just worked there, but I loved it. I loved the feeling infused into every part of the place.

"What's your favorite part?" The whisper of his voice against my ear had me turning. No one was there, but I looked to the wall of crystals. In the afternoon, when the sun hit them, it became a wall of light. Part of why my perfect house would be one with floor to ceiling windows where I could see the whole world, not some dark, cramped little apartment that faced the brick wall of the building next door.

"It's beautiful." Like a ghost, he trailed his fingers down my

arm to take my hand. *"Show me your house?"*

It wasn't mine yet. Just a place. An idea.

"Show me." Command and request. Seduction and demand.

With a roll of my eyes, I retreated from the shop and walked out onto the deck of my cliff house. I could see it so perfectly. The salty air blew in from the west. The thrum of the waves a soothing soundtrack, even as birds called in the distance. He was indistinct, but he stood next to me as I leaned against the railing.

"Open...not very defensible."

I snorted. "I don't want to hide behind walls," I confessed. "I've lived in the shadows for so long. I want light. I want— this." Open skies. Open air. Light everywhere.

"Who kept you in the shadows, hellion?"

Life. What I was. Succubi didn't even want to be around their own kind. We separated from our families as soon as we could survive on our own. We dared not get too close. It was why I had to go.

"Shh...you don't have to do anything. Show me more."

I should tell him no. I really should. This was my place. I'd built it for me.

"Please."

The single word shocked me. I'd already wanted to show him, but now... Fine. I took his hand, threading my fingers with his, and guided him inside. The bedroom was exactly as I envisioned it. Huge, like the room I shared with Rogue, Maddox, and Fin. The bed was much bigger, too. So it was the same with a few tweaks.

He chuckled at the description as we moved toward the windows and looked out over the ocean. *"Magnificent."*

I thought so, too. It was why I wanted to be able to look over it. Always. "Just imagine the sunset over the water..." The light changed and played exactly as I'd wanted it to be.

"Show me more?"

The bathroom, the sunken tub and the oversized shower. Though images of the pools in the bathing room flickered in and out. Downstairs, I showed him the kitchen and dining areas, but they were the library. Piece by piece, my house turned into the keep and then changed back.

"It's all right, Fiona. Trust me."

Why should I? But he didn't answer the question as darkness crowded my vision, and then I was gasping as he lifted his head. We were in some room I'd never been in before, and Alfred gazed down at me, his lips red with my blood. He rolled me over so I lay breast to chest, and then he tucked my head to his throat. I knew what he wanted but I was so tired.

I didn't want to do this anymore.

"It hurts." It did. Everything hurt. Breathing hurt.

"You have almost no blood left," he told me as he stroked the hair from my face. "It is like pulling poison from a wound, Fiona. I have to cleanse it all, and I will cleanse it through me."

That didn't even make sense.

"You must trust me."

"Why? You bit me."

He smiled. "And you may bite me, hellion."

I didn't even know him.

"Not true," he whispered, cradling my face when I couldn't hold my own head up. My vision dimmed as my heart slowed. Somewhere, a roar punched through the hum in my ears.

Maddox.

"Will be fine. Fin and Rogue are with him. This is hard on the dragon," Alfred warned me. "Don't fight me too long, hellion, it hurts him."

I frowned. How was it hurting him? I didn't ask for this. I didn't ask for any of this.

"No," Alfred told me. "You didn't…now you must feed."

I hated him.

I hated all of them.

"I know," he soothed, rubbing my back as he nestled my face to his throat. The pound of his heart vibrated against my chest, and I licked at the skin. Just a trace of my tongue to gather the salt there, but it was far more decadent than salt, and I sank my teeth in. It took real effort to clamp down, and the hand on the back of my head urged me to keep going, even if it had to be hurting him.

The first gush of blood filled my mouth, and I closed my eyes, losing myself to the ecstasy. The pain receded as I drank.

Rogue led the way down the hillside. We had to move fast. The barbed spear fired by the ballista had hit the golden dragon's wing. It had crashed to the earth. There were so few of them left. If we didn't get there fast enough…

I had never moved so fast, only to seem like it wasn't fast enough. The dragon's heart thundered in my ears. Pain echoed in his roar, and the clash of steel reached us before we made it to the clearing, leaping the downed trees he'd ripped out as he tumbled from the sky.

Ahead of me by two steps, Rogue unleashed a deadly volley of ice daggers. They sliced right through the opponents, and I continued on. There were easier ways to kill, but I wanted to get to the dragon before further harm had been done to him. My blade cleaved through necks and severed heads. I was already on to the next before the first body fell.

The dragon's wing dragged the ground, the spear having torn the delicate membrane of the wing. He snapped and ripped one soldier in half with a chomp of his teeth and consumed the two past them with a flash of white-hot fire. Their screams rent the air and then faded as they tumbled, burnt and blackened to the ground.

When the dragon swung his head to face me, I raised my hands, sword angled down. In my grip it was still dangerous, but my posture was non-threatening.

"I've come to help you," I told him. "You can kill me." Or try anyway. "Or you can let me free you. There are more of them coming. They've gotten very skilled at killing your kind."

The dragon glared, rage and pain radiated from him. The sound of running steps behind me had me twisting, and the head of the latest raider sailed from his shoulders as I stepped up to meet the assault. Rogue was soon at my side as we cut through the attackers.

When the last body dropped, I faced the dragon again. He'd been at our backs the whole time, and while he could have burned us, he hadn't. He stared steadily, and I passed the blade to Rogue.

"I am going to remove the spear," I informed him as I moved with purpose in his direction. "It won't heal as it is, and you won't be able to get off the ground."

Dragons were formidable creatures, but they were more vulnerable on the ground. The beast's pain beat at me. I could smell it in the air and feel it in the thunder of his pulse. When the dragon made no threatening move, I darted forward and gripped the spear. With a yank, it came free.

He roared, and my heart ached for him. I wanted to put a hand on him to help, but I had to move to avoid the snap of the damaged wing and the clack of his teeth coming together mere inches from my head.

Not a real attack. A warning.

"You're going to want to keep him, aren't you?" Rogue asked, his tone dry, and I shrugged.

In truth, I'd only wanted to help him. If he wanted to be a companion, I would not be opposed. "I think he likes me," I said with a grin, and Rogue laughed.

"I like you, didn't stop me from wanting to kill you."

This was true.

"Then you and he should get along well." I clapped Rogue on the shoulder. "Clean up the bodies, or leave them for him to eat?"

We eyed each other, then the dragon, who stared at us a moment. When he dipped his head to the bodies, I swore he smiled.

"Let him eat," Rogue agreed with me, and we withdrew to give him space.

Fingers in my hair tugged me away from his throat, and I met Alfred's dark gaze. Though his eyelids were half-lowered as though he was sleepy, I couldn't look away from the dangerous intensity housed there. The feeling of battle still surged in my veins, and the pleasure at saving such a magnificent beast.

Maddox.

He'd saved Maddox.

He'd saved Rogue, too. That was different in some ways. He'd saved Rogue for himself as much as for Rogue. But Maddox? He'd fought to get to him. Fought to keep him alive. Seeing him in the sun was so different from seeing him in the prison. He'd been majestic and proud. My heart wrenched to see him so hurt.

I licked my lips and then kissed Alfred. He let out a hum of approval as his tongue swept against mine. I lapped at the taste of my blood in his mouth while his coated mine. It was the strangest sensation and so absolutely right in the same breath.

The stroke of his hands along my sides had me arching, his cock nestled against my labia, already slick from how wet I was, and I ground against him. His chuckle vibrated through me as he fisted my hair tighter, the tug lighting up my whole scalp. The desire eddied there, a constant thrum against my senses, but it wasn't hunger but true want. True need. I sucked against his tongue and dug my fingers into his shoulders.

When he rolled me over, I wrapped my legs around him, arching upward to tease along his thickening girth. Breaking the kiss, he nipped at my lower lip, and I groaned.

"Do you want this, hellion?" The question startled me. "Do you want *me*? Or are you responding to your hunger?"

Hurt struck like a slap, and I blinked. I wasn't hungry at all, but he was like holding onto a storm, all sizzling zaps to my senses, and he'd saved Maddox. I wanted…

"Shh," he shushed me with a nuzzling kiss that took him to my ear and then to my throat. "I have to know, because I will not take from you as the little coward did." The press of his lips ghosting over the marks he'd made had me shuddering. "I will wipe him from you, but you have to want me to be in my bed."

Wasn't I already in his bed? Despite my best efforts, the words wouldn't leave my tongue. The graze of his teeth had me clawing at his back as the panic bubbled up inside of me. Darkness edged my vision, and Alfred sighed.

Had I disappointed him? Fuck. Why did I care?

"When I get my hands on that demon, I'm going to have his entrails for garters." With that cryptic, if brutal statement, he bit me again, and this time I didn't pretend not to scream. It was like I was being burned from the inside out as he began to suck. The pleasure faded entirely to pain.

We were standing on the beach. The house was above, but I didn't look there, I kept my gaze on the water. "You keep killing me." It had taken me a moment to put it together, but the agony racing through my veins before clarified it.

"Yes," he told me. Well, at least he didn't sugarcoat it. "You don't want me to make it sweet."

I almost laughed. Twisting, I met his dark-eyed gaze. I

really couldn't tell if his eyes were that dark because he was full of shit, or if his pupils had swallowed the irises. The corners of his mouth tipped up. "Why?"

"Because, Hellion…" He said the nickname like he had Fiona, and it sent a shudder through my whole system. "You fed on a shadow demon for weeks. You never fully transitioned. You basically slowed your own death, but death comes for everyone."

"So you're killing me? How does that logic work?"

"I'm turning you. I'm clearing away the stamp of the fool who tried to and the taint of the shadow demon who wanted to own you."

Anger flash-fired through me.

"Have no fear, Hellion. No one else will be able to claim you." He stroked a finger down my cheek.

"Except you."

"Except us," he corrected. "Fin is right. You do belong to us, but we also belong to you."

I rolled my eyes and jerked away from his touch. "I didn't ask any of you for this."

"I know."

"But you're doing it anyway."

"I can't let you die." The admission should make me feel something. Wanted. Needed. But all it made me feel was…

"That isn't *your* decision to make." I glared at him, and he gave me another of those faint smiles. It didn't quite reach his eyes though.

"It is very much my decision," he said. "As modern people are fond of saying, the buck stops here. I will make sure you have what is due you. The vengeance on those who harmed you."

"I can get that on my own."

"I have no doubt." At least he sounded like he meant that part. "Just as I have no doubt that I will very much enjoy helping you. The crimes done to you are numerous, and no one hurts what is mine."

I moved away from him, but I couldn't escape. He was there, like a shadow in my step. A pulse under my skin. He was pulling all the blood from my body.

Again.

"The pain is real," he murmured. "I can block most of it. But this is the best way to ease your transition."

"Wow, I'd hate to see the hard way."

He didn't comment. I focused on the ocean, on the foam of the sea as it rolled in and how the air tasted. I loved the ocean so much.

"Why?"

"What?"

"Why do you love the ocean?"

"Can you at least pretend to not read my mind?"

"Not right now, no," he said. "I am taking all of you into me, and then I am having you take me into you. You will know me as intimately as I know you when we are done."

Resentment sliced through me. "You turned Rogue without his permission."

"He hated me for a long time."

"Why did you do that?"

"Because he was my friend, and I did not want him to die."

"But he didn't want to live like this." Did Rogue and I have that in common? And I thought he was such an asshole to me.

"No," Alfred admitted, moving to stand next to me. I was tempted to lean my head against his shoulder, but I resisted it.

Barely.

"He didn't think it natural. Elves are—they are very attuned to nature. He was—is a frost elf. He thrives in winter, it is his favorite season. His magic is a part of him. When I turned him, he lost some of that. He gained more, but…that took time for him to grieve and to acclimate."

"And you feel no regret for it." I dared him to lie to me. I'd been in that memory. I'd been there when he turned him.

"I do not regret saving my friend. Nor do I regret giving him the time to make his peace with it."

"Generous."

He shrugged.

The light faded, and it was getting darker. I sat abruptly. The sand was warm beneath me, even if the breeze was cold.

"I could just not drink."

"I cannot let you do that," he told me, and he sounded almost sorrowful. But he wasn't. He didn't regret doing this to Rogue, and now he wouldn't regret doing it to me.

"Did you force Fin, too?"

But even as I tried to focus on him, he faded. Through blurred vision, I found him hovering over me. His mouth was red with my blood. He pressed his lips to mine, a teasing kiss, and then ground his hips gently against me.

I refused. Even if my body wanted his, I refused.

I closed my eyes and blocked him out.

"Hellion," he whispered. "You have to drink. Take back from me what I have taken from you."

"No."

His sigh filled the room.

"Fiona," he commanded, and my name settled on me like strings attaching themselves and jerking me to move. I opened my eyes to find his throat right there. He rolled onto his back, pressing my face into his throat, and then he dragged a hand down to my ass, massaging it. "Drink."

I scraped my teeth against my lower lip. The pain had gone past the point I even cared about it. Breathing was hard, and my heart grew more sluggish. If I refused, if I turned away, this could all be over.

At the same time…

"Do you really want to die, Hellion?" Alfred squeezed my ass. "You'll take Maddox from us."

What?

I forced my tumbling eyes open.

"Possibly Fin, too."

I swallowed at my dry throat, and it burned. All I could smell was Alfred. His scent filled my nostrils, and I ached. Even as I told myself no, I began to roll my hips. His cock bumped against my clit, and a spear of pleasure darted through me. Licking at my dry lips, I tried to pull away, but he kept my face at his throat.

"Maddox has already let you claim him, Hellion—you're his mate. Do you hear his roars?" I had, though I'd tried to tune them out. The room seemed to vibrate from them. "He will tear this place apart to get to you if you do not drink."

I could almost hear him, pleading with me. *Drink, Kitten.*

You can hear him, Beautiful. Fin's voice slipped in. *You have to drink.*

I was so tired.

"You are almost done," Alfred promised. But that could be a lie. What did I know?

Beautiful, trust us. Please. You're ours. I asked you for time, and you said you would give it to us.

The tears in his voice threatened to gut me, and I squeezed my eyes shut. Maddox's roar thrummed through me, and I pressed my mouth down against Alfred's throat.

I hate you all.

A pause as I sank my teeth in, and that old blood rushed in to soothe all the pain. I clamped down faster this time, even as I sank down on his cock at once. The pleasure lit me up as his power flooded into me.

We know, Beautiful. Fin sounded so damn sad.

Then I heard nothing as I began to move, every thrust sending me higher as I drank, and Alfred stroked me through it. When his memories swam up to swallow me, I fought them off, focusing on the way he stretched me and how my nipples scraped against his chest.

I drank until he went lax beneath me and came with a shout, my own orgasm staggering me.

Then and only then did I lift my head.

Meeting his gaze, I waited. His cock was still buried deep, and his eyes gleamed. "Yes?" he demanded.

And I finally understood the question.

He offered me himself, but I had to give in return. I had to give willingly.

Fine, if that was the only way out of this prison—the only way to be strong enough to defeat them all—then I'd take it.

"Yes."

Pleasure flared in his eyes, and Maddox's roar changed. Fin brushed his thoughts to mine, his regret and triumph tangled too tightly together for me to separate. Then they all faded. The only one I didn't feel or see was Rogue. Perhaps he understood my decision best of all.

Alfred gripped my hair and flipped me over, then struck.

As his teeth pierced me, I surrendered.

It looked like I was going to be a damn vampire after all.

Fiona may have surrendered this battle, but the war has only begun. Alfred, Rogue, Maddox, and Fin will have their hands full when we return in Succubus Unchained.

To keep up with Heather and all her series join her reader's group:

https://www.facebook.com/groups/HeathersPack/

USA TODAY BESTSELLING AUTHOR
HEATHER LONG
SHACKLED SOULS BOOK 2
SUCCUBUS
UNCHAINED

NP
PARANORMAL
PRISON

SHACKLED SOULS BOOK 2

SUCCUBUS UNCHAINED

SHACKLED SOULS BOOK 2

Nightmare Penitentiary

I'd become a damn vampire after all.

I never wanted or asked for this. What began as a one-night stand earned me a stint in prison, the attention of a shadow demon, and rescue by three devastating—to my system—males along with the declaration that I was their foretold something…

Yeah.

No.

To win this war and regain my freedom, I had to give up part of who I am and become something *other*. Now, Maddox calls me his mate, Fin labels me his lady, Alfred has declared I'm to be his queen. But I'm with Rogue on this one.

I'm trouble, and they have *no* idea what I'm going to do.

"The most dangerous animal in the world is the silent, smiling woman." - Anonymous

Seven weeks, six days, and something like fourteen hours since I made the worst mistake of my life. Arguably, the last mistake of my *life*.

The little fucker was still out there, somewhere. I didn't obsess. Not aloud. Not where any of *them* could hear me.

It was just narrowly four weeks since Maddox appeared in my cell and thrust me onto the next hellish level of my journey. The worst part? I liked him.

More than I cared to admit.

A scant few days with him, Rogue, and Fin, and then *Alfred* woke up. And in the three plus weeks since then, I'd not been out of Alfred's sight for longer than a few moments. Even then, I was pretty sure the ancient asshole had eyes on me. Like right now, I sat on a rock in the middle of the garden and a dozen crows fluttered about or perched. They'd arrived as soon as I had.

It didn't matter that Alfred had been 'asleep' when I dragged myself from his bed or that Fin had been sprawled on my other side. It wasn't until this week that Alfred even let me spend any time with the others.

The fact that I'd started to miss them just aggravated me even more.

I'd lost count of how many times I'd *died* over the last few weeks. Something had changed. Irrevocably. Something he had to know because this morning, I'd also woken to clothes waiting for me. Alfred's chambers were large, fit for a king. Furnished, it was filled with comfortable sofas and lounging chairs. My favorite—not that I had any interest in it mind you—was the fainting couch placed in the perfect position to look out the oversized windows toward the valley.

Toward freedom.

The sun streaked in through that window for several hours a day, and I could doze there and pretend to get a tan. Not that I imagined I'd get one. I hadn't really tanned before.

The clothing had been new. The long-sleeved Henley and jeans had been like a gift to slide on after weeks wearing a rotating selection of robes and kitten slippers. Occasionally, I'd been able to steal a shirt.

Occasionally.

It never lasted.

They, more often than not, shredded the shirts in their lust.

You might think it weird that I complained about that part. Succubus and all that, but even I had my limits. Not even a wrinkle of hunger pinched at me. I'd never been so full.

The fact that I craved any of them at all must be put down to the dementia formed by being trapped.

I despised Fin for his cheer and playfulness. I despised how he teased and dared me to play with him. I despised that even when I told him I detested him, he looked at me with sad, adoring eyes. I despised him for plucking at my thoughts, until I'd finally managed to push him out and keep him out. Even mid-orgasm, he couldn't secret his way in anymore.

I detested Rogue for his icy demeanor and all-to-knowing eyes. At least he didn't make promises only to break them. He didn't pretend to like me, either. Worse, he pitied me. Bastard.

I hated Maddox because he made me care about him. He loathed that the others hadn't kept his word. Not enough to help me escape them, but he'd promised all I had to do was listen and then they'd let me go. At least he had the decency to feel guilty about it. Not that I'd admit it aloud. Mate. He'd mated me or I'd mated him. I could pretend I hadn't been involved, but I hadn't forgotten the day he wanted me to bite him and I'd given in, or how it had unlocked something inside of me.

I didn't want to care. I hated him for making me feel that way. Relationships and succubi did not mix. Not long-term. Now, I was his mate?

The dragon's roars the day Alfred—that asshole—began my true "transition" echoed in my mind every time I considered my escape like the real bars on the cage they'd constructed around me.

Rubbing a hand against my neck, I sighed. The scar there had flattened and gone almost pure white against my skin. Even paler than the rest of me. The ridges, once defined and puffy, were smooth. The bites littering my arms, breasts, abdomen, and thighs had also faded, healing as if they hadn't been.

The sharpness of my canines couldn't be missed. Though

they were hardly as sharp as the guys', mine could pierce skin —Maddox's, Fin's, Rogue's, and Alfred's. The night before had also marked the first time since my arrival I hadn't been drained nor needed to feed on any of them.

My transition or whatever was complete.

Not that Alfred—the *asshole*—had said a word. He'd merely cupped my chin, then stared at me for a long moment before he'd nodded and left me alone. Not a single sentence or utterance.

Fin crept in when I'd been working out my next steps, and he'd curled around me, asking for nothing, and even as hard as I tried to ignore him—it made me feel like the bad guy.

Why the fuck did I feel even an ounce of guilt over these guys? They didn't deserve it.

What little loyalty I'd been cultivating died a swift and painful death the day Alfred found me in this garden. Not once had he bitten me anywhere but my neck. The flattened scar pulsed at the memory.

I hated him for that, too.

Aggravation struck flint inside of me, kindling a whole new fire. The door opened, the creak of it the only warning before the scent of coffee teased at my nose, but I didn't bother with turning to look.

The rough scrape of denim over rock rasped in the bitterly cold air as the dragon settled next to me. The heat rolling off him buffeted the chill I'd been ignoring, and it took everything I had not to lean into him. Then he cheated and held the oversized tumbler of coffee in front of me.

Half of my grumpy fled when face to face with the giver of life. Shut up, I was more than aware of the irony. Yes, I was a vampire and a succubus, and coffee was the secret key to my soul.

Tipping my head to the side, I met his quiet gaze and did

my damnedest to ignore the hope flaring in his eyes. The barest hint of a smile touched the corners of his lips. "Good morning, Kitten."

My fingers collided with his as I took the tumbler, and he didn't pull away as we both lifted it to my lips, nor did he look away as I took a long swallow of it. Of the four of them, Maddox was the one who'd been kept away the most. Alfred blocked him time and again.

This was the first time we'd been alone together since Alfred woke. Sighing, I lowered the tumbler and leaned my head against his shoulder. Maddox half-sagged as if someone cut the string on all his tension. He wrapped his free arm around me and pulled me close.

"You're better," he murmured, pressing his lips to my crown. It wasn't a question. I was better. The soreness and the exhaustion were both gone. The sting from so many half-healed bites had been erased along with their marks on me.

"I suppose," was all I'd comment on that, but I couldn't help the "Missed me?" I added on.

"Yes," he answered without hesitation. "I'm sorry I wasn't there for you."

It wasn't his fault. He didn't even have to explain it. Alfred —the asshole—controlled everything. Apparently, even them. Though he didn't throw Alfred under the bus.

"I'm here now," he offered. "What can I get for you?"

Since he brought me coffee, I really didn't need anything else. Well, at least nothing I would ask him for. I wanted to leave. But anytime I brought that up, there were always reasons I couldn't.

I needed to finish transition.

I needed to have the shadow taint purged from me.

I needed to accept what I was.

I needed to be a vampire.

Well, mission fucking accomplished. But a million dollars

said they wouldn't let me leave now. Not with all the changes to the keep going on. It was open and airy now. Fires burned in many of the fireplaces. A generator had been added, and Fin even brought in a huge screened television and DVD player. No digital, not yet.

I guess WiFi was hard to get in Shangri-fucking-la.

"Nothing."

"Kitten," Maddox prodded gently, pressing another kiss to my hair and igniting a wave of tenderness I fought to ignore. I would not go soft on the dragon. I didn't ask for this. "Tell me something I can do for you."

The note of pleading wormed its way under my skin, and I scowled. I pictured his face when I slammed my knee into his nuts in that cell. The anger in his voice when he caught up to me, and the rumble of his growl when I sat in the corner and ignored him in favor of building my house.

My house.

A shudder went through me, and Maddox squeezed me. "What's wrong?"

"Nothing," I said again. Maybe if I denied it enough it would be true. My house wasn't really mine anymore. Alfred had pulled the whole thing apart and explored every inch of the construction when he fed on me, and then submerged me into his colorful and bloody history while I drained him. I knew too much about him now—the manipulations, the control, and the power he wielded without a second thought. His bonds with Rogue, Maddox, and Fin meant everything to him, and while Fin was more a son than a brother, Rogue and Maddox were definitely his brothers.

It went beyond fondness and friendship. They were family, and no matter how they bickered, they would never choose me over each other. Not even Maddox, who promised I didn't have to stay.

His word only held value if his brothers backed it. That

helped to insulate me from the tenderness swelling inside, deflating it.

A growl rumbled in his chest as I pulled away, but the arm locked around me loosened, even if he didn't let me scoot far. I drank the coffee and kept my gaze fixed on the blue sky overhead. The scent of snow floated on the air. It was crisper, sharper, and more intense, just like everything else. Colors were deeper and richer. Scents far more provocative. And tastes? I could dissect every part of the coffee if I focused.

Fin had tried to tell me being a vampire wasn't so bad when it added so much to my senses. Unfortunately, I could taste all the bullshit he layered onto those sentiments, too.

"I should probably eat," I said, aware that expressing any kind of desire was the fastest way to getting Maddox to let up. I didn't look at him as I slid off the rock. In addition to clothes, I'd also scored shoes. These were more like hiking or combat boots—all function and no style.

That was fine.

They were an improvement on kitten slippers.

Maddox was my heated shadow all the way inside. He trailed me up the stairs to the library where, as with every other day, a virtual buffet had been set out. There was always bacon. Since the first morning Fin brought it back to me, bacon had been included in every breakfast. I filled my plate and carried it over to my favorite chair near the fireplace. It had become my favorite because none of them could sit next to me.

Though Maddox settled on the floor right in front of me with his back pressed against my legs. I bit back a reaction and focused on eating. If the day followed pattern, it wouldn't be long before my other keepers tracked me down. They often convened here each morning. Like me, Maddox ate. Fin had to have already been up since the food was here, but since I never saw it come or go, who knew how it arrived.

The shuffle of an unfamiliar step, however, jerked me forward in the chair, and I cut a look behind us toward the room.

A man I didn't know made his way through with a cloth, wiping things down.

"That's Anton," Maddox said, as if the name alone explained everything. "He will serve as librarian here. There will be more retainers arriving. Some came in last night."

Retainers.

I tracked Anton's progress. As if aware of me, the brunet paused to meet my gaze, and there was a flash of teeth as he smiled.

Vampire.

At Maddox's rumbling growl, however, Anton dropped his gaze and bowed to me.

Oh for the love of…

I turned my back on him and glared at the fire. The 'retainer' continued his task of wiping things down.

"They will not bother you, Kitten," Maddox told me as if that was my concern. "They know their place."

Did they now?

"Good morning, Beautiful," Fin called as he strolled in. I took a sip of coffee and said nothing before returning to my food. He hummed as he stopped next to my chair, and his gaze rested on me like a soft weight. With care, he waited until I lowered my fork and then pressed a kiss to my temple. "Not talking to me today?"

The barest hint of a wounded tone crept into his voice.

"She's hungry," Maddox said with a scowl. "Leave her alone."

I didn't need him to fight my battles for me. "I also have

nothing to say," I tacked on, and then took another bite of bacon.

Feathering his hand over my hair, Fin tugged one curl. "You look better."

I grunted.

He lingered for another couple of heartbeats, and then his hand fell away as he moved to collect his own breakfast. The sudden chill prickling over my skin warned me of the new arrivals, even if their silent footfalls didn't. Rogue said nothing to me as he gathered his own drink and food. Alfred bypassed all of it and plucked me out of the chair despite Maddox's snarl.

The dragon rose to follow, and the two glared at each other as I balanced both my plate and tumbler. Fortunately, neither fell. Honestly, I didn't have time for this. I just wanted a meal in peace.

"You've had her for days," Maddox said. "Leave her alone."

"I'm not harming her," Alfred countered. "Your mood, however, is far more dangerous."

The smoothness in the words demanded we side with him. The asshole didn't even have to try and compel me, it clung to every syllable and nuance. The stare-off continued until Rogue said, "Give her to me."

Give me? What the fuck was I? A damn object to be passed around?

I'd struggle, but that would just end up making a mess. I wasn't as strong as Alfred, no matter how much strength I'd gained. I wasn't as strong as any of them for that matter. If they wanted to pin me, I wasn't going anywhere.

The air crackled with agitation, then a second set of unfamiliar steps punctured the tension. This time, a woman made her way across the library toward us. Though, 'made her way' was too pedestrian a description. She practically glided. Dressed in silk and lace with a waterfall of pure midnight hair and eyes so dark I half-expected there to be stars glittering in them, she was probably the most beautiful woman I'd ever seen.

Ruby red lips parted as she smiled. "Alfred, my love…"

The ice plunging through the air completely smothered the fire. Alfred all but thrust me at Rogue. Well, at least he put me on my feet before passing me that way. Fin let out a low groan as Alfred faced the woman.

"Eleanor," he intoned as he moved to meet her. Maddox settled a hand against my lower back, but it was Rogue who tugged me back toward the chair.

The woman paused three steps from Alfred to dip into a curtsey that nearly took her to her knees before him. The lace and silk sheath of a dress left nothing to the imagination. Her dark nipples strained against the fabric, already peaked and pebbled. As she straightened, we all got an eyeful of shaved cunt.

"I have missed you," she said, her lyrical voice that of a siren as she stepped toward him.

It wasn't my imagination as she cupped his face and rose to kiss him that her eyes flashed toward me. Our gazes locked as she pressed her lips to his, and it wasn't a fraternal kiss of any kind. It was an open-mouthed, tongue twisting, wet kiss that bordered on the obscene.

She also made too much noise as she let out a little moan. I raised my brows because while her lust might be rolling like a cloud around her, Alfred's was a cloudless day of disinterest, though he certainly didn't push her away.

When she pulled away to offer him her throat, I rolled my eyes and moved back to my chair. Let him play with the vixen. I wouldn't kick her out of my bed, except she was trying *way* too hard and that beauty didn't extend past the surface.

As I settled, I found Maddox and Fin staring at me

intently, and I raised a piece of bacon with a smirk and took a bite of it. The hiss of breath suggested Alfred had taken the offered bite and hadn't been remotely gentle about it.

Good.

Hopefully, it fucking hurt.

Rogue let out a grunt as the woman's liquid voice spilled over me. "My lord," she whispered in a breathy 'please fuck me' voice. She had her hands on him, and he stared down at her with an unreadable expression. So much for turning my back on her, since she planned to continue her show in front of me.

Blood trickled from the wound on her neck. It was a trace amount. Negligible, yet she still arched her back to press her breasts to his chest and bare her throat. With almost practiced boredom, he bit her. There was no movement of his hands to cradle her as he sank his teeth in, and I doubted he had much time to drink before he lifted his head.

He spared me a look of distaste, as if finding my observation tacky. Too. Fucking. Bad. If they wanted to put on a show in front of me, let them.

Eleanor wasn't done. She went to Fin next and slid her arms around him. He scowled, no pretense in his expression at all. When she pressed her lips to his ear, he moved his head, then caught her hand and lifted her wrist to his mouth. He bit down once, and she let out a moan, but he didn't hold her there and, like Rogue, finished in scant seconds.

The apology in his eyes surprised me, but Maddox's snarled, "Go the fuck away, Eleanor," distracted me.

The woman paused in front of him and, as with Alfred, she went almost to her knees, but he ignored her.

"Have I offended you?"

Alfred moved into my line of sight, his expression utterly unreadable as he studied the pair.

"Just go away," Maddox said, motioning her to rise.

"But I am here to serve as always." Woman apparently didn't get the memo of disinterest, because she all but flung herself at Maddox. His expression darkened, and heat ballooned out as he shoved her away without any care, then she landed on her ass right in front of me.

Surprise, hurt, and then rage slid over her gorgeous face, and she lifted those dark eyes toward me. Challenge flooded her expression, but she shuttered it at Rogue's clipped, "Take the blood offering, Maddox, and then Eleanor can go."

"I don't want it," Maddox argued.

"It's not a matter of want," Alfred stated. "The offerings are coming. All will be accepted in due course. Eleanor is merely the first." He looked at me, and I lifted a middle finger while I picked up a piece of bacon.

Fin bit back a laugh, and Maddox's furious expression turned amused. None of these reactions lasted as Eleanor moved to her knees and then almost *crawled* to Maddox.

"Just get it over with," Rogue advised, and Eleanor's back stiffened. I crunched the bacon, even if my appetite had gone away. More offerings were coming? Retainers were filling the keep?

Did that mean their isolation was ending?

Those distractions might give me the time I needed. The stand-off lasted another three blazing minutes. Maddox looked at me finally, and his expression made all kinds of promises I didn't want him giving me. Like Fin, he went for her wrist, but rather than bite her, he just licked one of the drops of blood dribbling there and then dropped her hand like it burned him.

He hadn't wanted her blood. At all. Disgust rolled off of him in waves, and anger coiled in my gut. Alfred shouldn't have forced him. Still, my dragon moved away from the woman, who remained on her knees.

Undeterred, Eleanor rose to her feet and started toward

Alfred, only to stop when he raised a hand. He motioned for her to twirl and then nodded toward me.

If I'd thought her spine had stiffened before, that was nothing on it now. She turned to face me.

Oh. Fuck. No.

The earlier rage rekindled in her eyes. Rogue had moved to stand next to my chair while Maddox bracketed it on the other side.

Smoothing the emotions away from her expression, Eleanor dropped to curtsey before me and then tilted her head, though every part of her seemed to vibrate in rejection.

Yeah.

Not happening.

I met Alfred's gaze over her head, and he raised his eyebrows.

Ignoring Eleanor, I rose from the chair, and before I could put my plate or tumbler aside, Anton swept them from my hands and also offered me his throat.

Fin shook his head. *Beautiful...*

"Save it," I told him. "This...isn't happening." With that, I turned and moved away from all of them. They wanted to trap me here, turn me, and keep me isolated, fine. Whatever.

"Fiona," Alfred said in a tone that demanded I obey.

I paused at the doors to the library, but I didn't turn around. "You know I wouldn't take the warden's blood bags either."

Silence crashed through the room, and I shoved the doors open. What fondness for the library I'd developed died in front of the fireplace.

I wouldn't take a meal in there again.

If they planned on having a parade of these fuckers coming to offer their blood, I'd rather be back in a cell.

I doubted they'd give me long, but I descended the steps

and headed for the other wing. There were dozens upon dozens of rooms in the keep.

On the steps, however, I paused to glance into the great hall. There were easily half a dozen people moving around, setting up torches, chairs and huge tables. The floors had been cleaned and tapestries hung.

How were the retainers getting here?

Aware of someone watching me, I met the gaze of a younger vamp, his expression rapt.

I could use that.

I smiled slowly, and his own lips turned upward.

I could use him.

Because one way or another, I was getting out of here.

<h1 style="text-align:center">CHAPTER 2</h1>

"Sooner or later, everyone sits down to a banquet of consequences."
- Robert Louis Stevenson

When Maddox said more retainers were coming, he hadn't been kidding. Over the last three days, the keep flooded with new arrivals. Most were consigned to a different wing. I'd also earned my own room. Look at me, all fancy.

Then again, Eleanor had arrived, so Alfred didn't need a bed warmer any longer, and I was all transitioned and shit. Lucky me. The chamber assigned to me was tucked directly between Rogue and Maddox's rooms.

Like everything else in the keep, it had received a makeover. My windows didn't overlook the mountains. Stained glass framed the eight clear panes in the center, so the sun gave my room a dappled look. Like every other suite, a huge bed decorated the center of the room. Two lounging sofas had been added in a V around the fireplace, and my favorite fainting sofa from Alfred's room had been moved here.

Well, good to know I didn't need to return to his rooms. Ever.

The closet was packed with items, but I ignored most of them. I needed to pack light. My room also boasted a huge copper bathtub, but it would take forever to heat the water for it. So I didn't bother. Apparently, the bathing room downstairs was reserved for us alone, particularly after the first morning I'd been lounging there when one of our guests wandered in to join me.

The vampire's name was Jonathon, and he was exceptionally polite, though easily enamored.

Maddox bodily threw him out.

Still, the crush burgeoning in the young vampire's eyes hadn't been remotely dissuaded. I caught him watching me as I wandered the keep. I kept myself aloof, anytime I dared to strike up a conversation, one of my keepers appeared.

Despite having my own room, I didn't sleep alone. Maddox appeared that first night and slid under the covers as he wrapped an arm around me. I half-expected him to pounce me, but was pleasantly surprised when he buried his face in my hair and let out the longest, most profound sigh.

I hated him for that, because guilt began to nibble at me relentlessly. Didn't stop me from keeping an eye on Jonathon. Or from studying everyone else who arrived.

Vampires. The lot of them.

I'd never seen so many in one place.

The dress that appeared, hanging on the four paneled room divider with an ocean scene painted across it, served as a slap in the face.

Maybe I read too much into it. Maybe I didn't read enough. But the collar on the dress was comprised of golden links and fell in a straight train down the back like a leash.

The rest of it—what little there was of it—was forest green. It would hug my breasts and hips. A cutout triangle in the center would bare my midriff, and it had zero back to speak of and would probably give a hint at my ass.

In a word, it was exquisite and a shackle.

More. Damn. Chains.

"Do you like it?" Maddox asked, and I wanted to kick him, then myself, and then him again.

"It's beautiful." Not responding with the acid burning on my tongue took everything I had. I wanted them lulled to complacency. They were all so preoccupied with all the arrivals. Alfred had been accepting offering after offering. They were practically queued up in the main hall. Anytime I made an appearance, he tracked me with his gaze as he sank his fangs into every single one who presented him or herself.

It was a sea of lust in that chamber night and day. Bloodlust. Lust for power. Sexual lust. Straight up greed. The base hungers were there—particularly where any of the guys were concerned, but especially with Fin. It was almost adorable how they panted for him when he utterly ignored them all with a faint smirk on his lips, as if he knew I watched him.

Maybe he did.

I didn't spend a lot of time on it. I'd rather they were distracted.

The more distracted they were, the better my chances at taking advantage of all the comings and goings.

Outside, the cold wind blew and snow kissed the ground. It was almost postcard picturesque, even in the barren garden populated by my black-feathered friends each time I stepped out.

The garden, like the bathing room, had become a private domain. No guests ventured out. Guards had been stationed.

Those were annoying. But they didn't speak to me. In fact, they never even looked at me.

So they weren't there to keep me in so much as to keep others out.

Warm hands settled on my shoulders. "Fiona…"

I turned my head slightly, catching him in my periphery but saying nothing.

"I know you're unhappy."

Not a newsflash.

"And I cannot make up to you my broken word."

No, he really couldn't.

"But I promise, now that you have transitioned, it will get better."

"You shouldn't promise," I told him, and then took a step away from his grip. To my surprise, he let me go. "You cannot offer any promise that Alfred is guaranteed to keep, nor Rogue for that matter."

"They do not rule," Maddox said. "Over others, yes, but not over us."

I snorted, but I turned to face him and folded my arms. It was better than exploring the strange tug to look after his feelings. The rawness in his eyes cut me. "If that were true, then you would have made sure I could leave after you three told me your tale and I said I wanted to go."

Chin dipping, he said, "The circumstances were different then."

"Oh?" I raised my eyebrows. "So if I want to walk out the door right now? Would you stop me?"

His lips compressed. "You wouldn't get far."

It wasn't a yes or a no.

"You have to understand…"

"No," I told him simply. "I don't." But I understood more than he realized. Maybe more than any of them realized. Just because I'd avoided vampires for more than casual fun and feeding didn't mean I failed to understand them. They thrived on power and politics. The power in blood, and the games in politics. They loved to manipulate and control.

Alfred was far older than any vampire I'd ever met. It wasn't that he lusted for power. No, he *was* power. Disobedience just didn't register with him. Arrogant asshole.

"You truly hate us, don't you?" The sadness in Maddox's voice plucked my heartstrings, but I ignored that discordant sound. The dragon shouldn't have picked me in the first place.

"Yes." It wasn't entirely true, but I still meant it. A muscle ticked in Maddox's jaw, and he didn't call me on the fib.

So maybe he didn't sense it.

Good.

I'd been practicing diligently for days. Betray nothing. Not my thoughts. Not my feelings. Nothing. Let them see what they wanted to see.

"I understand," he murmured, then met my gaze. "I will make this right with you. I will earn your forgiveness." It was another pledge.

"I told you. No promises." Time for a change of subject. "I suppose you all expect me to wear this tonight?"

"If you do not like it, we can find you something else." Poor dragon. He was truly trying, and I was the bitch who didn't want him to succeed.

"It's fine," I told him, cutting a hand through the air. Then against my better judgment, I asked, "Why aren't you down there taking offerings with everyone else?"

Save for Eleanor, I hadn't seen him taking blood from any of the so-called offerings. Alfred was always there. I suspected Rogue was there as well, ever Alfred's shadow, which in and of itself was odd. Rogue had seemed the power here before Alfred awoke.

Fin? He'd been amongst the crowd, but I'd never lingered to see if he took any libations. Maddox hadn't, of that I was almost dead certain. The only times I'd seen him in that hall had been when he followed me, and then he'd stayed with me as I weaved my way along the fringes of the crowd.

I never stuck around. I didn't want their offerings or their blood.

Instead of answering me, he turned and walked toward the doors of my suite. But rather than exit, he closed them and pressed a hand to the doors. There was a whisper of sound and a small flash, just like when we'd been in the cell. Nostalgia crawled through me at an alarming rate.

I needed to shut that shit down.

Turning, he faced me. "The offerings are because of who Alfred is. They offer to all of us because he demands it. Protocol dictates we all sample their blood. Alfred must because of what he learns, but for us? It's merely a play of politics. Politics I have no desire to play."

Ah.

"So it means nothing?"

"No," Maddox said slowly, narrowing the distance between us until I had to tilt my head to continue holding his gaze. "Kitten, it's an important facet of ruling. Alfred has summoned many retainers...and the current leadership holding sway over vampires throughout the world."

Oh really.

Eyes narrowing, I studied Maddox. He hesitated for some reason. "Isaac is coming, isn't he?"

A huff of breath, and the dragon cut his gaze away. "He has been summoned." The Prince of Dallas. The one who'd sent me to Nightmare.

That son of a bitch would be at the party.

Well...wasn't that special?

"After such a long sleep, Alfred must remind those who have ruled in his absence that they are not the ultimate power."

"He's just one vamp," I reminded him. "Older than dirt or not."

A faint smile curved Maddox's lips, and he brought his hands down to my hips. The dragon wanted contact, and reluctant or not, I wrapped my arms around his neck. At the first touch, he picked me up and cradled me to him. When he buried his face against my throat, I didn't jerk. After days of Alfred biting me over and over, I was still not a fan of teeth at my neck, but Maddox had kept his word to never bite me there.

I could give him this.

He let out a shuddering sigh. "I hate the politics of it all," he grumbled. "I always have. But this is how they rule. How they make their power plays. He'll put them all together and make them prove their loyalty. Not everyone will survive. Particularly once he has their blood and takes their measure."

Their memories.

A light knock on the door prevented me from asking my next question, but I didn't really care whether Alfred got his teeth into Isaac or not. If the prince was coming here, I was going to kill him myself. I owed him that much for dumping me in a prison cell when I'd gone to him for help.

Two assholes did not make a right.

A growl vibrated against my throat at the interruption. I smoothed a hand over his hair and down his back. Poor thing seemed to need the comfort. The sound eased a little, and his muscles gave a faint tremble as he shifted his stance toward the door.

"It's Fin."

I'd guessed that. But I was going to do Maddox a solid since he'd done something to the door himself. "Do you want him to go away?"

Surprise rippled through him. Pulling his head up, he searched my gaze, but all I did was raise my eyebrows. At the moment, Maddox had offered me more in the last fifteen minutes than the rest of them combined about the circus they were currently conducting. Contrary to their popular opinions—and how much knowledge I'd gleaned from Alfred despite my best attempts—I didn't get nor did I give one flying damn about vampires and their politics. Once I got out of here, I planned on having nothing to do with them ever again.

Hybrid or not, I'd make my own way just as I always had.

"Is he not your favorite anymore?" The barest hint of teasing in his voice as he called the words out loudly made me smile.

"Hey!" Fin protested through the door.

"He was never my favorite," I reminded him, matching his volume with my own. The corners of Maddox's eyes crinkled.

"I *heard* that," Fin called before he hit the door again. "Open up."

"But you did like him better," my dragon—no dammit, not mine—reminded me.

I rolled my eyes and then wiggled to be put down. "Fine, I'll let him in."

I didn't even make it two steps before I was hauled back against his chest and his arms were around me as he pressed his lips to my jaw. "I haven't answered yet," he reminded me, his breath teasing me with little puffs and the faint rasp of his stubble grazing my skin.

"True." Rubbing my hand against the back of his, I almost smiled. "So what is your decision?"

Maddox didn't answer immediately, as though he needed the time to ponder it.

A pop of displaced air preceded Fin's arrival as he stepped out of the ether to stare at the pair of us. "Seriously?" A scowl tightened his beautiful face and his dark eyes gleamed with suppressed amusement as he planted his hands on his hips. "After all I've done for you? You have to *think* about it?"

"What have you done, exactly?" I asked, playing along. A smirk toyed with his lips as he dropped his gaze from Maddox to me.

"Coffee," Fin said holding up one finger before adding a second. "Bacon."

"Oh," I mused, head tilting back to glance up at Maddox. "He's right."

"I am not biting everyone who shows up," my dragon argued, and he also had a point. I met Fin's gaze daringly, and the druid smirked.

"I'm not biting them all either." He took another step toward me. "Is that bothering you, Beautiful? That we're taking the offering?"

"I don't care who you bite," I told him, blithely uncaring at the lie, because obviously I cared or I wouldn't be kicking up such a damn stink about it. But I didn't *want* to care, and that was nearly the same thing. "It's a good reminder that this place is filled to the rafters with vampires."

I might as well have said rodent dung. Lips quirking, Fin studied me as though he could pull the truth from me, but I met his gaze blandly even with the dragon wrapped around me. Leaning against him was far too damn comfortable. It really was long past the time I left.

"True, we're all vampires here," Fin told me. The lightest of verbal slaps.

Yes. I was a vampire. Thanks for the news flash.

But I said nothing, and the druid sighed. "I didn't come up here to fight."

"Why are you here then?" Maddox asked. "I thought Alfred set you a task."

Oh, had he? "What was that about him not being in charge of you three?"

"He isn't in charge of us, Beautiful," Fin told me. "We're a brotherhood, but some of us are more suited to some tasks than others. I'm the most charming, so I get most of the diplomatic jobs."

Maddox snorted.

"That said, I won't be at the party tonight." His expression bordered on resentful.

It took everything I had to contain my glee. One keeper down. That only left three to avoid. Arguably, Alfred would be busy receiving all his offerings, so that only meant Rogue and Maddox.

This could truly work to my advantage.

"You should be there," Maddox argued.

"Not necessary. Rogue isn't accepting offerings either, and since you've all but decided to abandon the practice, it would look wrong if I was the only one helping." Fin gave a shrug. "I don't want them anyway."

Even more interesting.

"Good," Maddox grunted. "When this is done, Alfred will likely stop as well."

"Right," Fin said with a snort and a smirk. "Anyway..." He looked to me again. "I won't see you in your dress tonight, Beautiful, and I may be away for a couple of days. I thought I would come to see if you've forgiven me enough for a farewell kiss to tide me over until I return?"

Hope nestled in those words. What I should tell him was he could hold onto hope in one hand and shit in the other and see which one got full first, but I swallowed the words.

Distraction.

I wanted them all distracted.

"Maybe," I told him instead.

"Really?" Surprise fluttered in his eyes and he smiled. "That's better than I thought I was doing." He took another step closer and raised his hands, but hesitated before touching me. Maddox wasn't moving away, so I gave Fin the tiniest of nods.

He cupped my face and then let out a harsh breath as his shoulders sagged. "Beautiful, if you can forgive me, I will never ask you for another thing." Then he kissed me. The brush of his mind touched me, but found no purchase. The constant hum that I'd perfected kept him out, but I parted my lips to his and drank in his kiss, even as he pressed me back into Maddox. The grind of his hips to my ass reminded me of just how much the dragon wanted me.

Well, if this was farewell… I wrapped my arms around Fin's neck and stroked his tongue with mine. The temperature in the room skyrocketed as Maddox began to kiss against my throat and stroke his hands along my sides.

The clothes didn't make it through the first kiss. The tearing sound went straight to my pussy, and I was already hot and slick and ready for them. Fin's groan as he sucked against my tongue sent another pulse through my system.

I could lie to myself and say I was hungry, but touching them had nothing to do with feeding. Between them, they shuffled back to the bed, and Fin didn't let go of my lips as he stripped off his clothes. One light push broke our kiss, and he fell backward.

I stroked my gaze over his body. The lean muscled perfection. The smooth, heavy ridges of his skin. He wasn't thickly muscled like Maddox, or tensely corded like Alfred, or even lean and powerful like Rogue. Fin's body was like a finely tuned weapon, elegant and slim, yet possessing a wealth of power.

Wrapping my hand around his cock, I pumped it twice, even as Maddox slid his hand down to my ass. I knew what was coming before two damp fingers pressed against my anus. Heated oil that was kept in a jar by the fire eased his passage up to the first knuckle.

The burn of intrusion had my eyes rolling, but I straddled Fin's lap as Maddox pressed me forward and then guided his cock into position so I could sink down on him. It wasn't the first time I'd had Fin in weeks. Like I'd said, he'd come to find me in Alfred's bed, but this was different somehow.

The stretch of him filling me had my head tilting back. He ran his hands over my chest, teasing and tweaking my nipples. One he smoothed and caressed while he pinched the other brutally. The sharp nip of pain amidst the pleasure sent lust spiking through me.

Maddox mouthed at my shoulder, the graze of teeth a tease and not a sting. He worked his knuckles deeper, stretching me for him. And I'd need it—the dragon always knotted me.

Mates, some distant part of my mind reminded me.

Rogue knotted me, too.

But I shoved that little bitchy voice away. I didn't know what Rogue was beyond an elf, and I wasn't asking.

The dragon was already too much mate for me.

Hopefully, he would forget in time.

Fin snapped his hips up, his cock striking deep and sparking pleasure to consume the errant thoughts tossing around in my head.

"Here with us," he commanded, and I met his gaze as I began to roll my hips. Maddox had three fingers in me now, stretching me, and the burn had increased to a forest fire of need raging through me. I wanted more than his fingers.

"Yes," Maddox whispered against my ear. "You will have it, Kitten."

Fuck, I'd said those words aloud.

Another harsh pinch sent pain rioting over my nerves and jerked my attention to Fin, as Maddox pushed me forward and tilted my ass up. Fin caught my breath in his kiss as the fingers in my ass eased away, and then the hot head of Maddox's cock pressed against the entrance.

It was so much larger than his fingers, but he didn't shove in all at once. He rocked forward, easing his passage. The heated oil added another sensation to the sparks exploding through my system, and I groaned against Fin's mouth. Digging my nails into his shoulders, I rolled my hips back to take more of Maddox, then forward to sink down onto Fin.

I writhed between them, and then Maddox filled me to bursting and my whole body lit up. Panting breaths escaped me, and Maddox wrapped a hand around my throat to turn my face to him. The scorching flame in his kiss branded all the way to my soul as they braced me, and then they began to pound into me. We found a rhythm that just drove me higher and higher.

Skin sliding on skin added another layer. I traced my tongue against the sweat trickling down Fin's face, then buried my mouth against his throat. He let out a little shout, bucking harder against me, his grunts echoing Maddox's.

"Bite me," he ordered. "Yes, Beautiful. Bite me."

I didn't want to, and at the same time, their refusal of the offerings was linked to me. I'd have to be a fool to dismiss the fact that they were making the attempt. Biting him would be cruel when I planned to leave. Maddox's fingers bit into my hips as he began to move me forward. The pace he set was punishing and driving the thoughts in my head to scatter against a haze of pleasure.

Fin's pulse throbbed beneath my lips, and I sank my teeth in. His ragged shout of my name sent a burst of pleasure through my system, even as his taste flooded my mouth. His orgasm detonated my own, and I clamped down on him and Maddox both. The swelling in my ass grew almost unbearable as the pleasure pushed me up and over the edge, the grind between them pulling orgasm after orgasm out of me, and I drank until I damn near blacked out from the raw pleasure.

We collapsed in a pile of naked limbs, bodies tightly intertwined, and they rolled onto their sides to keep me pinned between them. Fin didn't knot, but he didn't soften much, and seemed trapped within me thanks to Maddox's knot. There was something so fucking decadent about that.

Tiny kisses rained down on my face and shoulders. The whispers and loving words cosseted me, but I burrowed deeper away from them. I already cared too much.

I couldn't afford to care more.

But I could give them this goodbye.

They deserved that much.

CHAPTER 3

"Sometimes you put walls up not to keep people out but to see who cares enough to break them down." - Socrates

The party began before sundown and well after Fin left. I refused to say I missed him, though I did notice his absence. Maybe even more because the keep teemed with people. Maddox arrived at my door to walk me down to the party. Well, better stated, Maddox crossed to his room and changed before he returned and watched me get ready. I'd have complained, save for the avid sparkle in his eyes as I slipped on the dress.

Much to my disgust, it was comfortable as well as stylish, though I loathed the chain around my neck. I considered all the ways I could remove it, but I'd have to skip this dress entirely if I did. At least it wasn't heavy, and no magic sparked off the metal as it draped my skin.

At my doubtful look, Maddox said, "I wouldn't have

261

allowed any enchantments. Not after what happened to the shackles."

I made a face, and he shot me a rueful grin.

"I haven't forgiven you for those yet."

The slit of his eyes went pure dragon, and he gave a careless shrug. "It just means I must work harder. I have never minded a challenge, Kitten."

The last bit of the dress was a pair of killer heels. If I didn't know better, I'd have said someone had raided my closet. Though if Fin had been right, nothing of mine remained at all. Likely, it was all swept away by the same hand that dismissed me to Nightmare and tried to pretend I didn't exist.

Something else I needed to stab Isaac for.

As for my erstwhile escort, I really couldn't complain. He wore black jeans and a loose green silk shirt. It matched my dress perfectly, so it was no accident. Despite the fact that the clothes were an upgrade, he looked as comfortable as he had in the black guard's uniform he'd worn when he arrived in my cell. Which was to say, he also looked gorgeous. His hair fell neatly with its asymmetrical part, and the glint in his hazel-green eyes seemed equal parts a promise for playfulness and a warning.

Telling me not to do something was almost always a surefire way to make me do it, if for no other reason than to spite the person trying to control me.

Yes, sometimes I wasn't all that complicated.

He held up one last box as I faced him and propped it open. Inside were emeralds. Gorgeous, stunning emeralds fashioned into a bracelet, a ring, a pair of earrings, and a necklace. I raised my eyebrows and then looked at him.

"For you—no magic," he murmured. "I promise."

"That's too much," I told him and went to close the box, but he caught my hand and slipped the ring onto my finger.

It was set amidst a smattering of diamonds, and the band was an infinity loop, twisting dark and light metals together. The ring itself was warm on my skin. It slid right over the index finger of my right hand.

"Wear one?" he asked, his tone cajoling. "This one?"

The index finger wasn't a matrimonial or mating sign, right? Or was it for dragons? Fuck. I didn't know anything about dragons, except mine could be grumpy and sweet. It was an irritatingly attractive combination. "Is there some meaning to wearing this ring?"

"Yes," he answered, his smile slow and sly.

Eyes narrowed, I glanced from the stunning gem to him, then back. The emerald was near flawless from what I could tell. They all were. There had to be hundreds of thousands of dollars' worth of gems. I wasn't an expert. I liked shoes and clothes, but jewelry and I weren't that well acquainted. "Will you tell me if I ask what the meaning is?"

"I collect precious things," he told me.

A dragon with a hoard? I'd tease him, but it was kind of adorable.

"These remind me of your eyes."

"Poetry, Maddox?" I couldn't help tweaking him for that. Just a little.

He scowled. "Facts, Kitten. Not poetry. They do remind me of your eyes." He caught my hand and then stroked his thumb over the emerald. "Your index finger is a finger of power. It draws the eye. Though everything about you does. This is a symbol of status. Everyone will be studying you when we get down there. They will want to know you—are you a pawn? A player? A power? This ring answers those questions."

Huh. "What does it say? Property of and do not touch?" I'd only been half teasing, but his sudden smirk and rise to his feet made me scowl.

"I don't need a ring to stamp my claim, Kitten," he murmured, then kissed me before I could argue. "However, there are only a handful of emeralds in the world this flawless, and I own all of them." He tapped the box to his thigh before he tossed it to the center of my bed. "Or I should say, you do. They will know you, and they will respect you."

Uh huh.

"You're adorable." I patted his cheek and then headed for the door before he convinced me to say to hell with the party. It wouldn't even need much of an argument. I didn't want to go to this dog and pony show, save for the opportunity to map my exit.

I had an idea, one that having so many people—read, vampires—around would be very helpful with. At the door, I hesitated. If my plan proved fruitful, I wouldn't be returning to this chamber this night or any other. I wouldn't see any of them anymore. Maddox settled his hands on my bare shoulders. "No one is going to hurt you." The rough promise made me smile.

I wasn't worried about anyone hurting me.

Not when I was going to be the one inflicting the damage.

"Going to eat them if they try?" I asked, tipping my head back to look up at him.

"Going to make me gargle with bleach if I do?"

A laugh rolled out of me. "I wondered if you'd actually heard me."

A real grin softened his face, and he traced his fingers down my arms. "I heard you." Then he winked. "I also didn't belch."

Another laugh broke free. Dammit. I really didn't want to like him. "Stop being adorable. You need to go back to grumpy and bossy."

He snorted, then gave me a sharp slap on the ass. "Behave, Kitten."

That was better.

'Cause fuck, that hurt.

Ass still stinging, I preceded him out the door. We were alone in our upper wing, but the sound from below was a constant hum interspersed by a faint throbbing beat, like all of them together created one dysfunctional heartbeat.

When Maddox offered me an arm, I shook my head. I'd rather have my hands free. As it was, I'd only been able to strap a knife to one of my thighs. The boys didn't have a lot of weapons lying around. I'd stolen the knife week two—or week three? Somewhere in there—from Alfred's room and kept it.

No one asked for it back.

Not that a knife would be effective against a vampire, but it would definitely make a statement. The noise level increased as we descended the stairs. As with the bathing room and the doors to the garden, there were sentries standing guard at the base of the stairs.

A show of power? Or was Alfred truly worried about someone getting too close to me? A snort escaped me before the thought even fully formed. Maddox would worry, not Alfred. He'd barely spoken to me since I'd completed my transition.

Admittedly, my campaign to avoid him seemed to be paying off in spades. Not that I didn't find the weight of his gaze the moment Maddox and I stepped into the great hall. The dais at the end now boasted a damn throne, but it wasn't alone. There were four other thrones, placed two on either side.

I shook my head. Subtle, vampires were not. This was a show. The conversations rose and fell around us like a tempest striking the sea. Maddox became a firm fixture at my side as I drifted, but I didn't lock gazes with anyone.

Instead, I skipped from face to face, memorizing a quick sketch before moving on.

More, I searched.

But I didn't want to appear to be searching. Alfred stood near the dais, his attention seemingly focused on the bevy of retainers and courtiers all queuing up for his attention.

And offerings.

Gag.

Maddox put a hand to my back and nodded toward it, but I stared at him and then shook my head. I was not going up there to be on display or watch Alfred throw his weight around. He wanted the attention. Let him have it. Servants streamed through the throng. There were so many bodies crushing into this space, it made the cavernous hall seem tiny.

I couldn't imagine Rogue enjoyed this at all. I caught a glimpse of him keeping watch from just beyond Alfred. For a split second, our gazes clashed. His expression never shifted, but I swore he gave me the barest shake of his head.

Whatever. I didn't want to be up there anyway.

When one of the servants passed close enough to me that I could snag one of the flutes from it, I tested the alcohol with a sniff.

Champagne.

Oh, we were definitely celebrating. I put a hand on the servant to keep him still as I drained the first glass, then I returned the empty and lifted a second. "Thank you," I murmured. The man's pupils dilated to the point of swallowing all the color from his eyes, and I raised my brows. The lust rolling off him slapped me like an icy breeze.

He tilted his head back and presented me with his neck.

Fuck.

No.

Maddox let out a little growl as I released the man and

moved away, only to face three more males, all of whom bowed their heads first, then tilted their faces away, giving me their necks.

Were they for real right now?

"Go," Maddox ordered in a rumble that scattered the throng closest to us and pushed them away. I sucked in a deep breath, but the scents of so many bodies combined with all the lust in the air made it cloying and sticky. The champagne wasn't near strong enough for this. Did they have an open bar at this thing?

Cupping his hand under my arm, Maddox drew me back to him. "We should move up to the—"

"No," I told him flatly, and avoided meeting his gaze. I didn't want to see hurt or recrimination or—worst of all—sympathy. "I may have to be here for this, but I'm not standing up there on display."

Not when I had other things to hunt in this crowd. Maddox didn't argue with me. Whether he didn't want to risk a fight in front of so many or he didn't disagree with me, I had no idea. As it was, I took another mouthful of champagne and swished the chilly, bubbling liquid around my tongue. Anything to get rid of the flavor in the air.

Why the fuck did they all stink so much? Fruitier scents, too sweet and sickening, wrapped around some, while others were musky, earthier, and irritated my nose. The worst smelled like a damned distillery.

Lips against my ear, Maddox murmured, "Breathe only through your mouth. It's your senses. They are heightened, and you need to acclimate."

Thrilling. One more pin to stick into the 'I didn't want to be a damn vampire' poster I should have hung in my room.

Not that I'd be staying in that room much longer. I needed to shake Maddox's hovering. As it was, I let him move with me as I searched faces. Breathing through my mouth did help.

More surprising than an entire gallery hall filled with vampires was how many of them sported colorful clothing and hair. There were more dressed in jeans, like Maddox, than in tuxedos, like the grim count eyeing my progress. He was definitely a count, or at least some kind of aristocrat. He had that look about him.

When he stepped into my path, I barely spared him a glance.

Then he took my hand, and Maddox had him up by his throat.

Well, my dragon was definitely useful for dealing with irritations.

"You do not touch what you have not been given permission to touch," Maddox informed him in a voice so cold and deadly, it actually gave me chills. The vampires around us scattered again.

Then the count scowled and struck, raking his hands down Maddox's face. The metallic scent of copper twined with the spark of fire as he broke skin. Rage perfumed the air, and I glared a beat at the count. The distraction was exactly what I needed, but the fact that he'd harmed Maddox incensed me.

Another vampire raced at them, but I stepped in his path and locked gazes with him. He hissed, but a second later, he slammed into a wall and I didn't have to do anything. Rogue stood where he'd been.

Eyebrow cocked, he said, "Go to the dais before I have to kill half of this room."

I snorted. "No."

The count's feet were kicking in the air, and try as he might, he couldn't break Maddox's grip. Fury and bloodlust filled my dragon, even as Rogue put a hand on his shoulder.

"Let him go, Maddox. He's learned his lesson."

"No," Maddox gritted out. "He shouldn't have touched her."

That earned me another glare from Rogue.

The scattering of voices rose in volume. "Maddox," Rogue attempted again. "Let him go."

Alfred hadn't moved from the dais. I didn't have to look to know it. His presence danced over my skin like an electric wave when he approached. The vampire had slowly begun to stop fighting. They didn't need air, per se, but there was a very good chance his vertebrae were shattering.

Really, all he'd done was touch my hand.

Taking a deep breath, I drew Maddox's bloodlust into me. It was sharp, piquant, and very spicy as it spilled into my veins like liquid fire. The stiffness in his shoulders eased, and his jaw unlocked. When he opened his hand, the count fell and landed on his ass, fine clothes be damned. The man coughed and sputtered, but Rogue actually looked relieved, albeit briefly, before even that expression vanished.

"Be clear," Maddox informed the downed vampire, then he swept his gaze over the others. "You keep your hands to yourself unless granted the approach."

"They understand," Rogue assured him.

With a pained look and a flash of rage in his eyes—right at me, because yeah, I did all that, fuck you too, buddy—the count moved to his knees and offered obeisance. Everyone in his party went down, then rose one at a time to offer their throats.

Maddox let out an aggrieved sigh, and Rogue murmured something to him.

I could probably guess.

They'd exerted authority, so offerings had to be made and accepted.

The cuts on Maddox's face had already begun to heal.

Leaving them to it, I slipped away into the crowd, leaning into the one part of my nature few seemed to understand. Succubi fed on lust. We craved it above all other emotions to fill a blatant hunger. It wasn't that we didn't long for caring or even friendship, but we didn't feed on those things.

Everyone believed succubi were always in lust, always a half-step away from dropping our clothes. It happens, don't get me wrong, but it was all about feeding the hunger inside of us—the biological imperative to survive. That said, we could also feed the lust in others. Inflame it. I'd done it with Rogue, and I could do it with this noisy crowd. They were all eager for something, hungry for it, desperate in some cases, and in others, already enraged that they had to ask for what they believed should be theirs. It didn't always work, but the partial frenzy in this crowd and the eagerness to win notice with the others helped.

I drifted, sipping my wine and weaving through the crowd in an attempt to lose myself in the throng without any of my keepers on my ass.

"Children," Alfred said, his voice carrying over the assembled and sending a ripple of apprehension and desire up my spine. "Settle." Everything in his tone demanded absolute obedience.

The quiet rolled through the room, silencing the voices both protesting and otherwise. Twisting, I moved between two taller vampires, both dressed in business suits and looking almost too corporate to be here in this ancient setting. Course, they fit in a little better than the rock star wannabe with the rainbow hair four feet away.

The crowd shifted, and I focused on that agitator. He *hated* being here. Hated it because he wanted what Alfred had.

"Why should we?" he demanded all of a sudden, surging forward and dragging the attention of the rest. "Why should we bow and scrape when you've been gone for over a century?"

"You don't have to do anything," Alfred informed the detractor. "If you truly wish to break your covenant with me, just say the word."

Oh, he sounded so reasonable.

And bored.

"Well I do, I have—" We never really did learn what he had. Alfred separated his head from his body and then resumed his place on the dais without so much as mussing his hair.

The vampires nearest the fallen one had been soaked in his blood, but all Alfred said was, "Anyone else want to lodge their objection?"

A smile threatened to escape me. There was something sexy as hell about someone so at home with their power that they didn't have to make a show of it. Getting a lot of vampires killed didn't bother me in the slightest, but I wanted them distracted, not enraged.

"Excellent," Alfred continued when no one else spoke. The silence was so profound, every heart beating in that room pulsed against me. Some sluggish. Some faster. More than one pounded with a hint of a skip. You could almost trace the anxiety by following the metronome of their hearts.

I didn't listen to Alfred's speech. I didn't care. It was time to revisit old bonds and renew old allegiances, blah blah blah. That shit bored me on a good day, and today was not one of those. As the crowd shifted, leaning in to listen and pressing closer together, I slipped further to the fringes.

There was no sign of Maddox or Rogue, but I didn't strain myself to hunt for them. It was enough to be walking around in the dress and jewels... The ring on my finger seemed almost too heavy the moment my thoughts skipped to it.

I was almost to the doors the servants slipped in and out of, when the applause threatened to deafen me and cheers went up. Well, look at that. He'd appeased the mob. Alfred was their favorite again.

At least, their chosen flavor of the moment. That would work for me though. Focusing on the threads of thrill amidst the lusts for power, blood, and sex—yeah, sex was always a factor—I just dialed it up a notch.

Or twelve.

Time to make it a real party...

A woman's groan spilled through the cacophony, and two of the males nearest me seized each other in a frenzied kiss.

Oh, that was more like it. I fanned those flames and then headed for the door. A servant had stopped right in the entryway, staggered. "You're fine," I told him. "Go find her, lover boy. You know you want to."

The empty tray in his hands fell away as he all but bolted up the hallway. I followed him, moving with a lot more confidence on the stone in these heels than I expected. Maybe I got improved balance and motion. I'd take it.

The hall, apparently, led directly to the huge kitchen and preparation area. Hell, I hadn't even realized they had one of these. The scents of coffee, meat, fruits, and other delicacies as well as copious amounts of liquor filled the air. Two of the cooks were currently fucking away on one of the metal surfaces.

That could not be sanitary.

But the hairy butt pumping away into the woman had her clawing his back up as she screamed.

They *weren't* vampires.

No. Those were shifters.

Oops.

I tried to siphon some of that heat off of them, because really, that could be messy. But they paid me no attention.

Skirting the orgy about to break out, I headed for the hall on the far side.

If my calculations were correct, this would head outside the keep because they had to bring supplies in somewhere, and we were well and truly into the far wing where the guests had been housed.

I hadn't explored over here as much.

Halfway down the hall, it curved and descended, almost becoming a tunnel.

Down? Really?

The last time I went down, that hadn't ended well.

Well…okay, it hadn't ended *bad*, but it hadn't ended the way I'd hoped.

This time?

This time, I wasn't letting anything get between me and freedom.

The stone turned slippery, so I shed the shoes and carried them in one hand.

What? They were really nice shoes.

I picked up the pace. The lust I'd fired up there wouldn't hold forever. Granted, the guys had extreme stamina. But not all vampires were made the same. The tunnel curved again, and I crossed my fingers as I followed the low lamps lighting the way.

A great door stood at the far end.

Yes!

Not bouncing—or counting my escapes before they were hatched—I picked up speed and ran for that door. It was locked from the inside. Throwing up the bar, I pushed it open and the icy chill of winter air flooded in. Snow crunched under my bare feet as I stepped out—not into the garden—but along the hillside. There was a small clearing with multiple vehicles of different types staged.

Helicopters.

Oh, note to self—take flying lessons for the next time I had to escape.

But there were also snowmobiles. Those couldn't be any harder than a jet ski, right?

My breath frosted in the air, and I didn't have time to mentally debate this. Sooner or later—probably sooner—they were going to notice I was gone. Nothing ventured, nothing gained.

I raced over the snow to the closest snowmobile and checked for keys. Oh, luck was on my side. I'd just swung my leg over when a hand clamped down on my arm and dragged me off of it.

Dammit.

I impacted against Rogue's hard chest, and he glared down at me in the darkness, his eyes incandescent and so blazingly blue, they hurt to look at.

Arguing with him would be pointless.

"You created a mess in there." He damn near clucked his tongue at me.

I gave a shrug. "I don't care."

"I know you don't, little *sváss*." With a sigh, he lifted a jacket with his free hand. It was a heavy one, and he helped slide me into it. Shock went through me. "Lift your feet." The order had me lifting one half-frozen foot from the snow at a time as he set boots down. With a slide of his hand, he scraped off the snow and then helped me into them.

What was he…?

Straightening, he drew a cap from his pocket and then tugged it over my head and flattened my hair, but my ears were a hundred percent warmer.

"Rogue?"

"You want to leave, don't you?"

Without a glance behind us, he climbed onto the snow-mobile and then gave me a look.

"Why are you helping me?" Where was the trap in this?

"Do you really care, little *sváss*? Or do you want to go before Alfred and Maddox figure out that your absence is more than just a recalcitrant tantrum?"

The word 'tantrum' irked me.

"I care if it ends up with me in yet another cell."

"I will get you to the city. It's a couple of hours from here by this device and over some treacherous country that you don't know in the dark. From there, your freedom will depend on you."

Tension coiled in my stomach. Even in the almost total darkness, I could read his expression. When Alfred turned him, he'd given Rogue no choice. Rogue hadn't wanted to be a vampire anymore than I had. Like me, he'd had his own will overridden. Only this time, he'd been one of those determined to take that choice from me, too. Eventually, Rogue had left him and tried to kill him several times. Somehow—somewhere in there—he'd forgiven Alfred.

Or had he?

I hated Alfred, but I didn't want to kill him.

Or Maddox.

Or Fin.

My heart twisted.

This was going to hurt them. But I'd known it would when I said goodbye, even if they hadn't understood the farewell.

Succubi didn't do relationships.

I, personally, was terrible at them.

Licking my lips, I swung my leg over the snowmobile again and tucked myself against his back. The engine rumbled to life beneath us.

"Keep your face against me," Rogue cautioned. "I will keep the cold from hurting you too much."

"Rogue?"

"Yes?"

"Thank you." I squeezed him once. I thought he might have sighed, but he said nothing as he accelerated away from the keep.

And I didn't look back.

CHAPTER 4

"When brothers agree, no fortress is so strong as their common life."
- Antisthenes

Fin

Isaac wasn't in Dallas. He'd declined the invitation to the gathering—a faux pas in a young vampire, but a grave insult from one of Isaac's age. The prince was more than old enough to understand not only the futility of such a denial, but also the swift punishment that would surely follow. No one denied one of the original seven. The invitation had come from Alfred directly.

Studying the room around him, Fin took a seat at the bar and poured himself a drink. Half the occupants would never rise again. As for the other half? He had to wait for them to wake up. Perhaps they'd be more willing to answer his questions rather than just attack. Idiots.

A glance at his watch made him scowl. Even as he sat there nursing the brandy—cheap knockoff brandy at that—he let out a little sigh. The party would be in full swing at the keep. It might be midday here, but it was evening there. Fiona would be wearing that stunning green dress, and she'd own that room from the moment she walked into it. Maddox would have his hands full keeping the willing from throwing themselves at her feet. Amusement curved through Fin. He wished he could be there, not only to enjoy the show, but more because Fiona had been so unhappy earlier.

She hid it. Maybe more than most would be capable of, but Fin had spent the last few weeks getting to know her. Pretense wasn't really in her nature. For all that she could be playful or cutting with her remarks, she rarely lied. If anything, she spoke her mind, and Alfred must enjoy it because he didn't normally allow anyone to speak to him as Fiona did.

But the moment her transition had been completed, she'd walked away from Alfred and he let her go.

That was going to be a problem. She'd been too close to the edge when he woke. Too close to slipping away between the faltering transition and the taint of a shadow demon. Diplomacy, however, had never been Alfred's strong suit.

He'd saved her. For that, Fin would always be grateful.

But the wedge it had created seemed to widen rather than narrow as time passed. Even today, as he spilled himself in her while she writhed between he and Maddox, she held herself aloof. The fiery, seductive nature of hers was a radiant flame, hot and all-consuming, yet she kept it banked. Maddox had to feel it. He'd been in a dreadful temper for weeks that not even her recovery and certain survival had soothed.

The dragon had mated her. If she left them now…

A groan pulled him from the darker thoughts, and Fin tossed back the drink. When he returned from this mission, he'd broach the topic with both Alfred and Rogue. Being old and set in their ways didn't excuse colossally bad manners. They could hardly expect her to fit all her expectations into the way they'd lived their lives for so many centuries without trying to adapt themselves.

"Then again," Fin commented as he set the glass on the bar and rose. The groaning vampire looked up at him through bloodied eyes. "What do I know? They still think I'm too young and impetuous." Hauling the vampire to his feet, Fin dragged him over to the small stage. The night club apparently liked to host performances. It was also the least littered with body parts and blood.

Tossing the man onto the wooden platform, Fin pulled a handkerchief out of his pocket and wiped the blood from his fingers. At a prowling pace, he circled Isaac's second. A vampire named David, one of the few in the room who'd actually recognized Fin when he entered.

"Seriously, I'm not *that* young. I suppose it's all relative. I've been the youngest for so long, they really don't know how to treat me any differently." A simple fact, one he could even accept. "However, I'm also the one closest to her in age, and I think that makes me far more qualified to give advice. Let's face it, they're two hermits and one guy who might as well be a hermit. He checked out right after World War I, utterly done with the rest of us. Not that I can blame him."

At least World War II hadn't woken him up.

Pausing, Fin studied David as the vampire groaned and began to twitch. "The trick here is that where it used to be okay to just take what you wanted and then let them spend a few decades getting used to the idea, I'm not all that enamored of it now. I also don't think it will work in this case."

If anything, Fin rather doubted they understood the will Fiona must possess. She'd survived for weeks in Nightmare Penitentiary while sitting on the precipice between life and death. Not only had she survived, she'd held onto her sanity as a shadow demon feasted on her and in turn fed her. No, she would not just 'get over it' or 'accept' this new status quo. They were going to have to win her over.

Of all of them, perhaps Maddox had come the closest in claiming her. There was a softness to her where the dragon was concerned. A softness, Fin suspected, she would not care for… "Then again," he muttered. "What do I know? We've barely gotten to know her these last few weeks, and then only the pieces of her she's deigned to share." But what she had shared, he'd enjoyed a great deal.

The humor. The wit. The sly assessments. The utter lack of fear when she'd stabbed Maddox through the hand.

"She really loves bacon," Fin mused. "She seems to enjoy that I've made sure she has it every day. But one cannot truly express romance through bacon. Can they?" Certainly, there was the coffee as well. The world had changed, most assuredly it had, but could it really have changed that much?

The vampire pushed himself up with agonizing slowness as Fin paced around him.

"Whether you can or not, I suppose is a moot point. Because I know there are other ways, and one of those is to right that which has wronged her. Do you understand my meaning, David?" Fin put a foot on the vampire's back and slammed him back down to the wood. The pained groan he released as more bones cracked under the force Fin exerted echoed around the club. "I can't hear you, could you speak a little more clearly?"

"You're such an asshole," David managed to wheeze out, and Fin chuckled.

"I can be. I would remind you, however," Fin continued,

before easing his foot off of him and kicking him over so he was face up, "I did ask quite politely the first time. I even observed all the social niceties of announcing myself. Your men—"

"Are young," David said with a wet cough.

"I was going to say stupid, but we can go with young. Maybe too young to have the positions they are in. After all, who else would remain behind when their prince flees an invitation from Alfred?" The rules hadn't been written yesterday after all.

"Isaac didn't want to die," David protested. Or maybe it only sounded like he did. Coughing up a lung did have a way of turning a man's tone wheedling. Fin would let him have that one—for now. "He knew…he knew that you had taken the succubus from the prison."

"Hmm, did he?"

"The warden contacted him."

Squatting down, Fin met David's agonized gaze. "And what did the warden tell him?"

"I didn't hear the whole conversation," David admitted. "When Isaac realized it wasn't just that she'd escaped, but that Rogue and Maddox had been seen there, he began making plans to vanish."

Well, maybe Isaac had more brains than Fin had credited him with. "I won't be insulted that my presence there didn't give him pause." After all, it would be rather inconsiderate at the moment to lord that over them. At. The. Moment.

There was always later.

"Fearing Rogue and Maddox is very wise. That does not explain declining Alfred's invitation." The prince hadn't just 'not shown up' or 'not answered.' He'd sent an answer. His answer had been in the negative, along with the head of the retainer who'd carried the invitation to him. A young vampire, a very young one. Someone Fin had adopted twenty or thirty years earlier. A baby really. "Did you know Emilios was a friend of mine?"

"No, my lord," David wheezed. "I didn't. I would beg forgiveness, but you will grant it or not as you see fit."

"This is true. But I'm listening. Why did he decide to decline the invitation?"

A vampire on the other side of the room had made it to his feet and staggered in Fin and David's direction. The idiot's leg was still broken, and his arm was bent backwards at the elbow. He really stood no chance, yet he tried to rush Fin anyway. Rising smoothly, Fin caught him by the throat and lifted him with one arm as he held David's gaze.

"I do hate to repeat myself."

"He did not tell me," David said slowly, his expression a rictus of discomfort. "But I would imagine he expected to be executed upon arrival. So he ran."

"Well, we wouldn't have done it right away." His death was a gift. It would be rude to open the present before Fiona was there to enjoy it.

David tried to smile. It didn't really work so well, though the blood speckling each of his breaths began to diminish. Probably not permanently harmed. Maybe. Well, forty percent chance of it. Perhaps only thirty, because he coughed and had to turn his head as more blood spilled from his mouth. Definitely a punctured lung.

Very uncomfortable.

"He may not have told me, but I know all of his holdings, even those he thought he hid from me."

"Delightful, now you are speaking my language." The vampire in his grip kept struggling and struck Fin's arm once. Then twice. Bored with him, Fin spared him a brief glance before he wrenched his neck and broke the vertebrae, then dropped him on the floor.

"How would you like the list?" Smart boy. David might yet survive this encounter.

"In detail," Fin informed him, then bit into his own wrist before lowering it to dribble a couple of drops into David's mouth. The vampire swallowed convulsively, and his back bowed as Fin's blood hit his system. He wouldn't give David much, because the vampire had definitely deserved the pain he'd received. Another of the remaining vampires began to stir and tried to get to his feet. "Just don't," Fin told him. "If you lie there and pretend to be dead, I might actually let you live."

Intriguingly, the other appeared to consider it, even as he still gripped the broken edge of the bar itself to try and get to his feet. Either he couldn't make it or decided against it, because he collapsed in a heap. Attention on David, he waited.

Another swallow before the vampire began speaking. His list was indeed detailed, and it appeared Fin wouldn't have to kill any more in the bar that evening. Perhaps another day, but not this one. Seven different locations, and all of them in different areas of the world. All of them on the edge of another powerful prince's territory. Clever.

Not clever enough, because Fin didn't give a flying fuck who ruled where, he'd go as he deemed fit. Still, he supposed the prince deserved some points for effort. Points he immediately lost because his insubordination and inconsiderate actions cost Fin an evening with his lady.

That he'd take out of Isaac's hide, personally.

Only when he was certain David had told him everything did Fin clean his hands once more. The self-inflicted wound on his wrist had long since closed. The wounded vampire wasn't going anywhere fast—the blood had helped, but it hadn't been enough to heal him.

"You should consider consolidating your position here,"

Fin advised him. "If you're successful and you receive an invitation from Alfred in the future, my advice would be to accept it."

"I'll do that," David wheezed.

"Good. You have five survivors." He'd had to kill two more that tried to interrupt their conversation. "Perhaps a lesson on manners wouldn't be amiss, either."

"Understood, my lord."

The corner of Fin's mouth tilted. "How much do you hate me right now?"

David didn't say a word.

"Oh it's fine, you're not going to hurt my feelings."

"I don't hate you," David admitted, and it was the truth. Huh. Fin wouldn't have guessed that. "I am afraid of you."

He allowed himself a real smile. Well, maybe they'd finally talk about him with the same reverence they reserved for Rogue and Maddox. Not that Fin really cared. "Fear is good for survival," he said, then paused. "Before I go...one last question."

The other vampire swallowed.

"Where is Dimitri?"

"I wish I knew," David admitted. "I'd have killed that fool already for what he did." Nothing but honesty there.

"If you find him, don't kill him. Send word to us. His death is not yours to mete out." He leveled a look at the would-be prince. The vampire stood a very good chance of taking hold of power here. If he could think beyond his immediate needs.

With that, he left David, the wreckage of the bar, and the various remnants of the vampires he'd torn apart along with the handful of survivors. Outside, the sun was near setting. Fin scowled. It would be deep into the night at the keep. In all likelihood, the party was in full swing and the presentation done.

They'd wanted to give her Isaac tonight. Dimitri should be hers, as well. Though after what Fin had learned about him, he wouldn't mind just taking him apart and being done with it. He debated reaching out to them, but distracting them with so many others on hand wasn't a prudent maneuver.

Fine, he'd go hunting. If he went in the right order, he might make it back to the keep before dawn. Then he would be there to wake Fiona with the sunrise. Grinning at the idea, he reached for the root system and whisked himself away to his first destination in northern Canada.

Odd choice, but it had been a while since he'd gone to the great white north. Maybe he could pick up some poutine for Fiona while he was there.

THE NIGHT PASSED WITH AGONIZING SLOWNESS AS FIN traveled from location to location. David had given him explicit directions, and Fin didn't doubt the veracity of them or the honest intention behind it. David was not a fool. If he'd tried to mislead Fin, he had to know Fin would find him again. Fear, as Fin had told him, was a powerful motivator.

But Isaac was in none of the detailed locations. Frustration moved like an itch under his skin as Fin stepped out of the last bolt-hole not far from Istanbul in an area known as Kumkoy on the shores of the Black Sea. A handful of vampires had been inside, all retainers, most of them old enough to understand exactly what he was when he entered. Three were sun sensitive, and they'd suffered burns at his abrupt arrival. The sun had already climbed here, so he had less than an hour if he were lucky to make it back to the keep.

The interrogation took him little time. Isaac's disobedience of Alfred's summons earned him no friends among these retainers. They promised to capture and hold him should their former master make an appearance. Former, because if they continued to swear loyalty, Fin would be obliged to remove their heads. Everyone understood the potential threat and remained honest.

Still, a weariness Fin hadn't felt in a long time crept through him as he left the compound behind and twisted his way along the paths back to the keep. As much as he wished to have attended the party with Fiona and introduced her to a whole new world, the task Alfred had given him was equally vital.

Also, Fin was the least likely of the four of them to shed much blood. He'd at least left survivors.

Maddox and Rogue would have left none.

Fin could also travel farther, faster than both of them, and Maddox did not want to be separated from Fiona. A situation that seemed to concern Alfred more and more. There was nothing they could do about it. Nothing they should do about it. Fiona was theirs. Fin had known it from the moment she'd begun to change. The ringing bell of clarity had gonged through him. The knowing that all their long years of waiting for the promise of her had been fulfilled.

Now they just had to not mess it up. Destiny had a tendency to slap back.

The multiple vehicles that had decorated the exterior of the keep were gone. Most of their guests had probably been dismissed following the gathering. They came in early if they wanted time to petition or give an offering.

Ugh. Fin paused and tilted his head back as he stared up at the keep's windows. Most of them did not allow a view inside, though once upon a time, they had. Each could be shuttered and bolted. The keep itself could withstand cannon fire and had.

Updates had been made, mostly by Rogue. It was what he did with his time when they didn't pull him away for hunts or other issues.

The offerings.

The look on Fiona's face in the library. It had never occurred to Fin the offerings would bother her. Yet, the disappointment in her eyes had slashed at him. Refusing them hadn't been a hardship, though it had irked Alfred, particularly after Maddox's staunch refusal following Eleanor's ambush. Rogue stepping in to say he would prefer to avoid them this time around had been a surprise.

It also saved Fin from an argument with Alfred. He'd been asleep for a long time, and upon waking, he'd devoted every ounce of his energy and attention to bringing Fiona across. The problem was that while they'd bonded through blood and sex, Alfred had most assuredly *not* become her lover, and Fiona's anger had only intensified every time they came together.

I hate you all.

The whispered thought, raw and potent, haunted him. He'd known. They'd all known. Rogue had cautioned him and Maddox both from the beginning, but they couldn't let her die. To save her, she *had* to transition, to become a hybrid.

If that meant she hated them…well, they'd just have to repair the damage. They had *time* now. Time to court her properly.

Inside, he found Anton waiting for him. The vampire bowed once. "My lord, Lord Alfred says you are to attend him immediately upon your return."

Of course he did. "Absolutely. Is Her Majesty in the bathing room or the library?" Not that she'd returned to the library once in the last few days, but now that the guests were gone, maybe she would?

Not meeting his eyes, Anton said, "Forgive me, my lord. I was instructed to tell you to attend Lord Alfred immediately and to say nothing more."

Impatience creeping through him, Fin threw up his hands, and Anton immediately took several steps back. Yeah, he wasn't going to hit the retainer. Even if he'd been nursing a little crush on Fiona. Most males were going to. Some females for that matter. Just like they were attracted to Alfred's power, Maddox's spirit, Rogue's aloofness, and to Fin's own wild magic. They were all captivating and alluring.

Fin didn't care if they wanted her. They could want her all they desired. They would never touch her. No one was taking her from them. She was theirs to protect and to care for, even if she loathed them. They could take that heat until they won her forgiveness.

Hopefully, Alfred hadn't pulled an Alfred and made the situation worse. The fact that she'd allowed Maddox and Fin back into her bed had been a win as far as he was concerned. Fin hadn't missed the sweetness and the longing in her kiss. Even if she held her mind and heart back, she had given a piece of herself to Maddox, and if Fin were right, at least a sliver to him.

He'd earn the rest.

"Where is His Lordship?"

"In the library with Lord Rogue and Lord Maddox."

"Wonderful." Hopefully, that meant Fiona was there, and Fin could see her and find out what Alfred wanted at the same time.

He didn't bother with the stairs, too eager to see Fiona after what felt like a long absence. The irony that a few hours —not even a full day—could seem like forever when he measured time in centuries wasn't lost on him. As he stepped out of the fold into the library, three things struck him at once...

Rogue bled heavily from a slice across his chest that had shredded cloth and flesh alike.

Maddox's eyes were pure dragon, and the air around him rippled with the barely suppressed fury of his change being held off by a hairsbreadth.

Alfred…

Alfred was furious, standing between them, though he had his back to Maddox and his attention locked on Rogue.

Fin couldn't recall the last time he'd seen Alfred so ruffled.

He hadn't even twitched when Fin blew up a portion of the newly excavated bathing chambers trying to improve them.

It had destroyed weeks of work.

"Where did you take her?" Alfred asked. "I tire of asking the question."

"Then stop asking," Rogue told him bluntly. "My answer is not going to change. I didn't take her anywhere."

He was lying.

"You're lying," Maddox stated, his voice pitched low, a growl vibrating every single syllable.

Frowning, Fin swept his gaze over the library. The four of them were alone. There wasn't more than a trace of her scent in the air. Turning his attention to the keep, he swept it mentally, weaving the magic to find her.

"Where is she?" he demanded abruptly, and Maddox wheeled to face him.

"Gone," he roared, and Fin frowned.

Alfred's question registered with him, and Fin looked at Rogue. The elf met his stare with one of his own, calm and placid, despite his injuries. "I won't tell you anything more than I have already told them."

"What did you tell them?"

"She took one of the snowmobiles and made her escape

during Alfred's speech." True. "I noticed her absence from the great hall and followed her trail through the servant's hall to the kitchens." Also true. "I was unable to stop her, though I did follow."

That didn't quite ring true.

Finally, Rogue shrugged. "Sooner or later, she would have run. She doesn't want to be here. She has transitioned. What she does now is up to her."

"No," Alfred said with a snarl. "It isn't. She's still wanted. Isaac isn't in our custody. She has to feed both sides of her nature…"

"Then she'll feed. We all managed." Rogue folded his arms, though there was a faint tightening of his jaw as he pulled at the ravaged skin.

Maddox let out a sound that sent all the hair on Fin's body to stand on end. It was tortured. Furious. Hurt. Lost. Then angry again. He lunged at Rogue, and Alfred blocked him bodily, but Rogue didn't flee.

"You cannot kill him," Alfred told Maddox.

"He *helped* her to leave. He might as well have told her we don't want her." His accusing gaze landed on Rogue again. "You didn't want her here no matter how often you took her to your bed."

Instead of responding, Rogue merely waited out Maddox's tirade. Alfred finally got the dragon to back up, but the temperature in the library had turned almost sultry and steamy. Sweat decorated Rogue's face. The frost elf wouldn't die from the heat, but he would be uncomfortable.

Alfred turned his focus on Fin. "You have a new mission."

Find Fiona.

Dallas. If she wanted to go back to where she came from, she would go there.

But that wasn't all she wanted. She wanted to kill Isaac,

and like Fin, she would have to start where she knew the territory. Unfortunately…

"What?" Alfred demanded, and Fin raised his brows.

"You seem most disturbed for someone who did not care one whit for her feelings when you finished her transition."

"Don't start," Alfred said with a slice of his hand. "She's mated to Maddox, and he's not going to be able to think of anything else. If Rogue didn't care for her, he'd never have stood against all of us to help her escape. You can't stop thinking about her right now. *One* of us has to keep our head."

It wasn't him. The anger in his voice, the tension around his mouth…

Fin almost wanted to smile.

Alfred's emotional distance had done them no favors. His age had proven more of a handicap than a help.

Perhaps Fiona's flight would serve two purposes—allow her to regather herself and understand she needed them as much as they needed her, and to wake Alfred and Rogue up to the fact that they would *have* to change. This could work out well.

"Now you're smiling," Maddox stated, almost in accusation. "What do you know, druid?"

"Oh, big guy, I know so many things. We've had this discussion." He spread his hands. "But I will go and find our lady, since you've all so carelessly misplaced her." Slanting a look at Rogue, he considered him. "How much money did you give her?"

"Why do you presume I gave her any funds?"

"Because you call her your beloved and you would not let her flee with nothing but her skin when all she had in the world has already been taken from her. So how much?"

"If I did give her anything," Rogue conceded, "it would be

enough so she would never have to worry about her finances again."

So an account. Rogue had given her an account.

All Fin had to do was figure out which one.

Alfred rubbed a hand over his face. "Just find her."

"I'll go with you," Maddox announced, but Fin shook his head.

"Big guy…"

Eyes narrowed, Maddox just glared. "I can find anyone. If any of us finds her, it will be me."

"Maddox," Alfred began. "I need you here."

The dragon's glare promised acid at Alfred. "You broke this. You tried to break her. You kept me from her throughout the transition. This is your fault."

And that is part of why I helped her. The thought from Rogue pulled Fin's attention from the fresh battle brewing between Maddox and Alfred. *She is not our possession. It was not our decision to make.*

Yet you didn't argue against it either.

No, Rogue admitted. *I am just as guilty. I didn't want her to die.*

Well, that was something. *I'll find her.* Fin flicked a look to where Maddox had slammed Alfred against the wall. *Should we do anything about that?*

Rogue walked over to pour himself a drink. He moved stiffly, probably hiding more injuries. *No. Alfred is angrier than he's been in a long time, and Maddox is a wounded animal. Let them take it out on each other.*

That seemed reasonable. *I'll check in.*

Fin?

Yes?

Be kind to her. For all her bravado and strength, she is very much alone now.

We have all been that alone.

The only ones of their kind.

Rogue nodded. *Exactly.*

She's ours.

It was the only answer Fin had to that. He would protect her with everything he had.

Even from ourselves? Rogue's last question lingered as Fin reached for the paths and twisted away. He'd already been around the world once. Now he would return to Dallas and wait for her.

And plan.

He'd already wanted to win her back. He'd just have to be creative about it.

CHAPTER 5

"For Aphrodite engenders more mischief in the clever." - Euripides.

Three weeks. It had been three weeks since my evening escape from the keep. When I straddled the back of the snowmobile behind Rogue, I half-expected him to turn us around and bring me back. To trick me in some way. Loyalty, it seemed, existed only between the four of them, with all three deferring to Alfred. To my surprise, though, Rogue had taken me down the mountain and then across the wildly unfamiliar terrain to the edge of a small village before pointing me toward the train depot.

"The minute they realize, they will look at the airlines. You need to make your way to Germany from here." He handed me a card. "Speak to this man, and only if he is alone. Hand him this card, then tell him the name you wish to be known by. He will prepare the human identification you need." Then he pressed a second card into my hand. "The pin code is three-four-four-six-two. Repeat it to me."

I had, but confusion flooded me when I locked gazes with him. With care, he tucked one of my red curls beneath the cap, then brushed his knuckles down my cheek.

"They will look for you."

"But you won't?" I didn't know why I blurted out the question, but I didn't understand.

"No," he promised me in a solemn tone. "You have to decide what you want and where you want to be. They think they understand. They don't." Cupping my face, he held my gaze. "You need to feed on me before you go."

I wasn't hungry.

"Little *sváss*, you will have to learn to hunt and to have care, to feed both of your natures, and without us there, it will be more challenging for you."

I grimaced.

"I have every faith in you." He stroked my cheek, roving his gaze over me. "Now…feed." With that, he slipped his hand to my nape and tilted his head back. We were in the deep shadows of the building.

Stepping in to him, I pressed my hands to his chest and then rose up on my tip toes to nuzzle his jaw. The barest of smiles flickered against his lips as I kissed a path down to his pulse point. "Why are you helping me?" I had to ask.

"Because once upon a time, little *sváss*, I was you. Alfred… you will have to figure that part out on your own. I did as well." Then he dipped his face, and his lips just barely brushed mine as he continued, "You are always welcome, and if you need me, call."

"Are you in the phone book?" I couldn't help the tease. I hadn't seen my own cell phone in almost two months. Who knew what I had to go back to in Dallas. I doubted my landlord kept my apartment. Fin had indicated it had been cleaned out. Whether it'd been the landlord or Isaac was anyone's guess.

"Ah," Rogue answered with almost a wry chuckle, and the sound captivated me. He was always so standoffish and aloof unless he was intent on turning me inside out. Then... I shook off the thought. We didn't have time for that here or now. He dug into his pocket and pulled out a phone. "I purchased this last week along with a second one. I programmed my number into it—that would be the second phone."

"Did you program my number into yours?"

"No."

That was...

"I told you, little *svÁss*, this is about you deciding. If you need me, call. I will come for you anywhere. On that, you have my word."

Moisture burned in my eyes, and he went hazy for a moment as I had to blink back the tears. "Thank you, Rogue."

"You are welcome," he said, then gave my nape a gentle squeeze. "But you will feed before you leave me. You will give me this one last obedience so I know I sent you off full and with all that I could."

Pressing a swift kiss to his lips, I dug my fingers into his shirt. He tipped his head up and back, then I struck. No hesitation. I didn't want to hurt him, and they'd told me time and again, the swift pierce stung the least. His cock hardened against my belly as the taste of him flooded my mouth. I almost groaned.

I wasn't hungry, but at the same time, I craved this. The heat. The taste. The essence of him filling me. He massaged my neck as I swallowed again and again. Finally, I pulled back, nuzzling the bite with a few careful licks until the blood no longer trickled.

Tilting my head back, I stared up at him. His pale eyes

seemed to shimmer in the darkness. Then, he was just…gone.

They all moved so fast, but this was like one moment there, and the next, he blinked out of existence. I knew he'd run. The snowmobile had been left behind. Hopefully, they wouldn't hurt him for helping me. I carefully stowed away the phone he'd given me and the cards.

Less than thirty minutes later, I was aboard the last train heading for Germany. I persuaded the one person who asked me for identification that he wasn't interested in me, amplifying his lust to be done with talking to passengers and back to the book he was currently reading.

Child's play.

Rogue's blood hummed in my system as the train rolled through the night. I didn't dare sleep, my eyes focused on the shadows as I half-expected one of them to step out like some cosmic joke had been played on me.

Three weeks later, I still watched the shadows, but sitting on Elias' deck overlooking his backyard while his cats lazed with me in the sun and I drank a beer, there were no shadows to fear. I'd not seen or heard from any of them.

True to his word, Rogue hadn't called me. That didn't mean he couldn't trace the phone. I kept it, despite all the reasons I should probably have gotten rid of it.

The sliding door to the house opened, and Elias stepped out. His close-cropped dark hair glistened from his shower. He'd only thrown on a pair of shorts, leaving the rest of his dark brown skin bare. He held two fresh bottles of beer in his hand, and without a word, I drained the last of my first bottle and accepted the second.

He settled on the chair next to me and leaned back. "You ready to tell me what the hell is going on yet?"

I'd been with him a week. Shown up on his porch in the middle of a thunderstorm, drenched like a wet cat and smelling about as good—at least according to him. His eyes had narrowed though as he dragged me in for a hug. It lasted all of five seconds before he'd slammed me back against a wall and stared at me.

"When the fuck did you become a vampire, Red?"

Yeah. That conversation hadn't been fun. Not that you could call it much of a conversation. I'd given him the absolute bare minimum of facts. I'd made a mistake going home with a vampire from the club. Things got out of hand. I'd done a short stint in prison and escaped. I'd been trying to get back ever since.

All of it was absolutely true, just edited for public consumption. I hadn't breathed a word about Maddox, Fin, and Rogue, or he-who-could-go fuck-himself. After, I'd just asked him if I could stay there until I figured out what I was going to do.

Fin had been right. My apartment was gone, already rented out to someone else. Everything that I'd ever owned gone with it. A stop by the shop revealed they'd even hired someone new. Life had gone on.

It was like I'd never been there. No trace of me lingered.

The hollowness inside at that revelation had left me wallowing in bed for two days.

That was all Elias allowed me before he'd dragged me out and made me go running with him.

Did I mention he's a wolf?

He can fucking run.

I'd been in pain afterward, lungs burning and strained while I discovered muscles I hadn't even known existed. They hurt so bad, I'd barely been able to walk. I really didn't get how this shit was supposed to work. I was dead, right? Vampires died, then came back. That was how it worked. But my lungs *hurt* and my legs…well, I was half-convinced amputation with a rusty saw would have been better.

That was before I woke the second day and could barely move.

Elias, the backstabbing traitor, laughed at me and dragged me out again.

That was four days ago.

We'd gone running every day since.

He insisted it would get better. I insisted he was insane. We agreed to disagree.

Every evening, after a run, we returned to his place and took a shower—separately—then met out here to while away the evening hours before he fired up the grill. The man lived on a steady diet of steak, steak, and did I mention steak?

He should have been a cattle rancher.

Why raise when he could rustle? That was his usual response. I tipped the beer up to take a long pull. It was icy cold and didn't do crap to slake the thirst that had begun to plague me over the last couple of days. I hadn't fed since I'd taken that last bite from Rogue.

The absolute lack of appetite had been a gift. Maybe they'd all been wrong. Sure, delusion and denial weren't that far apart. I was a vampire. Okay, but I was a *hybrid*, so maybe that just meant I didn't *need* to feed. Not the way I had been before my transition completed.

It could happen, right?

"Fi?"

I dragged my maudlin thoughts together and cobbled them into something resembling coherency before I shrugged. "Nothing to say. I don't know *what* I'm going to do. I can't just…go back to what I had." Particularly when I didn't have it anymore.

"You haven't been to a club once this week." It wasn't a question. I hadn't left Elias' house since I'd arrived, except to go on his torturous runs with him.

Twenty miles. And he'd told me he'd been holding back.

Tomorrow, we were supposed to go forty.

He was a sadist.

I wasn't entirely sure why we were friends.

"Okay, pity party, table for one. You've been called, seated, served, and now it's time to pay the check."

Oh right, we could both be assholes when the occasion called for it. I lifted my middle finger in his direction. His teeth flashed as he smiled. "Wow, that was weak. Your game falter that much, Red?"

"Maybe," I said, shrugging again. Long before the thirst hit, longing had already sunk into my bones. I'd started dreaming about them. It was like I could feel them, as if they were right there with me. I'd even caught myself reaching for them a couple of times when I woke. The last time, the ache had been so profound, I'd gone into Elias' bedroom and crawled into bed with him. He'd only given me a curious look and then wrapped his arms around me.

Surrounded by his scent and his heat should have been enough to chase away the dreams. But it didn't work. They followed me like plague locusts. Elias hadn't commented the next morning, and neither had I. Though, I'd avoided fleeing in there again. We'd been friends for a long time and never lovers. I was so not his type. Too high maintenance—his words, not mine—and too much red hair. Probably why we got along so well. We wanted nothing from each other but companionship.

By all rights, he could have kicked me to the curb when I showed up. His dislike for vampires was legendary, but he hadn't. He'd just moved me into the guest room and let me wallow, however briefly, before beginning my torture.

"Fiona," Elias said, sitting forward abruptly and pinning me with a look. "This isn't like you. Do you need to feed?"

I shook my head. Even if the thirst was a constant scratch at the back of my throat, something that water, beer, and

coffee couldn't slake, I wasn't *hungry*. "No, I'm not, I'm just…
I'm just at a loss for what to do right now." That also wasn't
like me, and I wasn't so lost in all of this that I didn't recognize it. I'd fought to hold onto myself every single day in that
prison.

Clawing for every inch of my routine and reality until
Maddox walked in and…

I shook my head. Even after they got me out, I kept fighting. I wanted my freedom. I wanted Maddox to keep his
word, to let me go. After Alfred woke up, the only thing I
could fight for was to keep one piece of myself hoarded
away, boarded up and safe.

I'd finally gotten Fin out of my mind. Now I had everything I'd wanted.

I was free.

So why couldn't I even *enjoy* it?

"What do you want to do? You already said you couldn't
go back to the shop, and I haven't been able to get a line on
what happened to your things."

Those were a lost cause. "Thanks for trying though." I still
had Rogue's card hidden away, along with my new identification and the burner phone. I usually had them both on me
when I ran, but when I returned to Elias' place, I hid them
away. They were my armor out there in the world, not that I
was facing the world.

"Red, you know I love you like a sister."

"Nah, you'd like a sister."

"No," he said after a beat. "I really don't like either of my
sisters. You've met them. They're mean."

I grinned. "Point taken, because I'm never mean."

He snorted, but widened his eyes as though mocking me.
"Sweetness and light, that's you. Butter wouldn't melt in your
mouth."

Yep, that got him another middle finger. "Anyway…you were saying I know you love me like a sister."

"Right, I do. But this shit? This wallowing and pity party that you have going on? It's not doing anything for anyone, least of all you. I'm not kicking you out—"

"But it's time for me to go," I finished for him.

He shook his head. "Not quite, but close. If I thought you staying here was helping you, I wouldn't say a damn thing. My alpha isn't thrilled you're here, but he trusts me to handle my own business." That was something.

"Your alpha has never been fond of me."

"Red, you banged him, rocked his world, then walked away without looking back. The man might be good, but he's no saint and he does have an ego."

I laughed, and that earned a real smile from Elias. His alpha, Varick, was a big bruiser of a guy, darkly bronzed skin etched with sexy tattoos, and a firm grip on wanting to please a woman. I hadn't even realized he *was* Elias' alpha the night I met him, or I'd never have done it.

"He got attached. Too fast, too much." I shook my head. "But I can write him an endorsement if he wants it. I had no complaints that night."

My best friend stared at me a beat, then grinned this slow, evil, and wicked smile. "Please write the letter. Just write up all your ratings and leave it with me."

Yep. See, this was why Elias and I got along. "I would like him to still let me speak to you in the future. The fact that he took me dumping him—though I object to that categorization, because a one-night stand does not a relationship make—well enough the first time is not a reason to test him even if it would be funny."

"Buzzkill."

I laughed again, and Elias leaned back, a satisfied look on his face before that smile fell away.

"I'm worried about you, Red."

"I'm worried about me, too." The moment the words slipped out, I wanted to cram them back in and swallow them. I grimaced. "But you're right. It's probably time for me to go." I'd lingered here for over a week. If they did come looking for me, they might come here. Fin had wanted to know who Elias was, but I'd never told them. I'd tried to section that part of myself off.

I didn't know if the asshole who didn't deserve to be named managed to pull it from me or not, but if he did, I didn't want to lead them to him.

What would they do if they came looking for me and I was gone already? Would they leave him alone? Or was that wishful thinking on my part?

Fuck, why was I *thinking* about them? I gave myself a hard shake. "You know, maybe I do need to go feed."

Something akin to relief crept through his expression. "Where do you want to go? I'll come with."

"You hate when I feed."

"No, I hate the assholes who think they're winning the lottery because you deign to look in their direction. I hate that they treat you like a piece of meat."

"Exactly."

"But you need to feed, and you need someone to watch your back. If I'd been there that night you met that fucker…"

Dimitri. "I still need to find him." That had actually been at the top of my list when I left the keep, right below get the fuck away from them and reclaim my life, and slightly below gut Isaac like a fish.

"I've got a few of mine out looking for him. He's gone to ground." A growl threaded the words, and Maddox's face flashed before my eyes. Dammit. "He's a well-known player. I put the word out to some other packs. They know to contact me if he's spotted. Then we can go pay him a not so social call."

I chuckled. "This happening to me wasn't your fault, Elias."

"Yeah, but you should have called me the moment you woke up."

"In my defense? I was a little out of sorts. Dying isn't fun."

Lust for blood rolled off him in a heady wave, and I let it keep going. "Trust me, I'll make sure it isn't fun for him, too. I can make it last a long time."

I did trust him. "I still don't think you should go with me." It was a lot to ask from someone I'd already asked so much of.

He glared at me.

Two hours later, he was my shadow as we walked into the Bon Vivant. If a speakeasy, a strip club, and a burlesque joint got together and had a mafia den's baby, you'd get the Bon Vivant. The club had opened a couple of years earlier and gained traction with the nightlife in the area. Particularly with other supes, but also humans out for a kinky good time. It wasn't big with the vampires, though.

Or it hadn't been.

Maybe I just hadn't noticed them before. Easily half a dozen were scattered amongst the crowd. The dancers on the various platforms rolled their hips and swayed to the beat. One adventurous lady did a beautiful job of working the pole, while at another raised platform, the young Adonis holding court was down to a tiny scrap of fabric over his dick that couldn't be comfortable, because the thong in his ass left his muscled cheeks on display.

Aesthetically pleasing, but far too oiled for my taste.

Elias said nothing as we weaved our way through the crowd. I took a table near the pole dancer. She had the most patrons sitting close, more than half of them focused solely on her, and the lust perfuming the air was intoxicating.

Or better put, it should've been. I found it a little cloying and sticky. When the waitress came by, she bumped Elias' shoulder with her hip. "You show up after a month with some chick on your arm? What am I going to do with you?"

"Take me home and screw my brains out?" Elias suggested. "I'll even promise you the first four orgasms."

She snorted. "Henry would not be pleased."

"Then toss him over and run away with me."

I ignored the banter. The flirtation was open and sweet, and didn't include an ounce of real interest. Though Elias was clearly fond of her.

"What can I get you to drink…?" The waitress faltered a second when I met her gaze. Her wolf flashed in her eyes, and Elias wrapped an arm around her waist and pulled her against him.

"Beer for both of us, Mellie, and keep your cool." The direct command in his voice was a contrast to his sweet tone.

"She's a vampire," Mellie hissed out between her teeth. "Why are you fucking around with a bloodsucking leech?"

You know, I felt that in my bones.

"I'll be back," Elias told me as he rose and tugged Mellie with him. "Stay here." I didn't comment on the order or give him my agreement as he hustled Mellie to the other side of the bar.

Wolf politics. Not my business.

Elias hadn't even been gone a full minute when a vampire dropped into the seat across from me. I didn't recognize him. I also didn't have a drink to sip and ignore him with, so I flicked my gaze back to the bar. I had no interest in making friends.

Or new enemies. My dance card was a little full.

Unfortunately, my *guest* didn't get the memo.

"David wants to see you, Fiona."

Oh yay, he knew my name. "And I give a fuck what 'David' wants why?" Who the hell was David?

"Because when the Prince of Dallas demands your attention, you give it."

I spared him a look. Two more vampires had moved into my line of sight. That suggested the others present in the bar were covering behind me. Or perhaps coming at me from that angle. I couldn't see Elias at the moment, but I believed him when he said he was coming back.

"The Prince of Dallas is Isaac," I said idly.

"Was," the vampire answered with a smirk. "Things change. Now come before your mongrel comes back. I don't have to put him down, not that I'd mind."

I studied the vampire opposite me. He was tall, lanky, and in desperate need of a haircut. Vampires were often portrayed as the absolute best of the best. Sexy gods and goddesses, all with impeccable grooming and looks to die for. Apparently, someone skipped hitting him with the sexy stick during creation. His nose was a little too crooked, like it had been broken so many times it couldn't possibly heal straight. He had a kind of blunt jaw, not square but not oval either. His lips were too full when compared to his eyes, and he really lacked any kind of symmetry.

"Did you get beat up a lot when you were a kid?"

The vampire blinked at me. "What?"

I motioned to him. "Just wondering if you came that way or if someone took a board to your face one too many times. I'm leaning on the latter."

His eyes narrowed, and he reached across the table to snag my wrist. His grip was bruising.

Okay, well, his grip *would* have been bruising, except I wrenched my arm out of his grip without trying.

Oh. That was nice.

Surprise flickered in his face. What? Did he think I was going to roll over for the new Prince of Dallas any more than I had for the last one?

Fuck. That.

"You will come with me now," he ordered, his eyes going murderous.

"Or what?" I raised my brows. Did he want to start a fight right here? I was willing. In fact, I was almost eager. Energy surged through the malaise infused in my cells, and the only thing I wished was that I had a drink to knock back before I knocked his teeth out of his head.

I hadn't been in a bar brawl in a while. This idiot wasn't Dimitri or Isaac, but I could do with breaking his neck in their place for right now. It might even be therapeutic. The pair of vampires behind him started to crowd closer as the idiot opened his mouth to… Well, whatever he planned to say, I didn't get to hear it. His whole demeanor shifted, and he leaned back in the chair as if trying to put distance between us.

It was only when he flicked a look behind me that I braced for a possible attack…

One that didn't come.

Without a word, the vampire scraped his chair backward in his haste to leave. Wow.

How very anticlimactic.

A drink slid onto the table in front of me, and I froze, every nerve cell I possessed lighting up as the chair next to me was withdrawn and Fin took a seat.

"Hello, Beautiful," he murmured, his expression almost tender. "Miss me?"

CHAPTER 6

"Everything in the world is about sex except sex. Sex is about power." - Oscar Wilde

A smile flirted around the mouth of Fin's angelic face as he studied me with his nearly pitch-black eyes with the barest ring of gray around them. His dark hair fell in a messy tousle, as though he'd just rolled out of bed, and the longing skulking through me suddenly let out a clarion call. It was so fucking loud, I almost jerked at the cacophony. Hunger waged a second assault, and I seized the glass he'd placed in front of me with a surprisingly steady hand and tossed back the full measure of it without regard for what it was.

The whiskey went down smooth and blazed a path to my belly. Setting the glass down, I met those much-missed eyes. "No," I lied, because I'd cut my own tongue out before I admitted the attachment had burrowed deeper inside me than I'd realized.

"You wound me," he murmured, though his own nonchalance didn't betray any such thing. He rubbed his thumb along his lower lip, and I tracked the motion before forcing my attention back to his eyes, then away from them and to the dancers. "But then, you knew that."

I didn't respond. It was better to not rise to the bait.

"I missed you," he continued. The dancer I'd been watching swung around on the pole and locked gazes with me. I let one corner of my mouth curve upward. I admired the athleticism, but she was a far more practical soul, and while her audience might be drooling for her, she wasn't remotely interested in them. However, the spark in her eyes suggested I might have better luck.

Amusement curled through me until the dancer's gaze slid past me and she blanched. Much like the vampire had earlier, she jerked her attention away and nearly fell.

"That was rude."

"Was it?" Fin was a picture of innocence as I glanced at him. "I didn't do anything."

"Of course you didn't." I needed to go, preferably before Elias came back. If he noticed Fin here, he would come to defend me, and I didn't need any of them having his face or scent. I'd call him later and apologize.

So much for my continued hiding at his place. It was time for me to go anyway. Elias would never throw me out, but he'd been right earlier. I needed to do something. The longer I sat here, however, the more I realized I didn't need to feed on anything this place could offer me.

Well, save for the one who'd taken a seat next to me and threatened to send me up in flames.

Definitely time to go.

I pushed my chair back, but Fin had already moved to ease it away as I stood. Ignoring him took considerable effort. I hadn't really dressed up for the club, just wore jeans and a halter-necked tank top that left my back bare. The flat-bottomed boots were better for fighting or running if I had to do either. With a toss of my hair, I headed for the door.

"Are we done so soon?" Fin asked, even as he set his palm lightly against my waist, but his thumb skated over the bare skin the top left open. "You just had the one drink, Beautiful."

"Go away," I told him.

"But I just got here." He almost sounded like he was pouting. "It's been weeks. I'm not even chastising you for leaving me without the courtesy of a note."

We were almost to the main doors.

"Is this asshole bothering you, Red?"

Fuck.

I pivoted and slid between Fin and Elias. "No," I told him, and locked gazes with my bestie. "I've got it. Go talk to Mellie and work on your game. It's definitely gotten rusty if that's what you call flirting."

"Bite me," he snarked right back, but his hard gaze never left Fin. "You aren't leaving with him, right?"

The warning drenched in worry underscoring the words washed over me. "No. I'm leaving period." Blocking Fin's mental reach had become second nature at the keep, and I'd still been harmonizing, thankfully. Blocking out his physical presence was far more challenging, especially considering the hunger gnawing away within me.

Stroking his thumb back and forth along the edge where the top gave way to skin, Fin said, "So this is Elias." Smugness populated his voice, and he curled his arm around me as he studied my best friend. Elias narrowed his eyes.

"Red, you know what he is…"

"I do," I told him and jabbed my elbow into Fin's gut. He didn't even budge, despite his exaggerated and amused 'oof.' It also shouldn't be remotely attractive, but awareness of Fin hummed along the surface of my skin like the electric energy of a storm about to break. "Thanks for hanging out with me tonight."

Eyebrows climbing, Elias snorted.

I met his gaze steadily while all I wanted to do was tell him to fucking play along.

Of course, he didn't.

Instead, he narrowed his eyes. "You always have a place with me. And you don't have to go anywhere you don't want to go."

I wanted to punch him.

"No," Fin agreed, then pressed his lips to my bare shoulder, and the sensation branded me. "We can continue to hang out with your...friend? Pet?" The last word came out soft, low, and almost taunting. As long as...

The warning growl sounding beneath the throbbing beat of the music as a new set kicked up on the stage promised me I hadn't been that lucky.

I tipped my head back and stared at the ceiling. The dancer on the center stage moved with hypnotic grace, and it was almost soothing how her hips undulated and the muscles of her stomach rolled.

"Look, asshole, I don't know where you think you are, but look around...there's only one of you here." The threat vibrated off of Elias. He wasn't one for posturing.

"Correction," Fin said. His tone seemed almost relaxed and playful as he spread his fingers against my abdomen and settled me more firmly against him. "There are two of us. I know you didn't just threaten...Red?" The last he whispered against my ear, and it took everything I had to not stomp my foot down on his.

The contact of his chest to my back was not doing me any favors. The earlier need stretched open like a maw inside of me. The utter lack of hunger and desire had transformed to a raging demand.

It was really pissing me off.

Elias shot me a look, the question in his eyes damn near audible. Did I want him to intervene? Because he planned to get involved whether I wanted him there or not. The last thing I needed was Fin deciding to tear into Elias. I had every faith in the wolf, but despite some of the hazier pieces of my recollection, I'd been there when Fin and Maddox had torn through the hordes of guards, trolls, and other unmentionables during the flight from the prison.

If you hurt him. I will kill you. I focused that thought at Fin, letting that mental block fall away. The sense of him flooded me, and he tightened his arm around me.

As you wish, Beautiful. The words were a whispered caress, and I damn near groaned at the contact. I didn't want him in there. I didn't want to let him in.

But I'd be damned if I let him hurt Elias.

"Perhaps we should have a drink with your friend," Fin suggested, all conciliatory and diplomatic, as if why not?

I really have missed you.

Dammit.

The music changed, the throbbing beat increasing in tempo, and the temperature inside the club seemed to drop precipitously. Skin prickling with apprehension, I dragged my gaze from the dancer back to Elias, who wasn't looking at me or Fin. His attention focused on the front doors I'd been heading for earlier.

I half-twisted against Fin and followed Elias' glance. A whisper of Fin's breath brushed my shoulder as he half-sighed.

"David," he murmured. "This is a terrible idea."

Despite the pounding beat and rattle of conversation, I had no trouble picking up Fin's words, and I had to guess, neither would 'David.' Wait—the so-called new Prince of Dallas?

The vampire who'd approached me was back, along with a dozen more. And there were still more filtering through the door behind them.

"This isn't personal," one of the vampires said. Maybe 'David.' Maybe not. I really didn't care.

Chin dipping, Fin pressed a kiss to my shoulder. "Beautiful, I know you wanted to go. Will you go back to your table for me? Just go and enjoy the show that lovely dancer is putting on. I can tell she wants your attention."

A little shiver cascaded down my spine. Yes, the dancer did want my attention. She was a stunning brunette with more muscle control than the average dancer, and she definitely had her eye on me. More than impersonal lust rolled off her. Maybe not the best plan.

The tension climbed a notch as Varick put on an appearance. Elias snarled, moving to insert himself between me and the new arrivals. Since that would also require separating me from Fin, he just put Fin behind him.

Weird.

Now I really couldn't go back to my table. He was counting on me to watch his back, and I couldn't absolutely guarantee Fin wouldn't sucker punch him.

You're wounding me again, Beautiful. You said you didn't want him harmed. I won't harm him. I could almost *feel* his attention shift from Elias to Varick, who seemed to spend as much time glowering at me as he did at the cadre of vampires invading the club.

He's harmless.

Fin snorted. He didn't believe me.

Well, too bad.

Not even the exquisite dancing kept the patrons from noticing all hell was about to break loose. More and more wolves poured out of the back. Bon Vivant wasn't neutral territory, it was owned by Elias' pack, another reason I chose it. They tended to be a little looser on the rules for guests, but apparently, not tonight.

In sheer numbers, the vampires outnumbered the shifters by nearly three-to-one. More than one patron abandoned their table and headed for a rear exit. The dancers leapt down from their platforms and poles, including miss seductive muscle control.

Her eyes flashed wolf, and she gave me a toothy grin.

Yeah, okay, she was cute.

Under other circumstances…

Beautiful, keep eyeing her like that and I won't be responsible for what I'll do next.

I snorted and slapped his shoulder. He was so full of shit. The fact that the wolf was eye-fucking me turned him on.

He sighed and slanted a look at me.

"David," Varick spit his name out. "You're asking for trouble."

"I didn't ask for your opinion," David told him. "And I have no fight to pick with you. This is vampire business. Stay out of it."

I studied David. He seemed vaguely familiar, but I couldn't quite place him. Granted, my visit with Isaac had been hella brief and I hadn't had a chance to memorize everyone there, but I swore I knew him from somewhere.

His dark eyes tracked to me. Malevolence filled them.

Huh.

Hate like that said I'd done something to piss him off. Pity I didn't remember what it was.

"This is my club," Varick reminded them, mouth twisting as though the next words were distasteful. "Inside my club, they have my protection."

Le sigh. Fine, I'd apologize to the big galoot later. I thought he got the score. But since he was going out of his way whether he wanted to or not and his wolves had now encircled me and Fin in this little cone of protection, the least I could do was apologize.

Right, I'd put that on a list.

Somewhere.

"You get between me and the target, you will have only yourself to blame for the consequences." The implicit threat couldn't be interpreted any other way.

"I couldn't have said it better myself," Fin said, his tone idle and relaxed, damn near bored. "This is a mistake, David. Walk away. I will offer no further opportunities."

Bravado or stupidity? There was such a fine line between the two concepts. But David focused on me again. His expression menacing. "This does not involve you, Lord Fin, but a private matter that must be handled. Just give us the succubus bitch, and we can all return to our lives."

The silence in the club expanded, like too much air pressed into a balloon threatening to pop and still more poured in. The steady slam of wolf hearts thudded like its own beat. The near rasp of air being forced in and out as the vampires gave the illusion of continued life provided the counterpoint. Most did it out of habit, not necessity.

To be honest, I'd always thought fight club things were kind of gross. Too much blood, sweat, and tears. Frankly, broken, jagged bones erupting out of skin were probably the least sexy thing ever.

What I had enjoyed about fight clubs was the pungent bloodlust that flooded the place. I could get high off of it and had. The buzz of sexual lust inside the club rapidly dissipated for the rising temperature of fury and rage.

Both sides wanted the standoff to tip. Currently, Varick and David were locked in a staring contest, going all primal and shit on each other.

What was kind of funny was they were both ignoring Fin. He was clearly the largest threat in the room.

Aww, Beautiful, you're going to make me blush. Are you sure I can't convince you to go back to your table?

Does she look like she's dancing anymore?

The particular wolf in question stood less than a foot from me, all sinuous lines and taut muscles. At my glance, she shot me a wink, and I couldn't help it. I smirked.

Sue me, she was very much my type.

Or had been.

Just, not now.

Ugh.

That thought took root, and I glanced away to scowl at the vampires blockading us. Had they brought an army?

Maybe they were taking Fin seriously after all.

The air was electric with the need to spill blood. Primal. Demanding. And beneath all of it—rage.

Pure, unadulterated rage.

The hunger snapped at me, licking along my flesh like a huffing beast in the darkness.

Hunger.

This was more than lust perfuming the air. It was real hunger, and I recognized it. The posturing and verbal threats faded to the background hum of heartbeats, panting breaths, and buzzing from electronic equipment. What few humans had been in the place had all evacuated. There had been a table of witches celebrating something, but they were gone, too. No one really wanted to get between vampires and shifters when fights went down.

It just wasn't good for the health.

The anger in the room climbed a notch, and despite the icy temperature, it only seemed to get hotter.

I ignored David, Varick, and the others. I registered Fin and Elias. The dancer. Mellie. One by one, I noted and discarded the others.

Something else was in the club with us, and it wasn't any

of these fools getting ready to tear each other apart. Any other time, I'd probably grab a glass of wine and go find a comfortable spot on the bar so I could soak up the lust. I could probably fill my need for weeks in the sheer volume roiling amongst this crowd, but it broke as it rolled over me, parting like I was a stone in the middle of the raging stream.

The splash of it left me damp, but unmoved. Like water, if I stayed here, it would eventually erode through the surface levels, but I didn't want to consume this ferocity. Not at the moment.

Not when someone else already feasted on it.

And was still feasting…

Beautiful…

Not now.

To my shock, Fin only spared me a single studying glance before he nodded and focused on the enemy in front of us.

And they were the enemy.

I didn't make the mistake of thinking Varick's whole pack was on our side. They were protecting us because we were in his bar. Elias was my friend. He'd protect me regardless, the same way I would him. That they were extending it to Fin was just politics.

Fuck it, I didn't need to sort that shit out. I needed to figure out what was feeding on the rising bloodlust and magnifying it. The rising tide of the argument needed only one spark to strike. The taste of magic in the air curled up like smoke from a cooker.

Witch?

Wizard?

No…

Demon.

Scorch lay heavy under it. Brimstone. Fire. Battle.

Daevas.

A daeva was here.

I hated daevas. Greedy little things. They were minor demons. Old functionaries. They fed on one thing or another, but whatever it was they lusted for, they could magnify a thousand fold. They enjoyed nothing more than chaos.

Don't get me wrong, chaos had a time and a place.

It wasn't here.

It definitely wasn't now.

The moment it registered, all hell broke loose. David lunged, as did Varick. The clash of wolves versus vampires sprayed blood across the room, but I turned away from the battle. Three of the vampires had come straight for me. Two lay literally in pieces, and Fin held up the third one, his expression mild, almost bemused.

I pivoted, searching the battle of violence for the one feeding on it. Because even as they waded into each other, slamming fists and raking claws—the first roar of a wolf's war howl rose.

Fuck.

The wolves were turning.

Time for you to go, Beautiful.

"Don't," I told Fin. Putting a hand against him when he pulled me to him. He could just whisk us away, but this fight started because I was here. Guilt nibbled at me a little.

"We can't stay," Fin murmured. How I heard him over the ruckus, I didn't focus on too closely. The scent of blood —old and new—threatened to overwhelm me. I wrinkled my nose in distaste, because the smell of it was rolling my stomach.

"There's something here," I told him, still searching the shadows. One moment, we were in the thick of the fighting, and the next, we were on the stage. "I hate when you all do that."

He chuckled, then nuzzled a kiss against my ear. Fuck, I

caught myself leaning into it before I gave him a shove and turned. At least from up here, I had a better view.

The absurdity of our current situation struck. "Why aren't you fighting?"

With a shrug, Fin curled his arm around my waist and pulled me back against his chest. "Because they are handling it and I'm of a mind to just kill them all. It's what Rogue would do. And I already killed half of Isaac's cadre—well, David's now."

"He's really gone?"

"Sorry, Beautiful. He had to know we were coming for him. Alfred summoned him. When he declined the invitation, Alfred sent me to deal with him."

That was why he wasn't at the party.

"And you slipped away on us." He pressed another kiss to my shoulder. "You'll notice I am not spanking you or yelling at the moment."

"At the moment?" Wolf. Wolf. Vampire. Wolf—oh, dead wolf. I winced. Vampire. Shredded vampire. Wolf.

"We'll revisit the issue when we have more privacy, but for now, I'm just grateful to be with you again."

The earlier guilt resurged, and I scowled. "I'm not."

"And I choose not to be insulted. You've had a difficult few weeks. You're probably hungry..." He kept it so conversational.

Wait...

"How are we just standing here? I thought the vamps showed up for me?" Fin had dispatched three of them, but we were just standing on the stage—okay, cuddling on the stage and I wasn't pulling away, yes, I was aware—while the fight raged on, and none of them came for us.

"Magic," Fin whispered against my ear, a soft chuckle darkening his voice. "I wanted you to myself anyway. You're the one who wanted to stay. This way, we both get what we want."

"If I got what I wanted, I wouldn't be a damn vampire." I winced at the curt words the moment they slipped out. His soft sigh was so full of regret.

"I know you're angry… In time, that will pass." And that killed any misgivings I had.

"Don't patronize me," I snarled.

"I'm not," he insisted. "Transition is difficult. We all have to adjust."

"Well bully for me, I've transitioned. I'm all maladjusted and ready to go." Irritation swarmed through my blood, like stinging nettles raked over my flesh. I couldn't find the daeva, but the bloodlust in the room climbed.

Except for Fin. I twisted to glance up at him and found his dark eyes filled to the brim with concern and sadness. My heart twisted.

Fuck.

But wait…no bloodlust.

How was the daeva feeding it in the others and not in Fin? I started forward, but Fin's grip didn't loosen and he kept me firmly trapped against him.

"Let go," I ordered him.

"Beautiful, I will do anything for you, but I can't let you go." The lingering remorse there didn't make the pill any less bitter to swallow. He pressed his lips to my shoulder again. The barest scrape of his teeth, and liquid heat clawed through my system in demand.

The earlier thirst redoubled. I curled my fingers into my palms and dug my nails in. "Fin, there's a daeva here." The words gritted out between my teeth.

"So?"

So?

I glanced up at him again, and his gaze fastened on my mouth. The lust curling off him intensified.

Oh. That little...

Jerking my head around, I stared at the dancer I'd been fascinated with earlier. She wasn't in the fight at all. Instead, she leaned against the bar and stared right at me.

With a little pinky wave, she grinned. Before I could respond, Fin's hand closed on my nape, and he turned me to face him. His mouth closed over mine in a savage kiss that I longed to answer. Fuck, did I want to, and for a moment, I let myself get lost in it.

But this wasn't Fin.

Don't ask me how I knew it, but I did. Fin cared a lot. He might laugh, tease, and cajole, but he wasn't Nero. He didn't fiddle while Rome burned. The sharp sting of his teeth scraping across my lower lip sent blood welling up between us, and his arms were like steel bands locking me in place.

Want you... His thoughts tangled with mine. *Need you...*

I groaned as he pushed a thigh between mine. It had only been a few weeks, but I had missed him.

Them...

I ignored that little voice, then lifted my hands to grip Fin's face. I wanted to whisper sorry or to at least offer some soothing comfort for what I was about to do. The daeva was driving them all mad.

The wolves.

The vampires.

Fin.

His lust had always been a potent thing, but it seemed to have fanned from raging fire in the hearth to forest fire out of control. I sucked it out of him.

Every.

Damn.

Drop.

I sucked it until my head was light and my soul giddy. Fin jerked his head abruptly, breaking the kiss. Blood flowed from the fresh set of injuries he'd left on my mouth, but I didn't care.

Fuck me.

There was so much power in what I'd just pulled out of him. His eyes narrowed on me, then focused on the room beyond. His pupils had blown, and even his expression seemed a little lost. "What the hell…?"

If he'd been a lesser vampire, what I'd just done to him would have dropped him where he stood.

"She doesn't get to have you," I told him, and he yanked his gaze back to me. The words slurred a little on my tongue, and I stumbled as I turned away from him and focused on the daeva.

Shock rippled across her features, and I grinned. Between the blood and my teeth, I had no doubt it wasn't a pretty smile.

I could almost read the words she mouthed as I charged off the stage.

You bitch.

Yeah.

I was a bitch.

Oh, it was on.

I lunged.

CHAPTER 7

"In the midst of chaos, there is also opportunity." - Sun Tzu

The battle raging around us in Bon Vivant polluted the air with the stink of blood, fury, and fur. A host of other scents assaulted me, but I ignored them as I dove across the room for the daeva. Damn shame that the dancer I'd admired started all this shit. Then again, maybe that was why I admired her.

It was certainly not my first bar fight.

She hissed when I struck. I learned a long time ago to not curl my thumb into my closed fist. I also avoided hitting bone, like you found along the jaw. Joint shots really fucking hurt. Slamming my fist right into her boob though?

Not only had the air whooshed out of her, but her whole body shuddered. Grimacing, she bared her teeth at me, and I couldn't help the smile curving my own lips as I seized a handful of that gorgeous hair and slammed her beautiful face into the bar top.

Once.

Twice.

And on the third, her wild shriek of defiance sliced through the air. The glamour around her began to break apart, and at least some of the fighting behind me faded to silence. Eyes darkening to near soulless voids, the daeva tried to wrench free of my grip.

But look at that—I could hold on even as she raked her claws down my arms, leaving bloody furrows in her wake. She snarled at me, and I slammed my head forward. The collision of our skulls left my ears ringing, but she staggered dazedly.

If I hadn't had her hair looped around my closed fist, she probably would have collapsed. Too bad for her, I wasn't done yet. Something sharp raked down my back, but the attack didn't last longer than a split second. I caught sight of Fin via the mirror behind the bar as he tore apart the vampire who'd been about to grab me.

Dismissing both from my mind, I focused on the daeva again. Her fierce need to amp the chaos in order to feed her bloodlust couldn't just be channeled elsewhere. I had to break it apart and shatter the possessive hold she exerted on all of them, whether it was with pain or amping up her own natural lusts.

She wanted rage?

She wanted blood?

I had it all in spades.

The blackness of her eyes seemed to expand until it swallowed all hint of color. The feed had left her near staggering drunk, but the more pain I inflicted—I punched her in the boob for a second time, and if those babies weren't natural, they would have popped like water balloons—the more her focus locked on to me.

Daeva, like succubi, fed off the emotions. Hers were just a

lot more specific than mine. The rake of her need scoured against my skin as she fought for purchase.

"Oh honey," I murmured as I dragged her away from the bar and fended off the hooked claws of her fingers as she tried to grab my hair in retaliation. "I'm not playing."

Gaze fixed on her, I smirked. The fact that she fought to latch onto me to feed left her wide open, and I found the lust, the hunger driving her so desperately and fanned it as I locked my arms around her neck. Wild need like that could cloud the mind, and it also threatened the control.

I'd been starving once. Desperate. It hadn't been pretty.

A lot of bodies had fallen that night, and I'd sworn to never let myself tumble down that rabbit hole again. The daeva writhed back against me as I locked my arms tighter. Now my gaze was on the room. The bloody and the injured filled my vision. Somewhere in that mess was Elias. There were innocents caught up in this, too, but Elias was my friend.

That she'd involved him was bad enough.

When she dragged Fin into it, though, it tipped me over the edge.

I needed her tentacles out of all of them before I killed her. Otherwise, the whiplash might very well overwhelm them and make a bloody mess even worse.

A flash of movement, and my dark angel ripped another vampire in half who charged at us. Like puppets on a string, the daeva's power lashed at them to reel them in to protect her, but I'd cut off her oxygen. She was fighting for every single breath. I wasn't worried about assault from any other direction, not with Fin prowling around the edges of my own fight.

The fact that he didn't interfere scored him some major points with me. Not that I needed to focus on that at the moment. The sudden snap, like a board being broken, warned me a split-second before the daeva's violent need focused one hundred percent on me.

I inhaled the headiness of the near desperate wantonness. It did nothing for my own hunger. I survived by feasting on the lusts of others, so hers was merely an appetizer. But I focused on drawing it into me, even as she tried to magnify my lust. It didn't work.

Laughter bubbled up in little bursts of glee as she scrabbled at me, clawing at my arms and trying to throw her head back to hit me, but I avoided it and ignored the blood slicking my skin as she dug her nails in deeper. Now I could cut off her oxygen entirely.

Gradually, the struggle went out of her, and then she flopped, a doll on the end of a cut string, and I released her to fall the rest of the way to the ground. Straightening, I met Fin's gaze. My own breaths came in short, sharp little gasps.

Why the fuck did I need to breathe again?

I really didn't get it.

The fighting had diminished, but it wasn't totally done. The ferocity had dimmed. Fin raked his gaze over me, his teeth flash as he grinned. "Enjoy that, did you?"

I shrugged. "I told you, she didn't get to have you. I hate little bitches who feed on drama." It was an oversimplification, but it was also as much about territory as anything else. I couldn't let someone else wander in and start feeding on what belonged to me. That was like inviting them in to try on your shoes, and you just know those bitches were going to ask to borrow them.

The corners of his mouth curled upward as he glanced down at the daeva. "She's still breathing."

I shrugged. "I didn't need to—"

He snapped her neck, then wrenched her head right off. The spray of blood left me a little nauseated. Not because it was gross—okay, it was totally gross—but the smell of her blood was repugnant. Kind of like the way I reacted to Sambuca. I used to love the black licorice liquor, until I got puking drunk on it.

Now, even the thought of black licorice made my stomach rebel.

Fin grimaced at my expression. "Breathe through your mouth."

Ugh. "I'm fine," I lied. My arms hurt. My head hurt. My plans for the evening had been ruined. Fin had popped up like a bad penny I'd been desperate to see.

Yes, desperate.

I could admit my own damn short comings.

The worst part, though, was I was still hungry, and Fin eyed me like he could consume me. It was enough to make me burn with the urge to climb him like a pole.

Fuck, I did not have time for this, not with a bloody, headless corpse at our feet—the aforementioned head still in Fin's hand—and the wounded and dead piling up on the other side of the bar, where the pitched battle finally gave as both David and Varick called it.

Well, that was refreshing.

"Get out," Varick snarled.

"This isn't over," David warned him, but the newly christened prince—fuck, newly christened. That was right, Isaac was still out there somewhere!—glared while his people dragged away a few bodies. Some were missing limbs.

Did vampires regenerate them? Or were we going to be dealing with one-armed vampires? I really couldn't remember.

As if skipping a stone across the surface of the water, Varick glared right at me. The moment my gaze locked on the alpha, I knew we were in for a world of shit. His pack just bled for me, and he hated my guts. This was not going to end well.

Fin stepped between us, cutting off his line of sight, and I blinked as he tossed the head casually to land at Varick's feet. Despite his vampires evacuating, David maintained his stance. Vamp had balls, I'd give him that. "You want to blame someone for the trouble, blame your own employee, wolf." The arctic tone brooked zero arguments.

"If that bitchy little succubus—"

Fin was a blur across the room, and then he had Varick in one hand and David in the other, both by the throat, both hefted like they weighed nothing.

Okay, that was a little hot.

Totally lying—it was exceptionally hot, and a thrill went up my spine, even as my earlier hunger surged back to the surface. Every other creature in the room froze, including Elias. I caught his gaze as he focused on me. He flicked a look to Fin, then to me, and then to the bar behind me with a jerk of his chin.

He wanted me to go.

Now.

While Fin was distracted.

That was…

…an excellent plan. My raging hormones were incredibly not onboard, but I sincerely did not give a fuck. I left the keep for a reason. Fin finding me here didn't change that reason. If anything, it proved my point. I flicked a look back to Elias. I wanted to say goodbye. Something.

He dipped his chin a fraction. Understanding flared in his eyes. We didn't need to say it, but dammit, the fist in my chest tightened as I took a single step toward the door. Fin was still focused on the remaining vampires and the wolf pack while he held the lives of their respective leaders in his hands.

Nothing in this room was a threat to him.

Not anymore.

I didn't overthink it.

I just left.

The air outside slapped me with humidity as I hurried into the night. The stench of blood was all over me. I encountered a pair of eager vampires ready to swoop in and steal me away.

Fuck.

Them.

I left their broken bodies propped next to each other, and now I was wearing a lot more blood than I should be for a night out on the town.

Like enough that if the human police caught sight of me, I'd be spending a few hours cleaning up that mess.

Arms folded, I kept my head down and hurried away from the club. I needed to get out of the bloodied clothes, clean up, and do something before Fin tracked me again. It was the looking down that did me in. I slammed right into a hard wall of a body and damn near bounced off of it.

Snapping my head up, I stared into Rogue's too blue eyes. His lips were compressed in a thin line as he swept his gaze over me. The hunger I'd been wrestling with on the walk away from Fin flash-fired through me.

"You're hurt." It wasn't a question. I was going to tell him 'no.' I was going to say the blood wasn't mine. I'd already half-forgotten the furrows the daeva dug into my arms when I'd been fighting her. If anything, their discomfort could hardly compete with wretched need burning within me.

"It's nothing…" But he slid an arm around my waist and tugged me to him.

Oh, yes please.

My hands rested against his chest. He dipped his head and rubbed his chin against my hair. "You reek of blood and death."

"You smell like peppermint farts and rainbows," I

returned drily, and that earned me a sharp slap against the ass, but I still smirked. "What are you doing here?"

"It's been a few weeks, I wanted to check on you." We stood in the shadows between two buildings, but we couldn't stay here. Though I was loathe to pull away.

Fuck me. First Fin, now Rogue. I *left* them for a reason. I did not need to get sucked back into their orbit.

"I need to go, Rogue," I told him, and tried to ignore the groan underscoring my words. He really did smell good. Better than the nasty blood I wore.

"Where do you need to go, little *sváss*?"

Fuck.

"Away." I forced myself to step back, but he didn't let me go. Not even when the blood I wore began to soak his shirt. Great, we were both going to be disgusting. "Rogue, stop. Fin's here, and if we linger…"

I didn't even get to complete the thought. Rogue moved. He lifted me against him, his hand wrapping against the back of my head, and he ran. It was like when he took me from the prison, only I was a hell of a lot more aware this time, and the air that seemingly shredded my skin before barely stung now.

Well, mark one point in the pro-vampire column.

It still had a long way to go.

Face buried against Rogue's neck, I filled my lungs with the scent of him. It helped to clear out the cloying sticky nature of the blood in my nostrils. It washed away the taint from the earlier fight. It even chased away the bitter bite of loneliness that had crept in like a thief over the last few weeks.

Rogue didn't slow until salty air brushed my face. When he stopped, I lifted my head and stared at the sandy beach revealed under the half-moon above. The light was dim, particularly when you took into account the clouds and the promise of a storm in the distance. Lightning flashed, dancing across the horizon.

It was perfect.

Rogue lowered me to my feet and then settled his hands on my hips as I got my wobbling legs under me. My muscles protested how long I'd been plastered against him, thighs hitched to his hips as I held on. Not that I had any fear he would drop me.

"It's beautiful."

"I thought you'd like this…" Then he stroked his fingers over my bare shoulder. "You're still covered in blood."

I wasn't alone in that. I tossed him a look over my shoulder and raked my gaze over him. "It's a good thing we have all this water then, isn't it?"

I'd never been shy, and I didn't give a damn what most people thought. At the same time, it was like I'd been possessed by a giddiness I'd never experienced. I toed off my shoes, then stripped out of the top before peeling out of the jeans. I removed it all down to bare skin. Rogue's gaze rested on me fiercely, and he made no pretense about liking what he saw.

The erection straining the front of his pants would have told me that, but there was something far more raw and devastating in the way his eyes flickered from darkness to light. I didn't get him. Not really.

He hadn't wanted me, not when they'd stolen me from the prison. His body had been more than accommodating to my needs, but he'd kept his mind and his emotions in check. Not something Fin or Maddox had done.

Maddox.

My heart squeezed, and I dragged my gaze off Rogue before I gave myself away. I wanted to ask how he was. The question was right there on my lips and it burned on my tongue, but I refused to give it voice. I hadn't asked Fin, and I'd be damned before I asked Rogue.

If I asked anyone about Maddox, it would be Maddox himself.

With a sway of my hips, I marched toward the water. I didn't look back. The cove was relatively private. I didn't see or hear anyone else—not that the presence of others would have slowed me down. The rush of the water surging up to meet me sent it flowing over my toes and ankles. The wet sand squeezed between my toes as I ventured out into the dark sea.

I'd just reached wading depth when a splash alerted me to his following me. Hooking his arms around me, Rogue dragged me back to him as a wave crashed into us both, and a laugh tore out of me. The water wasn't warm. Far from it, but I didn't shiver so much as sigh. While the waves couldn't extinguish the heat burning away inside of me, it did cool it some.

Another wave struck. As we bobbed with it, I laughed again. "I love the ocean," I admitted, offering that little piece of myself freely. I couldn't explain it if he decided to ask. But I'd dreamed of the ocean for years. Even if most of the homes I'd known were landlocked. I'd had to make do with lakes and ponds, but they had nothing on this.

This was perfect.

"So I see," Rogue murmured, his body steadying mine as the waves rolled back. We were half-floating in the salt water, and it seemed to foam ahead of the wave rushing at us. With a powerful push, Rogue shoved us toward it, and then we had water crashing over our heads. The force of the water pushed him away from me. I was flat out laughing my ass off when I surfaced and shoved the damp hair from my eyes. I searched around the moonlit water, but Rogue wasn't there.

What the hell?

Then another wave hit me, and I rode with it, half surfing on the force of it back toward the shallower waters where I could put my feet down. A splash pulled me half-around, and I gaped. A bear lumbered in the water toward me.

A *bear.*

A *freaking bear.*

"Rogue?"

The sleek white beast flowed through the water until it reached me and then stared up at me with a twinkle in those blue eyes. He was *massive.* Delight curved through me.

"You're a bear."

No wonder he knotted. The thought sent a shiver through my traitorous system, and my earlier hunger redoubled. He pushed his head against me, knocking me back a step, and I landed on my ass in the water. At this depth, it was almost to my neck. The wave rising up would have crashed right over my head, but he stood up abruptly and the water broke over him instead and flowed around me. Then he dropped back down and butted his head against me again.

With care, I put my hands against his fur. "Are you flirting?"

The flat stare the bear gave me had me snickering. Still, it was cute. The force of his head and the sheer size of it kept me off balance each time he rubbed against me. He stared at me, then out to where the waves rolled in, then back to me again.

Oh.

"You want to go farther?"

One sharp nod.

"Long swim?"

Just a steady stare.

I bit my lower lip.

I didn't know why I pretended to hesitate. The only thing

waiting for me on the shore were our bloodied clothes, and Rogue was a freaking bear.

The frost elf turned into a solid white, gorgeous polar bear.

It was…adorable.

Yeah, maybe I'd keep that last part to myself.

Maddox was a dragon. My heart squeezed.

Rogue a bear.

Did Fin turn into a tree? The random thought had me snickering all over again like I was drunk, and I was pretty sure that Rogue had grown tired of waiting for me to decide. He pushed against me again, and I wrapped my arms around his neck as he maneuvered to get under me. Then I was on his back.

I was riding the bear.

No, not like that. Don't be a dirty bird.

I'd save that riding for later when Rogue was Rogue again.

Even I had some limits.

Ahem.

Anyway… I clung to his back as he turned out to deeper water and began to swim. It was like he undulated against the water, slicing through it neatly and evenly. The farther from shore we traveled, the quieter the waves and the more the silence of the night wrapped around us. I divided my attention between searching the darkness of the water for the stars overhead.

This was a far cry from Bon Vivant. From daevas and vampires and wolves. It was even further from the stone walls of the keep with its broody master, hotheaded dragon, teasing druid, and aloof elf. Maybe not so aloof now?

Still, the whole of it captivated me, and the hunger plaguing me earlier quieted as I filled my soul with the journey. When the waves picked up again, we were riding them toward another shore. It had to be a different one because I swore we hadn't turned around. The sand *glittered* when we reached this shore, and I slid off of Rogue's back. My legs were a little tired from clamping against him, much as they had been when we arrived at our first beach.

It took me a moment to get the wobbling under control, and I followed him up onto the shore. He paused periodically to glance back at me as he padded across the sparkling sand.

The sparkles were pretty, but they were actually sharp little rocks. Betrayed by beauty again.

Fuckers.

I picked my way carefully. The breeze was cooler here, and my nipples were jagged, hard tips all on their own. Goosebumps rippled over my skin as the shore gave way to grass, then heavily treed and natural foliage that obscured the paving stones Rogue paced toward easily.

I followed him quietly. It could be a trap. It could be just about anything. The last thing in the world I should be doing was following Rogue on this little magical, mystery adventure tour, and yet, here I was, and I didn't give a damn.

Currently, I wanted to see where he was taking me. The dense foliage gave way to an arch of trees, stretching out to each other and entangling themselves, and on the other side…

A house.

It wasn't huge or fancy, just a beautiful little villa tucked away in a jungle glen on an island.

There were lights on around the flower beds that lined the front of it. Not terribly bright, but enough to make out the blooms. Night jasmine perfumed the air. That and honeysuckle. I could still taste the salt, but that might've been on my skin.

The walls of the cottage were a sand color, but there were

dark wood accents, like a fairytale cottage or some shit. It was…adorable.

There was even a fucking porch swing.

"Is this yours?" I had to know, and I looked to where the polar bear just watched me, waiting. The air sharpened and crackled, even as a breeze hushed over my skin. Then he began to change. It wasn't swift and brilliant, like Maddox's violent change to the dragon, or the way he compressed himself down to assume his human form.

This was almost elegant, slow, and brilliant as his body reshaped itself, and there was a dazzling after-effect where between one blink and the next, the bear became the man.

Well, elf.

I dropped my gaze to his erect cock, and a laugh slipped through me. I would never call it an elfhood.

Not for all the money in the world.

But I might tease him with that.

Dragging my gaze upward, I found him half-smirking at me. But only half. There was caution in his eyes and…

"What's wrong?" I took a couple of steps toward him, the pull magnetic and inevitable. The dark ink of his tattoos flowing over his arm and shoulder reminded me of the twisting vines, but here they were, almost like shadows escaping the faint glow of the moon.

"I've never brought anyone here," he admitted. "None of them know about it. You should be safe here to rest for a while. There are clothes, and I can bring you more. Give you the time to decide what you want to do…"

He kept talking, the words washing over me as I fixated on the way his mouth moved to shape the syllables. We were both wet. His longer hair flattened down much as mine was, soggy from the sea. The brine in the air a reminder that we really hadn't washed, but the copper stench was gone and I could only scent him.

Rogue.

When I halted just in front of him, he paused mid-sentence and stared at me. "Little *sváss…*"

"Rogue?"

He raised his brows.

"Shut up and kiss me."

I slid my hand up to his nape, but I didn't have to ask twice. All hesitation erased as his mouth clamped down on mine.

Fuck.

I'd missed him.

"The art of seduction is knowing what she really wants and slowly giving it to her in a way that takes her breath away." - Unknown

Rogue

"I*'ve never brought anyone here. None of them know about it."* The confession alone was tantamount to betrayal, but for the first time in centuries, Rogue didn't care. Save for a handful of years, he'd given his whole loyalty first to Alfred, then to Maddox, and finally, Fin. He'd looked after them, protected them, and when the need demanded it, he'd delivered the required discipline to knock them out of their own bad moods.

He'd done it all.

Helping Fiona flee? It hadn't been anything more than showing her the same loyalty he'd so freely given the others, whether she understood or not. Standing there, on the tiny little island he'd claimed centuries earlier in front of the cozy little house where he allowed himself to pretend the intervening years and his own turning hadn't happened, he sank into her kiss, desperate for the taste of her.

The heat of her lips on his burned through the chill around his heart and rattled all the supposed ice running in his veins. Frost elves were not cold-natured, they were just more comfortable in the snowier and icier regions.

Correction—Rogue was more comfortable. There were no others that he'd been able to locate. War, famine, disease, and time had wasted them away, cutting their numbers through attrition. Some of the bloodlines mingled into the other races until they were all but diluted.

In Fiona's kiss, however, he found home again, the brand settling on his soul. Make no mistake, it was a claiming. She'd demanded the kiss, and he'd given it. The last few weeks of separation had been uncomfortable at best, but Fiona needed to find her feet. She needed to choose them for herself, not because they trapped her or compelled her.

Certainly not because Alfred would chain her to his will until she stopped fighting him, and that would make them both miserable. His fury over Rogue's perceived betrayal had led to more than one icy confrontation. Rogue didn't let it bother him, especially not with her tongue dueling his as she fisted her hands into his damp hair.

The salt on her lips only added to the sweet spice of her taste. Letting her go had been a challenge, but it had nothing on staying away from her. Fin had been circumspect in his contact, saying only that he was tracking her. Maddox, however, had been in a rage from the moment he discovered she'd left until about ten days earlier, when he'd simply shut both Rogue and Alfred out.

The dragon had pined and grown morose.

Another reason Rogue had come to check on Fiona. Maddox needed to know she was all right. Fiona's groan vibrated against his mouth as he deepened the kiss. Plastered to him, the heat from her body infused his, and his cock stiffened past painful. Need stormed through him as he cupped her jaw, then tilted her head back further so he could deepen the kiss.

The breeze teased cooling eddies across his skin, barely noticeable when compared to the stiff peaks of her nipples pressed to his chest or the heat of her pussy teasing the base of his cock. The slide of her leg up his hip had him dropping his hands down to catch her thighs. Hoisting her up easily, she let out another groan, one he answered as she wiggled a hand between them to grip his cock.

Pleasure raked fierce claws through him as she stroked his tip against her wet labia, and he bit down on her lower lip. Eyes open, he met the radiant green-eyed gaze with her blown pupils and mouth swollen from kissing. Want was an angry beast inside of him, snapping all civilized veneers away. He'd never wanted anyone the way he longed for Fiona. Equal to that desire, however, was the need to see her free.

One of her hands was still fisted in his hair, while the other stroked him from tip to base, then up again. Each squeeze had him hissing as need pounded in his balls. He longed to taste her, to bend her over and fuck her until she shook from the orgasms rattling her system, until he'd fed every part of her nature then spent himself inside of her, only to harden and take her again.

Face flushed, Fiona let out little sharp pants as she licked her lips. "I'm hungry, Rogue."

"Then feed, little *sváss*," he offered, stroking his thumbs against her skin as he strode forward. As long as he had the power to move, he would get her somewhere more secure. She tended to blow out his synapses. The day in his bedroom when she'd fed on his lust for her, it had only forced him to shed what restraints he'd managed to put into place.

He hadn't been gentle, but one thing he'd learned about Fiona was that she didn't necessarily *want* gentle. Inside, the air was a bit musty, but he ignored it as he strode through the simple room to the stairs and up to the bedroom. The bed there was nothing like the oversized one at the keep, but it would do for this. With each step he took, she kept stroking him, until every drop of heated blood seemed to surge into his cock and he threatened to swell past the pain he was already in.

But fuck if he didn't want this pain.

Her tongue skated over her teeth a split second before she leaned in to kiss him. Whisper soft and gentle, she nuzzled at his lips, and the near blinding desire bubbling in his system cooled a fraction and cleared the cloud from his thoughts.

If he were absolutely honest, fucking her had been in the top three items on his list for why he wanted to find her. Not the very top of the list, but definitely in the top three. The ache of loneliness he'd lived with since the last of his kind passed eased when she was there, and he refused to examine that too closely.

Fin lived for the tale of her being their very much fated mate, foretold in a vision and through prophecy. Maddox had been so gone on her, he'd demanded she claim him and he'd forever chained himself to her. Rogue found himself jealous of that connection. His other half had wanted to claim her that first night. From the moment he'd knotted within her, it had been a foregone conclusion.

Yet, it was another complication they didn't need.

He didn't have to claim her to feed her.

"Feed, little *sváss*," he encouraged her as he held her poised over his cock, but made no move to take her. His lust was a potent force. If she wanted the rest of him, all she had to do was take him. Head tipped back, she stared at the ceiling and groaned.

"This can't change anything, Rogue." The strain in the words pulled a reluctant smile to his lips. "I left for a reason."

He knew, but he said nothing. She fisted his cock tighter, and he gritted his teeth against the urge to thrust into her hand.

"You want to shackle me again…"

Anger flashed through him, and he glared at her. "I will *never* shackle you."

Head snapping down, she met his glare with one of her own. "You already tried."

"I didn't," he disagreed. Then, banding one arm beneath her ass to keep her in position, he lifted a hand to clasp her throat so she wouldn't turn away. "If I did, I opened them and threw away the key when I took you away from the keep. I have not tracked you, nor have I looked at your expenses."

Eyes narrowed, she focused on him. "Then how did you find me?"

He shrugged. "You won't like the answer."

"Then tell me anyway."

"You went home," he murmured. "It was why Fin waited for you in Texas." Despite the druid's protests, that was exactly where he'd been. "You went to your friend Elias."

Her teeth flashed at him in a mockery of a smile.

"And the vampires want you out of their city…"

"David."

He nodded once. "And Elias' pack owns that club. It wasn't that hard to find. All you have to know is you."

"Fuck."

"If you wish," he said with a slow smile, very aware that wasn't what she meant. "I'm quite ready to fuck you until you come on my cock a few times."

The bald language had once been anathema to him. He'd spent far too much time with Maddox and Fin. Silver-tongued or not, Fin could be as bawdy as a tavern wench on the prowl for her evening silver.

A throaty chuckle escaped her, and then she kissed him again, even as she ground her hips downward, and with one thrust, seated him deep inside her heat. It was all the permission Rogue required as he dropped her to the bed and pulled her legs up until they were over his shoulders. Her back arched, the action giving her breasts ample display. Gaze riveted on her eyes as she stared up at him, he gripped her hips and began to thrust.

There was no gentleness in his pace. He filled her sweet heat in relentless fashion, shifting his angle until she began to let out little cries with every strike. There she was. His Fiona was fierce in her pursuit of pleasure, and the sense of her feeding began to tug at him, honing his desire to a fine point. Wanting her was not a problem.

Her body stiffened, and she clamped down on his cock as the first orgasm ripped through her, so he paused his motions, gritting his teeth against the flutters of her inner muscles stroking him. He let the pleasure wash through her, and when her eyes opened to look up at him, he pressed his thumb against her clit. Two simple strokes, and she let out another scream as she came again.

Dampness flooded her thighs, but he kept her in place, mercilessly impaled on his cock as he teased a third orgasm from her, and when she hit her fourth and clawed at the covers, he began to stroke into her again, giving in to his own need to have her.

His whole body leaned in to hers as he drove into her over and over, and then his knot threatened, and he spread her legs so he could surge down to claim her mouth and swallow her scream as he pushed over the edge. His knot swelled, his dick felt like it would burst, and then he came in a rush of pleasure and pain.

She kissed along his jaw, mouthing damp, hot presses as she locked her legs behind his hips as they both shook. Then her teeth scraped against his throat, and he closed his eyes and tilted his head. She sank them in without further invitation, and need flashed through him again, his balls dragging up as he stayed seated deep in her.

He swore he came again as she began to drink from him, and she ran her hands up and down his back as though alternating between clawing at him and stroking him. They clung together, suspended as she fed and he settled, satisfaction unfurling in him.

Fiona was safe and sated. His mission accomplished. Even if he had to leave her to her travels again, she would last another few weeks before she would need one of them. Had she discovered that yet? What had she learned in their time apart?

Though he found himself longing to ask her, he kept his questions to himself. She released his throat and leaned back, boneless in his arms as he rolled over so she could sprawl atop him. They would be connected for some time yet. They lay in near replete silence. His hair was tacky from the sea, and hers mussed, but he wouldn't budge for anything unless she asked.

When she finally lifted her head to look at him, she did the unexpected—she offered her wrist. At his quirked eyebrow, she gave a facsimile of a careless shrug. "I fed, don't you need to?"

Need? No.

Want desperately? Yes.

His hips pushed up of their own accord, and the motion rocked his knot inside of her, leaving them both hissing at the over-sensitized connection.

She licked her lips. "You feel so good."

"So do you," he promised her, and stroked his hand down her back to her ass. Her curves were a delight for him to pet and fondle, though right now, he was more focused on her eyes. The pupils were so blown, he could barely make out the rich green of their irises. He had missed those eyes. Missed the faint pout to her lips. The quickfire nature of her temper, and the biting wit in her cutting tongue.

He'd missed her.

"Then feed… I don't know what the term would be for you, since you call me little *sváss*."

"What do you call me in your head?" Curiosity had always been his downfall.

"Asshole," she admitted, then grinned as if to rob the word of its power. "Though he-who-doesn't-deserve-to-be-called-by-his-name usurped that title."

Alfred could have it. Rogue chuckled, then caught her hand to press a kiss to her palm. "So what is my new title?"

Nose wrinkled, she said, "I don't really have one. I thought of you as a Viking, and now I know you're a frost elf and apparently a *bear*."

His smile was his own as he bit down on the heel of hand, not enough to break the skin, but definitely enough for her to feel the pressure of the contact. The fact that she didn't pull away pleased him. "You never asked me."

With a roll of her eyes, she squirmed a little, but every motion sent pleasure ratcheting through both of them as his knot stretched her. "I don't think we were really having a lot of get to know you conversations," she admitted on a sullen note. He thought she would continue, but she went quiet.

Smoothing a hand through her still damp hair, he waited her out.

She let out a sigh. "Why did I get memories when Asshole fed me?"

Ah. "Because that is who he is."

Eyebrows arched, she stared at him a beat. "Well, that wasn't helpful at all."

Rogue chuckled, and the action made them both groan. Fiona let out a little gasp as she began to squirm. Need stamped its way over her, and he slid a hand between them to tease her clit. In no time, her panting came in sharper, faster gasps, and she spasmed around him as she cried out. When she collapsed against him, he lifted his fingers to his lips and cleaned them off one at a time as she stared at him.

Studying her, he said, "Alfred is one of the seven."

"*The Magnificent Seven?*" Her voice was a little slurred. "That's a movie."

He barked out a laugh. "No, little *sváss*, the original seven vampires. He's one of the seven."

Fiona blinked at him sleepily. She was content like a cat and every inch the kitten Maddox called her.

"His blood carries memories, and he takes memories from blood. When he fed off of you, he would have learned all about you, and in turn, he gave you his when you fed from him." Smoothing her hair down again, he added, "It is an honor to take the blood of one of the seven. They are all different. They each possess a different talent. Alfred's... Alfred's is to keep our history." It also made him oddly vulnerable, though few saw it the way Rogue did, and despite his own irritations with him, he shied away from revealing that to Fiona.

A little frown tightened her brows. "So all you have to do to get a history lesson is feed from him?"

"Crassly put, but yes." Tracing patterns against her back with a finger, Rogue debated how much he should tell her, then shrugged it away. If Fiona was ever to truly trust them, they had to trust her with their secrets. "But he only shares his blood with a select few."

"Lucky me," she murmured, and her eyes grew heavier. "I don't want to talk about him anymore."

"Then we won't."

"Are you going to feed?"

"I am well enough," he promised her, no matter how much he longed for a taste. He could go much longer.

"Lost your taste for me?"

The question cut at him, sharper than a dagger, and he lifted her hand to his mouth, then moved to her wrist and sank his teeth in. The first rush of her taste across his tongue threatened to leave him drunk for more. He forced himself to only take a small measure, enough to quiet her concern. Her happy little sigh betrayed her, and Rogue sighed as she drifted off to sleep. He licked the wound closed, then settled her hand against his chest as he turned his gaze to the ceiling.

When his knot relaxed, he would tuck her in and go about readying the house for her occupancy. He welcomed the weight of her, his heart slowing to beat in tandem with her own. The taste of her on his tongue lingered like the finest of nectars. He hadn't been kidding when he said Alfred only shared his blood with a select few.

The seven were notorious in their privacy and for establishing their will. So much so, they faded to myths and legends until it was time to remind the peasants of their presence. Such was the case now, as Isaac defied him.

Another problem to be dealt with. All the princes needed to be reminded they held power only as long as their presence pleased those of the seven that granted it. While the others might be quiet, Alfred was awake and showed no signs of planning to sleep again any time soon.

His reaction to Fiona's defection, however, was even more telling. He'd summoned the princes to him—all of them. The ones who hadn't shown up were marked, and they knew it. Some, like Isaac, had run. Others had dug in.

It wouldn't be long before Maddox or Rogue would be paying them a visit. If Alfred went himself, there might not be anything left of the cohorts when he was done. His patience had worn thin. Though Rogue suspected it had far more to do with Fiona's rejection than anything else. The vampire had never been so resisted before, save for when Rogue had done it himself.

Dropping his gaze to Fiona, he studied her as she slept. Her relaxed features and gentleness seemed almost a disguise for the biting humor and sharp wit she wielded like a scalpel. The succubus wanted to control her own destiny, and she didn't trust any of them. He suspected she didn't trust anyone, which was why he had to win that trust, no matter how much he might want to steal her away and keep her safe for eternity.

Fiona was not a possession. If she was what Fin declared her to be, she had to be their equal and treated as such, or it would never work. That battle might be the hardest one to wage.

He softened slowly, and she let out a little whine in her sleep as he slipped free of her. The loss was profound for him, and he eased her into the covers and pulled one over her before he rose to deal with the house.

At the door, he glanced back at her and then around the room. It lacked much personality, as he'd decorated it more for his old home. Simple lines, with a touch of nature. Even the walls bore his art, with snow-coated trees on a landscape of white. The great north had been home for many years before humans began to trespass and forced his kind to draw even deeper into the wilderness.

Rogue had grown restless—and curious—so he traveled to meet the humans in their cities and explore their culture. Eventually, he'd met Alfred, and though he'd never have imagined a single drink in a tavern could change the course of his existence, it had.

Shaking off the maudlin thoughts, he went to deal with the house.

Fiona slept for hours. He checked on her infrequently while he prepared food and stocked the fireplace. It was hardly cold outside, the temperatures too mild to really call for a fire, but if she wanted one, he would light it.

Fin had reached out to him a few times, but he'd ignored the probing calls. Alfred had tried to call him once, and Rogue had simply shut him out entirely. The generator had started with only a little coaxing, and he'd gotten the pipes flowing. He showered, then dressed in fresh clothes before settling outside to wait her out.

It was just after dawn when movement upstairs told him she'd woken up. Trusting her hearing, he said, "The water is available, and there are clean clothes in the chest at the foot of the bed. If you're hungry, there is food laid out on the sideboard in the kitchen."

She didn't acknowledge him at first, the quiet telling, then she said, "Thank you."

It was another hour before she put on an appearance. She'd pulled on a dress, the simple gown one that had a full skirt that gathered at the waist, long sleeves, and a square neck. The green suited her coloring, and it most closely matched her eyes.

Feet bare, she walked outside with two cups of coffee. It was his turn to raise a brow at her, but she merely held one out to him wordlessly. Accepting the peace offering without comment, he inclined his head, and a faint smile flirted around her mouth.

The moon drenched clearing before the house had brightened under the sunlight. The flowers along the house bloomed even more fiercely than they had the night before.

The magic of the place called to him, and while he wasn't Fin, who tangled with the power of the earth itself, he did invest himself in every place he lingered. Here more than others, perhaps, because it was his alone.

"Thank you," Fiona said, breaking the silence.

Surprise kindled in him, and he slanted a curious look at her. "For?"

"For getting me away from there. For letting me go. For feeding me. For this place. Take your pick."

"You do not have to thank me for looking after you. You would do the same for me." It was what they did for each other.

She let out a little sigh. "I don't know if I would."

Well, at least she was being honest. Except… "You insisted I feed," he reminded her.

Her nose wrinkled. "Well, you did give me seven or eight orgasms. It seemed kind of fair."

A snort escaped him. "You never have to pay me for those, little *sváss*. That truly is my pleasure to give you."

Eyes narrowed, she faced him, and he let out a reluctant little sigh before he met her gaze. "Why?"

Why had he helped her?

Why was he still helping her?

There were many questions represented by the simple word. He chose not to misunderstand her meaning. "You said Alfred shared his memories with you."

A single nod.

"Did he share his memories of me?"

Eyebrows raised, he waited.

"You didn't want him to turn you."

He nodded once.

"You tried to kill him."

"For many years," he told her. "It took me a long time to forgive him for doing this to me."

"But you did forgive him." She frowned. "He was greedy and selfish, and took away your choice. How do you forgive that?"

"Because eventually, I understood why he did it, and I understood what it meant to him." Rogue shrugged. "It was a long time ago, and time has dulled some of that anger. Because of him, I am here now. So that is something to appreciate. Yet…I know you did not want this life."

"No," she said slowly. "I didn't. Not that any of you listened to me."

"I know. I am as responsible as Alfred."

Her absolute snort of derision made him smile. A true one, and her eyes brightened. For a moment, her lips curved, and a true grin settled on her face. The effect was breathtaking.

"Don't get me wrong," she said, still smiling. "I hate you all for that. But that son of a bitch didn't even try to understand or talk to me. He just bit the ever-loving fuck out of me and drained me over and over."

"I know."

"And then…days of that…when he was done, he moved on."

The bitterness in those last three words made Rogue frown. How had Alfred moved on?

She did a careless wave with one hand before she drained her coffee. "It doesn't matter anymore. I just—I have things I need to do."

"You said."

"And I won't be trapped there."

"No," he agreed, and she frowned as she studied him. Rogue didn't hide himself away or try to shut her out.

"You're being very accommodating." That faint note of wonder in her voice and the relaxed manner was a gift. The soft tumble of her red curls framed her face as she watched him.

A prickle along his neck was his only warning before a new voice joined the conversation. "He is, isn't he? It's only taken him a thousand or so years to foster a fresh rebellion. What have you done to my brothers, Hellion?"

Alfred.

Fiona's eyes shuttered, and her shoulders went rigid.

Betrayal etched into her very posture as she turned to where Alfred leaned against a tree at the edge of the clearing. Rogue sighed.

This was not going to go well.

CHAPTER 9

"People can be lovers and enemies at the same time, you know." -
Willa Cather

The fact that Alfred stood there shouldn't have shocked me. Yet, I'd believed Rogue when he said none of them had been here. That he hadn't told them how to find me. I'd let myself believe he meant it when he said he wanted to help me.

"No fierce words for me, Hellion?" Alfred the Asshole asked as he straightened and began to stroll toward me.

There were any number of answers I could offer him. None I was willing to give though. I just stared at him and kept my gaze off of Rogue.

"Alfred," Rogue began, but he didn't finish the sentence or add anything more. Asshole pinned him with a single, unreadable look.

Irritation flared through me. "Why are you here?" If anyone got to demand an answer, it would be me. "Why don't you go find Eleanor? I'm sure she would be more than happy to keep you company. Based on the sheer number at the party, I don't doubt you could have a wealth of companionship. Why me?"

Eyebrow quirked, Asshole stared at me with those enigmatic eyes. "You belong to us." Like that answered everything.

I snorted. "I *belong* to no one."

"You solve nothing by running."

"You presume I want to solve something." I really didn't. All I wanted to do now was leave. If he was going to be here, the chance of successfully fleeing and evading them both was nonexistent. I would simply have to bide my time. Again.

But I didn't have to stay here and talk to him. I turned away, but he caught my arm and tugged me back to him. "Hellion," he said. "Why are you angry with me?"

"Are you for fucking real right now?" The burn in my veins turned to acid. Still refusing to look at him, I fixed my glare on the house. It was a really nice house. It hadn't done anything wrong, but better to stare at it than him.

"Very," he murmured, his voice dark like it had been dipped in chocolate and danger. He stroked his hands up and down my arms. "Tell me why you are angry. You abandoned the party and fled before you could be presented. I understand you wanted to insult me. Message delivered. I forgive you..."

The acid eating away at my insides caught fire, and I wrenched myself out of his grip. Well, to be honest, I did try to wrench myself out of his grip. One of the things I'd learned over the last few weeks of freedom was that my strength and speed had increased infinitely. So not only did I know how to fight, I could seriously back it up.

Score one point for being a badass.

Didn't matter a damn against any one of them. They were faster. They were stronger. It sucked.

"You forgive me." While I didn't growl, I did grit out each word through clenched teeth.

"Yes," Asshole told me. Definitely Asshole. So much Asshole. "You are still acclimatizing, so running is normal. But it isn't safe for you yet."

"I was doing *fine*."

I was the one who took out the daeva. I was also the one who took out the assholes in the alley. If Fin hadn't shown up with the vampire posse on his ass, I would have been fine at the club. I had *friends*.

Fine, I had one friend. The point was, I didn't *need* them.

"Dallas' court is now a blood-soaked massacre."

"That's not on me." I'd be fucked before I let him pin the blame on me.

"No," Asshole agreed with me. "Not at all. Fin has cleaned house. After their attack at the club, he followed them back. Cleared the whole nest. Then brought me David."

Well, bully for Fin.

"He also told me you were there and fled, albeit far too swiftly for him to follow or track."

"So you assumed I'd taken her." Rogue's quiet words reminded me he was still there. With the iron-walled Asshole at my back, I didn't dare turn to look at my Viking elf. The curl of disappointment at his betrayal eased. He didn't sound any happier about Asshole's presence than I was.

"Correctly presumed." Asshole stated it as a fact without any heat in his voice. "You facilitated her initial journey. It did not require a great deal of consideration to wonder if you participated in the second."

"He didn't know Fin had found me."

That much I was certain of.

"Fin didn't tell you he found me immediately, either."

Asshole stilled. "Hellion, what are you afraid of?"

Afraid? "Nothing." I pulled at the grip he had on my arms, and this time at least, he released me. Taking three fast steps away, I pivoted to face him. Rogue stood a couple of feet to his right and back. His expression was far more remote, and his eyes glacial. They weren't pinned on me, but on Asshole.

Trouble in paradise?

"Then what is the problem?" Asshole dragged my attention back to him, and I curled my lip.

"You."

That wasn't quite what I meant to say, but it's what came out. The word flew like a bullet fired from a gun, and it struck him at velocity.

His dark brows gathered together, and he canted his head. I imagined that the look he wore was the same one he'd had when he'd first seen Maddox stranded and wounded by a spear—calculating and cold.

He's one of the seven.

Yeah, I didn't give a fuck. Vampires at this point gave me hives, and I wasn't going to be impressed by their myths, their legends, or their boogeymen.

If he didn't like it, he could just…

I'd been about to say bite me, but I wasn't issuing that invitation.

"How have I offended you?" What the hell? Why did he sound genuinely puzzled?

"Would you like me to go alphabetically or in order of occurrence?"

The placid, unreadable expression rippled as he lifted his brows. "In whatever order pleases you, Hellion. I have indulged this need to run long enough. It is not safe for you to be in the open."

Before I could spit back about his fucking indulgences, Rogue said, "We're not in the open here."

"You have no defenses here." Asshole cut a look at him.

"Maybe because he's not a prima donna with a god complex." My teeth clicked together as I snapped at him.

"The defense is no one knows of this location, though clearly I must rethink that if you found it so easily."

Asshole sighed. Genuinely exhaled a long, almost aggrieved breath. "So you defend Rogue from me now?"

"Sure, why not. He at least didn't want to hold me hostage." Well. He had, but he got over it. I wasn't going to split hairs on it now.

If I did, deal with it. Like I'd said before, I was complicated.

Asshole hummed. "We can debate that in the future." He swung his head to pin me with his gaze again. "Tell me what I have done that has so earned your ire."

"Let's see—you bit my neck over and over without so much as a by your leave. You woke up like some creeper from a horror movie and attacked me."

The memory alone sent a shudder through my system. Not even an altogether unpleasant one. Something inside of me had to have been cracked while I was in that prison. Or maybe it had been Dimitri's attack and the shit storm that led to me ending up in that cell. Asshole's possessiveness had been a heady, overwhelming experience.

Didn't change the fact that he'd bitten me there.

"I had to change the bite that made you," he told me patiently, as if that explained everything.

"Is there a Complete Idiot's Guide to understanding what the hell you're talking about?" Aggravation struck sparks in me again. "You know what, don't answer that. I don't want to know. You asked me what you'd done to offend me? Let's start with you bit me, then you drained me, then you fed me your blood, and you did it over and over and over again."

The memories he'd conjured in me, the emotions he'd

threaded through my system, had tangled with my own complicated feelings where my dragon—fuck me, he wasn't my dragon. Yet he was. But where he was concerned. Where Fin fit in. And Rogue.

As if drawn by the thought of him, I flicked my gaze to where Rogue stood. He no longer glared at Asshole, but studied me with a far gentler expression. The hint of affection in his icy blue eyes sent another shiver rippling over the surface of my skin, and I licked my lips.

He'd been every bit as dominant and possessive with me from the beginning, but he'd avoided my throat after I'd made it clear I didn't want to be bitten there. He'd also at least *tried* to explain things. But it wasn't just that… The agony in his eyes when I didn't listen to him and turned him —no, not me. Alfred.

Asshole, Fiona, I snarled internally. He doesn't get to be a name. Not here and not right now.

I needed the distance.

That was the confusing part. The anger and the self-loathing gleaming in his eyes in my memories superimposed over him now. None of those emotions were directed at me, however, and it just made it more difficult to reconcile.

Fuck, I did not sign up for this drama. I added it to the long list of reasons why I wanted to skin Dimitri alive.

"When a vampire makes another, the mark they leave from that kill is permanently etched into the flesh of the child." Asshole snared my attention again.

Gross.

"Some believe it is both a physical and psychic link between sire and offspring."

Yeah, yeah. "Whatever, he couldn't control me. That was what they were all worried about. Isaac tried." I bared my teeth in more of a snarl than a grin. "That didn't work out so well for him."

The barest of smiles softened the edges of Asshole's mouth. "You are far too strong-willed to succumb to just anyone."

"Thanks for the tip." The Sahara had nothing on the dryness of my tone.

"However, you are ours. Mine." The possessiveness in that last word locked me in place as surely as if he'd snapped a chain on. "You will not wear the mark of another. Few can change that of a sire."

"But you're special." It came out more snark than sarcasm.

He shrugged. "I am me." Closing the distance between us, he curved his finger under my chin and lifted my face so I would meet his gaze. Fuck me, the reaction skating over my skin left my nipples peaked and my body slick and soft. I did not *want* to want him. Somewhere, my body failed to get the memo. "You will wear our marks. You are *ours*. Erasing him from your flesh did not erase him from life. I will give you that as well."

I jerked my chin away, grateful for the autocratic haughtiness in his demeanor. It reminded me why he was an asshole. "I'll deal with him myself. I don't need you to do a damn thing."

"You needed us to purge the demon," he scolded me lightly as he trailed a finger down my throat to the mark, pink and faded against my skin. The mark of his mouth, and electricity went from tingling to zapping my system like I'd touched a live wire. "You needed to finish your transition."

No matter how soaked my thighs were, those last six words helped dry me right out. "I never wanted to be a vampire." I slapped his hand away from me.

He sighed. "You're being childish."

"Then fuck off, Daddy-o. You wanted to be a sire to a *child*, this is what you get."

Eyes narrowed, he raised his hand, and I braced for his

next touch. Shockingly, or maybe just to me, I wasn't worried about him hitting me. Far from it.

I was far more worried he'd kiss me and my traitorous body would jump on board, ticket or no, to ride the happy train.

Fuck. I yanked my thoughts off that single-track path. I didn't *want* to be a vampire. I definitely didn't *want* Asshole.

Liar.

Fin's tease made me groan, and I closed my eyes. The air around us all seemed to change as he arrived, even my goose-bumps got goosebumps. The sudden nearness of not just Rogue and Alfred, but Fin and... I turned toward Maddox, and when my gaze collided with my dragon's, guilt surged up through the rage to claw at me.

His beautiful eyes were slitted as he stared at me, his expression haunted and his jaw locked. "I told you," I said quietly. "Succubi don't do relationships. It's...just not a good idea."

The anger drained out of me as I moved away from all of them and retreated toward the house. I didn't flee so much as fling myself down to sit on the steps. I set the mug aside. I didn't think I could stomach even the idea of it at the moment. All of the good intentions I'd poured both cups with had long since soured.

Fin whistled slowly. "Yeah, the tension here is giving me a headache. Why don't you two take a breather and let us talk to her?"

I didn't have to look up to know who he meant. Rubbing my hands over my face, I tried to gather together the shreds of myself and my complicated feelings. I'd kill for a drink right now, and I didn't care what time it was. The four of them didn't say anything, but when I finally lowered my hands, I was alone with Maddox and Fin. The dragon waited until I looked at him before he crossed to where I sat.

The need to apologize to him vibrated on my tongue. I'd left him. He'd given me his word to let me go in that cell. It had been Rogue and Fin who'd made him a liar. Then it was Rogue who gave me the keys to my freedom. But I had left him.

"You're well?" His tone was brusque, but there was a dark heaviness to his words.

"I was," I admitted. "Kind of went sideways though."

With care, he eased to sit on the steps next to me. His thigh was close enough to brush against my own, but he kept a careful space. Fin, surprisingly, said nothing. When I stole a look at him, he gave me a careless little shrug, then nodded to Maddox.

Ah.

Swallowing, I focused on Maddox again. "Are you well?"

"No," he told me bluntly. "I will survive, however."

Probably not a good track to pursue then.

"Good." Because, really, what else was I going to say? Sorry? I get that you want me to be your mate, but that's not me? That seemed particularly cruel. Fuck my life, I didn't want to hurt him.

You know, beyond the fact that I'd kicked him in the balls twice back before I got to know him.

"If you were so unhappy, why didn't you tell us?" Maddox asked. The quiet question pressed a firm pause button on the guilt eating me up.

"How would you have imagined I wasn't unhappy?" I demanded. "I didn't want to be there. I didn't ask you to keep me chained to all of you. You stole me from one prison and then promptly locked me up in another."

Fin clucked, but we both ignored him. Maddox's eyes flared. "You were not a prisoner."

"Could have fooled me. I wasn't allowed to leave. One of you was always watching me. You told me over and over I had to feed. Then apparently, King Asshole woke up, and I was the first thing on the menu. I wasn't given a *choice* about turning."

"Fiona..."

I glared at Fin. "If you say he did ask me and I finally said yes, I want you to recall how many times I said no. How many times I said I *didn't* want this life. How many times I told you I *wasn't* a vampire." He opened his mouth, but snapped it shut abruptly, a scowl that looked halfway to a sulk settling on his angelic face.

"Kitten," Maddox murmured, jerking my attention back to him. "If you wanted to leave, all you had to do was tell me. I would have taken you anywhere."

Would have?

"I'll still take you anywhere you want to go."

I groaned internally.

"I know you didn't want to be a vampire, but I didn't want you to die. You are not like the others, any more than we are."

Right. Hybrid.

"Maddox, you're missing the point."

"No, I'm making my point." He held his hand up toward me, palm facing me. While he made no move to touch me, the look in his eyes was a dare. He wanted me to take his hand. Why? What did he think it would prove? Not that I gave voice to the questions, instead, I pressed my right hand to his left.

The surge that went through my system had me tingling from head to toe. His eyes damn near glowed as he stared at me.

"You feel that." It wasn't a question.

"You're hot," I told him, without an ounce of shame or regret. "I think I've made it pretty clear I enjoy you."

"This isn't about sex, Kitten." The hint of gravel in his

tone made him just the tiniest bit of a liar on that one, but I let it go because it was also kind of adorable.

Dammit.

"No?" It was my turn to dare him as I pulled my hand away, but the buzzing sensation remained and then redoubled when I pressed it against his and threaded our fingers together.

"No." Then Maddox lifted his chin, baring his throat to me and the mark there just over the pulse point stared back at me like an accusation.

"Is that Alfred's mark on you?" Mouth dry, I knew the answer without even asking the question. I just asked it to buy myself some time. He hadn't had that mark when we'd been in the cell. He hadn't had it when we first got back to the keep or the first dozen or so times he bedded me.

"No," he answered me simply, then dipped his chin as he tugged my hand to his throat and pressed my fingers to the mark. The tingle of our hands touching had nothing on this. A bolt of lust streaked through me, but it wasn't just heat and wanton desire. No, it was a vicious kind of need and affection. "You claimed me."

"I…"

"I know you didn't understand it." His voice was a delicious rumble. "But you did claim me, Kitten."

I closed my eyes and dipped my head. "I'm sorry."

"I'm not."

"Maddox, I shouldn't have done that."

He kept my hand pressed over the mark. "I wanted you to do it."

The library. When he'd asked me to bite him. Fuck.

"Maddox." I glared at him. "Why would you do that?" Then. "Fuck, you didn't claim me, right?"

"No," he said softly, his voice a croon that chased away the jagged bits of my irritation. "I would in a heartbeat, but I won't take that choice from you in the heat of the moment." Now, he cupped my cheek and smiled at me. "Are you truly well, Kitten? Fin told me of the incident at the club. He also told me you were fierce in his defense."

I tried to shrug it off. "I was fine, I stayed with a friend. I was trying to figure out my next steps." Though that had been my first night out since I'd escaped, and that had just gone swimmingly.

"Well, you were my hero," Fin drawled as he came to lean against the railing, a faint smirk on his lips. "You saved me from the big bad demon trying to dominate my passion."

I rolled my eyes. "Daevas are neither big nor bad."

"But they are demons," he teased. "And she snuck in when I was trying to protect you." Distaste settled in his expression. "She wanted me to hurt you."

"But you didn't." Fuck, why was I offering him comfort? Maybe it was the forlorn look on his face.

"No, I would have tried to overwhelm you though," he admitted. "Wanting you is a part of me now, Beautiful. You're my lady."

"Stop," I pleaded with them. "I can't be your mate," I told Maddox, and tried desperately to ignore the flash of hurt in his eyes. "Or your lady, or Rogue's…whatever it is. I can't."

"Okay," Fin said slowly, folding his arms. "I'll bite, Beautiful. What's the problem?"

I huffed out a breath and tried to pull away from Maddox. To my surprise, he allowed the retreat. Not looking the gift dragon too closely in the mouth, I rose, then paced away, not far, just enough to get some air around me that didn't hum and crackle with their power.

Or need.

Or the fact that I kind of wanted to bite them both.

Ugh.

"I'm a succubus," I reminded them. "In all your great and

vaunted wisdom gathering, have you never met one of my kind? Do you not understand us?"

"You feed on lust," Fin said simply. "It's a beast that you have to feed as much as Maddox has to hoard, or I have to make things grow, or Rogue needs to escape into the solitude, or even Alfred needs to shield and protect us."

I stared at him. None of those things were like the other.

"I am a solitary creature, Kitten," Maddox said while I still fought to find a response. "I understand the desire to be alone."

"I'm not, but I've learned to adapt. If you need space, all you have to do is tell me," Fin assured me. "We want you to be happy."

"Succubi don't do relationships." I needed to get it printed on a t-shirt. "They never end well. None of them. They don't even co-parent. We were…"

"You were?" Maddox prompted me, and I tilted my head back to stare at the sky. I didn't want to have this conversation. If anything, I just wanted to go and forget about them before I did any further damage. Claiming Maddox…

"Can it be undone?"

"Being a vampire?" Fin said, squinting at me. "No, Beautiful."

"No, the claiming Maddox part."

Oh, I regretted the words the moment I spoke them, because Maddox's whole demeanor shifted. His eyes glowed, his jaw clenched, and the softness vanished beneath a mask of fury as he surged to his feet. "No," he growled as he lifted me off my feet and banded his arms around me. I could do little more than rest my palms against his chest. Even beneath the fabric of his shirt, the muscles bunched and tensed. "You cannot undo it. I won't allow it. I've waited centuries for you, Kitten, and I want to be claimed by you. You may make me work and court you to earn the privilege of claiming you, but I will not let you discard me. Ever."

I gaped at the raw ferocity in his tone. Every inch of him pressed against me vibrated with raw need, and I slid my hand up into his hair and gripped it. He needed no further encouragement or urging before his mouth slammed down on mine and everything around us disintegrated as I went up in flames.

Fuck. Me.

"I intend to," he growled against my mouth. I hadn't meant to say the words aloud, but I suddenly didn't care. I couldn't get enough of touching him. I didn't look up, even when he marched away or when he tore his mouth from mine to snap, "Fuck off," to Fin. Then he kissed me again, and no amount of scrabbling let me pull my reserve back together.

So I just stopped trying.

I wanted him.

Fuck everything. I wanted Maddox. I wanted him desperately. No matter how bad the idea was, he *wanted* to be mine.

Damn it all. I stopped fighting.

"Friendship isn't about who you've known the longest. It's about who walked into your life, said I'm here for you, and proved it." - Unknown

I had no idea how far Maddox took us until he planted my back against a tree and ground his hips into mine. The dress was no obstruction to the weight of his erection. The fact that he never let me up for a breath began to make my lungs burn. Fisting his hair, I gave it a jerk. Not enough to hurt, but to get him to let me suck in a single gasp. That's all he allowed me before his mouth took possession of mine again.

Demand assailed me with every sweep of his tongue, as though he wanted to stake out his territory. Fuck me if I let him do just that. I wasn't a possession. I couldn't be his. He shouldn't fucking be mine. This was all a terrible idea. But he had his thigh thrust between my legs and ground me down against it until my vision began to white out around the edges.

Maybe his kisses were drugs, or maybe I'd gone soft in captivity. This was stupid. Why was I letting myself get swept away on the rising tidal wave of wanton desire flooding through me like a firestorm? With sure hands, he stroked up and down my sides, then over my breasts, pinching and twisting my nipples through the fabric. It was just enough pain to set my teeth on edge, and the moan I released was fucking embarrassing.

I didn't give a damn. I was so close, my orgasm dancing just out of reach, when he jerked back and pulled his head up. Shock had me staring at him, riveted as he flicked open his jeans freed his cock, then he gave me a slow smile and twirled his finger.

"Turn around, Kitten. Brace those claws against the tree."

"Fuck you," I snarled, but I turned and gripped the tree, because damn if I didn't want exactly what he offered.

Then the dragon did something I did not expect. At all. Instead of lifting my skirt and getting down to business, he leaned forward, bracing his hands over mine on the tree and then pressing his face into the crook of my neck. After a deep inhale, he pressed his lips against my throat with such absolute care, that I had to close my eyes. Another press of his lips, and he kissed just over the pulse point. He traced the mark there with his tongue, but no teeth scraped my skin.

The sheer fact that he remembered and behaved accordingly had me going soft, and I sighed.

"Did you miss me, Kitten?"

I wanted to tell him no and to fuck off and just get on with it. I had zero problems with his cock, and he definitely knew how to use it.

"Yes," was what I said, however. "I didn't want to. But I did."

He rubbed his cheek against my temple. The faint rasp of his skin was a tease and soothing in the same breath. "So much of what you didn't want has happened." That was the truth. "I'm sorry for that. I'm sorry I couldn't keep my word to you. I'm sorry that you had to transition because I couldn't bear to lose you. I should have taken you from Alfred and done it myself."

I didn't point out that he and the guys had been trying.

"He's an arrogant bastard," Maddox continued. "And I will be forever grateful to him for saving your life."

I sighed.

"But I will leave him today if it will get you to stay."

I twisted to face at him, shock piercing the lust-filled haze. "You've…you've been with him for centuries." Easily, if not longer.

"I don't care," Maddox stated, his hazel eyes with their gold flecks sober and intense as he met my stare. Even with his swollen pupils, he seemed grounded. "He is my friend, my brother. He has made many calls over the years that I haven't agreed with. But you're my mate. If staying with him costs me you, then I won't stay."

Fuck me.

The weight of that revelation settled heavily on me. This… "Maddox," I exhaled, and he dipped his face closer. His hands remained braced on the tree behind me, and his heavy cock was still out. I swore the vein on it throbbed almost in time with the one on his forehead. I dragged my gaze over him and then focused on his eyes. "This is why succubi shouldn't do relationships."

I wouldn't comment on the lack of conviction in my voice or the empty note at the end.

"It causes no end of problems."

"What you are," Maddox said slowly, "is mine. You are not

wholly a succubus anymore, nor are you wholly a vampire. You are both."

"And we don't even know what that means," I admitted, sagging against the rough bark and tilting my head up. He slid a hand down to wrap against my throat, no pressure, just resting there. Yet he used the tips of his fingers to nudge my chin up higher so I focused on him.

"We'll learn," he told me in a dark, heavy voice. "We'll learn whatever it is we need to know. But my first loyalty is to you."

How could he…

"Trust me." It was a request, a demand, and a plea.

A few weeks earlier, I'd slammed my knee right into his crotch and taken him down before fleeing him deeper into the prison. Maybe he was right. Maybe who I'd been wasn't who I was anymore. That Fiona had finally died, irrevocably ended by Alfred, and there was only the Fiona I had become.

"I can't take you away from your family." I closed my eyes as much to gather my thoughts as to escape the intensity of his gaze burning through me. His breath was a whisper on my cheek as he trailed kisses to my jaw and then down to my throat while he eased his hand away. Trusting him meant not stiffening as his lips touched the skin there. Trusting him meant not pulling away at the first scrape of his teeth over my pulse point. "Maddox…you're a dragon."

The silence that followed my statement had me opening my eyes, only to find his shoulders shaking with barely suppressed laughter. His breath huffed against my skin. "Yes, Kitten, I'm aware."

I punched his shoulder. All I succeeded in doing was hurting my hand. "You know what I meant."

"No," he said, still laughing softly. "I don't. Enlighten me, Kitten." Despite his continued mirth, he truly sounded like he was trying to sober up. I threaded my fingers through his hair, and my heart gave a little fist bump against my ribs. I really didn't want to care about him. Them. Any of them.

It was impossible not to.

"Dragons, or so I was told, are only solitary outside of their chosen grouping."

The stroke of his tongue sent liquid heat through my system. "This is true."

"The guys are your chosen grouping."

"They're my brothers," Maddox agreed. "But you're my mate." He lifted his head, and the dragon stared out at me from his slitted eyes.

"I don't want you to regret this," I conceded, and his smile was damn near blinding.

"I won't." He lifted me up easily, his large hands under my thighs, flipping the skirt of my dress out of his way. With one finger, he shredded my panties, and I laughed. His every action was deliberate and endearing.

Panting, I wrapped my arms around his neck as he wasted no time rocking his cock into me. The first press of the thick head had me biting my lip. I couldn't look away from him if I'd wanted to.

And to be blunt, I didn't want to. Legs wrapped around him, I levered myself down, and we both groaned as he filled me. Maddox went to his knees, never once breaking our connection, and when he reached for my dress, I fisted his hair.

"Don't rip it."

I kind of liked this dress. I liked the color. The fabric.

The fact that Rogue had picked it out.

What? I've said it repeatedly—I was complicated.

A growl rumbled in his throat as he lifted the dress, and I raised my arms so he could strip it up and off. That left me in a lacy little bra and the scraps of panties that he'd already shredded. The band on the panties didn't last another second, and I arched my back, brows raised as he looked at my bra.

"You want to rip it off me, don't you?"

He grinned. "Yes."

Arms spread wide, I licked my lips. Impaled on his cock, I wasn't going anywhere fast, and I flexed my inner muscles around him. He let out a little hiss with every squeeze, and then he hooked his finger in the center of the bra and snapped it open.

I dropped my arms to let it fall off and then reached for his shirt. But he was already stripping it up and off. His jeans were still on, but he made no move to remove them. And I got it. It might mean letting me go.

Suddenly, I didn't want to be let go. Arms wrapped around his neck, I pressed a kiss to his jaw. A single one, then another, tracing the stern line of it to that twitching muscle and laving my tongue against it. I kept flexing those inner walls against him in time with each kiss. The stretch of him threatened to split me open.

What a way to go.

He stroked his large hands down my back to my ass and then up to my hair.

"Kitten." The light tug had me pulling back to meet his gaze.

The emotion in his eyes warned me to shy away. The responsibility of it. The need in them. At the same time...I didn't want to leave him. "How does this work?" I swallowed once. "Succubi don't mate so...this is new to me."

The heartbreaking grin on his face was like the sun coming out. "You've already claimed me," he whispered. "Now, I just have to claim you."

He stroked his thumb against my throat. Claiming me meant biting me. "It has to be the throat?"

"The pulse point," he whispered, drawing his fingers

down to where the cadence of my heart seemed to throb. It increased in pace at the light touch of thumb. "Heart's blood."

Somehow, I suspected that last bit had little to do with anatomy. But again, I wasn't a dragon, so what did I know? The unspoken question hung in the air, even as I remained straddling his lap. Neither of us moved beyond the lightest of touches, and yet I could feel him in my soul.

"I can wait," he told me, the rumble of his voice vibrating through me. "You've claimed me. It's enough."

It wasn't. Yet, he told me that lie to let me off the hook. Need flared in his eyes. Need. Want. I could taste it all in the lust rolling off of him. Yet, it wasn't so heady it drowned me under it.

Huh.

I put that aside for now. There was only one other question I really had…

"What about the others?"

The corner of his mouth quirked up. "I have no objections to them," he said carefully. "As long as they are what you want. No one else, though, mate. Anyone else touches you, and I'll kill them." He stroked his free hand down my back, even as he tightened the one in my hair, keeping my gaze fixed on him. Not that I was trying to look elsewhere. "We can feed you. You will never be hungry…"

I hadn't been hungry. Not really.

Not until Fin walked into the bar.

Not until Rogue stole me away.

Not until Asshole arrived with his arrogant glare and dominating manner.

Not until Maddox…

Then… "And the so-called offerings?"

He snorted. "Eleanor has never been my lover." That wasn't what I asked. "I never wanted her. I will take blood from no one, if that is your wish. Only you."

Okay, that might be going a little far. Still, there was a thrill rioting in my system at his words.

"You have no reason to be jealous of her."

Seriously, the fact that I was currently riding his cock told me that. "I wasn't jealous." What the hell did I have to be jealous about? Sex was sex.

"Kitten," he murmured, then nipped my shoulder. The bite more a promise than an actual bite. "You hated her the moment she walked into the library. That was the moment you turned away from us."

"Not entirely," I said, making a face and lifting my hips to slide upward, only to surge down. The moment I was seated again though, he gripped my hips and held me still.

"Yes," he argued "It was. You were angry before. But you withdrew the moment she appeared."

"It wasn't just her," I snapped. "Are we really having this conversation right now?"

"Yes," he said, grinning slowly. "I want more than just your body, Kitten. I want your heart and your mind. I am not driven by my lust, no matter how insane you make me."

Something akin to wonder flared through me.

"You do not want the offerings." It wasn't a question.

I shook my head. "I don't even understand them."

"Alfred," he began, smoothing his fingers through my hair. "He reads blood, he takes memories. They don't always know that. The offering lets him check on them all."

Oh.

"He likes control," Maddox offered by way of explanation.

"No shit." I'd already figured that out.

"The offering," he continued, his tone dipping closer to soothing, "is a part of that control. He only included us so that we were held at the same level of reverence as he. It's also why he wanted them to make the offering to you."

I glared at him.

"It's true."

"I don't want to drink anyone's blood." Okay that wasn't entirely true. "I mean, I like yours and Rogue's and Fin's." Fuck Asshole. I wouldn't add him to the list if he were the last one left on the planet.

The corners of Maddox's lips tilted. "I like yours, too. And I am more than content to feed you, Kitten. Feed you *anything* you need."

I let out a little sigh.

His eyes darkened, and it was like the storm clouds gathered. "Have you fed since you left?"

Oh, there were lots of ways to answer that question. But right now? "No, well…yes. Rogue." Focused on him, I didn't miss the wordless question hanging between us. "No one else. I didn't…I didn't want anything else. Or anyone. Even when I began to get restless and thirsty and a little agitated."

Relief slid through him, and the tension bunching all of his muscles vanished. "Good. Then you weren't suffering from hunger either."

"No." Apparently, the wild cravings from the beginning were gone now. Or maybe I only needed them. Fuck, I was not going to look too closely at that. I didn't want to be that bound and yet… "Maddox, if you want to claim me…"

The flare in his eyes held me captive. "There is no *if*, Kitten. I *want* you." Then, as if to make his point, he claimed my lips. With one hand still holding me still, he began to move his own hips, pulling away and thrusting upward. He moved me on his cock, and we were both hissing. He hadn't softened an inch while buried inside of me, and I seemed to have grown even more sensitive.

Every stroke lit me up, the angle striking sparks, even as he ground into me and teased my clit. It was too much and not enough. I couldn't breathe for the sweeps of his tongue tangling with mine. I dug my nails into his shoulders, the struggle real as I wanted to roll my hips and meet his every thrust, but he kept control of me. The brutal pace he set taunted me, keeping me right on the edge but not letting me slip over.

An honest fucking growl escaped me, and the bastard tormenting me *laughed.* I bit down on his lip hard enough to draw blood. The next minute, I went from riding him to flat on my back, his cock still buried in me while he leaned close. He kicked off his jeans, shifting the angle of his thrusts as he shoved my thigh higher. The position should be uncomfortable. There were bits of rock in my back. The grass was damp. The air cool. None of that fucking mattered.

His gaze fierce and locked on mine, I let out a moan with every strike. My eyes closed, only to snap open at his snarled, "Look at me."

One hand planted next to my head, he leaned down until we were nose to nose.

"Focus on me, Kitten. I want you here with me." Where the fuck else would I be? I could feel him pounding into my cells with every stroke.

And the 'why' of it crystalized in me as he kept me right at the edge of madness. His own pleasure twisted his expression tight as I raked my nails along his back. When he let me come, it was going to shatter me. I could fight it. Fight him.

But the need for battle drained away, and I went soft beneath him as I held his gaze and then tilted my head back to give him my throat. Muscles lax as pleasure continued to ramp up and pool in my center, I gripped his nape, and at my tug, he dropped his head until his mouth rested at my pulse point.

Maddox stilled.

"Claim me." Two words.

Probably the hardest two words I'd ever spoken. I understood what it meant. I hadn't understood when he'd had me bite him. I did now. This would be as irrevocable as my transition. But where anger and grief had boiled in me at that decision, I experienced none of those emotions.

If anything, there were tears in my damn eyes as he pressed a tender kiss to my throat and then raised his head to meet my gaze. "You're sure?"

"Yes," I promised him, and then he seared my mouth with his kiss as he rocked into me. The tempo shift was unmistakable as he kissed, nipped, stroked, and thrust. I gripped him, digging my hands into his shoulders, his hair, and laving at his lip as he pushed us both up and over. The orgasm that detonated in my system had me screaming against his mouth.

He shoved me right through that one and into the next one. And still he was relentless, the overstimulation had my vision whiting out as he triggered a third, and I writhed, curling my fingers into fists to pound against his shoulders as I came. Then he struck, his teeth sinking in deep, and all I knew was pleasure.

It unfurled in me like a firestorm, consuming every drop of oxygen. The world shattered. I shattered. The stretch of his knot swelling as he claimed me just added another level of delight. His roar resonated deep in my bones, and I could see his dragon in the walls of the prison, striking out at the corpsesnare. Then again, when he battled those hunting him, even if that memory was through Alfred's eyes.

But the feeling of wings snapping out to catch an updraft and wheeling through the sky as I flew? That was all Maddox. We soared, spiraling and diving. It was utterly intoxicating, and I swore I orgasmed again before he released my throat and lifted his head.

We floated there a while, and it took time for the sounds of the woods around us—everything really—to filter back in. The breeze through the trees, the birdcalls, the rasp of grass beneath my bare back and the warmth of our combined orgasms trickling along the insides of my thighs. He was buried so deeply within me, there was no separation, and I didn't want one.

"I love you." I whispered the words that tasted foreign on my tongue. They were almost impossible to form, and yet I managed it. Maddox lifted his head abruptly and stared at me, wonder stamped across his features

He looked as dragged out and broken as I felt. The dizzying speed of his flight seemed to still be humming through me. It was like how the world still seemed to rock after you left a boat and you didn't have your land legs back yet. Just lying beneath the delicious weight of him, I still flew.

Would he actually take me up?

The thought struck sparks in me. Could I ride him as he flew through the sky? That would be...*awesome*.

A giddy little laugh escaped, and I found Maddox still gazing at me.

"What?"

"You said you loved me," he answered in a deep, rasping tone. Disbelief and delight tangled in the huskiness of his voice.

"I do," I admitted, suddenly uncomfortable under the way his gaze pierced me. I shifted beneath him, but the movement tugged at his knot, and we were both left gasping.

No, he wasn't softening anytime soon.

And I had nowhere to go to escape his penetrating scrutiny.

"Say it again," he beckoned, cradling my face in his large hands.

"I love you." Yep, still foreign and a little coppery on my tongue. The mark on my neck where he'd bitten me was different from Asshole's mark. It throbbed, and when

Maddox traced his fingers over it, spikes of pleasure radiated through my system.

Oh, shit.

I stared up at him, and he grinned. "Did you feel that?"

I nodded, mute.

"That is how I feel about you loving me." He stroked the mark again, and I swore I splintered completely apart and shuddered around him. He closed his eyes, and something akin to bliss filled his expression. When I could catch my breath, I touched the mark on his throat. The one I'd left. It sent tingles radiating up my arm, and his bliss almost seemed to intensify.

"You do love me," he whispered, almost hoarse. "I don't deserve you, Kitten."

I snorted, and he snapped his eyes open to look at me. "Too late now, Mad-Dragon. You're stuck with me." And I was stuck with him. Here was hoping when all the pleasure wore off, I was still happy about it. But I couldn't find it in me to regret this choice at the moment.

Not even a little bit.

I didn't know how long we lay there. Maddox rolled onto his back and cradled me against his chest. It seemed to take longer than ever for him to soften, not that I was complaining. My body ached from our play. Yet at the same time, I could have run a marathon or danced. The energy surging through me nearly as intoxicating as the man—correction, dragon—beneath me.

Tracing his fingers against my back, Maddox murmured, "You're smiling."

"Am I?"

"Hmm-hmm."

I hadn't realized, but when I dipped my gaze to him, I found a similar smile curling his lips. "So are you."

"I'm smiling because I have you."

"I could be smiling because I have you," I teased, and he chuckled. He palmed my ass and then gave it a squeeze.

"Could be?" The barest hint of warning teased along the words.

I chuckled then nipped his jaw. "I already said I loved you and I asked you to claim me. I think you've had plenty from me for today."

"She's not the only one," came the douse of icy water in the form of King Asshole himself.

And he sounded pissed.

I spared him a look over my shoulder. His expression matched his tone.

Unforgiving. Unbending. Unhappy.

Fuck.

Him.

CHAPTER 11

Maddox

Alfred's anger rolled through the little glen Maddox had found like a torrential storm unleashing its fury. It crackled and lashed at him like a cat o' nine tails sporting barbed tips. The knot had begun to release, slowly, but Maddox didn't rush as he fixed one of his oldest friends with a steady look.

The rage wasn't wholly focused on Maddox though, it was directed at the beautiful woman wrapped in Maddox's arms. "Change your fucking tone," he warned in a flat voice. "She doesn't deserve the brunt of your temper."

A temper he rarely displayed. Kitten had dug her claws into him deep.

Good.

It was time something brought him back to life.

Fiona let out a little sigh as Maddox finally softened, and as reluctant as he was to leave the snug warmth of her body, he still surged to his feet and brought her with him. The trickle of his release down the inside of her thighs made him puff his chest a little. She carried his mark now. She'd let him claim her. They'd sealed it.

Kitten was his.

Moving her behind him, he kept his focus on Alfred.

"So you have chosen her side?" The clipped syllables slashed at him, but Maddox rolled his shoulders back and smiled slowly.

Alfred was jealous.

He wanted Kitten's attention and, instead of engaging him, she ignored him as she gathered up her dress and began to tug it over her head. "Would you expect anything different?" Maddox challenged. "My *mate* will always come first with me."

Though Alfred didn't respond, Maddox swore he could hear the grinding of his teeth. "We need to talk," Alfred said finally, and his gaze landed on Fiona where she ran her fingers through the riot of red hair to free it from leaves and other debris. As if aware of his scrutiny, she glanced at Maddox and very pointedly didn't look at Alfred.

"So talk," Maddox told him, snagging his jeans and dragging them on. He'd had boots somewhere, but he didn't care. Fiona handed him his shirt, and he threaded an arm around her to pull her into him before he nuzzled his nose into her hair. The fact that she not only leaned into the contact, but spread her hand against his abdomen settled any elements of disquiet aggravated by Alfred's behavior.

Fiona had chosen Maddox, and even if they weren't drunk on each other right now, she wasn't retreating. The dragon would take the win where he could. For now, he kept his focus on Alfred.

"Go back to the cottage," Alfred ordered, his attention on Fiona. "Wait for us there."

"Go fuck yourself," Fiona retorted, leaning into Maddox, and the dragon chuckled softly.

"You know, I don't think any of us want to watch that," Fin commented as he strolled out of the woods like he had just been on a nature hike. Then again, it was entirely possible the little shit had done just that. Though he dressed in his traditional black, he wore a short-sleeved shirt and jeans. Even his scuffed sneakers were a far cry from his normal, formal attire. "Nothing personal, Alfred," Fin told him with a most insincere smile.

Maddox wasn't the only one enjoying Fiona's snapping back at Alfred. He'd been high-handed from the moment he woke up. Not that Maddox had expected anything different, but he had hoped the old bastard would mellow some. Fiona wasn't their possession. Nor was she a subject to be dismissed.

Alfred barely spared a glance toward Fin, his tolerance for the smart remarks and teasing developed over countless decades. "It wasn't a request, it was an order. Go back to the cottage."

Making no move to leave, Fiona tilted her head back to look up at Maddox. "Want to take a walk with me?"

A single solitary twitch in Alfred's cheek betrayed him. Maddox managed to control his response. Fin didn't bother. He burst out laughing. "Oh, Beautiful, you continue to delight me. If Maddox doesn't want to take a walk with you, I will. Hell, even if he does, I may tag along."

Sparing the druid a smirk, Maddox said, "You're more

than welcome if Kitten doesn't mind." That earned him arched brows from Fin, then a smile of such enormous satisfaction that Alfred let out a disgusted scoff.

"So you're choosing her, too."

"Alfred," Rogue answered before Fin could. "Be careful. We have survived all these years because we all choose to listen. You are not at the moment. Of course they are both choosing her." Arms folded, he took a position halfway between Maddox and Alfred, facing the vampire they could all argue was their maker on some level. "So am I."

Shock rolled through Maddox at that declaration. In all the years he'd known Rogue and Alfred, *all of them*, he had never seen the pair at odds. Not truly. Their disagreements were more debates, mild and often over minutia. This was not that.

Alfred's narrow-eyed gaze confirmed it as he focused on Rogue. "Et tu, Brute?"

The frost elf gave a careless shrug. "She's the one. You accept it or not, that is your call. But she is one of us. You helped as much as we did to get her through transition."

"Not that she gives a damn," Alfred spit the words.

"Oh fuck you," Fiona snarled into the fray. "I didn't *ask* you to do this. I didn't *want* you to do this."

Those dark eyes fixed on her, glaring. "I gave you the choice."

"You told me I had to say yes, and that if I didn't, I'd take Maddox with me."

She hadn't wanted to say yes. That revelation hit Maddox like a brick. While he'd already been aware of her desires, it was something else to hear it aloud.

"So you said yes for him?" Alfred challenged her.

"Does it matter so much to you if I did?" Defiance was etched into her every syllable, and she lifted her chin, her green eyes blazing. Maddox tightened the arm he had around her. Between one pump of his heart and the next, Alfred narrowed the space between them, and Maddox shifted her behind him so that he was chest to chest with the angry original.

Fin and Rogue moved to clasp Alfred by the arms, even as Maddox braced for the fight. Between them, they could take him. One on one, Maddox suspected he could take him, too. Either way, he would not be allowed to menace her.

"She's one of us," Fin reminded him. "We wanted her to say yes. *All* of us, and if you could get over being a contrary dick for five minutes, you'd appreciate the fact that not only did she say yes, she came back to us."

Alfred snorted, his gaze cold as he looked past Maddox to where she stood. Fiona hadn't retreated, if anything, her presence was a blazing warmth against Maddox's back. "No, she didn't. She ran from you while you were distracted. Then Rogue helped her escape to here. If I were to gamble, she would already be running if I hadn't come."

"You really are an insufferable asshole," Fiona stated before the others could cut in. "You want me to stay gone? Or are you just pissed that they found me when you couldn't?"

Fin was the first to take the brunt of Alfred's blow, and Rogue the next. They went flying in opposite directions, but Maddox braced himself to face the one he'd called friend long before he called him brother. But the lunge never came, he merely glared at Maddox with such icy control that Maddox read the war waging within him clearly in Alfred's eyes.

He didn't trust Fiona. But *she* wasn't the problem...

Straightening, Maddox stared at him. "Start talking, brother. What's happened?"

"The others are waking," Alfred warned, and Maddox

rocked back on his heels. "I am not the only one she has awoken."

"I didn't wake you," Fiona protested. "I didn't want anything to do with you."

"Kitten," Maddox said, glancing over his shoulder. "If Fin's vision is to be believed, the moment the vampire drained you and fed you his blood, it would have sent the tremor that began the waking process."

Her rolled eyes didn't do Maddox any favors, but he offered her a faint smile.

"If?" Fin muttered, dusting himself off as if he hadn't been flung several yards. "She's here. She's a hybrid. She's *ours*. She claimed you, remember? You told me yourself after you met her—she was ours."

This was true, and even when he shot an apologetic look to Fiona, she gave a careless shrug, arms folded. "Prophecy aside, who cares if the others are waking? Unless they're as big a bag full of dicks as Asshole here." Maddox winced.

"Kitten, can you just call him Alfred?"

She stared at Maddox like he'd sprouted a second head. "No, I can't. He doesn't deserve it. He's treated me like chattel from the moment he met me. The first fucking thing he did was bite me, then he dragged me off to his room where he killed me over and over again. I think Asshole fits."

And on that particular point, Maddox couldn't argue. He'd not been thrilled when Alfred ordered him out, and Fin and Rogue had to keep him out. Especially when he'd felt her die the first time. It had been agony. Not even his faith in Alfred had sustained him. Not at first.

It wasn't until she agreed. Until she began to fight…

He sighed, and his shoulders dropped. She'd chosen what she hadn't wanted for him. His mate had chosen him twice. Cupping her face, he rested his forehead against hers. "Thank you," he murmured in a low voice, ignoring Alfred's near silent oath as the other paced away from them.

"Don't thank me yet," Fiona teased. "I told you succubi don't mate and we aren't good at long-term relationships. I haven't figured out this hybrid thing, and I definitely know how to hold a grudge."

Fin's laughter echoed Maddox's own. "Not seeing a problem with that, Beautiful. For your Mad-Dragon, or for me."

She glanced past Maddox to Fin and then over to Rogue before she looked to where Alfred had his back to all of them. "If it's important enough he won't talk to you in front of me, I can find my way back."

"No," Maddox said in the same breath as Rogue and Fin. Grip firm on her nape, Maddox shifted to stand next to her, even as Fin slid an arm around her waist. "We do this together. Or we don't do this. We cannot demand you be one of us, then treat you as any less."

The words were every bit as much for Alfred as they were for Fiona. Maddox had waited endless centuries to find his mate. Even when he thought Fin had lost his mind, some part of him had held out what he believed to be a futile hope that Fin had indeed seen the woman who would be theirs. Though she wasn't a dragon, Maddox couldn't hold that against her.

There were no other dragons.

Not golden, anyway.

He was the last.

But she was *his*, and that was all that mattered to him. They could figure everything else out.

"The seven," Alfred began, facing them once more, all his earlier frustration and forbidding demeanor erased from his expression as though it hadn't been there in the first place.

"The original seven are those that sired all vampires. All lines trace back to us."

Though he half-expected her to make a snarky comment, Fiona just leaned into Fin, though she let her nape rest in Maddox's grip. The nascent trust demonstrated in her actions steadied him.

"Okay," Fiona said, no snark present. "So you and the six other dwarves are all awake. Does that make me Snow White or something?"

Well, so much for the theory that there was no snark present. The corners of Maddox's lips twitched, but it was Rogue's chuckle that broke the silence following Fiona's question. Alfred's jaw snapped shut, his teeth clicking as he stared at her.

"It's pathological with you, isn't it?"

"If you mean my charm and good looks?" Fiona shrugged. "It's a gift."

Fin's snickers joined Rogue's, and Maddox allowed his own grin to come out. "It is that, Kitten."

Shaking his head slightly, Alfred said, "They are not dwarves, nor are they cuddly. Most are not even as tolerant as I."

Before she could say the next cutting thing on her mind, Maddox added, "Rarely are all seven awake at the same time. It's usually safer for everyone if they aren't. They do not play well with others, and the last time all seven were awake at the same time, it was a war."

"Oh, joy." She sighed. "And this is my fault, how?"

"You are a hybrid," Alfred informed her. "One promised in prophecy. Your presence means the world will undergo another change. They will not want the existing power structure to change."

"Then it will be war," Rogue said flatly. "Because their only alternative would be to kill her."

Possessiveness threading through his veins, Maddox glared. He understood what Alfred wanted from him now. "You want me to find them."

A single nod. "You are the best suited. Take Fin with you…"

"Hey," Fin argued. "I just got back from my last task."

"Fiona will stay with Rogue and I, for now," Alfred continued as if Fin hadn't spoken. "There are things she needs to learn that you will both just be in the way for."

The insult bounced off Maddox, because he agreed on some levels. But he hadn't just claimed his mate to have to leave her. And he really hadn't done it to leave her with Alfred while he was still hell bent on being an asshole. The last thing he wanted was to return and find that not only had they not gotten along, but Fiona had abandoned them…again.

"Maybe she should come with us," Fin suggested, his own worried expression suggesting his thoughts had traveled a similar path.

"I will look after her," Rogue assured them both, but he looked to Fiona. "If she is willing to stay with us. If not, we can make other arrangements, little *svàss*. The cottage here is but one holding I have."

Maddox had plenty of his own. Not all of them were shared. Fin had plenty of bolt-holes as well for that matter. But Alfred sliced a hand through the air. "The hellion and I need to work this out between us."

Firming his jaw, Maddox glared at Alfred. He couldn't shake the mild suspicion that Alfred didn't want this to go well.

"You boys figure out what you want to do, then someone tell me what we're supposed to do when you figure out where the other six are. Kill them? Make a treaty? Something?"

That was a different task altogether.

"We will decide that once they have been located," Alfred stated, his tone declaring it wasn't open for discussion. "Until then, you will train with Rogue and with me. Maddox and Fin will move more efficiently without you there to slow them down or distract them."

"You agree not to be a big bag of dicks, or at least to take the log out of your ass so I can beat you with it, and I'll consider your *thoughtful* invitation. But be warned, I have my own tasks that need to be accomplished." She folded her arms, the glint of determination in her eyes making Maddox smile.

"I told you we would kill him for you," he reminded her.

"Yes, you did, and Fin has said the same thing…except that son of a bitch is mine to kill." The heat scorching each word made it clear she wasn't changing her mind, and if he were a wise dragon, he wouldn't insist on defending his mate, even if that was exactly what he should and *would* do.

"How about a game?" Fin suggested, his eyes brightening with delight. "A little wager amongst us."

Rogue's prolonged and exasperated sigh earned a genuine smile and a soft laugh from Fiona. As captivated as he was by her, Maddox didn't miss the snap of Alfred's attention or the way he focused on her when she laughed.

Jealous.

There was no other word for it. The old vampire had discovered something he wanted that he couldn't compel or order to do as he bid.

It could be good for him. "What's the wager?" Maddox prodded Fin, wanting to dig Alfred's hole a little deeper. Sometimes, the best way to catch the prey was to run until it let you catch them.

"Whoever gets him has to deliver his head to Beautiful

here, and she agrees to a week away wherever we choose. A little one on one time never hurt anyone."

Fiona snorted. "I just told you I wanted to kill him myself. What makes you think I'm going to agree to that?"

"Because..." Fin said, his grin growing more sly. Maddox already regretted backing this idea. "If you get him on your own, then we agree to do *your* bidding for a week. All four of us."

Alfred shook his head. "I will not agree to that."

"Then you lose out on all the fun and forfeit a week with Fiona all to yourself." Fin's expression was smug. "More for us."

"I still haven't agreed," Fiona countered. "But I would consider this wager if you include the proviso that if you *help* me, or at least don't *prevent* me from taking my target, the week I spend with you will include a day where *I* will be the obedient one."

Fuck. "No," Maddox growled. "You'll be with Rogue and Alfred, they automatically get a leg up."

Both Rogue and Fin chuckled, pair of assholes, but it was the faint smirk on Alfred's face as he focused on Fiona. "Four days."

"Excuse me?"

"If I help you get both of them and put their lives in your hands, you give me four days of that week to be perfectly obedient."

She sniffed, chin lifting. "This presumes I need your help."

"No, Hellion, it presumes I allow you to complete your hunt without interfering. You want them, you'll have to play this game of Fin's."

"Except *you* aren't playing," she retaliated, folding her arms.

Ha. This couldn't be going better if I planned it myself.

Maddox spared Fin a droll look. *You did plan this yourself.*

I did, didn't I?

Rolling his eyes, Maddox shook his head. "If this is the case, then Fiona should go with us. By cutting us off from her, we're already out of the running."

"Maddox," Rogue tsked. "You don't think you can't catch the prey and bring them back to her? An offering of your own perhaps?"

This was true.

And if you agree to split two of those days with me, or at least just let me play along, I'll help.

Smug little shit stirrer.

Thank you, I try.

"If I agree to the terms," Alfred countered, ignoring all of them for Fiona, "do you agree to the four days?"

"Does that mean for three of those days, you have to obey me?"

"It could be arranged," he said slowly. "Within *reason*."

Her smirk delighted Maddox on a whole other level. "Then I'll agree to the same, *within reason*. Because the moment you put caveats on it, Asshole, then it's game over. There's no reason to obey at all."

Alfred's smile was both slow and dangerous. "I would prefer if you would call me by my name."

"And I would prefer if you would go to hell, but we're both doomed to disappointment."

"So," Fin said, clapping his hands in glee. "We have a wager?"

He glanced at them each, one at a time. Maddox nodded once. As did Rogue. Alfred and Fiona stared at each other, neither refusing to bend, and finally, they both offered curt nods.

"Fantastic," Fin celebrated, then swept Fiona up. "Let's kiss on it." Then he wrapped her in his arms and kissed her. The move caught her off guard, but when she wrapped her arms around him and sighed a little into the kiss, Maddox's cock stiffened. Fin made no pretense of grinding into her gently. When he finally did let her up for air, her already swollen lips had darkened, and she scraped her teeth over her lower lip.

Rogue caught her next, his kiss surprisingly simple and gentle. Yet, she clasped her palms to his cheeks as they nuzzled and tested each other.

After she stepped away from him, Maddox held out a hand to her, and she turned to him easily, making his dragon huff a fiery breath within. His mate, their mate, wasn't pulling away. He kissed her gently, savoring the contact as he wrapped himself around her. "Try not to torment him too badly," he pleaded, but honestly, whatever happened, it was Alfred's own damn fault. Maddox just didn't want her hurt.

"I'll be on my best behavior," she said with a devilish grin. "Almost as good as when we had to share that cell."

Laughter burst through him and he kissed her again. "Be safe, mate."

"Hmm, you too." Then she nipped his lower lip. "Bring me back a present?"

"Or two," he said with a wink.

With great reluctance, he stepped back to join Fin. Rogue moved up to take his place next to her, but Maddox's last sight of Fiona was her giving Alfred a dismissive wave before turning her back on him as she said, "As if I'd kiss you…"

Then Fin yanked him away as they raced along the druidic paths.

A part of the dragon wanted her to cooperate and at least give him a chance.

The rest of him? The rest of him hoped she gave him absolute hell. Alfred wanted to fight their fate, to control it as he had everything else.

It would be a fine battle.

"I hope we don't miss the best part," Fin said as they appeared—where the fuck were they? Oh, Argentina.

"The best part?"

"Hmm-hmm," Fin said with a grin. "The hate sex when they get there is going to be epic."

"They have had sex." She'd fed off of Alfred, something that had left Maddox a little puzzled by the cratering distance between them.

"Not the same thing," his brother told him, clasping a hand to his shoulder. "Let's find you some shoes. The sex was to feed her then, but he was still trying to control everything. She didn't have the wherewithal to withstand him. She does now, and he wants her to choose him."

She definitely wasn't on board with that.

Ah.

Maddox sighed. "Let's get this over with. The sooner we find the six assholes, the faster we get back to her."

"Oh, we're not here for the assholes," Fin said, his grin widening. "I got a lead on Isaac. Thought we'd bag him up and put him away for her first."

Impressed, Maddox nodded. "I like this plan."

"I know," his brother was all smugness. "It's my plan."

CHAPTER 12

"Love is more cruel than lust." - Algernon Charles Swinburne

*I*t shouldn't have come as a surprise that Asshole relocated us back to the keep. What was it with me and being stuck in prisons? Granted, it had changed significantly since I first arrived to the dark, dusty, and hollow chambers.

"I do not pursue others," Asshole informed me when I gave him a look after we'd stepped off the plane. "They come to me."

Well, la-di-fucking-da.

Still, Rogue carried me after we left the airport, and they ran all the way back up to the keep, ignoring the snow and the colder temps the higher we climbed. As when Rogue got me out on the snowmobile, he shielded me from the cold.

I needed to ask him more about who and what he was, but there hadn't been time. While Alfred didn't *pursue* others, he had no compunction about sending them. Maddox and Fin had been absent since our return, and he'd dispatched

Rogue twice. The last time just as Rogue had tumbled me onto his bed.

Asshole seemed determined to earn his name.

At least the changes to the keep were welcome enough. Tapestries decorated the walls. Furniture filled the various rooms. The fireplaces were always alight and fires fed regularly. Servants moved through the hushed hallways, sometimes so silent, I could forget they were there.

Not always though.

We still had guests, too.

The majority of the sycophants had left, but there were still a few in residence—including *Eleanor*. Why she had to be there, I had no idea, and I sure as shit wasn't going to ask. Within an hour of our arrival, she'd come seeking he-who-can-go-suck-a-dick and they vanished off to who the fuck knew where. Other than his cock blocking with Rogue, I hadn't seen him, and I didn't want to.

Hopefully, wherever he sent Rogue, it didn't involve him bringing back my targets to Alfred. Though if he hoped giving me them would earn genuine obedience from me, he really should have considered his wording. The bargain involved 'within reason,' it didn't stipulate whose reason.

I'd lounged in my bed past sunrise. Honestly, there was no reason to get up. Nothing to do. Breakfast, as always, was served in the library. Yet, I refused to return there after my last trip. The first three days I'd been back, I'd just had breakfast brought to my room. Asshole cut that off with one of the nervous servants informing me that I joined them for breakfast in the library or I didn't eat.

Starving sounded delightful.

I didn't have breakfast all week. Not until I found someone had set food out for me in the bathing room. Instead of breakfast, I went there and lounged for an hour. It was the one hour I could be certain no one else would be there. Then the food started showing up.

Midday meals were served in the great hall as was supper. As long as I could have breakfast, I avoided those meals, at least until Rogue fetched me. When he brought me, I went. When Asshole sent him away, I skipped.

Breakfast awaited me when I arrived like it had each morning, and I dropped the dressing gown, picked up a croissant, and took a bite as I sank into the hot, steamy water. The food was laid out close enough I didn't even have to leave the water to eat. Pretty decadent.

It wasn't loads of food, simple fare really, but I preferred it. Nothing would quite top the bacon Fin brought to me that first morning. I'd been so damn hungry after nothing for so long. Meats. Cheeses. Bread. Fruit. Those were my staples for breakfast. The doors opening pulled me from my musing as I took a bite of the apple.

The vampire entering wasn't Asshole.

Nor was he any of my others.

That was unusual enough to get me to sit forward. The guards placed before my exodus were still present. Certain areas of the keep were off limits to everyone, save a handful of servants that I never saw.

Especially in here.

Anton, on the other hand, had been the retainer serving us in the library that fateful day. The young vampire—how I knew he was young I had no idea, maybe the better question was why I thought he was young when arguably, I was the newest—gave me a bow before closing the doors and crossing the room to stand on the opposite side of the pool I reclined in.

Not once did his gaze drift below mine until he looked at his own feet. I took another bite of the apple and waited.

Clearly, he'd come here for something and the guards had let him in.

Five hundred dollars said it was something for Asshole.

He didn't pursue, people came to him. Except, he had pursued me to Rogue's little cottage retreat. Fuck, I kind of missed it now. We really hadn't gotten any time there. Maybe I could talk him into running away there whenever he got back from his current task.

They said they didn't answer to Asshole. Apparently, they did on some level.

Maybe that was why he didn't like me—I wouldn't do as he said.

I was nearly done with the apple, and Anton continued to stand there, staring at his feet. Pursing my lips, I debated whether I wanted to continue until he either gave up and spoke—or left, either was fine with me—or end this impasse so I could get rid of him.

Finished with the apple, I rose from the water and set the core to the side for disposal and popped a square of cheese in my mouth. I chewed it thoughtfully before taking a sip of my coffee. Nudity didn't bother me, and a glance at my guest showed his gaze so firmly affixed to the floor, I imagined he could court it now.

Or describe it in detail.

A chuckle wound through me, and I climbed out of the water. There were huge bath sheets hanging on the wall. I could just wrap one around me, but the torture was much more fun. So I took my time drying off. My hair was still damp from washing it, but I could just let it dry on its own. I'd wrung most of the water out of it before I settled in to soak and eat.

Finally, I lifted the dressing gown from the hook and pulled it on, then tied it at the waist before facing my visitor.

Yep, he was still staring at the floor. But he was also sweating.

Profusely.

Rolling my eyes, I asked. "What do you want, Anton?"

Now that I'd acknowledged him, he lifted his head and a faint smile curved his lips. The expression seemed carefully staged with one foot firmly planted in flirtatious and the other somewhere closer to humble obedience.

It was fucking disturbing.

Arms folded, I raised my brows to indicate I was still waiting, but I refused to say another word until he told me why he was here. It'd better be good. The one thing I liked about this damn mausoleum besides three of its residents, all currently absent, was the bathing pool and my time soaking in it. Time, he'd interrupted with his presence.

"I have not had a chance to welcome you back to the keep, m'lady."

Uh huh, and I was the Queen of England. "And that required you intruding on my bath?"

One corner of his mouth curled upward as he circled the pool to approach me. "You have taken to hiding in here in the mornings, though I have waited in the library each day as instructed to serve you. You never come."

I shrugged. "Not planning on showing up there anytime soon, so don't hold your breath."

He hummed a little, tracing his fingers along the edges of the pool. The rock glistened, but there was just something off about the whole thing. His dark eyes for one. They were almost pitch black. Few people had truly black eyes.

Demons had them.

Not people.

Vampires fell somewhere in the middle ground, so not impossible.

At the same time... I shook my head, tracking his every

movement as he narrowed the distance between us. Vampires were predators. Only idiots forgot that.

Yes, I had been that idiot. Trust me, I wouldn't make the same mistake a second time. I barely trusted the ones I liked —grudgingly. Fine, I loved Maddox. I had no idea why. It was an uncomfortable fucking emotion that I would prefer not to have to deal with, and it made me worry about him.

Worse, it made me miss the bastard.

Fin and Rogue? I didn't have a word for them yet. Trust might be a stretch, and yet, I trusted Rogue. He'd proven it to me more than once that he would do exactly as he said, and so far, he hadn't deliberately lied to me. So points in his favor.

And Fin hadn't betrayed me to Asshole the moment he found me. He was also absolutely adorable.

Anton halted just two feet away, and I snapped all my attention to him rather than let myself wander off to moon over those who weren't here. With absolute care, he pressed a hand to his chest and then bowed. The move put him far too close to me for my taste, but I didn't dare back up a step. Three things that were true when dealing with any predator whether vampire, shifter, or demon—they could smell fear, they were always looking for weakness, and if you ran, they chased.

I didn't know how old Anton was, but I'd need the element of surprise to take him down, and this close, I wouldn't have much time.

"I am here to offer myself formally," Anton intoned, still bowed.

An offering? Was he fucking kidding? "Pass," I told him bluntly.

As he straightened, his expression tightened, and though the flicker was barely perceptible, it was definitely there. "M'lady—" he began, and I held up a hand.

"Let me stop you right there. I'm not your anything." In fact, the longer he stood there, the more I wanted him gone. "If that was all you had to say, there's the door."

The puzzlement flashing in his too dark eyes faded fast, and a slow, almost cruel smirk replaced it. "You haven't changed, Fiona," he said, but that wasn't Anton's voice. The chill lacing my spine turned into pure shards of ice. "I worried they would corrupt you, but you remain irresistibly stubborn."

Fuck.

Me.

"Dorran," I exhaled. Anton's expression shifted, almost like a mask, into some form of pleasure that looked way more like pain. "Wasn't expecting you."

He chuckled, then Anton's hand was around my throat and I was pinned to the wall. The strength in that arm was iron, and the grip on my neck equally inflexible. "But you hadn't forgotten me."

"Not likely," I told him, feathering a hand over Anton's wrist. The steady cadence of his heart hadn't changed once. If Dorran was truly pulling his strings, the actions didn't affect his pulse. I had no idea if that was a good thing or a bad thing. "Hard to forget my keeper, even if he was a *shitty* host."

Anton—fuck that, I couldn't think of him as Anton at the moment. Dorran leaned in, running his nose along my jaw to just behind my ear, and he took a deep breath. "I miss your scent, Fiona. But you're warm from the bath, and there's a flush of color to your cheeks." Another deep breath. "Are you wet for me?"

Tucking my tongue against the inside of my cheek, I bit back my first response. I needed the Dorran occupied Anton to move his head back, so I settled for an indelicate snort. "Not even a little bit."

The insult resonated, and he snapped his head up to stare at me. The darkness in those eyes drilled into my soul. Demons had eyes like that. Dorran was a shadow demon though, and they weren't known for possessions, but corruption?

That they could do.

The hand gripping my throat tightened, cutting off my oxygen.

"We can fix that," he practically purred. "Your cell is waiting for you, and I will make sure you are tended well."

"Thanks," I gritted out. "But I'd rather suck on a power line."

The taunt worked to pull him back into range, and I slammed my head forward. It cracked my forehead off of his. Pain radiated out from the strike like I'd taken a hammer to my own head. I locked my hands on his throat, even as the pressure had darkness edging my vision as oxygen deprivation actually seemed to mean something to me.

"Hybrids," Dorran murmured before he fucking licked my cheek—*ugh*, "have a few weaknesses to exploit. I will have fun devouring yours."

Even fighting for air, I had no chance of strangling the actual vampire before he took me down. Beneath the skin, two presences existed, and they weren't in any kind of harmony. The lust for power, for control, for dominance was all Dorran. I knew him. He wanted to feed on me, and I swore I could feel him panting at the first brush of contact. The second presence wanted to be free, but was suffocated under the weight of the shadow demon that had strip-mined him as if for parts.

I felt bad for the kid.

Lust was a funny thing...too much could impair judgment, make a person reckless, drive them mad.

The absence of it, though?

Apathy.

Malaise.

Ennui.

I dug into the shadow demon's lust and pulled on it.

All of it.

I'd fucking consume it if I had to. I wasn't remotely hungry, but that didn't stop me from dragging at him. His laughter chased me into unconsciousness as the world faded around me, even as I pulled and pulled.

It wasn't going to be enough.

Dammit.

Power surged through me. A roar of pure fury followed by a flood of strength like I'd never felt. I dug my fingers into his neck, teeth gritting as my fingers rent into his flesh. It did nothing to dislodge him, so I grasped the wrist of the hand he was using to strangle me.

And I shattered it.

Anton's shriek twined with Dorran's until both threatened to pierce my ears from the volume, but I kept dragging it in, the raw, unfiltered, and untamed lust like a bad case of acid as I inhaled it. The moment shredded when Anton was suddenly yanked away from me and flung across the room.

There was a sickening crack of bones as his whole body hit the rock face. Gagging both from the crushing bruise on my throat and the intemperate emotions burning in my system, I could barely make out the remote and unforgiving expression on Alfred's face before he turned all of his attention on Anton, who was currently picking his broken body up and staggering to his feet. The click and roll of bones grinding on each other in unpleasant ways echoed across the steamy room.

"Not Anton," I rasped out. Fuck my throat hurt.

"I'm aware, Hellion." Alfred's presence seemed to fill the whole cavern as he faced off with broken puppet currently limping toward him, more dragging his right leg than actually using it to walk on.

I leaned against the wall, waging a battle to get my rioting system under control. My skin crawled from the amount of corrupted lust I'd taken in. If there was a way to vomit it out, I might be tempted to purge. But there was only riding out the worst of it. I'd done it before.

I could do it again.

"You overstep yourself," Alfred—yes, I know he was still an asshole, but showing up when he did scratched him out a point, for now—didn't look remotely disturbed. If anything, he seemed almost relaxed, and that was somehow a hell of a lot more unnerving. "There is a protocol to these things."

"Is there?" Dorran smirked, but his puppet struggled to stay upright. Vampires could heal a lot of damage, but I didn't want to think about how many broken bones Anton probably had at the moment. "The protocol would seem to be break in and take what you want. Why else do you have *my* prize?"

A soft chuckle slipped from Alfred, and I swore all the hair on my body stood up and my panties would probably have burned up—if I were wearing any.

"Your prize? I think not. Do you not see the mark, demon?" Conversational, almost droll Alfred was really doing something for me. I could practically taste the blood scenting the air. "Think you have a greater claim than a dragon?" He paused and shifted to stand almost sideways so he could glance at me. The weight of his gaze drifting over me was like a physical caress. "Or my own?" The last three words were leaden with meaning as he faced puppet-Anton.

A scowl darkened his expression, and I swore I could actually see Dorran's own features for a moment. "I had her first."

"I don't care."

"I'm not a fucking bone to be fought over by the biggest dicks in the room," I snapped, even if every single syllable grated like I'd swallowed gravel to get it out. I'd been sick of the conversation long before it got started. Now it was just insulting.

Dorran looked past Alfred to stare at me. "You're going to come to me, Fiona. When you do, I'll be waiting."

The inky darkness seemed to cut at me, even from as far away as he was, the lash of it stroking down my arm. I jerked away from it just as Alfred pulled me to him and then flung something. Anton shrieked, the sound so awful, I cringed and fucking hid my head.

Yeah, call me a coward. It actually sounded like he was having the skin torn from his body, and I'd seen that before.

It wasn't pretty.

Not even a little bit.

Alfred covered my ears with his hands, tugging me into him as the sound intensified around us, only to cut off abruptly as the scorching scent of sulfur stunk up the air. When I would have lifted my head, Alfred kept me still. I gritted my teeth against the devastation of how silent the room had gone save for the lap of water against the rock pools.

"Don't look," he advised me. "Turn and walk out, go straight up to my room."

"What?"

"My room has older, more inflexible wards on it. We will be improving all of them, but it is there or my crypt. I thought you might prefer my room."

That even managed to sound reasonable. But I hadn't been back in his room since that last morning when they'd declared my transition complete.

He still wouldn't let me turn my head. I wasn't squeamish. Admittedly, a part of me was feeling guilty. I had the sense that there was no Anton left at all. Or if there was? It might be kinder to put him out of his misery. Atop all of that, my skin still buzzed and crawled with the sense of other I'd pulled out of the Dorran-slash-Anton whatever it was. I didn't think possessed was the right term.

"Is it safe to go up there?" was the only question I landed on, and it came out even raspier than before. The pain in my throat intensified.

"Yes," Alfred promised me. "He wasn't here long. Anton wasn't supposed to be here at all. He left weeks ago, and apparently, he returned a day before we did."

Oh. Someone was not happy about that.

"It won't happen again." The danger licking along that promise sent another thrill up my spine. "Now go, I will come to you when I am done here."

Arguing was in my blood. I hated orders. I sure as shit didn't like orders from assholes.

I had to wonder who was more surprised at my obedience—Alfred or me?

I didn't stop until I was at the doors to his room, and I pushed them open without a second thought.

It was just as I remembered it. The sofas framing the currently dormant fireplace included a pair of colorful throws now, both in deep green. The bed lay in the half-shadow of the room. Apparently, the skies outside were dark and stormy. I had to wonder if it would snow again. I hadn't been out to the garden since our return.

Closing the doors behind me, I leaned back against them.

The room even smelled like Alfred. Cool. Crisp. Aged whiskey, like you'd find in the old cask barrels. Leather. Something indefinable.

I closed my eyes as shudders of reaction rocked through me. My skin still crawled. My insides burned. And my throat could probably not feel worse if he'd slashed it open.

Pushing away from the doors, I stumbled toward the window and away from the sprawling bed. Unlike the rest of the keep, this room was hushed. Like the silence was deeper here. The wards, most likely, since he said they were stronger here and in his crypt.

That would make sense. I supposed.

Touching my forehead to the glass separating me from the rest of the world, I winced. There was a bruise forming there. Or whatever it was vampires did after injuring themselves.

The mark over my pulse point burned, and a sensation crept through me, chasing out the chills. Covering it with my hand, I could almost feel Maddox. It was just a sense of him. A flash. Intense anger. Worry. Then just as intense relief.

Had he felt what was happening?

Dorran had been choking me out. Would that have hurt Maddox if he'd succeeded?

Beneath the shivering and the disgust roiling through me came a much more potent emotion.

Fury.

That was where the energy had come from. Maddox. Stroking my fingers against the mark, I tried to focus on him and the sense that I was all right.

I had no idea how this worked. The other mark on my throat seemed to burn, and when I touched it, I could feel Alfred's approach. He was only steps away. I turned to the doors just as they opened. The tense and forbidding expression on his face eased a fraction when he locked gazes with me.

After closing the doors behind him with a soft, if ominous *click*, he crossed to where I stood. In some ways, it was a violent déjà vu to the morning he found me in the garden. The fixed look in his eyes, the tension in his jaw, and the sense of rawness that just emanated from him.

Only this time, he didn't collide with me and strike with a bite.

This time, he just raised two fingers to my jaw and gently nudged my head up so I'd show him my throat. His eyes darkened as he studied it. How bad did it have to look for his expression to turn so forbidding?

"How are you?" The gentle words and tone were utterly at odds with his expression.

"I'll live," I croaked out, and then grimaced. I sounded worse if possible.

"Yes," he agreed, then trailed his fingers down to my throat, and I didn't flinch so much as wince at the cool touch there. "He must want you badly, Hellion, to risk coming here."

"I have no clue why." I didn't owe him any explanations. None. Yet, I wanted to tell him. "I definitely didn't invite him."

"I know," he soothed, then wrapped his hand around the side of my neck. The coolness was almost heavenly against the ache there, and my eyes fluttered closed. Cool lips pressing against my forehead should have startled me, but I just leaned into the contact. "He hurt you. That will not be forgiven."

A shiver raced up my spine.

"My only question for you, Hellion, is will you let me help you?"

Will I…?

I blinked slowly and met his gaze. Was he asking my permission?

Holy shit.

CHAPTER 13

"It's not enough to conquer; one must learn to seduce." - Voltaire

A dozen answers formed and died unspoken on my lips. Alfred and I were not friends. I wouldn't even classify us as lovers. Yet, his presence calmed me in the most unexpected way, even as his touch eased the pain radiating from the bruises on my neck. The cooling caress of his palm as he wrapped his hand around my throat soothed when it should have threatened.

Hadn't I just been choked out by someone holding me the same way?

The difference, however, was in the way he tipped his head and how he watched me as he moved his fingers lightly into place, as though he were laying his hand into the impression left by Anton's grip. I swallowed once and almost instantly regretted it. Pain flash-fired along the inside of my throat. Just how much damage had Dorran done?

Alfred waited. He didn't ask me again, and he didn't press.

No, he simply held my throat and waited for the answer to his question.

"How?" I managed to croak out. Maybe it was my imagination, but I thought there was a hint of concern in his cool eyes as he studied me. "More blood?"

"It would be the simplest method," Alfred admitted. "But I have some other skills."

Surprise flared through me. "Other skills?" Okay, I needed to stop talking. It was like my voice grew more hoarse with each attempt. Or like I was still being strangled, just infinitely slower. Even the air getting into my lungs seemed too thin.

Eyes narrowing, he closed the last bit of gap between us. "Hellion, is it getting worse?"

I wanted to tell him no and to back off. But it was... "It's getting harder to breathe." I'd rather have my fingernails pulled one by one than admit I needed his help. "Can you help?"

"Yes," he said, sliding his free hand to cup my cheek. "You won't like it."

"Blood then."

"We'll try this first," he murmured, his eyes darkening as he dipped his head. It had to be a testament to how bad I felt that I didn't see what was coming until his lips brushed mine. Just a brush. No real contact. The coolness of his lips touching mine were there and gone again. He flicked his gaze to mine as he used his thumb to tilt my head, and then his mouth closed over mine.

The firmness in his kiss demanded an answer. I covered his hand on my throat with my own as I opened my mouth to the invasion of his tongue. Tingles radiated out at the contact as he pressed his fingers into the marks on my throat. White-hot pain sizzled along my nerve endings, but it was almost craven how much I wanted it.

There was no room to breathe in the kiss as he kept control of my head, and then I was against the window itself. The cold seeped in to combat the heat, but was losing rapidly against the fire as his tongue swept in, staking its claim. There was no mistaking it—the kiss burned all the way down to my soul, the imprint searing into my bones as he threatened to consume.

All of my oxygen cut off, and my eyes flashed open. Alfred's stare held mine, even as his pupils seemed to swell. Then he pushed air into me, the white-hot pulse against my throat cutting away what felt like barbed wire digging into my flesh. When he slid his thigh between mine, I gasped in another breath as he exhaled it into me, and then the shadows around us began to writhe.

Anchoring myself by holding on to him, I tried not to get swept away in the torrid passion igniting liquid heat to spill into my veins, but the hotter I burned, the more the shadows in the room began to dance. It was only when they began to rip out of me and I screamed under his relentless touch that it hit me.

There was no fire lit.

There was no reason for shadows when it was so dark outside.

Alfred didn't let me go as my head snapped back, and I exhaled a darkened cloud that swirled above us like a tempest. It geysered out of me, leaving everything raw and shaken in its wake. Horror rippled through me as the shadow spewed out like some kind of oily cloud of evil. It churned above us, agitating in a cyclone effect as lightning began to skitter over it.

Gagging, I clung to Alfred as he pulled me into him and held up one hand. "Close your eyes," he ordered, and I buried my face against him. Even through my closed eyelids, I didn't miss the sudden flare like sunlight that filled the room only a hundred times brighter. The sizzle of ozone filled my nostrils, and the dark cloud screamed.

Then the light faded, though I kept my still dazzled eyes closed. With one hand on in my hair, Alfred tugged gently until I looked up at him again. He stared down at me, and even with the glittering spots occluding my vision, I couldn't miss the quickening intensity in his gaze as he raked it over my face. He slid his hand back to my throat, and the earlier pain was absent. The stroke of his cool fingers left tingles in their wake that chased out the sticky barbs of pain.

I took a deep breath, half-expecting to choke on it, and then let out a shuddering sigh. The air seemed almost too cold on my raw insides, and more than just my throat hurt now, but it wasn't anywhere near as bad.

"Better?" The careful question pulled my attention to the present and the vampire still holding me.

"Yes," I admitted. "Still…hurts though. Like someone pummeled my insides and then clawed them up for good measure."

He lifted me up and carried me over to the sofas. Not his bed. There he settled and cradled me to him. "Then you need blood now."

I hesitated. Not because I had an issue with blood. No, I'd apparently gotten over that one in the last few weeks. The hesitation didn't come from shying away from the act itself, but because it was Alfred. When I drank his blood…

"I can control it," he told me as if he read my mind. "Or you can use it to get to know me more if you want."

"Have you ever heard of having a conversation?" It still came out a raspy croak, but it at least it didn't feel like I gargled glass anymore.

"Words can be misconstrued," he told me, his tone gentle as he traced his fingers along my thigh. The robe wasn't much for keeping his touch at bay. "Interpreted so many different ways. I am learning the new subtleties the different languages have developed since I was last awake. These don't always translate well."

Curious despite myself, I raised my brows. "Such as?"

"Such as when I take a woman to my bed and feed her, sate her body and her bloodlust, opening myself to her, I expect a closeness to foster. That did not happen with you."

I opened my mouth, then snapped it shut again, the audible click of my teeth earning me a faint smile.

"As evidenced by your continued reaction. You hate me for some reason." He danced his fingers along the outside of my thigh. "You weren't running from the others—you were running from me."

"Don't flatter yourself," I snapped. "I was leaving all of you. I just didn't regret leaving you." The harshness of the sentiment didn't make it any less true. Alfred nodded once, the stroke of his fingers on my thigh not so much eliciting goosebumps as soothing.

Yeah, I didn't want to look at that too closely at the moment.

"Tell me what I did wrong, Hellion. I have offered you great offense. Enough that Maddox is willing to break with me, as is Rogue."

So this was what bothered him. Losing his friends. Of course. The little kernel of hurt that swam up irked me. Why should his affection for them have anything to do with me? Of course they mattered more. We were *not* friends. Mutiny kept me silent though, because I wasn't willing to betray how much his words affected me.

It didn't make any damn sense anyway.

This whole conversation might be easier if I got off his lap, but he had an arm around me and he was both warm and safe. Maybe the attack had affected me more than I wanted to admit. I glanced up to the ceiling where the black cloud had been like a tornado in the room, and there was no evidence of it.

"It's gone," Alfred assured me, even though I hadn't asked.

"What was it?" Of all the things we'd discussed during my initial tenure here, we hadn't discussed what the hell a shadow taint was, and I didn't think it had anything to do with that inky cloud thing. *That* had been a first.

In all the fucking, biting, draining, and drinking, I hadn't seen one of those before.

With a sigh, Alfred glanced down at my thigh as he nudged the robe a little wider to give him more room to trace patterns against my skin. "Succubi are demons, yes?"

"Yes."

"Can you leave a little of yourself behind on someone you've fed on?" He glanced at me from beneath his lashes, and there was no hostility in the question, just simple inquiry.

"I can set off an orgy," I admitted, one corner of my mouth kicking up. Chin lifting, he stared at me a beat and then did something I couldn't have predicted.

He laughed.

The sound came right up from his belly and radiated out like a fountain of warmth. My smile grew as his expression lightened, and he squeezed my leg. "You are why the reception turned into a wild hunt's worth of fornication."

"And I'm not even sorry about it." Except... "Hopefully, whoever you got laid with..."

He snorted. "Laid is the word for sex? For fucking?"

"More or less."

"Then the one I wanted wasn't there, so I didn't indulge."

Huh.

"It did make for some amusing explanations as my guests came back to themselves. I do believe there were a few who didn't expect to find themselves entangled once more or ever." A careless shrug. "However, is that leaving a piece of yourself there?"

"In a manner of speaking," I said, a little curious about who ended up together. Then I thought about those shifters in the kitchen and skipped right on past that. In a few months if there were little ones running around, it might be better if we forgot about my consensual non-consent. Though it really wouldn't have affected them if they hadn't wanted to do it. I just removed the inhibitions. "I don't get it back, that piece, it's just…like lighting a match. The spark travels, feeds the fire, and poof…" I made a motion like an explosion with my hands. "It's gone."

"Then you do not do as some other demons do. Not all demons are equal."

He didn't have to tell me that, but I nodded. "I tend to avoid other demons. Succubi aren't really considered that high on the scale of things." Too often we were treated like whores there to service their pleasures. As unfair as that was, a lot of succubi were content as long as we could feed. It was a really narrow ledge to walk along.

The morality of the situation didn't faze me in the slightest. The presumptuousness, however…well, they could go fuck themselves. I said as much to Alfred, and he spread his fingers out over my thigh again, stroking slowly almost like he was petting me. "I had a similar presumption," he admitted. "I did not see why you would rebel when I could feed you pleasure upon pleasure. When all of us could."

"Because I'm not a fuck toy," I told him drily. "No matter how I'm drawn on paper. There's more to me than that." It took everything to keep the wounded note out of my voice. Particularly since he'd been delving through my memories when he drained me. "Or was that all you saw when you fed on me?"

"I saw your house," he told me as if I was being ridiculous. "The shop where you worked. Your friend Elias."

Fuck.

"I saw your loneliness, Hellion."

I snorted. "I'm fine."

"Now," he agreed. "You weren't then. You were isolated, alone, and fighting to survive against everything and everyone, including us. Or maybe…" He eyed me for a long moment. "Maybe especially us."

"I didn't want to be a vampire. What does this have to do with what that thing was?" Because really, I wanted back off this subject before it pissed me off all over again and he reminded me what an asshole he was. The fact that he was being so nice to me was really throwing me off.

The corners of his lips twitched as if he were privy to some joke he didn't plan on sharing. "Shadow demons can leave a piece of themselves behind, they can implant it in a person, let it continue to feed their misery, aggravate them, and in turn, that misery gives the demon pleasure."

"Implant it?" Disgust curled through me. "Like the critter in *Alien*?"

'Cause that was fucking disgusting.

"When you all said taint, you meant I still had some of Dorran in me."

He inclined his head in a slow nod. "Yes. Infusing into your cells. Shadow demons can, if given enough time, consume their prey until they are a mere shadow of themselves and then…then they become like them."

I'd been turning into a shadow demon.

A full body shudder crawled over me, and Alfred tightened his grip to pull me closer, and fuck if I didn't just lean into that grip. "I didn't want to be a vampire," I said, gritting my teeth to get the words out. "I lost that fucking battle. I would rather *die* than be a shadow demon."

His gaze sharpened on me. "I will not let you die," he told me, ice in his tone. Inflexible. Arrogant. Haughty. Asshole. There it was. I needed to hold on to that. "I will not let the shadow demon take you either."

"Why the fuck does he want me?" Seriously, I was not that great. "I'm pissy. Temperamental. I do not like most people. I would rather just do my own thing and ignore the rest of the world. I'm no great catch."

Another of those laughs escaped Alfred, warm, heady, and masculine. It left my pussy soaked and need clawing up through me.

Fuck. Me. *He's an asshole.* I had to remember that.

Though it grew difficult when Alfred studied me with soft, enigmatic eyes and the color seemed to shift in them. Darkening and then growing lighter again. Like they were a stormy gray shifting and changing with the weather.

"You're stunning, Hellion," Alfred stated as if it were fact. "Stunning. Powerful. Unique. Taking you now would be next to impossible. You were already fighting him off when I got there. More, you were fighting his possession of you, even though he pushed himself into you again."

I wrinkled my nose. "Is he dead?"

"Sadly," he continued, sobering. "He is not. What was done to Anton is what he wanted to do to you."

"Wait, he infected Anton, and he was possessing him that way?" It hadn't felt like a real possession, but Alfred nodded regardless. Sucking at the inside of my lip, I shuddered again. "Poor Anton."

"He will be properly avenged," Alfred said. "I will deal with the shadow demon myself so he understands there is no claim on you he can make."

Avenged. I kind of felt bad about Anton. I didn't know him, hadn't really wanted to know him to be honest, and now he'd been... "What did you do to him?"

"It doesn't matter," Alfred said. "We have strayed from the initial point."

"Um, it kind of does matter, because you did something in here, too. When the inky heartburn cloud from hell showed up." I studied him, looking for any twitch or change in his expression. "You said you had something else you could try, then you kissed the hell out of me."

I paused for a second as he began to chuckle and then groaned. I hadn't meant to make a pun. Stroking my thigh, Alfred's touch climbed higher with each pass, and when he drifted his touch to where my thighs met, I slid them apart.

"Pleasure is anathema to a shadow demon," he told me. "They need pain and torment." Dorran had definitely taken pleasure in me in the cell, but he'd also inflicted pain. It kind of sucked because on some levels, I'd actually liked Dorran. Granted, he was a means to an end.

Alfred slipped a finger along my labia and traced the slickness. Shivers radiated through me that had absolutely nothing to do with the cold.

"We were discussing my offense," he reminded me, probably a good idea, because he added a second finger so he could trace around my clit and down. The touches were far too gentle to give me more than a tease, and it took effort to keep my hips still and not chase his fingers.

"Hmm," I said, keeping it noncommittal. "We have discussed a lot of things."

After another teasing pass over my clit, then he plunged both digits into me, and the stretch was pleasant. When he curved his fingers forward and traced them inside, the little detonations of pleasure began to tighten into a chain. Fuck.

"We have," he agreed, skating his thumb over my clit. "If I continue to pursue your pleasure, to ease you after what you experienced, will this continue to cause offense?"

What?

"You don't know?" The outrage lost a bit of impact as he continued to thrust his fingers and my hips arched to meet them. Fuck, that felt good. I was still tucked into his lap, and he fingered me with almost relentless focus, edging me right up toward orgasm, but not quite over. The chill of earlier faded, and I was hot.

Burning up in fact, and I wanted the robe off, but that might mean moving, and hell, he pressed his thumb down on my clit. Right there…

But rather than let me plummet over, he slowed his motion and then halted, three fingers now buried in me and his thumb a kinetic presence right over my clit. Not touching, but just there.

"If it will make you hate me more, I will stop."

I scowled, then fisted his shirt and dragged myself toward him. Somehow, I shifted to straddle his lap and hand, all without losing his fingers from where they were thrust inside of me. "I will be really fucking angry if you stop right now."

The corners of his mouth curved again, the fullness of his lower lip looking ripe and ready for sucking on. I could feel his cock, the thickness of the erection as I began to roll my hips and ride his fingers. He held perfectly still, and the angle was ideal. I ground down to get the clit pressure, and then up and down against him to drag his fingers over my g-spot.

Sweat beaded along my brow, and I shrugged out of the robe, peeling it off, and Alfred glanced down at my breasts and then up to my eyes. "Do you want to come, Hellion?"

"Yes." Stupid question. Simple answer.

"Do you want *me* to make you come?"

I slowed my own roll and leaned my head back. It bared my throat, but I swallowed as I thought about it. "You're really trying, aren't you?"

"Yes," he whispered, and there—just at the edge of the single syllable, there was an edge of urgency.

"You just bit me," I told him, my breath coming in gasping pants, and need a vibrant thing in my core as I clenched on his fingers, but I kept still otherwise. "You walked out into that garden and sank your teeth into me like I was there for your pleasure."

Alfred didn't look away when I dropped my gaze to his eyes.

"I didn't want my throat bitten. Dimitri damn near ripped it out when he tried to turn me. It terrified me, and you did it without regard for me. Then you plundered my mind. Drained me and forced me to drink over and over." My mouth went dry, and the knife's edge of desire I had been riding on teetered precariously toward the earlier anger. "You gave me no choice but to turn."

He nodded slowly. "When you said yes…"

I nodded. "I agreed. So I could get even. If it was the only way to escape that nightmare, then I would have done anything. Even fuck you."

Which I had. But I divorced myself from it. I didn't even really recall much of it to be honest. I hadn't wanted to remember it. At least with Rogue, he had been blunt about answering the violent need in me, and then I incited him, too. Maddox and Fin had been courting me in their caring. But Alfred…

"You think I only used you," he said, carefully turning the words over. "Like so many have treated succubi before."

I nodded. I didn't want to be a thing. "I'm a person," I reminded him. "There were things I wanted, things I needed, and none of you wanted to listen to me."

"But you let Maddox claim you. How is his helping steal you from that prison and trying to complete your transition any different from what I did?"

Sliding my hands to his shoulders, I leaned forward until our mouths were bare millimeters apart. "Because he asked. He made me a promise in that cell. A promise I believed. A promise he wanted to deliver on. A promise he regrets failing." And because… "I love him."

Something alien flared in Alfred's eyes. Jealousy?

Surely not.

"And you love Rogue and Fin as well?" His tone didn't change.

"I don't know, maybe. I know they care about me. They acted like it. They didn't just treat me as a possession." Rogue had helped me to escape. Fin hadn't turned me over the moment he found me.

Alfred glanced down at his hand where he continued to cup my pussy, three fingers vanishing inside of me. "And I do."

At first? Definitely.

Now?

It was…

The doors to the suite opened, and Alfred stiffened as I twisted on his lap. Eleanor stood there, and she stared at me for a beat before she dipped into a curtsey. "My lord."

"Get out," Alfred said, not bothering to look at her. "Never enter my chamber or any other in this wing without permission."

She paled.

Okay, maybe I was a bit of a bitch, but I rather enjoyed the look on her.

"I thought you would need…"

"Nothing," he clipped out. "Do not make me repeat myself."

No mistaking the genuine threat there, and she yanked the doors closed, slamming them in her haste.

With a sigh, he pulled his fingers from me, and I let out a little whimper.

"Hellion," he almost groaned. "I'm trying to do what you want here."

"Then let me come," I told him. "You can use your fingers, but your cock would be better."

Surprise flickered across his face.

"What?" I said, licking my lips and reaching for the ties keeping his pants closed. "You just kicked that bitch out, I was hot for you before. You definitely deserve to come now."

Puzzlement slid over his face, but I had his cock in my fist, and he gritted his teeth as he locked his gaze on me. "I do not want you to regret this."

"Do you want me, Alfred?"

"Yes." No hesitation.

"I want you," I admitted.

What? How many times do I have to say I was complicated? Get over it.

"More than you deserve," I continued. "Maybe more than I do." I gave his cock a pump, stroking him from base to tip.

"Will you regret this?"

"I don't know," I told him honestly. "Will you?"

Another stroke, and whatever tether he had on himself seemed to snap, because he gripped my hips and moved me forward and then impaled me on his cock. There was no gentleness in him as he slammed it all the way home. The stretch burned, but it was exactly what I wanted.

Hands locking me in place, he thrust up, filling me over and over, the angle setting my body on fire as sparks danced before my eyes. This was what I wanted—hard, fast, and... Fuck, he locked his lips around my nipple and sucked on it as he moved me. It was like he was trying to bury himself as deep into me as he could.

The first orgasm had me clenching down on him, and he

went still as I cried out. My vision splintered. It was as though all that denial just intensified the rush, and I could barely focus for how much I was shaking.

He smiled slowly at me as I fought my way back to the surface. "Are you with me again, Hellion?"

I licked my lips, because damn, his voice was delicious. I gave him the barest of nods, and he pulled me free from him and lifted me up as he stood. One moment, we were on the sofas, the next, at the bed. His clothes were gone, and he flipped me onto my stomach and then fisted my hair before he lined himself up and thrust back into me. The angle took him deeper, and I let out another cry.

"Still with me?" he demanded.

"Fuck yes."

"Then hold on, Hellion. I will make it up to you." I could barely make out the words beneath the pounding thrusts that promised to fuck me right through the mattress. The fabric of the bed covers teased at my nipples, and I was scrabbling to fist the sheets to hold on, but he set a brutal pace that tipped me right over, and he kept slamming into me as he pushed me from one orgasm to the next.

When he pulled out and flipped me onto my back, I was damn near boneless and his cock still jutted out, thick and proud, glistening from being deep in my body. Alfred kissed his way up my thighs to my pussy, and then he buried his face there.

I was crying from the stimulation by the time he finished giving me another three orgasms. I couldn't fucking see straight for how sensitive I was. Every brush of his skin seemed to set mine alight. He kissed a path across my stomach to my breasts, then worshipped there for a while.

That was what it felt like—fucking worship, and I couldn't remember the last time I'd been so adored.

Before them.

Before Fin.

Before Maddox.

Before Rogue.

I'd never been this adored.

Alfred reached my throat, and when I tensed, he lifted his head and moved to kiss my jaw. Somehow, I grasped his hair and then tugged him down to kiss me. His face was slick from eating me out, and I tasted myself all over his lips.

He lined his cock up between my thighs again as I dragged my legs up to cradle him. Fuck, it was effort to move. I...I could feel the pulse of his heart.

"Can I bite you?" The question slipped from me between kisses. The dazzling smile on his face took what little breath I had left. Pleasure fountained through me at his delight.

"Nothing would please me more, Hellion." He offered me his throat, and I licked my lips. Did I want this?

The answer crashed through my system like a landslide. It was a resounding yes. I sank my teeth in, and he thrust into me again. Locked together, I began to feed, and the memories that spilled into me weren't from the past.

Well, not the distant past.

They were his memories of seeing me in the garden.

And the need it evoked in him.

This time when I orgasmed, he came with me.

CHAPTER 14

"If I cannot influence the gods, then I shall move all hell." - Virgil

Rogue

The walls of the club vibrated with the pounding beat of the music blasting from the oversized speakers placed throughout. The flashing lights strobed over the writhing bodies occupying the dance floor. The smell of sex and blood filled the air amidst the sweat and drugs. This was not any place he would have ever chosen to visit.

The server came over to him again, her fourth pass in the last hour, and the sheer scrap of cloth covering her midsection and breasts did nothing to disguise her nipples or the lack of panties. Her bare ass rubbed his arm, but one glance from him, and she backed up a step. "My lord..." The words slipped brokenly from her, but he had no interest in her offering or her service. With one jerk of his chin, he motioned her away, and she stumbled through a curtsey before she fled.

If she insisted on offering again, he'd snap her neck and she could explain it to her employer in the morning. The vampire was too damn young to be that oblivious to cues from her elders. Rogue didn't even bother with a drink as he studied the crowd. It had grown over the last hour, if that were possible, with more bodies, and precious few of them humans.

Catching movement from the corner of his eye, Rogue didn't react when the large man took a seat at his table. Despite his impressive size, Brandt moved with surprising lightness. He always had. Most facing him in battle expected a berserker, never quite realizing assassination had always been his forte. Not that it mattered.

"M'lord," he greeted Rogue, skipping the formalities of a bow which would only draw more attention. It was enough that Brandt had taken a seat at his table. When Brandt was in the club, no one bothered him unless he summoned them to him. For him to approach Rogue served as a signal to those of the younger generation, and the crowd on this level began to clear as they suddenly found the need to be elsewhere.

"I received word that Dimitri Sobolov sought you out for protection."

A long sigh escaped Brandt, but he only nodded. "Three months ago."

"Remove the protection," Rogue told him. It wasn't a request.

"He has gone to plead his case to Eamon." Even with the thrum of music pulsing through the club, there was no mistaking the apology in Brandt's voice. "If I'd known…"

Rogue waved it off. Brandt's loyalty wasn't in question. He served the seven. What favors he did for others was his own business, unless the seven ordered otherwise. "If he sticks his head up…"

"Would you like it delivered alive or dead?" Brandt's question had merit.

"Alive preferably," Rogue stated, though it wouldn't bother him in the slightest if he were dead. Fiona, on the other hand, wanted to deliver that death herself. His little *sváss* deserved to have what she wanted. "Maimed is fine."

Brandt chuckled, a snap of his fingers bringing a new server to their table along with two steins of beer. Though he hadn't asked, nor did he have any intention of drinking it, he nodded amiably to the other vampire. It was better to observe the niceties.

"I will do what I can for you, m'lord," Brandt stated, and it was as good as his bond. While he would not go into Eamon's hold to fetch the little shit, he would definitely deliver him if he put himself out in public. "I would request a boon of you."

Of course he would. The cost of doing business. Sparing him a half-glance, Rogue gave him a curt nod to continue speaking.

"Rumor says war is coming."

"Rumor often speaks out of turn and without informed consent."

Brandt grinned before slamming back the whole of the stein of beer that had been delivered to him. After setting it down, he wiped the back of his hand over his mouth before continuing. "Agreed. But if it is coming, I would like to request that you not ask me to choose a side."

Rogue eyed him in truth rather than a passing glance. As big as he was, the man still ducked his head rather than hold Rogue's gaze. Few could hold any of their gazes—another aspect of his little *sváss*'s personality that he adored. They didn't frighten her.

Pissed her off? Definitely.

Intrigued her? Quite probably.

Frighten her? No. Even when they triggered her fears, it was not them who provoked her terror.

It did not matter how many centuries he and Brandt had known each other, the assassin could not meet his gaze for longer than a few seconds.

"That's not a boon anyone can grant. Even if Alfred agreed, you would need the word of the other six." And any number of little rebellious factions who might try to take advantage of any battles.

"I am aware," Brandt admitted, casting a glance at Rogue's still untouched stein of beer.

With a gentle push, Rogue nudged it over to him. "How many have you already secured agreements with?"

In mid-reach to take the stein, Brandt froze. He had two choices—answer the question and admit how many he had been in contact with and risk offending Rogue, or deny he had any and risk offending them by thinking he could play this game.

There really was no win for him.

Another sigh escaped him. "Three."

"Who?"

"Would it be possibl—"

"No," Rogue told him. "I will not grant you this boon. I expect you to admit that you had seen and spoken to me if they or theirs came to you directly."

Though, of all of the seven, only Alfred shared his power with others. The other six were not so giving.

Or at least they hadn't been. It had been a long time since Rogue had to face one of them. He gave Brandt a moment to collect his thoughts as he scanned the club again. It wouldn't be a stretch to find one of them here. In the years since

Alfred went to sleep though, Rogue had only heard of two being active.

Eamon and Gemma.

Both kept to themselves. Eamon with his hoarding, he loved nothing more than to conquer the wealth of each new age, and amused himself by amassing and destroying whole fortunes only to amass another one. Gemma, however, was far more secretive and avoided the other six at all costs. Rogue had met her precisely once. She and Alfred had been dancing around each other over some inconsequential piece of land.

When Rogue had questioned Alfred about it, he'd only said Gemma needed an excuse. She was lonely, and the haggling gave her a reason to talk to him.

The negotiations went on for three years.

Then ended as abruptly as they began.

Gemma had been an odd guest, but Rogue only had to deal with her occasionally. She'd been fond of Maddox to a point, but that was also before Maddox had needed Alfred's bite. Shaking his head, he focused back on where they were.

The seven didn't get noticed unless they wanted to be, but they were also hard to hide if you knew what to look for. He did.

They weren't here.

At least not right now.

"Synove," Brandt said finally. "She came looking for Eamon a couple of weeks ago."

Synove was tricky. Rogue didn't know her at all, but Alfred had often warned about her tendency to play mental tricks and dabble in illusion. With that in mind, he swept a look over Brandt, who had finally clutched the stein Rogue offered to him but hadn't yet drunk it.

"Who else?"

"Eamon, obviously." Brandt grimaced. "He owns the club

now." Rogue slid him a look, and Brandt held up his hands in surrender. "He owns it, as a silent investor. You know how he is about coin."

If one of the seven owned this place, then Rogue shouldn't be inside it without their permission.

"And I am his host," Brandt admitted. "You have broken no protocols, and you will always be welcome in my establishments."

Pretty words. Dangerous subtext.

"The last?" For now, he would not allow any other reaction to leave him. Alfred had sent Maddox and Fin to discover where the other six were. They were all waking. Fiona's initial turn and final transition had stirred everyone. It had been a beat that roused Fin and eventually Alfred.

"Cyril." Brandt cast a worried glance at him, and well he should.

Cyril and Alfred loathed each other.

"All three have granted you this immunity?"

"They have."

Rogue shook his head. "Do not betray us."

"I would never," Brandt said. "I have offered no allegiances, and I will pledge none. You have asked for me for a service. You will pay handsomely, yes?"

It went without saying, and that he brought it up was tantamount to offering an insult. The other vampire grimaced, then bowed his head.

"My apologies, m'lord."

Rogue didn't respond. The vampire didn't deserve a response. Rising, he motioned for him to stay seated, even as the other vampire rose. The throbbing music, the stench, and the underwhelming lack of respect... No, not lack of respect...Brandt was just readying himself for the potential power shift if the seven went to war.

The last time had decimated vampire ranks and left them in sparse numbers for decades.

It had also damn near wiped out the dragons and Rogue's own people.

Ending a war before it started was the better idea.

Rogue threaded through the crowd, taking the path that led him directly through the throng. The crowd grew more frenzied. The smell of hot blood being spilled attracted his gaze, but he took only enough time to note that it was human and she was being fed on by three or more. They would have bodies on the floor before dawn.

Not his problem.

Humans came and went.

They would also pay the price if this went to full-blown war.

Outside, the cloying and humid air of the club gave way to the cool streets of Paris. The city teemed with nightlife. The more exclusive clubs, like Brandt's, were harder to find if you didn't know where they were located.

A sweep of the area let him pick out the watchers.

Four of them.

Only two were vampires.

They had chosen good vantage points. One even looked like a tourist. The shifters stood out more. Particularly the wolf.

Rogue's senses sharpened. They weren't trying to corral him. Most likely, they wanted to follow him. Find Fiona.

The keep wasn't a secret. But only those retainers who had proven loyal had survived their sojourn and the offering.

The others had been executed.

Brutal, but efficient.

Alfred had been furious with him for taking Fiona away. Particularly with the threat of the seven, but she was in far more danger with them than away.

Or she had been, until the idiots in Dallas decided they would punish her for existing.

Fin had given them some quarter after Isaac's abandonment.

There was no coven in Dallas any longer.

Rogue slid his hands into his pockets and started walking. He had no use for large cities or crowds of people, but he blended, half-fading from their perceptions as *too normal, average,* and *unremarkable.*

It worked better when he could blend into nature itself. Elves were not seen unless they wanted to be seen. Too many had forgotten that gift. His watchers hurried after him, one abandoning his pretense when Rogue faded from easy observation.

A smile creased his lips as a second watcher cursed and then strained to locate him, while Rogue made his way down an alley toward the boulevard with its midnight cafés and smells of wine and pastries. It was one thing to hunt them, to try and pin them down. It was another to remember that he and his brothers were not prey.

They would never be prey.

As soon as he left their direct sight, he moved swiftly, scaling a building and then stripping out of the loose shirt and slacks he'd worn to the club. The shift rippled over his skin, but instead of fur, he sprouted feathers and then he snapped out his wings as he alighted on a shadowy perch. The white plumage would definitely be noticeable if he moved into the light, but he was content to observe.

The two vampires tailing him raced through the alley. It was only after they hit the boulevard that they slowed. They hesitated, searching the crowds for any sign of him, but he had well and truly eluded them. Only the older vampires even remembered the hybrids, most still considered them myths and legends.

Fine by Rogue. It made them so much easier to pick off. If they had been able to maintain pursuit, he could and would put them down. They would not find Fiona on his watch. He maintained his vigil, then soared between the buildings, and the hunters now became the hunted.

They searched for nearly two hours before they finally gave up on their quest and retraced their steps to the club. Rogue found another shadowy perch as they moved to a car idling on the street rather than the club itself. The window rolled down, allowing them to give their report. From his angle, he couldn't see who was inside, but he had his suspicions.

"We lost him," one of the vampires said. "He was just strolling, then…"

"I have never seen anyone move that fast," the other said, as though apologizing. "We hunted, but we couldn't find his trail."

"Idiots," the voice inside was distinctly masculine. "Did you look *up*?"

"Y-Yes," the second one stuttered. "We took to the rooftops."

After an hour. Rogue almost snorted. It was pathetic. The fact that the first one's head went flying off his shoulders confirmed the one inside the car agreed with him. The second vampire startled and tried to back off…but not fast enough. The hand that locked on his throat kept him in place.

When the door moved, Rogue waited a beat.

Cyril stepped out of the vehicle, only switching which hand he held the vampire in as a concession to stepping free of the door. He moved with purpose, the second vampire strained against his strength, his feet paddling in the air.

"Do you understand that when you hunt the targets I give

you, that you cannot treat them like some idiot made in the last seven centuries?"

The vampire wheezed out an answer. It was barely audible because Cyril wasn't allowing him air. Rogue studied the whole interaction with a kind of dispassionate amusement. Unlike Brandt, who was built big and broad, Cyril was far more lean. If Brandt were a battering ram, then Cyril was a rapier—the blade in the dark.

He flung the vampire away from him and then stilled on the darkened street. The other clambered to his feet, still wheezing and looking genuinely terrified. Unlike him, Rogue didn't give into the urge to move, particularly when Cyril turned his gaze upward like he knew he was being watched.

Of all of the seven beyond Alfred, Cyril was the one Rogue knew the best.

He'd been the one who'd slaughtered half of Rogue's people.

Someday—and that day would come soon—Rogue would take his vengeance, Alfred's treaties with them be damned.

"Find the succubus," Cyril said finally without lowering his gaze. "Find her and bring her to me." Was he testing whether a threat to Fiona would make Rogue or any of them break cover, as if they were green warriors untested by true battle? "Alive, Roger."

The idiot's name was Roger. Rogue wished he could roll his eyes in this form. His little *sváss* would be so amused.

"Bring her to me intact and alive."

"Yes, Lord Cyril," Roger muttered, going to one knee. "I will gather our men. We will find her. The coven in Dallas had a lead on her, but they have all failed to answer any further inquiries."

Cyril snorted. "Go away."

Roger didn't have to be told twice. The vampire rushed

away without a second glance at his fallen comrade, leaving Cyril alone, save for his driver who had not left the car.

"If you're there," Cyril said slowly, pulling out a pack of cigarettes and tapping one out. He paused to light it, and then exhaled a stream of smoke. "Then tell Alfred I expect him at the castle before the next full moon. He would be advised to bring the succubus with him."

Politics.

They were so useless.

"Remember the last time I had to find my own target, Rogue." Cyril finished his cigarette, then flicked it away before he slid back in the car, and it glided along the street, leaving the headless corpse behind.

Rogue maintained his position for a little longer, letting the last sounds of the vehicle fade away before snapping out his wings and launching into the sky. He left Paris behind, turning east toward the mountains.

He would take the message to Alfred.

It was after dawn when he touched down at the keep. He could have traveled faster, but he paused twice on the way to investigate other sightings. If Dimitri had gone to Eamon, then there were a handful of bolt-holes the little coward might be stashed away in.

None of the vampires he'd found knew where the little shit was. Rogue made sure there were none left to tell the tale of who had been there. Particularly when they tried to snare him in a witch trap.

The bloodlines had to be growing weaker, because the progeny had become that much stupider.

The keep was quiet, the pre-dawn gray just giving way to the growing pink light on the horizon. He shed the feathers and wings for skin, cracking the vertebrae along his spine as he regained his height. The cold air wrapped around him like a familiar lover, but he strode to the entrance and let himself in, the locks giving at his grip as the wards recognized him.

Eleanor gave a jerk at his arrival, spinning to face the door as she pushed her hands into the pockets of her skirt. She half-stumbled into a curtsey, her eyes widening at his state of undress, but Rogue didn't have time for her or her need to curry favor.

Cutting her off with a slice of his hand, he said, "Not now." Then strode away. Her little strangled noise of objection followed him, but fortunately, she did not. He paused on the stairs to listen.

Fiona's heart was upstairs.

He needed to speak to Alfred, but he wanted to check on his little *svász* first. He ascended the stairs, then followed the steady cadence of her pulse not to her room—or his—but to Alfred's. Had the two finally found some kind of accord?

Knocking once, he let himself in. Fiona lay on Alfred's bed, red hair spilling everywhere, beautiful and perfect, with only a sheet pulled up to her waist.

"We had a visitor while you were away," Alfred told him as he tossed him a robe. Rogue caught it one handed and then glanced from Fiona to where Alfred stood by the fire. One he'd apparently just started. Dressed only in a pair of slacks, he held a drink in his hand. "The shadow demon sent a proxy. Anton is dead."

Fuck.

"We'll have to modify the wards." The shadow demon should not have been able to get inside, but if he'd managed to infect Anton, then he would have been a ticking time bomb, a Trojan Horse that allowed the shadow demon to piggy back inside on him.

Still, he took another step toward Fiona. Her chest rose and fell with the slow, deep evenness of her breaths.

"She's fine," Alfred informed him, and poured another

drink before he held out the tumbler to him. Rogue dragged on the robe before he took the glass and then moved over to the fire. "She fought him off, but he still managed to get a piece of himself into her."

"You got it out?" It wasn't really a question, yet he asked it anyway.

A single nod.

"And you've repaired things with her?"

The baleful look Alfred gave him only made Rogue shrug.

"You were the one who said you needed to find an accord with her."

"And you helped her run away."

The corners of Rogue's mouth curved. "She needed to run. We all do. She took far less time than any of us—especially me—if she is already finding it in her to forgive you."

They were both silent. Alfred stared at her. "She is remarkable."

"We knew she would have to be," Rogue reminded him. "Cyril wants to see you."

Alfred grimaced.

"He also wants you to bring her with you."

"Not happening." Inflexible. Immovable. Intent.

"Agreed, but they are all looking for her."

"She marks a change," Alfred said.

"It's going to mean war." He'd had this conversation with himself. "The seven do not want change."

"No, we don't. But if we do not change, we will die out. Already, we had grown complacent, fading in our interest in this world."

Not always a bad thing. "Brandt has asked to sit it out, to be neutral. He wants to give allegiance to no one. Eamon owns his clubs though. Gemma is on the move. Cyril is already hunting you."

"Then it is only a matter of time for the others."

Which was why Maddox and Fin were tracking them.

"You really don't care that this turns to war?"

Alfred cut him an impatient look. "Of course I care. I care that it affects you. It affects them." Then he looked to the bed. "That it will affect her. I don't care about the rest of them. Not anymore."

Tossing back the whole of his drink, Rogue considered his next words carefully.

"Ask."

He shook his head slowly. "It's not time yet for that question."

They'd known each other too long for Alfred to push him on this. Some instincts had never faded in Rogue, and this was one of them. In time, the question would be needed. They did not need it now.

"Are you two fighting?" The sleepy voice looped around him and pulled his attention to where Fiona sat up on her elbows.

"No, Hellion. We were not fighting."

"Not right now, anyway," Rogue teased her. "We were only discussing the news."

She wrinkled her nose. "Good news or bad news?"

"Both," Alfred said. "Would you like Rogue to curl up with you, Hellion, so you can sleep a little longer?"

Containing his own reaction, Rogue merely waited.

"I'd rather have both of you," she said. "Don't you need rest, too?"

"No," Alfred told her, but he put aside his drink and crossed to the bed anyway. "But I will stay with you if you'll have me."

When she flicked those green eyes to him, Rogue chuckled. "You never need to ask me, little *svász*. I will happily stay with you. Though I think if you and Alfred are finally getting along, I shouldn't intervene."

She rolled her eyes then held out a hand. "I'm just tired. Apparently, shadow demons give the worst form of heart burn."

Another chuckle escaped him, and he wasn't alone in that. Alfred slid onto the bed next to her, and she curled against him but kept her hand out to him. Shedding the robe, Rogue slid in on the other side of her, then cupped her face to press a kiss to her lips.

She searched his face, lifting her own fingers to his cheek. "What's wrong?"

Burying his concerns deeper, he shook his head. "Nothing." He could almost feel the weight of Alfred's regard, but Rogue kept his focus on Fiona. When Maddox and Fin first began their ridiculous plan to get her out, he'd not thought much of it or her.

Wild.

Unpredictable.

Untamed.

She was all of those things.

But she also had a heart, one she kept hidden behind traps and secured with her barbed tongue. Capturing her lips in another kiss, he poured affection into it, affection he hadn't let himself feel in far too long. He had a wealth of it carefully stored away, and he would give all of it to her.

Fin had been right. She was perfect for them.

He could almost hear her throaty laughter as she declared she was a succubus, it made her perfect for everyone, but there'd been an element of hurt in there, too.

Finally letting her have a breath, he met Alfred's gaze over her shoulder.

"Something is wrong," she said with a sigh. Lying to her was not the way to do this, but they had too much to explain.

Lips against her shoulder, Alfred solved it for both of them when he said, "Yes, Hellion. We will tell you after you rest and we sort it out from greatest to least important. Much of it is politics…"

Fiona made a gagging noise and flopped back dramatically against the pillows. "Vampire politics *suck*."

Mild surprise curled through Rogue, but when she let out a laugh at her very bad pun, he couldn't help but smile.

"Yes," he told her. "They do."

A yawn split her jaw. She faced him as she turned on her side, and Alfred pulled her back against him, molding her back to his chest. Mirroring her posture, Rogue studied her as her lashes dipped. "I'll need a scorecard," she mumbled.

"We'll try to do that for you." If it was what he was thinking it was. If not, Fin would explain it, or maybe she could. Almost too swiftly, she dropped off again, and Rogue narrowed his eyes. "How much damage did it do?"

"Too much," Alfred admitted. "But I think this is more. This is…trusting us." There was a hint of wonder there. "I don't know how well she slept in her absence."

Nor did Rogue for that matter.

Gathering her hand in his, he held it against his chest with his fingers just over her pulse.

"Sleep, brother," Alfred told him. "I'll keep watch."

Rogue didn't think he had it in him to sleep, there were too many variables to be accounted for, but the soothing rhythm of her pulse swept him away, and he let his eyes close.

For a little while.

CHAPTER 15

"Knowing your own darkness is the best method for dealing with the darknesses of other people." - Carl Jung

The seismic shift with Alfred awaited me when I woke the next day and seemed to grow with each day after. Absurd as it may seem, I didn't trust the change. Shocking, I know. Yet I couldn't escape the sense that more than just I had changed. Maybe that should comfort me, but I wasn't altogether certain I trusted it.

First, I'd woken after sleeping so hard, I was actually groggy when I awoke. Alfred stood near the window, sipping coffee as he stared over the landscape. The bed on either side of me was cool, so though I'd gone back to sleep sandwiched between Rogue and Alfred, they'd both risen before me.

"There is more coffee," Alfred told me without turning around. The broad lines of his bare back held my attention as I brought my sleep gritted eyes into focus. I wasn't sure I'd ever get the hang of being a vampire.

Or hybrid.

You know, whatever. I'd slept like I'd gone on a bender, drunk on…him? I grimaced at the thought. "I'd love some," I said, then winced at the croak in my voice.

For his part, Alfred didn't comment. Though he did move to where a tray had been set with a carafe and filled a large mug. He added cream and sugar to it. The temptation to snark at him scratched at the back of my throat, but fuck it. I wanted the caffeine too much. Well that, and the hot drink to go down my dry throat.

The faint quirk to his eyebrows suggested the swell of java-deprived lust flooding me was written all over my face. "Thank you," I said, still hoarse, like I'd been screaming my way through a concert. His fingers brushed mine as I wrapped my hand around the mug.

"You're welcome, Hellion. Shall I have breakfast brought up?"

I took a long swallow of the coffee and closed my eyes, in part to savor the taste and in part to block out the hint of tenderness in his gaze. Not quite up to that much of a shift, I would rather just down the drink and cobble my scattered braincells back together again. After the third swallow, I lifted my gaze to his stormy one.

Nope.

I wasn't there yet.

Another mouthful, and I shivered. My nipples tightened against the chill in the air, and I glanced down with a faint smile.

Still naked.

The sheet had gathered at my waist, and there wasn't a stitch of clothing on me. Running my tongue over my teeth, I tried to get my shit together. There was a little too much torrid emotion rioting in my system. Pushing the sheet back,

I went to slide out of the bed, only to have Alfred catch my arm to steady me and the coffee mug.

"Thank you," I repeated, and the words were odd on my tongue. He traced his fingers up my arm lightly, and those eyes of his saw way too much.

"You're hesitating with me again."

"I just woke up," I argued, pivoting to head over to the fire with my coffee mug cradled in my hands. "Right now, my only interest is coffee."

His soft chuckle traced over me like a caress as I stood in front of the fire. The heat left half of me warm. I should have expected it, but it was still a surprise when Alfred stepped up behind me and draped the robe around my shoulders and then helped me slide one arm, then the other into it. I took another sip of coffee as he tugged me around and then ran his fingers over my chest, then to my breasts and down to my hips, before he dipped his head and pressed a kiss to my forehead.

It was damn near sweet.

And not at all what I wanted.

Before he could straighten, I wrapped an arm around him and fisted his hair. I just caught the smirk on his lips as I pulled his mouth to mine. He tasted of the coffee he'd been drinking with just a hint of sweetness. His mouth moved against mine slowly. I might have asked for the kiss—fine, I demanded it—but Alfred took it over, one arm banding around me until I was pressed right up to him and the other, like me, keeping my coffee mug steady as he devoured my lips.

Consuming me was what it felt like, as though he couldn't take and I couldn't surrender enough to satisfy him. The hum in my system redoubled, and when he scraped his teeth over my lower lip, I let out a shudder and tilted my head back. He pressed kisses along my jaw and then down my throat.

A chill stole through the languid heat his kiss left behind, but then he pressed his lips over the spot he'd bitten me. The mark he'd left there. I suppose in some ways, just like Maddox, he'd claimed me. Only…

He traced his tongue over the faintly ridged marks, and a whole body shudder held me hostage. Sensation ping-ponged through my system, and if he hadn't caught the mug, the coffee might have been sacrificed.

"Fuck," I exhaled as he blew a breath over the damp mark he'd made, and a whole new set of goosebumps shivered over my flesh. My nipples, that had already been tight, now pinched to the point of painful.

"There is not always pain," he whispered against my throat. "No need for fear." Another lap of his tongue, and the zing of it went straight to my pussy. I groaned as I fisted his hair, not sure whether I meant to push him away or drag him closer. "This mark binds us—you to me, but me to you." Another stroke of his tongue, and need shimmered through me.

If he wanted me to beg, I was getting awfully close. The moment that thought surfaced, I growled, and he chuckled again.

The bastard.

Another kiss and a lick, then we moved. The air whispered around us. He had both hands on me now, gripping my ass and lifting me. I dropped mine to free his cock from his pants, and it jutted out toward me—hard, hot, and ready to impale me.

Oh. Yes, please.

Back against the wall, I hitched my knees to his thighs so I could get the right angle, and then Alfred continued to tongue the mark like he was eating me out. The pulse of conflicting sensations charged through me.

I swore I could feel his tongue on my clit, the hot press of his lips as he nibbled and stroked. At the same time, my pulse hammered a warning. Tendrils of icy fear crept through me, and even the prospect of terror galvanized my adrenaline and pissed me off.

Alfred raised his head, and then his mouth was on mine again, the kiss bruising and brutal. I wanted to slide down and take his cock into me, but he kept my hips still, denying me any freedom as his tongue swept against mine.

Over and over, he kissed me until I was digging my nails into his shoulders and clinging to him, more to stay on my feet than anything else. The whole world narrowed down to the contact where his mouth met mine. The thunderous cadence of my pulse meshed with a second, deeper beat. The caress of his fingers against my throat a moment before he wrapped his hand around it, and his thumb stroking over the bite mark had me floating.

A giddy, drunken sensation I'd never experienced without feeding on lust until I threatened to burst washed over me, and still my heart kept rhythm with…his heart. That was the second, deeper beat.

Alfred.

Again and again, he devoured my mouth, tongue stroking against mine, until I threatened to orgasm from the kiss alone. Still, I ached for more. How long we stood there, locked together just kissing, I had no idea. The gentle squeeze of his hand had me surfacing as little detonations of pleasure erupted in my system.

If this was what he could do with only a kiss, what the hell had we been doing wrong before? Because this was…

"Hellion," he murmured, the command in his voice

inescapable as it rolled over me, but it didn't sink into my bones so much as break like water rushing over rocks and submerging me in the heat of his need. Eyes open, I found him staring at me, the storm of gray darkening as his pupils expanded.

No words, but I knew what he asked me as he used his thumb to tip my chin up and my head back.

"No pain for you," he promised, and the silken thread of it coiled around me in invitation and request. "But I need you."

Surprise flared through me.

Need?

Some of it must have shown on my face because he smiled almost gently. "Yes, Hellion. Need. But I will not take from you again, nor will I demand you tell me yes."

I traced my tongue against my teeth. My whole body was primed for him, and at the same time, it wasn't hunger or lust, it was pure...*need*.

Even with my head at this angle, I could make out the column of his throat and the way the muscles moved as he swallowed. The mark of my teeth was still visible where I'd bitten him the night before. The memories he'd poured into me, of seeing me, had all been flavored by his awareness of me in the keep and of Rogue's warnings. Yet none of that had mattered a damn when he found me in the garden.

A singular thought had pulsed through him, territorial and autocratic. Then he'd bitten me and...

I flashed my eyes open again. I'd trusted Maddox at my throat, and since making my feelings abundantly clear, Alfred had listened to me this time. I licked my lips, the taste of him still lingering. "Please tell me I don't have to say something about an offering..."

The wickedness in his chuckle delighted me, and I blinked at him almost stupidly. They didn't laugh much. Fin did, almost all the time. It was part of his playful charm. Maddox did in between verbal spars, though I enjoyed it.

Rogue? Alfred?

They were far less inclined. Yet there was something utterly captivating about his soft chuckle, especially when he brushed his lips to mine again. "Hellion, offerings come from those who serve us, you are not here to serve me."

The words stabilized the sway of the room and locked my pulse in time with his.

"Yes, I heard you when you described how succubi are treated. That was *never* my intention," he told me. "I may be old and I may need to adapt, but you, Hellion, you are to be my queen and never my slave or servant. If anything, I will be yours." The declaration seemed to flame in his eyes, amplifying the heat beneath my own skin. "You ran from me —from us—because I treated you poorly."

An unexpected lump settled in my throat.

"I will never let you believe I will do that again. Even if I never taste you again, it changes nothing, Fiona." The way he said my name riveted me even more firmly than the storm unleashing in his eyes. "This world has not done right by you. I will change this world, and it will treat you better."

Holy.

Shit.

I...

He kissed me again, and I wanted to climb him like a pole. If anything, I fought against his grip on me to sink down on his cock. The sudden intrusion as he filled me to the hilt had us both hissing. Leaning back, I shifted the angle so I could ride him, even as he stood there, legs braced, holding me up as though I were light as a feather.

Every thrust seemed to bring us closer, but it wasn't just the pleasure. It was more than...

Fuck it.

I closed the distance and tilted my head back to bare my

throat, even as I gripped his hair. His hand spasmed against the column of my neck.

"Take what you need, Alfred," I whispered. The shiver of apprehension gave way to shudders of pleasure as he pumped into me with more force. Without a word, he spun around, and I landed on the bed, with him following without ever losing our connection. He had one hand braced against the covers to control his weight, but I wanted to feel him.

With one light squeeze around my throat, he pounded into me with a ferocity I found myself craving. Every stroke of his cock pushed the air from my lungs, and I stared up at his wild eyes. This wasn't transition. This wasn't change. This was…

Everything.

As with Maddox, the emotion in Alfred's eyes held elements of lust and need, but something far deeper that made the lump in my throat grow.

Adoration.

When I teetered on the edge of orgasm, his hand slipped from my throat allowing me to take a heady breath. With agonizing slowness, he dropped his face to my neck and kissed a path to the mark. His tongue began to lash against it as his cock did my pussy. I gripped his ass, writhing up to meet him.

I needed this.

Needed him.

Then his teeth pierced through the mark, and I went rigid as pleasure rolled over me in waves. If someone had put me inside a bell and struck it, I couldn't have vibrated more. I clung to him as the world splintered and fractured. My vision whited out, and I floated on an endless sea.

Slowly, I grew aware of his breath against my neck and the weight of his body holding me down. I was boneless. Liquid. Destroyed.

And when I opened my eyes, I smiled up at him.

I was whole.

What an unnerving fucking thought that was.

We lingered in bed for most of the day, toying with each other, kissing, and sometimes just being. It was altogether bizarre and somehow…

"Hellion, what are you worrying about?" The nudge of his voice pulled my attention up from where I had been stroking his chest. We were sprawled together on a thick fur in front of the fire. Food had been brought, a bit of a feast really.

"Where are they?" I flicked a look up at him. "Rogue was here and now he's gone again. I haven't seen Fin or Maddox since you sent them away on the isle." I hadn't even heard from Fin. That was unusual enough, and after weeks of absence, I found myself missing them.

He let out a sigh and spread his hand over my ass. Apparently, he'd grown rather fond of that part of my anatomy. He kept gripping it. "How much do you know about the seven?"

I shrugged. "Seven brides or seven brothers?" I mean I kind of knew a little.

One arched eyebrow, and I huffed out a breath. He didn't always appreciate my humor.

"In time," he said slowly, "I will adapt to your references. I will insist you teach them to me so I can join in your games."

The corner my mouth kicked up. "Fair. So…where are they?"

Because I didn't want to get distracted from what I needed to know. Right now, I did need to know, as abrupt as that seemed. Alfred wrapped his hand around my throat again, and I didn't even flinch. He'd bitten me twice more since I'd given him permission, always on my mark, and fuck if I didn't get off every single time.

Nothing more faithful than a convert, I supposed.

It helped that he'd meant every word about me not being

a servant. The stroke of his fingers teased me as he settled his hand into place. "Tell me what you know about the seven, first."

I sighed. "Not much. They're like the seven dwarves or something. Specific ancient vampires, of which, I'm guessing you're one. Which makes you one hell of a cradle robber." I paused. "Or me a grave robber, depending on how you look at it."

Laughter eddied up through me. That was a whole new kink to consider.

But the faint quirk to his lips and the flicker of exasperated impatience in his eyes silenced me. Probably sensitive about his age.

Guys were like that.

A snort escaped before I could stop it, and this time, he just exhaled.

"You are incorrigible."

"Yes," I agreed. "I am." But he'd asked a question, so I bent my knee and swung my foot back and forth in the air as I studied him. It was nice to just be sprawled over him, the heat dancing over our skin. I loved the way the light played against his eyes.

And I was officially turning into an orgasm-soaked sap. I needed to slap myself.

"The seven made all vampires, but they are a legend. Boogeymen. Or at least, that's what some vampires say when they are in their cups."

A single nod.

"You're one, right?" I didn't really need him to answer, but confirmation couldn't hurt.

"We were more than seven initially," he told me. "Only seven survived the last war."

Oh. "That doesn't sound ominous at all."

No smile or mirth. He stroked his thumb over my pulse,

circling his mark, but not quite touching it. Probably better not to have my brains leaking out my ears while he educated me.

"All of us drink blood," he said slowly. "But each of us is gifted in other ways. Gifts...that carried over."

"Does that make you a hybrid?"

"After a fashion," he said. "Though that is not the word we would use for it."

"Okay, we can play twenty questions, or you can tell me whatever it is you think I'm going to freak out about and I'll let my freak flag fly so we can both get over it." Largely because this verbal dancing suddenly made me nervy as hell. I didn't get nervy. Shit happened, I accepted that for what it was, but this? This was going to make me batty if he kept it up.

That, and I wanted Maddox here. My mind kept flitting to him. Like...

"Your freak flag is just a phrase, yes? You don't actually have a flag."

I opened my mouth to explain, but there was a glimmer of amusement in his eyes. "Great," I drawled. "Everyone's a comedian."

That earned me a slap on the ass and the sting sent a jolt of heat through my system. The answering flare in his eyes told me we'd be playing with that again.

Yes, please, and thank you.

Don't get distracted, Fiona. I gave myself a stern shake.

"I need to keep up with you, my queen," he murmured, and that sent an entirely different kind of jolt through my system. But rather than focus on that, he sat up, one arm around me to keep me in his lap as he met my gaze. "Twelve of us fell. We refused to take sides in a war for Heaven."

Wait...

...what?

"When our brother broke with our father, we were charged with holding the line. We would not draw on them, nor would we wage battle. At the height of the war, we were cast out and consigned to Earth."

I might not have gotten the best grades in math, but I understood basic equations.

"You're an angel."

"No," he said slowly. "No longer."

He didn't have wings.

As if anticipating my question, he gave me a small smile and slid the hand from my throat to face. "The wings burned when we fell. The intent was to kill us. But when we were created, we were created of celestial material and infused with the breath of life. Even consigned to mortality, we evolved."

Oh. "I bet your pops was pissed."

He gave a shrug. "I wouldn't know. We have heard nothing from him since that fateful day. Where once my brothers and sisters were numerous, then they became only twelve. The evolution gave us the taste for blood, and the gift of life—the breath of it—gave us the power to change others. To grant them immortality."

"You don't just trip over something like that," I said. "I mean, I can't imagine you woke up and went, huh, think I'll bite that dude and give him my blood and see what happens."

I don't know why I was trying to lighten this up, but the weight on Alfred seemed almost interminable, and to be honest, as real as I'd always known Hell to be, I really didn't want to think about Heaven.

Good girls versus bad girls and all that stuff.

Besides—hello, demon.

"I would give anything to understand your mind, and I think in a millennia, I will still be just as captivated," he admitted.

"That's sweet, and I'm very much a sure thing at the moment," I told him, aware of his cock hardening between my thighs. "I promise, you can impale me on that lovely dick of yours after we figure this out, because I think I'm going to need a scorecard."

He chuckled. "It is not that complicated, Hellion." While I loved how he said my name, I had to admit there was a thrill at the possessive way he intoned 'hellion.' "Yes, it took time to discover the ability. Some sooner than others. Some abused it, others refused to consign anyone to our fate. Not all were thrilled to find themselves earthbound, forever banned from all we'd known, and trapped amongst warring tribes of creatures, from elves to shifters to the humans in between."

"Yeah, I can see how that would suck." I coughed. "Pun not intended." Another faint smile. Look at me—scoring two in a row. "But you said there are only seven of you left. What happened to the other five?"

"I killed three of them," he said, and I stared at him. "We are hard to kill, not impossible."

Oh. Shit.

"Of the last two, they were killed by others. The battle lines had been drawn, and those five were the most fierce in the creation of vampires. They were intent on raising whole armies. They thought to settle the scourge of the earth by force."

The story he told was filled with blood and vengeance, terrible battles, and a mind-numbing death count. In some ways it was better—or worse, depending on how you looked at it—than that last season of *Game of Thrones* in terms of body count. It also sounded awful.

"Until Rogue," Alfred told me. "I'd never made another vampire."

That information floored me.

"What?"

"Rogue was my friend, and while the others consolidated power and rules, I wanted to learn about them. So I found a way to travel amongst them. To be 'normal,' and once upon a time, I could pass for human."

Bullshit. But I kept that opinion to myself.

Nothing about him was human. He would draw the eye of every person in every room. Power rested on him like a shroud. Even when he was an asshole, he was a powerful asshole.

"The creation of hybrids was forbidden, by all of us, to protect the races who were on the brink of extinction."

"But you've made hybrids."

He gave a careless shrug. "I was not building an army, nor trying to eradicate a people. I wanted to save men I cared about. Men who had become my companions. Then Fin had his premonition, his prophecy about you, and while I couldn't be certain, I understood that when you came into our lives, everything would change. Again."

"Yay?" I questioned it because he actually sounded tired.

"I have no regrets, Hellion. Nor will I, and I will allow nothing and no one to take you from me. That is where they are. Tracking the other six. Finding their bolt-holes. Because before they can launch another war, I want to deal with them. We have avoided most conflicts by avoiding each other, some of us sleep, others just burrow. The world has grown tiresome." He flicked his gaze over me. "Or it had, before."

I raised my brows.

"I find myself far more intrigued by it now than I have been in a long time."

As sweet as that was, I couldn't shake the apprehension in my gut. "That's why we're here, though, isn't it? And not out there? You said you don't pursue, others come to you?"

He nodded.

"So, your retainers and the other vampires who were here?"

"They pledged to me, and I afford them some protection."

"Okay, but you didn't make them?"

He shook his head. "My blood is powerful. The closer to the seven a vampire is, the stronger they are. I have only ever made four."

Oh.

Shit.

I stared at him.

His smile wrenched something inside of me. "I promise you, I never thought of you as a servant. It was my pleasure to fix what that idiot tried to break and bring you over. I can't regret it because it means you will live, and I have waited countless lifetimes for you."

Okay. Sign me up, I'd officially gone over to the sap side. I cupped his face and kissed him. "I'm sorry I ran."

"No," he whispered. "Rogue was right. I needed to dislodge my head from my ass and treat you better. You didn't want to be here, then you had to deal with the offering amidst everything else."

"It was a little much." But I was a big girl. I could handle it. Something in my chest tightened, and I pressed a hand to it. Alfred frowned at me.

"What is it?"

"Just... I can't shake the feeling something is wrong." Until I said it aloud, I hadn't even realized that was what I was feeling. His eyes flared, and then he touched his fingers to Maddox's mate mark and a dozen images assailed me.

That, and a dragon's pained roar.

"The healthy man does not torture others—generally, it is the tortured who turn into torturers." - Carl Jung

Alfred

Fiona all but vibrated where she stood next to Alfred, but he couldn't focus on her fully while he assessed the retainers in front of him. Both Fin and Maddox were missing. Neither had answered any calls. Distance could be a factor, but Alfred had no doubt that Maddox would not linger away from Fiona for too long if he had a choice in the matter.

No, something had occurred. Whether it was one of the other seven or not was the only question he had, followed shortly by *where* were they. Rogue had returned to them briefly, all too briefly, before he left to follow their path. He had some idea of where they'd gone. Or at least, where the seven were, so it would be a matter of tracking to each location.

Alfred's only regret was he had not acted sooner. If he'd paid closer attention, he would have noticed the lengthy absence and how out of character it was for both. They were neither cavalier nor leisurely when it came to tasks he asked them to do. And contrary to what his hellion believed, he had asked them. They just didn't observe what he'd *just* begun to learn were modern sensibilities, not too far from earlier centuries, where the language of a request required specific wording.

He and his brothers—and make no mistake, Rogue, Maddox, and Fin were his brothers, more so than the siblings he'd fallen with—had bled for each other. Would bleed for each other. They did not need the pretty words.

"My lord," Eleanor called, pulling his attention to the woman who had on and off through the centuries made herself a place in his court. At one time, he'd offered her shelter because the vampire who had changed her had done so in brutal fashion after murdering her entire family. Then he'd taken her and kept her. Her scars had been deep, but she'd healed, and over time, she'd regained her strength, her sense of self, and her place.

There was nary a shadow of the woman she'd been all those years ago, and no matter when or how long he took his sleeps, she had always come to him the moment he woke.

This was the first time he hadn't taken her to his bed, and that rejection stung. She would have to adapt.

"Not now," he told her. "Unless you have some word on Maddox or Fin." Unlikely as that would be. There were other retainers who were waiting to speak to him, and he had to put on appearances for the sake of possible spies. This was why he'd intended to present Fiona at the gathering, introduce her to those who sheltered under his banner as someone they would lay their lives down for or risk losing them.

Fiona's nerves continued to radiate, and he linked his fingers with hers. It pulled a startled look from his little hellion, and she flashed him a wan smile. The mating mark warned her something was wrong. Mates could feel each other. Another reason to kick himself. He'd been so distracted by needing to win her affection and trust, he'd failed his brothers…

"And what would you say if I were to tell you I did?" Eleanor challenged, and he shifted his gaze to the elegant beauty who stared at him—not at him, at Fiona with such daggers in her eyes. "Would my words be worth your boon then?"

When his hellion glared at Eleanor, fire in her eyes, Alfred tightened his grip on her hand to keep her at his side. If Eleanor wanted to play a game, he wouldn't indulge her. "What do you know?" A series of possibilities rolled out to him. Eleanor had not left the keep as far as he knew. She'd already found new rooms when she'd been forbidden from their wing. She'd tried to move in the first day of her return, and he'd sent Anton and Jonathon to make her comfortable elsewhere.

But she hadn't left. As with every other time he'd awoken, she set herself up to live in his court and to 'assist' however she could. He never needed her to be a hostess, but perhaps he'd indulged that fantasy for far too long. She definitely had not, nor would she ever occupy Fiona's place.

Eleanor cut a look to his hellion again. "Perhaps we should speak in private, my lord." Then she motioned to the reception hall. "It is a matter for you and I."

The tension in Fiona only amplified as she stared at Eleanor. He had little doubt if he released his hellion's hand, he would be picking up pieces of the other vampire. Though she was older by centuries, Fiona's blood came from Alfred directly and was boosted by his brothers. She would not make an easy target.

"Leave us," he instructed the room, but kept his grip on Fiona to make sure she understood it was not she who was being asked to leave. Her fingers spasmed against him, and he stroked his thumb along her knuckles. The trust between them was still in the nascent stages. Nothing could be left to chance where she was concerned.

Not again.

What few retainers had been waiting made themselves scarce. Eleanor's lips compressed as she flicked a look to Fiona, then to where her hand was in Alfred's before she glanced up at him again. As always, her eyes dipped as soon as their gazes connected. Demure. That was how he'd always thought of it. Very few could hold his gaze. Four others to be precise, of which, one of those precious few stood with him.

Having had her gaze locked on his—and even better, burning into his as she argued with him and defied him—he couldn't ever be content with anything less.

"Speak, Eleanor." The fact that he'd had to order it at all served as a raspy file across his goodwill. She should have told him the information already, rather than trying to enter a flirtatious bargain. If he had to take it from her…

"It would be best if you took the memory, my lord," she suggested. "I feel my words would be inadequate."

Fiona snorted. "Wow, you must really be desperate."

Eleanor shifted her gaze to Fiona again, and her eyes hardened. "My words and my memories are for my lord, just as my body has always been, no matter where he dallies now."

They did not have time for these dramatics or for Eleanor to irritate his hellion into the role of scorned woman. Before he could say anything though, Fiona perched on the arm of his throne, and he slipped his hand from hers to wrap around her. Both acts were natural, as if they had been doing it their whole lives.

Oh how much sweeter would the long centuries have been if he'd found her a millennia earlier?

"That's really scraping the bottom of the barrel," Fiona said, her tone so amused, Alfred found himself intrigued. The way her mind worked…it defied all conventional thought and fascinated him. "I mean, you're really stretching. So he's pounded you. Were you trying to piss me off? If so, oops."

"I doubted it would upset you," Eleanor lied and then smiled, her expression so patently false, it made Alfred's teeth ache just to look at. "Your type don't mind who they pleasure or who their partners pleasure…"

Alfred tapped a single finger against the arm of the throne, and Eleanor jerked her attention to him. Blanching and wild-eyed, she dipped to her knees. "Forgive my tongue, my lord. I have not cared for being replaced."

"That would suggest you had her place to begin with," Alfred stated. "You did not. Now, tell me about my brothers. If this was merely a vain attempt to strike at my queen, I will be cross with you." It was the only warning he'd give her.

Fiona glanced down at him, a faint smirk on her face. He stroked her side, an offer of comfort, but also petting her for his own pleasure. She trusted him to watch her back and took her eyes off the only potential threat in the room.

That pleased him on the basest and most primitive of levels.

"I literally can't tell you, my lord." Eleanor's pained statement pulled his attention, and he eyed her.

"Why not?"

She opened her mouth, but nothing came out. Defiance

flared in her eyes, and she tried again. Finally, she sagged. "I cannot tell you, my lord. Only that you must take the answers from my blood."

"Did you leave the keep?"

Not once had her gaze lifted to his. Nor did it now. If anything, she cut it to Fiona. "After the gathering, after you sent me away that night. Yes."

The fact that she remained focused on Fiona wasn't lost on either of them. "Can you tell me?" his hellion inquired, and he frowned.

Eleanor said, "I have a message for you, yes."

Tired of the games, Alfred rose. He gave Fiona a small squeeze of warning before he was in front of Eleanor and had her by the jaw. No more force was necessary. When he dragged her gaze up to him, she practically wilted.

"Enough," he ordered. "Tell me." Not allowing her any choice but to look at him, he compelled her obedience. The compulsion vampires could enact came from the blood they took from their creators. The spark of life in them—the divine he supposed, though he loathed the term—demanded respect and obeisance.

Face crumpling as blood began to run from her nose, Eleanor shook her head. "I cannot, no matter how much I might wish."

"You've been compelled already." It wasn't a question, and the woman nearly sagged in his grip, the relief flickering in her eyes as he withdrew the force necessary to make her obey him. "That is why you want me to take the answer from your blood."

One of his kin.

He cut a glance to where Fiona sat and studied her. "You do not care for the offerings," he said gently, as gently as he could when impatience crept through him. "If you wish—"

"I'm a big girl," she told him sternly, arms folded as she

descended from the throne. "I can handle it. But how do you know her blood isn't trapped or bespelled somehow?"

A fair question. He cut a look to Eleanor, but her tear-stained face revealed nothing. "There is nothing on this Earth that can poison me."

"But the ones who did this aren't from this Earth, are they?"

Still considering, he nodded once. His kin were not of Earth. Like him, they carried the same sparks of divinity. They'd traveled the same roads after they'd all blazed fiery trails through the skies, burning away their sanctity and leaving only their most base selves behind.

"But poison is not how we kill, Hellion."

"Very well, but if she kills you, I'm ripping her head off."

The corners of his mouth twitched, and he contemplated her with a long and steady look. He absolutely believed her. It was not loyalty or obligation that made her speak, but something far more rare in his life.

Passion.

"I will be quick, Hellion." Then because he needed it as much as she. He pulled her to him for a hard, swift kiss even as he held Eleanor away from them.

"I'll watch your back," Fiona promised, and he smiled.

"No doubt." He surveyed the room. They were alone. The closest heartbeats were in the farthest corners of the keep. Turning back to Eleanor, he pulled up her wrist and bit down. She still couldn't look away from him, even if she kept trying to push her gaze elsewhere. Disappointment gathered in her eyes, but at the first drop of her blood on his tongue, and the room seemed to spin away as the memory flashed to the forefront.

Synove regarded him, her pose almost languid as she leaned against the wall, arms folded and dressed in what he imagined was casual, modern clothes. The denim leggings were similar to what he'd seen Maddox and Rogue both wear. She cut a lean figure with her stunning fall of midnight hair and piercing topaz eyes.

"Hello, brother. I thought this would be the best way to speak as it is all too rare that we ever wish to be in each other's company. Your pets came looking for me. I considered sending you the druid back as a warning and keeping the dragon, but I care less about war these days. I suppose I have grown complacent in my years. I have slept for a long time. The world is much changed."

For a moment, she looked weary. Solitude, as much as they might crave it, was not good for their kind. Not for as long as they embraced it.

"No, I did not kill them. I did not even speak to them, though the boy speaks enough for a thousand men."

Alfred didn't chuckle, but he did allow the amusement to fill him. Fin could try even his patience, and there was nothing he loved to do more than poke at people until they cracked.

"The dragon is much changed from our last encounter, more settled than I thought his kind could ever achieve. Though, I suppose he is the last of his kind." She waved a hand airily, as if dismissing the topic. "This woman is one of your lovers, so I embedded the message in her to go only to you. It can only be retrieved through her blood, as you have discovered. You should know, she offered me the location of your keep if I were to take her into my care and keeping."

He almost wished he could be surprised by the betrayal.

"She would very much like to murder your latest pet. Consider that knowledge a gift from me to you."

And that was all it was. Synove could not stand deception. Whether she realized it or not, Eleanor had signed her own death warrant by even making the offer to her.

"Cyril is hunting you."

That he already knew.

"If you want to avoid a war—which I would very much appre-

*ciate, because the less I am forced to deal with our kin, the better—
then offer them her head, separated from her body of course. They
do not want the change she represents."*

It would never happen.

*"They have indulged your peculiarities for far too long, but this
one will not stand." Synove sighed and then turned as though she
looked directly at him. All he could see of her location came in to
sharp relief. She was in a city of some kind. It was night, and the
city beyond her was illuminated by lights.*

*"Aelfraed," she intoned his ancient name. "We do not handle
change well. They do not want it. They do not want her. Eamon
and Cyril are allied in this. They have sold out your pets and sent
them to a place where you may not be able to retrieve them." She
canted her head as though looking past him. "Gemma and Keeley
do not wish this fight any more than I do, but they will side with
Cyril. They do not want change. Wyman, however, remains as
always, a wild card."*

*She hesitated, the weariness he'd glimpsed earlier filling her
eyes.*

*"Do not reach out to me. I will not answer. I will not answer
any of you."*

Then she was gone, like mist. He pulled his teeth from
Eleanor and regarded her as she filled his view again. Paler
than earlier, she stared at him with hollow, knowing eyes.
Had she seen or known the content? Possibly both.

It didn't matter.

"Where did they send Maddox and Fin?" Because now she
had better damn well tell him if she knew.

The main doors burst open as Rogue strode through.
"They are in the prison. They've been turned over to the
warden and a horde of his shadow demons for keeping."

Fiona let out a wounded sound, and Alfred glanced at
Eleanor, who gave the barest of nods, utterly resigned to her
fate.

"You could have still been happy," he scolded her. "You did not have to get greedy."

"Will you forgive me then, my lord?"

"No," he told her bluntly. Then he snapped her neck. He spared her the pain of the death a traitor deserved, then twisted her head off. It was messy and the blood fountained, but he ignored it, discarding the head as an afterthought.

Rogue didn't even give the woman a passing look as he went to their hellion.

"Dorran has them?" Fiona asked, and Alfred sliced a hand through the air.

"He will not have them for long."

"No," Rogue said with a sigh. "But they have moved the prison again, and without Fin, we may not be able to find it."

"You already went." Of course he had. It was why he had been absent so long. "It does not matter, we will find them. Then we will deal with Cyril and Eamon."

"I can find it," Fiona said. Rogue stiffened at the offer. Alfred frowned. Did his hellion possess some magical gifts she had not made him aware of?

All at once, the shadow demon's words rushed back to him. *You're going to come to me, Fiona. When you do, I'll be waiting.*

Fury spilled through him, a rage he hadn't experienced in so long, he couldn't remember when. "No."

"I can't leave him there. I can't leave either of them there. Maddox is in pain."

"And he would suffer it a thousand times over if it kept *you* safe," Alfred said firmly. "You will not go. Rogue and I shall find the prison. We will bring them home."

"Alfred—"

"That is final, Hellion. You will not go." As much as he hated the pain flashing in her eyes, he would not risk her.

He would change the world for her, but he could not risk *her*.

Rogue pressed his lips to her temple. "We will find them, little *sváss*. I swear it."

But Fiona didn't look at him or at Alfred, her gaze was elsewhere.

They had to find them. If they didn't, she'd never forgive them.

Alfred would never forgive himself.

CAN FIONA TRUST THE NASCENT BOND SHE'S FORMED WITH Alfred and the deepening connection she has to Rogue? Or will she take matters into her own hands to retrieve Fin and Maddox? The warden did say she would come to him. Is she cursed or a Succubus Blessed?

To keep up with Heather and all her series, join her reader's group on Facebook.

USA TODAY BESTSELLING AUTHOR
HEATHER LONG
SHACKLED SOULS BOOK 3
SUCCUBUS
BLESSED

NP
PARANORMAL
PRISON

SHACKLED SOULS BOOK 3

"I am not afraid of an army of lions led by a sheep; I am afraid of an army of sheep led by a lion." - Alexander the Great

What the hell made him so great, anyway? Dude died when he was like thirty-something and not even in battle. Nope, he died from a disease. Or maybe someone poisoned him. Be kind of sad if he died by poison… well, for him anyway. Points to the poisoner, because you couldn't beat the asshole in a battle. Sneaky fuck for the win.

As it was, I stood outside the gates to Nightmare Penitentiary. Of all the gin joints in all the world… "Here I fucking am," I called. "Open sesame."

Nothing happened. Because of course it didn't. The locations to access the penitentiary moved. Or so said all of Alfred's sources. Rogue and he had discussed this at length. Fin had tracked it before. Fin had cracked it like an egg. Fin had been the one to send him the coordinates when he asked for his help.

Unsurprisingly, the entrance was *not* where it had been when they 'rescued' me. Not that I recalled much of the actual location. Rogue had been too busy racing me out of there for me to see much more than a puke-worthy blur.

Foot tapping, I eyed the alleyway. Of all the places for the prison entrance to be, a little used footpath in the center of a London park was not where I would have put it. First of all, it was a pain in the ass to even get in the country—okay, it wasn't *that* bad. But according to 'sources'—and I used that term loosely because no one was talking so much as Alfred and Rogue had to tear it out of them—they had sped up how often the entrance moved.

There was no guarantee it would be here…

I kicked an empty can, and it flew down the damp, dark alley, then bounced off something and came flying back at me.

First, I forgot how much force there was in my kicks. Second, fucking yes because there was something there. I dodged the aluminum projectile and danced forward, hands extended. It was one thing to hit the field with a can, it was another to crush my face into it.

When my palms encountered it, there was a buzzing sensation that radiated all the way down to my bones and up into my teeth. Fucking bizarre feeling. But it didn't hurt. Magic was so bizarre. Okay, I'd called in a few favors—ha, they thought they were the only ones with friends—but the witches I consulted told me three things.

One, no one could find the penitentiary and I was fucking nuts to even consider it. Well, no shit, but I was looking anyway.

Two, the prison was designed to keep *creatures* in, not out. Side note, did you know I qualified as a "creature" now? Check that out. So, it was designed to keep me in, not out. Since I needed to get "in," that worked for me. Besides, I was supposed to be in there, right? Inmate?

Ex-inmate.

Escaped prisoner?

Whatever.

Three, and the final little thing worth mentioning, people who voluntarily go in have more options for getting out. It was part of the magic of the place. I hadn't been there as a volunteer *before*, but I was all about it now.

Because on the other side of that field was my dragon *and* my druid. I wanted them back, dammit. I didn't tell anyone they could take them.

I applied some pressure to the field, and it seemed to stiffen under my touch. Huh. I knocked, and the air hardened to wood. Retreating a step, I studied it. There was nothing discernibly different. I mean, other than me doing a damn mime impression. I was still standing in this filthy, smelly little alley with the distinct odors of rotting food perfuming the trash and the damp, moldy kind of mildew that stone got.

What? It stunk back here.

Pinching the bridge of my nose, I sucked in a deep, smelly breath and then gagged.

Fuck that.

New plan.

I held my breath.

Better.

The more force I applied, the more resistance I met.

"You will not go after them," Alfred ordered me. *"Do I make myself clear?"*

"The words 'fuck' and 'you' come to mind," I responded. *"I can't leave them there."*

"Little sváss, *I know you're worried. But they will be fine. If I know them, and I do, they will free themselves."*

Rogue's words helped.

For three days.

Then the dreams grew darker and bloodier.

By day five, I was crawling the walls and Alfred locked me in my fucking room.

Day seven, I was out and on my way. I paused only long enough to let the bones in my legs heal—kinda no choice there—and to steal a phone.

Fun fact, I could survive a sixty-foot drop and do a super-hero landing.

Not such a fun fact, I broke both of my shins doing it.

Sexy? Yes.

Fun? Not so much.

I half-expected Rogue or Alfred to swoop in and drag me back inside, but I healed within an hour—yay—and was on my way an hour after that.

The speed thing was going to take some getting used to. I slammed into one tree and broke it. I hit another, and it nearly broke me.

Baby steps, I supposed.

But… I eyed the alley again, still not breathing. So far so good. I didn't want to pass out, and the smell wasn't making me wish I was dead.

It had taken me three days to make my way to London. At the moment, it was nearing a month since I'd seen them at all. Too damn long in my opinion. Even thinking about how long it had been distracted me.

Shaking it off, I focused as I squinted down the alley. I eased forward a step, and the resistance pressed back against me. But it stretched.

Oh, so it wanted foreplay.

I could do that.

I rolled my body forward, not stepping so much as sliding, and the field flexed and the view of the alley warped as I eased forward with agonizing slowness, step by step. But the field stretched with me, elongating the alley, and I had to fight the urge to shove or rush.

Seriously, I possessed patience. Alfred was so full of shit on that. I'd waited days, despite his ordering me to stay put.

Oh, I kinda wished I could have been a fly on the wall when he discovered that no, he couldn't compel me. I hadn't made that shit up when I said I wasn't worried about what my maker could or couldn't do. They'd *tried* to order me around. So had that dick Isaac.

Guess what?

I really did have an obedience issue and problem with authority.

So suck it Alfred.

The tiniest bit of guilt niggled at me. I'd left them a note. But they had to know I couldn't leave Maddox and Fin here. Yes, Alfred needed to protect me. It was violently sweet in a kind of psychotic way. Angelic way.

Psycho-angelic?

Yeah, I liked that.

Rogue? He definitely wanted to protect me, and I loved them both for it.

That thought froze me mid-step, and I just sort of stood there as the field was all kinds of warped around me.

I loved them.

I loved all four of them.

I loved them so much it hurt.

Huh.

The field popped with enough force, it was worse than the pressure of a plane on ascent or descent. Fucking ow.

I clapped my hands over my ears as the gates to Nightmare suddenly loomed above me. The darkened metal and twisted stone a thing right out of a...well, a nightmare.

Triumph slid between the cracks of dread those gates inspired, and I ran a hand over the front of the coat I was wearing. Lowering my hands, I took a tentative breath and some of my lightheadedness passed. Apparently, I could really hold my breath a long time.

Cool.

The air smelled more of mossy rocks and forests. There was a hint of something long-closed away. Kind of like sawdust and disuse, but it was hard to pinpoint. The path wound between huge boulders and led right up to the gates themselves, which might as well have been affixed into the side of a mountain.

I craned my head back. No might as well about it. It was definitely on the side of the mountain.

Okay, that would almost be neat, but I wasn't here to sightsee.

I half-expected the guards to rush out and grab me, but guess what? It was deader than a doornail out here. No birds. Barely any sunlight. It had been dark back in London, but we were definitely not in England anymore.

Another breath, and I rolled my shoulders back.

Apparently, I had to do everything myself. They weren't even going to capture me and drag me inside.

How damn inconsiderate of them.

Marching up to the gates, I glanced around for their version of a doorbell. If I had to actually break into the prison itself, I was going to report them all to the management.

Rolling my head from side to side, I gave a little shudder and shook off all the apprehension. The sudden influx of nerves wouldn't help anyone. And I had to find Maddox and Fin. I needed them more than I needed my next breath.

The moment I thought of them, the tug was unmistakable. Maddox was inside those gates. I closed my eyes—don't look at me like that, no this is not the best place, but I still needed to check—and the sense of him pulled me forward almost unerringly. I could find him in the dark without even trying.

I could follow that pull to the other side of the world if I had to.

I may never have asked to be a vampire or their mate, but…they were mine, dammit. I wasn't giving them up.

Ahh, Beautiful. You have no idea how glad I am to hear that.

Tears flooded my eyes as I jerked them open. But all I saw were the gates. Dammit.

Go back, Fiona. Yes? Go back for us and let Rogue or Alfred come. Or better yet, just wait for us. We'll get out of here sooner or later.

Are you insane? I demanded. *Seriously. I did not just jump out of windows, climb down a mountain, break every single nail I had, and figure out how to compel some schmuck so I could get clothes to cross a continent to get to London—where, I might add, I wouldn't have found if several witches didn't owe me a lot of favors—so I could just leave you here.*

I love you, too.

The declaration took a lot of wind out of my temper. But it didn't change facts.

I'm not leaving without you.

He didn't growl at me, but he did go quiet for so long, my heart squeezed.

All right. This is a terrible idea.

I'm very good at terrible ideas.

Yes, you are…

I could almost hear him grumbling, even as his eyes flashed with amusement. As much as he might complain… *You like it when I'm contrary.*

Yes, Beautiful, I do. I have from the very beginning. You're perfect just the way you are. Are you sure I can't persuade you to turn back?

I won't leave without you. I couldn't. The very thought was like a gaping hole in my chest. No, not only could I not leave, I wouldn't.

Beautiful, I plan to hold you to that for the rest of our unnaturally long and decadent lives.

Yeah?

I almost grinned, despite standing in front of these grim and gruesome gates.

Yes. I have a great many bad things I want to do to you.

And some good things, too, I hope. Because Alfred and Rogue are probably going to spank me until I can't stand, queen or not.

His mental laughter suffused me with such warmth.

I'll be sure to bring a balm for your rosy cheeks.

Ass.

But I was still grinning.

Deal.

Now, let's get you inside and that means...

Even as he filtered his ideas through, I could almost taste his weariness. He hid it beneath a veneer of cheerfulness and play. The flintiness in his voice though couldn't quite disguise the pain. Another reason I wouldn't leave him.

I wouldn't leave either of them.

Okay, so...I needed to make some noise. Gripping the metal gates in my hands, I began to shake them with all the force I could muster.

The metal actually screamed in protest, and metal shavings rained down on me. Magic suffused these gates, but thankfully, it didn't burn like those shackles Maddox slapped on me day one.

Hell, I'd almost forgotten about them.

I paused a second, and the sudden silence was almost jarring.

"Seriously?" I yelled. "What do I have to do to get a fucking guard out here? Hello! Dorran!" I slammed a fist against the gate and then yanked. The metal shrieked as it split, and I tore off a whole bar.

Oops.

A soft mental chuckle stroked against my senses. *Just figuring out how strong you are?*

Shut up. I broke a damn nail and my shins jumping out a window. If I'd known I could have punched my way out of the door, I'd have done that.

We'll teach you, Beautiful. Though in all honesty, I think we've all been waiting to see what you could do.

Yeah, I guessed they had. I gripped the gates and pulled, bending the metal as it screamed, and the magic buzzed like so many bees stinging at my skin, but it rolled off me more like a nuisance than a real irritation.

Oh, if magic didn't affect me anymore…fucking *yes*! I'd have to rethink my irritation at being signed up unwillingly, 'cause that was lottery worthy.

Not us?

Pfft. I had you before you finished forcing my transition. Don't play that card with me.

True, Beautiful. You did.

I grinned and stepped through the twisted and crumpled metal and headed toward the main doors.

I lifted a fist and slammed it against the door. That one didn't crumple. Nor did it buckle and blow inward. It did make a dreadful gonging sound.

"Knock knock," I yelled. "Avon calling."

Fin's mental chuckle warmed me.

The door began to crank, the roll of chains and pulleys announcing the locks being lifted and the drop gate pulled upward, even as the doors swung wide.

Dorran stood there, a black stain of shadow and darkness surging out to lick toward me. "Fiona," he greeted me. "My sweet pet. I told you that you'd come to me."

"Yeah, yeah," I told him as I strode forward. The shadows writhed toward me and back, never quite touching as I made my way inside. I had to go in willingly, right? Look at me, all willing and shit. "You also said you'd be waiting."

Wrapping his hand around my throat, Dorran loomed over me and dipped his head toward me as though he planned to kiss me. "And here I am…"

I really fucking hate this guy, Beautiful. Do not let him kiss you.

Really? That's your concern right now?

The shadow demon's lips barely touched mine, and a roar split through the silence of the prison, shaking the entire foundation.

Maddox.

I exhaled, jerking my head back, even as a stupid grin covered my face.

Told you. Fin sounded almost smug. *Go ahead. Let the bastard try to kiss you again and see what happens.*

You know. I just might.

CHAPTER 2

"I've learned so much from my mistakes, I'm thinking of making a few more." - Anonymous

FIN

A really long fucking time ago…

"*Fuil ár gcuid fola…*" the old man droned on, but Fionnbharr stopped listening on the third pass through the incantation. Gathered on the dark knoll, they waited for the last flicker of the sun's rays to sink into the west, consigning the earth to the longest night of the year. The bitter wind cut through his cloak, but the warming spell kept it from doing more than cool his cheeks.

Not all of his companions were so lucky. The older ones might not survive the vigil, but if the goddess wanted to take them this night, then to the crone they went and a beloved journey would they be wished. For the most part, Fionnbharr just wanted the sun to set so they could light the bonfires and open the mead.

There were many fine lasses waiting in the town. Waiting to stream out to find the druids and the vates. Pleasure in the darkest night of the year promised that warmth and light would come again, and he'd like to be balls deep in a few of those lasses and get on that sowing of seed.

There'd been a particularly fetching young maid just arrived from Europe as part of the new lord's retinue. Interesting sort, they'd hosted a feast for the surrounding villages, plied them with wine and rich meats, then offered plenty of work and protection.

Fionnbharr had attended, but had avoided consuming anything. They were the hosts. He was the guest. The law of hosting protected him, but in refusing their gifts, he kept his wits about him, even as the villagers and the other druids drank themselves into a stupor.

It was how he'd found himself in deep conversation with the lord, one he and Aelfraed had then continued each evening through the autumn. The new lord and two of his retainers would be in attendance after the bonfires were lit. Another reason Fionnbharr was eager to get on with the dirge to the sun's death and eventual rebirth.

He enjoyed those conversations, but he enjoyed the fine cunt on a lass far more and it had been some time since he'd been in one.

"Beannaigh dúinn an oíche seo...trí fhilleadh an tsolais a dheonú."

Finally, thank the gods. Fionnbharr flicked his fingers towards the huge pyre, with its wicker shaped effigies of the gods wreathed in dried flowers and fruited offers. The spell for fire rippled through him, and the sparks jumped from his fingertips to light the kindling. Even the stiff and steady breeze couldn't extinguish the flames as they began to cascade upward.

A mile or two away, on another knoll just like this one, the bonfire lit. Then another. Soon, the ring of light would blaze across the whole of the isle. Even in rain, they would keep them burning until the sun was reborn with the dawn.

Until then…

"And now we drink!" Fionnbharr called, and laughter raced through the assembled. Even the greybeards gave him a wry shake of their head as they chuckled. Popping the cork on the flask he'd brought for the occasion, he took a deep drink.

The solstices were the optimal time for visions. As a vate, Fionnbharr's gifts extended well beyond the earthly, and he needed strong spirits and stronger herbs to keep his mind grounded here.

Too many vates let their visions consume them, and he refused to be one of them. It wasn't long before the merriment poured out of the villages and toward the hills. Torches came to life in the towns as they would everywhere this night.

Everyone would be tasked with holding back the shadows and the darkness. For these long hours, they were alone in the battle until the sun god could be born once more. The crone spread her cloak across the land, and it was into her care that they consigned themselves. But the crone had a wicked sense of humor, though Fionnbharr suspected that he'd at least earned her amusement if not her favor.

Leaving the circle of the fire, he made his way down the hill, avoiding the natural trek of the road. The first girl on his list would be waiting for him in her warm cottage, her body naked and her legs spread. She'd asked for the blessing of the crone this night, and he would do his best to see it delivered.

It was the least he could do.

Another swallow of the mead in his flask, and the world shifted.

Fionnbharr paused. He was nowhere near the hill nor the village. Instead, the woods rose up before him, and he swore.

"Not tonight, dammit!" The boon he'd asked should have been granted, but a haze draped everything. The clay flask seemed impossibly heavy in his palm, and his hands went numb. The woods elongated and stretched before his eyes, and the darkness in them rushed out.

In true dark, away from any man-made sources of light, the world wasn't that dark at all. The sliver of the crone's waning sickle hung low in the sky. A glimpse of what could be.

The stars themselves twinkled overhead. So many stars, the jewels of the gods scattered across the sky and draped in their finery.

Turning in a slow circle, he staggered, and the clay bottle fell from his now nerveless fingers. It broke on some rocks. His heart thundered, the rush of his blood, and the world kept swaying as the earth shifted beneath his feet.

This time, he was deep within the virgin woods, untouched by the malignancy of man. The trees were dense, but instead of being trapped among them, he stood in the center of a clearing of a grove of old trees twining together to create an impenetrable wall.

"Fionnbharr," a voice whispered from everywhere and nowhere. He sank to his knees. Poison in his flask.

That was why he saw the shadowlands.

That was why he was here.

Irony, the longest night of the year, the night he would spread his seed to a new generation, and instead, he would die here.

Alone.

The crone always did have the wickedest sense of humor.

"Are you truly this dark and dramatic, or are you trying to impress someone?" The husky voice dragged his watering eyes upward, and he found the most beautiful woman in the world gazing at him. Her hair was the perfect color of the fire he lit, and her eyes a deeper green than the promise of spring. "I have to tell you, this really isn't a sexy look on you, Fin."

His name was Fionnbharr.

"Really? Pretty sure when I'm screaming as you drill your cock into me, Fin does just fine."

A laugh wheezed through him, and he choked on air and blood.

"No," she ordered, catching a hold of his face and forcing him to look at her. "You don't get to die, Fin. You promised me."

"*Cad a gheall mé duit, Álainn?*" At the moment, he would promise her anything. Give her anything. But his life faded. The shadowlands were there, and she was the bridge the goddess sent to him?

Maybe he could embrace his death.

"Drink, Fin," she whispered. "You've lost too much blood."

The strength in her arms cradled him, and he pressed his mouth to her pulse. Oh, he would die a happy man right here.

"You're not dying," she told him. "Do you understand me? You are not allowed to die. I did not come all this way to save you, only to have you die. You promised to put balm on my ass after Alfred and Rogue tan it, and what will Maddox do without you?"

Fionnbharr frowned and lifted his head. The vision of her splintered, and it was Maddox leaning over him. "It's poison," he said. "I can smell it."

Aelfraed replaced the knight—no, Maddox was no knight. This close to death, Fionnbharr could read the flames in his aura. The beast within him flared against his eyes. Rogue knelt on his far side, and the coolness of his hand eased the fever burning in Fionnbharr's blood.

"Where is she?" he demanded.

"Who?" Aelfraed asked.

"I don't know," Maddox answered. "He was alone." Their strange accents weren't so strange. If anything, they had become familiar. "I saw him leave the fire, and then he slipped away on his magic. I damn near lost his track the way he kept porting. If not for the poison, I think he'd be halfway around the world."

"We can try to drain it," Rogue said. "But his pulse is already weak and thready, and he can barely move. Whatever the poison is…"

"Nightshade and death goddess," Fionnbharr said. "There is no saving me. It's already trying to lock up my magic. Where is she?"

"Who?" Aelfraed asked him again.

"The goddess of flame and spring, she was here. I saw her. She talked of you, but she was here for me. I want to see her again…"

"Is he making any sense to you?"

"My lord," Fionnbharr tried, but he could find no strength in his limbs. "She wanted me to drink."

"He doesn't know what he's asking for," Rogue argued.

"Maybe not," Maddox said. "But he hears the spirits and the gods. If she wants him to drink, who are we to argue?"

Aelfraed said nothing, but he held Fionnbharr much as she had. His body was so cold. The fever leached away too swiftly.

"If I do this, Fionnbharr," Aelfraed said, his tone seeming to encompass all of his being, "there is no turning back. You will be one of us. A brother."

"I will be the best of you, but I have to drink from her." He wanted it.

"She is not here," Aelfraed told him. "Do you wish to live?"

Did he?

You don't get to die, Fin. You promised me.

"I have to live," he choked out, but his eyes were falling closed. "I promised her."

The world blurred, pain filtered through his body, and it was as though the magic in him tried to pull him apart and bring him back together again. She was there, the whole time, her fingers tight in his and her eyes filled with a canny intelligence and deep, almost soul sucking sadness.

"I'll live for you," he promised over and over as he waged his war against death. The lord, Aelfraed, waged the battle alongside him, and it was days before he woke properly, his body drenched in sweat and everything different.

The silent room he woke in boasted a single bed, a fireplace large enough for three grown men to stand in, and a heavy thatched rug in front of it. Light filtered through a single window, but it was gray and wintry.

He was alive.

Standing, he groaned at the pain in his limbs and the protest in his muscles. A beard coated his face, and his hair had grown longer. The tattoos on his hands had changed, melted away as though they'd never been.

The creak of a door had him turning, and when the chill in the room registered against his bare flesh, he called for fire and it whooshed to life in the hearth. The explosion of light and heat was intense.

Rogue stared at him for a moment and then the flames. "Good, you have not lost that talent with your transition."

"My transition?"

"We have a lot to talk about, Fionnbharr. Maddox is

bringing food, and I will bring the wine. Then we will sit and tell you everything before you meet with Aelfraed."

"Fin," he said abruptly, and Rogue paused at the door.

"What?"

"My name is Fin. Our goddess of flame and spring called me Fin and said that was the name I had when she came on my cock. She spoke of all of you. So whatever it is...I'll understand. But call me Fin."

He would live for his goddess. Just as she demanded.

Hopefully, she would come to him again.

Not so fucking long ago…

"I'm honored to meet you, Fiona MacRieve, I don't know if I said that earlier." Even casting himself across the prison, weaving his shadow against the prison's own magic couldn't diminish the simple joy in him at seeing her again. *Finally,* after so many years.

His goddess of flame and spring.

"No," she challenged in that delightfully husky voice. "Not really. But I'll bite, why are you honored?"

"You're the—"

"Fin." Maddox's snarl cut him off. "Later. For now, find us a route out of here preferably *before* Rogue arrives. This is an extraction, not a war." The grumpy dragon had never been any fun when it came to this vision of Fin's. No matter how many times he'd seen her or how the vision altered subtly year after year, she'd never spoken to him again as she had that first time.

When she'd saved his life.

"Eh," Fin said. "It's kind of both. Even you have to admit that. With the lovely Fiona here the prize at the center of the maze. We just have to get through all the mini-bosses to the big boss, and boom, we get the girl."

Now he had her name.

"Okay," she said, removing his shadowy hand off her thigh with two fingers. "Bored now."

"Ha." Maddox sounded far too self-satisfied.

"First, no one asked for rescue. Second, I'm not some helpless damsel. Third, I'm nobody's fucking prize."

"I can't wait to lay my real eyes on you when we rescue you," Fin said. "You're *delightful*."

She wasn't ready for him to declare himself to her. Not yet. They were at two different places in this journey, but she had always been his destination. Even as he snapped himself back to his own body and readied himself to move, the single glimpse of her could sustain him for another thousand years.

But his goddess was within reach, and he would steal her from this place if it was the last thing he ever did.

More like super recently, a.k.a. now...

PAIN RAKED OVER HIS BACK, AND FIN GRUNTED. THE FAE doctor, Brina, with her blood-red hair and too pale skin marred by a scar that bisected her left eye, paced in front of him. "You're distracted today, druid," she commented, studying him. "What holds your attention so firmly?"

"Definitely not you," Fin told her cheerfully enough. His goddess was there to save them, and that meant it was time to stop playing games inside the prison. They'd let themselves be taken in part to learn what arrangement the other originals had with the shadow demon running the place.

The demon's continued interest in Fiona was unacceptable. As was the blood bounty being placed on her head. Their goddess was not anyone's to touch. But she was here without Alfred or Rogue. Her fierce, impetuous nature and damn stubbornness put her in danger, but at the same time, a fierce pride filled Fin.

Fiona was strong. She'd always been stronger than even she realized. It was time to let her embrace that strength, but with the shadow demon trying to kiss her and Maddox about to beat the stones down, it was time for the games to end.

Fin snapped the chains holding him and straightened. Brina opened her mouth to cast, but he flung a hand out and her hair wrapped against her mouth like a gag, even as she tumbled across the room. She crunched into the wall and then slid down into a heap. Rolling his head from side to side, Fin grimaced at the stinging welts.

Nothing to do about them now, and his shirt was utterly ruined.

Another roar shook the foundations.

I told you... he began when Fiona's tart voice filled his mind with delight.

You dared me to do it again. Did you know that it actually burned him?

Oh.

Well, *that* was a twist.

Where are you? Her thoughts had a kind of breathless quality, like she was fighting. Oh, he wanted to see that.

I'm coming, Beautiful. Don't kill them all without me.

Snagging a key from the unconscious Brina, Fin let himself out of her chamber of horrors and studied the layout.

East.

Every cell in his body yearned east.

He couldn't slip through the roots inside the prison, but he could move fast. He made it to the main gates in time to see Fiona flip one guard, even as she tumbled into another. Blood spattered her clothes and her face. She had the look of a wild Celt at war.

A goddess of flame, spring, and blood...

How appropriate.

The shadow demon roared as he lunged for Fin, and Fin grinned savagely.

Yes.

It was time to dance, so he called the fire.

CHAPTER 3

"When everything seems to be going against you, remember the airplane takes off against the wind not with it." - Henry Ford

FIONA

Go ahead. Let the bastard kiss you again.

I had.

Only instead of dragging me closer, Dorran had roared in pain as light flashed out around us. With my sight still spotting from the brilliance of it, I blinked as Dorran yanked me away from him. The bite of his hands on my arms promised to leave bruises, but it was the dismay and the raw fury in his expression that captivated me.

That and the blistering around the corners of his mouth. Did I do that? Fascinated, I pressed my strength against his as I pushed forward. Locking my hands on his face, I dragged him down, and this time when he kissed me, I savaged him. The flare of light damn near blinded me. I'd be seeing the

499

afterimage for days, but Dorran erupted in my arms and the shadows exploded around me.

Wild laughter slipped free as I danced in a circle. The pull of those same shadows being dragged out of me by Alfred had left their mark. Now, as Dorran writhed along the walls, the shadows twisting and curling over each other but never quite touching me, even as they tried to surround me, made me laugh harder.

This was a delightful discovery.

I had no idea what that light was, but I liked it.

"Come on, Dorran," I taunted. "I thought you wanted me. Isn't that what you used to say? You were going to mark me and make me yours?" Hands on my hips, I surveyed the antechamber we occupied as his shadows licked over the area around me as though I were enveloped in a bubble. "I'm right here, big bad shadow demon. Come try and put all your shadows in me. I *dare* you."

Cocky?

Maybe.

Dangerous?

Sure, why not.

A roar shook the foundations, and the taunting smirk on my face slid away for something a lot more joyful. Maddox. Oh, I'd missed my grumpy dragon.

"Tick tock," I called out to Dorran and began skipping forward. "I am late for an important date."

The first guard swung at me, the shadows peeling apart to reveal his presence. I caught the fist he aimed at my face and damn near laughed again. It was like I was on speed or he was in slow motion. But it took me nothing to catch it, and I turned his arm until the bone snapped.

"Bad wolf," I scolded, and thumped him on the nose.

The shifter flew backwards and slammed into the wall with a crunch.

Holy shit, this was awesome.

At the sudden howling as guards rushed in, a sense of savage satisfaction filled my veins. Eagerness for battle flooded me, and I was already moving to rush toward one of the shifters myself. The wolf snarled, all teeth and claws. All the better to beat you with.

Maddox roared again, and I wanted to throw my head back and make the same sound, only I was a little busy dancing the kick ass fandango.

I told you... Fin scolding me was kind of hot, no lie. But I was a little busy right now. We needed to save the foreplay for later.

You dared me to do it again. Did you know that it actually burned him?

That shocked him.

Where are you? The question pinged through me, even as I seized another wolf shifter and slammed him into a second one. Their bones cracking shouldn't sound so cool, but it was kind of like bubble wrap.

Once you started popping, you couldn't stop with just one.

I'm coming, Beautiful. Don't kill them all without me.

I snorted. No promises. Maddox released another aggrieved roar, this one furious and demanding. Not agony.

No, he was pissed.

Pissed I could deal with.

I never wanted him to hurt. I was being pulled in two directions, however. At least the one from the west seemed to lessen, but the one to the east...

Oh, I needed to get that way.

The slick of Dorran's shadows still writhed about, slithering like an oily army of darkness. Another guard got in my way, and I knocked him off his feet and flipped him before rushing the next one.

Another sound split through the snap of bones and the meaty thud of bodies hitting the walls and the floor. The rich stink of copper filled the air with a near metallic haze. It made my eyes water and burn. There was zero desire to bite. It was like wading through a beer battle and I'd ended up in one of the vats.

The smell damn threatened me with nausea, and my stomach rebelled. All at once, the shadows slammed together and Dorran let out a near preternatural sound before he lunged at Fin.

Fin!

My heart swelled and I stopped to grin as he held up two fists ringed in fire and stepped into the fight with Dorran. Oh, my druid was littered with bruises and cuts, and one of his eyes was nearly swollen shut. It wasn't until he twisted and danced with Dorran, his back facing me, that I caught sight of the whip marks.

Whip.

Marks.

Fury was a potent thing. I'd once been told by a witch I liked very much that my temper was going to get me killed one day.

She'd been wrong about that. Lust had gotten me killed, not my temper. A snide little voice in the back of my mind reminded me it had been my anger that had me saying yes to Alfred and agreeing to that transition finally.

Potato. Poh-tah-to.

The point was, my anger was a powerful thing, and apparently, now, so was I. Whoever had put those whip marks on Fin was going to die.

I love you too, Beautiful. Big ugly on your back.

Fine. I turned and narrowly missed the fist aimed at my face, but it still managed to hit my shoulder. Fuck, that hurt.

Hitting the rocks as I skidded backwards and slammed into the stone wall hurt even more.

The roar from Maddox turned furious again.

"Keep your scales on," I yelled. "I'm working on it."

His bellowing fell off abruptly, and I glared at tall, mangy, and toothy, who glared at me from red-hazed eyes. The snarl had his lips pulling back from his fairly human teeth, though those canines were getting longer and his snout was growing.

Oh, he was shifting.

Ugh. I sent a mental apology to Elias and a kiss of thanks. He'd once explained to me how vulnerable shifters were in those precious seconds between reaching for their animals and when the shift came over them. On their human side, they were dangerous. On the animal side, fucking lethal. But in between?

I lunged off the wall, using my momentum to help me crash my fist right into his elongating jaw. His yelp of surprised pain served as all the encouragement I needed to rain blows down on him. The principles of fighting weren't lost on me. I did, actually, know how to fight. I'd even taken Krav Maga.

What?

It did wonders for my ass and my arms.

I'd never had any real effect against anything stronger than a human before. Okay, not totally true. There was this fae once, but that story was better forgotten and never told.

He would never forgive me for what I did to his hair.

Still, the strength coursing through my veins coupled with the speed vibrating my bones meant I was a fucking superhero. The last blow sent the guard tumbling across the floor, and he let out a rattling wheeze before going still.

The stink of blood coated my nostrils and clogged my throat. Spatters of gore had flown off the wolf as I tore into him. Even now, I was shaking little bits of stuff I never wanted to identify off my hands.

Shadow and flame danced in the antechamber. Some of the bodies had caught on fire, and the acrid scent of roasting flesh and burnt hair just added to the shitty Scentsy party.

Gag.

This was awful.

And…I was out of guards.

I took a step toward Fin and Dorran, when the shadow demon hurled backwards and shadows enfolded me.

Holding my breath seemed like a stellar idea. I did not want to take one ounce of him in by accident, 'cause, you know, gross.

Inky dark and icy cold draped me. A sensation akin to falling prickled over my flesh. The shadows pressed in even closer, mummifying and threatening to smother me. Thankfully, I didn't need to breathe—at least not right away. I curled my fingers against the insubstantial night. How much of it could I touch or affect?

It slid through my fingers like water. Great. The image of a wet T-shirt contest leapt to mind, and I couldn't help it. I had to laugh. How great would that be, to hear about the epic battle at Nightmare Penitentiary waged by a succubus versus a shadow demon in a wet T-shirt contest? I'd win the second my breasts were on display.

Men were so predictable.

Predictable.

I twisted around in the darkness, almost like I was swimming or trying to at least tread water, even without the sense of buoyancy. The shadows seemed to thicken, making it harder to move. All sound had blotted out like my ears had been stuffed with cotton. So annoying. Yet, men were predictable.

Even shadow demon males.

The thickest part of the darkness offered some resistance. Spongier. It pushed back.

A grin pulled at my lips, but I kept them pressed tightly together before I rammed my fist into that near solid, spongy mass. The darkness shuddered.

Another drive forward with my free hand into the same area, and the shudder turned to a vibrating pulse rippling through the darkness. Again and again, I struck until sparks danced in front of my eyes as my lungs burned in desperate need for air—mental or physical, who knew? I just knew if I dared suck in a breath here, it would open up another clusterfuck.

I, for one, was done with clusterfucks.

The ripples colliding into each other tumbled faster, like a whirlpool determined to suck me down, and somewhere within me, I swore Maddox roared again. As though demanding I do something. Damn, grumpy dragon. What the hell did he think I was doing?

The weight of Rogue's disappointment feathered over me. The image of him was a flash on my retinas, as though he stood just in the garden where the sun edged the cold, sleeping vines and the icy rocks. He wanted me to understand something, but apparently, I was being thick.

Alfred, hands in his pockets, stood in front of a blazing fire in the great hall. It was empty behind him, cold and barren. His anger was a palpable thing chilling the air, despite the heat from the flames. As though suddenly aware of me, he turned those dark rimmed eyes on me. Fathomless voids that held so much emotion, it threatened to suffocate me worse than the shadow demon currently holding me captive.

Currently.

Holding.

Me.

Captive.

I was no one's captive.

No cell would hold me again. Not one constructed by a vampire, demon, or angel. *Hear that, my loving asshole?* I sent the thought out there. *You're my asshole. I can accept that. But I will not be caged by any of you.*

And I would *not* be caged by this shadow demon, who, like everyone else, had tried to own me from the day he met me. How clear it was to me now. All those visits. All that steely affection laced with command. Forcing me to feed on him, even though I hadn't wanted it. Despite the fact he offered blood bags every day and I'd refused them.

The blood in those bags would never have sustained me.

I knew that *now*. Then? I just hadn't wanted them.

The scorch of heat flooded my veins. The thrum of power raced over my skin. My heart slammed a rhythmic tattoo against my ribs as I struck at the shadow demon over and over.

The white light from earlier pierced the darkness, and it seemed to shimmer out of every single one of my pores. One moment, I was encased in the darkness as I struck at it, and in the next, the darkness flooded with strands of silver and white, each vein creeping through the darkness to illuminate it, even as it began to separate it into a hundred different pieces.

Bursting through the cocoon of darkness, I stretched out my arms because the power seemed to swell through me, and it lit up the entire cavern. The surge of guards heading toward us turned back, shrieking as light filled every crevice and depression in the stone. They raised hands to cover their faces, and the stone just beyond them erupted as a dragon forced his way through.

The wild hazel green and gold eyes with their slits

focused on me, even as the pupils retracted at the brilliance of the light.

A pained sound pulled my attention, and I stared down at the warden now lying near my feet. He'd resumed his humanoid form, his dark eyes shot through with silver and his arm lifted as though to shield his face. Yet even as I watched, the grizzled parts of his cheeks turned almost ruddier and the light kissed over his flesh, softening him.

It was like the blur of a camera lens filtering out the harsher elements and leaving behind…

Surprise and wonder filled Dorran's eyes as he focused on me. There was color in those endless black pits. Shock and grief exploded through the surprise and wonder, and he let out a sound of agony so profound, it had to have shredded his throat.

A blast of heated breath hit me as Maddox roared, and I pulled my gaze away from the downed warden, his troubled expression already forgotten as I focused on my beautiful golden dragon. His scales shimmered in the light, and his huge head dipped toward me as I hurried across the buckled and crumbling floor with its litter of bodies.

Fin scooped me up a step away from Maddox and curled his thick arms around me as he pulled me close. "Give me a minute, Beautiful." Then he focused on Maddox when my dragon snarled a warning. "Mind your temper. She's *mine* too."

Before I could snap at either of them for arguing, Fin fisted my hair and dipped his face to mine. I cupped his cheeks, halting his descent as I studied him. Bruises marred his beautiful face, and there was blood on his lip where it had been split wide open and an ugly jagged slash through one of his eyebrows.

Worse, he staggered a little, blanching under his pallor. Pain.

He was hurting. Smoothing my hands down to his nape, I took care not to touch a single one of the stripe marks on his back. I paused only when I looked at my fingers against his chest where they seemed to glow against his flesh. Ignoring that for a moment, I flattened my palm over the beat of his heart.

It was sluggish.

Maddox's grunt of sound seemed to echo my own thoughts.

"Fin." Worry speared through me, but Fin ignored that and dragged me in for a kiss. Tears sparked in my eyes at the first brush of his cool lips over mine. Where I'd once tasted laughter and mischief, all I found was cold iron and ash.

Worse, deeper as his tongue stroked over mine was something more acrid. The blood from his broken lip flooded my mouth, and I jerked backward. It tasted *wrong*. Something darker slid through his veins.

He let out a mournful sound as I pulled away, and I turned him, trying to get a better look at his back.

"*Gheall mé duit, Álainn,*" he murmured. "*Tá mé ag fanacht le fada leat.*"

As beautiful as those words were, I had no idea what they meant. The marks on his back were dark and deep. They were radiating out in little black lines. Maddox let out another huff as he snaked his head around us, and there was a sickening crunch of bone and a meaty tearing of muscle and flesh.

I grimaced. Even as covered in blood as I was, that sound turned my stomach. "Something is wrong with him, Maddox..." I knew it. "And I love you, my dragon, but you're gonna remember the rules about kissing."

He huffed a laugh at me and then nudged me toward Fin as he moved to wrap around us both, then his wing slid over us like a shelter in the storm.

My dragon would watch our backs, and I cradled Fin to

me as he staggered. Turning his face to my throat, I slid my fingers through his hair.

"Drink, Fin," I whispered. "You've lost too much blood."

Cradling him close, I didn't miss his mumbled words as he mouthed a kiss against my pulse. "I could die happy here, Beautiful."

Thank fuck that was in English.

"You're not dying," I told him. "Do you understand me? You are not allowed to die. I did not come all this way to save you, only to have you die. You promised to put balm on my ass after Alfred and Rogue tan it, and what will Maddox do without you?"

The dragon let out a rumbling growl that verged dangerously close to a purr, and I smiled as I leaned into his side, even as I stroked Fin's hair. Even in the gloom cast by the shelter of Maddox's wings, I had no trouble seeing my damaged druid.

I was going to tear whoever did this to him apart.

Fiona... Nightshade and death goddess. There is no saving me. It's already locking up my magic. But you're here.

You don't get to die, Fin. You promised me.

I'd beg if I had to.

Please, my love, please drink.

Your love?

Yes, you impetuous fool, I love you, now drink...

Your throat... You don't like your throat touched.

You can have my throat. They all could. *I trust you.*

The hard strike of his teeth was instantaneous, as if those words unleashed the beast within my druid. The first hard suck had me shaking all the way down to my core. The fact he worked his hand right into my pants and had two fingers pumping into me registered distantly. All I could feel was Fin inside me, stroking me as though desperate to bring me to orgasm, wrapped around me like a cloak of the sexiest fur.

My whole body shuddered as he sucked and pulled and stroked.

Fuck me, I was going to come right here, and the release when it exploded out of me… I shuddered as I rolled my hips up to meet his hand, while his thumb kept pressure on my clit, and the pleasure just spiraled. When he dragged his head upward, the eyes shining down at me held mischief as he pressed his lips to mine, and I tasted my own blood in his mouth.

Drunk on the feel of him, I tore at his pants until I could wrap my hand around him and then began to stroke his stiff cock. The huff from Maddox registered distantly, as did the heat of fire and the screams of the dying, but I shut them all the fuck out as Fin tore my pants. Then he pushed into me, and I had my legs wrapped around him.

I sank my teeth into his throat, and he growled, a deep, fully bellied growl that was so like Maddox, I laughed. The acridness in his blood was a tang on my tongue, but I wouldn't be deterred. If the poison was in him, I wanted it out.

Nothing was allowed to harm him.

He dug his fingers into my ass as I drank and ground his cock deeper, even as he triggered another wave of orgasm with the pressure of his cock striking deep.

Lifting my head back, I screamed as I came, and then his teeth sank into me again. The light show around us left my eyes dazzled, but the heat of his seed shooting into me did something else to my insides. Molten fire in my belly spread out, like sunshine suffusing every single cell, and it was Fin crying out against my throat as his hips jerked, and I swore he came again.

We collapsed together against the surging side of Maddox's scales.

Shaken, I looked up as Fin pulled the bloodied strands of

hair from my face, and then he kissed me so fucking sweetly, my heart melted.

"Mine," he whispered against my lips, and I would deny him nothing. "My perfect goddess of flame and spring."

"Yours," I agreed, and fuck if I could catch my breath.

"My blood angel," he added, and I laughed at his poetry before I fisted his hair and dragged him down for a kiss.

This time when his blood touched my tongue, it was cleaner, earthier, and tasted of *Fin* and not poison. "You're mine," I reminded him.

"Always."

I stretched out a hand to run along Maddox's side. I hadn't forgotten him.

My dragon.

My druid.

Mine.

CHAPTER 4

"We need the tonic of wildness." - Henry David Thoreau

MADDOX

He canted his head at the next rush of guards and exhaled the fire he'd been holding in for the last several days. The whole point of their incarceration had been to learn more about which of the Seven were in league with the warden—the bastard who kept putting his hands on Maddox's mate. Puffs of smoke and fire erupted from his nostrils as the dragon swung his gaze around.

The warden had fled before Maddox made it all the way in here. Fucker had better run. But he would find him. He was never touching her again, even if she had scalded him so beautifully. Triumph and pride twined within him. His mate had grown far more powerful during his absence.

That absence left an aching hole within him. He'd felt her approach to the prison in his soul. Every step she'd taken, he'd been torn between scolding her for risking herself and the savage sense of rightness that his mate would fight for him. His brothers had, but now his mate—*their* mate would.

The smell of sex wafting from beneath his wing had him grunting. He could taste her pleasure and Fin's, but at least his brother's scent had changed. His kitten had been right to feed him her blood and to pull the poison from him. For just a moment, Maddox had hesitated, but her scent hadn't changed when she drained the poison. It didn't touch her, and that was enough for him.

For now.

The stroke of her hand against his scales urged him to lift his wing to glance down at them. They'd shredded their clothing, and he had to snort at that. Fin hadn't even pulled out of her, but her jewel-like green eyes locked on his and a pulse of love flashed along the bond.

He spared Fin a look. His brother's color was no longer ashen, and the wounds on his back had all closed.

"Don't growl," Fin told him in a brighter voice than Maddox had heard from him in a while. "I dare you to want to pull away from her in a hurry."

Fuck. You.

The focused thought landed well, because Fin threw his head back, laughing. "Yeah, yeah." It took them a moment to stand, but Fiona was now pantsless, not that she seemed to care. The tail of her shirt just barely covered her ass. Lifting his head, Maddox swept the huge chamber. The room had definitely heated, the rock had blackened—scorched from his fire—and the bodies were all unmoving. Nothing was going to see her ass.

Satisfied, he waited until Fin at least closed his pants and was fully on his feet and ready to defend her before Maddox focused and let his scales slip away as his body compacted. Then he stood on two legs and barely had time to brace before Fiona launched herself into his arms.

The feel of her slick heat against his bare cock was a welcome sensation as she wrapped her arms and legs around him. The sting of contact on his recently changed skin sent sparks raking over his nerves, but he ignored every one of them because the press of her breasts to his chest, the heat of her legs around him, and the fact she fisted his hair in one hand before she nuzzled a kiss to his throat made him groan.

He wanted to kiss her properly, but she had rules and he could respect that. Grinding against her, he slid a hand down to cup her ass and keep her steady.

"Outside, Beautiful. You too, Maddox." Fin slapped him on the back, and Maddox hissed at him with a scowl. The druid just gave him an unrepentant grin.

"Not yet," Fiona argued, and then wiggled out of his arms. He didn't let her go far, snaking a hand to her hip and yanking her back to him. Touching her settled his beast, and neither of them would be settled until they had her hell and gone from this place.

Fin swung around to look at her, but like Maddox, he scanned the room and kept a wary eye out. They were alone right now, but this reprieve wouldn't last.

"Kitten," Maddox said, and his voice came out rough and rocky. After weeks in his dragon's form, he hadn't had occasion to speak. Her sudden smile at him and the softening around her eyes had him dismissing the concern almost immediately. "We need to go."

"Someone hurt him," she said, the husky tone of hers wrapping around him like a caress. "I'm going to kill them."

Fin's grin was both savage and satisfied. Maddox didn't blame him. The possessiveness radiating from her was not something he'd realized he needed or craved. Yet he soaked in every dramatic ounce of it.

"They don't matter, Beautiful," Fin told her and caught

one of her hands. "Getting you out of here and taking what we know back to Alfred does."

"Then you two go," she instructed, recalcitrance etched into every stubborn inch of her gorgeous face. Even her eyes flashed, and for a split second, her skin began to glow. "I'll find them and gut them all. No one treats you like that."

Lifting her hand, Fin examined her arm and then slanted a look at Maddox. *Are you seeing this?*

He gave a slight nod. Fiona glowed. She'd burned the warden, and that sense of vicious vengeance in him unfurled. Hopefully, it stung the bastard for a long time. But even holding her, Maddox felt nothing beyond her.

Magic?

But Fin shook his head.

Fiona started to pull away again, but Maddox tightened his arms. "Kitten, they will wait. Unless Fin needs his vengeance now."

His brother snorted, then cupped her face. "I'm fine, Beautiful. And I'd much rather be with you than here a minute longer." Besides, they had information for Alfred and Rogue. It was better to get back.

A scoffing sound of protest fell from her lips, and Maddox pressed his mouth close to her ear. "Kitten, I need to get you out of here. I need you naked and wrapped around me for a few hours. Then I need to just feel you with me. More than all of that, I need you safe from this place. You have us, now take us home?"

It might have been fighting dirty, but some of the objection went out of her and she stole a look upward. "I'm coming back after them later."

"And I'll help." It was a promise.

"What the hell," Fin said before kissing her palm. "Field trip." Then, linking his fingers with hers, he nodded to Maddox. For the most part, Maddox didn't give a damn that he was naked or that his cock jutted out full and hard, as eager to be in her as he was. Still, he was more concerned about her lack of covering, not that either of them would let anything touch her.

Still, he should probably not have toasted all of the bodies. Outside, the cold air slapped against him and filled his lungs with something less charred. Fiona let out a laugh and glanced at him again. Speckled with streaks of blood, soot, and sweat, she was still the most beautiful woman he'd ever seen.

"I had to break in," she joked. "I'm afraid I wasn't subtle about it."

The magical wards pushed back against them, slowing them a step, but Fiona strode ahead, holding each of their hands in hers, and the pop of the magic fizzling out and away had Maddox raising his brows.

Yes, he could push through most magical fields and Fin could weave an opening into them, but Fiona had just erased it like it wasn't there.

Not erased. Recoiled. It literally didn't want to touch her.

He nodded to Fin. What the hell did that mean though?

And outside, under a night dark sky with no moon, Fiona's skin did more than just radiate light. It pulsed with health, vitality, and a shimmer that couldn't be mistaken for anything other than ethereal.

Suddenly, being out and in the open took on a new level of threat, and the urgency to get her to the keep and out of sight redoubled. As if reading his mind—and knowing Fin, he probably was—Fin picked up the pace. They had to get past the gates, then he could whirl them away.

The hum of the prison spells vibrated against his back, just as a scent he'd hoped to never smell again rushed him with the breeze. Digging his heels in, Maddox hauled Fiona

—and by extension, Fin—backward and tucked her behind him.

"Stay, Kitten," he growled when she started to move around him. Fin boxed her in though, pressing her right up to Maddox's back.

He didn't have time to appreciate the fact that she settled her hands against his back or that she didn't struggle. Not when the forest just behind the edge of the barrier had gone preternaturally silent. No birds. No insects. No ground creatures. Not even the leaves stirred.

One crunch of leaves. A deliberate foot being placed to alert them to the new arrival. "Do you require assistance?" Cyril inquired. "Or clothing?"

Of all the fuckers, it had to be him. Of the Seven, Cyril held the most animosity toward Alfred. They had never been friends. Diametrically opposed in every way. Leanly built and tall, there was nothing soft about the man. He was a razor sharp weapon, and even the most casual of slips could leave a person sliced and bleeding.

Maddox studied the member of the Seven as he strolled out from behind the trees like he was just out for a casual walk. Dressed in a bespoke suit, he looked more like he was on his way to a board meeting than a hike in the woods.

Wait...the smells were off for the woods. There was car exhaust and the stink of humanity on the breeze. The portal to the prison must be in a city somewhere. That explained the suit.

Not trusting Cyril for a second, Maddox never lost his focus on him. "I was unaware you had business with the prison."

It was a lie.

One that settled between them like a four-day dead fish, all rot gut and stinking.

Of course Cyril had business there. He and Eamon had

both set the shadow demon on the hunt for her. Maybe he didn't work for them directly, but they held some leverage over him.

Handling Cyril, however, was not Maddox's forte. It required diplomacy. He was more a gut first and rip their head off kind of guy.

"Lord Cyril," Fin greeted as he strolled out from behind Maddox. Despite the fact he wore a pair of loose pants only and blood spatter across his chest and arms added to his disheveled appearance, he was almost gracious. "I'm afraid you've caught us a little in flagrante delicto."

Maddox made a note to drown Fin, later. He ran a hand down Maddox's biceps, and it actually took force of will to keep his expression schooled and not roll his eyes.

"You two?" Cyril said with a snort. "Do I look like a fool to you, *boy?*"

"Do you really want me to answer that question, *buidéal pox?*" Butter wouldn't melt in his saintly mouth, nor would it diminish his smile. "If you don't mind, lover boy here is in a bit of a way, and he's been suffering for me so beautifully."

Definitely drowning the little shit.

Maddox gave a mock sigh, and if not for the feeling of Fiona's nails digging into his back, he'd be worried. His kitten was fabulous, but shy and retiring weren't anywhere in her personal lexicon.

Still, she didn't move away as Fin gave him a teasing wink. "C'mon, big boy, let's get home where I can take care of you."

"You're hiding the succubus." Cyril's cool tones held not a trace of amusement.

"We're hiding what now?" Fin's accent became more pronounced. "Have you gone daft, my lord? I know it's been a while since you were up."

Riding the edge between humor and insult suited Fin,

until the moment it didn't. Maddox braced himself, but he still didn't take his eyes off Cyril. The weight of Fiona's hands promised him she was right behind him, but there wasn't a peep out of her, and all at once, it hit him.

He couldn't smell her.

The stench of sex on Fin was still there amidst the blood, pain, gore, and magic. But not Fiona. He didn't dare turn his head, but what the fuck had Fin done?

His brother didn't supply any ready answers, but then Maddox didn't expect him to. Not with Cyril so close.

"He turned a demon." Cyril's tone was so frigid, ice slicked every single word. "You can't possibly want to protect the beast."

Beast.

Maddox snorted then folded his arms. Whatever Fin had done, their mate was hidden. Maddox eyed him. "Be careful who you call a beast."

Cyril pinned him with a look. "You should never have been made either, dragon. Don't think I won't still hunt you."

Her nails dug into his back. Oh, his mate didn't like that. So Maddox laughed, needing to defuse her temper. The last thing they needed was her shedding that protection to jump Cyril for him.

While the Seven were notoriously hard to kill...

They weren't impossible.

Maddox would put his money on him and Fin.

"Lord Cyril, the only reason you're still breathing at the moment is your treaty with Alfred," Fin cut in smoothly, all dulcet tones and easygoing manner. His smile was all teeth. Yes, Fin was their charming bastard. It was a mistake to ever think him weak, which a lot of the Seven did. They saw him as the pet. A feeling not unfamiliar to Maddox, because they'd done the same to him.

The original paused and snapped his head away from

them. A split-second later, Maddox allowed himself to smile. Alfred strolled in from beyond the trees, carrying with him the scent of the city. If Alfred was here, then so was Rogue. The lack of forest movement didn't mean he wasn't tucked away out there somewhere.

Cyril exhaled a low sound of disgruntlement. Aww, he didn't like being caught stepping over the line. Maybe Alfred would let them kill him now.

One could only hope.

"Aelfraed."

"Cyril."

The tension in the air thickened as power gathered between them. It had been a long time since he'd been close to any gathering of the Seven. When all of them were in the same place, it could be downright unbearable.

Another reason Alfred tended to want them to wait for him and not attend. Of all of them, only Rogue had never issued a complaint about being in their presence.

"Coming to join your lovers?" Cyril asked. "They seem to have interesting choices for recreational fornication."

"What they do that brings them pleasure is no concern of yours," Alfred informed him without a hint of intonation or smile. "Why are you cornering them?"

"You know why. If they don't have her, then you do or your other pet. I saw him recently, yet he's not here now. You never slip his leash, even when you were letting him play at assassinating you."

"If you have a point," Alfred said, "I suggest you get to it."

Cyril dismissed him and Fin entirely as he faced Alfred. "You know what I want."

"I don't really care."

The other snorted. "No, you would rather just do things your way and ignore the rest of us."

"I would classify that as a trait we all share, *brother.*"

Hands in his pockets, Alfred looked remote, untouchable, and like he belonged in this forest about as much as Cyril.

Spitting, Cyril snapped forward, closing the distance between them in less than a blink of an eye. "Do not play with me, Aelfraed. You cannot turn a demon, yet you have. She should never have been made in the first place. The demons were going to take her back, and then you liberate her."

Alfred's smile was thin. "I did nothing."

"Your pets did."

"Standing right here," Maddox reminded him. "And I bet I can still fry your wingless ass before you could get away." He was done playing nice. With Alfred present, he didn't have to pretend to be diplomatic. After all, he was the *pet*, right?

Alfred flicked him a look that said, *really?*

Yes, really. Maddox was tired of these games, and Cyril just confirmed their own information. It was indeed the others that had sent the shadow demon after her.

That alone was enough for Maddox to want to end him.

"You court war," Cyril continued, ignoring Maddox. "Bring us the succubus, and we'll consider the terms of our treaty satisfied. I'll await your answer."

He backed off a step, but Alfred said, "You don't have to wait for it."

Maddox stilled, and next to him, Fin seemed to turn to stone. If not for the continued weight of her hands on his bare back, Maddox would have twisted to find her and spirit her away now.

"I'm waiting," Cyril stated, his whole demeanor suspicious.

"The answer is no," Alfred told him, and while Maddox had believed Alfred wouldn't betray her, it still settled him as Alfred firmly aligned himself. "She's my queen. She goes nowhere."

"Then you want war."

"No," Alfred said. "But if you bring it, you should understand that you will not walk away alive from it. If any of yours come after what is mine, it will be the end of you."

Cyril took one step forward, and Rogue dropped from the trees, his whole body unfolding from his owl form to land in the grass without a whisper of sound escaping him.

Furious, Cyril shot a look from one to the other. But Alfred just gazed at him evenly. "You wanted my attention. Now you have it. Touch any of mine, and you will regret it. I have long wanted to repair this rift between us all, but I will sow the earth with your bones before I allow you to lay even a breath on Fiona."

Even anticipating it, Maddox wasn't quite ready for the shock of lightning being flung in all directions. It zapped him, pain lighting up every nerve ending as it danced over him and into Fin. He barely had a chance to brace at the second volley. A crash of sound thundered through the trees, and he didn't have to look to know Cyril had called in his forces or that Alfred had already engaged.

They crashed through the trees as Alfred drove him back. Fuck, that lightning hurt.

Rogue shot a look toward him that wasn't hard to read. Get Fiona out of here before he turned and took on the mob coming for them. Fin faced the other way, his magic already coming to fill his hands with fire, even as a windstorm lashed out to knock the vamps off their feet.

Vampires.

Hordes of them.

Maddox reached for his dragon but paused when the hands on his back vanished.

"Kitten," he snarled, but Alfred sailed through the air to hit the dirt and slid thirty feet, kicking up rocks, dirt, and debris before he slammed into a tree and it cracked from the force of his impact.

He caught the ancient oak as it toppled on him with one hand, and then flung it like a javelin at Cyril, who charged after him.

The other barely avoided being hit and tumbled into the grass as he ducked. But the worst thing that Maddox could imagine happened when Cyril snapped his head up and Fiona appeared in front of him, blazing white hot with shadowy looking wings extending from her back as though cast by her own light.

Wild.

Beautiful.

Perfect.

So not the fucking time.

Dammit, Kitten.

She faced off against one of the Seven, and Maddox had zero doubt she intended to fight.

CHAPTER 5

"They chose me, but I'm keeping them." - Anonymous

FIONA

I didn't know who the dick was, but based on Maddox and Fin's reactions, it couldn't have been anyone good. Maddox shoving me behind him had been the tiniest bit insulting. I mean, I'd just broken into the prison *by myself* and staged a rescue. Pretty badass if you asked me, course...they hadn't asked me.

Fine, fine. He was protective, and the growl pulsing along the mating bond was all kinds of hot. Even more, it turned my insides all soft and mushy. Not my favorite state to be in when standing on the edge of a prison, covered in gore, while my pants lay in shreds somewhere inside.

I'd told him over and over, succubi didn't mate. But I wasn't just a succubus anymore. I was very much his mate. He was mine. So was Fin.

When Fin crowded right up to my back and pressed me

into Maddox, I thought nothing of it. Nor did I think anything of the tingles of magic fluttering over me like a cloak settling on my shoulders. Fin's hands were warm, the breath of his kiss against my nape silken. I'd closed my eyes and sank into his touch, and just like that, the whole world had muffled. If not for my hands on Maddox's scorching hot back, I would have thought I'd turned into a ghost.

Fucking creepy ass feeling.

I could hear them, but it was clear after my first spontaneous, "Fuck you, buddy," they couldn't hear me. Or see me. I started making faces and cracking myself up. Okay, not so much, but I did stick my tongue out at the asshat a few times. Not asshole, asshat. The Asshole was mine, and this guy? He was just a dick.

Then Alfred and Rogue were there, and my heart fluttered. I hadn't seen either of them in a week. Yes, there was a little bit of trepidation. Alfred was bound to be furious with me. Then he said, "The answer is no. She's my queen. She goes nowhere."

Fuck me.

"Then you want war."

"No," Alfred said. "But if you bring it, you should understand that you will not walk away alive from it. If any of yours come after what is mine, it will be the end of you."

Possession swarmed through me, and the bite mark where Alfred had sealed my transition flared with warmth, the sensation of his lips passing over it. He knew I was here, and the stupidest smile pulled at my lips. Thankfully, whatever Fin's magic had done to me kept my expression hidden. My asshole didn't need to see me looking at him all dopey and lovestruck.

Nope, he did not—

What the actual fuck?

Lightning exploded out of the dick, and it hit them all,

including my dragon. The power of it shivered over him like eddies in a storm and then grounded without ever touching me. There was another wave of them, and then Alfred crashed into the dick and they vanished.

All hell broke loose.

Or heaven, I guessed, in this case.

This guy had to be one of the Seven, because he actually met Alfred swing for swing. There were vampires everywhere. Ice and fire flew as Fin and Rogue launched into the melee, but Maddox stayed right where he was, protecting me. Even though I'd dug my fingers into him, an intense rage I couldn't define slammed through me when Alfred skidded through the clearing and his whole body cracked into a tree.

No.

Just fuck no.

I let go of Maddox and stalked across the clearing, aware of the tingles bristling over me. Fin's magic itched now, as though clinging like static to my skin. A huge tree sailed past me, and *the asshat* ducked as it nearly caught him in the face.

Pity that.

It should have.

I felt more than heard Maddox's growled, "Kitten," but as much as I loved him, the rage demanded I act. With a shiver, like I was trying to shake off water, I shed Fin's cloak, and all the sounds in the clearing—the shrieks of attacking vampires, the sudden cutoff cries of the dying ones, the crackle of flames, the sharp smash of ice, and the crunch of bones—echoed through the air.

More, I could smell blood and fear. Maybe it shouldn't have surprised me that the fear came from the asshat. Fear and fury.

Right back atcha, buddy.

His dark eyes kindled as they locked on me, and I braced

my stance. If he landed a hit, it would probably hurt. So the plan was don't let him hit me.

Though I'd take that if it meant he didn't hit any of my guys with that lightning again, or throw Alfred into any more trees.

Eyes narrowing, what's-his-face—sorry, I wasn't listening when they said his name, or they didn't say it and I sure as fuck wasn't calling him 'my lord'—glared at me. "Succubus." The pupils in his dark eyes seemed to retract to pinpricks, or maybe it was the sudden flaring light in the clearing. Fortunately, it didn't bother my eyes in the slightest.

"Fuckface."

He frowned and his hand moved like a blur, but Alfred was suddenly there between us and he thrust the other away. "Hellion," he said without looking at me. "Go with Maddox."

"No," I told him. "We all go or we all stay."

Determination threaded through me like steel lacing my bones. I wasn't leaving any of them this close to the prison. Not Fin. Not Maddox. Not Rogue. Not my asshole.

He let out an aggrieved sigh as the other member of the Seven raced back toward us. It was weird. I could almost see him move. It wasn't a blur so much as he was just out of focus, like a stop motion shutter on a camera. Each click brought him closer and closer.

I slammed my hand out a split second before he got to us, and the light blazed like it had when Alfred purged the shadow taint from me the second time. Stranger still, the power pulsed right off my hand, and the former angel in front of us—right, all of the Seven were. Including my asshole. Alfred pulled me to him, even as Fuckface flew backwards and cracked through two trees.

The shouts around us grew louder, and I glared at the vampires swarming in. They were no match for my guys, but I could taste Maddox's fury, Fin's irritation, and Rogue's annoyance. All of them were so angry on some level, but nothing compared to how incandescent Alfred was next to me. I swore he glowed.

Glancing at where his hand wrapped on my arm, I stared. We were both glowing. I'd kind of done that earlier when I'd burned Dorran. Not a one off?

"Um…"

"Behind me, Hellion." Alfred thrust me behind him, even as Maddox let out a blistering roar and fire flooded the whole area in front of us. One moment, Fuckface was there, the next, it was a firestorm.

Rogue and Fin hit me from either side as they gripped Alfred and dragged him backward until the three of them formed a triangle around me. The air shimmered as Fin's magic bubbled, cutting out the sound of Maddox's roar, the smell of scorching bodies as vampires turned to ash as did trees, and fuck me, even the rocks cracked and split open just before they exploded.

Tucked right up against Rogue, I let out a breath. He cooled the air inside the bubble that had been sweat-drenching just seconds earlier. The blaze of red, orange, and yellow suddenly went blue, and I swore my eyes had to have rounded.

How hot did my dragon's fire get?

Very hot, Beautiful. His mate was about to take on one of the Seven. He could burn this whole mountainside down then take out the city, so let's take a beat and not rush into danger again.

I scowled. "I had it handled."

"Yes, little *svász*," Rogue said in an almost absently soothing tone. "You did very well, and we'll discuss the fact you took off on us—"

"Again," Alfred ground out.

"—later," Rogue finished, as though Alfred hadn't spoken.

"Discuss it all you want," I said. "I had to come get them."

"It's okay, Beautiful," Fin soothed and stroked a hand over my hair. "We need to go now."

"Maddox!" Alfred called, the command in his voice unmistakable as Fin tangled his fingers in my hair and tugged me toward him. Rogue's arms tightened around me, and Alfred didn't let me go much farther either, but then Fin kissed me and the heat around us eased almost at once.

"Really fucking funny, Fin," Maddox growled as Fin swept his tongue around mine and stole my breath. A glow inside of me just amped brighter with every contact, and then I was plucked from all of them and wrapped up against Maddox's chest, and I let out a laugh of delight.

Genuine delight speared me.

Except…

Arms around Maddox, I glanced past his shoulder to the devastated and scorched areas of blackened earth. Nothing moved. Very little was even standing.

"Closer," Fin urged, and he pressed to my side, even as Rogue and Alfred boxed in around me. Magic swirled in the air, but movement amongst the dark ash had me narrowing my eyes. Charred like a nightmare, the figure rose and opened its eyes.

Holy crap.

I opened my mouth to warn them but the world blurred around us as Fin's magic pulled us all along on a spiraling journey that dumped us from the smoky ruins beyond the prison to the snowy recesses just outside the keep. The frigid air had me curling closer to Maddox, who kept an arm banded around me.

Then he pivoted, pulling me away from them as he stalked toward the keep.

"Maddox."

Only his name and my dragon halted, his whole body

tensing. "Not now, Alfred. I need time with her before we have this discussion."

"We have to have it now," Rogue answered, not Alfred, and I twisted in Maddox's arms to look back at them. Both Rogue and Alfred stood like yin and yang sentinels in competing dark and light, with the setting sun blazing orange and red behind them. As much as I'd had to go for Fin and Maddox, I'd missed my asshole and Rogue.

Alfred caught my gaze, and for a split-second, I could have sworn he winked. But his expression remained unchanged, so maybe I just imagined it.

A growl rumbled in Maddox's chest, and I smoothed a hand over his shoulder. "I'm not going anywhere," I promised him. All of them really. "I have all four of you back now, I don't need to flee."

Fin sighed. "Bath. We can eat, bathe, and then you can steal her away after we're done, but they're right...we do need to talk."

I swore Maddox's growl deepened. "Fine," he snarled. "Get the food and the drink ready. We'll be there in a minute."

A squeak of sound escaped me as he fled into the keep, and then we were through the main hall and up to the wing where our rooms were, but he didn't slow until we were inside my rooms and he had me pinned to the wall.

"Kitten," Maddox said in a rough voice, and I hitched my thighs higher on his hips as I reached between us. His cock was hard and hot in my hands, and it took no urging for me to line him up, but when I would have sank down, he thrust in deep enough my toes curled. "I don't know if I can be gentle," he warned, and it was a battle.

The muscles in his neck were rigid, and his expression fierce. Despite all of that, he held himself completely still, even if he shook, and his grip on me—though tight—was not painful. Cupping his face, I ignored the smoky scent and the ash, blood, and sweat streaking his skin and probably mine, and kissed him.

Taut lips softened under mine and then his tongue swept forward, demanding access, and I opened to him. It took one roll of my hips, and he began to piston into me, not once letting go of my mouth as we fought to consume each other. I slid my fingers down to the mark at the juncture of where his neck met his shoulder.

Powerful emotion swarmed through me—love, longing, need, and even aggravation and irritation that I'd risked myself. Laughter tore out of my throat at the thorny emotions stabbing me, even as he swallowed the sound. I dug my fingers into his hair, fisting it as he began to swell, and when he finally released my mouth to kiss down my throat, I sighed.

The need to feel his teeth held me captive as much as the fact that he impaled me on his cock over and over again. Then a whisper of a kiss, a near silent plea. He wouldn't bite without me telling him yes, so I dragged him closer. "I'm yours," I reminded him. "You're mine."

My vision whited out as his teeth sank in and his knot swelled with his relief, and my whole body bucked against both as pleasure drowned me in waves. It was like the final bit of the puzzle settled where it belonged, and I floated on rapture, a contentment I'd never known filling my veins. Gradually, the pulls at my throat eased, and he pressed kisses along my skin to my jaw, then behind my ear, and finally over my closed eyelids. Whispering brushes of his lips to my flesh, and I smiled at the tenderness rolling off of him.

His knot loosened far swifter than it usually did and a sluggish part of my mind wondered, but he shifted his hold on me as he came free and I whimpered.

"Shh, Kitten," he murmured, his voice far silkier and

relaxed than earlier. The beast in him had been satisfied, and I had to smile. My dragon needed me, and what a terrifying thought that had once been. He carried me from the room, and Alfred leaned against the far wall, arms folded. I gave him a sleepy smile, and he let out a grunt of sound before reaching over to press a finger to my cheek.

"You need to trust us more, Hellion."

"I do trust you," I told him, head tucked securely to Maddox's shoulder as they fell into step side by side. The path we followed would take us to the bathing room, and I couldn't wait to get all the gore off. "But I had to get them. I told you they were hurting them."

All at once, the memory of the whip marks on Fin's back resurfaced and the endless days of feeling Maddox's roars deep in my blood.

"Tell her," Alfred said as he pulled open the door. Rogue stood near a huge table laden with food—oh, and there was bacon. My stomach rumbled.

"Tell me after I eat and have a bath," I suggested around a yawn. "I figure someone is probably going to try and spank me in there."

"No one is spanking you, Kitten."

Alfred snorted, but he peeled me out of Maddox's arms easily, and I tilted my head as he balanced me while helping Maddox strip off what was left of my clothes. I was utterly boneless and tired.

"Drink, Hellion," Alfred murmured as he tucked me close to his throat. "You fed both of them, and you've fought and not fed..."

"I don't want anyone else's blood," I reminded him with a grimace, even as I teased my tongue over the mark on his neck. The mark I'd given him. It was my turn to nuzzle his neck. If he wasn't going to scold me or rail at me, I could get on board with this. Why the fuck was I so tired?

"Drink, Hellion," he repeated, and this time, he cupped my head and held me in place. Oh right, he'd told me that before. I sank my teeth in, and at the first swelling drop of his blood, I sighed. Memories raced through me, not as powerful or visceral as the first time, but more like snapshots of battles.

A feeling of falling, of wings sheering away, of profound loss and agonizing pain. Tears welled in my eyes. Beyond all of that was the isolation as the twelve who would become the Seven faced each other, bloodied, wounded, and discarded from all they'd known.

Resentment swelled.

Grief thrashed them.

In the end, rather than pull together, they abandoned each other.

The first seeds of war planted...

A sob clawed at my throat because I hated that Alfred had ever felt this way, he eased my head back and frowned down at me. "I'm sorry, Hellion."

Words I'd never imagined hearing.

"You weren't supposed to see that, but..."

"You can't stop thinking about it after facing Fuckface."

Rogue spit out his drink, laughter erupting from him in a hot masculine wave that swept over Fin and then Maddox. Even Alfred's eyes gentled and a faint smile creased his face. "Cyril."

"Whatever," I told him, far more interested in that smile than I was in talking about Fuckface. "I'm happy."

"Are you now?"

"Yep," I said, then licked my lips. "Are you really mad at me?"

"I should be," he admitted. "I was absolutely furious when I discovered you'd bolted your door from the inside..."

"Hey," I countered, tapping his chest. "You started it. You locked me in my room like I was a child."

"No, I locked you in like you are something far too precious to lose because you're still very young and wildly impulsive and—"

"A lot smarter and stronger than you thought." I couldn't help it. Smugness invaded me. He was proud of me. It was right there in his eyes, and he shook his head as he carried me over to the bathing pool. He could have dropped me in, but he just settled me in the water.

"You are brilliant," he murmured, his voice so low, I thought I had to have misheard. "Your mind fascinates me, but what you did... The prison was bad enough, if the shadow demon got his hands on you..."

I sank into the warm water and laughed. "Oh, he did."

Then I ducked my face under the water to soak my hair, and as I emerged, I found a scowling, pissed off Alfred staring at me.

I don't know why it made me laugh, but this asshole really had endeared himself to me.

"Explain," he ordered.

Leaning back against the stone, I said, "He did get his hands on me. He even kissed me..."

Fin groaned.

The air went both icy and hot in the same moment and a growl rumbled from Maddox, but it was Rogue I stared at. His blue eyes had gone icy and shimmering.

"That wasn't an explanation, that was a provocation." Alfred's tone hadn't changed one way or the other. But there was a muscle ticking in his jaw.

"Beautiful," Fin said as he grinned at me. "Stop taunting them and tell them what happened. We just got back, and I don't want to have to deal with the fallout if Alfred and Rogue decide to level that prison."

A shiver went through me. "You'd do it, wouldn't you?" I searched both their faces, and it was Alfred who bent to the pool and braced one hand on the side and slid the other to my nape, forcing my head back so I had to meet his eyes.

"Yes, you're mine. Anything that touches you...I will destroy."

Okay, that should not make me feel so content, but I grinned. "I burned him, Alfred."

At his raised eyebrows, I glanced over at Rogue. He was preparing a plate, but had paused all motion and seemed riveted on me. So I explained about entering willingly so the prison couldn't hold me, and while neither of them rolled their eyes, they did look a little doubtful. The first kiss had startled him, but the second had lit me up and I'd burned him.

As I explained *that* part, Alfred's eyes narrowed and he glanced over to Maddox and Fin.

"Yeah, she glowed," Fin said as he stretched his arms up. "And you saw the wings."

"What wings?"

"Your wings, Kitten," Maddox grinned at me. "Shadow wings. Though the rest of you glowed ethereal light."

"We'll circle back to that," Alfred said after a moment. "What happened to the shadow demon?"

That was the best part, and I grinned. "I don't know what I did but I didn't want him hurting Fin, so I pumped all the energy I had flowing through me into him, like he tried with his shadows, and it seemed to break him—he went almost human and there was jagged silver in his shadowy eyes. I was kind of a badass. Rescued my dragon and my druid, and took out the warden. Or at least, hurt him a lot."

"Hmm, you were amazing, my fierce little hellion." Alfred pressed a kiss to my forehead. "But your druid and your dragon were right where they planned on being. So I don't know if your rescue went as you planned..."

"Wait," I said with a frown. "What?"

"You had to tell her?" Fin grumped. "Thanks."

"You're welcome," he told them as I stared from one to the other. "Next time you decide to go hunting for information and using yourselves as bait, *tell* her. I guessed. She didn't believe me that you would be fine."

"He's right." It was my turn to growl. "I didn't believe him. I broke out of here and ran away to get you, and you *wanted* to be there?"

"Kitten…" Maddox began.

Rogue slid onto the edge of the pool and held a drink out to me. "You need to eat, little *sváss*, then we will hold them so you can beat them for worrying you so."

Oh, there was going to be a beating. I glared between the two and finally locked my gaze on Maddox. It was his pain that tortured me. "Explain."

CHAPTER 6

"It's not what happens to you, but how you react that matters." -
Epictetus

ROGUE

Ignoring the dark look Fin shot his way, Rogue ran his fingers through Fiona's soaking wet hair. There were snarls and tangles he loosened with very little effort.

"I'm waiting." She snapped out the two words, her attention focused on Maddox. A reasonable direction for her anger. He was the one she'd mated first, after all. Mated. Trusted. And while Rogue understood the strategy and even the reasoning behind their actions, she didn't. Not yet.

Alfred and he had both tried to assure her they would be fine, but his little *sváss'* heart proved far too open, despite the prickly and biting exterior.

"Eat," he murmured almost under his breath. As fierce and warrior-like as she'd looked half-covered in blood and

539

soot from the battle, he hadn't missed the hollows in her cheeks or the over-brightness in her eyes. The battle had taken more out of her than she'd admitted, and she'd also fed both Fin and Maddox after their incarceration. It was why he'd agreed with Alfred she needed to feed on him.

Rogue would make sure she ate food, and then he'd feed her blood as well. A week. She'd evaded them for a week. He and Alfred had damn well known *where* she was heading, but the fact she'd managed to stay hidden had been a sharp if irritating surprise. If she could stay hidden from them, in all likelihood, she could avoid those hunting her.

But there was no doubt at all that Cyril and the others wanted her eradicated, and her going off on her own could have had far deadlier consequences. Maddox and Fin both knew this, yet they'd kept that crucial bit of information from her, and she was far too stubborn and headstrong to listen when compelled by a far more primal nature than any of them possessed.

Well, at least that they'd possessed any longer. Maddox would have been the same if it was his mate. Fin had proven it when he'd found out she was in the prison in the first place.

With a huffed sigh, Maddox said, "We needed to know who among the Seven sent the shadow demon after you. We knew it had to be one of them. We'd tracked nearly all of them..." He glared at Fin as if the druid were the one who'd had the insane idea. As likely as that was, Maddox still went along with it, so Rogue had very little sympathy for the dragon's predicament. "Between us, we decided that allowing our capture would give us a chance to see what they would do."

"Why?" Fiona demanded. "They could have executed you."

"Yes and no, Beautiful," Fin said, not pausing to let her argue that point. "We're a lot harder to kill than you might think for one, and for another..."

"They're leverage," Alfred answered for them as he joined them, a goblet of spiced wine in one hand. He held it out to her, and she wrinkled her nose like she'd smelled something awful, and he frowned. So did Rogue.

Last he'd checked, she liked the wine.

"Then they would have tried to use them against you?" Fiona asked, glancing up at Alfred this time as he set the wine aside. Rogue didn't bother to hide his smile at the twin looks of shock on Maddox and Fin's faces. Alfred had done a fair amount to win her over, though not enough, or she wouldn't have fled them. Then again, maybe she would have.

If nothing else, he had to accept that her very nature demanded independence. Still…

"Perhaps," Alfred told her. "They might have used it more to guarantee their distance should they try to bring the fight to me."

Nose still wrinkled, Fiona snorted. "You were hardly struggling against them today."

"Hmm," he replied almost noncommittally. "Then why did you rush to my defense, Hellion?"

"Because you're my asshole."

Alfred's pleased smile made Rogue laugh. Only Fiona could turn an insult into a compliment.

"Besides," she continued, expression sobering as she glared over at the pair in question. "I *felt* your pain." All at once, what humor there was to be found in the situation evaporated. There was no mistaking the very real anguish in her voice. "That's how I knew something was wrong, even before that stupid bitch brought the warning."

"Stupid bitch?" Fin asked.

"Eleanor," Alfred supplied. "Synove sent her with a message."

Maddox pushed away from his side of the pool and came straight to Fiona. Rogue didn't back off, but continued to work his fingers through the tangles in her hair. Periodically, he'd scratch his fingers over her scalp, and it would loosen some of her tension. Not all of it, not when she kept getting angry all over again.

"Kitten…"

"Were you really in pain?"

Grimacing, the dragon gathered one of her hands in his, but Rogue and Alfred both glared. She was barely eating anything, so he gave a near silent huff before picking up one of the croissants and offering it to her. The stare-off between the two was impressive, but she finally opened her mouth and took the bite, even as she rolled her eyes.

"The pain was necessary," Maddox said slowly, but there were lines etched around his eyes that told Rogue what he would say next before he even spoke the words. "I didn't imagine you would feel it."

"She's your mate," Rogue reminded him. "She claimed you, even before she allowed your claim. What part of mating had you forgotten?"

That earned him a baleful look that didn't impress Rogue. Nor would he back down from the implied challenge. "I would never have allowed her to come to real harm."

"But you did," Rogue reminded him. "Something we didn't quite understand because we worried she might be overreacting, but I don't think she was anymore." For that, he would apologize to her personally. But later, when they were alone.

"I'm aware," Maddox growled, this time at him. "I've never mated before, and it didn't occur to me she would feel it…" Rogue wasn't the one he needed to be saying this to, a fact he seemed to recognize himself as he looked down at Fiona again. "I'm sorry, Kitten. Truly."

She gave a little shrug, and it crushed Maddox some. If Rogue read her right, she was about to let him off the hook.

The dragon had made a mistake and now he wanted to make up for it, but her not allowing him to would be even a worse punishment.

"You not knowing seems fair," she said slowly. "After all, I told you succubi don't mate."

"You're not a succubus anymore," Maddox reminded her, disgruntlement in his voice and a sour look on his face that seemed more self-directed. Which was just as well, because Rogue did not believe that a fight right now was what Fiona needed.

Alfred, on the other hand, cleared his throat and Maddox scowled at him, all blazing heat and furious indignation.

"I wasn't scolding her."

"Good."

Fin bit back a snicker, and Rogue flicked his fingers and sent a jolt of ice right into the hot water. The druid's jerk brought his rounded gaze to Rogue, and the smirk on his face fell away.

Right, no laughing. I need to make it up to her as well.

Rogue nodded at him once.

For what it's worth...the vision. It all happened. Maybe not exactly as I saw it, but close enough.

Worry spiked through him, and though he continued to stroke Fiona's hair and half-listen to Maddox's quiet assurances and apologies, he focused on Fin. *How much?*

Enough. The wording seemed off, but I was hurt and poisoned.

Lifting his gaze to the ceiling, he sighed.

I know. The last time they whipped me, they must have laced the leather cords. Fin shook his head. *But she said the words, she wouldn't let me die, and then she fed me and drained the poison.*

Rogue slanted a look at the redhead, who had tilted her head as he combed his fingers through her hair. The dragon had fed her most of that stuffed croissant, and Alfred already had another ready.

Bring Alfred into this conversation.

The fallen angel glanced at him, then over at Fin. *Not here. Not in front of her.*

Fair.

Then after. We need to know.

He gave the curtest of nods, and Maddox shifted his focus to him for a moment and then scowled. "Kitten…"

"Not now," Alfred repeated aloud.

"Yes. Now." Maddox glared at him but almost immediately focused on Fiona. "No more secrets."

"I don't have any secrets," she snapped back and then bopped him on the nose. The act was so comical that even Maddox's fierce frown gave way to a smile.

"Not your secrets, Kitten. Ours."

Fin groaned.

"I haven't forgotten about you," she said, leaning to look sideways at Fin.

"Good," he retorted with a flash of a smile. "I'll present myself for you to tan my ass as soon as Alfred and Rogue are done with yours."

"Who said I was spanking her?" Rogue demanded, and Fiona glanced up at him, biting her lower lip. For a second, she looked so painfully young and earnest, even if her eyes sparked with pure mischief. "Little *sváss*, if you want me to spank you, all you have to do is ask. However, I won't ever do it as a punishment."

"Oh."

No, he could think of other ways to punish that would be far more pleasing. Though honestly, he had a small measure of a struggle at the flicker of disappointment in her eyes.

"I have to ask?"

"No," Alfred answered for him. "I'll take care of it."

Her laughter, warm and husky, filled the room and she sighed.

"Am I forgiven, Kitten?"

"Almost," she told him.

"Almost?" If a dragon could sound crestfallen, the noise Maddox made would be it.

"Exactly, consider almost your punishment for worrying me." Then she took any possible sting out of it with a kiss. But instead of stealing away with her, Maddox let her go after a slow, scorching kiss with a sigh.

"Then we had best discuss the rest in case I have more to make up for."

"Finish bathing, Hellion, then we'll take this somewhere more comfortable." Alfred's tone suggested there would be a real fight if Maddox or Fin argued with him. Rogue had no such objections. The bathing room was good for her, but between the hot pools and the fire, it was uncomfortable for him after a time.

More surprising than Maddox and Fin accepting Alfred's unspoken threat was the fact that Fiona didn't argue. She shifted to move for the soap and the shampoo, and he was forced to leave her hair alone. Instead, he examined his brothers as Fin rose from the water. The marks left on his arms and back had faded significantly, but even the pale pink of them suggested how bad they'd been.

For his part, Maddox looked tired, but he also bristled like his dragon was dangerously close to the surface. To be fair, he and his dragon were more often one in the same, the dragon in the human's skin and the human in the dragon's scales. But this was different.

Mating had changed him.

Changed all of them.

There was a peace to Alfred, a resoluteness that had never been there before. His reaction to her disappearance had been profoundly and dangerously quiet. They'd gone after her, and when they hadn't tracked her immediately, Alfred had simply cleared coven after coven of vampires—all those loyal to the ones allying against them.

Rogue had no objections. They'd gotten out of hand in recent centuries. It was more than time to cull back the worst of the worst. This hadn't been about culling. It had been about eliminating threats. The other members of the Seven had added a fresh bounty to Fiona's head. While vampires older than her might still find her a tough target, enough of them could overwhelm and that was not an option.

When she finished washing up and all traces of blood and soot were gone from her skin, Rogue swept a gaze over her as she rose from the water. He wasn't the only one looking for signs of injury. There was a hint of bruising along one arm and on her hip. No scrapes or broken skin. More, there was no hint of shadow taint on her to mar the shimmer. Even in the warm-lit gloom of the bathing room, she shimmered faintly.

Glowing.

Yes, he'd seen her outside the prison—the pure light she'd radiated and the shadow wings stretching out from her back. Even her deep red hair had taken on a more vibrant sheen, and when she'd looked away for the briefest of moments, her eyes had been purely luminescent, jewels given life.

Not that she hadn't always been beautiful, because she had. Beautiful. Stubborn. Irritating. She dug in deep, refusing to be dislodged with her hotheaded impetuousness. Now?

Now she was exquisite in a way Rogue couldn't even begin to define. Fin and Maddox both dressed in the clothes that had been left for them. It was Maddox who held out a robe and wrapped her in it before he scooped her up. She'd rolled her eyes and slapped his chest because she was fine, but he'd only nipped her ear and murmured something that had her laughing before he carried her up with the rest following.

They'd gone to the library, where fires awaited them, along with hot tea and more food. Fiona had only rolled her eyes as Maddox settled in a chair with her in his lap, and the rest dragged seats over to join them. Rogue plucked her away from Maddox when he was distracted and he scowled, but Fiona only wrapped her arms around Rogue and he curled her closer.

When he'd helped her escape, to spread her then metaphorical wings, he'd known where she was. Yes, he'd told her he wouldn't be able to track her, but he'd known exactly where she would go, just as Fin had. He'd been able to keep his distance and check on her—discreetly—even as Alfred and Maddox had raged at him.

This time?

No, this time, he'd had a taste of the cool gray over-whelming his world once again in her absence. He would not willingly return to that half-state. One he hadn't even real-ized he'd been living in for so long.

"So," Fiona said once Fin pressed a mug of tea into her hands and she snuggled back against Rogue. "What did you want to discuss?"

Maddox opened his mouth, but it was Fin who spoke. "The prophecy."

"Blegh," she said, her whole face screwing up. "I hate prophecies. I hate anything magic related."

"You don't hate me," Fin teased.

"For the moment," she snapped back, but the playfulness in her voice pulled a smile from all of them, even Alfred.

Smoothing a hand over Fiona's abdomen, he drew a light circle against the fabric of her robe. "Little *svász*, we need you to listen for a few moments and to hear us on this. While I agree, prophecies can be muddled and, as often as not, vague and open to interpretation, this one very much impacts you."

She twisted and met his gaze, searching his face for something. The little frown pulled her brows together. "How much does it affect the rest of you?"

"Anything that affects you will have to go through us," he told her simply, directly, and she let out that little sigh of impatience before making a face.

"Fine. I will listen and do my best to not interrupt. But I refuse to not roll my eyes if I think it's stupid."

"Why don't you like magic?" They'd never asked, and if they wanted her to believe in this prophecy even in as much as to help them with it, then they should know.

Slumping back against him, she made a pained sound, then laughed. "I don't like magic because witches are the most interfering creatures you've ever met. They have a spell for literally *everything*. Now, don't get me wrong, I have some very good witch friends. But magic and I? We haven't always gotten along. You know how they say a hybrid can't exist?"

She paused and glanced around at all of them, but it was Alfred who merely nodded and said, "They also say I don't exist, Hellion."

"Yeah, but they are kind of half-right about you," she pointed out. "You don't involve yourself in the world. You stay here, hidden away. You let them come to you so if they don't, then by that logic, you aren't a part of their world and thus you don't exist."

His mouth opened and then closed as he appeared to consider her words. A laugh worked its way through Rogue, and he wrapped a hand around her nape and turned her again. She met his kiss easily and lightly. Eyes lighting up, literally, Fiona leaned into him and then the tingle of her kiss spread through his whole body, and he wrapped her up tighter.

"And she's glowing again," Fin murmured in a low voice. Alfred leaned forward, and even Maddox studied her intently. As aware of them as he was though, Rogue let himself feel her. Something about her wildness had always called to him, from the moment he'd taken her from the prison and brought her to the keep.

The very primal part of her nature summoned his own to the surface—a part of him he'd long believed cut off. It was why he shifted again, something he hadn't indulged in over countless centuries. She'd done more than just push him, she'd brought him back to life.

Energy hummed off of her, but it was beyond soothing and he found himself wanting to cradle her, shield her light from any breeze that would extinguish it.

"I never expected this," Alfred said, running a hand over his mouth as he studied her.

That pulled her attention away from Rogue, and he exhaled a long breath. He could have cheerfully forgotten the rest and drowned in the brilliance of her.

"Spill it, boys. You're starting to freak me out."

They weren't. Not yet. But she tried to tease it out of them. Still, when she slid her hand over Rogue's, he threaded their fingers together.

"There's a prophecy," Fin said. "Borne from a vision I had of you...a long time ago. Now, while I agree with you—prophecies tend to be vague and open to interpretation—this didn't come from just any seer. It came from me."

That pulled her full interest, and Rogue could practically feel her leaning forward, even if she didn't shift a muscle. "Dun. Dun. Dun. *Dun!*"

Her intonation of the musical notes shattered the tension, and Alfred chuckled. The soft laughter carried through the whole library, and Rogue grinned. Maddox and Fin stared at them both like they'd sprouted second heads before they began chuckling, too.

"This isn't supposed to be funny, Beautiful." Fin's argument didn't hold much weight.

She shrugged. "You're an incorrigible flirt and you tease me constantly, and then you tell me in this super serious dark and sober voice that this 'prophecy' is something uber special because *you* saw it?"

With a sniff, he nodded. "Exactly." Then he grinned and another bubble of laughter escaped Rogue. When was the last fucking time he'd been *happy*?

He didn't have to see her face to almost feel the way she rolled her eyes. "Fine, I'll give this all the seriousness it deserves. What's the prophecy?"

Fin exhaled, then glanced at each of them before he focused on her. "When the female hybrid is born, the world will change."

She waited a beat. "It *will* change?"

He nodded.

"That's it? The world will change?"

"Hellion," Alfred began, even as Maddox said, "Kitten—"

But a sound tugged Rogue's attention. A sound and a ping on the wards.

It was the only warning he had before the first volley slammed into the building, but Rogue had already tumbled her out of the chair and over, shielding her as the explosion of light and sound rocked them.

CHAPTER 7

FIONA

The whole building shook. Books fell from their shelves. Artwork dropped off the walls. Even burning embers from the fire scattered as a bombardment of blasts slammed into the keep. Dust rained down from the rafters.

"Take her and go," Alfred ordered, even as Rogue tugged me up from where he'd folded completely over me. A sheen of dust clung to his blond hair and added a gray cast to his face. "Fin. Maddox."

He didn't say anything else, but the two were already in motion. Maddox paused only long enough to kiss me, then Fin did the same. I barely had time to process, and they were gone. Alfred wrapped a hand around my throat as he tugged me into another biting kiss.

"Behave for me, Hellion."

Oh, someone wanted a kick in the balls.

"Please."

Maybe not.

But before I could respond, he, like the other two, was gone.

Another series of blasts shook the whole building, and I glanced at Rogue.

"Trust us?" It was a request and not a command, and he held out his hand.

"I can fight," I reminded him.

"We know, little *sváss*, yet you should never have to. They will focus far better with you safe."

I wanted to complain. I just got them all back together, the last thing I wanted to do was abandon anyone. Still, I clasped Rogue's hand and let him thread our fingers as he scooped me up. The blur of motion as he raced through the keep threatened to upset my stomach. At least away from the windows, the light show no longer dazzled my eyes.

Though I half-expected Rogue to take us to somewhere more "secure," I didn't expect us to descend to the depths past the bathing rooms on a path that would take us to Alfred's crypt. FYI, the fact they even *had* a crypt remained creepy as fuck. And I still had to wonder whether it made me a grave robber or not.

Another blast slammed into the keep and Rogue slid to a halt, his shoulder just impacting the wall next to the great doors lightly, as though he didn't slow his momentum quite enough. The doors opened as he whispered a stream of syllables on a long breath. I didn't understand a single word, but the magic in the air shivered over my skin, not quite touching me as we passed through.

Rogue shot me a questioning look before he set me on his feet and pushed the doors closed. Then his lips were right next to my ear. "The wards also dampen sound and our voices are unlikely to carry, but for now, let us act as if they can hear everything we say."

Got it.

He tugged the tie on my robe, and I raised an eyebrow. Granted, it was all I was wearing and I had zero issue with being naked around him, except it was fucking *cold* down here and he just said we had to assume they could hear us.

My nipples tightened almost painfully in the icy air, and his fingers barely brushed my skin as he pushed the robe off of me. In the silence, it seemed to almost *thud* to the ground, even if it was a more hushed sound. One finger under my chin, he tilted my head back and then his mouth closed over mine, and the frigid conditions seemed to vanish as he half-devoured, half-worshiped my mouth. Rising on my tiptoes, I threaded my arms around his neck.

The fabric of his shirt scraped roughly against me, but when he slid his hands beneath my thighs and hitched my legs higher, I had to swallow a groan. The denim rasped against my skin as he walked deeper into the crypt. He never once let me up for air as the light around us vanished, plunging us into an inky darkness that might have bothered me, save for the burning eyes I met whenever mine fluttered open.

He didn't let up on the kiss for a single instant. Every nerve I possessed came alive, and I practically writhed against him. Light radiated beyond my closed eyelids, and I opened them to find us in a long tunnel. Rogue still had his arms around me, but he'd slowed his movements and he paused entirely when I broke the kiss and looked around us.

The light...

I lifted my hand and then glanced up to find him studying

me with an unreadable expression. The explosions. The sound of stone crashing. All of that had faded. Pressing close, I murmured against his ear, "Where are we?"

"About a mile from the keep," he told me in a soft voice, though he wasn't whispering. "Deep under the mountain. We're almost to where we're going."

"Besides the kiss," I teased, nipping his ear. "Why are we going so slow?"

"Because I don't want anything to damage this beautiful skin," he promised, sliding a hand down to palm my ass. "And because I'm enjoying myself."

It seemed almost wrong to be enjoying ourselves when the others were… Before the thought could fully take root, Rogue closed his mouth on mine, one arm still banded around me, while his hand fisted my hair to keep my head still. It wasn't until the soft thump of a door closing and the silence, punctuated only by my faint groans and the laps of his tongue against mine, changed that I managed to lift my head and suck in an unnecessary breath.

Beyond the circle of light given off by my skin, I couldn't make out much. Rogue slid me down his body to stand on my own feet, and I swayed a little. He waited until I was steady before vanishing into the darkness.

The cold suddenly invaded, and it hit me—the whole way here, he'd kept the chill off me. Arms folded against my hard as diamonds nipples, I tried to ignore the goosebumps prickling my skin. The air was cold enough to burn my lungs with every breath. In Rogue's absence, I glanced down at my hands.

Questions filtered through my kiss-fogged brain, and when he returned, holding out clothing to me, I raised my brows.

"Why am I glowing?"

"I don't know," he answered without hesitation or even a

hint of deception. He caught my hand with his and extended my arm as I gripped the clothes in my free hand. With careful fingers, he smoothed a path up my arm to my shoulder and down again. The touch had my nipples tightening, but the cold fled away again.

A frost elf was really handy for that.

"I don't recall ever seeing its like." He tilted his head, and I could practically feel the sweep of his gaze as he looked down at my body. As bare as I was, there was no missing that every inch of my skin had kindled the same glow.

"I have." The admission cost me nothing.

Eyebrow cocked, he glanced behind us as though listening, and I dragged on the clothes he'd found me. They were a little old fashioned and definitely too large. The pants had to be Fin's, they were narrow waisted like he was. I pulled the drawstring tighter to keep them cinched, then dragged the sweatshirt on. It carried a mustiness to it, but also Maddox.

He had a pair of soft boots in his hands, and as soon as I'd dressed, he knelt to help me in them. "When did you see it?"

"When Alfred helped me after Anton's attack." The flash of light. "It was very bright, but my eyes were closed and it still burned them."

Staring up at me, Rogue's eyes seemed to glow again. This time, I wasn't sure whether the intense blue came from him or his eyes reflecting the glow on my own skin.

"When Dorran had me at the prison, I pushed that light into him, too." I mean, I had said I would tell them later. It wasn't my fault we were under attack. I glanced toward the huge doors he'd closed when we arrived in this chamber. Closing my eyes, I reached for the sense of Maddox or Fin or even Alfred...

Rogue gripped my thigh, and it pulled my eyes open. "What happened when you pushed the light into him, little *sváss?*"

"You're distracting me."

"Yes," he answered me openly as he rose, and for the first time, that unreadable expression softened. "You said you felt Maddox's pain before. I don't want you to feel it now."

Did that mean…?

"They're fighting. There's always some sense of pain involved. I promise you, little *sváss*, no one will take them. This is the other Seven testing our defenses. They are hoping to catch us weak and distracted."

I frowned. "Have they *met* Alfred?"

A soft chuckle came before he cupped my face and kissed me. "Are you warm enough?"

"Yes," I promised.

"Then tell me what happened to the shadow demon when you pushed the light into him."

I gave a little shrug. "He seemed…less somehow. Almost more human. There was silver threading the darkness. Even his eyes changed."

Rogue exhaled a long breath. "The world is not ready for you."

"Then they better buckle up," I reminded him. "Because here I come."

His eyes softened. Or maybe it was my light dimming, because the room did seem to be growing darker. The kiss he gave me this time was far sweeter and filled with just the faintest hint of regret. A deeper emotion filled the contact though, one he seemed intent on pouring into me, and I lapped it up like a kitten with a bowl of cream.

Maybe I was Maddox's kitten after all.

The luminescence of my skin grew brighter as Rogue pulled away. Yes, dressing had hidden some of it, but I could see the outline of my arm beneath the heavy fabric of the sweatshirt sleeve. That was how light it was.

"Emotion."

"Hmm?"

"Strong emotions provoke it." He stroked my cheek with his thumb. "I need you to calm yourself as much as you are able and lock it down. Can you do that for me little *sváss*?"

"We're escaping again, aren't we?"

A prickle raced over my scalp. I didn't want to leave them behind.

"Yes." No lies. Not even an attempt to hide it from me. "They will find us. Fin can track us both. Alfred will always know where we are..."

"He will? 'Cause you know, that might be kind of creepy."

A hint of what might be a flush touched his cheeks. It was kind of adorable that he could be embarrassed. Rogue traced a finger in a figure eight around the twin marks on my throat.

"So he knew where I was when I left? When you helped me?"

Rogue sighed, then captured my hands and pressed a kiss to each palm. "Yes. The same way he knew where I was all those years I tried to hunt him. He let me be, and I thought he would you as well. I didn't count on the need to see you. The need I shared."

"That doesn't make it *less* creepy," I admitted, hardly mollified by the fact he just expressed how much he needed to see me. "Though...I kind of like that you missed me."

"I love you, little *sváss*." He said it with such ease, and at the same time, there was no mistaking the glimpse of surprise on his face. "It's not something I thought myself capable of...yet I do. So yes, I needed to see you, as did he. I don't doubt Fin and Maddox both did. We have been alone for a long time."

"But you have each other..."

"Family." He nodded once. "Brothers. Sometimes friends.

Oftentimes antagonists. And with Fin…well, he was the baby for a long time."

"If you call me the baby of the family, I'll make sure your balls are blue before they ever touch me again." That was bullshit, but he gave me such a solemn look, I couldn't help but smile. Even when I really shouldn't. This wasn't a good situation. We were alone down here, while the others…

"You are ours," however, was all he said, and it swept all of my objections aside. Ugh. When did I become such a sap? "That is all that matters to us."

"That and the so-called prophecy." Something they hadn't really explained beyond the serious vagueness above.

"Prophecies change," Rogue said, his tone growing fiercer. "Sometimes in a race to avoid one, you make it happen. But the circumstances they are forcing may lead to the doom they think you will cause."

The light vanished, leaving us in darkness. I was supposed to cause their doom?

"I'm sorry, little *sváss*," he murmured before he swept me up against him again. "I need you to keep the light out as much as you can."

Apparently, thinking about shitty things did that.

"Fine, I'll focus on what an asshole Alfred is." Only a glimmer reappeared. Rogue chuckled, and I couldn't help it, so did I.

"I'm afraid that your feelings on that shine for us."

Ugh. I groaned, and the light went out again. "Remember when I said succubi didn't do relationships?"

"Hmm," was his response, but we were moving. Thankfully, he could navigate in the dark, so I just tucked my face against his throat and held on.

"I'm kind of glad that I do," I admitted, and he tightened his grip on me. That was about as sappy as I was willing to get as we raced away from the others.

Safety was really fucking overrated.

~

WE EMERGED FROM THE TUNNELS NOT FAR FROM THE TOWN he'd taken me to on the snowmobile. At my glare, he grinned.

"You can't blame me for wanting to feel you against me for a while, little *sváss*. Especially when I had to let you go."

I snorted.

But he didn't set me down until we reached the edge of the town itself. It was just a little before dawn. How long had we been moving? Granted, he hadn't run nearly as fast as he had on other occasions, but once we'd gotten moving again, he hadn't stopped.

The air was still cold, but as long as he kept a hand on me, the chill remained at bay. Threading our fingers together, he led me through the side streets almost a silent wraith, until he reached a bakery. The smell of fresh bread, pastries, and more perfumed the air, even as little clouds of flour escaped through one of the gratings.

Not going inside—even when I pouted—he guided me up the stairs in the back and then into a door that he had a key for.

Because of course he did.

Inside, it was a tidy little apartment. Just three rooms plus a little bathroom, which I made a beeline for because I really had to pee. I hadn't said a word while we were moving because I didn't want to create a problem.

I was just checking my bedraggled appearance in the mirror when his voice drifted toward me.

"Two hours. Not a moment longer," he ordered. The tone was so cold and ridiculously inflexible. It sent a tingle straight up my spine. The woman in the mirror staring back at me had wild curls out of control and tangled together while she wore a shirt that was far too large and made her eyes seem way too big.

There was a smile on her face.

My face.

The call ended. "Are you hungry? We need to stay here but…"

I met his gaze in the bathroom mirror.

"What is it?"

"Are we mated? I mean…I know Maddox and I are. Fin bonded himself to me. And I'm pretty sure Alfred did…or if he didn't, I'm a little terrified what bonding is going to feel like after that. But are we? You and me?" The surge of panic slid through me like some snake sliding up my spine. It left me shuddering and uneasy. I didn't even know where it came from.

Rogue stepped right up to me and wrapped a hand around my throat as he tugged me back to him. Not once did he take his gaze from mine, and I didn't dare look away from him in the mirror, no matter how exposed it made me feel.

"My people always choose their mates. It was an act of the heart and the mind fusing to what the soul desired." He nipped at my ear. "If I hadn't chosen you, I would never have been able to knot you."

The shudder of apprehension turned to one of delight, even as disbelief welled up in me. "You didn't even like me when you knotted me."

"What the heart and soul desire is not always impacted by what one likes or dislikes, and it was never you I disliked, little *sváss*. I acknowledged who you were to me from the beginning…" He kissed the spot just behind my ear, even as his fingers tightened on my throat. No fear threaded through me, he wouldn't hurt me, and the possessive grip was to illustrate his point.

I swallowed.

"Little beloved," he whispered. "You destroyed centuries of ice, shattered a millennium of gray, and filled my life with color, even as you woke me from a slumber deeper than any Alfred ever took."

Tears might have welled in my eyes. It could've been the cold, or it could've been the depth of the emotion in his voice.

"I said you were ours," he continued. "And I meant it. Whatever ceremony you need, we can do. But I chose you then. I choose you now. There is nothing I won't do for you. Even help you escape us."

And he had.

Finally, I closed my eyes and leaned into him fully. "Thank you."

He chuckled. "You're thanking me for loving you?"

"Why not?" I countered. "Before the four of you, only Elias was ever so free with his affection."

His hand flexed against my throat, and when I peeked, I caught the sharpness in his smile.

"Elias is my *friend*. You don't get to hurt him because you think he might be competition. He loves me like a sister, not a lover."

Rogue grunted, but then he turned me around and we were out of the bathroom and on the bed. He made short work of my clothes, and I laughed as he cupped my breasts, then gasped as he closed his mouth over one nipple, even as he pinched the other.

When a cry slipped from my throat, he moved his hand over my mouth. "You have to be quiet, beloved. Can you do that?"

I stared at him. Was he serious?

A slow grin creased his lips. A smile that beckoned me to play with him. But the others... He bit down just below my nipple, and his teeth sinking in sent a bolt of heat straight to my cunt. I fought the groan, even as he kept his hand locked over my lips. I couldn't move because of the weight of him pinning me down, and he licked and sucked at the wound briefly before returning to suck at the nipple.

Back and forth he went between them, like he had all the time in the world, and I half-thought he was determined to make me come just from playing with my nipples. I dug my fingers into his shoulders and his hair. He wasn't even naked. A sound of protest escaped me, but the slickness between my thighs belied any real objection.

When he finally lifted his head, my nipples throbbed they ached so much, and just the act of his blowing a kiss of icy air against them sent a wave of heat crashing through my system. Everything coiled taut, and then unleashed. I swore my vision whited out, and by the time I surfaced, he'd flipped me over and lifted my hips. With one hand on my throat and the other on my hip, he drilled into me.

The first thrust of his cock sent sparks through my whole system, and I was already spasming around him as he drove into me over and over. There was no time to catch my breath or to do anything but hold on. I fisted the covers as we rocked together.

His breath was hot in my ear as he whispered in time with his thrusts. "I love you, little beloved. I choose you."

Over and over again until my earlier tears returned, and I sobbed as he triggered another orgasm. I needed him. I needed all of them. And he seemed determined to prove to me that he wanted and needed me.

That he chose me.

Hot tears escaped as he locked his hand over my mouth, smothering my screams as they escaped, and everything went up in flames inside of me as he slammed home once more and then began to swell. His knot stretched me and sent aftershock after aftershock through my system. He moved his hand so that his wrist was there, and I bit down, lapping at the blood he offered, and I swore I could feel his smile against my damp cheek as he nuzzled my face.

Almost as soon as his knot inflated, it released though. Exhaustion swarmed me as I lapped the wound on his skin closed. When I stole a look up at him, the wonder on his face made me smile. The tired fled, and I twisted, pulling free and flipping him so that I could lean over him. He stroked the damp hair away from my face, even as I closed the distance to kiss him.

We still had some time to kill…

CHAPTER 8

"You may kill me, but no one can make me go back." - Anonymous

It wasn't even an hour after we arrived at the little apartment that our madcap escape took on a different intensity. Being assaulted by the twin forces of sweetness from the bakery below and Rogue's scent all over my skin might have left me a little drunk—also hungry—but it was Rogue's brief vanishing act and returning with clothes in my size that left me almost schoolgirl giddy.

No lie. I used to mock girls in romance movies. The stupid little smiles. The happy little giggles. Blech. Who *did* that? Love—that four-letter word was not a factor in my existence. Not really. No, my four-letter word was L-U-S-T, and that was always about survival. Or had been. Not that lust was a problem with them, but that wasn't—

I sat down abruptly on the edge of the bed, Maddox's sweatshirt in hand. I hadn't consumed lust in a while. Not the same way at all.

I hadn't needed it. Had I?

"Little *sváss*," Rogue said, his quiet voice carrying, or maybe I just heard him better. "We need to go."

I stood and dragged the sweatshirt on, but an odd sound had me pivoting toward the windows. They overlooked an alley behind the little bakery, which also happened to be where their grates were located and tormenting me with all their sweetness.

The glass shattered, and I retreated to the door, narrowly avoiding the flying shards as a woman landed in the center of the destruction. Blazing eyes filled with—I would have said *hate*, but seriously, she looked more like one of those crazy ass shoppers who are determined to get the last item in a Black Friday instant sale—way too much insanity, the new arrival hissed. Legit fucking *hissed*.

I barely caught a flash of teeth before she lunged at me, only she never connected. Rogue slammed into her from the side, and she crashed through the wall—all the way through it—with an explosion of plaster, snow, and splintering wood.

"We have to go, little *sváss*." The words had barely left his lips when our visitor returned, and this time, punted him through a wall.

Liquid fury spilled into my veins. Even with the competing plumes of dust and a swirl of snow riding the icy breeze now whistling through the room, I couldn't miss the cloying scent rolling off of her like she'd bathed in some floral perfume. It clogged my nose and coated my throat.

"Hey, bitch," I snarled as I hit her. We flew together out the first hole she'd made when she crashed through the window. I had a fistful of her hair, and she raked my back trying to grab mine. We rolled against the brick building next door, dislodging several and sending them raining down on the alley.

A cat let out a screech as it vacated the warm spot on the grate at our battle. I crashed my forehead into hers, and while that shit looks awesome in movies, fuck me. I swore I saw stars and little dancing forest animals that said, *well, that was stupid.*

We landed against the ground in the alley. All the air whooshed out of us. I found her glaring at me as we lay there for what felt like endless seconds before she darted forward to seize my jaw in a bruising grip, and then she slammed me back against a wall.

Yeah, I was over that.

I kicked the bitch right in the cunt.

Newsflash, a ball shot hurts guys. Ask Maddox. A cunt shot definitely hurts girls. Especially if you have pointy boots.

Nothing could have prepared me for the shriek or the slap that left my ears ringing.

Bitch.

I narrowly avoided the next hit, and when I punched her, I went right for the boob. Look, was it fair? No. Fighting wasn't supposed to be *fair*. Her scream shattered glass, and she tore through walls, and she'd hit Rogue hard enough he hadn't come back yet.

I managed a second punch, and this one rocked her head back and she spat out blood. Oh, I felt that all the way through my arm. It was like punching a wall. Only I could crack a wall apparently. Rogue landed between us, and he caught her next fist and twisted her arm outward before it snapped audibly, and then he exhaled what looked like pure frost in her face.

"Go, little *sváss*," he ordered me. "This is Keeley." He shot a look toward me. "I'll hold her, you go…"

"Hell no," I snarled and pushed off the wall to lunge at her as she raced toward Rogue. I would not let her hurt him. I wouldn't let any of them be hurt. Not again. Not if I could stop it. The snow continued to fall from the leaden skies into our dark little space littered with bricks and blood. But the light from my fists intensified.

Light.

I had no idea who the hell Keeley was but what I'd done to Dorran flashed through my mind, so instead of hitting the bitch, I seized her by her shirt and slammed my mouth down on hers. The kiss was fury and snarls, teeth and blood, panic and desperation. She raked her fingers down my face, but I didn't let her go, not even when she tore some hair out.

Bitch.

The light poured out of me and into her, and I fed the light into her like I would have devoured the heat of lust from another. I didn't know where the idea came from, but it demanded to be unleashed so I let it out. Her blood was sour on my tongue, and I refused to consume it. Her screams grew frantic against me as she tried to pummel and claw and I didn't let up.

I gave her everything, and the world seemed to brighten like a summer's day beyond my closed lids, and then all at once, she ripped away and Rogue tugged me backwards. The hard feel of him against my back, the hot and cold combination, steadied me. I opened my eyes in time to meet the bitch's shocked gaze while her body turned almost blazing white as cracks and fissures split across her skin.

"What did you do?" she shrieked at me. But the spider webbing damage spiraled out, and then she incinerated in a cascade of fire and light.

Gone.

Poof.

Wow.

Silence rushed into the void of her disappearance, but a gasp pulled my attention to the side and I stared at a woman who stared at us. She had a phone in her hand, and her eyes were the size of saucers.

She was also very, very human.

Oh.

Shit.

Um…

I grinned at her and pushed away from Rogue. The lady took a halting step backwards, and I froze. "Sorry," I told her. "New special effects for that new series coming out next year, so hush hush."

Wonder edged the suspicion in her gaze, and that phone continued to point at me. Telling the whole world about supernatural creatures was just not a good idea. Every single time word of our existence got out into the world, some new series would kick off, from *Great Mystery Solvers* to *Monster Hunters*.

Really, just some tacky shit.

"You know *Make Magic*?" I was totally bullshitting. With a hand, I reached up to wipe the blood off my face. The gouges stung, but nowhere near as much as they had earlier. "See, fake skin. It looks like I tore it open, but nada."

Lowering her phone slowly, she gave me a trembling nod. "Oh. That's…" Excitement flared in her eyes. "That's so wonderful. Are you an effects artist?"

No honey, I'm a master bullshitter and I just fed you a line.

"Actually, she's our top-secret ringer," Fin offered as he strolled around the corner, and my heart did a swift squeeze. He was all right. His dazzling smile snared the human's attention so effectively, she completely pivoted away from me. Wow, even I was impressed, but then I'd rather stare at Fin too. "I'm sure you'll understand that we just can't risk that footage getting out."

Charm rolled off of him in waves, and she handed over her phone with the dreamiest of smiles while I had to bite back a grin.

"Thank you so much," Fin told her as he went through it

and made some adjustments. "Truly. You have no idea how fantastic this is, and because you're helping us out, I'm going to make sure you get something special. Okay?"

"Oh, that would be lovely, and I won't tell anyone. They probably wouldn't believe me anyway."

Another brilliant smile, and he handed her the phone back. A light touch to her shoulder had her moving away, and she walked kind of dreamily. I ran my tongue over my lower lip until I tasted the blood and grimaced before turning and spitting it out, then swiping a hand over my mouth. Maddox and Alfred stood on either side of Rogue, their gazes locked on me.

"What?"

I glanced down at myself. The outfit was a mess. She'd torn Maddox's sweatshirt. Ugh, that just aggravated me all over again. Running my fingers through the tangles of my disheveled hair, I winced when I came to the raw patches on my scalp. Yeah, she'd definitely pulled out more than a few strands.

"Hellion," Alfred said smoothly as he closed the distance. It wasn't until he caught my hands and pulled them from my hair that I realized there were charred bits of ash and flesh tucked under my nails.

Gross.

"I was behaving," I told him. "I was inside. She broke in." I pointed to the damaged walls above. How the hell were we going to hide that?

Alfred cupped my face and brought my gaze back to him. The lightness in his fingers as he traced over the skin she'd raked reminded me it was still sensitive, but the pain was minimal, if at all.

"We need to go," Fin said from behind me. "We repelled that force, but there will be more. As soon as word gets out about Keeley, you won't be able to call off the others."

Maddox cracked his knuckles and growled a laugh. "Let them come. Losing her is not an option. They should learn it now, then we can settle in peace with them gone."

Them.

The Seven.

Wait…

But before I could ask, they were all gathered in around me and Fin whisked us away. The magic pulled us along, and I clung to Maddox and Alfred, even as Fin kept a grip on me and I could almost perceive Rogue there. It was the strangest feeling, and my gut dropped as soon as we reappeared. The cold air no longer bit at my cheeks and the sweatshirt—or what was left of it—was almost too warm, but it was damp and there was a fine mist of rain sprinkling down on us.

Tilting my head back, I glanced toward the stone edifice we'd arrived at.

"A castle."

Fin shot me a grin. "It's not all that, more a fortress, but much more defensible than the manor house. While they are throwing themselves at the traps on the keep, this will suit our purposes fine…"

He dropped a kiss on my nose.

"I'm going to scan the perimeter." Then he loped off, whistling.

Rogue grunted, then dropped a kiss on my lips before shooting an enigmatic look at both Maddox and Alfred. "I'll help him."

We didn't linger outside. The interior was far more rustic than the keep. It had apparently been built back when years were three digits instead of four.

I wasn't judging.

Apparently, grave robber was a title that I just had to get used to.

Eh, worth it.

Maddox pulled me to him and wrapped his arms around me, while Alfred built up the fire in the hearth. We'd moved into the tiny kitchen, not that I was sure it was a kitchen, but it had a heavy table and bench seating and something that resembled a stone oven in the wall, and there was a hook in the hearth to hang something from.

We were as far from glamping as you could get, and I really wanted to get fast forwarded back to the decade I came from. Because I didn't think I was built for long term roughing it.

Yeah, yeah, first world problems.

When Maddox settled me in his lap as he took a seat, I curled up against him. Tired hit me like I'd been struck by all the falling bricks in that alleyway. I smothered a yawn, but Maddox stroked my back and I caught Alfred studying me from where he tended the fire. The corners of his mouth tipped into a smile, and that was the vision I took with me as I closed my eyes for just a few moments.

"Keep it down," Fin cautioned in a clipped voice. "You don't want to wake her."

"We're not waking her," Maddox's voice rumbled beneath my ear. I was still curled up against him, the heat from his body soaking through me. "She's not all the way asleep or all the way awake. Listen to her breathing."

"Just talk normally," Alfred suggested. "She keeps dropping off."

I must have, because they sounded a million miles away and right there at the same time.

"She killed one of the Seven, Alfred."

Wait...

"I'm aware. We arrived just as she tore her apart."

What?

"They're never going to let this go." The wariness in

Rogue's voice made my heart hurt. I stretched and tried to shift, but one hand stroked my leg and another my back.

"Shh," Maddox soothed and pressed a kiss to my hair. Sinking back into the heat cocooning me, I yawned.

"Don't want Rogue to worry," I said in and around the stretch of my jaw.

"He's not worrying, Hellion," Alfred told me. "He's planning. We all are. You used a lot of energy, that's why you're tired. Do you need to feed?"

I turned that idea over and must have dozed off thinking about it, lulled by the heat and the soothing stroke of Maddox's hand.

CHAPTER 9

"Change is the only constant in life." - Heraclitus

ALFRED

Clearing out the horde of vampires and the witches they'd dragged along to test our wards had been more of a nuisance than a fear. Still, removing Fiona from the situation had been vital. Maddox had no restraint when she was close or under threat. Not that Alfred seemed to possess much. He'd known the vampires. They were more of Cyril's get. While they hadn't discussed it with Fiona yet, he highly doubted Cyril was dead.

Alfred could survive Maddox's fire. It was particularly unpleasant, but he could survive it. There were too many questions about Fiona, and now that her transition had settled, she also seemed to be coming into her own and that was a dazzling sight. He would allow nothing to interrupt it.

But the last thing he expected when they tracked her and Rogue down was to find them mid-battle with another of the

Seven. Keeley. It had been centuries since the last time he saw her, and he doubted he would ever see her again. Fiona had filled her with angel fire. Or at least as close to angel fire as Alfred had ever seen outside of himself. It was a rare talent among his own kind, and never had he seen it in the hands of his brothers, not even Maddox.

The threat to her was immeasurable now. How long it would take word to reach the others that one of the Seven had died, making them the Six, he had no idea. Yet, he also held no illusions. They'd wanted Fiona dead before. Even Synove might abandon her desire to stay out of the fight.

For Fiona to possess it... A fierce kind of pride flooded him. Yet the exhaustion worried him, even if it didn't surprise him. Angel fire came from the soul, and it depleted the body swiftly. Maddox held her close and seemed unwilling to part with her. The dragon would take time to settle down. Each time he'd had to separate from his mate, stress had marked the occasion. While Alfred couldn't blame him for his concerns—he was the last of his kind—he was also not alone and he needed to understand that...

Still, Alfred could content himself with studying her and how peaceful she looked wrapped up against Maddox. Her vibrant red hair seemed to glow of its own accord, as did her skin, though the illumination had dimmed as she slept.

"She's pregnant."

Everything in the room halted, and his wasn't the only heartbeat to stutter.

When the female hybrid is born, the world will change.

Fin pushed out of his chair and extended a hand toward Fiona, even as Maddox's eyes flashed a warning, but Rogue just stared at all of them, arms folded. He seemed rather calm for such a pronouncement.

"Why do you say that?" Alfred refused to leap to some impossible conclusion. In how many thousands of years had they never fathered any children… She hadn't been pregnant before, had she? No, he would have known. Maddox would have known.

The dragon stared at Fin, but his arms were locked around her. They weren't dislodging her anytime soon.

"Because my knot failed."

Alfred flicked a look from Fiona to Rogue. He'd never inquired about their sexual practices or appetites. The knotting he'd heard about from others but… "And that means she's pregnant?"

"Yes," Maddox rumbled, but still, he stared at Fin. The druid had a hand over her abdomen and his head bowed as the magic seemed to hum off of him. "The desire to procreate has been riding me since I met her. Even mating couldn't quite quiet it."

"Transition kills." It always had. It was another reason he didn't extend that offer of life to many, because it was not the life they'd known. He'd been selfish with Rogue and to an extent with Maddox. Fin had been different, but he'd also asked for it. Asked because of the woman in Maddox's arms. Still…she had fought them all, and they'd pushed it. Alfred had pushed it because he couldn't risk losing Maddox, and ultimately, he had not wanted to lose her either.

"She was a succubus," Rogue reminded him. "That was always their objection. Not just that she would be a hybrid like us, but a demon hybrid. Do you even know what the spark of life does with a demon?"

"Succubi aren't high demons," Alfred argued. "They're barely demons at all." Particularly when one considered how they were treated among their own kind and why Fiona had objected so strongly to their possession. She didn't want to be a toy or used only for her hungers. Controlled.

Yet she hadn't even realized what a force of nature she was *before* he completed the transition.

Unmoved by the argument, Rogue said, "She's pregnant, which changes *everything*."

In that, he wasn't wrong.

Fin glanced up at him, and he saw the truth written in the druid's eyes.

Dammit.

Cyril already wanted her head. Eamon and Gemma had sided with him. Synove withdrew, wishing to be left alone and for her neutrality. That left Wyman. While Fin and Maddox had said nothing of him, he would be the most difficult to find, but Alfred had a suspicion of where he might be.

"What about Isaac and the whelp, Dimitri?" Those were the two lives they owed her.

Fin's expression tightened. "That's your question?"

"Yes," he informed him. "Her security and balance are the issues. Eliminating those who hurt her before is a priority."

"And no one else will touch a hair on her head," Rogue stated, arms folded. Maddox rumbled with another sound, but it wasn't a growl and his eyes were pure dragon.

We'll never get him away from her now. The observation from Fin earned a faint smile from Alfred.

No, but I'd rather he is with her. Very little can get past any one of us, but a dragon with a clutch?

No, nothing would survive to get past Maddox, and in his soul, Alfred rather hoped that child was Maddox's. The dragon had given up so much, and the thought that even a child with some dragon blood would be in the world? It would do his old friend good.

The soft snort from the druid suggested he had more to say, but he kept it to himself.

"Eamon's hiding them," Fin admitted. "We got close, that's when we realized that one of the..." He paused a beat, flicking his gaze back to Fiona. "That one of the *Six* had to be hiding them. They have to be using witches to try and mask the trail, too, or I'd have already found them."

"Stay with him," Alfred ordered, and he pivoted on a heel. The old fortress was located deep in the wilds of Wales. Its age would afford them some protection. It also held some of Fin's finest wards and lay within the cross section of two ancient stone circles. He could whisk them away before anything got close.

He barely made it a half-dozen steps before Rogue and Fin both blocked him. Only Maddox hadn't moved.

"What?" he demanded.

"You find out she's pregnant, and you want to move now?" Rogue asked. "You aren't even a little curious…"

"It's likely Maddox's. He was her first lover, first mate. It makes sense…"

"He wasn't actually," Fin said, and nodded to Rogue. Alfred frowned.

"Then that is as well… You both deserve it."

"Alfred," Rogue said quietly. "She has spent the most time with you, particularly after her transition."

"I'm not…"

He frowned. Procreation was not impossible *before*. Before the fall. But after? How many lovers had he taken on and off over the years? While there might have been long stretches in between…

"It's not just you," Fin said it almost gently, but Rogue held none of that kindness in his eyes as he pinned him.

"She said you used light to purge the shadow demon taint…"

Alfred stilled. He had. When the demon attacked her through Anton. He'd…

"That was the second time you did it," Rogue reminded him, the clipped tones held recrimination. "A shadow demon trying to transform her mid-transition, then you purged the taint even as you pushed…angel fire into her?"

"It wasn't angel fire," he admitted slowly. "It's the spark. It is the light that is the antithesis of the dark and yet fathers it at the same time."

"Because the moment you add anything to the light, the shadow has been created." Fin made a face. "Makes sense." Still, he looked thoughtful. "I think Rogue might be right—she glows. The wings? We saw what she did to Keeley. All of us are hybrids, but it was our natural talents that were enhanced. Hers…hers seems to have shifted fundamentally."

Unmade her.

Remade her.

Reforged her.

Alfred nodded. "Then we will have to address all of it later. For now, she must be kept hidden and safe. And I need to deal with my brethren."

Because they could not be allowed to harm her. *Ever.* A possessiveness threaded through him. He'd loathed the touch of the shadow demon on her already. And wanting her had never been a chore. But the others like him did not want change, and that was all Fiona had been—a detonation of light, color, and sound in the middle of their stone shrouded world.

A part of him wanted to take her, take all of them, and secret them away, far from the politics and the wars of his brothers and sisters. That would never happen though, because Fiona did not want to be hidden away. He hadn't even asked her yet, and he knew she didn't want to be.

The look on her face in the alley when she told him she'd behaved and that Keeley had started it more or less had been endearing, even if Keeley attacking them at all had filled him with a reasonable amount of dread.

"Whatever you're thinking right now," Rogue said, pulling

his attention to the present, to the one who had been his brother for longer than either of them could remember and to the younger one who had become a son and baby brother in equal measures. "This war isn't yours alone. We do this together. All of us."

"This war is between my brethren and me. It has never been about you."

"Wrong," Fin argued. "It has always been about us. Since you turned Rogue and Maddox. Long before you brought me over. They were furious about me, too. I haven't forgotten those attempts. Gemma was very determined to end me if she couldn't seduce me away."

Alfred sighed. "This should not be your battle. For most of you…it wasn't a choice." He looked at Rogue, and his oldest friend chuckled.

"That water has long since passed the bridge, my friend. We are not those people anymore. And for the first time in memory, I am grateful for your stubborn decision."

Fin's grin widened as he slapped Rogue's shoulder. "Fiona is worth it."

"Indeed," he agreed, and then they both looked at Alfred.

With a combination of a frown and impatient sigh, he eyed them both. "I claimed her. What more do you want from me?"

"Alfred…"

Leaving them, he strode back into the ancient kitchen where Maddox still cradled Fiona. Only her green eyes were open, even if the rest of her seemed to radiate exhaustion. There was still a glow to her, an ancient light he hadn't seen in a long time. Her smile grew when he entered, and then she stretched and Maddox helped her sit up.

"What's wrong?"

"Nothing, Hellion," he told her with a sigh. While he would withhold the information, he didn't dare. She needed to know she was pregnant. More, she needed to know why they couldn't allow her back into the fight and why the others were coming for her.

Damn them all. If they would only leave her alone...

But they won't. Fin's quiet voice tapped at the edges of his mind. The druid knew better than to intrude too deeply and trusted Alfred to not blast him for even this much contact. *They're afraid. They've been the big bads for eons. Most of you still think you're better than anything on this plane. Now she is a threat to them...*

Is she the threat, Fin? Or is our child?

The moment he claimed ownership, it settled within him as though it belonged there always. The world did not want them to have her, then the world would have to change. If that meant eliminating the others until only he was left, then he was prepared to do that. Before, he'd always resisted the idea and killed them only when he realized there were no other options.

Not this time.

Cyril had already shown his hand, as had Eamon. They both needed to die. There was a sliver of a chance Gemma could be reasoned with. Synove might yet keep her word. But he had to find Wyman.

"Do you still want Dimitri and Isaac?" The question was not the one he meant to ask, but the words still fell from his lips. Maddox scowled at him and Fin snickered, but he ignored both.

"Yes," she answered without hesitation or prevarication. All at once, she perked up. "Do you have them?"

"No, but we know who is hiding them. Once I end him, their safety will be compromised and Fin should be able to track them, or Maddox."

Her smile lit him up inside, and he reached for her. Maddox grumbled but surrendered her as she slid off of his lap and then wrapped up against Alfred. He passed a hand over her hair and then down her back. A part of him had to know she was intact. There had been blooded wounds when they first found her, but most had already closed.

Maddox rose from the table as Alfred cradled her. The castle was ancient and safe, and Rogue and Fin were right, he couldn't leave them behind, even with Maddox to guard her. Her shirt still had blood on it. Blood. Dirt. Ash. Dust.

She needed a bath and likely a meal.

"Something is still wrong," she murmured. "You're all staring at me."

"Nothing is wrong, Hellion," he assured her, though he supposed that depended on her point of view. In this instance, she may not agree.

When she gripped a fistful of his hair and tugged, a smile pulled at his lips. Acquiescing to the pull, he lifted his head to meet her gaze.

"Then tell me what is troubling all of you. Is it because of that girl I killed? Seriously, I don't even know how I did it. Just—I remembered what I did to Dorran and then did it to her."

"No," he said slowly. "Though we should discuss that."

"Is it because I kissed her? Are you going to get weird about that?"

A laugh rumbled in his chest. "No, Hellion. I don't plan to get weird about that." Then, because he couldn't help himself, he stroked her lower lip with his thumb as he cupped her chin. "Just know that whomever you kiss that is not us will die. Because if you don't kill them…"

"We will." Maddox nodded once, then folded his arms. But his attention never left Fiona. She might adore her dragon, but she'd never had several tons of angry dragon standing between her and the rest of the world. Nor a dragon desperate to keep what was most precious to him safe. They would be inseparable, and Alfred preferred it that way. He wanted her safe with equal ferocity.

Fiona rolled her eyes. "Trust me. I've got plenty of lustful energy right here and all the dicks I could want. I didn't mind some breasts now and then, but we're fine. Just remember the same goes for anyone you kiss, male or female."

"Noted," Fin said, almost lazily, but the smile in his voice harkened back to when he was far younger and more carefree. "I'm almost excited to tempt your jealousy, Beautiful. You're exquisite in all your aspects."

"A constant delight," Rogue murmured, but the soft sound of his hand slapping Fin upside the head filled the room and Fiona burst out laughing.

The sound bubbled through Alfred.

Even Maddox smiled.

"Okay, so it's not the killing or the kissing." She gave his hair a sharp tug, enough for the sting to send a ripple of need through him. "Then spill the beans, Asshole."

It was his turn to laugh. "That is not my name."

"But you're my asshole and you like to indulge me."

She wasn't wrong there.

"Let us get you something to eat, and I will tell you. Then we will discuss what must be done. There is a war to wage, Hellion. A war that we cannot avoid, and I would prefer you were not a part of." Almost instantly, rebellion flared in her eyes, but he pressed his thumb against her lips to silence the torrent of words surely swirling in that magnificent mind of hers. "But we cannot keep you from it as much as I might desire otherwise. So you need to know everything, and I need you to trust us when it comes to making battle decisions."

Her eyes narrowed. Likely, she didn't think he was being wholly honest. "What if I think they're stupid decisions?"

"Like going down rather than up?" Maddox asked, and she groaned and tilted her head back.

"Okay, you do it *one time* and now I never hear the end of it?" Still, the humor in her eyes and the love filled him with a lightness he really hadn't had in all the time since his wings fell away.

Burned.

Destroyed.

Cast out.

But with Fiona? It was like he could almost feel them.

"Hush," he ordered when Maddox went to retaliate. "You two can debate this later, for now, we have to discuss a great deal, starting with the fact that you're pregnant, Hellion."

"*What?*"

CHAPTER 10

"If it doesn't challenge you, it won't change you." - Anonymous

FIONA

"Y ou're pregnant."

"*What?*"

What had he just said? Alfred's dark-eyed gaze locked on mine. "You're pregnant, Hellion."

Nope.

I shook my head, then pulled away from him farther to sweep a look over each of them. Maddox's stare was wildly intent, and Rogue's guarded. But Fin looked at me with so much hope in his eyes, I whirled back to Alfred.

Yelling at him was easy.

"What. Did. You. Do?"

For the barest second, amusement flickered in his eyes and in the curve of his too sexy mouth. Then he seemed to reconsider that maneuver. "We're not sure yet... Hybrids are different. We discussed this."

Arms folded, I glared at him. The first question on the tip of my tongue was to demand how he'd gotten around the birth control spells I'd paid *excellent* money for. But the question died unspoken.

"You asshole, you killed me."

He huffed out a long sigh. "Hellion…"

"Kitten," Maddox interceded. "This is a gift."

Head tilted back, I transferred my glare from Alfred to the ceiling. I wasn't quite ready to dash Maddox's hopes, or Fin's for that matter. To be honest, I didn't want to think about this at all. A full transition required dying. To be honest, Dimitri had probably started it when he killed me.

"I really want to kill Dimitri now." More than that, I wanted him to hurt. All my earlier tiredness fled, and when Maddox curled his fingers around mine, I let out a sigh.

"Kitten," he murmured and tugged me around. "This is a gift."

For them. Maybe. "We've got a lot of other things to worry about right now, don't we?" Yep, denial was not just a river in Egypt. Please excuse me while I start paddling my happy ass at top speed. "The others? The people who keep attacking us."

Beautiful, you can tell us. The soft encouragement from Fin nudged me. But even he couldn't keep that hopeful note out. They were all happy about it. It being the bun in my proverbial oven. Though, did I have an oven? Of course, I did. Succubi weren't exactly *hatched*. We carried young like everyone else, we just didn't get attached because as soon as possible, we booted them out. Then again, I wasn't really a succubus anymore. Why the fuck was I even thinking about that?

Get out of my head, Fin. I didn't need him dredging these emotions up. Alfred still watched me with that calculating almost knowing gaze. He didn't seem to share Fin and

Maddox's simple joy, and I'd missed Rogue's reaction. When I twisted to search him for it, his expression was carefully shuddered. Then again…he'd looked at me with such wonder before.

Fuck.

Double. Fuck.

You're afraid. Fin's mental voice soothed. Would it be as soothing if I gave him a black eye? *Absolutely,* he promised, his lips twitching. *But hear me, Beautiful. You're afraid because you don't want to get attached. I understand that. Maybe more than they do. Right now. But you're not a succubus anymore, Fiona. Remember?*

Huh.

I wasn't. Not really. "We still don't know what I am," I said aloud, and when Maddox tugged me back against him, his chest to my back, I leaned into him and sighed. "And I really don't want to talk about this. I'm starving. I want to kill Dimitri. So who do we have to kill to get to him?"

"Alfred and Rogue will bring him," Maddox began, but Alfred gave a sharp shake of his head.

"No, we will stay together."

The silence in the room was almost tangible, as was the sudden tension coursing through Maddox. I swore the mate bond downright *throbbed* with fury, and the heat at my back turned my skin clammy and the shirt began to cling to me.

"She is not going into battle," he snarled.

"Alfred," Rogue said slowly. "We may not know the extent of her capabilities, but we know they will all be coming for her."

"And keeping us all together is the safer way to protect her. We're stronger as a unit," Fin offered with a saucy wink toward me. "She loves being the center of attention, and she can definitely handle us."

Incorrigible flirt. I wrinkled my nose at him rather than

stick out my tongue though. He'd definitely see the latter as an invitation.

"No." One syllable ground out through his teeth like he'd bitten off a rock and chewed it up to pebbles and dust.

"Don't start," Alfred cautioned, but his gaze wasn't on me, which was good because I was about to be offended. I wasn't the one who made the insane announcement. Really. Who just dropped a bomb like that? Oh wait. I forgot I was talking about my asshole. Affection flared inside of me, and I stuffed that little bubble of joy back into the box it kept trying to leap out of. I was supposed to be irked with him, not wanting to cuddle him.

Emotions sucked.

Anyway, Alfred wasn't staring at me. No, he stared just above my head at Maddox. My dragon's arms tightened around me.

"Maddox."

"No." The heat along my back bordered on scorching. I was in no danger of burning, but I might sweat to death. Tilting my head back, I found his furious eyes focused on Alfred, while his expression turned stonier by the minute. "We're not risking her."

"We would risk her more if we're apart." There was something almost soothing and almost lulling in Alfred's voice. "Think before you react."

Well, it was lulling before it became a tad condescending.

"I am thinking," Maddox snarled, and the rough growl in his voice sent tingles radiating over my skin. "And I said *no.*"

The world exploded around me, stone shattering and tumbling down, even as the heat grew almost unbearable. Only we weren't under attack. The grip around me flexed, and then we were airborne.

Holy shit.

Maddox shifted.

More, he'd shifted and taken off.

The cold air washed over me and around me, rapidly cooling the sweat slicking my neck, though it had the effect of also yanking my hair against my face. I tried to shove the hair away and look back. There was a dragon-sized hole in the stone edifice we'd just left. Not that I got a good look, it shrank rapidly as Maddox angled away. Tilting my head back, I stared up at the golden scales that glimmered under the moonlight—'cause there was no sunshine—and then back down as we continued to gain altitude. The air turned frostier, but from where I was wrapped in his clawed hands, I was almost toasty. The chilly air helped.

This was kind of cool actually.

I was flying.

Like legit fucking flying.

I might have squealed.

He snaked his huge head down to look at me, and I grinned. The pulse along the mate bond was like a tickle and a kiss all at once. I swore he winked one huge eye at me and then lifted his head back to focus on where we were flying.

Holy. Shit.

I was totally gonna have to yell at him for that seriously melodramatic exit. I hoped the guys were okay. Surely they were fine. Maddox might be in a testy mood, but he loved them, right?

Right.

Yeah, he loved them.

I wiggled a little to spread my arms out and then whooped again as he did a little spiral.

So. Fucking. Cool.

Yep, yelling could come later.

～

"Are you serious right now?" I demanded, and why yes, I did raise my voice.

I told you yelling would come later.

Welcome to later.

Maddox grunted. So far, he hadn't shifted from his dragon form since we arrived—I shot a look around the oversized cavern—in this giant warren of caves. Actual caves. It was damp, a bit musty, and the air was getting warmer and more humid the longer we were here. There were also stacks upon stacks of old casks, chests, and more than one broken open with gems and gold coins and items.

You know the old idea of a dragon's hoard? Pretty sure we'd found Maddox's, and not that I wasn't impressed because well, shiny. He even had books. Though, he'd put those in these temperature-controlled cases, and they were locked. Not that I hadn't tried to open one or two.

Fine, I spent some time poking around all of it.

"Maddox," I warned.

But my dragon just gave me a look and went back to watching the entrance. Anytime I'd headed that way, he'd blocked me with his tail or his wing.

Arms folded, I tapped my foot. A grunt of noise escaped him, almost like a whuff, but he didn't look at me.

"Maddox, do not ignore me."

Another pulse along the mating bond, this one full of adoration and sweetness.

"Yeah, that's not going to work either. I love you too, but you can't just bring us all the way here and then not let me out."

He flicked a look at me, and I swore I could practically hear him say, *watch me.*

Exhaling, I stared up at the ceiling. Well, what I could see of it, which wasn't much. It was pretty dark up there. He'd lit some sconces when we first arrived with his flame breath—

yeah, that wasn't getting old. It had definitely been welcome after the flight—that wouldn't get old either. Finger combing my hair, I turned back toward the hoard and the back wall of the cave.

All of this was tucked into this nook where the stone had been smoothed, almost polished. It gleamed under the torchlight. Pivoting in a circle, I studied the layout.

"You don't have a chair, Maddox. Or a bed. Or anything comfortable to sit on."

He extended his tail and it curved around me, gently knocking me right in the back of the knees until I was sitting on it. Then he pulled me toward him right under his wing until I was tucked up against his side.

"And you think this is enough?" Granted, I was tired after the flight. I'd been tired earlier after the fight at the prison and the raid on the keep. But this... "This isn't okay."

Another huff of sound, but for all the world, he might have just grunted at me as he tucked himself in to go to sleep. As it was, he curled his head around and tucked his nostrils just under the wing so his warm breath filled the area and chased away even the sense of a chill.

What? We were supposed to just nap here?

Yeah.

No.

I thumped him on his nose. "Bad dragon."

His wing arched as he pulled his head back. Okay, maybe I hit him a little harder than I meant to, but he deserved it.

"This is not how this works." Hands on my hips, I glared up at him. "Change. *Right. Now.*"

Another long-suffering sound, and then the air around me crackled with energy as his whole body began to shimmer. How something that *huge* became Maddox defied any conventional understanding of physics or science. And I said that as someone who didn't do well in either class, but I had seen plenty of sci fi.

Then again, I was dating a fallen angel, an ancient druid turned vampire, an even older elf turned vampire, and well… big, gold, and hot-tempered here.

When Maddox stood in front of me, naked, skin steaming, and his eyes blazing, I glared at him and folded my arms.

"That's better. Thank you. Now, explain why we are *here*."

"Because *here* is safe," he informed me, even as he stalked forward. Violence seemed to shimmer in the air around him, but it wasn't anger or danger. It was something far more primal. And it was kind of hot.

Like him.

Sue me, he was really sexy. As it was, I stopped his forward progress with a hand slapped to the center of his chest. "Here is also missing three people that you *dropped a castle wall* on."

"It wasn't that much, and trust me, Kitten, they're fine." He ignored my hand and slid his arms around me until he could drag me close. "And you're right, I need to furnish this. I'll get it taken care of, but for now, I can shelter you."

"I'm not going to stay here."

"Yes," he said. "You are."

Digging my nails into his shoulders, I rose up on my tiptoes to try and meet him eye to eye. He really didn't help my case by just picking me up. "Maddox," I snapped. "I can't stay here. It's a *cave*."

"It's a treasure room," he huffed. "It just happens to be in a cave." That was what he was going with?

"No—"

"Kitten." He gathered a fistful of my hair and angled my head gently before pressing a kiss to my nose. "You're pregnant. Already, there were those hunting you."

"Nope," I argued.

"You are."

"Not agreeing or disagreeing, but we are not having this conversation here, nor are you locking me away…"

"It's for your safety."

"I was in a *prison*, Maddox. Have you forgotten that?"

He blinked.

Aggravation raked through me. "And I don't accept that I'm pregnant just because you four say so. But even if I was, welcome to the twenty-first century. Women do not get hauled off into caves and locked up by the overbearing and brutish patriarchy because they feel like it."

"I am not overbearing nor a member of the patriarchy."

I glared.

The corners of his mouth twitched. "Kitten, you are the most precious thing in the world to me. And Rogue is right, you are pregnant. As long as you are…I cannot allow anything to happen to you."

"What's going to happen to me?" I demanded. "What?"

"As you said," he challenged. "You were in a prison, and you're right, I should have thought of that. I will make this much nicer. I promise."

I would not roll my eyes again. I would not. "That's not the point. I'm also *not* in a prison. I broke you and Fin out, remember? I waded through how many of their guards?"

Instead of persuading him, it only seemed to irk him more.

Oh for fuck's sake.

The rumbling in his chest seemed to grow louder. Grasping his face in my hands, I kissed him. Only instead of playing with the light or anything else, I just kissed *him* until the growling all but subsided and he began to relax. I pushed my love into him. Granted, I wasn't good at this love business. I'd never had feelings like this before, and certainly not so consuming. But when his snarls turned to groans, I pulled back to study him.

The hard lines of his face had softened, and the golden cast to his eyes had faded back to the hazel-green they'd been in the prison, with the golden flecks scattered like his gold coins across his irises.

"I saved Fin in Dallas. I saved myself from Dorran this time. I saved myself in that alleyway. Maddox, I got away from you in the prison when you came for me that first time. I've never been helpless, and I'm not starting now. I chose you to be my mate, and while I may not be very good at it, I don't think that means you get to lock me up with your *loot* and keep me hidden away."

He scowled. "Kitten, I'm the last of my kind. Rogue is the last of his. Fin...he might as well be the last of his. Even Alfred's brethren are whittling away."

"There's still six others..."

"Five," he corrected. "The one you killed in the alley. She was one of the Seven."

My stomach bottomed out, and for a moment, I had the most horrifying image of throwing up on him. I managed to swallow back the sense of nausea. Still, he shifted his grip on me and carried me over toward the boxes, uncaring of his own nudity, before he perched on one and settled me on his lap.

"I thought the Seven were hard to kill."

"They are," he told me. "They are very difficult to kill."

"But she wasn't that hard..." I mean, what had I done? I'd kissed her like I had Dorran, and I pushed the light into her. I thought it was because she was a vamp. Dorran just got more human, but she'd utterly come apart.

"You are a threat to the others, and I don't know how long it will take them to recognize it, but they will keep coming for you..."

"Then all the more reason I should help. You guys thought they were hard, if I can take them out—"

"No," he snapped. "Absolutely not. I will not allow you to go into battle with them. I wouldn't have allowed you that confrontation with Keeley had I been there..."

Not allow?

Not. Allow.

I shoved my way off his lap. He resisted at first, but when I growled, he actually let go of my hips. Rising, I smoothed my sweatshirt—still his—and stalked a few feet away.

"Kitten."

"Don't you Kitten me, you over-sized, ego-inflated, golden-scaled, lizard-brained jackass."

Fin chose the moment I turned to glare at Maddox to arrive. He had an apple in his hand, and he glanced from me to Maddox and then back again. "Problems?"

"Yes," I snarled.

"No," Maddox argued. "And I told you not to let yourself into my vault." The last he said to Fin, who just shot him a middle finger before he strolled over to me.

"Hey, Beautiful. Alfred and Rogue will be here any minute. I left them outside to cool off and came in here to make sure he was behaving himself. But I have a feeling you and I should make ourselves scarce for a little while."

"You're not taking her anywhere..." Maddox began, even as something on the far side of the cave gave the most powerful crack, and then a huge stone slab fell and Alfred stalked inside.

Holy shit.

He radiated black fire, and his expression was like hell had opened up.

"Maddox!"

"Or we could just stand here and pretend we don't exist," Fin muttered out of the corner of his mouth as he slid an arm around me and tugged me backwards. "I don't think they're gonna kill each other, but we might want to give them some room."

Wait.

"You don't *think* they'll kill each other?"

"All's fair in love and war, my ass." - Fiona

"You don't *think* they'll kill each other?" The words came out far screechier than I intended. As it was, the rage in my blood had turned almost incandescent. Yes, I was *pissed* at Maddox. But I didn't want to *hurt* him. Okay, maybe hurt him a little, but like bruises and things that would heal, maybe a little sexual torture, 'cause that would be fun. But I definitely didn't want to kill him.

As for my asshole wreathed in dark fire? Holy shit, that was hot and sexy and did all kinds of things to me, but I didn't want him *dead* either. A little pain was good for the soul, and honestly, I'd probably enjoy it if they dished it out. But that wasn't the point.

I started forward, but Fin hooked that arm around me and dragged me farther back.

"No, Beautiful," he said against my hair, even as I struggled. "Let them deal with it."

In the flickering shadows behind him like a blade of ice, Rogue stalked out of the darkness, and I might have drooled a little. Okay, that's a lie. I drooled a lot. Rogue had always had this kind of intensity about him, calm, unflappable, and steady. His gaze tracked from where Alfred and Maddox glared at each other, power pulsing around them both, to fix on me, and the tension around his eyes and mouth both eased a fraction.

I blew him a kiss because…well, at least he looked at me. Alfred was too busy getting ready to thump Maddox to notice.

"He noticed, Beautiful," Fin murmured against my ear as he kept me pressed right against him despite my squirming. "But Maddox and he need to sort this out."

"I don't want them to hurt each other."

"Shh," he soothed, his arms locked around me, holding me steady like we'd developed deep roots. "I know, Beautiful. It's going to be okay." *Trust me?*

I hesitated and then dared a look up at him. He still held the apple in one palm, but he had both arms secured around me and pinning me to him. His eyes held so much kindness and hope in them, and I sighed.

Please trust me?

"I do trust you," I whispered, and the minute I said the words, I sagged against him. I did. I trusted all of them. Even when they frustrated me, I trusted them. He pressed his lips to my temple and murmured something in a language I didn't understand. But I didn't have to understand it to feel the swell of emotion bundling around me or the very real bubble that suddenly appeared as Alfred and Maddox actually came to blows.

One minute, Alfred and Maddox were glaring at each

other. The next, Maddox flew through the air to crash into mounds of gold and jewels. The avalanche of it might have been hilarious, if we were in a cartoon. As it was, I cringed.

Fin kept rubbing soothing circles against my abdomen, but the magnetic effect of the dark fire surrounding Alfred and then Maddox's rippling transformation from man to dragon held me in place. When he belched out a plume of pure fire, I was pretty sure I let out the most inelegant of screams.

Fuck inelegant.

It was straight out of a horror movie.

The flames utterly engulfed Alfred, and for a second, I lost sight of him and Rogue both. Then Rogue appeared, taking up a position between where Fin and I stood and the battle. The heat must have stirred up a breeze, because his long hair blew back from his face. Then the fire vanished, and my dazzled eyes struggled to see in the abrupt darkness.

"Are you done?" Alfred demanded, and everything about his cool, biting tones sent relief cascading through me. He dusted off his shirt like he hadn't just been swallowed in a swirl of fire. The black flames dancing over him seemed to flare back like wings, and all the breath backed up in my lungs.

Maddox's roar escalated in volume, and his wing span was incredible. I'd seen him in the prison. Then I'd had a lot of time to study him after we arrived here. But he'd been curled up almost like a cat.

Right now?

Well, he looked pretty badass.

Then so did Alfred with his fiery wings.

Did he even know they were wings?

"Don't take that tone with me," Alfred reprimanded like he wasn't facing down two tons of angry dragon. I squeezed my thighs together at the desire spearing through me. It really was fucking hot that Alfred just stalked forward like he wasn't remotely scared. "You took her. You ripped her out of the safety of the four of us together and flew off like she was some sheep to be stolen away from the farmer's pasture."

Sheep.

Pasture.

Yeah, okay, fuck you very much. "I am not a *farm animal!*"

A huff and a smothered snicker from behind had me twisting to glare at Fin. His eyes danced, even as his lips twitched. "I'm not laughing at you, Beautiful, I promise."

He was lying. He was absolutely laughing at me.

Incensed that even he would be cavalier enough to find this funny, I slammed my elbow back into his gut, even as I caught one of his fingers and bent his hand free of me. He let out a grunt as I shoved him off, but I rebounded off the bubble.

Dammit.

When I turned on him, he held up both of his hands. "Beautiful. I know you're upset. But we have to let them sort it out."

"Let me out." Bad enough Maddox dragged me halfway around the world or wherever we'd flown and secreted me away in some cave—as it turned, out not so secret, since Alfred and the others found us—but still. "Now."

"Little *sváss*," Rogue said, and I glanced over my shoulder to find him holding out a hand. "If you want out of that safety, you still have to stay close to us. No one here wants anything to happen to you. Alfred and Maddox must work out this difference, but it would kill them both if you got caught between them."

I nodded once. "I won't get between them right now."

His smile grew a tad wider. "Not good enough, little *sváss*. Right now ends as soon as the barrier is dropped. Allow them the opportunity to settle this, and if they cannot reach an accord, then I'll help you negotiate with them."

"So will I," Fin promised.

Okay. That was a little better.

Across the cavern, Alfred blazed up at Maddox and the dragon's whole expression was absolute fury. He wasn't backing down.

Neither of them were.

"I told you why we had to stay together. The others will not come one at a time, so it will require *all* of us to keep her safe. Or are you so selfish you would rob us of our chance with her because you are so careless?"

Ouch.

Arms folded, I bit back my salty response at needing to be "protected." Foot tapping, I held Rogue's gaze as he waited, even as Alfred pressed forward.

"You are *not* the only one who has waited for her."

Behind me, Fin snorted. "None of them waited as I did. Not that I'm going to throw that into their argument."

"Probably a good idea to keep it to yourself." Rogue nodded, never looking away from me. "Well, little *sváss*?"

"Fine, I'll stay out of it, but I don't want them to hurt each other and I really don't like this fight." At all. I shook on the inside like I'd been hopped up on way too much caffeine when, point of order, I hadn't had coffee in forever.

My stomach also took that moment to growl. As the bubble around Fin and I dissipated, he held out the apple to me once more. A gentle smile graced his lips as I took it, and then I leaned up to brush a kiss to the corner of his mouth. "Sorry I elbowed you."

His grin grew. "I love whenever you touch me, Beautiful. And I'm very sturdy." He winked as he nudged me closer to Rogue, who lifted an arm and gave me an inquiring look. Yes,

I tucked myself up against him and then took a bite of the apple as Maddox and Alfred continued their glare-off.

The sweetness from the apple flooded my mouth, and my hunger seemed to redouble. Rogue rubbed my shoulder gently while we waited them out. The barely restrained violence pulsing in the air left chills racing over my skin. The dragon shifted abruptly, then it was Maddox, skin steaming and expression fierce, who glared at Alfred.

"I will not allow you to take her into war."

There was that word again.

"I don't recall *asking* your permission," Alfred retorted, his cool, precise tones utterly at odds with the fierce, dark image he painted. "She needs *all* of us, Maddox. Or did you think she only belonged to you?"

"Standing right here," I muttered. "Not someone's luggage."

Fin let out a little laugh next to me, but he dodged my elbow this time. Rogue gave my shoulder a squeeze before he slapped Fin upside the head. Did that dissuade the druid? Not even a little. He just grinned, all cheeky and shit.

Assholes.

The lot of them.

I was almost done eating the apple. Man, that went quick.

"She's pregnant," Maddox snarled. "You cannot expect me to let her…"

I started keeping score. Because they were starting to really piss me off with these declarations.

"I expect you to trust me, old friend," Alfred stated as he narrowed the distance between them. While the dark fire still writhed over him, stretching back to create the sense of wings, it had diminished a fraction. "I expect you to honor the bond we've shared for so long. Have I ever failed you?"

Maddox's shoulders bunched so tightly, they made me ache. When I was down to just the core of the apple, Fin plucked it away and discarded it, then offered me another with a flirty smile. I rolled my eyes but took it, and leaned up to kiss him in thanks before taking another bite.

"No," Maddox admitted. "But it's been so long, Alfred."

"I know. I remember when the last of your kin fell. I was too late to prevent it."

Tears burned in my eyes for the depth of sorrow in Alfred's cool tones.

"How could you have made it when I didn't tell you?" Maddox argued. "I didn't trust you to stand against your own kind."

"You are my kind, Maddox." Alfred had made it the last step, and he braced a hand against Maddox's shoulder. "My friend. My brother. She is your mate, but she is also my queen and Fin's lady and Rogue's chosen. We will all lay down our lives to protect her, but had I disappeared with her…"

Maddox glared at him. "You did."

"To transition her, yes, and you couldn't see straight for how she fought it. You knew that part of transition required death, but it was hurting you. So yes, my friend, I did keep her from you then, but you always knew where she was."

The kindness in the way he said that, like I was some bone that they negotiated or shared, was almost sweet. Almost. I mean, I liked the kindness, I did.

Not sure how I felt about being a bone.

"But Fiona is not our possession, Maddox."

Three points to Gryffindor. I grinned at Alfred. I was so proud of my asshole.

"No matter how much it drives us all to protect her, we cannot treat her as such."

I'd take it. I must have let out a pleased little sound, because they both paused to glance over at me. "Oh, look, you remembered your bone was here. Please, don't let us interrupt your moment. I need you two to kiss and make up before I thump you both. Well, thump Maddox. I might kiss Alfred."

He chuckled. "Hellion, I will absolutely kiss and make up with you, though I wasn't aware we were fighting."

"Oh, I'm sure we'll come up with something." In the meanwhile, I leaned against Rogue.

"The last time a real war broke out amongst your kin, Alfred," Maddox said, his smile sad and strained, and all at once, my heart just hurt for the echo of loneliness and anguish resonating through him, "they eradicated so much."

"I know," Alfred said slowly, his gaze leaving me for Maddox, and I swiped at my eyes before I looked too weepy. "That is what I plan to avoid this time. Those losses happened because we were apart."

"And I didn't trust you," Maddox admitted. "I could not see you choosing my people over your own."

"Yet I would have because you are my people. We didn't know it then. We also didn't have Fin."

"Ha," Fin declared with a pleased little grin. "I make everything better."

"Shut up, Fin," both Maddox and Alfred said at the same time with equal amounts of exasperation, and I laughed.

They all loved each other so much. I stole a look up at Rogue. His stoic expression hadn't shifted as he watched them.

"Alfred, if I lose her—"

"If any of us lose her," Alfred corrected him. "Or if she loses us."

My grin faded, even if a part of me soared that Alfred had noticed.

"She left us to retrieve you, Maddox," Rogue said softly, the vibration of his voice thrumming through me. "She left us and security, risking possible capture and death, to retrieve you and Fin."

"And did a kickass job, thank you very much," I reminded him.

"Yes, little *sváss*, I know." He pressed a kiss to my temple before looking at Maddox once more. A pained look tightened around his eyes. "If she needed you so badly then, what would keeping us away from her accomplish? Would you torture her to satisfy your need?"

All at once, Maddox sought my gaze, and the horror etched there had me forgiving him. "I'm okay," I told him, and I *would* rather they were here. Even if Alfred arrived all badass and scary.

His wings were gone, as was the dark fire.

"Wait…" I said slowly. "You're not burned at all."

He shot me a small smile. "I was ready for the fire. But even if I hadn't been, I could have survived it, Hellion."

An image of the crispy figure staring back at me from outside the prison when Maddox unleashed on Cyril and his hordes flashed through my mind.

Cyril was still alive.

That was a problem.

Still, I shoved that aside and focused on Maddox. I squeezed away from Rogue, and when he didn't try to stop me, I hurried over and gave Maddox a hug. He folded me close and rubbed his cheek against my hair. "I'm sorry, Kitten. I wasn't thinking. Just reacting."

Alfred exhaled a long sigh, and when I stole a glance at him, all I found on his face was relief. How worried had he been about fighting with Maddox?

"A dragon with a clutch is the fiercest creature on the planet," Alfred told me quietly, even as Maddox kept me close. "That was why Fin came in to get you out of the line of fire. Maddox would defend you to the death."

Great. I filed that piece of knowledge away. "Do I get a say in this?" Though I glanced from Alfred to Maddox, I was really asking all of them.

A long sigh escaped Maddox. "I don't even know if the child you're carrying is mine, but it will be mine, regardless of which of us gave it to you."

"Skip the baby talk. I'm still firmly on Team Deny Deny Deny with that one. I'm talking about this—secreting me away and locking me in rooms or hiding me in treasure troves. Do I get a say in this?" Because there was only one correct answer.

With a long, almost pained sigh, Maddox said, "Yes."

Alfred nodded once. Then I glanced over to Fin and Rogue. Rogue inclined his head, but Fin just grinned. "I'm all about equal rights, Beautiful."

I exhaled.

"But you cannot deny your state too long, Hellion. None of us knows what it means. So we need to make sure your needs are met, whatever they might be."

I made a face, but it was Maddox who pulled back and tucked a finger under my chin to tug my gaze up to him. "Why are you so upset? That is the part I don't understand. This is a miracle."

"Yeah, I'm not big on those," I told him. "I shouldn't exist, right? The whole hybrid thing and the whole demon thing and now the whole angel thing. What even *am* I?"

"Ours," Alfred said softly, and his hands came down on my shoulders. "Everything else, we'll figure out. From this new power of yours…"

Oh for fuck's sake, I was glowing again. Just stick a fork in me and call me a damn fairy.

Maddox released me as Alfred drew me back against him, and then he buried his face against my throat and took a deep breath. The last of the tension cording through me eased. Wait…that tension hadn't been all me.

I stole a look at Maddox, who'd moved away and seemed to be searching amongst the crates and chests for something. The move of his muscles flexing along his ass and thighs had me clenching. It didn't help that Alfred nuzzled at my throat or that everything in me yearned for more than just the cuddling.

Don't get me wrong, the cuddling was amazing, but I wanted so much more…

Heat suffused me from multiple sides, and Maddox shot a look toward me that was all need and desire. There was an element of chilly adoration, and along with that came Fin's soft laughter and the brush of his mind against mine.

It wasn't just my desire.

Not all my feelings.

But this wasn't lust, and I wasn't *hungry*, I just…

I twisted to look up at Alfred and ask, but then his mouth closed over mine and the room faded away.

Well, it did until the sound of flesh slamming into flesh and the flash of pain broke the heady spell. I pulled back to find Maddox on his ass and Rogue straightening as he flexed his right hand.

"Don't do it again." It was all he said before he turned to look at me.

"Are we done with the fighting part?" I had to know because the need was still right there, and based on the hard length of Alfred's erection pressing against my stomach, I wasn't the only one feeling it.

"Oh yeah," Fin said and headed straight toward us. "But I think we need some place more defensible than this if we're all going to play."

Oh.

Hell yes.

CHAPTER 12

"Just make sure that the make-up sex always lasts longer than the fights." - Anonymous

From the dark and gloomy confines of Maddox's cave—after they replaced the huge stone slab Alfred had taken down—to the sunnier location of the island with its sweet little cottage that Rogue had taken me to before, we whisked from one side of the world to the other. From winter to almost a balmy kind of summer. From cold to warm. From night to day. Or maybe it had been day there. My hours were all sort of running together.

Alfred lifted my hand and pressed his lips to my palm before he said, "Sweep the island, check the security. Fin, reinforce the wards with Rogue. Then come find us."

While none of them argued, Maddox grumbled a little. They hurried away, and for the first time since I fled them, I found myself alone with Alfred. He let out a slow breath and then met my gaze. "Worried, Hellion?"

Lifting my chin, I shrugged. "Nope."

He raised his brows. "Really?"

I swore my toes curled from the sheer amount of sensuality he managed to imbue in that single word. When he slid his hand around my throat, I smiled. "Really. If you want to spank me, spank me. If you want to scold me for taking off on you, scold me. If you're going to give me hell, bring it. I can handle you."

Laughing softly, he tightened his grip without actually squeezing and tugged me to him. "Yes, I think you can." When his mouth covered mine, I let out a little sigh, then his tongue swept in to duel with mine. Despite the gentleness of his hand on my throat and the way he leaned into me, possessiveness threaded that kiss that demanded obedience and offered so much. Heat sizzled through my system as I leaned into the him.

Around us, the breeze pushed at me, and where I'd been chilled before in the sweatshirt, now I was too hot. I tugged away, and he frowned as he lifted his head, but as soon as I started to lift my shirt, he smiled and pulled it up and over until I was just in the tank top. In the dappled sunlight beneath the trees, my skin didn't seem to be glowing, but then it brightened as he traced his fingers down my arm.

"I really don't get this," I said, and then extended both arms in front of me so I could turn them back and forth. The glow intensified as he ran his hands down my arms and then caught my hands in his. The dark fire sparking over him earlier surged back into the present and wreathed him once more.

The effect made my skin tingle everywhere we touched. "I've only ever seen this on other angels, Hellion."

Angels.

I snorted.

At the inelegant sound, he chuckled and pulled me to

him. Wrapping me in his arms, he lifted me up, and the tingling seemed to vibrate over me like we'd been dropped inside of a bell. The sensation swirled around us as I stared behind him at the wings of fire stretching out. And fuck it, I reached for one, and Alfred froze in place when I ran my fingers along the edge.

There was no heat, just...I wanted to say electricity. It sizzled against my palm, but there was no pain. His whole expression shifted as I teased my fingers over what almost felt like a bone and yet wasn't. "Does this hurt?"

"No," he said slowly, but his eyes didn't carry the same message. If anything, he looked...stunned.

The wings flexed, and he tilted his head before he slid a hand up my back, and I swear it was like playing the game of Operation. The *bzzt* of sensation that went through me had my eyes widening, and I shivered.

"Does that hurt, Hellion?" The amusement in his voice as he tossed the question back at me helped pull me out of my stupor as I shook my head. "But it feels strange?"

"Very... Do I have wings?"

"You do," he murmured. Then stroked his hand over something again, and that shiver seemed to resonate through my system and I swore the air around us brightened. "Beautiful wings of shadow and silvery flame."

"Alfred...what the hell am I?"

"Ours," he reminded me as he began walking again. Only this time, there was no rush and he kept me close. The longer he held me like this, the more the current seemed to settle. "I told you that already."

"I meant *what* am I? You're mine and I'm yours." The possessive flare in his eyes at my admission made me smile. "Yes, I'm stubborn, but I can say it. I even feel different now. But the point is...what happened to me? I don't seem to need to even feed as I did before."

We had arrived at the little bungalow, and I was ridiculously happy to see the place. I'd been here, what? A handful of hours? And still…it felt like coming home, even if it wasn't the keep.

"Tell me about the need to feed," Alfred prompted me as he carried me inside. He didn't slow as he made his way to the bedroom. Unlike the keep, the bed here hadn't been as large, but I was less concerned about the where than the who to be honest, so I let Alfred make the call on this. He set me on the bed and began pulling off my shoes. I barely even remembered putting them on.

"It's just different. I mean…I know you want me, I can feel it. But the lust that would usually leave me hungry, it's… just not there. Which is a little strange." It was a lot strange.

"Hellion." The soft command in his voice had me raising my eyebrows, but the gentle stroke of his hand up my calf soothed as much as his demand irked. "When was the last time you fed?"

"From you…" I thought about it. Maddox and I hadn't… had we? It all kind of blurred together.

"You fed from my blood. When was the last time you fed on lust?"

He reached for the pants I had on and began to peel them down as I squinted at him. Honestly, I wasn't sure. There had been a time I'd never seemed so full. Yet even when I'd left, the hunger hadn't plagued me. Not like it had before. Still, I'd been able to ignite it in others, such as I had during my escape.

"The daeva," I said slowly as he skated his fingers along my sides to my abdomen and then paused, one hand over it. "When I was in Dallas, when Fin found me, there was a daeva and it incited a huge fight. It was trying to cloud Fin, use him… It doesn't matter. The point is, I was a lot stronger, and I fed on it and fed it back to itself."

Essentially.

"Did you feed on it properly though?" He still knelt next to the bed, his right hand curved against my abdomen, and more than once, his gaze dipped to it.

"You're excited." Probably not the answer he was looking for. His dark eyes lifted to meet my gaze as he spread his fingers, and the tingling awareness of him prickled over me. "About the…you know."

"Baby?" He cocked his head to the side as though trying to understand me. Good luck with that. I didn't understand me at this point, or why my eyes kept getting hot. I was not a crier by nature. The fact that tears kept trying to escape was making me a little crazy.

Okay. A lot crazy. "Yes, the baby." I stared at him. "I had a birth control spell. This shouldn't have happened, and then boom, you kill me to make me better and faster and stronger than before, then bing, bang, boom, Bob's your uncle, there's a bun in the oven and I'm glowing like some solar power day pop." The words spilled out of me in a rant, but Alfred didn't laugh at me.

If anything, he just continued to look at me rock steady and gorgeous as he stroked my stomach with his thumb. "I think you're beautiful." He said it so simply, like we were actually discussing the weather. "Beautiful. Over the top. With a mind I can't parse and I hope to never fully understand, because you delight me."

Goddammit, the tears swelled up again. "Stop it."

"Stop what, Hellion?"

"Stop being nice. Be my asshole."

He chuckled and then scooped me up and moved me higher on the bed before settling me down and then leaning over me. The weight of him coupled with the faint roughness of his clothes settled me more than I cared to admit.

"But I'm trying so very hard not to be, Hellion," he said in the most sensuously soothing tone. "You've been through a great deal, and I forget sometimes how difficult the transition can be. For me, it was so long ago."

"And now you have wings again." They'd faded while we spoke, and even mine seemed to be gone. Which was probably a good thing. I didn't want to think about crushing them while lying on them, or worse, having them fall asleep or wake up. How fucking weird would that be.

His expression shifted minutely. If I hadn't been watching for it, I might have missed it entirely, but the lines at his eyes tightened and his mouth firmed.

"That's a good thing, right?" He'd described how he lost his wings. How he'd fallen. The way they'd been seared from his body.

"I don't know, Hellion," he admitted after too long a silence. Long enough, I reached up to press my hand over his heart. "I don't know. I am…amazed that they are there. Yet they are different. So perhaps not a bad thing at all."

"I think they're beautiful." No lie. His arrival in Maddox's cave had been epic. The way the dark fire had danced over him… A shiver radiated up my entire body as I smiled, and I swore the light in his eyes began to shimmer.

"You're glowing again," he murmured, and I rolled my eyes.

"That's gonna get old."

"No," he whispered, cupping my cheek in one hand. "I don't think so… Tell me though…does it hurt? At all?"

I shook my head. "I feel good. Confused maybe. No maybe…" Wow. The words just slipped right out like I had to amend even the idea I might be lying immediately. It wasn't a lie. "I feel…weird. But not bad weird, just bizarre weird, like there's all these feelings and I don't know what to do with them. I love you."

Yeah, that was just right out there.

"I love them and I love…I love being with all of you, but that's not me. Or it used to not be me. Maybe it wasn't me because you weren't there and I didn't want to be this. I fought it so hard, and now I'm happy with this." I frowned as his whole expression softened. "Don't look at me like that. I'm still mad that you did it the way you did it, even if I get it. 'Cause I'm stubborn and I didn't want to listen and if I had my way, I'd have never gone through with it and I'd probably be dead or a shadow demon right now."

I shuddered as everything in me went icy at the thought, and the light in the room vanished.

"I would never have let that happen to you," he promised me with such ferocity, I believed him.

"But that's just it, you did this to me for you—for them. But you didn't do it for me. Or maybe you did." A tear splashed out of my eyes as I squeezed them shut, but I didn't want to let go of him long enough to wipe them away. "I don't know. I don't even know what all of this is. This…life used to be simple."

The fact that his smile grew at that last comment made me growl, but I didn't get another word out before he kissed me. This wasn't like earlier kisses where he demanded and took control. No, this was full of decadent sweetness. I swore my heart grew with every stroke of his tongue. When he slid his knee between my legs and then eased himself down until I could cradle him, the sheer gentleness threatened to overwhelm me.

Then I was fucking crying again. Alfred didn't say a word, just kissed the tears away, and when he gazed down at me again, there was an astonishing amount of tenderness in the black flames of his eyes. Holy shit, there were black flames in his eyes, and the room brightened again. I didn't even have to look to know it was me.

With careful thumbs, he wiped away the tears. "I've never

felt this way about anyone, Hellion. Not the way I feel about you."

I swallowed, but when I would have opened my mouth to say something, he pressed his thumb to my lips. I wrapped my mouth around his thumb and sucked it lightly. His smile edged a little wider and his eyes flared, but he schooled his expression.

There was my stern asshole.

"I will never feel about another the way I do about you. You are stubborn. Impulsive. Wild. Reckless. Beautiful. Fierce. Adorable. Perfect."

I raised my eyebrows, even as I nipped his thumb. He may not want me to respond, but that was a whole lot of tenderness spilling out of him.

"I have no idea how to deal with this either," he admitted. "But I'm not going anywhere. So if you need to cry, you cry. If you need to rage, rage. If it involves clawing me up or me fucking you until you can't walk, we can do that, too."

Laughter erupted at that mental image, because yes please and thank you.

"Just know that we will figure all of this out, and while I will never tell him this, Fin is very skilled with emotions. So I'm sure he will say the thing that will make this all better."

"See," came Fin's voice from somewhere behind Alfred, along with a thump sound like he'd smacked someone. "I'm the glue. I get this. Fiona's in love with us, and while she's been a succubus her whole life, attachment is not something she's ever allowed herself to have. But she can have it here. In fact..."

He appeared at the edge of the bed and grinned at me over Alfred's shoulder.

"I insist you be attached, Beautiful. I've waited so many lifetimes for you. There's nothing we won't do for you or the baby you're having. Bets on it being mine?"

Alfred sent his gaze skyward, then said, "I promise, it seemed like a good idea to transition him at the time."

"Holy shit," Fin gasped out, grabbing at his chest. "Alfred's making jokes."

Maddox's laughter, deep and booming, rumbled through the room. He wasn't alone. Rogue's chuckle was there, and Fin's smile grew as our gazes locked. Alfred let out a soft grunt and then rolled off me, but before I could get too chilly, he settled on the bed and pulled me into his lap until my back was against his chest and he could nip my throat gently. It was the barest scrape of teeth.

My nipples tensed, whether from the cold or the fact three sets of hot-eyed gazes scorched over me, I had no idea. And I really didn't care. I swore the light in the room grew brighter.

"She loves us," Alfred said simply, and Maddox's smile turned to a full-fledged grin. Rogue seemed content, but Fin was smug.

"Of course she does," he said, as if it was clear as day. "She's radiant with it."

I groaned and struck out with my foot. It caught him in the chest, and he slid back a couple of feet, still laughing, the little shit. Rogue chuckled. "Not as taken by your charms as you think," he taunted gently before catching my foot and taking a seat on the edge of the bed. "Little *sváss*, I don't care what the prophecy says or what your life was before, only as long as neither ever hurts you."

My heart squeezed.

"I have no idea how to parent nor do any of those here. We'll figure it out." He stroked my calf. "I know you're scared, all the bravado in the world can't hide that from me." His pure blue eyes held me captive. "But you're not *just* a succubus any longer. I don't think you ever were. You fought your own nature to be more. You stood up and demanded to be counted. You have never let anyone put you in a box."

Well…I wouldn't go that far.

Closing his hand around my ankle, he pressed his thumb to my pulse. "We can handle anything, but you have to let us help you, whether it's rescuing those idiots or addressing your fears. Or defending us all."

I ducked my chin at the last. The need to protect them was a fierce flame inside of me. More, I just wanted to be right here with them. No more fights, no more separations or threats. But if they came for us…

"Agreed," Maddox said, his gaze seeking mine when I looked up. He stood at the end of the bed, arms folded and looking every inch as ferocious and grim as he had the day he walked into my cell. "I won't take you away from them again, Kitten. I'm not leaving your side, either. Some things… I cannot change."

"I don't want you to change." Stretching out a hand to Fin and then to Maddox, I waited until they moved to grasp them before I glanced at Rogue, then back up at Alfred. "I like the fighting and the making up and the pushing and the passion and the craziness. I even like that you're an asshole."

He sighed at me, but it was far more indulgent than it was aggravated. "Good. Because I rather doubt I can change all that much, Hellion. Though for you, I'm willing to try."

"And on that note," Fin said. "We're just going to say we witnessed a moment for the ages—Alfred saying he will try something he isn't positive he'll be good at."

There were groans and laughter, and then Fin let go of my hand to grasp my cheeks. He kissed me, slow and sweet, then released me before Maddox swooped in to kiss me. His held a bite and heat and an element of apology that filled my eyes with tears again. Finally, when he lifted his head, Rogue studied me.

"It's us," he murmured.

"What is?" I asked, licking my lips.

"What you need," he said slowly, and my heart did a little fist bump with my ribs. "You need us."

Alfred tightened his grip on me. "What did you tell me about succubi? They only fed on lust, and they couldn't form lasting relationships because of it?"

I swallowed, and then nodded. "We're terrible parents." My chest tightened. "And not great mates—I mean, we don't mate."

"But you do, Kitten," Maddox rumbled, and there was something so pleased in his voice and possessive that I had to laugh.

"You're a hybrid, Beautiful. You're not a succubus only anymore. I don't think you ever were. I think you were always meant for more." Then he went thoughtful.

"Meant for us," Rogue said. "Nothing was certain until we found the brat there." He nodded to Fin, who just gave an airy wave.

"You're welcome."

The tension split wholly as laughter rolled through all four of them, and something clenched so tightly inside of me unlocked. They were okay. They were safe. They loved me, too.

And oh shit...we were gonna have a baby.

"You know..." I said, latching back onto the denial life vest. "I'm very naked here, and I'm not used to vomiting up my feelings like this."

"Would you prefer some orgasms, Beautiful?" Fin teased, but the appreciative look in his eyes didn't go unnoticed.

"As long as we're secure?" Yep. That was me. Hopeful and dedicated to security. I could be both.

Rogue chuckled. "We're secure, though I don't think we should linger here too long."

"Then we need to be efficient," Alfred ordered, and all at once, he tilted my head back and his lips swept down to mine. "Fin, I believe your lady had a request."

His mouth hadn't even closed over mine before Fin's hand slid along my thigh. His mouth kissed my pussy a second later, and my whole body lit up again.

See, I told you I liked it when he assholed.

CHAPTER 13

"Dreams can become reality." - Anonymous

Fuck me. When Alfred told Fin to get to work, he hadn't been kidding. Rather than let me go, Alfred had simply spread my legs wide for my druid to work his tongue along my labia and then around my clit. He took the carnal kiss deeper until I squirmed against Alfred, but my asshole kept me locked in place, not allowing me to escape. The prod of his erection at my ass was a secondary tease, in combination with the twin stares from a pair of hot and cool elemental gazes raking over me.

At the first release pulling me taut and then splitting me apart, Alfred cupped my throat and turned my head to him, and then he was devouring my mouth. The kiss left no room for thought or even breath. It took the pleasure already assaulting my body and deepened it somehow. So close, their breath teased my flesh, a soft masculine laugh rolled over me a split second before a hot mouth latched onto my nipple.

If they'd attached electricity to me, I couldn't have felt it more. Fin worked his tongue inside of me, alternating between thrusting against the clench of my too empty channel and swirling it around my aching clit. It was too much and not enough. The pulse of soft sucking on my nipple left me wanting more, and a cry of protest escaped my throat. Then teeth sank in over my other breast, and I came. Fuck, I came so hard, I swore I saw stars.

It wasn't the lust boiling inside of them that threatened to drown me. I could taste the want in the air, the musk of arousal, and the sheer heat of their desire, but something much richer flooded me. It swelled up like a rising tide of heat that filled my system, and even with my eyes closed and my mouth locked on Alfred's as his tongue lapped at mine with delicious strokes, the brightness flooded my eyes.

The pressure of two fingers spearing into my ass had me crying out again, but Fin didn't let up as he pushed me from one orgasm to another. The hot pull of the mouth on my breast sent another tendril of need to curl through my system. They were all touching me, teasing me, filling me with...*worship* from Fin. *Tenderness* from Maddox. *Adoration* from Rogue. *Delight* and *devotion* from Alfred.

It was too much. Sobs tore from my throat as the pressure on my cunt eased, but before I could catch my breath, the fierce pressure of a cock filled me and I dug my fingers into Rogue's hair where he sucked at my breast, just lazy pulls. It wasn't feeding, it was intimacy. Maddox caught my other hand in his, lacing our fingers together as Fin thrust into me, every stroke lighting me up, and there was no choice. I came in a rush of heat and a torrent of emotion I couldn't suppress.

A crack splintered inside of me, the breaks spider webbing, even as I arched my hips and wrapped my legs around him. Fin's grip on me tightened, and I tore my mouth from Alfred's to meet Fin's hot stare. It was like that was all the impetus he needed for his own release. Somewhere along the way, he'd shed his shirt, but he still wore his pants. The muscles on his chest flexed as he buried himself deep. His throat convulsed and his eyes scorched me and there was no distance at all. I could feel him in my mind as he flooded in, the pure weight of his love shattering through the barrier.

Mine. A single word but it resonated through me, and the heat bursting within lit me up for real. The air itself around us seemed to brighten, and the grip they all had on me grew more ferocious as I arched forward and met Fin's kiss. The soft exhale of Alfred's breath teased along my back, and then his mouth traced kisses as Fin's tongue twined with mine.

Love.

Little sváss.

Kitten.

Hellion.

Their voices all seemed to collide in me, and the tears I'd shed earlier returned in full force. The depth of emotion rushing in was too much and not enough. Hands shifted over me, and then my head was turned and it was Rogue's mouth locked on mine. I could taste the hint of blood from where he'd fed, and my whole body went liquid once more.

Teeth sank into my wrist, and my mind went awash with color. Hands on my hips lifted me, and the spongy head of a dick pressed against my ass and then, with a thrust, filled me until I groaned. Rogue released my mouth, only to move between my thighs. The heavy weight of his cock pushed at the swollen flesh, and he sheathed himself with a gentleness that sparked a fresh round of tears, even as it pulled a groan from me and from Alfred.

Head back, I half sprawled against Alfred's chest as they slid me between them. The dark fire dancing over his skin seemed to enfold me, shadow on light, and when I turned my head, I found my dragon gazing at me. The want in his eyes was matched only by the twin flame of love burning in him.

For a moment, I swore the man and dragon occupied the same space. He stroked his hand over his cock, and I licked my lips as I looked at it.

He needed no other inquiry, and as one, both Rogue and Alfred adjusted so he could press in. At the first brush of his cock, I opened my mouth and took him deep. The weight of him was heavy on my tongue and tasted like pure heaven. Rogue and Alfred rocked me between them, and Alfred's teeth pierced my throat as Maddox began to rock his hips.

I forgot everything but the feel of them as they moved. The friction of Alfred's chest against my back. The spark of his flesh on mine. The chill of Rogue's deeper thrusts, a counterpoint to the boiling heat already simmering inside of me from Fin's release. The salty tang of Maddox's pre-cum on my tongue. The sharp pierce of teeth in my wrist and in my throat. Then a fresh bite to my neglected breast.

Bite me, Kitten.

I opened my eyes to find Maddox's golden, slitted gaze meeting mine. He wanted me to bite him. He'd fisted my hair and pushed deep into my throat. The tears rolling down my face were as much from the pleasure of them taking me apart as from the way my throat convulsed around him.

Bite me.

The command laced with the request sent a shiver right through me. The last thing I wanted to do was hurt him. No matter how tempting that idea had been earlier.

Laughter huffed around me, chokes of masculine humor and gasps of pleasure as their delight exploded within me, and I clenched around Alfred. He swore against my throat, and the first hot pulse of his cum rushed me as I scraped my teeth as gently as I could, eliciting a small welt of blood that had my eyes rolling back as I came.

Rogue slammed deep and held still, his cock thick and fully rigid. I could feel the tremble in his muscles as he fought against the spasming of my body around him, because Maddox had begun to thrust against my throat with a fervor that had my jaw aching, but when he let out a small roar, it vibrated the room around us and the hot taste of him spilled across my tongue. I lapped it and the blood up at once.

The burning inside of me turned into a full-fledged conflagration. Sweat slicked my body, and at some point, Alfred released my throat and Fin my wrist. When Maddox's knot swelled gently and then released against my puffy lips, I sagged back only to find myself straddling Rogue as he rolled onto his back.

I gasped at the sudden absence of Alfred and that the only hands on me were Rogue's, but the weight of their presence was all around me, inside of me, and when I looked down, Rogue stared up at me with unabashed love in his eyes.

"Ride me, little *sváss*, take every drop of pleasure I can give you."

How could I say no to that?

Even exhausted and trembling, I rocked my hips and arched my back. Alfred lay against the headboard, watching me. His eyes, once unfathomable to me, held me captive and I never wanted to escape. I dug my hands into Rogue's shoulders as he thrust up to meet my downward cadence. Every single touch just overloaded my system.

I couldn't stop shaking, but I didn't want to stop moving. Maddox's broad hand stroked down my back, and Fin touched a finger to my chin and turned my head. His smile was so sweet before he kissed me with such gentleness, I was crying all over again.

Fucking tears.

Then he moved my mouth to his throat, and I sank my teeth in without him having to ask. The first hot pulse of his blood across my tongue filled me with renewed strength. I clamped down on Rogue, and he let out a grunt of sound along with a stream of language I didn't recognize, but the images filling my mind translated for me.

Love and lust twined beautifully as he began to move me himself. A fist in my hair pulled me from Fin's throat and turned me to Alfred. His cock was already reddening and hard again, but it was his throat he moved me too and I struck without further urging.

Memories filled me. All of them. Every night they sat around a fire, laughing and teasing each other. Some where they were weary from battle or covered in wounds, others where they looked lazy and bored with the partying around them.

Always, the conversation would turn to Fin and he would recount them with the tale. Maddox would often snort and shake his head, indulgent with the kind of affection one showed a youth who was too enthusiastic about their sharing of a fantastical tale. A similar expression would often fill Rogue's face, but when he thought no one noticed, he would stare away pensively. As though he didn't dare hope.

Alfred held onto the thought, the idea of the goddess of flame and spring, even when he thought it nothing more than an impossible dream, a vision produced by a man dying of the poison filling his veins. He slept with thoughts of me filling his mind and wondered what I would be like if I ever existed.

I shuddered as he pulled me from his throat and came at the love in his eyes. "Better than a dream, Hellion."

Rogue dug his fingers in as he let himself go. I sagged, my whole body lax and shuddering with too much feeling. It buzzed under my skin and seemed to burst over the edges and cascade around me. With care, Alfred laid me down until I draped Rogue and then tucked my head at his throat.

My head fell forward, even as he tipped his neck back. The thrum of his pulse drew me, but I was suddenly elated and exhausted in one. One swipe of my tongue, and I pierced the spot to drink. Three, four pulls, and his coolness washed through me, helping to abate the flames licking me up from the inside.

"I love you," I mumbled against his neck as I lapped the wound closed.

A brush of lips to the top of my head. A wordless kiss to my hand. Another to my shoulder. Then Rogue tightened his arms around me.

Their love kindled inside of me, without language or reason. Their thoughts were as clear and vibrant as the emotions themselves.

My queen.

My mate.

My lady.

My chosen.

Mine.

That singular feeling threaded through all of us, and I smiled. Never alone again. Never taken for granted. Never a possession.

Always treasured.

"Our word," Alfred said aloud to their murmurs, and then I dropped right into sleep, cocooned between them all as they somehow fit all four of them onto the bed. It should have been impossible, but I was buried beneath so many naked limbs and I wouldn't have been anywhere else.

Ever.

THE AIR WAS COLD WHEN I OPENED MY EYES. COLD ENOUGH I could see my breath. The bodies around me didn't move. Didn't breathe. If anything, they were so still, it was like death had crept into the room with us.

I reached for Alfred, his face was the closest to mine, but his eyes were closed and his skin hard and cold. All the color had leached from him. Worse, he was like a statue shaped around me. They all were. One after another, I twisted amongst them, looking for some awareness or wakefulness.

The air grew more frigid. Teeth chattering from the cold, I tried everything to wake them, but not even the hot tears scalding my cheeks worked. I wiggled between them at the sound of something beyond the room—a door slamming.

Someone was in the cottage.

They were helpless, and someone was here.

It took some maneuvering, but I slid out from beneath them and then stared back at the bed. They were so still, it wrenched my heart. My skin tingled though. Even in the frosty air leaving my skin prickling with goosebumps and my nipples so taut they threatened to break off, my skin seemed electric.

Magic.

The brush of it swirled around me, and I glared at all four corners of the room. Another thump of sound.

Footsteps.

Pivoting, I faced the door to the bedroom. It had closed sometime between when we came inside and collapsed onto the bed. I hadn't really paid attention to our surroundings, my focus wholly consumed by the men currently rendered helpless. I snagged a shirt from the floor and pulled it over my head. Better to not face an enemy naked.

While it was distracting for them, I didn't want to invite the groping. I might actually rip something off them if they touched me. A ferociousness unfurled in me, and the dark room brightened with a blue-white light that made my loves look even more cold and lost. Fury turned my blood hot, and when the doorknob turned, I braced to launch across the room.

They'd messed with the wrong fucking girl.

The door swung inward, revealing a mountain man of a being standing there. He wore old jeans tucked into motorcycle boots of all things and a heavy leather jacket over a ripped T-shirt. His expression was fierce, a pair of glittering eyes hidden beneath a cascade of dark hair and a heavy beard.

Everything about him was menacing. Dangerous. He practically exuded threat.

I shifted my balance onto the balls of my feet as the light on my hands intensified. A flicker of flames, silvery and bright, flashed in the corner of my eyes, but I didn't look down at them.

"Well," the man said in a voice that echoed more like gravelly rocks grinding and tumbling against each other, "you must be the one all the hullabaloo is about. Not sure what I was expecting, but you were not it."

"Fantastic, then turn your big, hairy ass around and leave before I turn you into a flaming pile of bones."

Not that I was sure I could set him on fire, but I didn't dare let him get near Alfred or the others while they were helpless.

He stared at me for a long moment and then laughed.

And laughed.

And laughed.

The fucker was still laughing when I slammed into him and not only knocked him back several steps, but right through the wall and into the grassy clearing beyond the cottage. He rolled over and then came up to his feet before glancing down at his smoking leather jacket.

"You have a redhead's temper," he murmured. "Noted."

"I told you to go."

I didn't know who he was or what he was. But he was huge. He'd easily match Maddox in size and breadth. He had all of Alfred's presence and the quiet threat Rogue always exuded. But if he thought he held a candle to Fin's charm, he was sorely mistaken.

While I regretted the damage to Rogue's cottage, I needed this guy gone.

"Little girl has bite," he said as he dusted off the jacket and put out the hint of embers burning on the leather. "I suppose you'd have to in order to lure that surly bastard out of his keep in the mountains."

I glared at him. "Are you hard of hearing?"

He grinned, the slash of white teeth amidst his beard almost fiercer than his scowl. "Make me leave."

I just had, but if he really wanted a test… I flew at him. Literally fucking flew.

I don't know who was more surprised, me or him, but I struck him full in the chest again, and this time, his whole jacket caught on fire before we crashed into the trees at the edge of the clearing. I narrowly avoided one landing on me as it cracked around him.

He launched upward, far more spry than a man his size should be, and latched one hand around my arm. His grip barely closed on me before he yanked me toward him, but then he released me with a sharp curse as the scent of sizzling flesh scorched my nostrils and my stomach revolted at the scent.

Laughter erupted from him again as he tried to snare me, but I avoided him. One moment, I was on the ground, and the next, I was airborne again. He actually swung a tree at me.

A whole damn tree.

And I narrowly avoided it. When I hit the ground, he tried to pin me and a scream ripped through me, even as a blast of pure white light erupted like a beacon, flooding the darkened clearing.

Then I snapped upright on the bed. Alfred, Maddox, and Rogue were on their feet, their eyes open and their expressions fierce. Fin still curled against me, but he snapped his gaze from me to the room around us and then back.

My heart hammered as I tried to process it.

We were all still naked.

All still in the room.

They weren't still like statues, but warm and alive.

The sun shone outside the windows.

Who the fuck was that hairy bastard? A nightmare?

Fin let out something that sounded like a growl, and I stared at him wide-eyed.

"Wyman," he said in a breath, and Alfred exploded out of the room. A split-second later, a crash sounded outside.

CHAPTER 14

"A friend is one who has the same enemies as you have." - Abraham Lincoln

FIN

Fiona shimmied out of Fin's arms, the glow on her skin undiminished, despite the ferocious expression she wore. Maddox already had the door blockaded, and Rogue stood by the windows. Dragging himself up, Fin caught the pants Rogue threw at him, even as Maddox tugged his own shirt over Fiona's glowing skin.

"Can you dim it, little *sváss?*" Rogue asked her as he tucked up behind her. Outside, another crash sounded and there was a boom of familiar laughter. Fin had only met Wyman briefly, very briefly, when he'd still been human.

The old bastard had drunk him under a table and then poured him back into his chamber at the end of the night, leaving Fin to wake with the worst hangover he'd experienced in his whole life. At the time, he'd truly thought he would die.

Then the bastard did it again the following night.

Good times.

The radiant luminescence from Fiona gradually faded until she was just her normal radiant self, right down to her sharp eyes, swollen lips, and flushed face. Fuck, he did not want company. He just wanted to drag her back into the bed and spend the next several hours figuring out all the ways they could make her scream. One thing he'd already noticed —she responded differently to different stimuli. It wasn't just their desire and lust she needed. No, she needed *them*.

Loving her had been inevitable. He'd loved her long before he'd put his own eyes on her, when she'd been nothing more than an ephemeral dream. The woman had been so much more. Alfred had been correct when he said she was much better than the idea of her. From her stubborn denials to her reckless behavior to her ruthless defense, she was absolutely perfect for them.

Besotted didn't begin to cover his feelings.

Dwarfed by Maddox's shirt, she glanced around the room as though searching. Her leggings just peeked out from the end of the bed, a dark spot of fabric against the paler color of the comforter. Tugging them out, Fin held them up, and her smile spread.

Another crash sounded from beyond, this time accompanied by the shattering of glass. Rogue sighed. They were being quite unkind about his secret hideaway. Fin would make it up to him later. Maybe he and Maddox could swing some repairs.

When Fiona caught her leggings, he tugged her forward into his arms. "Let them go beat up Wyman and we'll stay here," he suggested as he cradled her close.

To his enormous pleasure, she wrapped her arms around

his neck and nuzzled his chin before he kissed her. But the sharpest little sting at the end of her scraping her teeth over his lower lip had him sighing. No, they could not coddle her no matter how much they wanted to, and as if summoned by the very thought, her mind opened to him as she smiled up at him.

I'll let you all hit him first. The dream she'd just experienced filtered through Fin, and his eyes narrowed. Wyman had that ability.

We'll hold him for you, love. He promised. *Then you can beat him silly if you wish.*

Her smile redoubled in force, and it knocked all the air from his lungs. Yes, besotted just didn't cover it. Catching her pants, he went to one knee and pressed a kiss to her abdomen before he held the leggings so she could step into them.

"Suck up," Maddox grumbled with as much humor as he did disgust. Probably annoyed Fin had thought of it first.

"Stick with me, brother," Fin advised him. "I know how to treat our lady."

Rogue snorted and cuffed Fin lightly on the back of the head as he tugged her leggings up over her hips. She smelled of them, but also of herself—alluring and devastating to his senses. He wanted just a few hundred years to learn everything she enjoyed.

Maddox slid a ring onto her finger and a necklace around her throat. The gems barely held a candle to her brilliance, but she scoffed as she curled her bare toes. "I'm hardly wearing the right clothes for these."

"They're yours," he reminded her, all gruff and stern. It was killing the dragon to not lock her away. Every part of him just wanted her safe and as far from any potential harm as possible. Definitely not adding Wyman to the Christmas card list once Maddox found out about the dream raid.

Another crash, this time more wooden with splintering, and Fin sighed. "Does he ever visit without making a mess?"

In one voice, Rogue and Maddox said, "No."

"I don't like him," Fiona announced when Fin stood and offered her his arm. She chuckled, then threaded her arm through his and pressed a kiss to his bare bicep. He wasn't the only one who hadn't bothered with a shirt. He rather doubted Alfred had even remembered the pants before he'd rushed out there.

Maddox stalked ahead of them, and Rogue closed in behind.

"See, we're the most precious among them," he murmured in her ear, and her laughter eddied over him like a caress.

"And it has absolutely nothing to do with the fact that you can spirit me away at a moment's notice." The dry tone delighted him.

"Absolutely not. Though, if you're saying you want to run away with me, I'm all in. Where would you like to go? New Zealand? Madagascar? India? Belgium? Norway?"

"Maybe later," she teased and pinched him. "No one is leaving anyone right now."

The rigid muscles in Maddox's back eased. Yes, Fin's lady knew exactly what to say to settle the dragon. The man had a tight control over his more primal side, but it was a near thing and they all knew it. Recognized it, even before he'd stolen away with her.

It hadn't changed any of their reactions. Alfred's fury had been a wild storm, and Fin hadn't ever seen him that angry. Rogue's reaction had been far more silent and guarded, but there'd been no mistaking the cold rage flowing through him. Tracing them to Maddox's vault had only taken them a little time, but Fin decided against taking them directly in while they'd both been in a state. To his surprise, Alfred had agreed with him and sent him ahead to secure Fiona.

Now they had another interloper to deal with. It was time to eliminate all possible threats, then the dragon could settle in and so could Rogue and Alfred. Once they all quieted, Fin and Fiona could go back to having fun before the child arrived. Oh, and when he or she did…

Outside the bedroom, they found an enormous hole where the front window had been, and the door was completely off its hinges and lying half down the steps on the porch. Outside, Alfred and Wyman were laughing and both men were bloodied, though Wyman looked like he'd gone back to some native Viking roots with his wild long mane and beard. Well, if Vikings turned into bikers.

"Hellion," Alfred called as they arrived. "I have someone I want to introduce you to."

"We've met," she said in the iciest tone Fin had ever heard from her. He glanced down at their love with surprise, but she'd already unhooked her arm from his and started around Maddox as she stalked toward Wyman.

He pushed to his feet as Alfred shot him a look. Ah, so he hadn't confessed his little trespass, had he?

"Ah, don't get snooty on me now, hot stuff. You were a fine, fiery little minx, all teeth and claws in defense of your men." That jovial tone was very much him and probably going to get him killed. Fin debated how much he cared and then thought hard on the near month-long hangover the old bastard had left him with.

No, he couldn't say he'd mind too much if they all delivered a few blows to him. Both men had signs of blood on them, but neither was openly bleeding. Wyman had a hell of a black eye though, so Alfred's welcome had definitely been the bruising kind.

"Wyman," Alfred warned, and the other man held up his hands, laughing. Not an ounce of shame or remorse there.

"The prophecy about this one has been around a long

time, Al, you and I both know that. More, rumors about her are racing around the world with a hurricane force gale. I wanted to see what the fuss was about. No surprise you've already claimed her."

"She claimed me," he told him in such a stiff tone, even as Rogue moved ahead with Maddox to bracket her. They hadn't stopped her from approaching, but when Alfred held out his hand, Fin had to hold his breath. Yes, a great deal had changed since they'd broken her out of the prison, and her love and affection for them was without question.

He believed she trusted them, but Alfred needed her to show that trust and choice right now. Not that Fin should have worried. She padded past the guys to slide her hand into his, and Alfred drew her right to him. One thing Fin had always loved about Alfred—he'd never had an ounce of shame. Rogue actually had a pair of pants for him in hand, but Alfred kept his right arm free as he slid his left around Fiona.

"I saw that. She wasn't letting me get anywhere near you either." Wyman sounded altogether too smug.

"Stay out of her head," Maddox growled.

Seemingly without care, Wyman laughed. "Leash yourself, Goldie, or I'll do it for you."

Fiona started forward, but Alfred dragged her back. He mouthed something, but the syllable was too low for Fin to hear. Probably wait or trust me or something. Or maybe just give it a minute. With Alfred, it could be anything. But she didn't try to rip his balls off, so whatever it was, she seemed willing to listen for the moment.

"Wyman," Rogue said. "Don't start fights. You and Alfred enjoy tormenting each other, but our lady is not here for your pleasure or entertainment."

The wild card of the Six shot him a sly look, then grinned. "Good thing she's already entertained me, then, right?"

"Do you truly want to die today?" Alfred asked, his voice deceptively calm. The dark fire he'd been sporting reappeared, dancing over his flesh, as did a pair of wings, both seemingly composed of the same fire. Nothing moved in their little clearing, save for some birds in the distance utterly unperturbed by the drama unfolding below.

The beauty of nature, it held no interest in their short-term issues. For nature was always there, something Fin had taken a great deal of solace in over the intervening centuries. Now though? Even their nature had changed. There was a peace inside of him he'd not felt since realizing someone had poisoned him. A peace within himself and with the world around him.

All traces of humor fell from Wyman's expression as he stared at Alfred and Fiona. Maddox shifted his weight. It was imperceptible, but Rogue had already moved. He now stood on the other side of Wyman, slightly closer to Alfred and Fiona. They were caging him in, and Fin tested the air for magic.

No spells gathered around the wild card, but still, he'd be wary regardless. Nothing was allowed to touch Fiona. Alfred's arm around her was as protective as it was possessive. He had his palm flat over her abdomen, and without a doubt, he'd fold over to take any hit coming their way.

"You know she hardly needs your protection," Wyman said slowly as he stared at Alfred. "She handled my 'approach' just fine."

"You shouldn't have approached her in the first place," Alfred told him a clipped tone that brokered no arguments.

"Brother, the day I don't look after our interests is the day you spread my ashes in the wind. I hear about you shacking up with some demoness—no offense, little miss. You're hot and I can see the appeal, but a succubus is a succubus is a—"

He never finished the next part of the statement. Alfred

went from holding her to knocking Wyman clean off his feet and back several yards until he crashed through the trees, felling several of them along the way.

Rogue sighed as Alfred stalked after his 'brother.'

"I'll fix them as much as I can," Fin assured Rogue. They were damaging his lovely little island getaway. The sad truth was they were pretty hard on any area when they fought. They'd wiped out whole cities before, leveled civilizations. It was why Alfred worked to keep the peace.

Only, he wasn't so interested in that right now.

None of them were.

Fiona started after them, but Rogue intercepted, even as Maddox shifted his weight forward, but Fin held out a hand. "Give them a minute. Wyman's here for a reason, and I don't think he came to hurt us."

Oh, that earned a baleful look from Fiona. "He threw a tree at me."

"A dream tree," Fin soothed, though he glanced to where Alfred and Wyman had disappeared. "Though, he really shouldn't abuse you or the trees."

Her snort made him smile, and he snuck a look at her. Exasperation and humor filled her eyes, a brief flash, before anger glittered in them again.

Beautiful, Wyman is a bit of a bastard, but I don't think he means any real harm.

"You don't think?" she asked in that deliciously husky voice of hers. With her hair mussed and her lips swollen, all he could think about for a split second was spreading her out in a sunny patch and reacquainting himself with her sweet cunt.

"Fin likes to see the good in people," Maddox grumbled.

"I do," Fin agreed. "It's good practice for how much time we spend together." The little dig landed and the dragon growled at Fin, but he also laughed too. Fiona's smile reappeared, and some of the tension gathering around her eyes eased.

Over the next fifteen long minutes, Rogue had to persuade Fiona twice to stay. Maddox finally stalked inside and returned with a mug of hot coffee. Fin wasn't sure she was supposed to have that. There were rules about pregnancy. Or so he'd heard on some show he'd been watching at one point. He might have to brush up on that.

But from the way she cradled the mug in her palms, he'd die before he let someone take it from her. "Bacon?" he offered. It wouldn't take him long to go and arrange a meal.

Everything about her brightened at the offer. "I'm starving."

"Then I'll…"

Of course, that was exactly when Alfred and Wyman returned. Both were bloodied again and the dark fire on Alfred had vanished, but Wyman had ditched his jacket and pulled his wild mane up. It was hard to miss the scent of singed hair.

"Of course you'd wear a man bun," Fiona said with such disgust, Fin made a note to never do that.

"Aye," Wyman agreed. "I am. And on that note, little miss, your lordship here has decried that unless I'm willing to pledge myself, I'm not allowed to stay around you."

Maddox folded his arms, a slow smirk forming.

"Nothing personal against the rest of them, or even to Alfred himself, but give me one good reason why I should pledge to you?"

Alfred's gaze went skyward, 'cause no, Wyman couldn't make it simple.

Rogue's expressionless face betrayed nothing, but Fin suspected he wasn't as put off as he behaved. No, like the rest of them, he was just protective and Fiona wasn't happy at the moment. The narrow-eyed look she favored Wyman with didn't promise that would change any time soon.

You don't like a lot of people, do you?

While she didn't look at Fin, he knew he had her attention. A part of him wanted the closeness to keep Wyman from sneaking behind her defenses again, though he suspected the being needed a weak mind or true sleep to accomplish such a task.

Fiona was not weak minded.

Most people treat me like I'm a succubus.

He almost smiled at her.

My love, you treated you like a succubus.

That earned him a glare but without any real venom. *Not anymore.*

No, he agreed readily enough. *Not anymore.*

Do you trust him?

Did he?

"Are you two quite finished discussing me?" Wyman asked, almost bored. Alfred didn't slug him, though Maddox might. Rogue tossed pants to Alfred, who pulled them on while they awaited Fiona's verdict.

"No," she told him acerbically. "We're not. Be quiet."

Wyman's eyebrows climbed, but he surprised Fin by doing as she asked.

I don't mistrust him. Just never drink with him. I swear his leg is hollow.

A faint smile curved her lips as she met Fin's gaze, and her whole countenance brightened as her skin glowed.

Dammit.

The smile dropped off and so did the glow, but it was too late.

"I'll be damned," Wyman said slowly, then pivoted away from her to face Alfred. "No wonder they tried to take her out."

"No one is touching her, Wyman. I meant what I said, pledge to her or go. If you try to stay without offering her your bond—"

"I am *not* bonding with him," an incensed Fiona interrupted, offended as hell, and Fin couldn't help it. He laughed. Not that he would share her with Wyman. Ever.

Nor would Alfred or Rogue or Maddox.

But they'd just sealed their own bonds, so of course she'd…

"He does not mean bond to him, little *sváss*," Rogue assured her with a dark look at Fin. "He means for Wyman to swear his allegiance to you, to die in your place and to die should anything happen to you, to pledge his loyalty and to kneel before you as a queen."

"Oh." She wrinkled her nose as if the idea was distasteful. "I thought the Seven were equals."

Wyman gave a careless shrug. "That's always been their mistake, little miss, but we fell because we followed and we survived because we followed and we flourished because we followed." He cut a look at Alfred. "She's your queen?"

"She is."

"What the hell," Wyman declared. "You only live once. I'll offer you my pledge," he told Fiona and started to bend his knee, but she stopped him with a scoff of sound.

"Never said I wanted it," she informed him, then tossed back her coffee. "But you could begin to negotiate this pledge by fixing Rogue's lovely cottage and then Fin's trees and maybe apologizing for scaring me to death by making me think they'd died."

And it had been going so well…

Maddox struck. Because…Maddox.

Fin groaned, but Alfred didn't seem bothered at all, nor did Rogue. Fiona looked pleased, and he really couldn't fault her. The dragon had flung Wyman away to crash into more trees that Fin would have to heal.

"It's good for him," Rogue said and pressed a kiss to Fiona's temple. "Do you still want Fin to fetch you bacon?"

That delighted smile she gave him resolved all his issues. "As my lady wishes," he told her with a wink. "I'll be back. Do try not to let them destroy the island."

CHAPTER 15

"A king is not complete without his queen." - Anonymous

FIONA

lfred had been serious about Wyman pledging to me. Worse, after he and Maddox tore another swath through the beauty of the island, I had to accept. Not because I particularly wanted the grungy bastard's allegiance. What the fuck was I supposed to do with it? Accessorize? Ugh. They needed a rule book, or at least a complete idjit's guide to being a hybrid queen.

Maybe I should write one.

Yeah, that wasn't going to work. I could barely focus on the construction of my house anymore. Kind of bothered me, though now and then, if I unfocused my eyes, I could see the sea beyond the windows as the sun set.

"Kitten," Maddox murmured as he draped a soft, furry cloak over my shoulders. The entire hall was close to freezing, though Fin nearly had the stones back in place to repair the gaping hole

647

our visitors had left in the wall. Apparently, the battle at the keep had involved a great deal of damage from their magical bombs.

You have access to magic that can do fantastic things, and you make bombs? The world was populated with monsters.

I tilted my head back as the dragon wrapped me up and then settled behind me on what was left of the dais and pulled me back against his chest. To be honest, the whole hall was freezing, but the cold hadn't bothered me as much. They'd all promised the bathing rooms hadn't been hit, but I hadn't been allowed to see the library.

That was Rogue's request, and I found it almost impossible to tell him no.

Wyman's booming laughter came from the servants' hall, and I swore my upper lip curled. He was such a loud bastard, constantly telling the worst jokes and flirting with me like it was his occupation. Maddox grumbled and Rogue gave him cool looks, but it remained mostly harmless.

"There you are, Your Majesty," he called as he appeared, summoned as if drawn by the very thought of him.

Kill me. He'd also taken up that address because little miss and hot stuff had Alfred hulking out with dark fire.

The dark fire was hot in so many ways.

"They've been putting together a supper for all of us now that the hard work is done."

Fin's scoff from the entrance where he manipulated the stones as Rogue literally held back the icy wind made me smile. "You mean now that *we* have done all the hard work?"

"Takes lots of work to look as good as I and Her Queenness do."

Maddox groaned and rubbed his cheek against my hair. He'd gone almost catlike in his need to touch, and to be honest, I wasn't saying no because it soothed me nearly as much as it did him.

"Fiona is effortless in her charm," Alfred announced as he entered, dressed once more in a dark shirt and slacks and looking absolutely devastating. Every cell in my body vibrated to life, and his eyes flicked to me as if sensing it. The huff from Maddox told me my desire was definitely in the air, and I didn't care.

I could eat Alfred up.

You're drooling, Beautiful.

I know.

I also didn't care.

The curve of Alfred's lips made me wiggle back against Maddox, and his very interested dick thickened against my ass as he tucked me more securely into his lap.

"I don't think she's even listening to me," Wyman complained, but I ignored him, because I definitely wasn't listening. Instead, I tracked Alfred's progress as he inspected the newly finished wall and then helped to actually secure the new doors. To my immense shock, Wyman, the lazy bastard, helped as they maneuvered the spelled doors into place.

"Well, she must be getting to know you already," Alfred said. "Brilliant and beautiful."

"A deadly combination."

Maddox huffed a laugh next to my ear. "He's trying to get you to like him."

I wrinkled my nose. Somehow, I doubted that.

"He doesn't generally talk to people he doesn't like," Maddox soothed as he began running his hands up and down my arms. "Do you need anything, Kitten?"

"I'm good," I promised him. We'd dined on a huge spread of food, including several pounds of bacon that no one else touched until I'd had my fill. Then Wyman had made good on my demand and gotten to work on repairing Rogue's cottage. At least until Rogue banished him away from it because he'd rather do it himself.

After Fin tended to the damaged trees, we'd returned here to dig in. Alfred had also sent emissaries to the rest, informing them of the new rules. Something my asshole had apparently left out in his tales of how the Seven were equal and made their calls, was that he'd been their leader *before* they fell and he'd blamed himself.

What I hadn't figured out was whether he'd purposefully cut himself off so they could have freedom they might not otherwise get, or if he'd never been moved to create a whole plethora of sycophants and followers.

I leaned toward the former truthfully, despite how it had looked when he first awoke and the courtiers and admirers had flooded these halls seeking their favor. A lot of it had begun to make sense to me.

"Are you really calling in all who swore allegiance to Alfred?" That question had been troubling me since we left the isle.

"No," Alfred answered for me as he strolled over to join us. His new shadow moved just a pace behind him. I hope the new pet, as feral as he was, understood when I had the boys put him out of our rooms at night. I didn't even want someone else up in that hall.

The rather startling thought crystalized more firmly after they made the decision to return here. Alfred brushed his knuckles down my cheek, and I smiled up at him. The reaction was instinctive, needing the shine of his attention as much as I wanted to give him mine. I searched his face for any sign of weariness, but all I found was deep acceptance.

"I know this is difficult, Hellion," he told me. "But we've decided to summon the remaining Six. They can choose or not to bring their forces. If they do…"

Wyman cracked his knuckles. He'd taken the news of

being only Six pretty well, all things considered. Though they'd failed to mention my participation in the removal of Keeley. Even without Fin's well-meaning *let us have this please, Beautiful* and Alfred's hidden but very firm wink, I'd already chosen to hush. I had nothing to prove.

Not to any of them, and I didn't give a single fuck what Wyman thought, as long as he didn't betray Alfred. If he did that, I'd kill him without a second thought.

The being in question caught me staring at him, and he raised his hands. "I didn't do it."

"Yet," I tacked onto the end for him with a smile. Then there was a clang as the last door settled into place. I flicked my gaze over to where Rogue and Fin examined their work. The library was next on their list, or so they'd said, but first, our defenses.

"Tough audience," Wyman commented, though he didn't sound too put out by the observation. "I'm going to check out your staff and see if they'll feed me, unless you want me to stick around here."

Leaning my head back against Maddox, I asked, "Are you really on our side?"

The whole of the room hushed. Even if the sound of work had quieted, not even the heartbeats of those servants still present intruded. What, did everyone hold their breath?

"Are you challenging my word?" Wyman asked. Maddox didn't tense behind me, so either he didn't perceive a threat or he wasn't concerned about what threat might exist.

"Your word doesn't mean anything to me," I told him as simply and honestly as I could muster. "Your loyalty has value to Alfred and to the others. I just want to know that you're truly on our side. Or if it is the five of us against the five of you?"

Scratching his beard, Wyman contemplated me for a

moment, then slanted a look at Alfred. "She's worth it." It wasn't a question.

"I know," he told him.

"Yes, Your Majesty," Wyman continued when he faced me once more. "I am on your side and theirs. It will be at least the six of us against three of them. Synove wants nothing to do with this fight."

"So she says." Alfred's mild tone suggested he felt otherwise.

Work complete, Rogue and Fin wandered toward us. Fin's grin was both lazy and playful, but Rogue was far more content if watchful.

"Synove doesn't want war, Alfred," Wyman said, sounding weary for the first time since I'd met him. "She lost her lover in the last one, and it turned her stomach for war. This battle…this battle is a pointless exercise to cling to a past we carved out in blood and tears because some are afraid of what change will bring to their lives."

With a shrug, Alfred said, "Then they will lose. They only see Fiona as a threat to their consolidated power, and they've made their intentions clear. I will not suffer a single hair to be harmed on her head."

Not the time to bring up my split ends.

Fin's eyes flashed as he sent me the cheekiest grin, and I winked at him.

"Well, we can try to negotiate—" Wyman cut himself off as he yawned, then added, "But that's boring and they won't go for it. We're all too stubborn and unchanging. Set in our ways." He paused a beat, then glanced from Alfred to me and back again. "Or some of us were. Apparently, you can change, Your Majesty."

"For her?" Alfred sent me a look that warmed me all the way to my toes. "I'll change everything. So when you reach out to them," he continued, speaking to Wyman without ever releasing my gaze, "make it clear there is no negotiation, only capitulation. Before they attacked, I would have let them be. They made their first mistake when they moved on her before we'd even found her. They made their second when they came here after her."

The heat in my chest bloomed so fiercely as his dark eyes held me captivated.

"There will be no other chances for them." Only then did he look to Wyman. "And I want the two called Dimitri and Isaac. Alive and in my hands."

"Incentive?" Wyman asked almost lazily.

"No," Alfred told him. "A demand."

"Understood."

With that, Wyman gave an almost mocking bow that he ended with a very real salute before he strolled away from us.

"He's a real asshole sometimes," Fin commented. "But I like him."

"You would," Maddox said with a chuckle.

"It's why we get along," Fin teased, his grin growing, and the warmth in my chest continued to spread. Of all of them, though, Rogue remained guarded. Twisting against Maddox, I pressed a kiss to his jaw before I slid out of his lap. He gave me a little squeeze but seemed more intent on wrapping the blanket around me. I passed Alfred and Fin and went to Rogue.

His quiet smile as I tucked up next to him did little to lift the reserve in the rest of his expression. "Yes, little *sváss?*"

"Is the bathing room secure?" It was the first place that came to mind. I'd prefer the garden in some ways, but it was frigid outside and they didn't want me exposed. Besides, it might give Alfred and Maddox time to talk war.

Already handling us, Beautiful?

Maybe.

But Rogue made me laugh when he swung me up, tucked

my face to his neck, and ran. The swift passage of air promised we'd relocated from the main hall down to the bathing room, if the hot, steamier air wasn't a giveaway. Inside, I didn't need the heavy fur, but Rogue set me down gently before going to get the fire lit.

I sometimes worried about him in the intense humidity and warmth of the room, but nothing in his demeanor changed. It was still careful and guarded.

"What's wrong?" I asked as I stripped out of the clothes I'd mixed and matched from borrowed and mine. Despite the warmer air, my skin pebbled. I'd grown very fond of this dark little chamber with its grotto like hot pools.

The room had seen me through a myriad of changes over the last few months. Had it only been a few months? Hot on the heels of that came thoughts of Elias. I needed to warn him. He had to know a bigger battle was coming, then again…if they came for us here, they wouldn't be going for him there.

"War is never pretty, little *sváss*," Rogue answered me after I slid into the water and he stripped his own clothes to follow me. I loved that he didn't pretend something wasn't wrong or try to humor me and lull me with a different set of security.

Also, the minute I sank into the water, I groaned. I hadn't realized just how much I needed a bath. I still carried all of their scents, not that I objected, but at some point, the skin did begin to itch. Pushing away from the side, I moved to where he sat. He'd dunked his head under as soon as he'd climbed in, and it plastered his beautiful blond hair to his head.

Lathering shampoo into my hands, I began to run my fingers through his hair. He gripped my hips lightly and tugged me forward until I straddled his lap. After, he ducked his head to grant me easier access.

"I can't imagine it is. But we've already waged a few battles."

He nodded, then moved to dunk his head again, rinsing out the shampoo without ever releasing me. After I conditioned it, he gave me an almost sweet smile before he urged me to dunk my own head so he could return the favor.

"War always demands a price, often in blood. My people paid one such price, as did Maddox's."

His fingers scraped gently over my scalp, and I wanted to purr at the caress.

"I will not allow you to be the price paid in this one."

Eyes half-closed, I studied him. "To be clear, I won't allow any of you to pay that price either."

Not now that I'd found them.

"I may not be good at this or even understand it most of the time. But before you, only Elias ever seemed to care about me for me. I adore him, but those feelings do not hold a candle for what I feel for you or Maddox or Fin or Alfred."

"Even when he infuriates you?" It was the gentlest of teases, and I smiled.

"Especially then," I admitted. "Or when you're bossy and domineering or Fin is flirty and fun or Maddox is growly and possessive."

Fingers digging into my hips, Rogue dragged me closer until my breasts brushed his chest. "You should remember we're all possessive."

"Right back atcha," I told him, then brushed my lips to his. It wasn't about passion or demand or sex. If anything, it was more about affection and caring. From the moment he stole me from Maddox and Fin to the first time he'd claimed me to answer the wild hunger inside of me, he'd always been controlled and dominant. But there'd been something else there, always. A softness I doubted anyone else got to see.

And I was extremely possessive of that.

He chuckled, then urged me backward to rinse my hair and I took my time, arching my back so my breasts were on full display for him. He stroked a hand over them, a soothing petting motion that demanded nothing and offered everything as I sat up, then he squeezed the water from my hair.

"Little *sváss*…"

Oh, that tone was serious.

"I know just how strong you are."

"I'm going to hate this, aren't I?" I didn't have it in me to be angry, even if I half-suspected what he was about to ask me.

"Probably, but you carry all of our hearts, and more, you carry the future we never expected to have."

The squeeze in my chest grew tighter.

"Should the tide turn, one of us—likely Fin, if I have my way—will take you from here. I need you to promise me you will go."

"I won't abandon you," I argued. "You all made me run before when you and I went. Then she found us in that town."

"I know," he admitted. "That is a risk, but if they begin to overwhelm us, we need to know you are safe. If I die—"

I clapped a hand over his mouth. "Don't. You. Dare." Anger turned incendiary within me. "You are not allowed to die. Do you understand?"

He kissed my palm, then peeled my hand from his mouth. "Nor are you, little *sváss*. Nor are you." This time when our mouths fused together, it was as much battle as love. I wouldn't let him go, nor, it would seem, would he release me. "Will you promise me?"

The quiet need in that one question threatened to destroy me. How could I promise to leave them? Any of them?

"I will see," I told him. It was all I could do. Because in truth, I did a thing called what I wanted. What I wanted was them. This time when he kissed me, he shifted our angle, and then his cock filled me with one thrust and we never let up for a breath as I rode him.

We needed together.

We soared together.

We'd win this damn thing together too.

"War does not determine who is right – only who is left." -
Winston Churchill

A part of me had expected—well, dreaded really—that Alfred's invitations would either be ignored or bring hundreds to the doorstep. Wyman had vanished from the keep for a couple of days. Though Rogue had been circumspect, I'd caught him returning from some mission very early one morning when I'd snuck up to the library. It truly had been half-ruined. Many of the books on the shelves showed some scorch or water damage, what few books remained. The art had also vanished from the walls, along with more than half of the bookshelves themselves.

The walls were blackened in places, and magic seemed to be keeping the weather out, but there were huge open swaths where the valley was quite visible. The chair I often used by the fire had gone totally to pieces. There was a hint of a water-stained cushion and a few bits of wood that had formed the legs. The cold fireplace just seemed a sad echo of the sunnier room.

It was only turning my back on that destruction to stare out at the sunrise that I caught Rogue's return. He descended from the sky as this great owl and then reformed as a man when he touched down. I didn't mean to hide, but I pressed close to the bit of wall that offered some cover as he straightened.

Exhaustion hung over him like a shroud, and I swallowed a sigh that wanted to escape. How many things were they all handling while I swanned about this building? Surely there was something more I could be doing for them.

His request from the baths a few days earlier had been ever present in my mind. If things turned against us, they wanted me to flee, preferably with Fin. I'd turned that over and over in my mind, refusing to dismiss it immediately, even if a part of me would prefer to just stay here with them. To fight alongside them.

I could fight. I thought I'd acquitted myself well, but they'd also been fighting together for centuries, longer even. A rational part of me expected that was another reason they wanted me to flee. We really didn't know all I could do, and it could take a few decades to rein in my new abilities. I was running on instinct and impulse.

While Alfred hadn't scolded me, he had expressed a reservation, particularly in light of the rugrat currently setting up shop in my body. None of us knew how far along I was. I mean, there was something of a swell there but not like an actual bump, and my boobs didn't hurt like they could. Fin had told me about that one.

Okay, correction, my boobs didn't hurt when one or more of the guys weren't playing with them until I came or they sank their teeth in. I was pretty sure that didn't count.

Ugh. Okay, that was tomorrow Fi's problem, today's Fi had to figure out what to do.

A tingle of awareness glided over my spine, and I sighed as the rich scent of green and forest threaded around me a moment before his arms did. The kiss he pressed behind my ear settled some of the disquiet.

"I didn't think you'd be awake yet," I said in lieu of good morning. The rasp of his unshaven cheek against mine actually made me smile. I loved that he'd rolled out of the bed and come in search of me. Though I had my own room, we'd all been sleeping in Alfred's in the enormous bed he had. Usually, they tucked me in the center and took turns on who slept on my immediate sides, with the others rotating to the outside. It settled Maddox's dragon and seemed to be soothing all of their protective instincts.

"The moment you moved, I woke," he told me, the sweet lilt in his voice making me smile. He could probably read to me from the phone book and his voice would do that to me. How fun would that be? "I wanted to give you some time to yourself, but then I started missing you and I just wanted to see you. I was going to leave you be, but you looked sad again. Why are you sad, Beautiful?"

"I'm not sad," I admitted, leaning into him and running my fingers over the backs of his hands where they cupped my belly. They were all doing that, sometimes consciously, mostly subconsciously, or so it seemed to me. One of them always covered my stomach as I went to sleep. Fin kissed it with reverence. Maddox would nuzzle it with his cheek and sometimes rumble that near purring sound. Even Alfred wasn't immune to the little touches, as though reassuring himself.

And one night, we'd all gone quiet because there'd been the faintest echo of my heartbeat. I had to try and slow mine, but it was there. A gentle little *thump-thump*. Faint, almost imperceptible, and yet present. Since then, Maddox had become even more watchful and solicitous. Fin teased him nonstop, and it had definitely made all the smothering more bearable. Rogue and Alfred were a little more subtle in their attempts

A little.

Not that it said much. One of them or all of them offered to help with my hair or bathing me. Even sex had gotten gentler, sweeter, and sometimes so achingly tender that I thought I would lose my mind or sob from it.

Sometimes both.

While I wasn't complaining—well, not much—it remained a constant series of adjustments. I had no idea what each day would bring. As I'd told Elias when Fin arranged for me to call him—he snuck me out of the keep and secreted us away to a distant city where he had a luxury apartment. It might have been Prague. But the view had been stunning, and he promised to bring me back. Anyway, as I'd told Elias, I wasn't even sure who I was most of the time, but I was happy with the change.

The only thing I hadn't told him was about the baby. Fin had made a sound argument that our child was going to make a huge change in our world. Right now, that child was enormously vulnerable. The ferocity that awoke in me had only made him smile. "And that right there, Beautiful, is what we all feel when we think of someone trying to harm either of you. Secrecy keeps the baby safe. I'm not telling you to not trust your Elias. He seems a good enough man and a kind friend, but he's not family. Not here. Not yet."

And my reluctance at the charge fled when he said 'yet.' I might not know anything about being a mother but I did about being a friend. Reconciling those concepts helped. I wanted to tell him. Fin's 'yet' promised me I would be able to, eventually. That helped even more.

When pressed, I'd had to admit that the constant restless-ness and hunger I'd lived with my whole life was now absent. The absence alone would be disconcerting, but filling in that gap was a satisfaction and pleasure I couldn't define.

He'd tried to understand but it was clear in his voice he didn't, so he demanded to know only one thing. While Fin had afforded me some privacy, I knew he could hear every single word spoken, so I'd just glanced over to find his gaze steady on me.

"Ask," I told Elias. "I won't lie to you."

"Nah, you never do. You just tell me to shut up and mind my own business." The gruff acceptance sparked fresh tears, but I grinned.

"You know me well."

"That I do, Red. You tell me you're where you want to be and with who you want to be with and I'll back it, every step of the way."

I smiled, and those damn tears burned in my eyes again. "I love you too," I told him, and Elias' stunned silence only made my grin grow. Yeah, I wasn't the touchy feely type. But I did love him. He'd been my best friend for a long time and put up with me at my worst. "I'm exactly where I want to be."

Clearing his throat, he said, "Are one of those assholes right there?"

"Yes," Fin had answered for me. "Feel free to threaten us. Trust me, we'll destroy ourselves before we let anything happen to her."

"Just so we have an understanding."

"Agreed."

Men.

I'd huffed and rolled my eyes. After, Fin had cuddled me close as I let the stupid tears out. He didn't seem remotely disturbed by them. Though he was a bit of a bastard and laughed at my mournful complaint of, "Am I going to be a weepy mess the rest of my life?"

"You're beautiful, even when you weep, love. It will be fine. Trust me, it just gives me incentive to chase the tears away." And on that note, he did his damnedest to drive my tears away, and he was more than successful. It seemed forever since it had just been Fin and I alone, not that I objected to the others being there.

Okay, caveat, not that I objected anymore. I loved them all with a kind of fierceness I hadn't expected to ever be capable of. But like my time with Rogue in the bath or with Maddox before the party, and honestly, with Alfred after he finally listened to me, I needed this time with each of them. Fin never once complained about having to share me. If anything, he exulted in it.

The gentleness in his hands coupled with the depth of emotion in every kiss was a drug to my system. Even after our heartbeats slowed and the sweat had begun to cool on my over-heated body, I was in no hurry to move. I sprawled over him, and he traced his fingers up and down my spine. The glint of the emerald on my finger twinkled back at me. I'd gotten used to just keeping the emeralds on no matter what I was wearing.

Maddox's sheer pleasure every time he saw them made me want to. But Fin continued to trace his fingers lazily along my back as I explored one of the Celtic knots inked along his shoulder.

"Are we going to get in trouble for being gone so long?" We hadn't really made a big deal out of our sneaking out. Yet after Maddox "stole" me, there'd been no mistaking how they kept a closer watch. All of them.

"No, love, I promise. They know where we are, and at the first sign of danger, we're away. But I needed some time with you." At that, I lifted my head and smiled at him.

"I'm glad we came."

"Me too."

Then we just…talked, for hours, about everything and nothing. Talked about where he grew up and what it was like for him. About the things he still wanted to do and what he hoped for the future. It was probably the deepest conversation I'd ever had, and when he'd asked me similarly hard questions, I hadn't avoided the answers.

I told him about my mother. I'd never known a father. She didn't keep men around all that long. Never dip too often into the same well, she'd always advised. When I was fourteen and the first pangs of real hunger began to hit me and I earned the notice of the men she courted, she spent a year teaching me how to coax out lovers, get what I needed, and get away.

Then one morning, she'd just been gone.

Fin's scowl deepened with every word, and not even me sprawling against him and telling him it was perfectly natural could dissuade his temper. He wanted more details, but it didn't take me long to figure out what he really wanted—a target.

And I didn't need her to die. I didn't need anything from her. She'd done what all succubi had done—she'd raised me until I could survive on my own, taught me skills, and then gone. It was my own fear about the child I carried now. Would I not be able to bond? But I pushed that fear aside for now. I wasn't a succubus, and I had to make that my mantra or I would go mad.

That day at his Prague apartment had been three days earlier. Our return had been welcomed and not scolded, much to my relief. Maddox and Alfred had both stolen me away for similar time spent, though we didn't leave the keep. The only one not seeking me out so far had been Rogue, but

I'd counted his absences and they seemed to happen in and around the others stealing me.

As amusing as the game was, I wanted to know what he was doing that they thought I needed to be distracted from.

"You're worried," Fin said softly.

"You're all keeping things from me again."

"Not on purpose," he answered. Well, at least he wasn't denying it. "We're getting a feel for where the others are. Wyman can move more freely, but Rogue has the greatest stealth because his animals can slip in and out nearly undetected."

Nearly.

"It's still a risk."

"Yes, love, it's always a risk." He pressed his cheek against mine as he hugged me tighter. "You'll have to forgive us for being overprotective for now. We're still getting used to what it means to us to even consider risking you."

Rubbing the back of his hands where he linked them over my abdomen, I didn't smile. "Fin, why is it all right for you four to conspire because you are so worried about risking me, yet you risk yourselves?"

"Because there are more of us than there are of you," he answered me simply. "Because we have waited for thousands of years to have you in our lives, and I don't want to wait another thousand years on the chance you'll come back to us. Because we're selfish pricks raised in a time long before chivalry, when men made war and the women were the ones we protected, or stole. That last part doesn't really help my argument, does it?"

"No," I told him, but I couldn't suppress the grin trying to break through. "Not particularly. And not all old cultures kept women at home barefoot and pregnant."

And yes, I might've been curling my toes, because I was a damn example of the latter.

"No, they didn't," he admitted.

Tilting my head back, I gazed up at him. "And just because there are more of you doesn't make it all right for me to lose any of you. I won't choose who I need more or want more because there's not one among you I want to risk losing."

He grinned. "But I'm still your favorite, right? It's fine, you can totally tell me. It'll be our secret."

I pinched him, and he laughed.

"I promise, Beautiful," he said, his voice pitching lower as he sobered. "None of us will leave you willingly. And all of us will fight for each other as much for you."

That made me feel better on some level. Perhaps it shouldn't have, but it did. I half-expected Rogue to join us, and was about to suggest we gather breakfast and build a fire and maybe spend the day together just the five of us, when movement flashed on the horizon. The sun had begun to inch its way up on the horizon, all pinks and purples with the promise of a new day across the pristine snow.

But the movement was a dark smudge. A shadow against the light.

"Fin..."

"I see it," he told me, arms tightening around me.

That was a lot more than just the five Alfred had summoned—the five that included Wyman and Synove.

Alfred appeared beside us as if summoned by the thought. Only the breeze stirred by his movement pushing at my hair alerted me to how fast he'd arrived. He wore slacks only, hastily pulled on and not buttoned.

Similarly, Maddox stood there, in jeans and bare feet looking rugged and primal. And my hormones were up for it. Holy fuck, between the two of them and the fact that Fin was wrapped around me, I wanted to forget there was an army approaching and just get naked.

What had I been thinking about a day together?

"Wyman is with them," Rogue answered an unspoken question as he came to stand on my other side. When he held out his hand, I clasped his. The look in his eyes held the question he'd pressed me to answer days earlier. Would I go? Would I leave them to this fight and flee the danger?

"We expected that," Alfred said. "He would have to ingratiate himself, but he's given his word and his bond. He won't break it."

"That's a lot of trust, Alfred," Maddox commented. "I'm not saying you're wrong, but what if you are?"

"I've known them all since we were children in another time and another place. I knew them when they were truly my blood brothers and sisters, when we fought together. I knew them when we fell. They would not be here if not for me, for my choices—"

"And theirs," Rogue said, not letting Alfred finish that thought. "They chose to follow you, as we do."

The stiffness in Alfred's shoulders rippled as he seemed to settle into himself.

"He's right," Fin said casually. "If they got their panties in a twist over where they ended up, that's not your fault. I don't have a single regret about following you." He punctuated the last with a kiss to my shoulder before moving to take his place between me and Alfred. Yes, he still had my hand, and the weight of his regard struck me.

Would I let him secret me away?

I still didn't have an answer for that beyond I didn't want to leave them.

"Even if we did," Maddox said abruptly, "no one can mistake our choice for anything else."

"Except Rogue." Alfred's tone held just a single note of guilt.

"It's long done, brother," Rogue told him. "I am exactly

where I want to be, and I forgave you a long time ago. Without you, I'd never have known my little *sváss*. It's enough."

"And now that we've gotten the maudlin portion of battle prep out of the way...what do we want to do?" Fin rolled his head from side to side, then cut another glance at me.

I exhaled and then looked at them, one at a time. Maddox's gaze was pure dragon and raw fury. He was ready for this fight. Fin was no less wild in his countenance, but his expression held just the faintest smirk. He'd already decided we were winning and he wouldn't accept any other outcome.

Rogue didn't flinch, but he seemed equally resigned and yet hopeful regarding my decision to stay or go. Finally, I looked at Alfred.

Did I do what I wanted, or did I follow what they needed?

What if they needed me?

"If you stay, Hellion, you fight at my side. You stay with me for the entirety of the battle."

My heart squeezed. If I stayed... He was giving me the final decision. Fuck, I loved them.

"We'll never leave you," I whispered. "And I'd follow you anywhere." Fuck those who fell with him. I'd fall every time, no question.

"The two most powerful warriors are patience and time." - Leo Tolstoy

ROGUE

War. He'd told Fiona that war was never pretty and it always came at a price. Of course, the remnants of the Six would not let this go. While they had no way of knowing whether they'd learned of Keeley's death, it was possible. Rogue had taken responsibility for it, because while they were already gunning for Fiona, he'd prefer they brought their revenge plans to him. Never had he experienced terror as he had that night in the alley.

Not since the massacre of his people. Then, he'd been numb. The destruction had left his soul a bleak place. When Alfred had "saved" him, his fury had known no bounds. How dare Alfred take from him the chance to journey to his people in the afterlife? That cold rage had fed his soul while he sought his revenge, and it had kept him alive.

Alfred allowed it because he wanted Rogue to have a reason to live. It had taken him far too long to understand it. By then, his anger had faded like so much else. Following Alfred had been a choice at that point, but not one Alfred ever asked of him.

But Fiona had brought light and color back into that world. For all of them. She'd given Rogue a reason to hope. A reason why Alfred had forced this life on him so long ago, and he could be grateful. Even if they hadn't known then, everything had been building to this moment. Every blood-soaked, painful moment.

Losing her was not an option. He knew damn well the others felt as strongly, but the moment Alfred gave her the option, he'd known what her answer would be.

Of course she wouldn't leave them. She'd done it before, and danger had followed. So maybe, maybe she was right. It didn't make the decision any more palatable. Together. It was what they'd told Maddox after he stole her. What Fin insisted on the moment he'd felt the ripple of her presence in the world.

Together.

"You stay at my side, Hellion. We won't have much time before they get here," Alfred said. "Maddox, put her in the armor."

The dragon nodded and held out a hand to Fiona. She clasped it and then glanced at Rogue and Fin before going with him. The armor was something they'd been working on.

"What is the plan?" Fin asked as soon as they were out of earshot. "I've sent the servants into the catacombs." Yes, most of the retainers were not prepared for this battle, and while there were many who had sworn their loyalty, they would be conveniently late if they showed up at all. Alfred had not summoned them.

He did not relish the killing, even if he'd once served as the Deathbringer.

The Angel of Death, who'd refused to wage the war on his own kind and was cast down because of it, would now wage war on those of his kind who'd survived. Not for himself, but in service to those he cared about.

In her name.

A soft huff of laughter escaped him as he tracked the movement of the force coming at them. They wanted to be seen, so they took their time crawling up the mountain like a dark shadow. Proof that their numbers were so much greater than Alfred's. That was the thing that Cyril and Eamon had never understood. It wasn't about numbers.

It was about conviction.

They were all devoted to each other and to her—his little *sváss*, with her cutting tongue and wild temperament.

"Enjoying yourself?" Alfred asked him as he pulled on a shirt. Fin had summoned their own armor to them, allowing them to prepare while keeping an eye on things.

"Actually…" Rogue told him as he buckled on his own armor. It seemed a long time since he'd even bothered to do more than wear a leather coat. So very little could truly hurt them. In some ways, this battle exhilarated because it was not a sure thing, even if they couldn't allow any other outcome. "Yes, I am."

Alfred and Fin both glanced at him, and the shock on their faces would have been insulting if it didn't amuse him so much.

Fin didn't wear more than some light armor because the chain messed with his magic. The cloth and leather wouldn't give him much defense. Of course, they'd have to put their hands on him, and he tended to be slippery at the best of times.

Alfred didn't bother with much, though he had strapped

on his sword. His shirt he left open and loose, and the dark fire dancing over his flesh just added to the low level of menace he gave off. Frankly, Rogue didn't disagree. He was thoroughly tired of their home being attacked. The keep may not be perfect, but they'd maintained his sanctuary for centuries and it had been invaded and disturbed multiple times.

"We're going to have to replace the books," Rogue said as he checked his weapons. Two knives. He didn't need anything else.

His hands would be faster.

"And the art," Alfred agreed. "I'm sure we have something in the vault or in Maddox's hoard that would do the trick."

"We could let her pick out what she likes," Fin suggested, and Rogue chuckled. "Maybe take her to a few museums if there's other types of art she's interested in."

Alfred eyed him. "Planning a heist?"

"Why not?" Fin shrugged. "We only live once, and when she wants to redecorate, we can take it back. Besides, there's a good number of artifacts in the British Museum that belong to me. I just let them borrow them because it was cheaper to store them there."

Rogue laughed for real and shook his head. "Of course you did."

The approaching army had *slowed*, but Rogue assumed that was for more affect. Gemma had to be with them. Melodramatic bitch.

The scrape of a boot had him turning, and he grinned at the sight she made.

"Ah, Goddess of Spring and Flame and Blood," Fin declared, the Gaelic in his voice strong. "Welcome to the battle, my lady."

Damned if Fiona didn't look beautiful in the blue-green and golden-scaled armor. It had taken some doing, but they'd worked on it over the years, sometimes more as a lark. They'd harvested the scales from Maddox himself, and it had been imbued with Fin's magic and the measure of Rogue's as he worked with it to shape it. He'd only done the final changes in the last couple of weeks fitting it to her.

It was perfect.

She really did look like a goddess.

"She needs a crown," Alfred said.

"We'll make her one," Fin volunteered, and Fiona threw her head back and laughed. But Maddox stared past her to the army beyond, and his expression darkened.

War was never pretty.

MADDOX

Fiona threaded her fingers with his as he hurried her down the steps to her rooms. The armor would be stored there. They'd gathered it piece by piece, refitting it to her shape. They'd had the base ready for a long time, only needing to find her to match it. Fin had been pretty accurate in guessing most of it from his visions.

Or maybe his visions had just been that accurate. It didn't matter. Maddox wanted her in the full body armor if she insisted on going into battle.

"Hey," she said as he pulled down the trunk they'd stored it in. Fin had spelled it so only one of the five of them could open it. "I've been in fights before, Maddox."

"I don't care," he told her grimly as he unpacked the armor. "This is not just a fight. This is war. There's a thousand people out there who want your head, and three in particular who won't stop until they take it or lose theirs."

He would find them first. Alfred likely had a similar plan. Everything else was cannon fodder.

"I can't leave you," she said in an almost too steady voice, and he paused in the unpacking of the armor to find her stripped down and pulling on the cloth jerkin and soft pants that would serve as the lining under the armor. "Please don't ask me too."

And in that request, even his dragon settled. "You will stay at Alfred's side?"

"Like I've been super-glued."

It was enough. It had to be. He buckled her into the armor, and he didn't miss the way she looked at it or how perfectly it conformed to her body. It wouldn't in a few short months, but by then, they would not need to wage war.

They would see to that.

He chuckled. "Kitten, do you remember what you said to me in the cell?"

"I said a lot of things." The spark of humor in her vibrant green eyes filled him with a near indolent pleasure. "Which one?"

He finished tucking the last bit of armor into place, then nuzzled a kiss to her jaw. The armor shielded her throat so he couldn't touch his mark, but he did place two fingers above it before licking her ear ever so gently.

Laughter swelled out of her. "If you start licking me again, I'm going to tie a knot in your dick so tight, you'll be screaming when you take a piss."

"That's it," he said with a grin as he leaned back. "That spirit right there. Fight with that, yes?" The glow from her skin had deepened and the hint of those wings was back, but he really only had eyes for her. "You're a dragon's mate, never forget that."

"And you're my mate," she told him as she gripped his

shirt and tugged him down for a real kiss. "Don't you forget it."

He grinned against her lips and then kissed her with every ounce of caring in him. Gentle wasn't in his nature. Or maybe he'd forgotten over the long centuries, but dragons were ferocious beings. That ferociousness was very much alive in him, but so was the need to protect her. Forehead to hers, he closed his eyes and filled his lungs with the scent of her.

"Some day," she said, "I want to go to the beach and hold hands and walk in the sun as the water rolls in. Maybe get a tan. Though…I'm a redhead. I usually burn or get freckles."

Laughter swelled in his chest. None of this was funny, and yet, she made it better. "I will make sure that happens, after I've swept the beach and removed all obstacles."

He wasn't totally serious, but it was absolutely worth her roll of eyes. Still, he had to admit, dragon scale armor looked delicious on her, and the natural sway of her hips had him thinking of anything besides battle.

Maybe he'd just set the whole lot of them on fire and then bring her back and spread her out on one of the beds. Or the floor. Or the wall. Truthfully, he wasn't picky. No, she was pregnant. Definitely a bed.

"Stop staring at my ass," she tossed over her shoulder as she climbed the stairs.

"No."

She grinned back at him, and then they were with the others. Rogue looked somewhat stunned, as did Fin when they saw her in the armor. Alfred gave her an approving look.

"Ah, Goddess of Spring and Flame and Blood," Fin declared, the Gaelic in his voice strong. "Welcome to the battle, my lady."

"She needs a crown," Alfred said, and Fin quickly offered

to make her one. But even as his mate threw her head back and laughed, she never lost her focus on the approaching army.

"So I stick with Alfred," she said slowly as she sobered. "What are you three going to be doing?"

"Killing them all," Fin said cheerfully enough. "Hopefully before lunch, because I know what I'd like to spend my afternoon doing."

Maddox snorted.

"You're assuming my intentions are less than pure." How the druid managed to sound truly offended and sarcastic at the same time was a gift.

"I'm not assuming anything," Maddox told him. "Focus now, play later."

"Pfft." He blew Fiona a kiss. "Dibs in the bath? I'll scrub your back?"

She grinned. "And my front?"

"If you insist," he replied with an almost courtly bow.

But the time for teasing was over.

"Go," Alfred said. "Get into position."

It wasn't the first time they'd fought together, and they really didn't need words. Fin connected them so they would each only be a thought away, but they all had their parts to play, and Maddox relaxed and let his dragon out.

Thankfully, the roof was already gone.

FIN

Maddox didn't even wait for them to break off before he shifted. The massive dragon filled the demolished library and earned a wild grin from Fiona before he took to the skies.

"Show off," he muttered, but Alfred just gave him a look.

Yeah, yeah. He was going. Ugh, he'd had plans today. And they just had to go and show up on their doorstep with an army.

Of course, they'd retreated to the keep for a reason. At least here if they leveled anything, they wouldn't take out a whole city.

Maddox roared.

Maybe?

Not waiting any longer, he slid between the wards and out into the fields beyond the keep. Without the muting effect of the reinforced protections, the sound of so many feet marching echoed toward him. The drama of it all was ridiculous. Was this supposed to inspire fear?

Really?

Kind of reminds me of Helm's Deep.

Fiona's voice tickled the back of his mind, and he was hard-pressed not to laugh, because wait for it...

What is Helm's Deep?

Alfred's deep baritone echoed through him, and it was Rogue, of all people, who snorted mentally.

It's a movie.

And a book, Fin tacked on helpfully.

About a group of humans...

And elves! Fiona added, and Fin cast his gaze skyward.

There were no elves there in the book.

Yep, that was Rogue.

Well, I like the movie better anyway. The point is, big battle, ugly orcs, lots of boom boom, orcs die, and humans win.

Fin grinned. *Sorry you asked, Alfred?*

There was a beat, then a mental shrug. *No. If it delights my queen, then we shall have to see this movie.*

Movie marathon! Popcorn. Chocolate. Snuggles. We can skip the Gollum parts.

The laughter escaped him, and thankfully, he kept it as

silent as possible. Still, they really did have an army of vampires marching on them, and he could see the likeness to the orcs.

Mental fingers crossed, he blew another kiss to Fiona. *Stay with Alfred.*

I will. You focus on keeping your beautiful ass in one piece.

Ha! Smugness filled him. *I knew you liked me best.*

He could almost taste her grin, and then Maddox let out a roar.

Playtime was over.

Now the fun began.

CHAPTER 18

"To be truly great, one must stand with people, not above them." -
Baron de Montesquieu

ALFRED

One by one, the others left. Maddox took to the sky. There was no mistaking his dragon form. He might be the last of his kind, but Eamon and Cyril would be expecting it. So would Gemma for that matter. Their followers, however, would taste a fear in his roars that could petrify the soul.

Rogue vanished swiftly, moving on fleet feet. He could transform, but he likely wouldn't. He preferred to fight with his own two hands, and he served destruction with a ruthless kind of efficiency. Fin was the last of the three to depart. His gaze flickered to Fiona once, then back to Alfred.

He inclined his head. Nothing would touch her. Not as long as there was life in his body. She was the target. His brethren would be coming straight for her. It was why he'd taken the position at her side and wanted her next to him at all times.

Even with the banter and Fiona's playfulness, her tension was palpable.

"How long do we stay up here?"

"They come to us," he told her, and the corners of her lips quirked.

"You really do mean that literally."

He inclined his head. "I've only gone to you, Hellion. I will only ever come after you."

"Well," she said, the pleasure in her voice tickling him, "I went after Maddox and Fin."

"I know." Further, he understood better now. In the future, this would not happen again. Fiona craved their nearness. Not their lust or even their touch, though she had no objections. She craved *them*. Her feelings had deepened, and the transition had shifted something fundamentally within her. "And I came for you."

"You did," she said with a pleased note. "Didn't you?" Light as air, she brushed a kiss to his cheek as she rose up on her tiptoes. "Thank you for coming for us."

"Always," he promised. In all the many centuries since he fell, he couldn't recall feeling like he belonged as much as he did now. He belonged. He had a purpose. A family. A home. The foundations had been there, shakily built through selfish decisions and hasty actions. Though in truth, the real impulse had always been Fin.

The final bit of their puzzle. He'd kept them grounded and tethered to this world long enough for Fiona to be born.

Beyond, Maddox roared. He tired of this waiting game.

Be patient, Fin counseled. *Let them do their song and dance for our amusement.*

I'm not amused.

No, on that point, Alfred agreed with Rogue. He'd much

rather be figuring out the rest of their lives and what it meant that Fiona carried a child. Was it because she was a hybrid? Was it the spark? Was it just her?

The dark fire flickering along his hands intensified. Like Fiona, his own emotions seemed to dictate the return of it. He'd had the ability once, long ago, to rain fire down when the battle required it. When he had to smite a whole city or village. It had been that ability he'd been ordered to use against the angels who'd rebelled.

And he'd declined.

Not only had he fallen with his whole wing, but that very fire had stripped away their wings as it was torn out of him.

Having it back now?

Did it mean he was forgiven? Or that his decision had finally been accepted? Or was it simply Fiona? She changed them. All of them. The presence of his wings was a familiar weight on his back, both tangible and intangible. Somehow, he suspected it was Fiona. She had taken out Keeley...with love. And he had no idea if she understood what she'd done yet. She'd done something to the shadow demon who served as warden, something he intended to investigate further later.

Fiona had done that, driven by instinct alone. She bounced from her heels to the balls of her feet and back. Restless energy danced over her. Demons were not all the same. Just like angels weren't or vampires. Isolating any species and putting them into a box of sameness was a mistake, and he had found himself guilty of it. But Fiona? Primal? A little ruthless? Utterly beguiling and daring him to think and live outside of that narrow box?

There wasn't anything he wouldn't do for her.

He'd saved the display of his wings for this confrontation. Saved them because they wanted to slay Fiona because they feared what changes she might bring. Fearing change did not prevent it. His world had already irrevocably changed, and their pursuit of her destruction would end theirs. A part of him wanted them to see reason.

It was why he'd sent Wyman. His booming laugh and congenial temperament might do what Alfred could not. He didn't coax. It just wasn't in his nature, particularly not when they'd already tried to kill her without remotely attempting to speak to her or even understand first.

"Do you really use swords?"

He glanced to his right where Fiona continued to bounce forward and back. "Once upon a time," he admitted. Not that he'd needed them in a very long time. The blades themselves were pristine, sharp, and polished. The metal didn't come from this world, but he'd only picked them up once before since the fall. He had no doubt Eamon would have his. Cyril would, too, most likely. He'd made the mistake of attacking them outside the prison without his blades.

Alfred doubted he would make such a mistake again. If he did? Well, he would die that much quicker.

"I'm sorry you have to fight them for me. They were angels, too, right?"

"Yes, Hellion, they were, but none of us are angels any longer."

She flashed a grin at him, and the faint glow of her aura began to brighten like a beacon. "Tell that to your wings, my lord."

The tease edging around the address pulled a chuckle from him. "I thought I was your asshole." As incensed as the insult in that word had been in the beginning, he'd grown rather fond of it, especially when she got possessive.

"You'll always be my asshole, don't worry!" Laughter eddied up out of her, but she sobered nearly as swiftly as she looked out through the hole in the wall. "I just wish…"

When she shook her head and didn't finish the thought, he frowned. "What do you wish, Hellion?"

"If Heaven is a real place, then so is Hell...and I kind of wish I'd been born in the other instead of where I was, I guess. I mean, I'm pretty sure I was born here on Earth...but it makes ya think maybe things would be easier for everyone if I'd been born something else."

"You were born perfect," he informed her, even as he closed a hand on her nape and pulled her around to face him. He pivoted in order to shield her so her back would not be facing the approaching army, and the flex of his wings brought them forward, as much to shield her brilliant light as to surround her with his own dark fire. "Hellion, Heaven and Hell are human concepts. Yes, there are demons and angels, but they come from different planes not primordial concepts such as you might have been taught. If anything, the fact that you think that tells me you are of this Earth, this place, as much as Maddox or Fin or Rogue."

Her nose wrinkled. "But you still call me Hellion."

"And you call me Asshole."

The spark in her green eyes grew brighter, and she pulled herself up, fisting his open shirt. The brush of her armor against his chest was hot and cool in equal measures, as supple and teasing as the woman it protected. "I love you," she told him fiercely, as if reminding him.

"I love you too," he promised. The words seemed paltry in the face of the torrent of emotion she unleashed in him. No more would he be distant from this world. Not with how she tethered him. The sound of the approaching army grew in volume. Maddox released another roar, and fire scorched the horizon as he cut a swath across the front of their lines.

Whistling of projectiles sailing through the air cut into his focus, but he kept his gaze fixed on hers. He needed her to believe him.

"I'll stay with you. I'll be right by your side," she swore, and something deep inside of him unlocked. She didn't just mean the battle. "And later…when we get this mess cleaned up…we're going to talk about decorating."

He chuckled. "Anything you want, Hellion."

Another whistle split through the air. They were trying to bring Maddox down. The moment it dawned on Fiona though, her expression turned violent and ferocious. She swiveled to face the opening, but he didn't release her nape. He trusted her and believed her, but her need to defend them was so damn powerful that he wanted to make sure she didn't give in to impulse.

"Maddox is fine," he assured her. The army had broken into disarray. Not that organizing that many vampires and whipping them into a frenzy served much purpose. The frenzy would shatter their control. The older ones might be able to stand up to the pressure, but not the younger. "He's playing with them, and the more frustrated they become, the more they break their own lines." With one thumb, he stroked the column of her neck. "See how they are turning back on each other and splitting apart?"

"Fin," she exhaled his name.

"Precisely, and soon, the screaming will start in the rear."

"Rogue."

He smiled. "We all play our parts well, Hellion. Trust them. They know what they are doing."

"And we're waiting for the others of the Six?"

It still pained him on some level that what was Seven had now become Six. Not that he had any regrets beyond wishing his kin had not acted so hastily. They'd fallen with him, following his lead. They'd formed cadres here, established themselves, and he'd always opened his home to them and refused to compete in their power politics.

With few exceptions, it had worked.

"Exactly."

And they were coming. He could feel it in his bones. All the noise and fanfare outside was a distraction.

"They're coming, Hellion," he murmured. His awareness of them growing by the second. "Stay close."

Her eyes widened a fraction, and for a moment, the pupils dilated. At first, he thought in fear, but then her expression hardened as she scowled. "We're gonna kick their asses."

"Yes," he said with a chuckle. "We are." He squeezed her nape once more, then shifted so he faced the doors at the far end of the library. They were coming up the stairs. As much as he wanted to continue holding her, he had to ready himself for the first onslaught. "They will target me first, Hellion, not to kill, but to wound and push out of the way. Do not react to my injuries. Protect yourself, but stay behind me as much as possible."

"That's not fighting," she challenged. "That's hiding."

"You say potato," he tossed at her, and her sudden laughter made him grin. Fin had been using that one a lot lately, and he rather enjoyed it.

The doors at the end of the hall burst inward, even as the floor *behind* them exploded upward. Shattered wood and stone flew like projectiles. Something sliced along his leg, even as he faced Cyril and Eamon. Cyril definitely looked worse for wear, his face still reddened and blistered as though even his healing had been slowed.

Like Alfred, they were both armed, and he blocked the first swing of Eamon's blade. Cyril thrust forward, and only a circular parry kept the blade from finding purchase against his skin. The dark fire he'd been coiling within unleashed, dancing down his arms and off the tip of his blade. A shriek from behind him beckoned for him to turn, but he didn't dare expose his back.

Eamon slid to a stop as the room brightened behind

Alfred, and it just seemed to intensify his shadow. His wings extended, and Cyril spit. Another shriek, and then…

"Do you want me to keep this one alive? Or can I kiss her into shutting the fuck up?" Fiona sounded aggravated, and she moved up beside him with Gemma in a head lock, her eyes dazzled as Fiona blazed brightly.

Wyman sauntered into the library behind Eamon and Cyril. "Oh, those are new," he commented as though a battle wasn't being waged in here or out there. Unlike their brothers, he was still dressed in jeans and a plaid shirt over a T-shirt that read *Hogs are life*.

Yeah, Alfred wasn't going to ask.

"H-How do you have wings?" Eamon's voice stuttered, a sound Alfred hadn't heard in centuries either. Dark to Cyril's light skin, Eamon wore his strength like a badge of pride. He'd scarred himself over the long years—lines for every war and battle he'd fought, burns scalded into his flesh until it puckered and twisted.

The self-mutilation had always been an expression of his own self-loathing, but Alfred had hoped that someday he would make peace with it. He and Cyril had built, destroyed, then rebuilt vast empires several times over. Maybe that had always been the problem. They repeated a pattern that brought them no satisfaction.

Much has Alfred had—or had he? Limiting who he turned, he'd only chosen those who had meaning, who could help deepen his life. Each connection he forged had cost him in some measure—with Rogue, he'd nearly lost his closest friend, and with Maddox, it had never seemed enough to make up for the loss of his kind. With Fin?

Fin settled all of that. He grounded them in the now, and though Alfred would still sleep some decades and centuries away, Fin was always a half-thought away and brought stories that he would tell. Half-remembered dreams to keep

Alfred company. Ultimately, he'd seen what they needed most of all.

"Because he's a badass," Fiona announced when Alfred failed to answer. There was a great swell of pity within him because there could be no other outcome to this conflict. Eamon and Cyril had to die. Likely, Gemma as well.

And it grieved him as it had all those years before when he'd been forced to slay others of their brethren to stop their madness.

Would he someday ultimately go as mad and need his family to slay him?

Cyril flicked his gaze at her. "You're the slut demon."

"You're the crispy fried jackass. Glad we could clear that up."

Sharp laughter escaped Alfred at her response. That earned him one reproachful look and another that verged on shock. "She must be a demon," Wyman drawled. "She got Alfred to laugh."

"It's not so hard," she replied. "Maybe the rest of you suck." Fiona paused a beat, then glanced down at the trapped Gemma, who wore an almost terrified expression.

Alfred barely spared the woman a thought, he kept his attention on Cyril and Eamon. They weren't moving, but that didn't mean the threat was done.

"Actually, let me rephrase that, you all *definitely* suck. Which one of you fuck nuggets had my ass sent to prison and then sicced a shadow demon on me?"

The smirk on Wyman's face promised he found Fiona amusing, but he wasn't looking at her so much as focusing on Cyril. Fine. If he wanted Cyril, Alfred would take Eamon. The latter was far better with his blades anyway.

"She's not a demon anymore," Eamon said rather unceremoniously, as though he hadn't even registered her question. "Look at her."

"Look at him," Cyril countered. "He's corrupted. Look at the wings and the dark fire."

"Now, boys," Wyman said. "To be fair, Al has always had that last bit. Just because you were always behind him in battle instead of at his side doesn't excuse you that lack of knowledge."

A snarl twisted Cyril's lips, but Eamon flicked a look to Fiona. "You should never have become one of us."

"On that we totally agree," Fiona said. "I'm definitely not one of you. Just look at me. Really? I'm in a class by myself. And my asshole is a hell of a lot better looking." She bumped her hip to Alfred's, and another soft laugh escaped him. "Also, the ex-chickie here is kind of heavy. Can I snap her neck, or is this more catch and release?"

"Snap her neck," Alfred agreed. It wouldn't kill her, but it would incapacitate her. Fiona wrenched Gemma's neck and then dropped her motionless body to the floor.

"Oh, much better. Thank you." Then she focused on their audience. "Also, I'm still waiting for an answer, boys."

"How dare you speak to us," Cyril began, then a blade slammed into him from behind. Alfred had barely seen Wyman move, but Cyril's whole body seized up and his eyes turned murderous as he half-twisted to face Wyman, who just waved all jovial like as Alfred shook his head.

Maybe letting Wyman hang out around Fiona had been a mistake. Then again, he'd always been something of a wild one. Cyril dropped.

Then it was just Eamon. Like Gemma, Cyril wasn't dead. Yet.

They had a few minutes before either would regain themselves.

"Answer my queen's question," he ordered Eamon, drawing the former angel and his once brother-in-arms' attention back to him. "Which of you ordered it?"

"Does it matter?" Eamon asked. "And you no longer command me, Captain. You gave up that right when you abandoned us."

"I did not abandon you," Alfred countered. "You chose to follow me. I would not have faulted you if you hadn't, but once we were here, we had a chance to be other. To build a different life. If I had led, you would have followed and we would be forever the same."

"So instead, you abandon us..."

"No," Alfred told him. "I treated you as equals. I respected your choices."

"Not all of them." Eamon rolled his head from side to side as he moved to keep Wyman in his line of sight. "And apparently, now you make deals behind our backs."

"Stop pissing like a little baby. You three were in cahoots. What, it's all right if you do, but not if he does?" Fiona challenged, and Alfred tilted his head to press a kiss to her temple without ever taking his gaze off Eamon. "Yeah, I know. I'll hush."

"Not at all, but he must pontificate and bluster for a bit longer if we want him to answer. Though if he has given shelter to Isaac and Dimitri, killing him will also open them up to our reprisals. Whatever my queen wishes..."

"You really have tied yourself to her." Eamon spit out the words as though he couldn't believe it.

"Yes," Alfred told him. "And you should understand that I will always defend what is mine. You should never have gone near her." Ever. But he left that last bit unspoken. Locking eyes with a man who had once been a brother to him, a comrade, a companion on this journey, Alfred let himself see all the things he had never wanted to before.

The sadness.

The loneliness.

The loss.

The greed.

"Keeley is dead," he told him. "As so many others were before her. We've been Seven for a long time. Now we are Six." A part of him truly wished his brothers would not push him to this, but there had been no other choice. From the moment they'd gone after Fiona in that prison, it had only been a matter of when, not if.

She was *theirs*.

"Then I suppose one more won't cost us anything." Eamon hadn't even finished his last word before he lunged. Alfred had expected it, and he countered immediately, one blade flashing up to block as he struck Eamon's right knee with the other.

Blood fountained from the wound. Fire licked along Alfred's arms as he met Eamon's furious strikes. Where Alfred had trained for efficiency, Eamon had always favored brutality. The clash of their blades sparked blue fire, even as the dark fire raced down his arms to engulf his blades. His opponent managed to land one blow to his shoulder and that sent one blade skittering free, but Alfred only needed the one he had left.

Back and forth, they waged the battle, and twice, Alfred went airborne as muscle memory dictated and he landed swift kicks to Eamon's face and sternum. They were both bleeding, Eamon more heavily than he, but blades were unforgiving and the punishment of this fight was something Alfred hadn't realized he craved.

He and the others should have been faster to get to her. He should have taken more interest in his people. In turn, they should have come to him before they decided to assassinate her. Worse, to consign her to life as a shadow demon. Fiona had done them no harm. In the reckoning of things, it was Alfred who had done the injuries.

Alfred.

Eamon.

Cyril.

Gemma.

Keeley.

Wyman.

Even Synove.

They were the Seven. It was on them to leave this world better than they had found it, even if all they did was not interfere. Caught up in the self-recrimination, he realized almost too late Eamon's strategy. He couldn't beat Alfred, and Alfred had held back out of pity. In maneuvering him through the fight, Eamon had gotten Alfred to move and left Fiona exposed. He knew what would happen a single second before he struck.

Eamon lunged for her. That blade would go through Fiona's armor just as his blades could pierce Maddox's scaled body. Alfred swung his sword and released the dark fire, but the sickening thud of a blade sinking into flesh and Fiona's startled shout echoed in his ears, even as Eamon's head flew off his shoulders and rebounded across the floor.

"You know what, this is my story so I'm gonna make my own quotes, and it starts with, 'Guys are assholes, but they can also be awesome.'" - Fiona

FIONA

The clash of blades colliding against each other echoed through the nearly demolished library. I wasn't looking at the big ass hole in the floor bitch-kitty had created when she launched through it. Seriously, scared the shit out of me for a second there until I got a good fistful of her hair. She was all clawed fingers and stab-happy with her play blade.

Fun fact, the armor deflected the little knife. Well, mostly. And I only called it little because Alfred and the other asshole had huge fucking swords. Still, despite my dragon-scale armor—I was not thinking about how they got the scales off Maddox and if he shed. There were just some things a mate didn't need to know. That definitely fell under 'don't need to know and really didn't want to find out in case it was gross and icky.'

Anyway, back to that original thought… Despite the armor, her blade had bitten into my wrist, but she got me at the wrong angle to open a vein.

Still stung like a bitch.

I wrapped around her in a choke hold because the minute my hands fixed on her, she'd gotten all crazy shaky. The guys didn't want kissing unless I killed them, and granted, I wasn't a fan right now, but I didn't think I should make the call on whether these guys died or not.

The crispy fried fucker? Him I had no problems killing. He'd dumped Maddox and Fin in the prison where they *whipped* Fin and *tortured* them. So yeah, he could go. I didn't know bitch-kitty, so I'd reserve it and besides, she was being all docile now. Don't ask me why. I kept my focus on Alfred and staying close to him.

I'd promised.

When Cyril insulted me, he hit the ground a second later, a quivering blade in his back. Man, how fucking hard did you have to throw a knife to do that—okay, wait. That was a lot bigger than a knife. Maybe a short sword.

Wyman shot me a cocky grin, and I considered flipping him off. But he had kind of done us a solid, so I settled for mouthing 'fuck off' at him, and he grinned even wider. The nutjob was kind of growing on me, or bitch-kitty had hit me a little too hard in the head.

I half-tuned out of Alfred's conversation with Eamon. The guy was a raging bag of dicks. When they let me break the bitch-kitty's neck, that was extremely satisfying. Wyman watched the interplay between Eamon and Alfred as though he couldn't make up his mind what he wanted to do. I got that, because Eamon, really? Whine, whine, whine. How annoying was that?

But then it was Alfred and Eamon sword fighting, and I had to admit, I might have swooned a little. Alfred had moves, and with his shirt open, I got to enjoy the ripple of muscle along his chest and shoulders. I might have even fist pumped when he leapt into the air and kicked Eamon in the face.

It was definitely badass.

Then again, sticking close to Alfred in this scenario didn't seem wise. Those blades were hella fast. The clang of the steel on steel, the hiss of the blades slicing through their skin. They were both bleeding. The scent of it clouded the air. I kept glancing from their fight to where bitch-kitty and the crispy fried one were out.

Neither moved.

Still, the last thing I expected was for Eamon to lunge at me mid-battle. Maybe I should have. Maybe I'd gotten too complacent. But it had been so vital to all of them that I stay with Alfred, and they'd wanted me out of the fighting as much as possible. I tried.

I really fucking tried.

Bitch-kitty's little letter opener had sliced my wrist, and I really didn't want to find out what that sword would do. Thanks, I liked my boobs and the baby. Yeah okay, maybe like was strong, but he or she was ours and no way was I letting him hurt them.

A body slammed into mine and knocked me backwards, and I tripped over bitch-kitty's prone form and landed on my ass with a startled cry, just as a blade was shoved through Wyman's body.

"No!" I launched to my feet as he crumbled in just enough time for the *fountain* of blood geysering from where Eamon's head used to be—and by used to be, I meant it was currently bouncing its way to the hearth, so we might have to burn this whole level at this rate—to soak me down.

So. Fucking. Gross.

Oh, and it *smelled* terrible.

My stomach lurched, and I started to put a hand to my mouth but it was covered in blood too. Oh, this was just foul. Shaking that off, I turned to Eamon, even as Alfred grabbed me. Fin appeared between one breath and the next...

I'm here, Beautiful. He paused mid-kneel to where Wyman lay and flicked a look over me. *Whose blood is that?*

"Eamon's," I answered with a shuddering grimace. "And it's in my mouth. This is *nasty.*" Okay, yes, I'd earned the right to whine. I didn't want any part of them in me anywhere, and I spit it back out onto the prone corpse.

Man, it smelled even worse up close.

Okay, time to stop being a pussy. "Is Wyman okay?"

"Oh, hot stuff finally remembers me," Wyman grunted. "Just had to take a blade for you right between the damn ribs. Pretty sure he fucking broke them with that."

"Stop your bitching," Fin told him with a thump of his hand against his back. "He missed your heart. Told you you lost it a long time ago."

"Fuck off, druid."

Alfred let out a little chuckle, and I exhaled a breath.

"Okay, he's fine. I can go back to freaking out about the smell."

"Let me—" Alfred began when a scrape of steel across the floor pulled him around. He barely got his arm up in time for the blade to go right through his forearm, and the point stopped just at my breast plate when a golden dragon head snapped Cyril's whole body in half.

Oh.

Yeah.

I puked.

Sorry, not pussying out, but that was fucking disgusting. What had I told Maddox about *eating* people?

It was for a good cause, Beautiful.

Even with Fin's cheerful words, I just couldn't. I brought up food and blood, and that couldn't be good.

Alfred moved away from me and yanked the sword out of *his arm,* and I winced. Nauseated and blood-covered just didn't seem to be on par with a sword going all the way through his arm, and it sounded like it scraped bone.

A distinctive *thunk* came from behind me, and seriously, I'd had more than enough. I didn't even jump. Rogue stood next to the now headless bitch-kitty. At least I didn't get her blood on me, but it really did stink.

"And then we were three," Wyman wheezed.

Alfred cut a look at him. "We're six—the five of us, and you have earned your place as family. Your loyalty will be repaid in kind."

"What about Synove?"

With a shrug, Alfred said, "If she keeps the peace, I see no need to disturb her."

"Does this mean I get a turn with hot stuff?" I really didn't know who hit him first, but his groaning redoubled and I snorted as Maddox glared wild fury down at him. "It was a joke," Wyman said, almost weakly. "Just a joke."

"It was a terrible joke," Alfred deadpanned. "You're not funny."

"I'm hilarious," Wyman said as Fin did something that made him groan. "Course, you've been out of touch for a while."

At that, Alfred locked his gaze on me. "Not anymore."

That was just…romantic and sweet. And I really stunk like blood and wanted to puke again. On that note, I was going to take a bath.

❧

One month later...

"You do realize that happy people are still asleep right now, don't you?" I demanded of Rogue as he led me down the steps. Just fifteen minutes earlier, I'd been sound asleep in the middle of the huge bed in Alfred's chamber. Well, our chamber, I supposed. All of us slept there now. Anyway, I'd been sound asleep and enjoying it. Then Rogue, the party pooper, woke me up and not even in a nice way.

He chuckled softly as he continued to guide me down the steps. "I will make it up to you, little *sváss*, I promise."

"You better," I grumbled. "I don't think having you fuck me awake is too much to ask."

"Not at all."

"I'd do it for you."

"And you have."

"Just so we're clear."

"Crystal," he said with a grin and kissed my cheek. "But this really couldn't wait."

Into the main hall we went. There'd been some renovations done over the last month, mostly cleaning. And I was right, they'd had to scrap what was left of the library level and start over. I did not miss the blood-soaked floorboards one little bit. As it was, the main hall had also undergone a renovation. It was less 'giant echo chamber, check out the big dick in the center on the dais' and more family friendly fare with multiple seating areas and the opportunity to actually talk instead of mill about.

I still wasn't a big fan of the dais—which stayed, along with a new chair added to it for little ole me—but some things weren't negotiable. This turned out to be one of them. So Alfred agreed to make the place a little warmer and more gathering friendly, and I agreed to the throne, even if I sat in one of their laps whenever I was up there.

Look at me, compromising and shit.

Three steps after I entered the great hall, everything went silent. Every conversation ceased. Fin leaned against the wall next to where I'd entered and he immediately joined me, whereas Maddox stood dead center in the middle of the room with Alfred, and at their feet…

"Oh!"

No wonder Rogue had hurried me out of bed.

"Am I forgiven, little *sváss?*" Rogue asked, amusement in his voice.

"Definitely." I stood on my tiptoes to kiss him. "I will definitely be blowing you later."

He laughed and returned the kiss with some ferocity before letting me go.

"What about me?" Fin asked, all mock wounded. "I may have had something to do with this."

I patted his chest. "You should have been the one to wake me up then. But I'll let you eat me later if you want."

He laughed, and there was some mild groaning over by one of the sofas. "Can you fuckers please get a room?"

Alfred glared at Wyman.

"Begging Your Majesties pardon and all that."

Alfred nodded, and I laughed.

We seemed to have earned a permanent houseguest out of Wyman—for the moment—and giving him shit had become one of my favorite past times. He also had the best stories of a young Alfred and could be bribed into sharing them. All I had to do was persuade Fin to bring in mead and ale.

That was fun too.

But I shuttled all of that aside for the moment as I stalked across the room to where Isaac knelt on the ground next to Dimitri.

"Hello, Micro Dick, and his friend, King Dumbass."

Isaac glared up at me and then let out a cry as Maddox stepped on his hand. "You don't get to look at her. You're lucky we're letting you look at her shoes."

I blew a kiss to my grumpy dragon, and he winked at me.

Dimitri didn't say a word, just stared at the floor like he was waiting for the executioner's axe. Well, in all fairness, he probably was. Still…if he hadn't been a fucking moron, I'd never have ended up in prison or been found by Maddox and Fin, then rescued and dragged here and completed my transition.

I would also probably not be knocked up, a reality that grew each day now that my stomach had begun to swell. I tapped a finger to my lips. What to do? What to do? I snuck a look at Alfred, who watched me with the most placid and serene expression. It warmed me all the way to my toes.

This was their gift to me.

Wait…

"Which of you caught them?"

"We're not telling you, Kitten," Maddox said, and I frowned.

"Why not?"

"Because if we all brought them, then we all get the obedience, yes?"

Oh.

That was sneaky.

"But if none of you fess up, then I get the obedience."

He grinned. "Already yours, Kitten."

"Ha," I laughed. Because they were as obedient as cats left unsupervised in a house full of breakables. Still, totally worth it. "How about a bargain?"

"No," Alfred said, his expression unchanging and his eyes still dark and warm. "We have arrived at our bargain. We have brought them to you. A deal is a deal, Hellion."

"Fine," I agreed, like this was really going to be a hardship. "As soon as I'm done with them, I'm all yours to do whatever you want with."

"Like she wasn't before—" Wyman muttered and then let out a grunt. The air next to me displaced and then settled again as Rogue returned. I didn't know where Wyman ended up, but he wasn't in the hall anymore.

"Much better," Rogue said, and Alfred chuckled. "What would you like to do first, little *sváss*?"

"I want to hear what they have to say, and I'll start with Micro Dick since he started this whole thing."

"You heard the lady," Fin instructed, and Dimitri let out a harsh breath as he mumbled something.

"What?" I bent a little so I could try to see him. My hearing had vastly improved. I was a lot faster and stronger. I was my own personal nightlight, and apparently, now I survived on love, the love of my four lovers—mate, chosen, king, etc. I also could convert it like a weapon, which was kind of cool. Not that I got to practice with that much because it required a lot of the contact it had as a succubus, and my guys just weren't keen on me making out with anyone else.

Which was fine.

Also turned out, I could only drink their blood. We'd done a few experiments. Everything else made me sick or nauseated. It was them or nothing.

So they were as much my life as I'd become theirs. Seemed an okay trade-off in my book. I mean, I was happy with it.

Still, I hadn't caught what Dimitri said.

"I'm sorry," he repeated, and I blinked. "I'm sorry." This time he looked up at me. "I was...an unmitigated ass. I thought... I don't know what I thought. I shouldn't have done it and I shouldn't have abandoned you. I swear I didn't know they'd put you in prison or that any of this would happen. I lost control, and then I was so scared I'd killed you. I never thought the blood would change you."

He sounded so miserable.

"Are you serious right now?" Isaac demanded. Despite his broken posture, his tone still sounded like he was a supercilious jackass. "You're apologizing to that abomination? It's bad enough you—" The rest of his words were muffled as he pitched forward into the floor. If I had to bet, Fin had done something to shut him up.

Sweet, but unnecessary.

Dimitri glanced from Isaac to me and then cast his gaze down, as if he remembered he wasn't supposed to look at me. "I'm sorry, Fiona. Truly."

And you know what? I believed him.

Yeah, maybe it was the hormones, but I didn't taste an ounce of deception on him. He truly was sorry. In the long run, I really couldn't regret it anymore. I mean, the sloppy technique and lack of really great orgasms, sure, but the rest of it?

"Kitten?" Maddox prompted, and I grinned at my dragon.

"Let him go."

Dimitri jerked a look up at me, shock all over his face. Alfred studied me a beat.

"Are you sure, Hellion?"

"Yeah. He apologized and he meant it. He's not even begging for his life, like he's resigned to the fact we could kill him." I glanced down at Dimitri once again. "Let him go. Just...don't screw up again, or one of us will find you and you won't like the result."

He damn near wept, and my stomach grumbled. I needed coffee and bacon. Before I could ask Fin though, Rogue cleared his throat. "And this one, little *sváss*?"

I glanced back at Isaac. "He's still a douche. Him, you can kill."

I was seriously starving, and I didn't want to wait.

Fin just held out a hand and I said, "Yay," and then we were away in a swirl. Isaac was dead before the room vanished.

Goodbye and good riddance.

EPILOGUE

Five months after the attack at the keep, we were moving. Not formally, as the keep would be our "home" for meeting with those liaisons seeking Alfred's advice or counsel with regard to matters affecting their cities. It was a whole lot of politics that I didn't want anything to do with. For the most part, Wyman's recovery had ended after seven weeks and he'd taken his leave, promising to check in regularly.

When we last spoke to him, he'd been on his way to annoy Synove, at least according to Alfred. Alfred had been quiet in the days after he left. He missed the others, even if he didn't want to say it aloud. I was almost getting good at this feelings stuff. I made a point of spending more time with him and picking on him.

It worked out really well for both of us, I thought.

But today, we were leaving the keep. There was no hiding my pregnancy anymore, not even the balloon skirts of France in the *Dangerous Liaisons* era could cover the massive baby bump. I was six months, they thought. Though, fun fact, gestation for each of them turned out to be a bit different, as did being a succubus, so we had no idea how far along I was.

Yeah, I was cranky about that too.

But the guys were very determined to make it up to me, and so far, me and the bump were getting along. I only drank their blood, and nobody else was allowed to bleed around me. Win-win.

"You ready, Hellion?" Alfred asked. I was inside the new library. It wasn't quite furnished yet. They'd only recently finished the installation of the new windows and bookshelves. Fin promised he had access to all kinds of volumes. I didn't ask. He didn't tell. They'd also installed a beautiful set of stained-glass windows to catch the late day light, and I rather loved them.

Oh, and the rose garden? It was in full bloom now. Even Alfred's crows seemed to be enjoying it, even if the little tattletales ratted me out every time I stripped off to nude sunbathe out there.

You'd think I was trying to get his attention or something.

"I am," I told him as I turned. Maternity clothes were at least cute. Fin and I spent three days picking out stuff from different cities around the world. I'd even gotten to go and visit Elias for a short bit. His reaction to the pregnancy still left me in stitches.

"A mini you? The world is doomed."

We were besties for a reason. He promised to visit after the baby was born, and the guys all agreed to it. See, we were master negotiators and solid at the compromise.

"Just feels weird to leave," I admitted. "I've kind of gotten used to living in this mausoleum."

He chuckled and tucked my hand into his arm. Wow, he usually played along with my taunts. "We'll be back, but we all agreed. We want to be somewhere no one knows to find us until the baby is born and perhaps even after. A place that is just ours, with no ties to this world."

"But *everyone comes to me, Hellion*." I deepened my voice as though I were him.

Ahead of us and down the stairs, Fin laughed. "She almost sounds like you."

Alfred shot me an amused look. "Precisely. They come to see Alfred, the King of the Vampires now." It was not a title he wanted. Not that I blamed him. Let me tell you how much Queen of the Vampires didn't tickle my fancy. But needs must and all that. "Where we're going, we are us—Alfred, Fiona, Fin, Rogue, and Maddox."

Maddox and Rogue waited with Fin, and they all wore matching looks of smugness. They really were up to something. They liked surprising me. I liked being surprised.

It worked for us.

"So what I hear you saying," I told him, "is you want a place where I can be naked all the time."

"Exactly," Maddox said with a wide grin. When he held out his hand, I squeezed Alfred's arm and then crossed to take it. Maddox wrapped me up close and then pressed a hand over my swollen belly. "And this little boy needs his mother to be very happy."

"That little girl will be fine," Fin countered. "She's as resilient as her mother."

"And they will never tire of this argument," Rogue said with a kind of resigned weariness. "The child, male or female, will be perfect."

"Exactly," Alfred said as he glared at both of them. "Enough, it's time for our lady's surprise."

"Yay." I would have clapped my hands, but they all gathered close and then we were off in a swirl of magic and the world shifted to a living room.

A sunken one.

With all the amenities.

A bar.

A television.

Big huge sofas. Oh yes.

And windows everywhere.

On a cliff.

Over the ocean.

It…

I turned and glanced up at the different levels. The stairs. The hidden nooks. There would be a huge bedroom up there with a sunken tub. And windows to see the sunrise in the morning, just as there were windows here to see the sunset at night.

It was my house.

It was everything I'd ever built in my mind, right down to the colors.

I burst into tears.

The sobs clawed at my throat as the heat rushed my eyes and spilled down my cheeks.

"I told you we should've warned her," Rogue admonished someone as he wrapped his arms around me.

"You didn't say it would break her," Maddox argued. "She obsessed over this in the cell."

"Fin, you proposed the surprise, fix it." Alfred's stern order almost silenced my tears entirely just so I could laugh.

"Well, I suppose now would be a good time to tell you that it's twins," Fin said. "A boy and a girl."

That stopped the tears all right.

And I almost slept alone that night, except I really loved my surprise, so I contented myself with yelling at them in between bouts of tears.

Fuck me, was I over the crying, but it seemed that came with baby bumps and they were all getting used to it.

Four months later—almost a year to the day it would

seem that Alfred finished my transition—I gave birth to a boy and a girl.

Both radiant with light and carrying the spark. Apparently, Alfred really was the daddy. Go angel DNA. Because they were perfect. More perfect was when Alfred cradled them both and murmured, "Now, we are eight."

Yeah. I cried again.

At least until Maddox said, "Dibs on being next."

THE FREAKING END
(Well, except for the bonus novella that comes next!)

No cliffhangers. No reason to throw your kindle or yell at me. I mean you can if you want. I'm okay with it. If I made you feel something, it means I did my job.

Farewell is never an easy and yet, somehow, this time, it feels fitting. I love Fiona. I love her snark, her fearlessness, and her indomitable spirit. I love her story and the men she falls in love with. From Fin's rakish charm to Rogue's quiet steadiness to Maddox's passionate nature and Alfred's stubborn assholishness that's an absolute match for her.

She's unique in how she takes on the world and writing her has been an absolute blast. I seriously never knew what would come out of her mouth. That was half the fun.

Thanks for coming along with us.

xoxo

Heather

P.S. Don't be a stranger! Also, because you got this super cool collection you get a bonus Fi tale! Just keep on turning the page

SHACKLED SOULS BONUS NOVELLA

SUCCUBUS SCALES

Once upon a time, the last thing I wanted to be was a vampire. I was a happy-go-lucky succubus who got lucky one night. Well, I ended up in prison as a hybrid, only to be busted out by a dragon and a druid, who were convinced I was their prophesied mate.

Surprise! I was. After a courtship from hell and some solid lessons in how not to be an asshole, the five of us—me, Maddox, Fin, Rogue, and Alfred are the perfect happy little family, along with our two demonic cuties. I don't care if they're angels, Mireille and Benedict were perfect little devils.

After three years, my darling little hellspawns sleep through the night and don't need to suck my breasts dry for sustenance. I was even getting back some of the old pep in my step. Succubi thrived on sex, bearing an angel's—fallen or not—spawn had done all kinds of whacky things to my system.

With our anniversary right around the corner, I had all kinds of plans for my men. None of which involved the development of scales.

Have I mentioned that my plans might now include *killing* one of my men?

CHAPTER 1

*Whoever said having children was a sign of bliss, never had kids. -
Fiona*

FIONA

Wyman stood in the center of a ring of destruction laughing his damn fool head off. Well, I should say *rings* of destruction. Not only were there three or four layers to the rings, from the ground blackened and cracked just below his feet, to the next ring where the earth was scorched bare to blackened and finally just wilted, but he was also missing most of his beard and a significant section of his hair.

Arms folded, I stared at the laughing fool as Mireille and Benedict danced in a circle clapping their hands. They'd called lightning.

Lightning.

Because Uncle Wyman was the *bestest*. It took everything

I had to not roll my eyes. He'd been absent for the past couple of years.

"C'mon, luv, don't look at me like that. They're angels. They're gonna have the gift. We know they have holy fire, but it's got some kick you know." He flashed another dimpled grin at me and I stared skyward just in time to catch Rogue transforming mid-air and hitting Wyman full force as a bear.

The kids squealed with laughter and scrambled back toward me.

Fin appeared in front of me, even as Alfred flashed in next to him. Maddox landed with an earth rumbling shake. He hadn't bothered to change, if anything his tail lashed from side to side disturbing the sand. The only good part of Wyman's insanity was he chose to do it on the abandoned beach, tucked between the craggy rocks and the sea.

Wyman's manic laughter continued even under Rogue's assault. The fallen angel had been one of Alfred's cadre before and he was still a member of our family, though at the moment, distant, mad relation seemed to be a better description for him. With a roar of discontent, Maddox transformed and launched into the battle and Fin let out a snicker.

The kids were cheering—Benedict for Uncle Wyman, because Uncle Wyman was his most favorite ever—but Mireille turned those incandescently green eyes up to her papa and my asshole, King of the Assholes, melted like paper thin wax. He immediately joined the fray and sent Wyman crashing into the cliff.

Chaos rained down on him as the kids squealed in reckless delight.

"I've changed my mind." With four words, the entire scene froze, and Alfred held Wyman pinned. "I'm not leaving them with him."

I scooped up my devilish pair and marched up the stairs

cut into the cliff that led to our escape. My beautiful cliff house that looked over the sea. No way would I trust the two most precious things I'd ever created to the lunacy of a former angel, who probably fit better in with the Hell's Angels, than he did in a nursery setting.

Even if my babies could explode things.

"Mama," Benedict complained, but one look from me and he hushed. Succubi were horrific parents. But as I'd been told time and again, I wasn't just a succubus anymore. These wicked little devils had grown within me and changed me. I still had some of the spark, though they retained nearly all of it. Someday, Alfred reckoned, they would be more powerful than him.

Some day.

They needed to survive that long.

"Kitten," Maddox said from ahead of me on the stairs.

"Don't," I warned him with a snap of a syllable and look. They were all ahead of me, even the half-demolished and still smoking carcass formerly known as Wyman.

"C'mon Hot Stuff, it was a game. See?" He gave himself a shake and some of the soot vanished. His hair was still a wreck, and so were the holes in his clothes, but the rest of him had healed. "They have to learn to use those gifts. We wouldn't want them accidentally toasting you."

"Not helping," Alfred declared, clapping Wyman in the back of the head. "Hellion…"

Nope, I wasn't listening. Both Benedict and Mireille clung tighter to me. The warmth of their little bodies filled me with a depth of affection I'd never thought myself capable of, but more, the power pushed the guys back a few steps if they tried to stop me. One thing we'd learned about the twins very early on, when they wanted me, they didn't always want to share.

They'd needed a steady diet of both my blood and milk.

We'd finally weaned them and to my relief, though I hadn't confessed it, they didn't need to feed on emotion. They might be sensitive to it, but where I needed lust still to a certain amount and I craved the love my mates gave me, they were not similarly crippled.

No one would ever be able to control them through those desires.

The doors to our home opened for me, well, they opened because Fin pushed them open with his magic. The interior was as bright and airy as it had been the first day they brought me here. The different levels offered differing views. I could see the sunrise and the sunset depending on where I stood. The library was filled with books. The chairs and lounges were comfortable. The fireplace was full and the bathroom was a dream.

Most of all, was the room at the crown of the building that was ours. The room where our bed allowed all five of us to sleep together. It was perfection. The added room for the twins was also secured inside of our room. There was no way for anyone or anything to come at them without coming through us.

For three years, we'd hidden their presence. They were our most jealously guarded secret. When duty called, one of us always remained with the twins. Most often me, since the others could hardly nurse them. But more and more of late, I'd been able to take little excursions with my mates, one or two at a time, while the others looked after them.

But our anniversary approached. Four years since the day Alfred turned me, three since the twins had been born. Three nights and two days away, that was what they'd asked me for, and they promised the best for looking after the twins.

Wyman.

The best.

I snorted.

We'd be better off taking them to Elias and his pack. They would always protect little ones. But that would mean revealing their presence to the world. So far, the only others besides myself that even knew of their existence were all in this house.

I didn't slow until we were in the twins' bathing room and then I set them down. Almost immediately, they turned those brightly lit, glowing eyes on me and I shook my head. While they might devastate the guys, I was apparently immune to the compulsion.

Thank fuck, or chaos would reign every day and since when did *I*, the succubus, become the most rational one.

I shuddered.

"Get out of those filthy things," I informed them, even as I began to loosen Mireille's braids. They had their father's rich dark hair, though somehow Mireille's had a hint of red amidst the black locks, while Benedict's were pure midnight. Their eyes, however, were all me. The deep green turned luminescent with their power. Eventually, they would learn to tone it down.

At least their wings hadn't come in yet. Yet. Unfortunately, Alfred had no idea when those wings would come in. He couldn't remember that far back. The perils of grave robbing to pick my mates. He was literally older than dirt.

I promise not to tell him, but if you do, please let me be there when you do, Beautiful?

Fin's words were as much a caress as they were laughter within my mind. I ignored him, but there was nothing but kindness and acceptance as he waited for me to give him even an ounce of attention.

Apparently, my words had gotten them all and now they were plotting. Being mated and bound to them meant I got some sense of them, even when I focused elsewhere. The children stripped gleefully out of their play clothes and right into the stone bath that filled from a warm fountain. It was shallow. As they had grown, Fin had allowed the pool to deepen. As it was, it was as much a part of the living earth outside, as the building they'd constructed for me was, layered in so many complex magics it made my skin tickle to enter and leave.

Restlessness had begun to invade our paradise and I couldn't be sure who it came from, me or them or maybe all of us? They were all older than dirt, really.

Mean, Beautiful.

I mentally flipped him off and his sexy mental chuckle made my cunt spasm.

I could take care of that.

Yes, he could. They all could. The kids squealed as they got into a splash war. Thankfully, most of the dirt, soot, and sand washed off whether they were splashing each other or actually washing.

The door cracked open an inch and Fin peeked in.

They always send you.

He flashed me a grin before teleporting inside and shutting the door behind him. *Because they know* I'm *your favorite.*

That did make me laugh, but the scent of coffee and the fact he had a hand behind his back gave away the rest of his secret gift for being my favorite. He knew that coffee and bacon were the quickest ways past my temper.

"Thank you," I murmured as I held out my hand and he strolled over to press the tumbler against my palm before fisting my hair and tilting my head back for a kiss. The sweep of his tongue against mine chased the acrid bite of my temper away and left a lingering sweetness. Hunger and need vied for my attention, but then he broke the kiss to the laughter of the children who, like good little rug rats, began flinging water at us.

"Play magic!" Mireille commanded. "Make big."

Her dark hair with its red streaks stuck straight up stubbornly in places and Fin pressed a kiss to my nose. "One moment, my beautiful lady. The second lady of the house is being demanding and bossy."

"I not bossy," Mireille declared a moment before Benedict dumped a whole pitcher of water over her head.

"Yes, you are! You need to learn to listen. Not boss. I'll be in charge." Every bit the budding asshole his father was.

Fin bit back a smile as the twins suddenly lunged at each other and then they were wrestling in the water, their demands of us completely forgotten.

Scooping me up, Fin took a seat and settled me on his lap. The sundress I wore wasn't much of an impediment to his wandering fingers, but even I had some standards.

I didn't fuck in front of the kids.

Anyone else? Eh. I didn't care. My mates did, but not me. But not the children. Maybe it was 'cause they were too attuned to me or maybe because it was just flat out creepy. Still, it didn't stop Fin from stroking his hand up and down the inside of my thigh.

"Wyman will be fine with them," he began. "They already adore him, and he will let them run wild for a few days..."

I opened my mouth, but he quirked a brow that asked for my acquiescence to his argument for the moment. Mutinous, I pursed my lips but then lifted the coffee he had brought me, and I nodded before taking a sip.

The slow curve of his luscious mouth was my reward. However, when I crossed one leg over the other to trap his hand from going any higher, he laughed softly and mouthed 'touche.'

"Hmm-hmm."

"Wyman's as old as Alfred," Fin ticked off. "He loves those children like they are his own." At my dour look, he shrugged. "He adores you, Beautiful. If you'd have him, we'd probably never get rid of him."

"You're not making the sale you want to make."

"Mama, do my hair," Mireille ordered.

"In a moment," I informed her. "And when you learn to ask nicely. For now, actually use the soap to wash the rest of you."

"Soap is boring," Benedict said, and the water caught on fire. "Fire cleans."

Fin snapped his fingers, and the fire went out. The water temperature must have dropped because they squealed. Rogue was just outside the door. The chill of his blown kiss brushed my cheek.

"Now," Fin said in a voice that demanded obedience and instantly soaked my panties. "Do as you were told. Enough trouble or you will be separated for the rest of the day."

That was the single worst punishment we could offer the twins. We reserved it for when their behavior truly demanded reparations. Almost immediately they went for their soap and began to wash and Fin worked his fingers a little higher to slip under my panties. His delighted smile made me flick him.

"Behave. Or you can be separated from me for the rest of the evening."

It was as effective a deterrent for him. His hand retreated, but it was still very warm against the inside of my thigh.

"We can return in a flash," he continued as if we hadn't ceased the subject. "We've worked them up to your absences, gradually. The last time when you and Alfred went away for two days to deal with things in Asia, they handled it beautifully."

But the twins had never been separated from all of us.

As if reading my mind, Fin nuzzled a kiss to my ear and whispered, "Which is why Wyman is perfect. He will indulge them, and yes they will be terrors for a few days when we get back, but we miss you Beautiful. We want to celebrate these days with you. Just you."

My resolve wavered and I looked over at the pair of children gradually appearing as they washed off the muck. They really were rather precious. The feelings swelling in my chest left me aching all over again. Love was not something I'd ever understood before my mates. Even then, what I felt for the twins was so powerful.

"Think about it?" Fin beckoned gently.

"Make Wyman understand what will happen to him if anything happens to them," I ordered.

"Done."

"And I want to slip back at least once a day to see them, to *know*."

Fin blew out a breath then nodded. "But only when they're asleep."

"Agreed." That was a term I could accept.

"Anything else, my beautiful fire rose?"

I glanced over at him to find the hopeful tenderness in his eyes ready to knock down the last of my objections. "Bacon, I'm starving."

His grin lit up the whole room and he kissed me hard and fast. "What my lady wishes, she shall receive." I groaned as he devoured my mouth with his own and he was so smooth as he settled me on the chair in his place before he glanced at the kids. "Behave for your mother, or the separation will last all day tomorrow."

"Yes, Dada Fin." They chorused beautifully. He shot me a wink before he vanished. The door opened as I started to stand, but Rogue slipped in.

"I heard there was a dark angel in here needing her hair washed," he said as he approached me with a sly smile. "Are you my dark angel, little sváss?"

"No Dada Rogue, that's me!" Mireille declared. "Wash my hair, pwease?"

"Ah," he said, grasping his chest like a true dramatic artist. "Two such lovelies in one room. I think my heart is forever bound."

Mireille laughed and pointed a finger at him. "You're silly."

"Yes, I am," Rogue agreed. But he got right down there and up to his elbows in the water. He washed both of them. While Benedict's hair was much shorter, he often seemed to get mud just everywhere, even at the roots. It was better to get it all taken care of. As if summoned by a thought, as soon as they were both rinsed, Maddox strolled in with giant towels and the soaking wet children leapt for their dragon daddy and he wrapped them up warm and tight to dry them off.

He winked at me as he slipped away. Rogue took my hand, pulling me to my feet, before he cupped my cheek. "What can I do to make your day better, little sváss?"

"You've already done it." The fact they loved the children as much as I did was something I knew, but it didn't hurt to be reminded. I wanted them safe, always. "Where is Alfred?"

"Describing in detail the Hell that awaits Wyman should he fail in any of his duties," Rogue told me with a grin. "Now, would you like your hair washed?"

Now that he mentioned it...

It was a good thing I'd finished my coffee, because he whisked us from the room and through the house at full speed, to our own private bathroom and the much larger hot tub that fit us all. My clothes were off and his cock was buried inside of me before I even finished exhaling. I groaned at the hard and furious pounding he delivered as I dug my nails into his back and clung to him.

Need swelled within me even as his knot filled me and

the first orgasm had me gasping, but he was far from done, and his knot hadn't locked him yet. Pulling free, he turned me around to face the mirror. The first plunge of his cock into my cunt made me scream. With one hand, he went to work teasing my clit until I was soaking both of us and with the other he pinched my nipples, working them until they were aching.

When he put his mouth to my neck, I exhaled his name and pulled his wrist to bring it to my lips. I sank my teeth into him as he buried his into my neck and the bond between us flared to life as orgasm after orgasm wracked my body. The swelling of his knot locked him so firmly inside of me I kept spasming. I was too sensitive and the hot taste of his blood on my tongue was a nectar.

He did get around to washing my hair.

Eventually.

CHAPTER 2

FIN

Kidnapping her was the only way we were going to get her away from the children. Wyman could handle them. He was fully prepared, or so he claimed. If he could handle war, famine, plague, and death, how hard could twins be?

By mutual decision, none of us told him. Those children were the very best of Alfred and Fiona. They were also their very worst. As long as Wyman kept them entertained, it should be fine, and he wanted to be *their* favorite uncle. Still, despite her agreement and several repeated conversations of the rules, the schedule, and the routine, Fiona kept putting off our leaving.

Rogue, of all of us, seemed far more inclined to indulge her. Then again, he didn't want to leave the little ones either.

None of us did. The thought of children had been a bit daunting in the beginning for everyone except Maddox, and the less said about his reaction the better.

Fiona's fears came from a real place. Her species, in general, weren't the best parents. But she was no more *just* a succubus than I was *just* a druid or Maddox *only* a dragon. We were more. We were hybrids. Those children were a product of an eternity-aged fallen angel and an angel-blessed succubus.

That said, Fiona loved them to distraction. The love she felt for them burned in her brighter and brighter every single day, and it just made me love her more. The fact she still found wonder in understanding love, in acknowledging *our* love for her? It was the reward of centuries upon centuries of waiting for her.

I couldn't have imagined the depth of love I would feel for her and had experienced from the moment we found her. From the delightful torment and sass she challenged Maddox with, to the way she fiercely fought Alfred for every inch she gave in. Nothing about Fiona had ever been easy, nor should it be. If we were to be worthy of her, we had to earn her.

Now, it was our anniversary and I would take my lumps for this, but I prepared the mead for our supper. Since the babies no longer needed to nurse—and that had taken some convincing, because they would climb up in her lap whenever they were hungry and latch onto a breast—I didn't have to worry about the drought affecting them.

I didn't let anyone else know about my plan. It would be better if Fiona were only furious with one of us. Besides, making things up to her was my specialty. If it were Maddox or Alfred, it could take us the whole of our three nights away to earn her forgiveness. Dinner was a fun affair. In deference to soothing Fiona's worries, we put Wyman in charge and we'd all made it very clear he could not fuck this up. Somewhere between the beach lightning, holy fire strikes and dinner that evening, he'd shaved off all of his hair.

The kids found his bald head fascinating and kept staring at the tattoos on the skin. Hell, I hadn't even realized he had tattoos on his scalp. With the whiskers gone from his face, he looked less like some half-giant from a kid's book and more like a fierce sorcerer or battle-hardened warrior angel that he'd been.

I kept Fiona's cup half-full, measuring out the dose so she would only get sleepier over the course of the meal. The idea was to get her to relax and ease the edge off her anxiety. Wyman performed spectacularly, even convincing the twins to finish all their food with the promise of telling them three stories at bedtime. When Benedict immediately demanded four, Wyman countered with two.

Both twins gaped at him and I had to hide a smile. They managed to renegotiate back to three stories, but only if they didn't argue further during the supper. When it came time for them to go to bed, not only did they clean up their plates neatly, but they did the circuit of hugs and kisses without much complaint, until they got to Fiona.

"Mama come up and listen to the stories too?" Mireille gazed up at her mother with the sweetest eyes. Sadly, most of us could deny her nothing, except Fiona. Somehow, our passionate minx could withstand even the most stunning adorable compulsion.

"No, my darlings," Fiona informed them. "Your deal was with Uncle Wyman and you agreed to the terms. Mama coming up was not in the terms."

Benedict and Mireille both scowled, but one glance at Wyman as he stood, then their mother, seemed to decide them. They quickly climbed up into Fiona's arms for tight hugs and kisses. Each whispered in her ear and I suppose we could all hear it, but we gave them the benefit of discretion. We had to model the behavior we wanted to see from them.

Absolutely logical.

As soon as they finished getting their snuggles, they headed up to their room, each with a firm hand in one of Wyman's. I wasn't the only one letting out a sigh of relief as Fiona leaned back in her seat with a hum of contentment. When I held out a fresh glass of mead to her, she lifted the glass and chuckled.

"You do realize you don't have to get me drunk, right? I thought we'd covered the fact I was a sure thing." The lazy warmth coiled in the air around her. It was like the first kiss of summer after too long a winter.

"I like seeing you happy," I teased.

"I like seeing you relaxed," Maddox rumbled.

"Agreed," Alfred said, though he gave me an enigmatic look. I had a feeling our fearless leader had figured out my plan. "You have spent the last few weeks worrying and we all want you to take the next few days to just be."

"Translation," Fiona said with a hiccup and a laugh. "You want me naked and wrapped around your cock or theirs or all of them."

"If it takes that much to relax you," Alfred said with a satisfied smile. "Then I would never deny my hellion anything."

Her laughter filled the room with a rich warmth. Rogue reached over and coiled one lock of her hair around his finger. It was the barest of tugs and she drained the mead before she leaned in to press a kiss to his lips. "Hmm," she murmured. "You feel good."

"So do you, little svàss, maybe a little too good." He shot me a look and I kept my face pleasantly neutral.

"Good enough to take you on," she said with a slow grin before nibbling kisses along his jaw. "All of you in fact."

"Good enough to run away with us then?" Maddox asked. We'd been careful over the last few days when she began making the excuses. As fearless as Fiona was, leaving her children, even with the safety of someone as powerful as Wyman to protect them, she'd hesitated. We didn't want to force the issue, well—Alfred did—but so far, he'd allowed us to outvote him.

This had to be Fiona's choice and if a little drought of something relaxing could ease her fears and let her make the choice she wanted? Well, I wasn't opposed to that, if for no other reason than her fear and hesitation hurt her, and I hated *anything* hurting her.

Leaning back, Fiona licked her lips slowly then looked at each of us one at a time, finally settling on Alfred. "You think I'm foolish because I'm reticent for all of us to leave at the same time?"

"Not in the slightest, Hellion." Alfred gave her a long studying look. "My queen, if this is truly something you cannot do, then we will simply wait until the twins have achieved their majority to take our time away as all five of us. But there will be some of us leaving for this anniversary and you will be one of them."

"My asshole has spoken," she intoned then sat forward, chin in her palm as she stared at him. "It would be dreadfully unfair of me to make two of you stay behind."

"But," Maddox said, answering before Alfred could. "We would do it for you, Kitten. We would do it for the twins. We all love them too. We would raze the world flat for them. Wyman, for all his bluster and irritations..." Of the four of us, Maddox liked Wyman the least. Rogue's half-grunt, however, reminded me that even our chilly frost elf had his issues with the angel. "He would die for them, Kitten. He would have died for you, as well."

Not that any of us needed that reminder of how close she

had come to being impaled on an angelic blade. Alfred's expression darkened and the heat in the room went pure ice. "Probably not the thing to say," I suggested. "Still..." Since I'd done the dirty deed of giving her the drought to relax her, I would volunteer to be the one left behind should she truly need that. "If it will make you happy my beautiful lady, then here I shall stay to keep watch over the twins and Wyman. I can still fetch you home to see them as you wish."

Surprise flared in Maddox's eyes as well as Alfred's. Rogue's lips compressed. Well, he knew then, but so be it. Surely by now, they had to know they needed me. I was the one that glued us together before we found our lady, and I would do anything to keep us all together, even if it meant easing her rougher edges.

I would gladly submit myself to her punishment later.

"No, I don't want to leave any of you behind," Fiona admitted. "It has been a long time since it was only just us and I know three years isn't much to all of you..."

Alfred snorted. "Every day with you is a gift, Hellion, never doubt that. But every day with our children has been a gift, too. We will be back in time to celebrate their birthday. We promise."

"Agreed," Rogue said. "We wouldn't want to miss that. Our little Mireille would be most cross with all of us."

"Can't have that," Maddox said with a boom of laughter. "She's almost as inventive as Fiona with her punishments."

"That sounds like a challenge," Fiona teased, and Rogue rose.

"No, little sváss, it most certainly was not." He held out his hand to her and when she took it, he pulled her to her feet. "If we're going to go then let us away."

Alfred stood, as did Maddox. All three of them, however, stared at me when Fiona swayed. She wrapped her arms around Rogue and murmured something in his ear. "I'm sleepy," she said. Then yawned. The rumble of Maddox's growl just made me grin as I rose as well. With a sweep of my hand, I cleared the table and sent everything to appear in a sink elsewhere to be washed. There wasn't much left of the food anyway.

Without a word, Alfred eased Fiona from Rogue's arms and she slid into his easily. He lifted her, cradling her to his chest as she tucked her head on his shoulder and her eyes closed even as she yawned.

Fin.

The growled mental call from Maddox had me spreading my hands. *She needed to relax. It will not last long, but it will help her cope with the separation anxiety. For all that she feared she would not love her children because it was not within succubi to share their lives with others, she's proven quite the opposite.*

Rogue sighed. "We won't protect you."

"Not even a little," Alfred agreed.

I inclined my head. "I'm content to be able to prove this to our lady. It will make other anniversary trips easier. For both her and the twins."

Since not a single one of them could dispute the point, I stepped in closer as they gathered to me and then my magic wrapped around us all. We were going to back to the Keep. We were rarely there, save for major events, and it was something of a nostalgia trip. It was, after all, where the five of us finally came together and sealed our fates. Technically, if we were doing a trip down memory lane, that should include a brief stop at the Nightmare Penitentiary.

But since I'd rather raze it to the ground and Alfred likely would, better we go to somewhere with memories we all enjoyed.

We're away. I informed Wyman. *Keep them safe.*

On my honor and soul.

And with your life's blood. I reminded him, despite the absolute certainty in his voice.

That too. His mental chuckle was the last thing I heard before I swept us away to the Keep. It had been repaired over the years, it was now quite festive and warm. No more long drafty halls. There was color everywhere. The library had been restocked. Alfred's suite expanded and access to the bathing pools more direct from his rooms. We could spend all of our anniversary here and not a single other resident of the Keep would know it.

For while retainers were often in residence, the royal quarters were cut off, by both stone and spell. As soon as we appeared in the royal bedroom, Maddox took care of igniting the fire and Rogue went in search of fresh sheets and blankets. We always made it up when we arrived, not when we left.

I slipped away while all three were distracted and made sure we had enough food in places I could steal it away. Then I went for the roses. Some from our garden itself, because they were the perfect red—the exact shade of her hair. Then I added to the collection with a myriad of colors. Some for rose petals to strewn about and others to just add to the beauty of the room.

By the time I returned, the room was cheerfully warm and Fiona lay in Alfred's lap, half-awake. She lifted those sleepy eyes to glare at me. "You're in so much trouble."

Going to one knee, I held up the roses in a show of supplication. "Whatever my lady commands of me."

Alfred stroked her arm as she considered me and when she shifted on his lap, spreading her legs to give me a glorious view of her bare cunt, I sighed.

"You may begin with your tongue," she commanded me. "I will let you know when I have forgiven you."

Alfred spread his own legs so that hers were even wider

and it made room for me to kneel between them both. Someone took the roses as I spread her labia wide and went to work servicing my lady. If she wanted to come on my tongue a hundred times, then I would die in the effort to give her exactly what she wanted.

The feel of her hand fisting my hair pulled me up short, the rich muskiness of her arousal made me salivate. "Oh, you will not die in this effort, my druid. But you may find that you will be eating what your brothers leave me with as much as you are eating me. I hope you are hungry."

It did not bother me in the slightest to pull their seed from her. Anything that came from her would be a bounty to my lips.

"And you may not come," she added with finality and my cock might have died just a little. "Not until *I* allow it."

Behind me, Maddox laughed in a low, dark chuckle and Alfred began to stroke her breasts through her top, though it had already been loosened and there was a spot of blood on her creamy skin.

"As my lady commands," I acquiesced, surrendering everything. "Now may I pleasure you, my lady?"

She grinned. "I adore you."

"I love you as well." When she released my hair, I resumed my approach from before and buried my face into her silky cunt. Her clit was already swollen, the hood pulled back and her pussy soaked with need. I lapped up every drop before sucking her clit against my teeth. When she came the third time, I sank my teeth into her cunt itself and she exploded her pleasure and the room around us became dizzyingly hot, but I kept my hand from my own cock. No matter how hard it was. I endured the moment she pushed me away and Alfred lifted her to impale on his own cock.

I locked my gaze on hers as she leaned forward to kiss me even as she writhed on his dick, hips rolling as he pounded away in her and she licked herself clean from my mouth. I could drown in her kisses and when she screamed her release, I accepted the pound of lust even as I scented Alfred's own release filling her.

The room went quiet, save for our panting and as Alfred slipped from her, she leaned back again, legs spread.

"Again, Fin," she ordered, and I buried my face between her thighs again, as eager to lap up their passion as I had been to sink my teeth into her.

I might die, but this would be a glorious death.

CHAPTER 3

FIONA

*D*awn arrived all too soon, considering how long they spent pleasuring me through the night, not that I hadn't done four times the work—I mean there were four of them. Not that I would really label it as work and Fin had long since earned my forgiveness for soothing me with a drought of whatever. My whole system hummed with pleasure. While they sprawled spent, and half-asleep in a room that smelled so heavily of sex I could probably get high off of it, I paced over to the doors that led down to the steamy pools below. Instead of following the long hallways or descending the flights of stairs, this was more of a spiral ramp.

Fin had manipulated earth and stone to form it and though it was several levels below it didn't take that long to reach. Inside, the fire already burned, and the heat of the room was like a blast furnace against my skin. It wasn't winter currently, but it was always much colder up here. I took the time to do a wash, but then climbed into the higher pool to float and soak.

For the first time in years, I was alone.

"Running away already, Kitten?"

Or not.

I lifted my eyelids to find Maddox staring at me. The adoration in his eyes just made me smile and I held out a hand to him. It took no beckoning at all for him to move to the bathing pool. He gave himself a quick wash, mostly cleaning away the sweat and the cum clinging to his skin, before climbing into the bigger pool with me. I was still floating, so I didn't mind at all when he traced a hand over my chest. A light caress to let me know he was there before he slid me up to rest with my back to his chest.

Stretching his much longer legs out as he sat, he nestled my ass against his semi-hard erection and we both kind of sighed. I leaned my head along his shoulder as he pressed a tender kiss to my temple. "Am I interrupting?" The rumble of his voice vibrated through my whole being.

"Not really," I murmured. "I was just thinking about being alone and the quiet. Then you were there."

A huff of laughter escaped him. "I can leave you alone again, Kitten."

"No, you're fine," I murmured and stretched. The combination of heat from the water and my dragon loosened all my muscles. "I think I'd forgotten what it was like to soak in a bath without one of the twins wanting or needing something." So odd. "They are so little and yet so loud."

He chuckled, drawing a lazy pattern against my abdomen. "That is why children are so precious, they fill in this space we didn't even know was there."

"Eh." I made a face. "I love them, don't get me wrong. But I kind of miss us being us..."

"You miss bandying words and arguing incessantly that you were not our mate and that succubi don't mate?" His arch tone was going to get him punched in the dick any minute now. Well, maybe right next to his dick. I was kind of fond of that massive cock of his. "Or perhaps it's hurling insults at us and arguing with Alfred the Asshole, I believe you called him."

"I called you a lizard-brained jackass, too," I commented, tilting my head back to meet his gaze. "Your point?"

His grin widened. "You did. You also used to get irritated at me for eating people."

"I still get irritated at you for eating people..." I hesitated and narrowed my eyes before turning half in his lap. "When have you been out eating people?"

"The only person I've eaten in over three years, Kitten, is you." His smirk was adorable.

"Good," I mock-growled. "I was about to be quite put out with my dragon."

"Definitely yours, Kitten." He clasped my hips and pulled me back to straddle his lap. His cock had already stiffened and I arched an eyebrow at him.

"So soon, Maddox?" Hadn't he fucked me solid half the night? Even for him this was impressive.

"I ache for you, Kitten," he admitted. "The moment you left the bedroom, it was like I had to follow."

Looping my arms around his neck, I smiled and kissed him gently. "Do you remember when you burst into my cell?"

"And you were the most stunningly beautiful raging brat I'd ever met, who was also covered in another's scent?" The possessiveness in his voice had my cunt aching and when he lifted my hips, I wrapped my hand around his cock. It seemed even larger than normal and between us we maneuvered me into place and I sank down, taking him to the hilt with one thrust that made me see stars. Thick and full to the brim.

"Yes," I said both in answer to his statement and to the feel of him stretching me. No matter how many times he took my body, I did not think I would ever get enough or ever fully used to him, and I didn't mind.

His eyes flashed, the pupils constricting as his dragon gazed out at me. *My* dragon and I dug my nails into his shoulders, I wanted him to feel the bite as I rolled my hips. His grip on me was bruising because no sooner would I pull away than he would slam himself deeper inside of me.

"Mine," he rumbled in that voice that was barely human, and I groaned.

"Yours," I promised and sealed it with a kiss as we rocked together in a near frenzy. Need unfolded in me like an inferno. Hunger sharpened the taste of him against my tongue and I don't know if he bit my lip or I bit his, but the mingling of our blood into the kiss sent a jolt through me.

Steam billowed from the pool as though the water evaporated faster than it could be refilled. Maddox surged upward, his arms tight around me as I locked my legs on his hips. Even as he moved, I kept our rhythm and then my back was to a rough stone wall and only his hand cradling my head kept me from slamming it into the stone.

Once in place, he sank his teeth into the mating mark he'd left on me so long ago and began to pound into me in earnest. The fire in his blood seemed to burn in mine and I screamed as the first orgasm detonated within me. But it didn't slow him one whit. The punishing pace burned and incited and I was coming again, spasming around his cock.

His desire was like a living thing, invading my body and claiming me, heart, mind, and soul. He lifted his head from where he'd bitten me. Blood stained his lips and his dragon stared at me, possession etched into his every feature.

"Mine," he demanded again. The dragon wanted my surrender, my obedience, and my pleasure.

Normally, I'd put up a fight, but holy fuck, everything inside of me strained to be with him and I struck, whispering, "yours," just seconds before I sank my teeth into the heavy corded muscle at the base of his throat. It was a vulnerable spot. One I could tear out and end his life. As it was, the fiery blood poured onto my tongue, and I lost all sense of time and place as pleasure flooded me.

The hard thrust of him driving into me over and over was all that existed. We had to be one. We couldn't stand to be apart. Then even as another orgasm ripped me in two, he came with a roar that shook the very stone around us as his knot expanded and stretched me even tighter.

It was just this side of pain and I drank from him even as hot jets of his seed filled me. The two fires met in the center, and I went up in flames. My last sight was his dragon's satisfied and possessive eyes locked on mine before I blacked out.

His.

The thought floated around lazily in my mind as I stirred. There was hot water buoying me, and a careful hand washing me, as though I were the most precious thing. The powerful scent of sex filled my lungs as I took a deep breath. More than that, was the taste of fire, smoke, and amber.

As my eyelids flickered upwards, I found Maddox smiling down at me, "Hello, Kitten."

I chuckled. He had every right in the world to look smug. It was rare that they could overwhelm me with their passion. I was drunk on his. Another laugh escaped me as he worked his hands over my abdomen and carefully between my thighs. I was sitting on his lap, cradled in the lower pool, though he was very intent on washing me.

My cunt was more than a little tender and I exhaled as he carefully washed warm water over it. Oh, how long had we been locked together? It felt like I'd pulled a muscle in a my vagina. Maybe all of them. The impression of his cock was still there and I spasmed at the thought of it.

Maddox bit his lip as he gazed up at me. "I didn't hurt you, did I?"

"No more than I wanted," I promised him. His tender kiss in reply settled something in me and the sleep that eluded me the night before seemed to be calling to me now. But I didn't want to slip away yet. This was nice. He worked diligently until every inch of me was clean. Finished, he lifted me and carried me over to the lounging chairs by the fire. A new addition, because I got tired of being fucked against stone. All earlier evidence to the contrary aside.

With careful hands, he settled me onto my back and then began a massage that started at my feet and I was gone before he reached my thighs.

The next time I opened my eyes, he was seated deeply within me, kissing me lazily until I woke. A laugh nearly escaped me at the pleasure waiting for me. It had been a long time since he'd needed me so much he'd gotten ahead of the fucking to wake me up with his dick.

Not that I minded.

I loved when they woke me with their dicks.

All of them.

Speaking of dicks...

I glanced around but we were still alone, save for the dragon's eyes looking down at me. "I need you, Fiona."

"Then have me."

He pulled out with such speed, it left me gasping and empty. But he left me only long enough to flip me over onto my belly and to drag my hips upward so he could get behind me. I braced for the first push of that massive cock and it wasn't enough. There was no patience in him this time. The slap of his balls against me added to the sound of his cock gliding in and out. Thank fuck I was soaked or even I would be struggling with his girth.

The press of his thumb against my ass was a singular warning before he slid his lubed up fingers into my ass and the pounding he gave my cunt sent shockwaves of pleasure through me.

With his free hand, he fisted my hair and then he locked his teeth against the mating mark and I went wild. His pleasure coursed through me like lava. I clamped down on his cock so tight, he had to fight for every inch he took and returned.

I bucked backwards, wanting to have him everywhere. He thrust his fingers into my ass in time, somehow managing that rhythm. The thrusting kept rubbing my nipples against the soft fabric of the lounger and I couldn't seem to control it. His passion spilled into me and magnified. I let loose with a scream that seemed to last forever, as his knot swelled and swelled. It hurt. It felt so good. The pain split me in two. The pleasure pulled me back together again.

Then it was like we floated down from some great height. He was still locked deep inside my body, even as he held fast to my throat with his teeth. He took lazy, slow pulls of my blood and my eyes were drifting shut. The world faded. Then hot blood filled my mouth and a snarl echoed from one of my mates to another. I could barely make out the words as I drank.

Alfred. My asshole. His spark flooded me as I drank. Then it was Rogue. The chill of his blood cooled wild ardor raging in my system. As tangy as his wicked personality, and I licked my lips when he forced my teeth from him. Then Fin, oh the sweetness of his blood and the earthiness of his magic cradling and soothing.

Between them all, I flushed with warmth and peace and what pain had existed vanished as if an errant thought. My cunt spasmed around Maddox's cock, still knotted and locked within me. But my head was in Fin's lap and he stroked my hair with his gentle fingers. The argument around me continued to rage, but I didn't care.

All I felt was loved. Needed. And full.

I didn't think I'd ever been so full in my existence.

"Sleepy," I murmured. "Shhh."

The argument around me ceased immediately and my asshole suddenly appeared in my line of sight. "I love you," I whispered and touched his cheek. The ferocious frown he wore eased and then he pressed his lips to my temple.

"And I you, my queen. As soon as Maddox's knot loosens, we shall put you to bed."

"That sounds nice," I whispered. "Snuggle with me?"

"Promise," Rogue said even as Alfred's smile turned even softer. My eyelids drifted closed again, but not before Alfred's gentle expression turned to rage again and it wasn't me he was looking at so, honestly, right now I didn't care.

But someone was getting an ass whoopin' and it wasn't me.

CHAPTER 4

"When I say I love you more, I don't mean I love you more than you love me. I mean I love you more than the bad days ahead of us, I love you more than any fight we will ever have. I love you more than the distance between us, I love you more than any obstacle that could try and come between us. I love you the most." –
Unknown

ALFRED

Our anniversary escape was for my hellion more than it was for any of us. After an eternity, what was a few days to us? But in the few brief years we'd already had with her—everything had changed. I wouldn't have it any other way. The twins were a gift I never dreamed possible. As were the return of my own wings. Flexing them now as I stood atop the keep, I stared out over the valley and the range we had made our own for the last few centuries.

There was peace amongst us again. Of the seven, there were only three of the original left. We were now eight and the outlier. Synove wanted nothing to do with us and though she tolerated Wyman, she had asked for peace with me and I'd been inclined to grant it.

Until three hours earlier when she called to one of my crows. Now...

"Alfred?" Fiona's husky voice pulled me from my musings, and I turned to find her walking across the rooftop in bare feet, wearing only one of—it had to be one of Fin's shirts. She'd found some oversized t-shirt with no buttons and some ridiculous saying on it.

No, you're right. Let's do it the dumbest way possible because it'll be easier for you.

The breeze caught her shirt and pinned it against the curves of her form, even as my gaze tracked from her bare legs up to her beautiful smile and sleepy green eyes. The mating mark Maddox had refreshed was puffy and swollen, but my hellion glowed. Moonlight or sunlight, nothing could compete. I flexed my wings and started to fold them back, but she held out a hand and I froze.

If she wanted to stroke my wings, then I would never deny her. The shadow of wings extended from her own back. They were like smoke and light danced together, ethereal, yet tangible. If I were to run my fingers over them, they would be as soft as the fresh down of new growth and yet they were far more powerful.

The lightest touch of her fingertips along my pin feathers had me shuddering and I bowed my head to my queen. The only person on or off this earth to whom I would bow.

"What's wrong?" She glided into my side, tucking herself under my arm and I drew a wing down to shield her, even as I hugged her close.

Lying to her wasn't an option. It no longer even occurred to me. For as demanding and high-spirited and fierce as she was, she was also smart and cagey. She saw options none of us did and her reasoning, while also convoluted, had worked out solutions to issues that had plagued the kindred my brothers and sisters had created. So many abandoned vampires struggled without powerful leadership, but I would not be Cyril or Eamon.

My laws were succinct. They were firm. There was little room for forgiveness. Only my queen might earn them that boon and she only intervened when she felt it right. We balanced each other beautifully. For all that she would deny it, her heart was the most precious of gifts. She had kept it deeply hidden, chained, and in the dark where nothing could harm it, nor could anything warm it. When I took her life, those bonds shattered, but only because she surrendered them to me.

In turn, I would give her everything. We would lay this world at her feet. Not that she had any interest in it.

"Alfred," she murmured and once again, my wandering thoughts returned to the here and the now.

"Sorry, Hellion," I murmured and pressed a kiss to her temple "Synove reached out to one of my crows and now I am pondering the why of it as well as do I care..."

"Ahh."

Such understanding in that single syllable. She didn't ask me for more information. Instead, she just leaned into me, letting me inhale her scent. She must have bathed again since waking, for there was the familiarity of her favorite soap and the shampoo she preferred. After Maddox let his own passion nearly drain her, we'd all let her drink from us. The restoration swifter than any before. It was hardest on Rogue and Maddox sometimes. The other sides of their nature, their beasts as it were, could be so damn possessive.

Yet where Maddox's passions could rage out of control, Rogue rarely allowed his free reign. The temperament of the elven kind, I supposed. Though when it came to his little sváss, he would challenge even me, as would Maddox and Fin, and in this the four of us were in firm agreement, I might be the king, but she was *ours* and no single one of us could claim dominion.

It kept us watchful and protective. "Synove wishes to speak with you," I told her finally. I'd turned the request over in my mind a hundred different ways and I found no misdirection or deception in Synove's blunt request. She had allowed for none. Instead, she worded it specifically.

"Me?" Surprise and skepticism twined in Fiona's voice and she leaned back a little to look up at me. The stroke of her hair against my wings sent content and lust to swim through my system. I needed my focus on the request, not on carrying my queen into the sky and taking her there. Flying was not something she'd practiced overmuch.

We would need to correct that.

"Yes. It would seem she's encountered an old—" I hesitated to use the word *friend* because the warden of the Nightmare Penitentiary had not been a friend or a companion. He'd been her jailer and her lover, he'd also tried to turn her into a shadow demon and for that alone I could kill him. But she had dealt with him and been satisfied in her own punishment. "Acquaintance," was the word I finally chose. Even that lacked something.

"Apparently not someone you're terrifically fond of, or you wouldn't sound like you'd just sucked on three day dead blood."

The very thought was disgusting, and I frowned down at her. She gave a careless little shrug.

"Something is vexing you, my asshole, so just tell me." The fact she'd turned an insult into an endearment pulled a reluctant smile from me.

"Dorran," I said his name with as little emotion as possible.

"The warden?" Surprise filled her eyes. "He's still *alive?*"

"So it would seem," I said, maintaining my neutrality a challenge. "Vastly changed if Synove's description is to be believed, and she wishes to speak to you about what you did to him."

Fiona's puffy lips formed a little 'o' but then the corners tilted upward and laughter escaped her. "The fuck if I know what I did." After giving me a squeeze, she took a couple of steps away, almost dancing along the roof until she reached one of the parapets, where she hopped up and spread her arms. The breeze caught her gorgeous red hair and it fluttered like flames, even as she balanced there.

"Tell me," I beckoned to her.

"About what I did?" she asked, casting a glance over her shoulder. At my nod, she gave a careless shrug. "I don't know. I mean, he was pissing me off and I wanted to get to Fin and Maddox." The sobriety in her tone hid the far more furious feelings she'd expressed at the time. We'd forbidden her to go which, of course, meant she'd flipped us off and gone after them on her own anyway. No one forbid Fiona. It was like waving a red bit of meat at a starving animal.

"And?"

"And...he was doing his shadow demon thing, trying to smother me in his darkness and I remembered what you'd said." With that, she pivoted and faced me. "About how he was trying to turn me and that day he did—whatever and you suddenly flooded light through me."

The spark. Yes, not even shadow demons could stand up to an angel. Even a fallen angel such as I. There was enough of creation left within me to erase their taint. He'd wanted Fiona for his own and I refused to allow him to shackle her soul. I'd purged him from her system.

What I hadn't known then, what none of us had known, was when she went after Maddox and Fin, she'd already been pregnant. Her body changing as she hosted the twin souls of Mireille and Benedict. Pride and love flooded me in such force, I was tempted to wake Fin to take us to them right now. But, we were on our little sojourn, and we'd gone to see them just a couple of hours earlier while they slept. They were exhausted, filthy, and very content.

Wyman looked like he'd been through a war, but he was alive so I didn't really listen to his complaints. Fiona had flat out laughed in his face, then removed the sting by kissing his cheek. His gaze filled with wonder as he followed her retreat and Rogue had reminded him, rather forcefully, that he could adore her from afar and that was it. Fiona was ours and I could wish my brother had found someone with half her fire and spirit so he too could be as happy as I, but not so much that I would share her affections an inch further than they already went.

Rogue and Maddox would likely kill him if the idea were even given voice. Still, his affection for Fiona did not go to those depths and so I didn't worry.

"I don't know what I did, I just know light splintered the dark and he changed—even his eyes changed."

His eyes. "How?"

"They were filled with silver, like it streaked through the darkness—a falling star. I couldn't put my finger on it and to be honest, I didn't want to. I wanted Fin and Maddox. I wanted them back and Dorran was not allowed to keep them from me. No one was." Ferocious heat flamed in her eyes. "He fled not long after that and I mostly just forgot about him."

That made sense. Fiona had done something remarkable though. Or maybe it was Fiona in combination with the twin angels she'd carried in her womb. For all that succubi were a form of demon, she herself was not demonic. Not now and I highly doubted before. There was too much heart within her.

Too much passion. Even now, she remained changed. Her wings were present and she filled an emptiness in my own soul I hadn't realized was there.

She'd also graced me with my own wings.

"So, I can meet with her if you want," Fiona offered, jumping from the parapet with her wings catching a bit of the breeze and I was after her in a heartbeat, my own wings stiffening as I launched. But she wasn't falling, if anything, she glided and the rapture on her expression kept me from interfering. Still, I stayed close. A moonlight flight had been on my mind, hadn't it?

"Perhaps," I said after turning the idea over a bit more. "We shall discuss it later. Synove has kept her own counsel these past three years."

"She talks to Wyman," Fiona pointed out with sweet reason, as she did a little twirl and laughed. She plummeted for a moment, off balance, before her wings spread again. Their shadowy form never failed to amaze me. As though they were the substance of dreams and thoughts—of faith itself—instead of body, blood, bone, and feather. Yet they were perfect for her.

"She does," I agreed, circling her once before nodding to the far mountains. "Think you can make it that far, my hellion?"

"Where we can see the snow? Or where it dips into the next valley?"

As I considered her questions, she blew me a kiss and raced ahead. Laughter filled me at her cunning. Not that she didn't need the head start. My wings were stronger, and I had far more practice. But I wasn't as interested in beating her as I was in keeping pace in case she weakened or tired. I should have known better.

My hellion loved a challenge and the fact I kept hovering was most certainly a challenge. She fought her own weariness with incurable stubbornness and made it to the ridge as the first rays of dawn touched it. Her sheer gasp at the stunning light climbing over of the ice and snow, sending up glittering rainbows, was all the reward I needed.

Still, when she threw herself at me, I caught her easily and cradled her cheek against my palm. Those depthless green eyes were those of a goddess. Fin was right. His green-eyed goddess who'd demanded he stay alive for her, centuries before she'd even been born. How tightly wound were all of our fates, I couldn't begin to fathom.

I'd long since lost my faith when I'd refused to war with my brethren and fallen instead, cast out from our kind forever. Twelve of us. Then war took us to seven. A second war I had not wanted, but did not refuse cut those number to three. Only three of the twelve still stood, but we were eight and if Synove came around, then perhaps we would be nine again, but I didn't worry about that for now.

I had my brothers, my hellion, and my children. I could ask for nothing more. The bounty and grace given to me were beyond measure.

"I love you," Fiona whispered, and my heart stuttered at the declaration. She was not given to sweet words or gentle emotions. Her love was a living thing, a fire that consumed all in its path and I would willingly burn in it for all eternity.

"And I you," I promised. "I always will."

"Even though you were an asshole, and I didn't want to be a vampire?"

I chuckled. "Even though. I will always be *your* asshole, for as my queen, I will be whatever you need me to be."

"Hmm." She looped her arms around my neck and leaned her head back as the light reached us. It lit her hair like it was the very fire I called her and just around her mating mark from Maddox, the skin had shifted in shade to bluish-black with streaks of red. He truly had bruised the hell out of her.

I moved to my own mark. The mark that turned her and I teased over it with my tongue, opening every feeling I had for her, opening my very soul, as it belonged to her, and the dampness of her tears landed against my cheeks like drops of rain.

When she tugged my hair up, I fused my mouth to hers and lowered her to the land. She deserved satin and silk, softness and feathers, but I found nothing beneath the shirt but her bare skin and she freed my cock from my pants wordlessly, one stroke was all I needed to lung forward and I filled her pussy with a thrust that left me basking in heaven.

"I love you," she declared again and this time it was her soul that opened to me as she sealed her lips over the mark she'd given me. "Feel me."

I did.

I always would.

"Feel me," I insisted and when her teeth sank in, I let my thoughts of her, my love for her, and my memories flow between us as I met her rising hips with thrusts of my own. I wasn't sure where I felt more pleasure, in my body or my soul, but she took it all and magnified it. The orgasm that ripped through me had my wings stretching out as though to absorb the light, and her mouth fused to mine once more, as I forgot how to breathe save for touching her.

The thrum of her heart beneath my palm as I shielded her with my wings and lay cradled between her legs, I had to ask, because I wanted to hear her say it.

I needed to hear her say it.

"Are you happy, Hellion?" I murmured. "Are you truly happy?"

Her smile filled me with delight. "I will deny it if you tell anyone else—but yes, my king." A title she rarely graced me with. "Yes, I am truly happy. I have a life I could never have imagined and I am not that furious girl who began a perilous journey in that prison."

No. None of us were who we were when we first met.

"You are my world," I told her. "You and the twins."

"What about Maddox, Fin, and Rogue?"

I grunted as if it was a chore. "Fine, them, too. But I draw the line at Wyman."

Her rich laughter filled the air and she ran her foot up and down the back of my leg. "Liar."

"Don't get me wrong, I love him like a brother. But he isn't my world."

"Now we are eight," she intoned in a voice intended to mock mine, but the reminder sent a bolt to my heart.

"Fine, but if you ever tell him, then I will deny it." I growled and her grin grew.

"Your secret is safe with me, my king. I swear it."

"And yours are always safe with me, my queen." This time, I kissed her just to kiss. The massage of her lips beneath mine sweet and the taste of her decadent as she parted to sweep her tongue against mine. My cock had already stiffened again, my need for her would never waver. Only we didn't rush, instead, we moved in slow decadent strokes. It was like flying, as we climbed with our pleasure, the only thing that mattered was right here as we rocked together. When the climax finally swept us away, it was like falling into pure decadence.

So much so, that I'd all but forgotten what had gotten me up earlier and I was loathe to return to the keep, except her stomach began to growl. My queen did not do well when hunger assailed her. As it was, Fin awaited us with a feast of bacon and coffee. She sat in his lap all through the meal and when she vanished beneath the table after, I had to chuckle.

Because the sound of her sucking Fin's cock deep into her throat had my own hardening. Fortunately for all of us, our queen was a generous woman and she treated us all to the pleasure of her mouth. The table didn't survive us all, either. It cracked from Fin, broke in two thanks to Rogue, parts of it began to char with Maddox and I splintered the rest as I spilled my seed down her throat.

Yes, they were all my world, but she stood at the very center of it.

CHAPTER 5

"Love is a thing that is full of cares and fears." – Ovid

FIONA

*A*ll too soon, our sojourn at the keep was over. Though I enjoyed it just being the five of us, even when they bickered, or Fin picked on them until he infuriated one of them—usually Maddox—I was eager to get home to the twins. Each night we'd visited, they'd been healthy and whole, sleeping like little angels.

Wyman, on the other hand, had taken quite the beating. His beard had been shorn before along with his hair. The tattoos drawn in swirling ink over his skull looked almost demonic, but they glowed with a pulse of their own power as though containing something—like an angel, I supposed. Alfred housed so much more power than was visible, but I didn't always notice it now.

Maybe because I was inside that circle of power. Or more like knot of it. The four of them with me formed a knot, like one of those Celtic patterns. It shielded Maddox's dragon unless he wanted to be seen and Rogue's more elvish nature, which was so far from human that he would stand out as would Alfred, himself.

Weirdly, of the five of us, Fin was probably the most normal and he could actually weave magic from the elements. This was our normal though. All of those wondrous powers, along with the responsibility to look after vampires around the world and their dealings with other supernaturals.

Politics *sucked*.

Alfred only involved me when it was going to be fun. Or at least it seemed that way. The last two times he'd had me go along, I actually got to kick the crap out of a bunch of dumbasses. It had been like the best bar brawl ever.

But even that wasn't enough to make me want to leave the twins. Wyman made himself scarce five minutes after we returned and about three minutes before Fin dragged him back. The twins were perfect, but the house was a wreck.

Nearly every single window had been blown out and I swore they'd burned concentric circles into the floor of the living room. The furniture had been blasted to bits, including my favorite chair. I debated tearing a strip off Wyman's hide for all of thirty seconds when Mireille took one look at our faces and then the destruction before she burst into tears and threw herself at Alfred.

His fury blazed through him as he cradled her close. Fin and Maddox turned on Wyman as one and I swore even Rogue was ready to do war. Unfortunately for Mireille's amazing acting skills, Benedict couldn't hide his devilish little grin. I put two fingers to my lips and whistled shrill enough to make all of them flinch and that put their focus on me.

Wyman owed me.

Big time.

"What happened?" I asked, pinning Benedict with a look.

Mireille sniffled and Alfred let out a growl. My asshole really needed to remember she was definitely *my* daughter too. That meant she was far from *innocent*. "We can tell—" Fin began but I cut him off with one look.

"I didn't ask you," I said, then focused on Benedict. Mireille was far better at her game face than he was. When he would have looked to his sister, I took two steps forward blocking his line of sight. Now all he could do was stare up at me. I raised my brows. "I'm waiting."

Benedict tried, I'd give him that. He fought to hold my gaze, but he couldn't do that and lie. The streak of honor in him was too strong. While they might have my mates—their fathers—wrapped around their little fingers, they could not compel me. For once, my succubi nature played into my own favor.

With a deep sigh, Benedict said, "We were bad. We wanted to play when Uncle Wyman said no."

"Benny!" Mireille shrieked, then she cut off with a little squeak of sound followed by a solid whap to her ass. I didn't have to look. Alfred's swiftness was legendary, and he didn't hurt her. The fact he'd spanked her at all would have stunned her silence. He'd only done it once before and it had been for this very thing.

A lie.

She didn't want to be in trouble so she tried to lie and we would not have that.

Benedict swallowed hard, then lifted tear-filled eyes to meet my gaze. He blinked until the tears themselves faded before he said, "Uncle Wyman said no fire in the house, but when we called it, we couldn't put it out. Then Mireille called wind and I thought water..."

Twin sighs echoed from Fin and Maddox.

It was Rogue, however, who stepped next to me and he eyed Benedict then twisted to look at Mireille. "Come here," he ordered her. She was full on snuffling when she joined her brother, face flushed and red, bright green eyes filled with real tears not the faux ones meant to earn sympathy.

One by one, their fathers gathered around them in a circle and it was Alfred who looked to me and then Rogue. "When Elvish children did this, their powers were bound."

"Yes," Rogue said. "Until such a time as they could be trusted with such responsibility."

"Then bind them we shall," Fin continued, again his gaze went to me and then Maddox nodded. "Though it will mean we shall have to invest in a true nanny for them."

Yes, a defender.

I had an idea for one.

"Mama," Mireille said, suddenly grasping at my hands. "Please don't bind us. We will be good."

"You are good," I told her as I knelt down in front of both of them. "But you are fiercely powerful, both of you and you are following your nature, acting without thinking, because you want to. Not because you understand. This..." I motioned to the destruction around us, letting my own hurt show. "I love this house. Your fathers built this for me. It was from my dream and you've destroyed it."

Benedict burst into real tears this time and he threw himself at me, as did Mireille. I held them close because they did understand now that they had been bad, but these tears were as much for the fact that they had to face consequences than anything else. So, I would not be deterred.

I met Rogue's gaze. "How do we do this?"

We will lock their powers, binding them with ours. His voice came to me through the link we all shared in Fin. *It won't hurt them and probably should have been done much sooner. They are far more powerful than we realized. They are nearly pure angel, little sváss.*

With just enough of their mother to make them interesting. Fin's teasing fell flat though. *And until today, I didn't realize how strongly they could compel us.*

Alfred nodded. *But not Fiona, she sees through them, because you, Hellion are a good mother.*

Those words meant more than he could understand. Or maybe he did. I'd told them so many times, I had no idea of how to be a parent. My own mother had only taught me enough to survive and to feed before leaving me. Succubi didn't particularly share well.

"We love you," I told them even as I pulled them back away from my neck where they were soaking my shirt. "We need you to survive and grow strong, to understand the power you can command and to use it wisely. Most of all…" It was my turn to sigh. "We need you to have the control to not hurt someone you don't mean to hurt."

That was what had gotten me in this position in the first place. I was also no saint, I'd done my share of harm before I learned to control how I fed. They were lucky, they did not need to learn that, but they did need control—period.

"We're sorry, Mama," Mireille told me.

"I know. This won't hurt a bit." *Right?* The internal question I directed to my mates, but Maddox squatted down with us, lifting Benedict into his arms.

"No," he rumbled to them, and my neck pulsed at his tone. The dragon was in his eyes. "This is to protect you," he promised, then focused on me. "To protect your mother, as well."

Fin scooped up Mireille. "You will, however, need to sleep a bit more. It's taxing when you don't have the whole world at your fingertips." He softened the blow with a raspberry blown against her belly. Rogue caught my elbow and helped me to stand, then Alfred joined us as we all hugged, forming a circle around the twins.

Only Wyman stood apart from us, his expression unreadable. The magic Rogue and Fin called pulled on me and I opened myself to what they needed. I didn't understand all magic nor spells. To be honest, I was in no great hurry to learn. I trusted them to protect the twins and if binding their powers would do that, then we would.

Maddox rumbled next to me, and I swore his dragon tried to shield me from sharing too much, but no one else protested, so I just elbowed him gently. That had about as much effect as trying to move a wall. Then again, I could punch through some walls, so even less effect.

Mireille fought the yawn pulling at her jaw, but Benedict was out like a light. Though her eyelids were heavy, Mireille struggled to stay awake. "Not fair," she said to Fin. "Don't like."

"I know, sweet princess," he murmured. "But they are safe and now so are you. Sleep, little one." He kissed her forehead, and she gave me one last plaintive look before she dropped off into sleep.

"We'll put them to bed," Fin said as he and Maddox carried them up, though Maddox hesitated when I didn't follow.

"Go on," I told him. "I need to talk to Wyman."

"Oh shit," Wyman said. "Look here, Hot Stuff, I thought we were on the good books now. I tried to keep them in line and if I'd realized a good spanking would do it, I'd have done that much sooner."

Rogue snorted but Alfred glared. "You don't get to spank them."

"Actually," I said, folding my arms as I looked at the destruction. "If you'll come back to us for a while and work as the children's guardian, you'll have my permission to correct them if correction is necessary."

Alfred and Rogue both stared at me, mouths open.

Didn't expect that, did you boys? But for now, I ignored them and focused on Wyman. He squinted at me like I'd gone crazy. "You're inviting me into your little love nest?"

"As their guardian," I repeated. "Not my lover."

"Damn straight not her lover," Alfred snarled, and I didn't roll my eyes but Wyman snickered.

"I mean if you wanted to sweeten the pot," Wyman suggested. "I'm a big fan of watching."

The house shook with a dragon's rumbling snarl and all four of us glanced toward the stairs. "The house is already a wreck, Maddox. Don't do any more damage." For fuck's sake. The shaking stopped immediately, and I refocused my attention on Wyman. "If you truly do not feel up to the task, then I understand, but I need the children to learn from others as much as they learn from us, and I want them protected."

Particularly now that their powers were bound.

Wyman ran a hand over his bald head and grunted. "Fine. I don't have much going on right now, but I need a few days off each month. All the sex around here and I'll need to find a pussy or three to pound myself or my balls will fall off."

I chuckled. "I'm sure we can give you that time and you don't always have to stay up in the house."

The relief on Rogue's face was profound.

"Since we're already going to have to fix it up."

"We'll take care of it, little sváss," Rogue told me as he slid an arm around my shoulders. "We will work through the night, you go and rest."

Amused, I let him guide me up the stairs, but I didn't miss Alfred yanking Wyman out of the house and then they were gone into the distance.

"Alfred doesn't need to threaten him," I pointed out. "He only flirts with me because it pisses all of you off."

"We know," Rogue said as he led the way into our room. Fortunately, this one seemed to have escaped the twins' wrath. Fin and Maddox stepped out of their room and closed the door. The magic on it would not allow anyone but us to open it. "But if he's going to be around the children more, he cannot speak of their mother that way."

I laughed. "You all have said far worse things."

"We're your mates," Maddox growled. "That cunt is ours to pound whenever we wish."

Fin groaned and he slapped Maddox hard. "Knock it off, or you're going to get us all grounded from her pussy."

Dropping to sit on the edge of the bed, I pulled off my boots. "I'm not kicking anyone out of bed. You're all being ridiculous." In fact, they'd all been ridiculous for the last two days, but I'd put it off to our celebration. "The anniversary was wonderful. But we're home now and we need a little more normalcy. So go fix my house and I will see you when you come to bed."

I was stripping out of my clothes and crawling up to slide under the blankets. Maddox took a step closer to the bed, but Rogue put a hand on his chest and just glared at him. Their conversation was a distant hum in the back of my mind. That happened when they cut me out of whatever mental debate they were having.

"Boys, if you want to argue, do it somewhere else. If the twins wake me up in three hours and I haven't had enough sleep, you won't like me grumpy."

With cross between a growl and groan, Maddox stormed out with Rogue behind him. I sat up and stared after them then looked at Fin and raised my brows. "You staying, lover?"

"Hmm-hmm." He stripped off his own clothes and then gathered up my discards making everything neat. I tracked his naked form as he walked a circuit around the bed. The circle he erected sent a tingle over my skin. "Just until they seal up the house and I can reassert the wards. Wyman is not guarding you and them."

"Ahh," I said as though that explained everything. "As if…"

"Exactly." He grinned at me before sliding into the bed and pulling me against his chest. I really was tired and I curled into him, soaking up his nearness. "Besides, I endured my punishment for the last three days without complaint."

"That you did, lover and I will happily return the favor if you need me to ride your cock or swallow it." Though he wasn't that hard. He cupped my breast and gave it a gentle squeeze.

"In the morning," he teased. "Make them all watch."

I laughed and he grinned at me all unabashed. "Hmm…how about I ride you first, then suck you off and only after you've had my ass, I let the rest of them play."

I swore his eyes glittered with joy. "It will drive them mad."

"And probably leave me too sore to walk." I'd nearly achieved that the last three days. Fuck knew, Maddox had left my cunt bruised as hell, but I had enjoyed it.

"Never," Fin promised, sliding his hand down to cup my pussy and warmth invaded me as he eased the bruising. "If you ever hurt too much you must tell us."

"I love the pain as much as the pleasure," I pointed out, though the tingling warmth spreading throughout me made my limbs heavier as though I were in an orgasm's wake. "I love you."

"And we you, my sweet goddess. But you are ours to serve and to protect. Never to harm. Never to be made to feel anything but wonderful."

Another laugh burst free from me, and I dragged him down for a proper kiss. "Keep it up, Druid, and we will not be sleeping and they will have to listen to your groans while they do all the work to repair the house."

He grinned wickedly. "You make that sound like a bad thing."

True.

I slid down his chest, but he pulled me up before I could reach his cock.

"In the morning," he said firmly. "Binding the children took more energy than you realize yet." Well, I was tired. Enough that I could work up the energy to blow him but I was fine with not, and when was the last time that happened.

Yawn cracking my jaw, I snuggled into him. "I promise to blow you in the morning."

"I look forward to it," he murmured. "Sleep my lady. Sleep and dream only good dreams."

He really didn't have to tell me twice, even if a dragon rumbled and grumped in my dreams all night long.

CHAPTER 6

"One word frees us of all the weight and pain of life: that word is love." – Sophocles

ROGUE

SIX WEEKS LATER...

As much as I hated to admit it, Wyman proved himself more than capable to the task of guarding the twins. He wasn't a *nanny* or so he insisted, yet he was. Once upon a time, when my people were still alive and Alfred new to our world, we'd shared many discussions about cultural similarities. Amongst the frost elves, the raising of the young was for everyone in the community. Our children were few and far between. They were always valued.

Amongst his kin, it was similar. The birth of angels was such a rarity that it was cause for great celebration and even the fiercest among them would volunteer to look after and train their young. It fostered powerful community ties and helped prevent our most powerful young from harming themselves or others.

For the last few years, the five of us had been more than enough, though Fiona had tended to their most basic need for food. We shared in their care and tending. As they grew older, though, they needed more instruction, and the binding of their powers should have happened sooner. We'd indulged them too much and it had nearly been catastrophic.

Wyman, thrilled to the challenge, despite all of his grumpiness and he only flirted with Fiona as more of a habit, than with any genuine interest. The fact she rarely responded to his comments shut him down more effectively than any of us had managed. If that wasn't humbling, I didn't know what was.

Speaking of my mate, I went out onto the deck and looked toward the beach. She'd gone out that morning to walk along the sand. Instead of taking one of us with her, she'd wanted to be alone. Since it wasn't often she made such a request, I'd thought nothing of it. But Fiona had changed the last few weeks and I wasn't the only one who noticed.

I was also no longer knotting when we fucked. That alone warned me of what had happened that night at the keep when Maddox entered the mating frenzy and took her with him. We'd brought them back from the edge, but it may have been too late. She'd said nothing and the only outward sign I'd seen was the bruise on her neck around the mating mark. It hadn't faded. If anything, it had deepened to a gorgeous shade of indigo and red, not that a bruise should be so pretty, but it was.

Also, Maddox had changed. He watched her constantly, even when she wasn't aware of him, he was always nearby—not quite hovering. Alfred had to all but drag him away on their latest visit to the South America. A couple of nests had gotten out of hand in a war for territory. The slaughter of more than a thousand villagers on the border between two countries had infuriated him.

Those nests would be purged.

Normally, that would be a task I'd have joined him on, but Maddox had been annoying the hell out of Alfred with his possessive behavior, so he'd taken him with him. Fin had gone to handle matters at the Keep since once each three moons we allowed audiences for those seeking our judgment and assistance in matters they couldn't settle themselves.

I'd rather gouge out my own eyes and the last time Fiona had taken the audiences, she'd damn near gouged out theirs. She had ripped out the heart of some vampire named Brad something and it had been a whole thing. When it became patently clear she would rip off the rest of their heads or their hearts, it didn't much matter to her, they shut up and the death of Brad became a moot point.

Politics were not our thing. So, I'd stayed with our mate while the rest handled the issues at hand. Wyman currently had the twins eating breakfast. We'd repaired most of the house, replaced the windows, and the furniture. Fiona had us leave the scorch marks on the floor in the living room though.

Every single time the twins saw them, they quieted a little and I admired the point. She didn't berate them or bring it up, but not everything they did could just be wiped clean. So the scorch marks stayed. Leaning against the railing, I watched as she wandered closer to the surf and the water brushed against her bare legs.

I wanted to know what she was thinking. What haunted her. What would make her smile. But since I had a feeling of why she was troubled, I also knew there was nothing I could do until the realization settled on her.

But if I were Maddox, I'd have confessed a whole lot sooner.

"Rogue," Wyman said from behind me. "The children are watching their show in the playroom." It had taken the twins some time to get used to being "normal" and "power-locked," but they were children. They adjusted far more swiftly than some adults. "Is Fiona all right?"

I glanced away from my little sváss to eye him. "Why do you ask?"

"The bruise on her neck. It's darkening and growing."

"Leave it alone for now," I advised him.

He frowned. "None of you have told her?"

"There's still a chance it will not take." The first few months were so critical. When we realized the first time, I didn't think it was real. None of us did. How could we? It shouldn't have been possible, but the twins in their playroom proved us wrong.

"There's a chance she's going to geld the lot of you," he grunted. "Just to be clear...I'll help her."

That made me turn entirely and I faced the ancient angel and raised both brows. "You mean that." I don't know why I was surprised.

"I do. She may not be my mate, but I love her and her spirit. She deserves better than to be caught off guard, particularly if the dragon is the one."

I held back a groan. Wyman wasn't wrong and dragons were so very different. It had been too long since I'd even seen a female dragon, much less one preparing for a child.

"She deserves to know."

I didn't disagree. "It's not your place."

Wyman stepped out onto the deck, narrowing the distance between us. The enmity between us went back too far for me to ever *like* him. I could respect him. I could accept him as a part of our extended *family* and as a guardian for the children. But we were not friends and he needed to remember that.

"If this is like with the twins, there will be no missing the signs soon." He locked his gaze on me. "If he cannot tell her himself, don't let her be caught unawares. This could be more brutal."

More brutal than housing the living spark of the angels? Something so fundamental it had not only been a part of the twins' conception but changed her in such a way that she was still different. Her wings had never gone, nor had some of her other angelic abilities. A portion of the spark still resided within her soul and if Maddox had managed to impregnate her, then there was a real chance it was because the spark was there.

The spark, and the fertility magic created when a druid and a succubus had bonded. I sighed and nodded my head. "I will take care of it."

To my surprise, he nodded. "Thank you. I know I'm over-stepping and that you hate my interference. But I like the little wench. She's got more spirit and spunk and given more life to you fucktards than anything ever has."

"She brought Alfred back to life," I said, and he gave me a curt nod.

"Yes she did and she brought you back from the edge. We may not like each other, but you are one of the few I enjoy fighting with."

At that I laughed. "Don't push your luck."

He grinned and pivoted to return inside. "And I plan on getting laid this weekend, so you boys should plan on watching your own spawn."

Right.

I ignored him and glanced down at the beach again. Fiona stood right in the water, the waves rushing up to wrap around her legs before retreating. It took me a moment to notice the steam though. Steam from where the water touched her skin and began to evaporate. It was a sunny day without a cloud in the sky and there was a fog beginning to form around her.

Fin.

I reached for our brother and though he was more than half a world away, he wasbored as fuck from the speed of his reaction.

Please tell me you need me back there right now.

I was almost sorry to laugh at him. I didn't envy him the assorted politics either.

Maddox needs to tell her.

Fin's sigh was so visceral he might as well have been in the room with me.

I'll talk to him.

I shook my head slowly even though he couldn't see me. *I'm almost certain that was why Alfred took him. But Wyman has noticed.*

The silence echoed along the connection.

I wish it was me. The softness of that thought made me smile. Because he was not alone in that desire. The idea she could bring our children into the world, bring back what for me would be the first elves in... no. I would not think on that for now. But I understood Fin's feelings. The problem was, dragons were different, and if she changed as much as she had with Alfred's—then she needed to know.

And she needed to know now.

I stared down at her and found her gazing up at me.

If he does not tell her tonight, we will. The decision was made. He may have been in a frenzy, her as well, but he had to know if we all did.

Agreed.

With that thought, Fin released the tether and I gripped the rail and jumped. I leaped from rock to rock, making my way down to the sand. I would not be separated from my little sváss by such distance. If she still wanted time alone, I'd go for a swim or a flight above.

No sooner did I touch down on the sand did she begin walking toward me. The steam rising from the water continued to drift out as though a fog rolled in. The warmth from the sun could be too much sometimes, but the water was normally much colder. The first drift of it across my toes told me it wasn't as chilly as it had been.

"Do you need more time, little sváss?" I asked as we neared each other ,but she launched herself at me and I caught her easily. The heat boiling off her pulled perspiration from my skin and I closed my eyes, pulling my own magic around us. The air cooled, the water temperature dipped, and she let out a deep sigh.

"Yes and no," she murmured against my neck.

"Well, I'm glad we cleared that up." The comment made her laugh and she pulled back. It gave me my first good look at Maddox mating mark on her neck. The color had deepened and grown patchy. She lifted a hand to cover it and met my gaze.

In that moment, I realized it was far too late.

She'd already figured it out.

"When do Alfred and Maddox return?" Her moods had always been mercurial, her passions swiftly shifting from anger to joy to sexual desire. Yet in that moment, I could read nothing from her. When I held out my arm, she tucked herself under it. As warm as she was, she wanted me colder, so I reached for that magic inside of me and there was frost forming on the sand that melted as we walked together.

"By nightfall," I promised.

"You all know," she said. It wasn't a question.

"We suspected." I would not lie to her. "Though, as with all possible pregnancies, it might not have taken."

She snorted. "Our anniversary weekend."

I just nodded.

Studying her as we walked farther, I asked, "Little sváss, you were very upset last time. None of us wanted to upset you until we were certain."

She snorted. "Last time—last time I was struggling with the fact I was a vampire hybrid succubus and the twins were filling me with angelic spark. So there's no definition for what I am anymore."

True.

"Now?" She cast a look up at me then ahead before she sighed. "Am I going to turn into a dragon, Rogue?"

I opened my mouth then closed it again because I literally had no answer for that. If she did turn into a dragon...

Oh, I would not be Maddox for all the jewels in his hoard right now.

"We will figure it out, little sváss," I promised her and kissed her temple. Somehow, we would figure it out.

CHAPTER 7

"Being deeply loved by someone gives you strength, while loving someone deeply gives you courage." – Lao Tzu

FIONA

"Ten years?" My voice climbed despite every ounce of my determination to *not* yell when Maddox and I had this discussion. "Dragons are pregnant for *ten years?*"

"It is not so long," he attempted to soothe me, but he was a smart dragon, he didn't get within arm's reach. "And we are not certain..."

I glared at him. "There's a lot you're not certain about." I reached up to cover the mating mark reflexively. It itched. The bruising around it had grown worse and worse. But it wasn't bruising. It was a scale.

Something I'd discovered in the shower that morning, before I'd taken myself out for a walk and put it together. Not only had Maddox managed to knock me up—hadn't he actually called dibs on being next?—he wasn't entirely sure what would happen next.

"Kitten," he murmured, taking his life in his hands as he moved closer. I was torn between kissing him and punching him. I might do both. As it was, anger billowed through me as though someone fanned the flames at some great forge. Irrational? Probably. Did I give a good fuck about that part? Hell no.

"What?" I asked, the syllable coming out a pure growl. It hadn't escaped my notice that Rogue, Alfred, *and* Fin were all present and while they weren't right out here on the deck with us, they were easily within earshot. To be honest, I wasn't sure who they were here for more—me or Maddox.

Wrapping his arms around me, Maddox tugged my stiff form against his chest. His body framed mine and he dipped his whole head so that he could bury his face against my neck. The brush of his lips against that scale where his mating mark *had* been and clearly still *was* beneath it, sent a wash of love through me.

"There has not been another of my kind in more centuries than I care to count," Maddox murmured. "The last female dragon I knew died thousands of years ago. This— should not be possible and yet you have made all things possible."

I made a face, but it was hard to stay mad at him when he actually sounded so—excited. Like Benedict and Mireille did when they discovered something new. The wonder and the awe in his voice...

"I should have realized it when the need to have you over- whelmed everything," Maddox admitted. "Your scent changed when the twins no longer needed to nurse, and it kept changing...I should have known that it meant you were fertile again."

Fertile.

Again.

"Wait."

I locked gazes with Fin through the windows to the living room.

Yes, beautiful. You are our mate in every sense of the word.

Which meant I really was pregnant with a dragon. "Don't dragons..."

"Lay a clutch of eggs?" Maddox said, pure delight in his voice. "Yes, they—"

Pivoting, I struck without a second thought. One fist right across his too happy damn jaw and shit-eating grin. If he hadn't gone flying backward toward the rail, my knee would have slammed into his dick. As it was, I rushed forward and kicked him square in the chest with both feet as I leapt upward. Rage like I'd never experienced exploded within me and Maddox's startled expression vanished as he disappeared over the edge.

Alfred wrapped an arm around me from behind. Hauling me backward even as I would have followed Maddox right over the edge. His wings snapped out and we were airborne and soaring *away* from Maddox. The rage inside of me went incandescent. I was a damn beacon in the gradually darkening sky as Alfred raced us eastward and away from the sea. I dug my nails into his arms, but it had little effect, in part because a distant part of my mind did not want to hurt him and at the same time, the killing fury held me in its grasp.

We flew forever. Until bit by bit, the cold winds cooled the flames of my temper and reason began to creep out of the corners and stare at me with wide eyes. I'd been pissed off before.

This was nothing like that.

Finally, Alfred let out a sigh as though he'd held his breath this whole time. Maybe he had, what the hell did I know? His descent was not nearly as rapid as the climb when he'd stolen me away from our home, but when we landed, the land around us was stark, frozen tundra with no heartbeats for miles. Not even animals ventured out here in the isolated wilderness of nothingness.

"Where are we?" I asked as he loosened his grip on me. Even though I was still dressed in the tank top and cut off jean shorts that I favored when on the beach, the icy ground actually felt *good* against the soles of my bare feet. Hints of steam rose up and I sighed.

It was the other confirmation I'd gotten from the waves. Pivoting, I glanced at Alfred and froze. His shirt was gone as were most of his pants. His skin had turned a dark reddish-black in places and blistered.

"Asshole," I whispered in horror and all at once the heat fled my body as I went to him. "I hurt you."

"Shh, my hellion," he whispered as he cupped my face. "You did not intend harm."

My stomach plummeted and tears flooded my eyes only to freeze as one tear drop landed on my cheek. Even as I stared at him, his skin had begun to repair. The charred bits flaked away leaving behind pink, flushed, new skin beneath.

Cupping my face, Alfred kissed the tear away. "Hellion," he said, his voice firm. "You meant no harm. This is just another challenge for us to get used to."

"Alfred," I said, stomping my foot. Yes, it was childish. No, I didn't care. "I'm going to turn into a dragon."

"We don't know that," he said, holding my gaze steady.

"I turned into something close to an angel."

"Yes, and you're still an angel," he teased. "My angel of hell, but still an angel."

I shouldn't have laughed but I did. "So now I'm going to be a dragon of hell? What does that mean? Scaley lizard queen?"

A shudder raced through me at the thought and I pulled

away as the heat in my system seemed to billow out. Kind of like how Maddox exhaled fire when we'd been in the prison. I'd seen him blast Alfred before, too. Alfred had survived and then...

Fists clenched, I fought to get my anger under control, but it wasn't just anger. I reached up to touch the mating mark. There were more scales. Eyes closed, I traced my finger around my neck, searching for where the change in texture ended. It was like a collar had formed.

That just pissed me off even more.

"Brace yourself, Hellion. Maddox doesn't know what's good for him."

My eyes snapped open as a torrent of air hit from above, the power of wings slapping downward and slowing the golden dragon's descent. He'd *followed* us?

Reason whispered in my ear as though my rage was being ridiculous. *Of course, he followed us. We are his mate.*

We?

No sooner did I latch onto that than Maddox landed. Wisely, this time, the great dragon kept his distance. Those solemn eyes focused on me and utterly ignored Alfred. Good, if he got all possessive and pissy with my asshole, we were going to have more than words. Hands on my hips, I glared back at him.

The dragon's eyes were slitted and unblinking. A rumble of satisfaction escaped him as he dipped his head to me and then lifted his wing as though offering shelter. I flipped him off and stretched my own wings. and while I didn't have Alfred's style, I caught a draft of air and used it to give me some lift.

Maddox roared and leapt after me. Only his wings were a lot bigger than mine and the surge of air they dislodged knocked me off balance. I would have plummeted if Alfred hadn't caught my hand and tugged me right side up.

"Behave," Alfred snapped at him. Oh good. For a second there... "And you, Hellion. I will not have either of you try to destroy the other. You have done something wondrous, and he is rightfully excited." Oh. I clenched my jaw. "However, you," he continued, glaring at Maddox. "Could have some tact. Fiona is afraid. You're celebrating her fear and her loss of control and the fact *none* of us know what will happen exactly."

We hadn't known before and while Maddox and Alfred glared at each other, all of us hovering in the air, it hit me. We really hadn't known with the twins. My whole world had been upside down. I'd been an emotional wreck driven by compulsions and needs I hadn't understood. It wasn't until much later the guys revealed the pregnancy and even then, fear had assailed me.

Succubi were terrible mates and terrible parents. We were solitary creatures, better suited to take what we needed and then move on.

But I wasn't solitary, nor was I a terrible parent.

This mating business however...

He *needs to prove his worth. Not us.*

The little voice of reason whispered in my ear again.

We are the gift. The reward. The prize.

Excuse the fuck out of you? The voice of reason could fuck right off. I was *no one*'s prize.

Fair. I misspoke.

Damn right you did.

Still, if a dragon cannot protect his mate, not take all that she can throw at him, then he does not deserve her.

Maddox was always trying to protect me.

So?

Yeah, okay.

"I need to think," I said finally, ending the glare off between the two. *Fin...*

My druid answered by appearing below us and Alfred descended with Maddox circling slowly as if uncertain of his welcome.

Good.

"Are you all right, Beautiful?" He held out a thick cloak and wrapped it around me as soon as Alfred and I landed. I leaned into him and the blanket, then glanced upward.

"I don't know yet. I don't know how I'm going to change or what's going to happen."

"None of us do," Fin teased. "We never have with you. It's most of the fun."

I glanced up at him and sure enough, his expression held elements of adoration and teasing in equal measure. "You mean that?"

"You are my goddess of flame and spring. You bring life to where none has been allowed to grow before. You are the gateway to races long thought extinct. But even if you were none of those things, you have held my heart since long before you were even born." That was a humbling thought. He pressed his forehead to mine. "The children are a gift. But you are the treasure. We are all possessive of you, we will always honor and covet and try to keep you safe whether it is Alfred elevating you above all or Maddox hiding you away in his hoard or Rogue who would build a whole new world or home for you wherever you wished it."

"And you?" I asked, more curious than anything else.

"I am the easiest," he swore. "I just want to be a part of your life."

"As do I," Alfred said as though Fin had somehow failed to include him and Maddox rumbled a sound that said as much.

I glanced toward them as Maddox finally landed and his dragon body shimmered, and folded, and tucked, until he wore the form of the man I loved. Not that I didn't love his dragon.

Approval echoed within me.

"What if you don't want me if I turn into some monster? I mean, Maddox eats people."

"I only eat the bad people," Maddox argued. "And it's more about eliminating problems before they plague us. You don't complain when I eat you."

I swore I could hear Fin roll his eyes. "Do you think Maddox or his dragon are monsters?"

"No." The answer flowed from my tongue easily and some of the fear leached from my bones.

"Then why would we ever think you were? You were great and fierce in your protectiveness of us, the power you housed while carrying the twins is still there. Changed, adapted, more you than them now, I suspect this will be the same."

For some reason, that made me feel so much better. I met Maddox's gaze—his—not his dragon's. His eyes held love, but also... "Kitten, I'm sorry. It never occurred to me that you would be afraid. It should have and in that, I failed you. You were right to smack me upside the head."

A little smile pulled at my lips. "I'm not really sorry that I did."

He chuckled and then held out his hand toward me. "Feel free to do it whenever you need, Kitten. I can handle your claws."

That wasn't arrogance. Well, it was, but he had proven that time and again. While I wore very little, he wore nothing at all. Fin loosened his hold as I went to Maddox. When I slid my hand into his, he raised it to his lips and kissed it gently. His gaze went from my eyes to my throat and almost immediately his pupils slitted as his dragon stared down at me. When he lifted a hand to wrap around my throat, a shiver went over my whole skin. The scales were so sensitive.

"Mine," he said with such possession I swore my cunt

soaked right through my shorts. His nostrils flared as though he approved, but then Maddox blinked and it was just him again. "We'll figure this together, Kitten. All of us."

Alfred and Fin moved in to buffet us, the only one missing was Rogue, but he was right there—in my heart. I closed my eyes and pressed my forehead to Maddox's chest. His relief filled the air with the sweet musk of male who wanted to rut.

Great.

Now I could smell his arousal.

But not only his. Alfred's and Fin's were there, maybe not as strongly, but their hunger for me softened me further.

"Ten years?" I asked again because the year I'd been pregnant with the twins had been a very long year, and sometimes even my own sexual appetites during that time had been impressive even to me.

"Among my kind," Maddox said. "The male fertilized the female and she carried the eggs for ten years before they were laid..."

Wait.

My head snapped up. "I have to lay eggs?" Somehow I'd managed to forget that part from earlier.

Collectively, they exhaled.

Oh, I wanted to kill Maddox all over again.

Lay eggs.

CHAPTER 8

"Love is like Heaven, but it can hurt like Hell." – Unknown

MADDOX

SIX MONTHS LATER...

My kitten slept late today, and Fin took the children off to play with others. The playgroup with human children had been Wyman's idea. First, to teach them manners and interaction with others, and also to impress upon them how to resolve difficulties without beating each other up. Without their powers, they'd taken to pouncing each other. Mireille more than Benedict.

Amusingly, Fiona blamed all of us—herself included—for the children's absolute lack of diplomatic skills. So, we sent the most diplomatic among us to shepherd them through the process. So far, Fin hadn't brought them back bound and gagged so it must be going well. Once they developed the interpersonal skills necessary, we would begin to introduce them to the supernatural community, but only in limited quantities of those we'd vetted.

Currently, there were only two on the list. Since we'd discovered our frenzy had impregnated her, we'd had to consider a lot of things that hadn't occurred to us before. With the twins, it had been a singular focus to protect Fiona and them. Now, they were growing up. Angels matured at their own rate, according to Alfred. They seemed to be maturing on an even scale, they were still children. Dragons could take longer to mature, as could elves, it was based on lifespan, I supposed.

Fin, for all that he was a druid, had been human. An empowered human, but human. His children with Fiona would likely be the same. So, we needed to figure this out *before* Fin got her pregnant. Also, the discussion of birth control was now an issue, and I would not argue with my kitten on this no matter how much my dragon and I would both prefer to keep her pregnant at every opportunity.

To have other dragons in the world would be...a longing ripped through me that I hadn't experienced for more than a thousand years. I'd forgotten what it was to have another of my kind. My brothers filled the gap and Fiona—she filled a space inside of me that I had long since believed a void forever.

The ruddy and indigo scales around her neck formed a perfect circlet and they'd begun to move down her chest. Though the scales continued to spread, her belly remained only slightly rounded. I longed to see it swollen and full, but unlike with the twins, her figure had not altered as much. Definitely not as much as her temperament or her scent.

Those jewel green eyes opened slowly to stare at me and for a split-second her pupils were slitted, more draconic than they'd ever been. My dragon slammed into me from within, staring through my eyes as we locked gazes. Her pupils dilated, fattening to their normal size and my dragon let out a forlorn sigh within, but not me.

Alfred had been correct as had Fin. They'd speculated that until she could safely shift and embrace her dragon, her pregnancy would linger and might even fail. The very idea that she could carry within her a clutch of eggs for us, a brace of younglings, but that she would be unable to lay them, burned in me like an ancient wound.

"Kitten," I murmured as I abandoned my perch on the chair to slide onto our bed. The lovemaking had also changed in the last few months. She'd always been demanding and open with her needs. Her sexuality as much a part of her as her hair color and her eyes. But there had been a greater need in her, an appetite it took all of us, sometimes hours, to satisfy and that was normal. A female dragon hoarding her eggs and preparing to lay them needed them well seeded.

I'd come in her so many times and I wanted to again, but until she shifted...

"You've figured something out," she said around a yawn by way of good morning. The sheet slipped down revealing the gorgeous scales that now sloped over her shoulders and partway down her biceps. Fiona wasn't sure what she thought of them, but I thought them beautiful. She would make an exquisite dragon.

Not golden, and that was all right. She was her type of dragon and that was even better. A one of her own kind and all mine.

"Yes," I admitted, unwilling to try and dance around a topic that upset her as often as it brought her pleasure. At least her mercurial moods had settled some. She no longer tried to kill me if I wanted to touch her. In fact, she invited my touch so often I didn't feel the need to ask anymore. The first time she'd slapped my hand away when I'd cupped her breast upon waking had hurt. But I didn't let it push me away from her.

No, that was the challenge of a female dragon. If her mate could not withstand her, then he did not deserve her, and Fiona had already been through so much for us already. Now I needed her to go through more.

"If I could take this burden for you," I swore to her. "I would."

A smile softened her puffy lips. They were still swollen from our kisses the night before. In fact, I'd passed out into sleep with my cock buried between those lips as she took me fully into her throat and drained me of every ounce of seed I could release. At one point, I'd woken to Rogue fucking her fiercely from behind as she rode Alfred and Fin was stroking himself, waiting for his turn. She'd only gone to them after she and I climaxed more times than I'd thought possible.

The lingering marks of their bites faded on her skin, everything healing swiftly. While their mating marks were present in places, only mine and Alfred's were visible. His as her maker and mine as her mate. She was Fin's goddess and Rogue's chosen. Their marks were on her soul and did not need to show on her flesh and yet they did from time to time.

"Tell me," she commanded as she curled into my arms and everything in me settled as she wrapped herself around me. It wasn't desire or sex that had her seeking shelter with me. It was love and affection. Mutual need. One mate's call to another.

"You need to shift, Kitten."

"Well, you make it sound easy," she said, the corners of her mouth deepening with her smile. "Just shift and all will be well."

I chuckled and flattened onto my back so she would be sprawled above me. All her soft curves fit me everywhere. If someone had carved her from my own flesh, they could not have made her fit more perfectly. "Well, for a dragon, it's quite literally the opposite."

She frowned. "What?"

"When a dragon is born, Kitten…"

"Hatched," she pointed out and I grinned at her.

"Yes, hatched. When we're hatched, we're dragons. We do not have *this* form yet."

Her eyes widened. "Then how…"

"We learn."

The frown tightening her brows deepened. "How long did it take to learn?"

"Forgive me, Kitten. I don't remember. It's been a very long time, in almost all ways, both forms are very much me. I cannot remember a time when I wasn't both."

She frowned, then pulled at her lower lip in thought.

"But these," I continued, tracing my finger over her scales and delighting at the shiver that went through her and the pleasure in her eyes. For a moment, the pupils slitted again and I wondered. The more I petted and stroked them, the more she appeared in them. Her dragon was in there and my heart caught fire as even my dragon held his breath. We hadn't been alone, not truly, since we found her. But it had always been *her* and now it was *them*.

Our mate.

"But these?" she prompted pulling me from this new wondrous discovery. My kitten, with her sharp claws could bleed me anytime she wished, had just given me the answer to prayers and dreams I'd never imagined.

"These scales tell me she's already in you."

Fiona's eyebrows rose as she pushed herself up and stared at me. "She?"

"Your dragon."

Her expression changed from puzzled to irritated to

curious then back to annoyed. I had to bite back a smile at the dance of emotion over her features. "The voice I keep hearing."

Now it was my turn to scowl. "Voice? You've been hearing someone else, and you didn't tell us?"

With one finger, she booped my nose. "Simmer down, lizard-brain. I've been thinking of it as the rational and reasonable side of my brain telling the rest of me to calm the hell down when I've been so furious and that it was okay to kick your ass."

I opened my mouth but one furious look from her and my dragon snapped my mouth shut. Female dragons were notoriously ill-tempered when carrying a clutch and not only was mine carrying our clutch, she hadn't been able to get out and confront *us* yet.

Silence was definitely the better part of valor.

"But if you're saying you can see my dragon..." The corners of her lips tilted into a lazy smile. "Okay, that's weird because I think of *you* as my dragon."

"We are." Without a doubt. "And always will be, Mate. We are always yours."

Her smile ballooned through me as she tilted her head. It almost looked like she was listening to someone else and her smile faded. Fin hadn't mentioned another presence, but then sometimes my druid brother kept things to himself until one of us was ready to understand it. The dragon might always have been a part of her. A part we awakened.

I rather liked the idea of that, to be honest. He'd seen her in a vision thousands of years before she was born. Known she was to be ours, and she'd saved his life then. She'd saved all of ours in different ways since coming to us. All the rules shattered. All knowledge given the finger, as she was want to do. One being should not be able to house so much and yet, in her, we found completeness.

"I need to see Elias," she murmured.

"Why?" I growled and so did my dragon. The wolf was her friend. Fine. Whatever. We didn't like how friendly he was with her, even if he didn't try to take our mate. She gave me another look and this time the boop on the nose actually stung a little. I growled again, then gritted my teeth and forced the sound back. "Why do you need to see him?"

"Because he learned to shift back and forth in the last century, so he's probably not so old he doesn't remember how."

My mouth formed an 'o' as my jaw dropped.

Her smirk went straight to my dick as she sat up and her breasts looked positively delicious. "No, you have to keep that dick of yours out of my cunt for the day. I'm sore and Fin's not here to fix it."

I grunted.

"But I'll call Elias and see if he's free for a visit. His pack isn't terrifically fond of me."

I'd eat them all.

"And no," she said as she climbed off me and wiggled that perfect ass on her way to the bathroom. "You cannot eat them."

Could too.

"Maddox."

"Yes, Kitten," I said as obedient as I could muster. It must not have worked because her laughter carried out as she turned on the shower. I preferred the bath, where I could ease into her and slosh the water about, but showers were nice too.

I followed after her to watch as she began to wash. The soap over her breasts just made my dick harder, but I could wait. Her gaze dipped and she chuckled. "Let me wash my hair and then I'll suck you off, I want you in a more mellow mood if I'm going to be around other men."

My mate was a brilliant woman, and her mouth was definitely heaven. No sooner had she rinsed her hair than I stepped inside, and she went to her knees. I should be down there worshipping her, but the first slurp of her tongue over the head of my cock and I was eager for the pleasure she offered. She controlled the pace, stroking my balls gently until the frenzy hit and when I looked down, her dragon looked back at me.

The strength of her suction eased as she relaxed her jaw and my mate—my dragon's mate—invited us to take her and I gripped her hair gently and fucked her mouth until tears ran down her cheeks and I roared my pleasure. Her orgasm followed us as she worked her fingers against her clit. Despite Fiona's earlier protests, she came with a roar of her own and the sound vibrated through my soul.

Yes. Our mate wanted us and for the first time since I'd realized she'd taken my seed, our mate had not only not rejected us, she'd invited us to take her and claim her. We'd proven something to her.

Finally.

And I didn't question it as I dragged her quivering body up and offered her my throat. She latched onto the mating mark with a ferociousness that had my cock stiffening again and Fiona climbed me, wrapping her legs around my hips as she took my cock in her hand. I would have gladly spilled to those strokes, but she lined me up and I thrust home as she drank from me.

I tasted her pain and her pleasure and I obeyed every command she gave as she encouraged my furious pace. This time, when I spilled into her, fire filled my lungs and she met my kiss with her own mouth and when I exhaled fire, she took it into herself. The water around us turned into nothing but steam as I came, filling her with more seed than she could ever possibly require, but her inner muscles milked me, even though I couldn't quite knot.

No, she was very pregnant. Her body just wanted mine and we were glad to give it to her. By the time we finished showering, I was near boneless from being replete and she carried my marks everywhere. The scales had begun to spread down her back and I licked my lips at the image I could imagine of her as a dragon.

Would she fly with me?

Would she allow us to take her mid-flight? A dragon's mating dance was supposed to be one of the most pleasurable experiences, and I'd never done it.

Didn't matter. My dragon wanted to quibble, but this time I shut him up. Fiona had us body, heart, mind, and soul. She was all we needed. If her dragon would have us too, then we would take our time. Until then, it was a non-issue.

I had a feeling she knew what I was thinking because she kissed me tenderly before we had to go and dress. Warm and relaxed from the shower and the sex, she was also cuddly and sat in my lap while we ate breakfast and she called Elias.

It turned out the wolf was an excellent source and after he stopped laughing at her which took a good hour, he actually gave some solid advice.

Maybe I wouldn't eat him.

CHAPTER 9

"I love you more than bacon, and other lies we tell ourselves." -
Fiona

FIONA

TWO MONTHS LATER...

Elias was full of shit. The twins would be turning four soon, and I was lucky my mates didn't object to the fact that I was mostly scales with red hair these days. He'd explained shifting to me both in concept and in practice. Mostly, what he'd said was that it involved reaching for each other and surrendering. To know that I was the dragon and the dragon was me. That I wouldn't be lost and she wouldn't be the only one left.

In fact, if the voice of reason inside of me was indeed my dragon, then she also insisted the same thing. She could not be without me. She didn't *want* to be without me.

Fine.

But she seemed as frustrated with the process as I was with regard to making this work. We'd meditated, fucked our mates until I was so satiated nothing could touch my relaxation and we'd fought, argued, run, swam, and pretty much everything else we could think of.

Beyond all of that, it was depressing.

It had been nearly a year since our weekend away and Maddox knocked me up and still beyond the barest sense of a rounded tummy, there was no sign of my pregnancy. Every week that passed without success had left me in tears. I refused to let them see me this way. Even the twins were upset at this point.

Mama was unhappy and they knew it. I was being a terrible, selfish mother, because I couldn't even allow my body to shift to free the children hidden within it. My dragon tried to talk to me but we didn't agree. She thought it was fine. We were who we were. Would she like to release her wings and soar? Yes. Would she also like to take a lump out of Maddox's ass for this? Also. yes.

But we were loved and we had a family and...

I pitched the glass I'd been drinking out of as hard as I could against the far wall where it smashed to bits. I was at the keep. In my current mood, I didn't want to be around the very breakable glass walls when the twins had been so diligent in their behavior of late. The only other one in the residence with me was Fin. I'd asked him to bring me then give me some space.

While he might not approve and was actually still somewhat present in the back of my mind, he was very much giving me the space and privacy I'd asked for. I'd gone down to soak in the bathing room, but it had done nothing and my irritation was simply growing. Like my skin wanted to itch off my body and it took everything I had not to claw at myself.

I wanted to fight.

I wanted to cry.

I wanted to scream.

I picked up the bottle of mead and stared at it. Alcohol wasn't good for children, then again the rate I was going I was the world's worst mother anyway, so I took a huge mouthful and then just spit it out. The exhale caught fire and I stared at it.

That was almost funny.

So, I did it again.

And again.

Until the bottle was empty and some of my nerves were a little calmer.

I was this uncomfortable when I'd gone into labor with the twins. It was the last time I could remember feeling this way. I threw the empty bottle into the fire place and set my hand over the non-existent baby bump and sighed.

I wanted to meet this child, hatched or not. I wanted to give that dream to Maddox. He told me the only thing that mattered was me. Over the last several months, he seemed to have made his peace with the idea. His love was a great comfort, but I was failing.

Restless again, I abandoned the bathing room and headed up the stairs. I wanted the walk. I avoided the main hall. No one could enter the residence unless they were with us, anyway. I kind of wanted to go out to the garden, but to get to it I'd have to go across the hall, so I kept climbing. Past the floor with our rooms and past the great library.

The sense of Fin was there, he was inside and stilled at my approach, but I kept going, following the round staircase to one of the ancient turrets and finally outside into the sunshine. The air was brisk, winter just around the corner. It always seemed colder here than where we lived now, but then again, we were high in the mountains. Rogue preferred the chill to the beach, but he lived on the cliffside over the ocean because it was my dream.

So unfair that any of them should have to give up on dreams for me. Or that I couldn't even do this one little thing that infant dragons could figure out and young wolves sorted all by themselves. Why couldn't I just...

Fists clenched, I threw my head back and just screamed and screamed and screamed. I needed to get the frustration out. My scales itched violently and without giving a damn for the consequences I raked my fingernails over them. My whole body was nothing but scales now. They even covered my face.

I just wanted them off or to change or something. I fought against them, but they didn't budge and I screamed again as hellfire seemed to race through my blood.

"Fiona..." Fin's voice came from so far away and I turned to face him. but my vision changed, flattening and elongating and I seemed to climb higher as my skin cracked and split. The pain was nearly as bad as childbirth, but I didn't care, it helped.

Holy fuck did it help, and I threw my head back to scream again and this time what came out was a roar and it echoed over the valley.

Startled, I stumbled and slammed a clawed foot down on the rock of the precipice knocking it clear and sending it tumbling to the earth below.

My clawed foot.

Holy. Shit.

I snapped my head around to find Fin staring at me with real tears in his eyes and a brilliant smile on his face.

"Hello, Beautiful," he murmured.

I opened my mouth to respond, and I trilled a sound that

seemed to come from deep in my chest. It was a hilarious sound and at the same time, almost pretty?

Musical. The smug voice of reason told me. Well, I told me because she was right, we were one and the same. Why had we felt so split?

Grow. Change takes time. You had to accept.

All the words Rogue, Fin, Maddox, and even Alfred had said to me over the last few months. Ugh. I hated it when they were right. I trilled again and it was like laughing. Just because they were right didn't mean I had to tell them that.

"I'm going to get Maddox and the others, Beautiful," Fin summoned my attention back to him. "If that's alright with you. They are going to want to see you."

I glanced down at my clawed foot again. I was not golden. I was more... *Am I a red dragon?*

I had to know.

Fin grinned. "Yes, you are, and indigo. If you stretch out your wings." At least this I had practice at, so I extended them but fuck they went a lot further than they used to. "You have indigo stripes along them, like your wings when you're in your angelic form."

My angelic form.

My succubi form.

My dragon form.

Hybrid.

They were all me.

"Yes, our goddess of flame and spring," he whispered but I had no trouble hearing him and I wanted to kiss him. As it was, all I could do was lower my head gently to the roof next to him and he reached out with a gentle hand and stroked it over my eye ridge. A purr went through me at the sensation that elicited. At least I wasn't itching anymore.

Though my whole body seemed swollen.

He pressed a kiss to my eye ridge then murmured, "One moment, my beautiful lady."

The flow of his magic tingled against me as he left, and it wasn't even a full moment before he was back with all my mates. Maddox's eyes lit up from within in pure joy as I raised my head. My system ached though, desperately actually, almost as if I needed to pee. But...

The eggs.

Fin...I need to lay this clutch. That I could even think those words was just—whatever. I'd make fun of myself later.

"Maddox, she's ready to lay the clutch."

"It's early," he said, my dragon mate's voice taking on a note of fear.

"It is what it is," Alfred said. "Where?"

"The vault," Rogue and Fin said in the same voice and the crazed look of fear on Maddox's face wrenched at my heart. "Where you keep your hoard. That will be safe for her and the eggs both."

Fin didn't wait for a response as he reached out and put a hand on me, I felt him touch inside my mind and I opened to him easily. The world spun as we whisked along the lines to the vault I hadn't seen since the lizard-brain jackass kidnapped me all those years ago when we'd found out I was pregnant with the twins.

Oh, it was perfect. Messy, but perfect. I nearly stumbled as I took two steps. The guys avoided my ungainly form because I was a lot bigger than I was used to being. Maddox spun around and then began to snap orders. My mates all moved swiftly.

They cleaned, they straightened. Fin left and returned with dozens of different items, and I realized what they were doing was building me a nest. There were clothes amongst the heavy straw and soft blankets. Familiar scents, all of them theirs and eventually, I tired of waiting for them to finish.

I settled into the center of the nest and my whole body shuddered as I relaxed and it wasn't pain that rippled through me but a sense of peace as though I'd released a part of my burden. Maddox made a sound, and I turned my head to look.

Well, look at that.

I'd laid an egg.

The sense of peace invading me grew stronger because while everything else had been confusing, this my body—or at least my new body—understood. Before the afternoon finished, I'd laid four eggs in total. All of them pulsing with life. Maddox was prouder than a peacock and he kept smacking Alfred on the shoulder about look what he'd done. Alfred had only given me twins. Maddox had given me quads.

Fin whisked him away before I snapped him in half. Because now that I'd done all of that, I was exhausted. The next few days passed in a half-dream state. I slept a lot. One of them was always with me. They brought me food. I should probably turn my nose up at the number of cows they brought, but I was too hungry to be picky.

At least I didn't rip anything in half.

Fifteen days after I'd laid all four eggs, I woke in my own form, shivering, but tucked up to Maddox's dragon body as he sheltered me and the eggs both. I glanced up at him and smiled.

"See what *I* did?" I had to point it out and he let out a huff of laughter that filled the cave. As much as I wanted to stay with my eggs, I needed to see my twins, too.

We had no idea how long it would take, but for the next few months, Maddox and I traded out each week. I would spend a week with the eggs and he would visit the twins, or he would tend the eggs, while I visited the twins.

We had to keep them warm. They were also very vulnerable, so we didn't dare move them. I was also getting pretty good at the whole transformation thing.

Three days after the twins turned seven years of age, and almost four years after Maddox *knocked* me up in the first place, the first egg began to hatch. The chipping sound roused me from my dose and I swung my head around to look. Sure enough, a golden nose peeked out against the egg and excitement flooded me.

Fin!

In almost no time, my mates and my twins were there. They loved Mama's dragon form almost as much as Dada Maddox's. It took most of the day for the first of the dragonlings to get free of his egg. And he was definitely a he, and a perfectly golden shade, exactly the color of his sire's scales. Love filled me. We couldn't help them, Maddox had cautioned. Just as my own dragon had to find her way into world so did our children and at the same time, I worried. What if they weren't all successful?

The first was so adorable though and he stumbled about as he found his footing. He studied the others and then would go to hide under my wing. It wasn't until the second egg began to crack a couple of days later that he ventured out to his father's coaxing. The second egg was also a boy and he broke through his shell with a lot more violence and intent. He was also the same reddish shade as my scales. I didn't want to hear it.

Fine, he had my temper.

Whatever.

Though the boys were both hatched, the last two eggs were nearly another week before they finally began to show movement, and the terror in my gut finally subsided. Maddox had warned me that not all eggs survived. But the last two hatched another golden, this one a girl, the only female amongst them, for the very last one was another male and he was neither red nor golden, but deep green like the springtime.

I glanced at Fin, and I wasn't the only one. A deep smile curved his lips and there was pleasure there. Pleasure and knowledge.

They were all perfect. Three boys and one girl. Mireille decided that the golden girl and she would be best friends and told her so. Of all the hatchlings, the little girl went straight to Mireille and leaned against her, not hiding with me.

Laughter and triumph filled the cavern and I nuzzled each of them, familiarizing myself with the scent. Maddox promised they would have human forms too. It would just take a little more time.

We had all the time in the world.

Now, I whispered into my mind. *We are twelve.*

Alfred turned, holding the green dragon hatchling in his arms and his eyes locked with mine.

"Yes, my queen. We are twelve."

To keep up with Heather ,and all her series as well as bonus content and sneak peeks, join her reader's group: https://www.facebook.com/groups/HeathersPack/

AFTERWORD

Thank you for reading the Shackled Souls trilogy and the bonus novella. Now it's your turn to let me know whether you want to see more in this world or not.

Like, we have Elias, who is still Fiona's best friend and a shifter, not to mention there's pack politics.

Dorran is still out there, the forever changed warden. Just what did Fi do to him?

Synove, the last of the fallen, is still wandering around out there supposedly minding her own business.

And we couldn't forget Wyman, our Nanny Angel with the really big—personality.

I mean, anything is possible. Right?

Thoughts?

Drop by my group on Facebook to let me know what you think or send me a note or even leave its n your review. Authors do enjoy a little love, too.

xoxo
   Heather

ABOUT HEATHER LONG

USA Today bestselling author, Heather Long, likes long walks in the park, science fiction, superheroes, Marines, and men who aren't douche bags. Her books are filled with heroes and heroines tangled in romance as hot as Texas summertime. From paranormal historical westerns to contemporary military romance, Heather might switch genres, but one thing is true in all of her stories—her characters drive the books. When she's not wrangling her menagerie of animals, she devotes her time to family and friends she considers family. She believes if you like your heroes so real you could lick the grit off their chest, and your heroines so likable, you're sure you've been friends with women just like them, you'll enjoy her worlds as much as she does.

Follow Heather & Sign up for her newsletter:
www.heatherlong.net

Marine under the Mistletoe

Have Yourself a Marine Christmas

Lest Old Marines Be Forgot

Her Marine Bodyguard

Smoke & Marines

Bravo Team Wolf

When Danger Bites

Bitten Under Fire

Boomers

The Judas Contact

Deadly Genesis

Unstoppable

Cardinal Sins

Kill Song

Chance Monroe

Earth Witches Aren't Easy

Plan Witch from Out of Town

Bad Witch Rising

Her Elite Assets

Featuring:

Pure Copper

Target: Tungsten

Asset: Arsenic

Fevered Hearts

Marshal of Hel Dorado

Brave are the Lonely

Micah & Mrs. Miller

A Fistful of Dreams

Raising Kane

Wanted: Fevered or Alive

Wild and Fevered

The Quick & The Fevered

A Man Called Wyatt

Going Royal

Some Like It Royal

Some Like It Scandalous

Some Like It Deadly

Some Like it Secret

Some Like it Easy

Her Marine Prince

Blocked

Heart of the Nebula

Queenmaker

Deal Breaker

Throne Taker

Lone Star Leathernecks

Semper Fi Cowboy

As You Were, Cowboy

Madison, The Witch Hunter

Every Witch Way But Floosey's

Songs and Sweethearts

Wolves of Willow Bend

Wolf at Law

Wolf Bite

Caged Wolf

Wolf Claim

Wolf Next Door

Rogue Wolf

Bayou Wolf

Untamed Wolf

Wolf with Benefits

River Wolf

Single Wicked Wolf

Desert Wolf

Snow Wolf

Wolf on Board

Holly Jolly Wolf

Shadow Wolf

His Moonstruck Wolf

Thunder Wolf

Ghost Wolf

Outlaw Wolves

Wolf Unleashed